Other books by David Fairchild

Award Winning:

The Exodus

Circle of Dogs:

The New Paladin
Wolf
Eulogies

On Writing:

Where's the Blood?
25 Creative Writing Exercises with
Motivational Anthology

BOOM

Fairchild

Four Doors
Publishing

Four Doors Publishing LLC
Spanish Fork, UT

Printed in the United States of America.

For my sister and friends, whose names
are too many to list here, who have allowed
me to see worlds beyond worlds within my own.

. . . and. . .

To that one friend in every group who
makes you ask, "Did he really just say that?"

Right, James?

Contingency Plan (Section FF)

In case of imminent global destruction:

Step 1: Read the signs and follow instruction. Even if you think a high leader is stupid, "run" means run. It's only possible to rub a wrong decision in someone's face if you both survive or die together. Hell is built on people who never got to say, "I told you so."

Step 2: Never follow the crowd. It never gets it right. If they run—stop, you're not supposed to run. If they stand still and laugh at the highest military leader—run, that's where the best seats are. People who sit in the best seats never go to Hell, unless you pushed and shoved to get them.

Step 3: If it's empty, take the gold ship not the standard issue one. The standard issue one is not the best seat. There's a special and separate place in Hell for people who create standard issue.

Step 4: Two seats means you can squeeze in three so you don't have to leave your friend behind, so long as the pilot can reach the controls. Hell's population is entirely made of people who lost control.

Step 5: Avoid bad math and close your canopy. Once people see you have the gold ship, they'll stop laughing and beg you for a ride. For every seat you have, they'll see ten. This will weigh you down and no one will survive. People who weigh down others burn the longest in Hell.

Step 6: Take off. Only those who think for themselves will get off the ground. The ground is where the fire is. First the slothful burn in the fire on the ground, then they burn in Hell. We're not sure if there's a break in there between one to the other, but we know they burn.

Step 7: When the green fire comes, don't worry. You tried. At least you're pointed in the right direction. The green will burn you once and then—oh hell, just keep flying!

1
▲
Reassignment

Hallways conceive war and rumor is the lewd weenie that puts it there. Its swollen ego sneaks in, spreads its lies throughout. Then—bada-boom, bada-bing—a bouncing bundle of joy measured in megatons jumps out and asks why everyone's on fire.

Merrecci, however, already knew why, and he marched through the corridors wishing someone would have chosen to terminate the rumors growing here, just like he had warned of their conception months ago. If these were his halls, he might have scolded caution a time or few at loose lips. He would have demanded others to entirely stop breathing life into the abominable creature he knew would come, but it wasn't his place. This was the storm before the strike that, like all war, shouldn't be born. Yet these were not his walls. So, he minded his own business and pressed mercilessly deeper into the halls.

Right now, he was more interested in delivering his fist to a particular face. The closer he drew to his friend's office, the tighter his fingers curled into his palm. His friend knew better. He's the one who gave Merrecci the moniker of Barbarian Captain, after all.

When Vincenti Merrecci chose you, it was forever or until either you or he died. It was typically you. Friends were tools and tools dulled, but Merrecci was never going to die. To be called to his service was a promise of death warrant, but it was also a guarantee to be revered or chosen first to lead the next big team. To leave or deny Merrecci for any other reason was career assassination. To stay in his service was reverence. He avoided these halls except upon return to port. He hated angry children and their safe cubicles.

Today, he was summoned, and he loathed to be summoned. He wouldn't have wended these halls for any other reason. With summons came orders and sometimes dismissals, and those pissed him off.

As he pressed forward, he was aware of the nods towards him that others made because they were not new; the glances away from those who were; and the gawking from those who worked for nitwits who should have left halls like these long ago. Then there were the smirks of those whom he believed thought he had finally fallen from his high rung. He ignored and remembered them at the same time. He would intrude upon these corridors soon enough again and watch those smirks change into low-to the ground puckers. Of that, he was certain, but when? His only concern now was parading this open hallway, filled with its little people; their large desks crammed against the walls; and their sealed doors to various offices filled with even smaller pencil-pushers with higher-paid self-grandeur. This hall took him to the lift, which took him to a narrower, cleaner and emptier corridor filled with logos on flags and entirely too much shiny.

It reminded him of a future he could have had if certain people in high places weren't afraid he'd do more damage with a pen than he could do with torpedoes. Truth is, he was pretty certain he'd have stabbed all those people with that pen if they ever forced one into his hand. The red and silver carpet he was following came to a cross-point, and he turned left.

Two women and a shield array acknowledged his approach. The women wore the blue suit and tie of the security staff. They appeared unarmed, but Merrecci wasn't that stupid.

While one held up a scanning board, the other stood with her hand poised to apparate a weapon into it directly from the arsenal locker.

"Purpose," the scanning guard asked politely.

"Just scan me already and find out," Merrecci replied.

He might have noticed a slight jolt to the second guard's stance. He might have taught her a lesson if she were his security.

"At the summon of Prime Admiral Shade," the scanner instructed. "You may proceed."

Yet, Merrecci hadn't stopped proceeding forward since he'd left the lift. Either the disintegration shield had calibrated for his passage, or it hadn't. What's the worse that would happen then? He'd burn in hell?

The surprised movements of the scanning officer and her fevered attention to her control board told Merrecci that they hadn't. He didn't care. She would have the shield down for him, or she'd be known as the woman who killed the greatest barbarian captain the Franchise ever had. He stepped through and felt his personal effects and naval-issued weaponry dissipate from his body. Without a word or nod, he continued past the security check.

The officer with the empty trigger finger, who had been waiting to summon her weapon issued lecture on waiting next time for the shield to drop.

Merrecci did halt for this and turned suddenly on her. She didn't budge, just as she hadn't done when the shield wasn't fully prepared for him to pass through.

"On your way, Captain," she said, and her hand turned from the position of receiving a pistol weapon to receive a stun staff.

"You sure you want to be so brave, Lieutenant," Merrecci said.

"Yeah," she replied. "An angry captain in a hall of admirals. Ooh! Scary."

Her eyes were bright blue, but Merrecci found them to be darkened in something other than color. He knew that look.

"As you were," Merrecci fired back, revoking her authority.

"Thank God for that," the woman replied. "I was worried I couldn't get back to standing in a hall."

The corridor offered a cross-point choice again, and he continued straight. A robot floated up beside him and traced him with a scanner as he pressed forward. The captain gave no heed to the knowledge of the mine the robot carried as a line of defense against assassins. If it blew, the walls would still stand, his blood and liquified bones would be all over them. The cleaners would remove it before the hour was up, and the mine engineer would never have a career higher than lieutenant, if that officer even went on to be the biggest hero the stars had ever known.

The mine eventually stopped following him. A wall appeared directly in front of Merrecci's path now, then disappeared as he walked into it head-on and past its holo-projectors. A receptionist appeared behind a plain platform desk and a second disintegration shield. She looked up, knew Merrecci and authorized his passage before Merrecci could reach it. Merrecci crossed through. He stopped a moment before her desk. Her eyes elevated to his, and she realized she had forgotten she'd been chewing.

"Is that gum," he asked.

"Yep," she replied.

"What flavor?"

"Blue," she said.

"Do you have another piece," he asked.

She bit down a tight and serious chew before she leaned back in her chair. She should have slid straight out of it, as she reached into the pocket of her tight leather skirt and dislodged a silver square. She took back to her seat and handed it to Merrecci.

He thanked her and turned to a red and oxblood ornate door, pretending to be oak. It opened before him, and he stepped into a glass-bubble office that dabbled in purple and black décor. To the far end was a short man who was once larger than this whole room, but now he was smaller than the shelf behind him that held about twenty copies of his latest book. They were all signed, no doubt.

The short prime admiral spoke silently to someone unseen and beckoned Merrecci forward. Merrecci approached right up to the silencing buffer that encased the prime admiral and his desk and then waited. The admiral laughed inaudibly, talked some more. Merrecci made a promise to himself that this would never be him.

The admiral's attention turned to Merrecci, his countenance changed to serious, and the hum of the silencing buffer ceased.

"Captain," Admiral Shade welcomed in a way that told Merrecci the scolding came first this time. "I trust you're re—

"Two years," Merrecci saluted, shouted, and remained respectful all at once. "You give me two years and have the gall to release me and order me back here two months later?"

The admiral leaned forward in his seat, barely returning the salute. He might have seemed taller to any other captain, but not to Merrecci. Vincenti was pretty sure his superior was in reach of a good, hard slap, which would be easy from his saluting position, but he wanted to punch the man, not slap him. Shade's jaw twisted into scorn while his brow said it would forgive Merrecci.

"Don't pretend you really thought we'd leave you out of the game for two full years," Shade said.

"Two months," Merrecci fired back, still respectfully and full of disdain. He dropped his salute and let the fist form.

"Yes. Well. Redtape," Shade replied unapologetically. Then he raised a fat finger and let it fall atop his desk. The entire surface suddenly filled with tall stacks of holographic folders and tablets. "I've gone back over and reviewed all your final mission reports again, Captain."

"Wow. You're a gracious turd," Merrecci replied respectfully. "Now, whose idea was it to reassign me command to a transport vessel? Because I want to know whose rear end to park it in."

"And I've reviewed your complaints," the admiral added, taking up one of the holographic tablets. This time his tone warned Merrecci about whose office he stood in.

"Is that what this is about, Admiral?"

"I hate extra reading, Captain."

"Have you seen how they run those prisons," Merrecci asked.

"Not those complaints, Captain. Nobody's desk is that big," Shade sneered. "Complaints from your last crew before they removed you from command!"

"Well, shut 'em up, and you won't have to listen to it," Merrecci argued.

Shade pursed his lips and sighed as though Merrecci had missed the hint.

"The admirals hate extra reading too," Shade said, and he stood. Better. Merrecci had a mean uppercut.

"I don't answer to them," Merrecci replied. "The only thing they know about space is how to attend orbital parties, and I never throw any. Besides, you and I both know Earth-bound admirals can't read."

"Would you prefer to command an academy school bus," Shade asked. His brow glistened with the rumor of tyranny that had once haunted Merrecci's academy days. "A bit's happened since you've been in exile. The Great Divide stands poised to bring us a war—

"Shame someone didn't warn you about it," Merrecci bellowed.

"I know," Shade suddenly yelled. "We all know! You're right. We're wrong. That's the only reason you're here."

"The only reason I'm here is because it's the only place I happen to be," Merrecci bellowed. "That doesn't mean I'm going to pretend you're doing me a favor?"

Shade's finger stiffened directly at Merrecci.

"It was still a gamble that you shouldn't have played with! Next time you choose to bet, don't pick such an ambitious crew set on being the first or the youngest to do whatever they—is that gum? Are you chewing gum in my office?"

"Two months," Merrecci replied, biting the gum as if it had been the one that decided to send him to prison.

Shade took a breath and allowed himself to tone his voice down. "We could possibly be entering a war that we need every person for, and we do not need you at the center of another mutiny."

"They wouldn't dare try it again," Merrecci scowled.

"You haven't taken a crew into war."

"The Viridian logged more combat experience under my command than any other vessel."

"Battles, Captain, not war," the admiral said.

"Only because I'm the one that kept it from getting that far," Merrecci retorted.

"Crews behave differently in war, especially when the captain may have to keep classified secrets from them. If our upcoming negotiations don't go well—

"Negotiations," Merrecci asked. "Have you listened to your halls? I'm out two months, and we're at war. These aren't negotiations; I don't care what you call them."

"Regardless," Shade said. "We may find ourselves in an even bigger conflict, and the last thing we need is one of our warship captains overthrown."

"How should you like me to kiss up to my subordinates and wipe their noses, Sir?"

Shade glowered up into Merrecci's face.

"I should like you to take the Viridian and accompany the Crimson and Jade to the Havanti sector two days from now to the peace talks with that Divide Coalition, but you no longer *have* the Viridian, do you?"

"So, give it back," Merrecci said. "I'll rebuild the crew."

Shade snorted. "The last thing peace negotiations need is a barbarian captain slamming down his hammer, and yet we need you in a ship in case things don't go well."

"I'll stay out of the way, Sir," Merrecci said.

"Of course, you will, Captain," Shade replied. "You don't have a ship."

"The Viridian is mine. You should have never taken it from me in the first place."

"It's never been yours, Captain."

"Sir, with respect—

"You lost it! We didn't take it from you. Your crew did," Shade snapped. "You lost it! You!"

"And turned out I was right," Merrecci reminded.

"I don't care! Name one other captain in this fleet who's ever lost their own entire ship!" Shade was yelling again, and Merrecci caught glimpse of the admiral gripping the edge of his desk as he did to keep himself from punching someone. Good! That meant Merrecci was cleared to throw a counter if the prime admiral followed through.

"And, unfortunately," Shade continued. "We need that crew to function right now, and they won't if we let you go back to the command chair for round two with a big, fat 'told you so' on your lips."

"So, they get away with it," Merrecci asked and wished Shade would just once lean forward, but he realized the prime admiral knew him just as well as Merrecci knew his old professor.

"Don't be stupid," Shade said. "They wanted the Viridian. Now, that's all they'll get."

"And when they decide to mutiny against the fleet next," Merrecci asked. "Did the admirals think that far ahead? Or are they not worried about their strongest ship turning against them too?"

Shade held up his hand to gesture silence.

Here it came. First the attempt to de-escalate, followed by the gesture to point out the carrot, then the lean in to gloat, finally one punch and broken teeth. Then Merrecci could chug two and half beers at Jackson's Barrel before the authorities found and took him back to prison.

"Do you really think I wouldn't have your back on this, Vincenti," Shade said, smirked and extended his fat, stubby finger to the sky. "Now, temper that fist, before I forget I'm one of the few people who likes you."

Merrecci realized he should have known better. His fist loosened, and he looked to the bubbled-glass ceiling. Peering to the heavens, he found the small black patch that Shade was pointing to doting above Earth. He knew what it was, that it had been under construction for the past two years. Even from this distance, he could tell it was larger than any other Earth ship.

Merrecci bypassed smiling.

"It's ready," Merrecci asked. "I thought the Brown was supposed to be Captain Torkin's ship."

"There never was a brown. We just needed a carrot until Torkin realized he was too old to keep commanding in space. This is better. That is the Onyx, Captain. It was always supposed to be yours."

Merrecci looked to the black patch once more and didn't speak.

"How didn't I know about this," Merrecci asked.

"Despite what you think, you've never had the highest paygrade around here," Shade retorted. "With the Paichu urging the Divide to declare war, it only makes sense to put our barbarian captain in command of our barbarian-class vessel."

"Barbarian class?"

"It's new, and it carries a lot. Enough that it could stay away from Earth for very long periods of time," Shade explained.

"How long," Merrecci asked.

"Long," Shade replied, insinuating that he didn't like the interruption. "The fabricators can actually produce torpedoes, and it has a few more raizer outputs. We've begun producing thirty more of these ships. They won't be as armed, as large, or as powerful as the Onyx; we have to cut some corners to get them into war, but they'll do the job of the Viridian at least."

"Meanwhile, who's got the Viridian, if I may ask," Merrecci inquired. "Commander, I mean, Captain List."

"What does a dock station commander know about battle vessels," Merrecci asked.

"Nothing but," Shade held up a silencing hand again. "His crew does, and he'll learn from them."

"His crew? I made that crew!"

"Not anymore," Shade pointed out. "None of them volunteered to follow you to the Olive."

"The Olive? Please tell me you're not making me audition for the Onyx by showing I can handle the Olive," Merrecci moaned, and he found himself leaning over the opposite ledge of Shade's desk, hoping that gripping it would work for him as it had for the prime admiral. "With respect, I wouldn't follow you to the Olive."

"Think we were going to tell them about the Onyx?" Shade snipped. He withdrew from the edge of his desk. Merrecci wondered if Shade recognized Merrecci was restraining himself just now as well.

"The audition wasn't yours, it was the potential crew's. If volunteers won't follow you to a transport vessel, we're not going to trust them with our new flagship," Shade explained. "Unfortunately, you'll have to build most of your own crew because our timeline got rushed."

"I have to build a new crew," Merrecci asked. "From the ground up? Me? I have to do that?"

Shade's face turned serious again.

"Give me some credit," Shade retorted. "Don't mistake this as a reward, Captain. Whether you were right or wrong, you were still found guilty of the crime for the time and information we had. You still lost your ship, and that can't happen again. You botch this command, and you won't be remembered as the barbarian captain, you'll be remembered as the screw-up captain. No one wants to work with you. The majority of volunteers we could find willing to serve under you are fresh out of the academy because they still think you're a legend. If you can't keep your crew happy and together this time, the highest career you'll find yourself reaching is in the classroom teaching Battle Tactic Theory to freshman. So, get your ship in order, stop torturing your crew and keep it that way or someone else will."

"Yes, Sir," Merrecci hissed. "When do we depart?"

"Three days." Shade now tossed the holotab he'd been holding to Merrecci.

Merrecci's wristband emitter immediately took control of the transfer, allowing him to catch it.

"It's pretty much empty right now as it's going through final analysis, pressure test and sealing. Then it's just a matter of running diagnostics," Shade explained. "The only thing on that ship at the moment are the bonding nanobots and a bit of precious cargo. It will be biologically ready for humans in twenty-four hours, giving you two days to let you and your crew get settled in and familiar with it."

"And I'd like my command staff to get to know the ship somewhere in there, hopefully before we take on crew," Merrecci added, still inspecting the pages of information within his tablet orders. "That's not enough time."

"That's what you have. Be glad you weren't part of the ship's construction crew," Shade said. "But you're right, that's why the admirals are giving you full authority to assign anyone not currently serving on an essential battle-ready vessel. We can't depend on volunteers anymore. You'll have to be persuasive. You'll find a list in—."

"I already have it," Merrecci said.

Shade didn't seem to be bothered by the interruption.

"On a good note, we have updated the bridge according to your Viridian preference, with a few slight alterations for obvious reasons when you get there. Any changes you'd like to add will have to be made after you depart. I imagine you'll have a few tweaks, but at least you don't have to deal with that right now," Shade said.

"Thank you, admiral," Merrecci said. He anticipated Shade's dismissal and had already begun to make his exit before Shade had allowed it. He abruptly stopped. "So, I do have full permission to fill the crew as I see fit?"

Shade nodded. "So long as they're not currently serving on a battle-ready vessel."

"From anywhere," Merrecci asked.

"You're the priority here," Shade said. "If they'll say yes."

"I won't ask," Merrecci said.

Shade was about to rebuke his approach, but he wasn't fast enough. Merrecci turned to exit the admiral's office. Shade quickly threw out a promise to find time to dine with Merrecci the next day.

At this, Merrecci spit his gum out on the floor and purposely stepped in it while he was still in the office.

"All right, but you should know," Merrecci said. "Once you retire, I'm knocking you on your ass. You've got it coming."

"I know," Shade replied.

From here, Merrecci passed the receptionist, who appeared to be primping her attire. She was civilian so her professional dress was not standard uniform. Merrecci wasn't sure exactly what she wore. He didn't care. She was definitely not an option to make crew, although he should just to dampen Shade's day. He approached the hologram wall, then returned to the two security guards and their shield. By now, only the last few remnants of gum on the bottom of his shoe continued to thread over the carpet. He hoped Shade would spend a long time appreciating the trail of stickies in his floor rather than a fist across his jaw.

Merrecci stopped and stared into the disrespectful security guard's blue eyes to be sure his inclination was right about them.

"Keep moving," Captain she said and held her arm for the stun staff once more.

Merrecci tapped at his holotab, and her wristband changed from Gold to black, while the crowns of her shoulders turned dark but remained trimmed in the gold associated with filling an essential role to serve admiralty until she was officially released from her current assignment. A holo image appeared from her wristband announcing high-class orders. The image turned into a holotab, and she immediately went to scrutinizing it.

"Congratulations, Lieutenant Issa Almma" Merrecci said. "You're being reassigned to my command."

"Sir," she asked.

"You have your orders and two days."

"Two days?"

Merrecci nodded. "It's always the captains."

"Sure, why not," she replied. "Now get your ass out of my hall. Your meeting has concluded."

"Not entirely," he replied and turned to the guard who operated the shield. He glanced at his tablet, then to the operator and back to his tablet. "Now, I'm done," and he exited through the shield to build the rest of his crew.

2
▲
Exit

By the time he had exited the administration wing, he had filled four seats of the 3,318 left that were necessary to run his ship at minimal operations. Families and civilian advisers would add to that number and give him a human resource pool if he found himself in need and out of range for more qualified replacements. According to his tablet, the ship could handle nearly sixteen thousand people. He wasn't sure why it needed to accommodate that much, but things were what they were. At least those extra bodies could act in case of state of emergency.

Merrecci spent the next twelve hours in the archives studying the rosters of ships, planet-side staff, and Earth's Mabbis space station, which filled five hundred posts on the Onyx. Unfortunately, no one who filled the posts were exceptional people. They were all rookies, underachievers, subordinates no one wanted or who had made their commanding officers all too happy to get rid of. Merrecci took them. He'd break them later.

He accessed files regarding reserve, retired or classified officers and filled four hundred more seats. Most of these seemed to be people who were happy to leave the service and were only coming back to get a steady paycheck again. In other words, no one exceptional came from that either. His next stop was the academy, where he added 1,500 crew members from students graduating within this and another 1,000 students who showed promise, but who wouldn't graduate for a year or more. It was authorized to be the most extensive study abroad program ever conducted. Merrecci hated it, but that's how it was going to have to work this time. Each department head was going to have to fill the role of a professor or Mentor. He also took two adjunct instructors who were all too eager to prove they could pad their C.V.s. He called in old favors and drew from private sectors. That filled forty posts.

Before forty-eight hours had passed since his meeting with Prime Admiral Shade, Captain Vincenti Merrecci had filled all, but his senior staff seats and one other department, none of which he could convince anyone to fill and leaving him to feel like he was scraping the bottom of the barrel. So, he scraped even harder.

*   *   *

Pawn Ashton hovered above the rest of the bridge. As soon as the alarm sounded, an anti-gravity shield encapsulated his being then hefted his body out of his chair and over his operational staff. This allowed him to monitor the personnel beneath him; ensuring everyone could hear his voice; and letting him see which tasks needed to be micromanaged. Before the simulation had turned to battle, he sat proudly in his chair, sure of his design. Rather, it was a throne that already loomed at a higher elevation from the rest of the consoles. The entire room was a good layout. He'd put a lot of thought into it and received what he was sure were the highest marks in his Leadership Design and Facets class.

A captain's bridge was his own creation, a partial demonstration of his command style. He wanted to be aware of everyone, communicate to them clearly. This program he created was a triangular room, opera house style to carry his voice. The lights were dim, and a grand and fluid chandelier floated in the center of it all and projected holographic imagery of Pawn Ashton's ship in its surrounding space near Mars orbit.

Within the holo was the image of an all too familiar alien vessel: a disjointer, a long Paichu ship that looked like a double-bladed dagger. It was designed for one purpose, to pierce and tear through enemy hulls. It was one of the Paichu's older discontinued models because it had a habit of self-destructing itself on impact, but the Russian academy had gotten a good deal on it for their own wargames training from less than desirable traders. Directly to its right side was a smaller funnel-shaped vessel. This was the one that Pawn Ashton was now commanding.

"Stay on its starboard," Ashton stated calmly.

"Setting course for the other side of the disjointer, Sir," the pilot stated from a console, one of many with other bridge crew that encircled below the chandelier-like hologram.

"Like you've never misspoke before," Ashton replied curtly. "Just stay where it can't joust us."

"That I can do," the pilot replied.

"Open communication," Ashton ordered.

The hologram of the two ships faded and a man who seemed entirely too pleased with himself appeared in its place. He sat proudly in his own chair.

"I am Pawn Ashton, acting captain of the Earth Franchise vessel Totoro," Ashton announced. "You have entered Mars training space, please—"

"Captain Ass Clown, we meet again," the holographic human head of a young, wavy-haired man announced, and laughter filled the enemy ship's broadcast.

"Mute transmission," a young woman at the opposite end of the bridge commanded.

"Acting commander," Ashton snapped. "As you were."

"Captain," the woman continued. "Recommend doing away with the pleasantries and firing torpedoes alternately against their bow and stern."

"We've never done that before, acting-commander," Ashton said.

"We've never won against them before."

"We can't waste torpedoes like that, Commander, and I'd like to end this without losing any lives," Ashton replied.

"Hello," the holographic captain's head called in a clear Russian accent. "I can no hear you when you is on mute, Mr. Ass Clown."

"Captain, he's here to humiliate you," the woman explained. "Firing the torpedoes alternately may rattle their ship, knock them out of their chairs, give us time to finish this quickly."

"Here is song I write for your crew," the hologram said. "Captain Ass Clown! Captain Ass Clown. You suck five eggs, all double yoke." When he finished belching his tune, he cried. "You like song?"

"Captain," the woman said. "They're just buying themselves time."

Now a chorus of belching erupted through the hologram from the enemy's bridge crew.

"Volley," Ashton ordered. "Ten torpedoes, broadside."

"Broadside? They'll hardly feel it in their bridge!"

"That's an order, acting-commander," the captain snapped.

The holographic head suddenly vanished, and the two sparring ships reappeared in its place.

Just as the first torpedo fired, the enemy vessel turned its bow towards the Totoro. Had the Totoro not happened to attack right then, the bladed ship would have swung too quickly for Ashton's to pull back.

The first mock torpedo registered against the disjointer. Shields flared red under the green diffusion, and the enemy ship stopped maneuvering as it simulated how it would behave under real-event circumstances.

"I said broadside," Ashton roared.

"The next torpedo struck the aft, and the barrage that followed rattled the entire spacecraft back and forth.

"Report," Ashton called out.

"Their shields are at twenty percent," a voice announced from the right of the hologram.

"Alternate shots again," The woman said.

"Those were not my orders!"

"We'll destroy them this time," the commander retorted.

"Why should we kill them when we can take their bridge and access their intelligence. There are things to consider here rather than just blowing everything up," Ashton rejected. "Prepare to hit them with raizer drains, then phase three boarding parties directly to their bridge."

"Drains prepared," a crewmember called.

"Captain," the woman interrupted. "If you lower our shields to phase parties over, they can do the same to us."

"Not if we act quickly," Ashton said.

"I swear to god, if you cost me another grade, I'm taking it out of your ass," The woman threatened.

"Launch, acting-commander" Ashton ordered. "That's an order."

Three mock spheres blasted from the Totoro. As they approached the enemy vessel, long legs unfolded giving them all the appearance of spiders. They grappled the enemy shield and lit it up in a red cocoon that flickered out.

"Shields down."

The commander was now sprinting across the bridge towards Ashton.

"Phase the parties," Ashton said.

As the commander drew her battle baton, three bright, yellow lights opened within the *Totoro* and within them several of its crew members raised and exited straight through the roof. The light carrying the crew members stretched towards the enemy vessel's hull and inserted its passengers into it.

Suddenly, the Totoro's bridge also filled with blinding light and the entire room erupted with weapons fire. Ashton suddenly fell from his hovering bubble and landed hard upon the floor.

As he lay there, he became aware of his commander who was pinned beneath his own bulk. The Russian captain knelt down over them.

"Why you always lose," the enemy captain asked. Then he abruptly turned and shot the commander with a stun blast even as she was trying to wedge her own weapon from beneath Ashton's limp weight. The Russian captain laughed in his mock victory along with the rest of his boarding party.

The lights went up. As the effects of the stun charges wore off, the Totoro bridge filled with groans and complaints, while the enemy team continued to celebrate amongst themselves. Then the transcender surrounded the invaders, and they rose from the bridge, as if ascending into the heavens, but returning to their own ship. A moment later, Ashton's own crew returned to their full faculties.

Ashton rolled off his first officer and began to rise to his feet.

"What the hell, Adrigga," he yelled. "Why can't you just listen for once?"

Ashton's commander was already standing herself.

"Oh, shut up," Cadet Adrigga Nandy snapped back. She turned her stun weapon on him and touched off the trigger, but this time it had been disengaged. The proctor had seen this game before, so she anticipated the event. Adrigga punched Ashton in the shoulder.

Ashton cursed the birth of his new bruise. "You're a psycho!"

"And your an—

"Captain on deck!"

The entire bridge of cadets snapped to attention.

"As you were," Merrecci allowed.

He entered from the proctor's office, which would have otherwise been a ready room on an actual, Earth Franchise vessel. The bridge was quiet as he looked around. He approached Ashton and Nandy and looked down to his holotab.

"I am Captain Vincenti Merrecci," he said coldly.

Whispers that had already began caressing the walls, now became mutterings.

"Quiet down," he ordered calmly.

He looked up from his holotab and took in the surroundings of the bridge and its officers. Then he returned his attention to the work in his hands.

"Do you know who I am," Merrecci asked.

Ashton and Nandy acknowledged they did.

"Have you heard I'm building a crew," he asked again.

They both acknowledged once more.

"Rumors do fly here, don't they," Merrecci said, all without ever looking up from his holotab. "I need a second in command for the most dangerous spacecraft anyone can get into, and it will greatly piss off my previous five choices to see that a cadet could do the job and surpass their ranks. Can I count on you to give me the same as I saw you do here?"

"Yes, Sir," Ashton and Nandy replied.

"Will you accept the post then," Merrecci asked.

"Yes, Sir," they both replied again.

"Cadet Ashton, until you can learn to glue your ass to the floor, no captain in their right mind would enlist you" Merrecci stated. "I'm speaking to Adrigga Nandy."

"I'm sorry, Sir. I thou—

Merrecci silenced Ashton with the simple maneuver of looking up at him from his holotab.

"An enemy ship knocks your bridge power out. What happens," Merrecci asked.

"I'd have it rerout—

"You'd fall and break your damned neck on your chair, or that railing, or the floor. I bet you'd do it flying across the room and taking out a control console in the process. Or maybe you'd do it just as you did, nearly killing your first officer who was trying to protect you from the attack she warned you would come. Now your ship's out a captain, a commander and control over vital access to operations, which now opens the entire fleet up to losing a vessel and any intelligence we don't want falling into other hands—all because you want to fly around and look down the pretty cadet's uniforms."

Ashton fell silent.

"And why are you in battle wasting power on non-essential anti-gravity toys anyway?"

The bruised cadet stammered.

"Costing your classmates points in here, leads to costing your crewmates lives out there. " Merrecci gestured two fingers throughout the bridge. "This is the most irresponsible bridge design I've ever seen."

"Well, Professor Martin gave me an A on it," Ashton said.

"What does Professor Martin know? He lost two teeth falling on my foot once," Merrecci replied and went back to his holotablet.

Ashton said something about how he thought his design was good.

"It's only good if you don't live long enough to see how bad it is." Merrecci mumbled.

"I respectfully disagree."

"Oh, shut up." Merrecci went on to ignore Ashton and studied his holotab before turning back to Adrigga. "It's your lucky day, Adrigga Nandy. Pack your things. You report immediately to Earth's new flagship. You're my new first officer." His face rose to meet hers and his crumpled in resignation. "Good god," he cursed to himself.

Nandy's wristband chimed to notify her of her new orders. Her shoulder crowns on her uniform turned black and the holo-emitter upon them presented her new commanders' tonks.

As Merrecci had already began walking away, Nandy called after him, "Sir?"

Merrecci stopped and turned, visibly annoyed at the delay in his busy schedule.

"I'm just a cadet. I don't graduate for another semester. Are you sure about this?"

"Think I'd be here if I was," Merrecci answered.

He warned her not to be late as he resumed his quick exit.

*　　*　　*

The information desk had sent Merrecci here. In truth, he'd never stepped foot into this wing of campus for the simple reason that it had no bearing on anything remotely to ever do with his studies, nor most people's for that matter. Many students didn't even know it existed, and most of those who did wondered why.

He once had a class with someone who spent time in this wing. He'd even thought about writing a paper for his personnel management class that would have suggested none of these people should be here, and not just here on campus. Parents could be absolutely irresponsible in not subscribing to common sense.

All he knew now was that he'd have to wait for the doctor who oversaw this whole mess. Currently, there were few chairs set up at the moment compared to what this rec-hall facility could handle. Those seats that had filled the room prior dissipated and were replaced with a circle of eleven that had been set off in a lonely corner. It was supposed to help make the meeting more private and let others know it was out of use to the public. Merrecci had been on his feet all day, so he resigned himself to sit in one of the eleven and suck up his annoyance as he waited.

The young woman sitting almost directly across the circle from him wouldn't stop staring. He caught her glance a time or two, and she never looked away, just stared through her squinted and misshapen eyes. He tried his best to ignore her and study on his holotab what he'd already studied and memorized hours before.

"There's only nine today," another young lady said from his left. She was perhaps a little older than the one across the circle, but she had the same eyes and flattened face.

"Pardon," Merrecci found himself asking.

"Pardon," the pudgy woman across the circle suddenly stated and stood from her chair with fists clenched.

"I said pardon," Merrecci said.

"What's that," she asked and stepped into an even more aggressive stance.

"Never mind," Merrecci said. "Just sit down."

"I'll kick your ass," the woman on the other side of the circle cried.

"That's Dawn," the young woman to Merrecci's left said. "Just ignore her. She's mean."

"What's that," Dawn asked again. Then she growled and snapped, "I'll kick your ass too!"

Merrecci tried to return to pretending to read what was on his holotab. If these had been any other circumstances, he would have told the academy village-idiots simply to shut up, but these weren't ordinary circumstances, and he really needed the next person on his list. That meant sitting here in the circle with people who shouldn't even have a seat at the academy to sit in.

"Normally, there are eleven," the girl next to him continued after Dawn finally sat down but wouldn't stop glaring at Merrecci. "But today there are nine because Mathew and that jerk Terry got into that fight yesterday, and—and what—what happened yesterday was Terry said Bria was a buffalo-butt-face. That's her right there."

The lady to Merrecci's left pointed about six chairs down to a person whose face had shriveled into itself. She had eyes and a mouth, but they all appeared to be molded beneath an inverted, pruned countenance that Merrecci could understand why Terry insulted her as he had. Truth was, Merrecci thought Terry was right. As if the faceless girl could hear the captain's thoughts, she looked into her lap where she pretended her cadet uniform pants needed to be straightened with her hands.

"So, when Terry said Bria looked like a buffalo-butt-face, that made Mathew jump up and say, 'You take that back, Terry from

Boulder Nevada','" the talkative cadet continued. "But Terry didn't take it back, and Mathew popped him in the nose with his unopened milk carton and made his nose bleed all over, but you couldn't tell until later because of how his milk exploded all up his face and stuff.

"Then Bill, the big Bill who helps the nurses, not the Bill who sometimes brings the little horse to pet. Anyway, the big Bill who helps the nurses, came in, and he asked Terry what happened, and tattle-tail Terry said, 'Mathew hit me with a milk,' and now Mathew and Terry aren't here today. By the way, did you know that if you pronounce Nevada with an A like you say in awful, every Nevadan wants to punch you because you just showed how stupid you are. It's Nevada with an A like in apple. Ne-vaa-duh."

Merrecci found himself staring at the lady to his left watching her mouth form the word correctly. The hologram in his hand kept him from slapping the annoyance. He was about to return to ignoring her when she took in a breath and started again.

"So today, there will only be nine. There's Bria that you heard of before. Don't be scared of what she looks like."

"I don't care," Merrecci replied.

"You'll care," Dawn yelled. "You'll care or I'll kick your ass until it looks like you care!"

"Neither of you have to be so mean," Miss never-shuts-up said. She pointed again to an even bigger attraction than Bria, two sisters joined at the hip. "That's Charity and Cora. Charity's really smart. She's some kind of doctor, but I don't remember what kind because she just got her license. She doesn't need to be here, but Cora does. Cora's pretty smart too though. She drools and draws a lot, and no one really knows why, so they both have to come to the circle. Charity said Cora used to draw really cool things once, but people came and took her pictures away."

"What did I say, Mirror," Charity asked.

"Oh yeah," the girl to Merrecci's left said. So, her name was Mirror. Her drivel continued. "You don't want me telling people she draws anymore. Sorry."

"Who took them away," Merrecci asked, turning to Charity, but only as a device to get the girl to his left to leave him alone.

"Your kind of people," Charity said directly.

"Your kind of people can bite me," Dawn blurted.

Merrecci realized that plan backfired. During his epiphany, his eyes settled on a twenty-year-old whose entire body rattled as if his seat was running an electric current right now.

"Stop staring at him," Dawn shouted.

"That's Allen," Mirror said.

Allen's hands rattled against his lap. His seat had extra spacing to his left and right. It only took a moment for Merrecci to understand why when one of Allen's elbows involuntarily popped to his side and might have jabbed anyone who might have been sitting in the space.

"He says he can't control it, but I think he just likes elbowing people in the ribs." She drew close to Merrecci's ear and whispered. "He's also a little weird about the number seven."

"Are you kissing," Dawn asked.

Charity sighed heavily.

"What was that," Dawn asked. "I will knock you out!"

Merrecci looked around the room for any sign of the doctor he had come to speak to.

Suddenly a creature stretched up into his lap and started barking in his face.

"Geez-the-hell-is-that," Merrecci asked, as a full-grown man in his early twenties was gnashing his teeth up at him.

"Bad, dog," Never-shuts-up Mirror chided. "He's a guest."

The barking man whined, smiled, and started wiggling his butt. Then, he pawed up Merrecci's front and began licking his face.

Merrecci shoved him away, and he yipped as he fell back.

"Mike," Dawn snapped. "Come here."

The man spun and ran across the circle, where he suddenly dropped on the floor at the side of Dawn's chair.

"That's Mike," Mirror said.

"He's our dog," Dawn warned. "You don't look at him."

"He's not really a dog," Mirror said. "He's like me and Dawn. People say we're retarded."

"You're retarded, Mirror," Dawn snapped.

Now the woman to Merrecci's left suddenly stood and screamed, "Doctor Wanship says you're not supposed to call me retarded anymore, you half-wit!"

"You said we were retarded," Dawn retorted.

"No, she didn't," Charity groaned. "She said people call you retarded."

"Who says that? I'll kick their ass," Dawn snapped. "We're not retarded."

"I know," Charity replied. "You're smart."

"I'm gonna kick your ass," Dawn erupted, leaping from her chair yet again.

Cora made some kind of strange noise through what might have been a smile, and she drooled over her and Charity's shoulders. Charity reached up with a tissue and wiped it off without looking. It was clearly second nature. When she realized Merrecci was watching, she threw him a "really?" grimace.

"Dawn memorizes dictionaries and things in databases for fun," Mirror said.

"Mike invents things," Dawn said.

"That guy invents things," Merrecci suddenly blared. "Him?"

"He designs stuff for starships, so they don't blow up," Dawn said.

"Hey," Mirror complained. "I was going to tell him."

"Well, I have heard it all now," Merrecci replied.

"You must be pretty dumb then," Dawn said.

Charity laughed.

"He's going to make a zillion dollars one day on his shoe laces that tie themselves when he gets around to building them," Dawn continued.

"Can he even tie his own shoes," Merrecci asked.

"Sometimes, he can," Mirror said.

Dawn's eyes narrowed on Mirror who was now sitting with her arms crossed to Merrecci's left.

"And Mirror's just a know-it-all. She thinks she's smart about everything, which is why nobody likes her," Dawn spat.

Dawn leaned back into her seat, proud, shoulders high. Her head rocked back and forth, drawing out a long smile over not a single straight tooth in her face.

Now it was silent.

Thank God!

Merrecci returned to his holotab, when tap-tap-tap came to his shoulder.

His eyes rose from his work, and he found they met Charity's who threw a silent "isn't this fun" snicker at him. As much as he didn't want to, Merrecci let his head turn back to Mirror and squared eyes with her to tell her to knock it off.

"Willis, really his name's William, but a lot of people call him Bill," Mirror said holding a matter-of-fact finger to Merrecci and letting it point past him to a lanky character smiling bigger than Dawn, but not as much as Cora, who just happened to be drooling again. "We call him Willis because we don't want the Big Bill to come running by accident if we ever say his name. We have entirely too many Bills here. Anyway, Willis loves everyone. You have to be careful around him because he hugs a lot, and it's kind of scary if he doesn't bathe, and what's worse is sometimes he'll never stop bothering you."

"I understand completely," Merrecci said.

Mirror's finger turned to another young man with dark hair, average build. He didn't actually look like he should even be in the room. The only item out of place with him was perhaps the lint roller he clenched within his lap.

"That's Pablo," Mirror said.

"I can introduce myself," Pablo said softly.

"She's doing it," Dawn erupted. "Now shut up before I—

Suddenly Pablo turned to Dawn and yelled, "Shaddup!"

Dawn was back to her feet, her fists clenched. Her chest heaved with threatening breaths.

"Anyway," Mirror said. "That's Pablo."

"What did I say," Pablo snipped.

"You don't have to be so mean," Mirror said. "I'm just being polite."

"Just because we have to talk to you, doesn't mean we have to listen to you," Pablo retorted.

Dawn agreed.

"He gets that way when he has to miss his game show," Mirror said. Then as if none of this had just happened, she continued to introduce Pablo. "He has the O.C.D. That's why he carries that little roller, it's for lint, because he always cleans everything up even if it's on you. He thinks everything has problems. He has really good focus though. But you can't play checkers with him, or anything for that fact." Again, she drew up to whisper in Merrecci's ear. "Everything has to be centered and hide anything that looks like a manual, or he has to read it."

Then Mirror was quiet again.

Merrecci looked at her, afraid to speak because it might set her off once more. He inhaled deeply. His eyes fell on the last person in the group who happened to be focused on some kind of puzzle in his hand. It was a jar filled with clear marbles, one steelie and water. He was carefully examining how close he could tilt the jar before its contents spilled.

"Who's that," Merrecci asked and then suddenly pursed his lips at his own stupidity.

Charity popped out an amused "tss" but didn't actually laugh.

"That's Drinker Bone." Pablo said. "They had a stroke when they was nineteen. It should have killed them they say."

"Yeah, and it's like he should be smarter than he really is," Mirror added. "But he's hard to understand sometimes. His brain can't always say the word he needs, and it fills it in with material."

Merrecci realized he must have appeared confused.

"They will say the word, 'material' in the place of other words," Charity explained.

"It can make him difficult to understand," Mirror said.

And that's when Merrecci could take no more of being patient with the slow class.

"Are we done," he asked holding up his hand to silence the rambling Mirror. "Anyone else you want to introduce to me?"

"Huh," Mirror asked. "No. I mean not unless you want me to go find some other people in the halls."

"Then shut up," Merrecci replied. "Good Lord, just shut up! You have me out of breath just listening to you."

"Oh," Mirror said. "Another person with anger management issues."

"I'm the only one with anger issues in this class," Dawn demanded and was out of her seat again. "Don't make me sick our dog on you."

Mike erupted into a flurry of barks from beside Dawn's seat.

"I don't have anger management issues," Merrecci scolded.

"Could have fooled me," Charity snorted.

"I'm a Captain, Cadet," Merrecci lectured.

Everyone in the circle stood upright from their chairs and snapped a salute except for Charity, who sighed because she was forced to stand up at Cora's behest.

"I'm not Franchise, you pompous piss," Charity replied. "My sister is, and she hasn't said jack to you."

The tapping started again.

"What," Merrecci bellowed, turning on Mirror again. "And will you people stop saluting," Merrecci chided to the others. He turned back to Mirror. "Well?"

Mirror startled and was tearing up when she asked. "I was just going to ask what was wrong with your brain?"

"It belongs to a jackass," a woman's voice answered from outside of the people already gathered in the circle.

"Thank God," Merrecci cried elatedly. He stood and turned to the woman in her early forties that was approaching the circle with entirely too much purpose.

"Prilla," Merrecci said.

Doctor Prilla Wanship was younger than Merrecci was, not by a lot, but definitely younger. He rushed across the rec hall to meet her.

"No," she said, pressing her way past him.

"Commander Wanship," Merrecci said, suddenly finding himself trying to keep pace with her. If someone said "no," he'd typically go to the next person on the list, but he had to follow her.

"The last time I was on a ship, I contracted Wanship fever and gave it to my husband," Prilla said.

"I know," Merrecci acknowledged.

"And then he died," she added.

"I know."

Wanship stopped, and Merrecci almost stumbled over her and knocked them both down.

"Why are you really here," Wanship asked barely catching herself and Merrecci from falling.

"You're the leading authority on overcoming long-term battle fatigue," Merrecci said.

"I don't play that game anymore," she said.

"And yet you're still the leading authority on overcoming long-term battle fatigue," Merrecci replied.

"No," Wanship said. "I just happened to be good at it. This here is my specialty now."

"What," Merrecci asked. "Working with the product of conspiracy theory, anti-DNA abort-nots?"

"Uh-uh. No." Wanship snapped, almost slapping Merrecci.

Merrecci rolled his eyes, "This again—

"That's right, Captain Barbarian. You can't guarantee if their lives would be better if they had been improved upon or erased."

"Well, just look at them, it has to be better than this."

Wanship now turned from Merrecci and made her way to the group of patients waiting for her in the circle of chairs.

"I don't have time for this," Merrecci said. "Are you, or are you not the foremost authority on methods of helping soldiers navigate long-term battle fatigue during war?"

"She is," Charity replied sharply. "And you can drop the strut in here. This isn't your ship, Captain."

At the word "captain," all but Dr. Wanship snapped into salute once more. Charity went for the ride is all.

"What is with you people," Merrecci asked. "I've never seen so many people saluting each other."

"It's what they do," Wanship growled. "That's all they do. Every cadet here could stand all day saluting everyone who's their superior, which is everybody. Or did you forget? And these cadets have to do it more since most of them are outranked by even their own classmates.

"Well, I'm not academy," Charity replied, urging Cora back into their seat. "So, believe me when I say I have no problem helping find a way for you to sit on this chair with it inside you."

"Got that right," Allen said. His foot stomped, kicked, stomped, and he punched before going back to shaking.

"That's not very Hippocratic of you," Bria said softly.

"I'm pretty sure Hippocrates wasn't above kicking a captain's ass," Charity said.

"Me neither," Dawn agreed. "Come on, Captain. Let's fight."

Everyone stood and saluted.

"Will you all please sit down," Prilla Wanship pleaded, waving her group to stop saluting and take their seats. "Trust me, the only salute this captain deserves is a bare butt."

"You mean like a moon," Mirror asked then started giggling.

Willis broke out laughing. Several others did too. Mirror and Prilla clapped hands.

"You find this all funny, cadets," Merrecci asked.

"Hey, I'm an Ensign," Mirror snapped.

"Me too," Dawn followed.

"How," Merrecci asked in disbelief.

"That's it," Charity said.

Wanship stood and held up a hand until all eyes in the circle were on her.

"Every time I think it's impossible to imagine you as a bigger ass than the last time I saw you, you show me wrong," Wanship said. "What would Mom say?"

"That's your brother," Charity asked incredulously. "That's the one who—

Willis stood from his seat across the circle and approached Merrecci.

"Stand down," the captain said as Willis approached and embraced him.

Willis let go and returned to his own seat as though he was having the best day in the world.

Merrecci huffed in.

"The answer's no," Wanship said. "You made that decision for me."

"Prilla," Merrecci said. "I'm disembarking tomorrow. I need you there this time."

Prilla Wanship said nothing.

"She said no," Drinker blurted without tearing his eyes off his jar of marbles.

The group began chanting, "She said no."

Willis laughed and shook his fists.

"Just go," Prilla said after failing to calm the group down.

With no other choice, Merrecci retreated out of the room and tried to recall the direction from this wing of the academy. He should have known better, had no reason to come here. Of course, she wasn't going to step foot on one of his ships.

Somewhere in his retreat, there was an information desk in a four-way junction where two cadets, a man and woman, were stationed behind it. When they saw Merrecci coming, they snapped to perfect attention as soon as they saw him.

"No one does that on a real ship," Merrecci yelled. "Which way out of here?"

The cadets wouldn't release their still salute, like statues. Hurricanes couldn't bend them.

He released them from their pose with an order, although he really wanted to do it with a hard slap.

The woman leaned up over the desk and yelled down one of the halls to where a group of three people were chatting and starting wars.

"Sara, can you show the captain out," she asked.

The small group snapped to perfect attention.

"Knock it off," Merrecci ordered.

"Sure," Sara called back after dropping her stance. She turned towards the information desk, just as a blast of debris smashed her and her conversation companions through the wall and into oblivion.

A burst of flames erupted farther down the hall, and fire surged towards the information desk and junction.

3
▲
Run

A deflector shield bubbled up around Merrecci and the two cadets behind the information booth. Flames, plasma, and debris spread quickly around them, pushing the shield of Merrecci's battle baton to its limits. When the burst of the attack had passed, flames and residual continued to burn the halls.

Automatic fire supressors attempted to control the chaos, but it was still warmer than Merrecci was comfortable with.

Raizer fire erupted, answered by gunfire. These weren't Coalition weaponry.

"Are you two armed," Merrecci asked.

The female cadet drew a cylinder, and it opened into a silver staff. The male flipped open a standard issue baton. Though not as technologically advanced as what Merrecci carried, they had some decent defensive capabilities in a pinch.

"I need to get back to the student Special Accessibility Center. You're my way out, and I'm your way out," he ordered and turned back for the way he had come.

The building shook under more blasts as the three rushed down the halls. The cadets directed Merrecci back down the corridors he had found himself lost in only a few minutes previously. They guided him through clear smoke and burning, rotten air—this meant only one thing, Jimmosheans. Where there were Jimmosheans, there were Didjians.

As they directed his path, Merrecci corrected their footwork with caution to help keep them alert and safe. They climbed through a trail of fallen and sizzling rubble, and flames breathed throughout their pathway back to Merrecci's sister. Merrecci activated his respirator, it unfolded from within his nostrils and covered his mouth. The cadets had to apply theirs manually, fumbling through their own ready-pockets to find what they never had to use beyond simulation.

Around the next corner, they observed their first crossfire. It took place at the three-way junction at the far end where three Didjians appeared and were shooting straight ahead of them at whatever forces Merrecci could not see that were farther into their cross-corridor. The invaders did not notice Merrecci nor the cadets approaching from the side. Although, he could see three Didjians, the blue reflective gear they wore meant there was at least a fourth behind them. They probably didn't expect anyone alive to approach from the burning hallway to their side, and they probably didn't expect anyone other than retired pencil pushers or their students to be who might be emerging upon them.

Didjians weren't much more than humans when it came to technological advancement or place in the universe. Their ships could be formidable in great numbers, but they left space battle mostly to their counterparts the Jimmosheans. Where the Didjians truly excelled was in their ground combat troops.

Merrecci stopped running for the Didjian soldiers and held the grip of the baton to his hand. A glass ball rolled into Merrecci's palm. He threw it. As it struck one of the Didjians, the glass exploded and tore holes through its suit and that of one of his comrades. Merrecci cursed that it hadn't struck all three.

Suddenly, Merrecci dropped behind some wreckage and held out his arms to signal the cadets to do the same.

One of the enemies, confused at the sudden breach of his suit, finally looked to his side to see Merrecci and the two cadets. The soldier yelled something urgent behind them to someone hidden farther down the adjoining hallway. Merrecci imagined it was something to the tune of, "Don't fire!" It wasn't soon enough.

A white-crown, capping what Merrecci knew was clear flames spit across the open end of the hall where the Didjians stood. The two damaged suits let white flames leak through the holes that Merrecci had just pierced open. What the enemy had been wearing, having burned out everything that was inside, fell into a pile, but there was no damage to the clothing that had once been protecting them.

The third, remaining enemy turned into Merrecci's hallway.

When he saw the captain, he posed to take aim with a rifle, but flew back as a spearhead suddenly grew out of the woman cadet's staff, and she hurled it. It plunged into the invader's chest.

Merrecci began running once more, this time having to rely on the two students to have the common sense to know how to follow his advance.

That was when the fourth Didjian wearing a golden suit stepped into the junction. This was a flame screamer, and it carried ten cannisters of waizle fuel. His job was to stand behind the front lines and unleash flames that would destroy anyone who wasn't wearing the blue protective gear. Merrecci let loose into a hell-bent sprint for the confused attacker.

The screamer took aim on Merrecci. He could have probably fired it off well before Merrecci reached him, could have ended this story right here, but he saw in Merrecci something that had frozen many people before. Waizle flame would never kill this human fast enough. The Didjian saw it in a face that wasn't afraid, wasn't angry, but was going to kill him all the same. By the time the flame-thrower operator overcame this strange shock, Merrecci had already jammed his baton down the barrel of the liquifying weapon, but the Didjian failed to see the maneuver that had just taken place.

"Keep running," Merrecci ordered. "Don't look back."

As Merrecci's small party rushed past, the fat screamer maneuvered all too slowly under the weight of the waizle cannisters to launch an effective attack. By the time he had taken back the flame thrower's aim, Merrecci had led the cadets over the incinerated bodies of what must have been academy students, security, or staff. In a few quick strides, Merrecci and the cadets ducked into the next adjoining corridor. Before taking the shelter, Merrecci turned long enough to hurl another marble that exploded against the flame screamer's suit just as the operator ignited the flame once again.

Merrecci tore the male cadet's battle baton from the male student's hand and ignited its shield as the area before them revealed another stream of white-crowned, invisible fire. The flames dropped, Merrecci could tell from immediate disappearance of vapor currents streaming before him. The roar of where waizle fuel spewed from the barrel of its thrower and mixed with oxygen also fell silent. Merrecci let the cadet's standard-issue battle baton's shield rest. The captain snapped a quick peek around the corner of the hall that held the flame operator. The last thing he needed was the waizle Screamer following them in case Merrecci's marble hadn't done the trick. There were no more living beings in the hall, just their protective clothes filled with liquified remains. The walls themselves continued to collapse and melt away. The student's baton had done its job of preventing the same from happening to Merrecci and the two information booth students.

"Where there's reflective suits, there's waizle flamethrower," Merrecci said, hearing when his own father had stated the same to him. "Remember that."

He continued on his path, keeping the cadet's baton; no way was he trusting one of these imbeciles with it to protect him.

Meanwhile, Prilla was trying to calm her patients in their circle of chairs. They huddled in the corner of the recreational hall, the part that wasn't on fire was buried in ceiling supports and construction material. Charity's attempts to take on some of the burden wasn't exactly relieving the situation.

Merrecci and the cadets pressed into their meeting room. The building shook again, allowing more bits of ceiling to fall.

"Are you armed," Merrecci asked.

"Of course, we're not armed," Charity replied. "This is a safe space!" Prilla shook her head.

"This is Captain Vincenti Merrecci requesting status on the attack on the academy," Merrecci finally spoke, activating his communicator.

No answer came.

"Again, this is Captain Vincenti Merrecci, I am in the academy requesting—

"Captain! Thank God," Admiral Shade's voice interrupted. "We need you in the Onyx now."

"Understood," Merrecci said.

Doors to the side of the room broke open as a small squad of Didjians rushed in and began to open fire. Merrecci summoned the shield once more, pushing the diameter to cover himself, the cadets, Prilla and the patients.

Prilla had already started directing those under her watch to huddle close behind Merrecci. This meant Merrecci wouldn't have to spend so much of the baton's power to make it cover greater distance.

"Merrecci to Onyx." He watched his cadet-grade baton warn that it was draining power more rapidly than he was used to with his own. Each metal Didjian round that struck it was slowly burning away before the eyes of the group. "Lock onto my location and transcend all lifeforms standing directly beside me out of here now."

He couldn't help notice that those huddling around him suddenly drew closer, enough to almost jostle him off balance, but he felt someone's hands on his shoulder counter the potential mishap.

A waizle flame screamer appeared in the doorway.

"Stay behind me," Merrecci instructed.

The flame thrower took its aim on the small group.

"Did I stutter, Onyx," Merrecci snapped.

The white mask of flame shot.

Merrecci turned the baton to focus his shield before him and adjusted it to an inverted cupping shape, causing the flames to disperse away from the group and hopefully back at the attackers, though it wouldn't work because of their suits. At least they couldn't see well enough to maintain their aim though. The flames ended. Only a moment enough later, the baton's power gauge fell dark. It would give no more protection.

The waizle flames instantly shot forth again and the area filled with light, but different from the white crown that passed now through the group of people clinging to Merrecci. However, there was no heat this time.

Merrecci felt the familiar reversal of gravity, pulling him and his entire group up, out of the room and through the construction materials that made up the academy. His cells slid apart and between the structural bonds of matter that would have acted as obstructions to his rescue and escape otherwise. He and the others were outside of the academy now. They all sped away from the burning building and the warzone beneath them. Their velocity increased the higher they rose into the atmosphere. Soon they were in the black of space.

One glimpse was all he got of a fleet of enemy ships attacking Earth's space docks. Earth Dock one had already collapsed, broken apart. Wreckage of lost ships on both sides of the fight floated aimlessly into what might be history. Perhaps a dozen Didjian fighters fired upon a lone vessel that was far larger than any other battleship that belonged to Earth, a black pyramid. With every hit it took, its edges pulsed with golden energy, yet it returned no fire.

In moments, Merrecci was standing in an egg-shaped room that he instantly realized could only be the Onyx as it was his usual bridge design, which resembled a baseball stadium. If he remembered correctly from what little he had read up on the Onyx, they should be four floors below the observation and botanical tip, which was the highest point of the vessel. He immediately found himself reaching for the nearest operator's console to help him maintain his balance under the continuous shaking.

"Oh, three," the cadet named Allen Being shouted. Merrecci didn't have time to care and ignored it."

"Captain," Nandy said, appearing relieved and standing before another control panel that she had just used to phase Merrecci onboard. She appeared more wearied than frazzled.

"Cutting it a little close," Merrecci said.

"I'm sorry, Sir," Commander Nandy replied. "You said to bring you up. I answered you, but you didn't hear me. I was calling to the ship, and no one was responding, so I had to do it manually myself, and I've only done it like three times, and I had to lower the shields so you could get in, but we were also getting hit, and I didn't know if I could get them back up and you up, then I had to get them back up even after bringing you in. It was like even the ship was fighting me. I thought we'd get boarded for as long as our shields were down." She barely took in a breath but continued her nervous rambling. "I wouldn't have even been in here, but I was trying to get a head start on knowing the ship, and since no one was here and—

"Wait," Merrecci yelled, after many failed attempts to interrupt his babbling officer. He took a moment to finally look at his bridge to see no one else sitting at any of the many consoles that it took to effectively operate the Onyx. "You're running the defenses and you brought us up?"

"Yes, Sir," Nandy said, then added, "I'm sorry."

More rattling.

"Alone?"

"I'm sorry, Sir," Nandy replied and appeared that she might have wanted to burst into tears right there.

"Well, you're not alone now," Merrecci said. "Open a fleetwide transmission. Let's see if we can get some help in here."

The Onyx shook a little more heavily this time.

"I don't know about you," Charity screamed. "But I'd sure like a weapon or something in case a landing party comes on board!"

"Their troops are too invested with the invasion. They just want to destroy us." Merrecci said.

"They don't have weapons," Nandy realized and suddenly became aware of the others in Merrecci's group. "Those aren't crew members. I thought you had crew members. How are we supposed to fly this without crew members?"

"Commander," Merrecci requested, trying to calm the shaking rookie as every inch, panel and rivet of the Onyx rattled around them. "Adrigga Nandy. Look at me."

She did as if in a daze.

"Six," Being announced.

"They're not the crew," Merrecci said.

"Oh, thank God," Nandy said.

"Excuse me," Charity asked.

"Nandy," Merrecci stated directly, avoiding discussion on the insult. "One thing at a time. Open a fleetwide transmission for now."

Nandy focused in on a holotablet in her hand.

"Comms aren't working for me. I can't raise any other departments. I can't send messages off ship. I get 'em, but I can't send them," Nandy said.

"What are other ships saying," Merrecci asked.

"Mostly calling for help and trying to organize." As if she

realized she might be on the verge of hyperventilating, she focused on something else. "Shields are holding at seventy-two percent, but it's taking everything I have just to hold them there because I can't access Onyx's autorouter. Luckily, only Didjians are focusing on us, probably because they've surmised we're unmanned. Their ships don't put up much blast, but if the Jimmosheans take interest, we might be done for."

At this, when the Onyx shook several times, Nandy almost dropped the holotab she'd been operating the ship's defenses from. Not just the ship's defenses, but the orbital thrusters too. The hologram flickered as she fumbled to catch it, but it became solid again once she had it.

"Okay," she said. "Now we have three more firing on us."

Several vessels, she'd observed, were now firing upon the Onyx in a way that was trying to force it more into Earth's gravitational pull. This was an issue because Nandy was not a pilot, she was a strategist with a pathway at the academy in diplomacy. She had basic knowledge of keeping a ship afloat, and barely enough understanding for that as it was. She just didn't know that math so well. Her science was in people's intentions, not how to keep ships from falling, but here she was doing it—not because of classes she took either, because of observing other students in their work during group projects and mock simulations. If a single person could do all the work after all, there'd be no need to have crews.

"If comms aren't working, can we figure out where our bridge crew is," Merrecci inquired.

"According to what I could gather, about four hundred personnel were on board when I got here. I don't know where they are now nor how many have arrived since then." Nandy explained and suddenly, as if she'd heard Merrecci's thought's ordering her to, she took a deep breath and came back with, "What's going on, Sir?"

"We'll figure it out," Merrecci said. "First thing's first. We need help."

Merrecci held his hand to the curved wall.

"Vincenti Merrecci, Captain. Welcome Captain," the room spoke.

"Onyx," Merrecci said. "Other than those officers already in this room, locate nearest bridge personnel."

"There appear to be no other bridge personnel currently on board."

The ship shook particularly hard this time. Merrecci stumbled forward into the wall.

"Uh, uh," Allen stuttered. "Two. We're back to two. It's two."

"Onyx, why are ship comms down?"

"Ship comms are not down," Onyx replied in a calm and clear demeanor. "Bridge and engineering have full ability to communicate with each other until diagnostics are at fifty-six percent."

"What about off ship transmissions," Merrecci asked.

"The Onyx is able to receive transmission only, until diagnostics reach fifty-six percent," the Onyx replied.

"What is the point of that," Charity cried. "Are we just supposed to sit here and hope we don't die?"

"You know what? That's a good question," Merrecci snarked. "Why don't you go find one of the engineers who wrote the bootup code and ask them. While you're at it, tell them to report to the bridge. We could use some people who know what they're doing up here!"

The ship continued to shake.

"Onyx," Merrecci yelled. "Where are my engineers?"

"There are no engineering personnel currently on board," the Onyx said.

"Well, we can't keep this up," Merrecci snapped. "The first Jimmoshean shipbreaker that sets sights on us is going to tear us apart."

"Agreed," Onyx said. "Recommend abandoning ship immediately to increase chances of survival."

"Like hell," Merrecci said. "Onyx, can you notify any personnel in engineering with any bridge experience to report here at once and inform them to pass the message on to anyone in the halls with such training to do the same."

"Yes," Onyx replied. Then came back with, "I have delivered the message."

"And," Merrecci asked.

"There is no one in Engineering, but I have delivered the message."

"And you can't contact any other part of the ship?"

"That function is not available yet," Onyx replied.

"Okay," Merrecci said. "Try locating any life signs on this ship and then use the transcender to bring them directly here."

A moment later, Nandy came back with, "It's not letting me, Sir."

"Onyx," Merrecci asked as though he were about to start yelling. "Why can't we use the transcender."

"Transcender has been disabled during stages B, C and E of diagnostics," the Onyx replied.

"So something can turn on and turn off just like that," Charity cried.

"Yes," Merrecci blurted. "Sometimes, things turn on and turn off during diagnostics in case one function might affect another's initial function. Now, go flip a light switch!"

Merrecci turned on Prilla now.

"You and your students go see who you can find on board," Merrecci ordered.

"You want us to wander the halls of a ship we don't know while it's under attack," Prilla asked. "You'll be scraping them all off the walls in five minutes."

"Yeah, that's a pretty dumb idea," Dawn agreed.

"Okay, Fine," Merrecci grumbled. His finger fell on the female student from the information booth. "What's your discipline?"

"Terraforming," she answered.

"You," he asked, turning his finger upon her male counterpart.

"Anthropology," this student replied.

"What am I supposed to do with any of that," Merrecci asked, then spoke to the ceiling. "Can you arm missiles, Onyx?"

"Missiles are only to be armed in the case of potential threat," Onyx replied.

"What do you think this is," Nandy shrieked, intent more on what was happening on her holotab than in the room at the moment.

Merrecci glanced disapprovingly at her, and she didn't even notice that she was getting visually reprimanded because her attention was locked on the small, artificial screen in front of her.

"Sensor data suggests we are in war game," Onyx replied.

"Onyx, what is the status of your sensor protocol," Merrecci asked.

"Diagnostic is at twenty-eight percent. Sensor protocol is at forty-percent and will be completed when diagnostic reaches ninety-two percent."

"What is this nonsense," Prilla asked.

"We weren't scheduled to disembark until tomorrow," Merrecci explained. "Sensors haven't been patched on what makes an enemy ship yet, so it thinks everything out there's friendly."

"But the shields are up," Prilla said. "How do we have shields to defend ourselves but not sensors to see what's attacking us?"

"Because that's what you do in wargames when you have a bunch of little rookie fingers on weapon controls," Merrecci snapped in a way that told Prilla to let him work. "Onyx, we are currently under attack by enemy vessels. Your sensor protocol does not know this yet. We need armaments."

"Armaments are offline at this time."

"Do you have anything we can defend ourselves with?"

"Shields are currently at seventy percent. Shields help prevent attack on hull structure from many physical, psionic and energy weapon attacks, and they can keep enemy forces from materializing boarding parties within its walls. Would you like to know more about shields, Captain?"

"Oh my god! They gave me a ship with a teaching computer," Merrecci replied sharply.

"You have an Alpha priority message from Admiral Shade," Nandy asked. "Would you like me to connect?"

"Yes," Merrecci snapped as if Nandy should have already known that answer.

"Sir, we are not all cleared for Alpha priority. Are you sure you should play it," Nandy asked.

The ship continued to shake.

"Put him through," Merrecci yelled.

A hologram of Admiral Shade appeared in the battlecron within the center of the room. The prime admiral was surrounded by rubble, but Merrecci could tell it was the administration building, the very halls he had been in only two days ago. His uniform was torn, he was covered in scorch, filth, and blood. He appeared to be in a group of people navigating the warzone of their hallways.

"Vincenti," Shade said.

Weapons fire intruded heavily on Shade as several guards helped to urge him forward. Shade's secretary was stumbling over one broken heel and no awareness to remove it after the other had fallen off. She struggled to keep up and appeared injured and dazed.

"At least I hope this is getting to you, Vincenti."

"It's me," Merrecci replied.

A burst of gunfire broke out from his guards.

"Are you sure this is—mitting," Shade asked, his own voice barely audible over the attacks. "Look, the transmis—is bad, I—see you. I hope you're getting this."

"It's not great," Merrecci stated, but Shade kept going.

"They're taking admirals—lockdown. We won't—able to—mmunicate. The talks were a trap. The Jade and Crimson have been destroyed. We have lost conta—the Viridian. The Onyx must survive—"

One of Shade's guards threw him to the ground, poised over his back and fired a rifle. The guard's arm slumped, and he swore before firing off another several raizer shots to end whatever skirmish they had just wandered into.

Merrecci used the time to attempt enhancing the signal receivers. He wasn't sure if what he had done worked.

Shade returned into view as he continued to fumble over debris throughout the hall he was in.

"Your mission orders have been up—to the Onyx. Review them soon as—ossible. For now, get out—here! Oh, and we are promoting you to—admiral. Do not relinquish—mmand—Onyx. Very important—be sure you—"

Prime Admiral Shade was suddenly being ushered through a door, and his transmission ended.

"Captain," Nandy announced, then corrected herself. "Uh, Admiral? Did I hear that right?"

"You heard what I heard," Merrecci said.

"A fleetwide warning has gone out to all ships to clear orbits," Nandy said.

"That's protocol for an invasion. Planetary shields are going up soon. We have to leave, or we'll be stuck beneath it," Merrecci said. "Onyx, engage autopilot to exit Earth orbit."

"Autopilot will be engaged when diagnostics reach eighty percent," Onyx informed.

"I need a pilot now," Merrecci demanded.

"You are a pilot," Onyx replied. "Your skill level meets the minimum capacity to operate thruster systems. Recommend finding more qualified pilots as soon as possible."

"Are there any more qualified pilots on board the Onyx," Merrecci asked.

"I will check. Please wait for diagnostics to reach fifty-six percent."

"What are we at now," Merrecci asked.

"Twenty-nine percent."

"We were just at twenty-eight!"

"We are almost at thirty. Recommend abandoning ship," Onyx said.

"Do we have any external sensors, Onyx?"

"Yes."

"Which ones?"

"The ones outside."

The Onyx shuddered.

"Receiving priority urgence to evacuate orbit," Nandy announced. "It's the last call to exit, Sir."

Merrecci turned to drop into a pilot's seat.

"The star maps are one of the first patches, so they should be working," Merrecci said. "If I can get us to Mars. We can re-evaluate."

"Everyone might want to take a seat," Nandy instructed.

Prilla agreed and began rushing her students to various chairs behind operational posts around the bridge.

"Switching to manual operation now," Merrecci said.

The Onyx began to move away from Earth.

The next attack was massive. Merrecci flew out of his seat. He struck the floor and felt it in his head next.

"Admiral," Nandy called after him.

"Warning," Onyx said. "No operator is at the helm. Disengaging engines."

Merrecci thought he had responded as he rose back to his feet, but he didn't. The bridge was dim to him, not black, but not entirely there. He forced himself up, stumbled and tried to keep going. Nandy held him. Prilla too was at his side.

"Attempting to engage engines now," Allen's voice announced.

"Stop him," Merrecci ordered weakly.

"Unauthorized pilot at the helm," Onyx stated.

"He's a pilot," Prilla said. "Give him authorization."

"He shakes," Merrecci complained.

"So does your brain," Charity snapped.

"He's not intellectually fit to serve," Merrecci said.

"Neither are you," Prilla retorted respectfully. "He just needs to get us out from under the shield zone, right?"

"thirty seconds, Sir," Nandy reported.

"Onyx," Merrecci said through some slur. "Assign Cadet—

But he didn't quite finish, so he pointed to Nandy to give his order.

"Assign Cadet," Nandy started, but suddenly realized, "What's his name?"

"Allen Being," Prilla identified.

"Assign Cadet Allen Being to full pilot status of the Onyx," Nandy said.

"Negative," Onyx replied. "Bridge members must be of ensign rank or higher. Recommend abandoning ship."

"Promote Allen Being to acting ensign on my authorization," Nandy said hotly.

Onyx didn't respond.

"Onyx," Merrecci ordered. "Promote—

Onyx thrusters engaged.

"Visual sensors are online," Onyx said. "Diagnostic is at thirty percent."

"Earth shields are up, Sir," Nandy said.

"Did we clear them," Merrecci asked.

Nandy nodded, but, at the moment, Merrecci couldn't tell a nod from her nervous shaking or if it was his own concussion that just made her appear to be rattled.

"Do I wanna know how close it was," he asked.

She shook her head.

"Hey no fair," Dawn shouted. "How come he gets to fly. I want to fly. I get to fly next!"

"You're not flying," Pablo Escobedo erupted.

Instantly, Dawn started screaming, "That's not fair!"

"Stop complaining, you're giving me a headache," Mirror retorted.

Merrecci snapped his fingers at his sister to fix the situation.

"Okay, everyone," Prilla said. "This is serious time. We have to listen to the admiral and his first officer."

"Fine," Dawn grumbled. "But I get to fly when we come back."

"If visual sensors are online, show me," Merrecci ordered.

A hologram of Merrecci's black pyramid and the surrounding battle suddenly appeared in the center of the bridge over the battlecron, the central hub that allowed holographic visuals.

Currently, the battlecron presented a hologram that counted three hundred ships from multiple enemy races attacking Earth. Forty were concentrating on the Onyx. Fourteen were Jimmoshean.

Jimmosheans typically weren't any more formidable of an opponent than their cousins the Didjians, but what the Didjians were to ground troops, the Jimmosheans were to space battle. The two races would often work hand-in-hand in war. Jimmosheans were well-known for carrying Didjians for invasion and providing orbit to ground support before turning attention on space warfare. Still, Jimmosheans knew Earthers were not the type to just roll over and take a beating. If the Didjians could invade Earth and keep its crews from reaching their ships, Jimmosheans would at least be fighting only partially manned enemy craft.

"Shields are at fifty-two percent," Onyx said.

On the hologram, the pyramid-shaped Onyx began to navigate through the battle and away from the Earth.

Merrecci tried forcing himself back into full awareness.

"This is only a temporary permanence," Merrecci said. "We need a real pilot."

The Onyx spun between a tightly formed group of vessels steering to join the attack upon it. Thirty-two enemy ships broke away from the main attack on to Earth to pursue Merrecci.

"Will you slow down," Nandy suddenly screamed at her holotab.

"No," Merrecci blurted. "Why would we slow down?"

"I'm sorry, Sir," Nandy said through a shaking voice. "I can't plot a course fast enough for the pilot, and the—the shields are going to build slower now that I can't use the power from the engines to re-energize them, and I think—but I'm not sure—but something is trying to divert juice from the rest of the ship."

"Commander," Merrecci said.

Nandy didn't appear to hear him though. Her breaths suddenly became heavier.

The hologram explained it all. There were just too many enemy ships giving chase and firing upon the Onyx.

"Captain—I mean, admiral," Nandy continued her ramble. "They'll wear our shields down before we get to Mars. I can't keep everything up."

Despite his concussive haze, Merrecci finally felt in control of himself enough to sit.

Prilla helped lay Merrecci back down and instructed him not to push his limits just now.

"Can you act like a doctor and give her something to calm down," Merrecci asked. "We need her."

Prilla immediately moved to a panel in a nearby console and opened it to remove an emergency med kit. She handed it to Charity who began familiarizing herself with its contents. Eventually, she pulled up a small canister.

"Desindanxtoxtalindin," she said. "Twenty milligrams."

The container produced a small opaque capsule. Charity loaded the pill into an injector and handed it to Prilla.

The Onyx dodged a volley of missiles through spinning and making several hard turns that would have broken any of Earth's other ships.

"Onyx," Nandy spoke in epiphany. "Do we have the ability to stealth?"

"Yes," Onyx said.

"Do it," Nandy ordered.

"Understood," Onyx said. "When diagnostic reaches eighty three percent, stealth will be engaged."

"Onyx," Nandy screamed and abruptly burst with, "Ow!"

Prilla apologized and withdrew the injector from Nandy's arm.

Nandy appeared to want to rebuke Prilla, but of all the thoughts running through the commander's head at the moment, reprimanding a civilian was not at the top of her priorities.

"Onyx. Do we have any functions immediately available to us right now that can help us evade our attacker," Nandy asked.

"Yes," Onyx replied.

"Will it help us get away?"

"It's possible."

"Apply this function now."

"Engaging encouragement sub-routine," Onyx said. "Keep going, pilot. You're doing a great job, pilot."

"What is this," Merrecci asked.

"You can do it, pilot. Fly me, pilot. Fly me really good."

Merrecci sat up again and looked to Nandy who appeared as confused as he did. He didn't really expect her to know.

"I think," Nandy stirred out, appearing a little less anxious and trying to cover that she was putting her own thoughts together at the same time, "Maybe her processing capacity is reliant upon how much diagnostic is completed."

"That's not how it typically works," Merrecci said. "Maybe they've adjusted how much power the ship has to draw on with this one."

"They'll kill us," Charity chided. "We should get off this deathtrap."

"Think we'll live longer in escape pods," Nandy asked.

"Earth's defense contingency is now fully engaged," Onyx suddenly announced at a startling loud volume.

"Good Lord," Charity cried, covering her ears as the others were doing too.

"Diagnostic has now reached thirty-one percent," Onyx announced.

"Onyx," Merrecci yelled. "Cut your communication volume by seventy-five percent."

"Okee dokee," Onyx screamed back. "Crew voice-environmental command will be applied when diagnostics reach thirty-four percent."

The bridge filled with complaining, some from Merrecci and his first officer, some from the cadets who had followed him, most from Prilla's patients.

The bridge hologram continued to show itself fleeing farther from Earth and reported that forty-two enemy vessels were in pursuit.

"Do we have any good news," Merrecci asked.

"Shields are at eighteen percent, Admiral," A soft voice spoke.

"Who said that," Merrecci asked.

"Bria's sunken face peered apologetically from around another console.

"What is she doing?" He just now came to realize that he wasn't standing. He thought he stood up a while back. Prilla was kneeling to his side. He had known she was there. Seen her, but only now registered that he was actually on the floor. Two other faces had been over him. One of them seemed intent on treating a head wound. The other smiled and drooled at him.

He felt that the fog had lifted, and he was no longer struggling to stay aware. He tried to stand.

"Let me finish this," Charity ordered and shoved Merrecci back down so she could finish treating a particular gash across his shoulder that he had not yet noticed was still spilling out blood.

"Prilla, get your student off my console."

"She's just sitting there," Prilla said. "She's only reading what the console is saying."

"That's it," Merrecci yelled. "Everyone who's not a member of this crew get off my bridge!"

"And where would you like us to go," Prilla said. "To our quarters? Or our stations?"

Before Merrecci could respond, Nandy announced that a volley of missiles were incoming.

"Sir, I believe I can get shield regeneration up faster if I can reroute some of our limited power," Bria said.

"You're not a member of this crew," Nandy snipped.

"I'm sorry," Bria replied softly. "I just thought I could help."

"Let us do our jobs," Merrecci ordered, then he turned to his sister. "This is what you wanted to turn down working on this ship for, Prilla?"

"With respect, Admiral, do you think the shields will last longer with or without a person sitting here to feed them power," Bria replied.

"I'm handling the shields," Nandy stated.

"You're barely handling yourself," Prilla said. "You need help."

Merrecci would have sworn at the fact that she had a point, but he refused to trust an idiot with bridge controls.

"I just need your authorization," Bria added.

"Sir," Nandy stated. "I have to strongly object. We have no idea if she even has the mental capacity and motor skills to hold that post."

"Well, she definitely has more than no one who doesn't have any at all, doesn't she," Charity retorted.

"Sir," Nandy quipped. "I don't need one more thing to have to clean up after."

"Name one ship where a first officer would have to operate this much, Vincen—Admiral," Prilla snipped.

"Fine! Fine," Merrecci relented, knowing he was going to regret it, but he also understood his first officer couldn't keep this pace up without help. "Your name's Bria, right?"

"Briata, Sir," Bria answered. "But yes, Bria."

"Onyx, promote Cadet Bria Leonard to acting ensign and make her a bridge crew member."

"I must go on record, Sir," Nandy said. "I do not support this decision."

"That makes two of us," Merrecci blasted. "But we make use of the tools we have, no matter how cheap they are. We can't fight, we can't hide, and, if we survive until the weapons come back online, I need you to not be worked into a frenzy. If they can help us run, then I'll take it!"

The ship shook.

The first time Merrecci had ever been hit by enemy weapons fire, he had been in a small craft. It was armed and eventually won the confrontation because of those weapons. The only reason this thought occurred to him at this moment was because when the Onyx shook just now, it was a hundred times worse than when he was in that dinky, cruddy little ship. Whatever had just hit here was something large.

"One," Being cried.

"Let's not do two," Merrecci grunted.

"We need a two," Allen said. "We need a two."

Prilla brought herself to her feet and moved up behind Allen. She kicked the back of his seat.

"Two," Allen said.

Prilla kicked it again.

"Three."

She kicked it four more times until Allen had counted to seven.

"What was that all about," Merrecci asked.

"It was seven," Prilla answered.

"I told you he had a thing for the number seven," Mirror piped in. She was currently sitting at another console without an operator. Her chair swung back and forth from boredom.

"Why do you ask such stupid questions," Dawn asked.

Merrecci wasn't quite sure what she was doing, but he left her to it. Dawn wasn't touching anything, just petting and reassuring mandog, who was currently curled around the swivel post of her seat and whining, that he would be okay.

Under any other circumstances, these people would have been escorted off the bridge and never allowed to see one again, but all the new admiral cared about now was that Acting-ensign Being had become focused on his flying, and the Onyx seemed to regain a steady course. In fact, Merrecci realized that Allen, since he had first met him, was no longer shaking now that he had control of the helm. His entire body appeared steady.

"Sorry about that," Allen Being replied. "I'll try not to let it happen again."

"That's because you're doing a good job," Onyx yelled. "You're doing very well!"

Charity held up a med-injector to Merrecci, whose first response was to attempt to bat it away.

"I need to stay sharp at a time like this," the admiral objected.

"This is going to help with the pain and boost your neural pathways," Charity said. "You're going to want to be more active than you are, but you're going to regret it later if you try. You have to take things slow, low energy, understand? You'll get about five minutes before a migraine kicks in. The more active you are until then, the more severe the migraine will be. Do you understand?"

Merrecci did, but he didn't have time to care.

Charity tapped his shoulder, and damn if Merrecci didn't think she made it more painful on purpose. These med injectors didn't have needles, but he could have sworn she went out of her way to swirl one inside of him anyway.

"Shields have risen to twenty-five percent, Sir," Bria said. "If we can keep from getting hit a little longer, I can get us back to full."

The bridge suddenly flashed red, a Jimmoshean shipbreaker had entered the pursuit.

"And there it is," Merrecci said. "It was only a matter of time."

"It's locked on, Sir," Nandy said. A moment later she announced, "Jimmosheans have launched an apocalypse Torpedo, Sir."

"Shields aren't enough," Merrecci said. "Suggestions?"

"Let me drive," Allen replied.

The Jimmoshean torpedo approached more slowly than most projectiles, undeterred by decoys, if the Onyx had any available at this time to throw in its path. It didn't move more slowly because it was hindered in any way. The Jimmosheans had used it as a method to frighten enemy ships more into giving up. It was their deadliest missile with a punch slow enough to help adversaries realize they had only one alternative to inevitable destruction. An apocalypse tended to destroy a great many vessels in one blow, those that could survive one, didn't survive two. If a ship could use the extra time to surrender, the Jimmosheans preferred to keep the resources and slaves rather than destroy them.

Merrecci was not going to surrender though, nor was he too stupid to waste decoys on torpedoes. There were other ways of dealing with apocalypse ship breakers. Of course, Onyx informed him that none of them were available until diagnostics had reached a variety of higher percentages.

If he'd thought the apocalypse sensors could be scrambled, he'd have done that, but they were immune to such defense tactics. The apocalypse's sole purpose was to seek an enemy's strongest power point, drill into it and detonate the ship from the inside out. If it decided it could not penetrate the hull, it would explode exteriorly and commit any other damage it was able to. Usually, it drilled.

Strong enough shields could keep the apocalypse out, but Merrecci knew back on the Viridian they needed at least seventy-five percent to fend off a single of these attacks, and Jimmosheans never launched an apocalypse at fully-powered defenses when they wanted to destroy something. He assumed they didn't care about burning Onyx down considering how weak she currently was. Still, he wasn't quite sure what his new girl could handle. So far, she seemed stronger, more versatile, but he wasn't willing to test any new ship's limits against a heavy hitter. Then again, he didn't really get a say in the matter right now.

"Shields are at twenty-nine percent," Bria said.

The dot in the hologram that was the apocalypse torpedo drew upon the Onyx and, before it could disappear, the entire vessel shook, throwing nearly everyone. Allen gripped the piloting controls, swearing.

"One," he groaned.

Prilla crawled quickly to the chair and smacked out six more rattles to Ensign Being's seat.

"Report," Merrecci requested, bringing himself back to his feet, realizing he was doing this a bit more than he would have liked today. He turned his attention to gazing over the operational console where Bria sat.

"Shields are at twelve percent," Bria said. Her fingers were moving quickly over diagrams of power lines throughout the ship. She hardly looked at her hands, but they became a blur as her digits moved to answer whatever riddle was on the screen in front of her.

"Can we get anything back," Merrecci asked.

"I'm working on it," Bria snapped then caught herself. "Sorry, Sir. It's different from the simulator. The console's a bit touchier. I just hope it can keep up better than the simulator."

"What do you mean keep up?" He found himself unwittingly mesmerized at her hands as they lightly danced across images on the console. Her fingertips floated over the input sensors rather than pressed upon them. He had never seen a person move so effortlessly at these kinds of controls. This meant only one thing: she was reckless.

Merrecci strangely decided he needed her full attention to stay on her work. He could have removed her from the seat and attempted the work himself, but his focus needed to be steered towards more than Buffalo-butt-faced Bria's conduct. He also doubted that his fingers could have moved as fast as what he was watching her do right now.

"Don't kill us," he said.

"She might not have a choice if they fire another apocalypse," Nandy said.

"You should abandon ship," the Onyx yelled.

"Maybe we've lost, Sir," Nandy said. "Escape pods don't get fired upon."

"You can't be serious," Prilla replied. "They get fired upon all the time, or we'd get enslaved instead!"

"Slaves can live to slaughter another day," Merrecci finally said. "We should abandon the ship."

"I can do this," Bria said.

"Anywhere you're still alive is somewhere you're not dead, Ensign," Merrecci replied.

Commander Nandy announced that the Jimmoshean shipbreaker had just fired another apocalypse. Her voice warbled at the sight of the large dots now flying across the arena shown in the battlecron's holo. She had no sensors to tell her, but she was certain just from the size and the speed.

"That's it," Merrecci said, "Abandon ship. Maybe the explosion will give us the mask we need to escape in the boats.

"I can do this," Bria urged. "Just give me a second."

"It's not sustainable," Merrecci replied sharply. "If we can get away, we can still carry out our mission, but it might be on a different ship."

"Just keep them off us, Allen," Bria said.

"What do you think I'm doing," Allen burst without looking up from his own controls.

"That's it," Merrecci roared. "You're both off—

"You should throw a probe," Drinker announced.

"You don't throw a probe, stupid," Dawn said.

"You material I mean," Drinker snapped.

Mike growled at Drinker, clenched his hands tightly, shaking his arms and head, and then he barked.

"You're starting to annoy me, Mike," Drinker snapped.

"I'll kick your ass," Dawn yelled back.

"Prilla," Merrecci said, after attempting several times to take control of the conversation again.

"You know how strong you'd have to be to throw a probe," Dawn asked. "Even in space?"

"I don't mean throw a probe," Drinker replied.

"You said throw a probe," Dawn said.

"I mean, fire a material," Drinker corrected.

"We should fire torpedoes," Mirror said.

"Quiet," Merrecci snapped, and he felt his head throb for a moment, stopping him from confirming his order to abandon ship and forgetting to continue ordering Bria and Being to step away from their consoles.

Charity nodded, reminding the admiral that she not only didn't like him, but that he needed to not get excited and feed the migraine growing in the wings of his brain.

It was here that Merrecci felt someone at his leg, and Prilla was suddenly interested in whatever it was to make it stop.

It took a moment for Merrecci to realize that Mike was at his feet and assuming a common canine position.

"Did he—," Merrecci burst. "Is he peeing on me?"

4

▲

Chub

Prilla pulled Mike away.

"He's wearing pants," Prilla replied. "He peed on himself."

"Better not have gotten any on my floor," Merrecci complained.

"Sir," Drinker said. "We should fire probes as soon as material."

"We don't have torpedoes," Merrecci said.

"Do we have probes," Drinker asked. "Not torpedoes."

"We can go count them together on our way to the lifepods," Merrecci quipped. "If our shields last that long."

"Yeah," Dawn said. "Probes are stupid, Drinker."

"No," Drinker replied. "Materials have shields. We don't need it to reserve material to go long distances. We can material all that power into shields."

Merrecci heard it and asked, "Onyx, can we fire probe?"

There was a pause, so Merrecci asked again.

"Probes are online," Onyx replied, and Merrecci thought he might have heard hesitation in her response as if she were trying to evaluate what Merrecci was up to. This is exactly why he hated being injected with anything during emergency situations.

"Target probe onto the approaching torpedo," Merrecci ordered.

"Targeting systems are offline," Onyx replied.

"Pablo can do it," Drinker said. "He can fire manually."

"Which one's Pablo," Merrecci asked.

Pablo raised one hand holding a lint roller and his other palm slapped it down.

"No," Merrecci replied and turned to the two information booth cadets. "Any help?"

They both apologized in the negative. She was a dietician. He was still in his generals. Both were worthless, which explained why they took seats behind consoles farthest away from Merrecci and the battlecron. He'd almost forgotten they were there, they'd been so quiet, and neither had volunteered to help.

"Of course," Merrecci cried. "The clean freak with involuntary impulse is the one who blows things up."

"He has OCD," Prilla chided.

"And slight Tourette's," Pablo shouted.

"Even better," Merrecci replied.

"Brace for impact," Nandy announced.

The ship shook, throwing half of the people on the bridge. This time, Merrecci held his post at Bria's console.

"One," Allen said. "One. One. One."

Prilla scrambled once more. She kicked the back of Ensign Being's seat, shaking it with each until Allen counted out seven repetitions.

"Report," Merrecci asked softly as he watched Bria turn a horrified brow to him.

"Four percent," she replied just as softly.

"They've fired two more apocalypse," Nandy said.

Two additional dots appeared in the hologram.

"Meatballs," Merrecci complained. "Had to get stuck with meatballs."

He then quickly made Pablo Escobedo an acting ensign as well just so he could fire a stupid probe.

Pablo dropped into another console.

"Shields will go down when we launch it, Admiral," Nandy said. "They'll be able to board us, Sir."

"Yes," Merrecci acknowledged. "This isn't one of your simulation matches with Russia. I know about damage that probes can cause bouncing around between shields and ship hulls. Doesn't matter though with only four percent shields."

"Eight percent now, Sir," Bria said.

"Hear that," Merrecci asked. "We have eight percent, we're ready to take a barrage."

"Well, I'd have more, but," but she didn't finish, just seemed deep in thought.

"But," Merrecci asked.

"Something called Special Quarantine is eating a bit of power we could use, and I can't divert it. Whoever's there is putting a strain on the Onyx's AI and our current energy resources."

A proximity alarm began blaring.

"Well, until we can figure out who it is, let's try to keep their rerouting options down," Merrecci instructed, then yelled towards Pablo, "Will you fire those probes already?"

"Launching probes," Pablo called out, then he suddenly spit on the screen directly in front of him. He immediately came back with, "I am so sorry, Sir!"

"Should I muzzle you, or can you keep it under control," Merrecci said.

"He can't," Charity snipped. "That's why he does it!"

Merrecci avoided having to respond and instead watched the two blue dots that had appeared on the hologram, each approaching one of the apocalypse torpedoes.

"Those missiles are designed to tear through ships," Prilla said. "How do you expect a probe will stop them?"

"Did I not order everyone to abandon ship," Merrecci fired back.

The first probe hit the torpedo, and the projectile exploded. A moment later, the second approaching apocalypse burst as well. The Onyx fled just ahead of its explosive blast range.

"What just happened," Nandy asked. "How was that even possible?"

"Who cares," Charity shouted. "Don't look a gift torpedo in its aft."

"The apocalypse arms after sensing that it passed a shield, any size of shield," Mirror explained. "Then it evaluates the strongest power sources of the craft inside, no matter how large or small, and detonates upon hitting it. It's all because of it's internal—"

"We get it," Dawn shrieked. "You don't have to always be a know-it-all."

"That's enough, Dawn. She's just helping," Prilla found herself speaking. "That's a very good explanation, Mirror."

"And it took a stroke victim who can't communicate clearly to suggest it," Merrecci grumbled. "They might not be fooled by decoys, but a shield would initiate their detonation process. How is there no record of someone thinking to do this before?"

"Guess no one was stupid enough, Sir," Nandy replied.

"Now, if only the fabricators worked," Mirror said.

"You would think of food at a time like this," Allen complained from his pilot's seat as he continued to steer the Onyx farther away from Earth.

"I'm not hungry," Mirror said.

"I am," Dawn said. "If the fabricators are working, I'd like lasagna."

"Will you shut up, Materialhead," Drinker yelled.

"Don't call me that," Dawn snapped. "Commander Wanship, Drinker said—

"Shut up, already," Drinker yelled.

"Torpedo volley incoming," Nandy announced.

The holo showed several projectiles begin their chase on the Onyx.

"Apocalypses," Merrecci asked.

"I don't think so," Nandy replied, scrutinizing the dots in the battlecron's center that were smaller than what the apocalypses had been.

"Those we can handle apparently," Bria said. "Also, shields are up to ten percent."

"Captain," Mirror said.

"He's an admiral, Mirror," Dawn said.

"You're an admiral," Mirror snapped back.

"You're a big mouth, stupid admiral," Dawn, said drawing back a fist.

"You're mean," Mirror replied curtly.

"You want your teeth in your mouth or your spleen," Dawn asked. "Cuz I'm going to kick your ass."

"If the fabricators are working," Mirror finally began to explain, avoiding Dawn's threat. "We could fill our probes' shields with Venunxian gas and launch them at the bad guys."

"Correct me if I'm wrong," Merrecci said. "I mean, clearly, I haven't been a genius commanding officer as long as you have, little miss Never-Shuts-Up—but doesn't Venunxian gas eat shields. We'd be putting our own, weak as they already are, at risk."

"The probes will be well past our own before they would have time to eat theirs," Mirror said.

"The gas wouldn't do anything other than eat the enemy's shields," Nandy said. "We don't have anything to fight back with even if the probe worked. It's wasted resource. Try again."

"Not necessarily," Merrecci found himself correcting.

The Onyx suddenly rattled, then shook even more.

"Sorry about that," Allen said.

"Diagnostics are at thirty-two percent," Onyx screamed.

"Probes aren't without defenses," Merrecci returned to his previous conversation. "They can self-destruct."

"If we hit a ship with one probe carrying Venunxian gas to eat through a shield and disarm the ship beneath it, a second probe filled with explosive Nanti gas could then get in close and give their self-destruct a little more kick," Mirror explained.

"Perhaps enough to breach the hull," Dawn clarified. "If we gave it a plasmic trigger, it would give it an even more productive blast."

"What in which hell just happened," Merrecci asked looking to Prilla for an explanation.

"This is what they do," Prilla said. "If people would just listen."

Merrecci abruptly turned towards the battlecron.

"We'd have to know right where to hit," Merrecci said. "Really," Escobedo asked. "I thought we'd just throw all the probes into a big potato sack, hurl it at the ceiling, and whichever ones God doesn't want, he'll throw for us."

"That's enough of that," Nandy reprimanded.

Escobedo apologized, and Merrecci silently accepted it, as Shade's words rang through his brain to maintain his crew.

"Onyx display schematics of enemy vessels," Merrecci requested.

"Okay," Onyx yelled. The hologram of an alien child's toy ship appeared in the battlecron.

Alien children praised excitement at the appearance of the toy as it broke apart into 250 pieces.

"Parents put it together again," a narrator announced. "Power incubators sold separately."

Charity broke out laughing. Cora might have too. It was difficult to tell.

"Quiet," Merrecci ordered.

Charity pursed her lips to match the narrow glints in her eyes.

"I know where to hit," Dawn said.

"This isn't a guessing game," Merrecci rebuked, realizing the migraine that was now unleashing upon him.

"I don't guess. I know," Dawn snapped. "I saw the schematic once, I know where to hit."

"Oh, good," Merrecci said, turning to Prilla. "She saw a schematic once."

"She has a photographic memory, retard," Mirror admonished.

"He's an admiral," Drinker chastised.

"Yeah, you call him Admiral Retard," Dawn added. "And then you punch him and win the fight and save humanity."

"You three," Merrecci said, drawing a finger from Drinker to Dawn to Mirror. "Help or get off my bridge."

"Please," Dawn said.

"Excuse me," Merrecci asked.

Prilla tried to intervene, but not quickly enough.

"You say please," Dawn said. "Or I'll kick your—

"Now," Merrecci yelled.

Dawn folded her arms in tight, huffed and turned away from the admiral.

"Vincenti," Prilla said. "You can't encourage them this way."

Merrecci held up his hand to silence her.

"Really," he asked. "While we're dodging torpedoes?"

Then he turned back on Dawn. "You're the one who said you knew where to hit. Now are you going to make it work, or are you going to let everyone on this bridge die because you think I should be nice?"

"You're so damned smart," Dawn screeched. "You know everything!"

Merrecci turned once more upon Prilla as if this had somehow been her fault.

Prilla shrugged at him.

"What a surprise," Merrecci said and considered a new tactic. "The genius can't do it."

"I can so," Dawn snapped.

She suddenly marched down into the heart of the bridge with the battlecron, purposely bumping her way past Merrecci, and she didn't apologize or anything to him. She pointed to the underside of the holographic toy ship's belly.

"Hit it there," she said and suddenly realized, "That's a toy!"

"Thank you, Cadet," Merrecci said.

"You didn't have to be so mean, you big stupid," Dawn screamed. "And I'm an Ensign!"

"Dawn, not okay," Prilla said.

"I don't care, he's mean," Dawn argued. "I don't want to play anymore. It's supposed to be lasagna day!"

"Tough," Merrecci said and then singled out Dawn, Drinker, and Mirror. "Since you three seem to get all of this, prepare my probes to attack those ships."

"He's not an engineer," Mirror said.

"Yeah, he's not that kind of smart, you big dummy," Dawn chided. "Only me, Mirror and Mike are."

Mike yipped at the sound of his name.

"Someone, get some probes ready," Merrecci demanded out of exasperation.

"We need fabricators," Mirror said. "Or did you forget that?"

"Onyx, do we have fabricators online," Merrecci asked, trying to keep his breath from boiling over.

"We have fabricators," Bria replied first.

"Fabricators are online," Onyx screeched.

Merrecci added three more people from Prilla's circle to his crew roster. He tried promoting them to ensigns so the Onyx would take their commands to make the fabricators create something more dangerous than food but was immediately reminded again they already were ensigns.

"Sir, six vessels are attempting to enter raizer range," Nandy said.

"Shield status," Merrecci requested.

"Back up to ten percent, Sir," Bria replied. "And that special quarantine siphon, whatever it is, isn't helping!"

"Pilot?"

"Don't you worry about me," Allen replied.

"Here's a novel idea," Charity said. "Why don't we engage the Nessla Drive."

"It won't work," Merrecci said.

"You haven't even tried it," Charity sneered.

"Onyx," Merrecci called. "Is the Nessla Drive online."

"Nessla Drive is not available until diagnostic reaches one hundred percent," Onyx yelled.

Merrecci now approached Charity and Cora, squaring himself against them.

"The Nessla Drive is always the last operation to go online so it doesn't accidentally trigger from another system short during the boot up and send the ship off God knows where," Merrecci realized he was now causing the conjoined twins to retreat as he continuously stepped into them. "The sooner you understand that this is not my first inning, the sooner I can—

"Admiral," Prilla pled softly and while pulling him away. "She's not used to this. She's a civilian."

"That's right," Merrecci said coldly. "She's just a doctor, what does she know about saving lives?"

His eyes pierced back into Charity and Cora. Cora's countenance might have been smiling and laughing.

"And she's the cadet?"

"Hey, you talk about my sis—

"I was only pointing out which one of you apparently got the brains."

Right there, he made Cora a member of his crew and promoted her to Lieutenant just to end the conversation with an exclamation that Charity would understand about who was in charge on his bridge.

"Shindan-ritsu wa san juu san passento," Onyx shrilled.

"What was that now," Merrecci asked.

"I believe it was German, Sir," Nandy said.

"Why is it speaking German," Merrecci exclaimed.

"It's Japanese, dummy," Dawn corrected.

"It must be diagnosing the translator," Nandy said.

"Well can't it do it in a language I know," Merrecci snapped, then apologized. "Just do your job."

He didn't notice Charity signal Prilla, who quickly asked, "The migraine's hit you hasn't it?"

"Who even speaks German anymore," Merrecci continued to stammer.

Charity and Cora approached and read him with a scanner. Charity withdrew and didn't speak, didn't have to.

"Are you fit to command," Prilla asked.

"Do I have a choice," Merrecci retorted. "Which one of you can do it?"

"Hey," Allen quipped. "Are we going to do something to get these torpedoes off of me or we just going to keep making me try to crash them into each other?"

Lighting in the bridge suddenly fluctuated.

"They're in raizer firing range, Sir," Nandy said.

"Shields are at twenty-two," Bria reported.

"Probes are ready for loading," Mirror announced.

"Finally," Merrecci said turning sharply back on the hologram to find the toy model still floating. He took in a deep, cleansing breath and suddenly yelled, "Blow something up! Onyx, will you show the bleeding arena already?"

The hologram shifted back to present the scene of the battleground. Two ships, known for quick pursuit had broken ahead of the cluster of over thirty already in chase. Merrecci knew these two at once. They were snips, common among many planets due to leaky intelligence and black market, junkyard retrofitting. The race that had invented them no longer existed as they destroyed themselves and their planet under their own crusade to develop stronger firepower. Well, they developed it.

Snips were small, but fast, carried no torpedoes, only energy weapons designed to drain shields and transport boarding parties. Merrecci knew better though. They were suicide squads with the purpose of distracting their opponents while the snips' more powered allies caught up to unleash the heavy damage.

He hated to say it, but had this been the Viridian, Merrecci probably wouldn't be worrying about his next maneuver. The Onyx was already showing what kind of a run it could make, and his previous ship, reliable as she had been, couldn't have made it this far, nor maneuvered this well.

"What happened to the torpedoes," Merrecci asked. "I thought they fired torpedoes."

"They did," Nandy said.

"I thought you said there were six vessels?"

"There were," Allen replied. "Now there are two."

"What happened," Merrecci asked.

"He happened, Sir," Nandy replied, nodding to Allen Being.

A fresh volley of missiles appeared in the holo.

"Okay," Being said to himself. "But I can't keep doing this, someone's going to catch onto me."

"Probes are loaded, Sir," Pablo announced.

"Launch them," Merrecci ordered and immediately recognized the missing subtle vibration that shields stirred upon the vessel as they dropped once more to let additional probes through.

Then the bridge filled with bright lights of materializing bio matter. Didjians used the tactic to gain surprise. That's how boarding parties worked, they sat there under their own engineer's eye waiting for that split moment that an enemy ship dropped its guard, and they always went for the bridge. They may have missed the previous time the Onyx dropped its shields to fire probes at the apocalypses, but they would be watching for it now.

Merrecci anticipated what would come next. The Didjians took tactical effort to protect their boarding parties by manipulating light waves, making their rematerialization process brighter. The theory was that just as the light of the sun can blind a flying craft to a foe hiding in its rays, enemies couldn't target apparating bio matter hidden in similar light. It was an effective method to blind enemy bridge crew.

Merrecci quickly retrieved a baton from the console closest to him, which happened to be his command chair. The weapon armed to life. Nandy turned, armed with two red batons.

Red batons were something only a rich daddy could afford to reward to his baby girl for getting promoted to commander before she'd even graduated the academy to serve under the Franchise's most notorious captain. Red was not the standard issue. The Earth Franchise allowed it, but only wealth could acquire it. It couldn't just be bought though. Its operator had to be certified in its use.

Every baton had an energy shield feature, but red could manipulate that energy to assist in hand-to-hand combat, even shroud the user's entire body in armor. As far as combat features went, there wasn't much stronger. Anyone who could get their hands on better, you watched closely, or you stayed away from, especially if it was black. If you see black armor, close your eyes because those users don't want witnesses. Red would protect her longer than any of the standard issue batons stored on the bridge—except Merrecci's, his was—

Eight Didjians appeared. They were slightly shorter than the average human. Unlike those that Merrecci had encountered in the halls of the academy on Earth, these weren't geared to spread destruction, but to quickly disarm and gain control of the enemy helm. There were no flamescreamers this time. This didn't mean these soldiers were weaker. It meant the lack of stronger weapons forced them to fight smarter and better, which meant higher caliber opponents. Their skin was already as tough as turtle shells, and their claws often made them the perfect boarding parties. Any skill added on to that made them a little bit more than annoying, which is what made them such great ground troops.

"Stay focused on your tasks if you have them," Merrecci ordered as he began to move towards one of the forming balls of light. "Trust us to defend you."

Prilla was the first to attack as she was closest to one of the materializing beings. She slammed a red hot baton into the Didjian. His shell, chest and torso boiled right out of existence the moment it attempted to appear in the first place. The blinding light had been effective on her once, but she'd seen too much of it now to know how to respond to it.

Merrecci clashed with another enemy now, but this one was prepared when he solidified. He instantly blocked the admiral's death baton with his own rifle-like energy weapon, even as it took form.

Nandy, however, disintegrated her opponent's head quickly.

As more of Onyx's probes fired into the holographic battle scene, another boarding party began to solidify onto the bridge.

This time one of the beings began appearing before Charity. She held her scanner to the forming molecules and triggered an effect that caused the particles to lose their bond and scatter throughout the bridge where they would dehydrate and die in moments. This was the very reason Earth used transcending beams rather than materializers. Materializers had too much of an opening to disrupt resolidification. It was one reason the Didjians hid their own process in blinding light. A third enemy boarding party began to appear even among the fighting. Fourteen Didjians now focused on how best to contend with the Earthers on Merrecci's bridge.

Merrecci found himself disarmed and watched the culprit swing a mace type weapon right upon Merrecci. The admiral slid to the side as the mace hit the floor, then he watched Prilla burn away his attacker's neck with her baton, severing his head from his shoulders.

Suddenly she was stumbling backwards, punched by another invader who now also swung a mace over his head. He swiped at Merrecci then Prilla, missing one then the other.

A shrill roar filled the bridge as Nandy leapt into the Didjian's chest, knocking the invader down. She held the two striking tips of her batons against each of his temples. A red plastic-type substance poured from the ends of her weapons and encapsulated every contour of her opponent's head, giving her batons the leverage she needed to twist his skull against his spine. Suddenly, the Didjian cracked, not just his entire outer protective shell, but his internal vertebrae. Nandy's batons drank back in the plastic-like substance. As this enemy fell, Nandy leapt into the back of a Didjian that had turned her attention upon Bria who sat innocently at her console, trying to do her job as Merrecci instructed.

In the chaos, Bria Leonard hadn't moved.

The faceless girl didn't flinch, Merrecci thought to himself as he observed Nandy stun Bria's attacker then stop him eternally and move to another. His first officer, however, continued to skip from one invader to the next, killing each with a single, devastating twist of the neck. Merrecci was certified in red baton. To use one demanded skill. Nandy wielded two and seemed to already be a master of cracking thick Didjian vertebrae, in one stroke. Whoever had taught her this leveraging technique had to have been one vicious bastard, Merrecci thought. This was entirely too clean of an approach for Nandy to have discovered in this moment.

Here, Merrecci noticed something that intrigued and upset him at the same time. Dawn was huddled beneath a console, and Mike was sitting on his guard, barking at an enemy that had come too close.

Merrecci used to run such a nice, sane bridge.

Drinker Bone, the cadet who had suffered a stroke cowered in a fetal position upon the open floor. Something about the way he sat stuck with Merrecci. Drinker wasn't crying, he wasn't rocking as the admiral had seen frightened soldiers do in the past. None of Drinker's behavior suggested he was afraid. Merrecci didn't see PTSD. This kid was hiding! That's it!

Wait. No. He wasn't hiding. He was tucking himself out of the way for those who were fighting to not fall over him. Yet, he wasn't covering his face. He was watching! Strange.

Willis, the one who laughed and hugged, now cowered in a corner, and covered his face. Unlike Drinker, he was shrieking.

As another boarding party began to materialize, Merrecci was aware of where each invader and bridge member carried themselves, many of the Didjian intruders were greeted by an anger that never gave them the chance to appreciate how fantastic their foe was.

"All probes are fired," Pablo finally said.

Merrecci blasted a hole through the backside of another invader. When he gathered himself this time for his next attack, he found Nandy was just adding death's finishing touch on the final standing fool to attempt to board his ship.

"Shields are back up," Bria added. "We are at thirty seven percent."

Merrecci breathed deeply then asked, "Are we missing anyone?"

"Sir," Nandy said and pointed to a body hanging from the side of a console.

It was the male cadet that had followed Merrecci ever since the information booth back at the academy. He shook as he cried and bled, the handle of a Didjian mace that had pierced into his back and through his chest now propped him from falling completely to the floor. Near his feet, his co-worker bled from her shoulder, arm, and neck. She gave a shaky thumbs up to the admiral, but he could see the belly wound seeping darkly into her cadet uniform.

Merrecci reached the two cadets even before Prilla could.

"Doctor," Merrecci called from the side of the male cadet, but Prilla stopped him.

What he had taken for crying was the young cadet's nervous system merely saying its last goodbyes.

Still, Charity and Cora evaluated him. Then they started into assessing his female counterpart.

"Just in case no one else was wondering about it, are there any more of those soldiers on this ship," Charity asked as she worked.

"Doubtful," Merrecci answered. "It's all about taking the command center, but if they're here, they'll storm in the next few minutes."

Then he stood.

"Show's over, we're not done yet," he stated flatly and ignored the instant repugnance that shaped the edges of Charity's eyes.

"Sir," Drinker said. "Both teams apparated in the exact same positions around the bridge. Probably gave the same rematerialization coordinates to all boarding teams. We can use that if we have to lower our shields again."

"You're sure about that," Merrecci asked.

"I saw it," Drinker said.

"That means they have a Paichu officer on board," Merrecci said. "That's one of their tactics."

"Diagnostics are at thirty-four percent," Onyx announced in English. Her volume was decreased, above a whisper now, having finally enacted Merrecci's order to reduce its volume."

"What," Merrecci yelled. "Oh, uh, return to normal volume, Onyx."

He turned back to the holographic battle scene happening in the center of his bridge.

"Did it work," he asked.

"We have twenty-one less ships chasing us," Dawn shouted. "Boom. Gone!"

"I don't believe it," Nandy said. "How did these bozos just disable shields on twenty-one ships and destroy just as many with probes?"

"Pardon," Prilla asked, and Nandy suddenly seemed interested in her holotab.

"What about those still pursuing us," Merrecci asked, too fixated on the remaining cluster of enemy ships giving chase in the holo to care to correct Prilla's response to his first officer. He couldn't help notice that a second ship breaker had joined them.

"Twenty-one's not enough ships for you the first try," Escobedo asked.

"Welp, she needs surgery," Charity informed. "I can do it, but not with these tools."

Now, Merrecci turned to Prilla. "You and the doctor get our cadet to the hospital."

Prilla nodded.

"I wouldn't have been able to find you if it weren't for her," Merrecci said. "You understand?"

Charity glared and nodded. As there were no med bots online until Onyx reached ninety-eight percent, the information booth cadets had to be moved manually. Prilla had requested to phase them directly from the bridge to the hospital but was reminded that the transcender was deactivated during phases B, C and E of diagnostics.

Instead, Prilla located the hospital on a ship map and had to use handheld tractor wrenches from the maintenance locker located beside the exit doors to allow her, Charity, and Cora to drag the two information booth cadets off of the bridge.

"Pilot," Merrecci asked, turning to his next priority. "Can you keep this up, I have a feeling this is going to last a while?"

"I kind of have to pee," he said. "But I can hold it."

"Wait a minute," Merrecci suddenly realized as he examined the holo map. "Where's Mars orbit?"

"Passed it," Being replied. "Thought we should keep going to put some distance between us and the fleet attacking Earth. The prime admiral said to get out."

"Keep at it then," Merrecci said, knowing that Ensign Being was correct. "Next time, run that decision by me."

Allen Being agreed.

"All right, everyone," Merrecci said. "We still have a long crawl ahead. We should probably get to Mabbis, but we're going to need more ideas like what we just had if we want to survive getting there and finishing our diagnostics."

"Sir," Nandy said, and her tone told Merrecci he didn't want to hear it. "We have another fleet of ships on intercept ahead of us."

"Adjust course, make them work for it," Merrecci instructed.

"Sir, incoming message from a Jimmoshean vessel," Nandy said.

"Let's have it on the wall this time," Merrecci replied. "I don't want to take my eye off this map for even a second."

The curved wall lit up with the torso of an energy-armored and decorated Jimmoshean.

"I am Master Cha of the vessel, Shilidrohn. This galaxy has been placed under the jurisdiction of the Great Divide Coalition. You will surrender your vessel and crew for relocation," the Jimmoshean master announced. "Prepare to receive me on your bridge."

"You're speaking to an admiral of the Earth fleet," Merrecci answered, then he dug deep into his diplomatic nature, pushing away all the responses he wanted to say. He was at war, and he didn't need to pour fossil fuel on the fire currently before him. War required affability. Putting his vindictive instincts aside, he spoke carefully and clearly.

"Go screw yourselves," he eloquently replied. "Earth has not surrendered. You are trespassing, and I'm gearing to rain hell upon your pathetic army for your crimes."

"We both know your words are pointless and bluffing," the master Jimmoshean replied. "Let me over so we can end this peacefully. You barely have the capacity to fight let alone flee in your obviously non-war vessel. We detect no signs of weapon power functions."

"What a coincidence, we didn't detect that your fleet had any either," Merrecci said. "We tried to probe your ships but twenty-one of them just blew up. We thought to be fair, we shouldn't probe you anymore, or we might destroy your flimsy fleet. Please tell me you have something stronger coming. I don't want to be known as the overpowered admiral who unfairly wiped out a weaker Jimmoshean and Didjian fleet with scanning equipment. Now, if you don't mind, we're trying to decide if firing garbage cans at the rest of your fleet would cause too much collateral damage on your end."

The Didjian captain huffed and leaned into his monitor.

"I would have your name, Admiral," the master sneered out the rank in hot contempt. "I will need to spell it correctly for the placard that will hold your head in my quarters."

"Admiral Vincenti Merrecci," the admiral replied.

"That's not possible," the master said. "The barbarian captain commanded the Viridian. I saw the Viridian in flames myself."

"I appreciate that information, and I've just given myself unlimited authority to kick your ass, Master Cha."

"Hey, that's my line," Dawn suddenly shouted.

"Diagnostic is at thirty-five percent," Onyx announced.

Master Cha's face twisted from concern to amusement.

"I see now," Cha said. "The great Merrecci is buying time before his ship falls. Tell you what, let me come aboard and take command of your vessel and—."

"You can't fall in space, stupid," Mirror yelled.

"Yeah," Dawn added. "There's no gravity."

Cha burst out laughing, and his image disappeared from the wall.

"Two things," Merrecci roared. "Onyx! Never interrupt me during a transmission."

"Understood," Onyx replied.

"And the only person who speaks to the enemy on my bridge is the commanding bridge officer, or you'll find yourself in the brig."

"But he was stupid," Mirror said.

"Look at who's talking," Merrecci fired back.

"I am," Dawn replied without taking her eyes off Merrecci.

Then her shoulders slunk. "This isn't fun anymore," she said. "I want my lasagna."

"Dying's not fun neither," Merrecci said. He turned to Nandy. "I could really use some trained staff right now."

"As soon as diagnostics allow, we can fix that," Nandy said.

"Diagnostics," Merrecci realized. "Obviously, we can communicate now. Onyx! Open a ship wide channel.

"That feature is not available until the ship diagnostic has reached fifty-six percent," Onyx said.

"What the hell," Merrecci complained. "Open a channel to the Earth fleet."

"That feature is not available until the ship diagnostic has reached fifty-six percent," Onyx replied.

"We were just using that feature," Merrecci was now yelling.

"No, you weren't," Onyx returned a moment later.

"Yes, we were, check the logs," Merrecci demanded.

"The ability to check logs will be available when diagnostics have reached fifty-seven percent," Onyx replied.

"That's screwed up," Merrecci blasted.

"Yes," Onyx replied. "You should abandon ship because of it."

"I need staff," Merrecci asserted.

"Would you like me to go search, Sir," Nandy asked.

"No. I need as many working brains on the bridge as I can get," Merrecci said.

He scanned over the room and settled his finger towards Drinker. "You."

"Sir," Drinker asked. He stood now.

"Go in the halls and tell the first member of the crew you see to report to the bridge," Merrecci ordered.

The ship shook.

"Sorry," Allen said. "Only one hit. I need two."

Merrecci looked instinctively for Prilla, but, realizing she'd left to find the hospital, he settled on Nandy to complete the task. Nandy kicked the back of Ensign Being's seat until he counted seven shakes.

"Shields are at thirty-six percent," Bria announced during the process. "Sir, these shields—they're not like previous ones our other ships have."

"I gathered that a little," Merrecci said.

"They can take a beating," Bria explained. "If we can get us back to eighty-five percent, I believe we can hold out as long as we can keep outrunning them."

"That seems a pretty big assumption to me," Merrecci said. "Are you sure? I mean, we're not really outrunning them."

"Provided we don't keep picking up more enemies and that Allen, uh, Ensign Being can keep us clear of other chasing projectiles," Bria replied.

"And apocalypses," Merrecci asked. "You have to consider all potential weapons. What if we run out of probes."

"We're replicating more," Mirror said.

"How long until they're ready," Merrecci asked.

"Three days," Mirror answered.

"I need the power for the shields," Bria said. "Sorry."

"How long would it take us to produce a probe normally," Merrecci asked, turning to Nandy.

"Ten minutes, Sir," Nandy replied.

"We can't beat apocalypses without the probes," Merrecci pointed out. "You think slowing down production of probes is the right decision in a time like now?"

"Well, I guess that's up to you, Sir," Bria replied. "I can direct all power build shields to full which will allow me to divert the same attention to building probes once we're full so that we can fend of apocalypses more, or I can build probes and let the smaller torpedoes peck us to death, so it won't take an apocalypse to kill us. It's your ship, Sir. You tell me if you prefer hovering around having no shields or having shields."

Merrecci prepared to yell, but realized Drinker was still standing at attention before him. "What are you doing here? I gave you an order."

"Sir," Drinker said. "I should stay. I have an idea."

"There's a surprise," Merrecci replied shortly. "Can it stop apocalypse torpedoes?"

"Well, not material," Drinker stammered.

"Not material," Merrecci asked. "Oh, I can see your stroke posing no translation problems here at all." He took a breath to remind himself to hear any suggestion his bridge had to offer. "What's your idea?"

"Get us to the material belt," Drinker said.

"The material Belt?"

"Yes," Drinker replied. "Get us to the material, and I believe we can material ourselves."

"I don't understand," Merrecci said.

Drinker nodded in anticipation. "We can material the asteroids."

"Asteroids?"

"If you can't understand him, Captain, maybe we can." Pablo said.

"Fine," Merrecci relented. "What's one more fool on this ship?"

He held back a tirade of complaints and cursings. To help him with his previous order to search the ship for help, Merrecci turned on Willis who sat in an empty seat smiling over the entire scene.

"You," Merrecci said, holding a finger.

Willis looked around, then pointed to himself to ask if the Admiral was talking to him.

"Yes, you!"

Willis's grin broadened, he stood and ran in a limply stride towards Merrecci.

"Go through that door and run through the halls. Tell the first person you see to report to the bridge on my orders."

Willis looked at the door then the admiral. He smiled.

"Do you understand?"

Willis blushed.

"You can't speak, can you?"

"He can moan," Mirror said.

Willis made a happy sigh and a smile of fake and strangely, perfect teeth popped through his lips to say, "hi!"

"Okay," Merrecci said. "Then go through that door, physically grab the first person you see and drag them back here."

"Sir," Nandy said. "The crew might not conform to him since he doesn't outrank them?"

This time Merrecci got half of a swear word out before silencing it.

"What's your name—what's his name again," Merrecci asked then quickly amended.

"Willis," Mirror said.

"Willis what," Merrecci asked.

"Willis," Mirror started but couldn't finish.

"His name's Willis," Dawn shouted. "She already told you it was Willis."

"I know it's Willis. Willis what," Merrecci inquired again.

"Diagnostics are at thirty-six percent," Onyx announced.

"It's not Willis What," Dawn answered. "It's Willis."

"I'm not going to debate baseball with you," Merrecci stammered. "What is Willis's last name."

"Willis doesn't play baseball," Mirror argued.

Merrecci pointed to Bria, "A little help—what are you doing?"

"I'm waiting for your order for what you'd like me to do," Bria replied. "Shields or fabricators for probes?"

"Keep us alive! God! Why didn't I just stay in bed all day? I could have slept in and avoided all this crap," Merrecci exploded with such force that his entire frame shook. His head felt instantly heavy, and he wanted to fall. He calmed himself and reattempted his inquisition. "What is your friend's last name?"

"I don't know his last name, Sir," Bria said. "Allen?"

Allen didn't know, neither did Drinker.

"Merrecci to hospital," he called to open a channel to Prilla, if she had arrived yet, but then remembered that he had no communication except with engineering, and there wasn't anyone there.

"Onyx, can you identify this cadet whose first name is Willis?"

"Not at this time," Onyx replied.

"How do you morons not know that," Dawn asked.

Merrecci tore off his uniform jacket and helped Willis dress into it, donning Merrecci's outdated Captain's tonks, as admiral level-tonks required a different type of rank-insignia holo emitter to cut down on counterfeiting rank insignias at that high of clearance.

"No one's going to argue with a captain. I am temporarily field-promoting you to rank of Captain, so others are more to obey you when you drag them back here," Merrecci stated, then issued the order to Onyx. "Thank God you can't speak! Now go grab someone and bring them back."

Willis straightened up, saluted, and ran off the bridge through a sluggish portal.

"Sir," Nandy said. "What if he gets lost."

"Oh my god," Merrecci complained, rubbing the front half of his head where it throbbed the most. "Ask me that before he goes, not after."

"He's going to get lost," Mirror said.

"He always gets lost," Dawn added.

"Hey, I think I got it," Pablo suddenly announced. "We should go to Kuiper Belt."

"Yes," Drinker approved. "That's what I was trying to material. Go to the material belt."

"And do what," Merrecci said.

The ship shook. Nandy kicked Allen's chair six times.

"Shields are at sixty-two, Sir," Bria said when she found Merrecci's face over her again.

"Keep going, Ensign," Merrecci said, then wondered why Bria was even with this group. Obviously, her face was deformed, but she seemed alert, intelligent.

"Sir," Nandy suddenly broke urgently. Although she didn't have to explain why, she did.

Merrecci turned to the hologram, as was his habit, and saw the bulky ship that had joined the fleet in pursuit. It was a chub, a cube that looked like a class of preschoolers had built it out of all the misshapen blocks that had been left from a set of toys which no one ever threw away.

From a battle standpoint, they weren't anything to be too worried about for the most part. They couldn't fight like most ships, had no armaments. They were fortresses found mostly in convoys or commercial transport. Their hulls were so heavy, they required no shields, and the most valuable cargo was considered safest within their walls. That's all they were designed to do: move and protect large amounts of cargo.

Chubs never entered planetary orbit, or they'd fall, and once they landed on any soil with decent gravity, they never left, not without vast amounts of help that wasn't typically feasible. No amount of any single, artificial anti-gravity device could compensate for its weight and bulk once a planetary body had caught it.

One had landed on Earth's moon once, and the only reason it was ever able to return to space was through cargo ships after the chub had been completely mined apart for resources. It took twenty years, despite the moon's home owner's association calling it an eyesore.

Another time, the Viridian had to track one down after a band of pirates infiltrated it by shipping themselves as cargo. The battle ended with the pirates steering themselves into a super sun after Merrecci used psychological warfare to convince the hijackers that someone aboard was a murderer and was going to take over the crew one by one. Pirates were kind of dumb that way. The Viridian might have been able to crack their hull open eventually if they could get another chub to keep restocking her torpedo supply. That's how it was on other Earth ships, they couldn't fabricate their own weapons. It was against protocol due to the demands the use of energy put on a ship to sustain itself in battle or retreat. The fact that the Onyx could fabricate its own weaponry was a point of interest that Merrecci would have to check upon later. He had his doubts as to fabricating during battle as he'd just experienced how it interfered with Bria's abilities to recuperate shield strength. None of this, however, had anything to do with Merrecci convincing a bunch of stupid pirates to fly themselves and their chub into a sun. He doubted this particular chub had crew stupid enough to fall for that trick here, especially since the only sun available at the moment was two planets away from Earth, and he wasn't going to risk that venture, especially in the Onyx's current state.

What chubs lacked in just about everything except hull and bulk was made up for in tractor beam technology. They could drag entire space stations and were initially designed in hopes they could tow unlivable planets that were rich with resources back into a safe orbit where its purchaser could mine it without having to set up expensive gathering routes. They had also been used to move moons or tow away stars before they could go supernova. It usually took several chubs to work in coordination to pull off such maneuvers though, which is what led the Jimmosheans to discover the true strength of these cargo vessels.

In battle, the proper formation of a few chubs could lock entire enemy fleets in place while the chubs' allies picked them apart. Additionally, a chub strategically placed between another ally and an enemy vessel was a nearly impossible shield to tear down. Other than that, the only other action chubs were good for was ramming. One hit had been known to annihilate entire smaller ships, throw larger ones, even crack apart space stations. It took a special stupid to want to attack a chub.

The Onyx shook. Then rattled. Merrecci stumbled forward even as the Onyx filled with deafening white noise.

"Brace yourselves," Allen announced.

Merrecci gripped the tactical railing encircling the battlecron in the center of the bridge. He nearly lost that hold when the ship rocked so hard that he was certain he'd have no choice but to give the order once again to abandon ship as he was certain there'd have to be hull breach.

Right as the ship settled and Merrecci was about to ask Onyx for a damage report, he fell away from the railing under another shattering. He caught himself before tumbling to his face. Then the floors shook again.

"Are we done," Merrecci asked.

Allen sat muttering something under his breath. He was pale, his eyes wide, his hands working feverishly at the pilot controls.

Three consoles away, and on the aisle facing Allen, Bria's terrified face was also lacking color.

"What happened," Merrecci asked.

"Sir, I," Nandy tried answering, but she appeared to be overcoming her own fall and loss of her command holotab. She scrambled to have her bracelet rejuvenate it in her hand so she could answer Merrecci better.

"You don't want to know, Sir," Bria finally said.

"Yes, I do," Merrecci demanded sternly. He turned to Nandy for her to pick up the answer instead.

"Six torpedoes hit," Nandy said. "Sixty-three did not. Our pilot got them to hit the chub."

"I suppose it's too much to wish it was enough to make it disappear," Merrecci asked.

"Ha," Nandy guffawed. "Right."

"And our shields?"

"Fifty-three percent, Sir," Bria said. "Now fifty-four."

Merrecci was finding himself aware of Allen muttering. Then he realized. He moved behind Being's chair once more and kicked. Through his stubborn will to command, Merrecci hadn't noticed that his bridge had been growing a little darker to him with each second that his migraine intensified.

Kicking the pilot's chair was all the admiral's brain needed to say, "That's it! This job sucks. I'm going to bed." Merrecci wasn't even aware that he didn't have a choice to comply.

He was, however, aware of his young first officer's voice calling out, "We're caught in the chub's tractor beam." He didn't feel the ship suddenly halt nor the floor punch his face.

5

▲

Asteroids

This wasn't the bridge. Everyone who had lived most of their lives living on one knew. This room was more lulling, designed to keep people at ease when they came out of sleep, or when they couldn't breathe and needed something to help them. Merrecci knew what a hospital bed felt like when he was in one.

The hospital! What was he doing in the hospital?

He sat upright before his eyes had even opened to take in the dim brown tones of the medical lamps, which had been designed to make dilation easier on the waking brain.

Hands wrested upon him, and he ordered them away. He demanded a report before the faces in front of him could take focus.

"Well," Prilla's voice said in a way that suggested she was about to skirt around an issue. "We're out of the tractor beam and currently in an asteroid field."

"And you brought me here," Merrecci complained and stood, but for some reason his right side of his body had forgotten to do its part holding him up and allowed him to stumble from his bed until he slammed into the wall, causing him to drop once again.

He was really starting to hate this ship.

Prilla and another set of hands, Cora's, helped him up.

"Brief me," Merrecci asked.

"Oh boy did you screw up," Charity snorted.

Merrecci snapped a warning glance at her, but she didn't care. Prilla's, she did heed.

"From what we know," Prilla started. "We got caught in a chub tractor beam. Mike, Dawn, and Mirror blew it up though."

"We have weapons," Merrecci asked.

"Not exactly," Prilla continued. "For some reasons, which I don't claim to understand myself, but umm tractor beams, as I'm sure you in all your illustriousness know, operate under the theory that intense light waves can pull an object towards the light source, add in some lasers to help channel it and some other—

"Why you wasting my time," Merrecci asked. "You know how I feel about this crap. Get to the point."

"Well, although light doesn't affect sound waves, apparently the same is not true for sound not to affect light, particularly when they have the appropriate lasers to act as conduits."

Merrecci huffed at Prilla.

My students-slash-patients blasted the tractor beam with something called Enter Sandman by a group called Magnetica."

"That doesn't sound right," Charity said.

"Whatever," Prilla redacted. "And it caused some kind of magna refraction nerd-shift-thing throughout the lasers in the intensified tractor beam light and blew up the chub's main tractor emitter.

"And then we used pissy thoughts to follow Peter Pan and Stinkerbell to this beautiful land of asteroids," Charity added.

"Just like that," Merrecci said.

"Yeah, uh, uh-huh," Prilla said.

Merrecci felt his eyes narrow, knowing Prilla understood he knew there was more.

Suddenly, Prilla was smacking Merrecci.

"What were you thinking," She started screaming amidst the barrage.

Merrecci tried blocking but felt himself falling again. Charity and Cora caught him this time before he might go out again.

"Stand down," Merrecci snapped.

"You're not my commanding officer!" Prilla shot back and extended a finger into Merrecci's face. "And you're not dad, so you don't get to pull that with me. Not anymore."

She suddenly retracted her hand and waited for Vincenti to start breathing again.

"If you're on this ship, you answer to me," Merrecci exploded.

"Oh yeah," Prilla scolded "Just for that, you can figure out the stupid you do on your own!"

"In the meantime, think you might want to get a reliable person in command of this ship," Charity asked coldly.

"We're alive," Merrecci said. "So, my first officer must have things under control."

Charity laughed.

"He thinks his first officer's in command," she chortled.

"You mean that first officer," Prilla asked, pointing straight past Merrecci.

Merrecci turned and found two more hospital beds. One held an injured information booth cadet who was recovering from her belly surgery. The other held Nandy, laying on her side.

"She was helping me lay you down in here when you fell on her and made her crack her head on the handrail," Prilla said. "Now, she's recovering from head trauma because you damn-near killed her."

"She brought me down here herself," Merrecci asked.

Prilla nodded.

"As if I don't have enough people falling down right now," Merrecci said. "Wait! Are you telling me your special ed brigade are running this thing?"

Charity started laughing.

"Why didn't you take command," Merrecci asked. "You're both doctors for damn-it-all sake."

"I'm not officially a member of this ship's crew," Prilla retorted. "And she's a civilian. You promoted Cora, not the doctor."

"That's not true, I made you a member of my crew."

Prilla shook her head. "No, you didn't."

"Onyx," Merrecci said.

No answer came.

"No internal communication yet," Merrecci asked, but didn't need a response.

Prilla mugged a smile.

"Did you find any other crew members to fill bridge posts?"

Prilla nodded in the negative. "Turns out our current bridge needs a lot of medical attention—surprisingly, all the ones who are supposed to be smart!"

"Get me to the bridge," Merrecci said.

"Please," Charity snarked.

"Now," Merrecci yelled and fully expected her and Cora to jump at his order. "You have been drafted." His palm, fingers fully extended wiped from Charity to Prilla. "And you are reassigned officially. Any failure to uphold your duties and responsibilities as I deem necessary until I release you will result in imprisonment for the duration of the trip until you can be tried for treason. Do I make myself clear?"

"That's uncalled for," Prilla said.

"Quiet! We'll discuss this later, but for right now you're my ship psychologist, and you'll retain your commander rank." Merrecci turned to Charity. "And you!" He struggled a moment with what he needed to say, but didn't have time to really contemplate how he wanted to handle the civilian doctor, so he just blurted. "You're the hospital chief. And because I don't have time to babysit the politics this could mean with the rest of whatever crew might be somewhere here on this ship, I should make you your department's commander until we can find ours."

"What," Prilla asked louder than Charity in surprise. "She's not academy."

"She's been stuck to that cadet, sitting in on her classes for how long," Merrecci asked. "Seems about as sane to do as anything else that's happened today! I'll enter it officially with Onyx when I get back to the bridge."

"Fine," Charity said. "Then I relieve you of duty out of fear you'll screw up again."

"I don't care how well you can aim. You'll lose this pissing match, Doctor," Merrecci said, a little friendlier, but no less sternly. "Despite what you think, Earth's survival doesn't depend on me not screwing up out there. It's all about you not screwing up in here because you fix the people I need to help me out there."

Charity pursed her lips. "I understand."

"Sir," Merrecci said.

"Sir," Charity replied coolly.

Merrecci tried standing once more and found Prilla sustaining him.

"You ever relieve me of command again out of spite, and you'll be your own next patient," Merrecci threatened.

"Yes, Sir," she replied. This time, she made it clear she didn't respect him, but understood him.

Merrecci didn't care, most soldiers don't fully respect those at the top. It comes with the game. He'd been on both sides plenty of times.

"God," Merrecci complained. "What a nightmare! Help me back to the bridge."

The first thing that Merrecci noticed, as Prilla began escorting him back to his command post, was that he hated the décor. Shag rug, brown shag rug, wood baseboards, although he was sure it wasn't really wood. He'd inspect it in private later. The walls were the same beige that he'd had in his bedroom during grammar school. Light came from overhead tracks.

"This place looks like grandma's house," Merrecci observed.

Prilla agreed.

Still, Merrecci couldn't help but notice how much quieter it was here than in the Viridian. Although he could still feel the engines, it was muffled. Probably because of all the shag. Merrecci couldn't be absolutely sure.

"I'll have to get the fabricators working on different carpet," Merrecci said mostly to himself.

"I like it," Prilla said. "It's a nice change from a cold ship."

"It's shag."

"Yeah, but you can walk barefoot in the halls now."

Merrecci shook his head in disapproval. "It's shag carpet! I'll bet Shade did this just to get back at me for the gum."

The touch panels in the walls that normally illuminated with room numbers, maps and computer access were all dark. He made the assumption they hadn't gone through diagnostics yet.

They reached two plain placards with "Bridge" and "Authorized Crew Members Only" markings. A dimly-lit rim of red lights traced the panel frame, signifying there was an off-ship transmission coming in, and no one should interrupt.

"Sorry about what I said," Prilla apologized.

"No, you're not," Merrecci replied and approached the entry to the bridge.

The door panels swung in towards the bridge. Here he found Master Cha's holographic head floating in the center of the room rather than on the wall, and Bria stood before it, gripping the handrail. She did not see the admiral enter.

"I will not ask again, little bug," Master Cha said. "Remove yourself from this asteroid field, lower your shields. Whether you like it or not, I and my soldiers are coming aboard."

"And I will say it again," Bria said confidently. "Do not linger here. Remove yourself and your fleet from this system or the consequences will be yours."

Cha laughed.

"Big words from something that will be so easy to squish," he said.

"Then why haven't you," Bria asked.

"Enough," Cha snapped. "I will not be talked to by a grunt found repulsive by the standards of even her own race. Where is your ship's captain?"

"Where is yours," Bria returned sharply. "All I seem to be dealing with is a fool."

Master Cha growled from within and suddenly burst with, "You insect! I have not come this far to—either let me on, or I will—

"Finish that statement and make it your last," Merrecci ordered as he forced himself away from Prilla. He moved carefully to the battlecron's railing, without looking as though he were struggling. Here, he stood beside Bria. Cha's head floated above eye-level so that Merrecci could give the illusion enemies were looking down on him and give them a false sense of superiority.

"There you are," Cha hissed.

"Remove yourself and your fleet from this system or I'll thump ya," Merrecci nearly repeated Bria's warning. He leaned into the railing, a trigger to cause the holographic head to now lower below his eye-level. This was now to put Cha on the intimidated defensive. "Else get to squishing." Now he turned to Bria and said, "We do not waste our breaths on lapdog captains. End this communication."

The head disappeared.

"Thank you, Admiral," Bria said.

"What the frunk do you think you're doing taking command of my vessel," Merrecci asked.

"Someone had to," Bria answered.

Merrecci said nothing. He stared, right into her eyes, only her eyes. This wasn't about testing her soul, his glare went no farther than her green eyes, and he held her gaze. She didn't look away as so many did who were ashamed that they had made a mistake. She was confident in her decision.

"Return to your post," Merrecci instructed. He summoned a captain's chair which rose up from the floor. It was a simple seat, ergonomic with armrests rated for sitting long hours. A captain's console unfolded to its side. "Onyx, promote Acting Ensign Bria Leonard to the rank of acting lieutenant-commander."

Here, Merrecci decided to take in a deep breath as cleansing as he could make it. He knew it would be the only one he got in a while.

"Onyx, open a channel to Earth fleet," he requested.

"That feature is not available until diagnosti—

"We were just using it," Merrecci yelled.

"No, we weren't," Onyx stated.

"Sir," Bria said. "I think we can only communicate in transmissions we receive at this time."

"Have we received any from our fleet," Merrecci asked.

Bria shook her head.

"Onyx, why can we receive transmissions from the enemy but not from our fleet," Merrecci asked.

"The enemy is closer," Onyx answered.

"What is the status of our diagnostic initialization," he asked.

"Diagnostics is at forty-nine percent," Onyx said.

Merrecci turned back to Prilla who was sitting in the wings, watching Merrecci's recovery.

"Can that woman handle the hospital on her own for now," he asked Prilla, who was even now observing Merrecci for any signs of mental fatigue that might shut him down again. Even as Prilla was nodding, he then continued with, "Will you please go find me some crew members with bridge experience then. They're probably trapped in some room somewhere because the doors don't work if diagnostics haven't reached four million percent."

"Probably right," Prilla said. "We had to give some encouragement on the door to open the hospital."

"If that's the case, please look for people who have opened a door on their own, I'd like the smartest ones if we can find them," Merrecci said.

Prilla nodded and left the bridge, but not without pursing her lips at his insult.

"Report," Merrecci finally asked turning back to his bridge.

"Shields are at a hundred percent," Bria replied. "We are holding position in the Kuiper Belt. I've begun fabrication of more probes. Our position's not pretty, but they're not coming in after us. They've tried shooting at the asteroids, but they just waste weapons, and we simply move. Our weapons are still not online, but we have been developing a means to fight back. It's dangerous and won't be fun nor accurate." She nodded to Dawn, Mirror, and Mike. "Go ahead and explain it to the admiral."

The all stepped out from three rows behind Bria's station which had been on the operations side of the bridge.

Merrecci's gaze fell on Mike.

"Him," Merrecci asked. "You're going to have him explain this to me? Him?"

"He's very smart," Mirror said.

"Oh, I'm certain," Merrecci said. "All right then, let's have it, Benji."

Mike growled, then Merrecci snorted and turned to Bria as if to ask if he'd just made a mistake in promoting her, which he already knew the answer to deep down.

"I thought how we could weaponize the asteroids," Dawn said.

Mirror gasped.

"You're a liar," she accused. "You didn't think of anything. Drinker thought of it."

"This was Drinker's idea," Merrecci asked.

"One of them," Mirror said. "He's always got ideas, you know. Though you can't always understand them on account of his—

"Was it your idea to blow up the chub's tractor array too," Merrecci abruptly asked Drinker, who was sitting at the back of the room folding his fingers into strange and entertaining contortions.

"That was Mike's idea," Dawn said before Drinker could answer.

"Nu-uh," Mirror said. "Drinker thought it up."

"Yeah," Dawn added. "With Mike's and my help!"

Mirror gasped again then whined with, "You're a liar! All you did was tell us what to do."

"Because it was the only way to get you to shut up," Dawn argued. "Besides, I chose the music."

Once more, Mirror heaved in then blurted out, "You did not!"

"Well, I would have, I wanted to listen to opera, but Mike made us use something called electric guitar," Dawn continued.

Mike suddenly started barking.

"Oh yes you did so," Dawn scowled. "You wouldn't even let me play what I wanted."

"That's enough," Merrecci snapped. "What's the idea, Mike?"

Mike reared back on all fours and grumbled.

"Oh, right. I forgot you're a dog," Merrecci said. "If you're a dog, speak!"

Mike whimpered and circled behind Dawn.

"What did I say about kicking your ass," Dawn suddenly shouted. "Now I remember why I don't like you on the bridge."

"You're mean," Mirror said.

"What's your stupid idea," Merrecci yelled, leaning forward in his chair.

Mirror startled and straightened instantly.

"We smack all the asteroids around us with our shields and throw them at the enemy ships," Mirror said.

"That's your plan," Merrecci asked looking back to Drinker. "And you think we can do that?"

Drinker nodded.

"See," Mirror started. "The way it works is—

"Ensign—Dawn is it," Merrecci interrupted.

Mirror corrected him.

"Let me explain something, Mirror," Merrecci replied coldly. "I don't care. Just because I command this ship doesn't make me a genius of every profession on board."

"Uh-huh," Mirror interjected.

"I did not take all your engineering classes. Why? Because name a single corporation or organization where an engineer has ever been the person fully in charge. It's always someone who's learned how to talk to other human beings or can get to the head-honcho's office faster than anyone else. Do you know how far away the engineering bay is? In a crisis, the cook is more likely to run to the bridge first; show their valor; and earn a promotion than the engineer can.

"I got here by playing baseball and kickin' ass because my background is in phys-ed and team management. Two disciplines I've already had to apply since we all got here. Sometimes, I might pick up a few things listening to boring engineers."

Mirror blinked at him and said, "Uh-huh."

"When I ask if something can be done," Merrecci continued. "I care only about three things: can it be done; when will it be ready; and will it blow us up? Other than that, I don't care. Do you understand?"

"Yes, Sir," Mirror replied a little more softly and less chipper than her usual self, but cautiously asked. "How did you ever get a job on a ship then if you don't know science?"

"Phys-ed is science," Merrecci replied curtly. "I directed the physical fitness department on my first tour."

"Oh," Mirror replied.

"So, Drinker," Merrecci asked turning his attention to the back of his bridge. "Can they do this?"

Drinker shook his head in the affirmative.

"Is it safe?"

"For us," Drinker replied. "Material."

"That's yes," Bria said.

Merrecci thanked her.

"Did you give any thought to how those asteroids might just sail towards Earth," Merrecci asked.

"It was just an idea," Drinker said.

Merrecci took a moment to consider whether Earth's planetary systems would still be in condition to defend against any stray asteroids that might find their way to Earth.

Then again, it might already be dead by the time any of the asteroids from the Kuiper belt got that far.

"How does it work," Merrecci asked, then caught himself before Mirror could say something to correct him. "I mean just the gist."

"We shrink the shields as close to the hull as possible without exposing it to too much shield slap," Mirror replied.

"Shield slap," Merrecci asked.

"Yes, shield slap," Dawn blurted.

"Then we suddenly expand them like a balloon while flooding the inside with repulsor particles," Mirror continued explaining as if she'd never been interrupted. "Should give everything within the reach of our shields a nice shove away from us."

"Sir," Bria added, "You should know to do this will mean rotating the frequency of our shields so that it gives them a bit of spongier effect, for lack of better term.

"Springy shields," Merrecci asked. "How is that possible?"

Bria pointed to Dawn, Mirror, and Mike.

"The problem is, while they'll act like a springboard to the asteroids, they'll still take damage from them, and they might not be great at stopping enemy projectiles from bouncing in and smacking the hull," Mirror explained. "Thus, creating shield slap."

"What is shield slap," Merrecci asked again.

"It's when the shields smack the hull of the ship," Bria explained.

"I've never heard of that before."

"Because no one's ever had springy shields before," Dawn quipped.

"How much damage could we take from asteroids during this whole thing," Merrecci asked. "It sounds like it's still damage to shields. Could we lose them?"

"Don't know. It's possible, we could knock our shields out completely on our first attempt," Mirror answered.

"So basically," Merrecci said, "We'd be blowing up a balloon within an asteroid field and whatever debris gets hit goes flying outwards? And we pray the balloon doesn't pop?"

"Duh," Dawn said. "That's what she just said."

"How do we aim the asteroids," Merrecci asked.

"You ever hear of someone aiming an asteroid," Dawn ridiculed. "Be happy we can make the shields spongy."

"We'll want to execute the action inside clusters of asteroids that would give us more projectile coverage," Bria suggested. "And it helps to allow their fleet to get closer than we'd like them to be."

"Fair enough," Merrecci acknowledged. "When will you have it ready."

"We've been ready for forever, but you never shut up," Dawn chided.

"We were going to test it, but then Master Cha hailed us," Bria explained.

"Battle grid," the admiral ordered.

The hologram of the Onyx and too many dots of ships and asteroids to tell them apart appeared."

"What happened," Merrecci asked. "They had twenty ships, I thought, before I blacked out."

"They got more. There are thirty-six now, Sir" Bria said, "Sensors still can't tell the difference, but we can see them enough to know what they are."

Merrecci grimaced. "This would be a lot easier if they'd stop being so difficult."

Then Bria's wristband chirped, she opened her hand to receive her holotab into it.

"Cha is hailing us again, Sir," she said.

Merrecci leaned forward in his chair.

"On the wall this time," Merrecci ordered.

The wall remained blank.

"Sorry," Bria said, fumbled a moment and lightly swore.

"The academy still teaches your kind of people about professionalism," Merrecci said.

"Sorry," Bria said. "Just getting used to where everything is still. Got it!"

Master Cha's head appeared on the wall.

"What the," Merrecci cried, standing from his seat. "You again? Oh my god! I thought we were leaving this channel open for people who were important."

Merrecci flounced back in his seat.

"Why didn't anyone tell me it was this buffoon again," Merrecci exclaimed, putting on a show of asking about the bridge. "Look. I'm sorry, Mister Chi. I don't have time to talk to you. I'm about to blow your fleet up." He leaned forward. "Or are you surrendering?"

"Let's drop the façade Admi—

"End communication," Merrecci ordered.

Cha's head disappeared from the wall.

Merrecci stepped towards the battlecron to investigate the holographic asteroid field hovering above it, in which the Onyx and its enemy fleet skirted.

"You sure you can do this," Merrecci asked.

"Why else would we suggest it," Dawn replied.

"Yes," Drinker responded.

"Leonard," Merrecci ordered. "Do it."

"Initiating," Bria said from her console.

The battleground hologram burst with a spherical explosion of asteroids from around the Onyx's position. Space debris sped away in all directions.

Moments later, the ship began to sway and toss. It pinged with electrical vibration and lasted long enough that Merrecci's arms grew tired of anchoring himself to the central railing. For a moment, he felt the artificial gravity waver.

"What was that," Merrecci asked, but doubted that, even if his speech was clear, anyone could hear him.

"Standby," Bria replied hotly, and Merrecci allowed it, fully understanding that she was the only reason the shields hadn't let the Onyx die yet.

Suddenly the ship bounced. Merrecci's feet left the floor, and he barely managed to clasp the railing to keep himself from falling away.

Pablo, however, fell from his seat. Allen gripped the pilot's controls, trying to maintain some sort of flight path. He did not fall from his chair.

Finally, the shaking stopped.

"Are our shields gone," Merrecci asked.

"Not so bad actually, considering," Bria said.

"What was that?"

"The first bout was shield slap from asteroids, Sir," Bria said. "The second bout was shield slap from exploding ships. I didn't expect there to be so much."

"How many enemy ships are left?"

"They have twelve."

"Master Cha's?"

"Survived, but low on power."

"He's hailing again," Bria informed.

"Put that master Putz on the holo this time."

Merrecci didn't really want it on the holo, but realized Bria needed the practice managing the communications.

Master Cha's head appeared. Electrical sparks fell in waterfalls behind him, and Merrecci leaned in.

"About that surrender," Merrecci said.

Master Cha made a gesture and groaned, which made it unclear what his intentions were. Although he did sound like he was requesting Onyx to lower its shields and prepare to be boarded.

"All right," Merrecci said. "Let's see what you say after another volley."

Merrecci ended the transmission once more.

"Diagnostics are at fifty-one percent," Onyx announced.

Now, the doors to the bridge swung open and revealed the familiar face of the spitfire security officer that Merrecci had recruited from Admiral Shade's staff the day he received the Onyx. Lieutenant Almma, wearing her new ship-specific uniform, stormed onto the bridge.

"One you all owes me silicone," she roared.

"Excuse me," Merrecci meant to roar, but found himself so elated to have another experienced officer on his bridge that he greeted her instead. "Glad you could join us, Lieutenant."

"Well, there'd be a lot more of me, but whoever's throwing this ship around just ripped my good ta-ta out," Almma greeted bemused and frustrated.

"That'll be enough of that, Lieutenant," Merrecci asked.

"I just went skidding down a hall made of shag carpet, and it wasn't on my ass," she shouted. "Someone's fixing these."

She abruptly stopped and adjusted her chest, which appeared no different than when Merrecci had first encountered her. Then she took in a breath and said, "Lieutenant Almma reporting for duty, Sir."

As she passed Escobedo's chair on her way to Merrecci's, she suddenly found herself stopped as Onyx's current navigator immediately stood into her path.

"Hi, I'm Pablo Escobedo," Pablo welcomed holding his hand out to shake Almma's. "I'm sorry about your boobs."

Almma hesitantly reached back to shake Pablo's hand, but he suddenly grabbed her left breast. He recoiled and buried his face behind his palms and fingers while apologizing profusely.

"To be fair, I can't say that hasn't worked before," Almma informed. She turned to Merrecci with a bewildered look meant to ask, "What the hell is this?"

Merrecci apologized to Almma and began scolding Pablo.

"He can't help it, Sir," Bria stated.

"And yet, I've still had worse," Almma said.

"Are there any others with you?" Merrecci asked, and he wondered how long until someone could replace Pablo.

"I don't know about any others," Almma replied. "Admiral Shade ordered me to a shuttle as soon as the attacks started. You know they had made me a farewell cake before this all started."

"Lieutenant!"

"I came alone," Almma continued. "We wanted Shade to come along, but he said it was safer on Earth. I think he was just annoyed that he couldn't take his sex doll secretary with him."

"Lieutenant," Merrecci scolded again. He made a mental note to speak to Almma about her bridge conduct.

"I arrived just before Earth's shields went up," Almma finished, then quickly added. "You owe me a cake. It was a damned good cake."

"You don't have to swear, you know," Dawn blurted.

"Seriously," Almma asked.

"You don't have to swear," Dawn insisted.

"Where's the pilot." Almma ignored Dawn and honed in on Ensign being, "And you owe me two C-cups!"

Merrecci quickly reprimanded her.

"Sir," Bria announced, "Master Cha's vessel is abandoning ship."

Merrecci turned to Pablo. "Ensign Pablo."

"Ensign Escobedo, Sir," Pablo replied. "Moron!"

Pablo clapped his hands over his mouth and began muttering about how stupid he was.

"Excuse me, Ensign," Merrecci snapped.

"Pablo's my first name," he corrected.

"Understood," Merrecci acknowledged. "I'd like some intel on our enemy actions. Can you lock a tractor beam on an escape pod? Or are tractors online yet, Onyx?"

"Tractor beams are online," Onyx replied.

"Can you bring me an enemy escape pod, Ensign and place it in the closest shuttle bay?"

Pablo shook his head.

"It seems your timing is fortuitous." Merrecci proclaimed to Almma. "Please go to the shuttle bay, recover whatever guest comes out of that life pod, and escort them to the brig until I—Onyx, is the brig operational?"

"The brig will be functional when diagnostics reach seventy-seven percent," Onyx replied.

"Sounds about right," Merrecci said before turning his attention to Almma once again. "Find something to lock him in and Guard him until you hear from me."

"You'll have to bring him to shuttle bay ten," Almma said. "That way I don't have to destroy another door."

"Say that again," Merrecci asked.

"I was locked in the bay," Almma said. "Couldn't even fly out to navigate to another one to see if any other people were in the same shoe. I had to focus my ship's thrusters to burn through the door to access the halls. That's not as easy as it sounds."

"Are you serious," Merrecci asked.

"Hey, I tried transmitting to the bridge, but no one answered," Almma said.

"But can you communicate with other shuttles that may also be trapped in shuttle bays," Bria asked. "We can't communicate with anyone else."

"Of course," Almma said. "That's exactly why I had to burn a hole through the door because I was able to speak with all the ship captains in space, and every one of those dipshits suggested I burn a hole in the doors."

"You don't have to be mean," Bria said directly.

Almma stiffened, then answered. "No, I haven't been able to communicate with anyone since I got here, well, except for the ship's A.I., and she sounds like an expensive prostitute—not the kind that is expensive, the kind that thinks she is."

"That's sounds about par for now," Merrecci said. Then he was about to excuse her to fulfill the duty he had just asked her to a moment ago.

"Can I go with her," Pablo Escobedo asked.

"Aren't you supposed to be catching me an enemy lifepod," Merrecci replied.

"Oh, right," Escobedo replied. A few moments later, he came back with. "Got one. Reeling it in now."

With that, Almma was only now taken aback as she visually scanned the bridge and its crew. Her brow crumpled.

"Today, Lieutenant," Merrecci said.

"Yes, Captain," Almma replied.

"It's admiral, Lieutenant."

Again, she was taken aback. "Oh, good lord! This is going to be all sorts of fun, isn't it?" Then she turned and exited, all while muttering something about how the pilot better hope she comes back with the same ass.

No sooner had she exited then Merrecci called after her to send any crew members that she might come across to him, but the port had already swung shut behind Almma.

"Sir," Bria said. "The enemy fleet is regrouping.

Merrecci watched the battle holo. The attacking ships began to cluster on the port side of the Onyx.

"Ensign Being, can you take us to a denser cluster of asteroids," the admiral asked.

"Of course, I can," Allen Being replied.

"Remember who you're speaking to, Ensign, this is Earth's flagship," Merrecci corrected. "Members of fleet can spend their entire lives working to sit in that chair. You shouldn't even be here."

"Sorry, Admiral," Allen replied, but Merrecci could tell that this was Ensign Being just being formal too.

Now, Merrecci noticed a strange silence in the ship. He felt the Onyx should still be shaking from enemy fire.

"Commander Leonard, what is the status of our shields," Merrecci asked.

"Eighty-two and still rising," Bria replied.

"Can we do that maneuver again? Find another cluster of asteroids?"

"It's hard to say, Sir," Bria replied. "Like I said, it depends on the havoc the asteroids wreak on our shields. Based on how that last execution went, I think so."

The disquiet was bothering him now.

"K, why aren't they firing at us?"

"They have been, Sir," Bria said. She nodded to Allen. "They don't send apocalypses anymore since we've shown we can trick them. They haven't learned their smaller torpedoes don't take much for us to recover from."

"That was not my experience on the Viridian," Merrecci said.

"Sir, with respect," Bria said. "I'm glad we're not on the Viridian. We'd be dead."

"You underestimate its crew."

"No, Sir, I don't."

Onyx informed the admiral that diagnostic had reached fifty-two percent.

Again, the holo showed a swarm of asteroids cluster around the Onyx.

Bria informed that the enemy fleet had stopped firing. Ensign Being announced that he was holding position.

"All right," Merrecci said. "If they get too close, we'll do it again."

Merrecci used this moment of waiting as opportunity to absorb more of his new environment.

Admiral shade had known him well enough to prepare the bridge to Merrecci's typical design. This command center was larger, had more consoles than the Viridian. His chair sat on a mound that reminded him of his days pitching baseball in youth up until he graduated the academy. It was an exaggerated bit of a hill, but it was home. When the chair wasn't needed, it disappeared to leave a mound of dirt. On slow days, Merrecci would often throw a few balls across the bridge and into a net that would appear to catch them.

This was the adaptive reflux technology of the bridge which allowed its egg-shaped confines to change its interior design according to whichever captain was in charge. It wasn't hologram. It was actual reflux material. Before his captain's zone sat the holographic battlecron. Many captains hated the holograph, it could prove distracting, particularly to new crew members. He knew of captains who laid out their consoles so their operators couldn't view the projection. Merrecci didn't do that.

In his early command years, he had been like those types of ship commanders. There were times when he had seen images on the battlecron that frightened even himself. He had thought in these younger days that allowing his bridge crew to see some of these images might dishearten or demoralize them. So, he designed his bridge to prevent his staff from seeing what he saw. He kept it that way until the day he was in communication with an alien race that lacked vocal cords. It instead had learned how to use the resonance of its own bile during self-induced regurgitation to make sounds which ship translators throughout the galaxy could understand. These aliens spent the bile from their stomachs into a tank, and a tube fed it back to them through their noses so they wouldn't run out of communication fuel.

During Merrecci's conversation with one of these aliens, an Earth Franchise ensign stood, turned to the hologram, and swore at the ghastly picture. The creature took offense, and Merrecci spent several days apologizing to it with gifts and empty promises. Eventually, the race invited him onboard to feast upon their rekindled friendship. The food was vile, and they purposely served it to observe Merrecci's genuine reaction. He'd never eat it again, but the alien race would never know that he had not only found it disgusting but had also spent the next 48 hours married to his toilet.

This was when Merrecci had decided that if his bridge crew members had been more accustomed to watching the battlecron, they wouldn't be as likely to react badly to the potentially horrific sights it could present. He decided bridge crew should be accustomed to the images if they were to perform to their best no matter what danger they were facing.

Now, his consoles all looked upon the holographic center in a baseball stadium structure. To his left were stations devoted to ship operations and defense. He was used to having six as that's what the Viridian had. On the Onyx, there were fourteen.

To his right was his first officer's station. It resembled a curved dugout that carved into the floor and was filled with easily accessible consoles. Although it was nostalgic to Merrecci, it actually set up his second-in-command to quickly take control of the ship or any post on the bridge should the need arise.

The roof of the dugout was designed to be an observation area for his tactical supervisor, this would be Almma's post during her shifts. From here, particularly during battle, she would be able to observe all aspects of the bridge. This station was designed to allow the tactical officer to oversee all operator consoles so that it could quickly coordinate with the defensive section during intense circumstances. The tactical post was typically not for an apologetic officer, especially when they needed to take over a slow-performing crew member's control panel.

Climbing above the tactical supervisor's station were bleacher-like consoles, twelve in all. They peered down, upon the battlecron, which was set where second base should be. Unlike the defensive side of the bridge, these consoles were all translucent. She could look up and see every weapon operator's face, look down to the operations and defensive side of the bridge and see each crew member there too. She could see the battlecron and the admiral. Directly beneath her feet, a clear floor doubled as the ceiling to the first officer's dugout. As far as perspective went, Almma would have no blind spots. She could control all weapons, calibrations and even self-destruct capabilities. With no one to currently helm them, they sat empty.

From the captain's mound, Merrecci saw less, and he liked it this way. For him, it was more important to cut out the noise. While seeing everyone's faces constantly was necessary to his senior staff, they could be a distraction when Merrecci had to make the tough decisions. The last thing he needed during these moments were second thoughts that frightened countenances could stir.

What mattered was that he could see his coaches: the tactical officer, the first officer, the pilot, and that they could report back to him. He did however, set the command chair on his pitcher's mound to face the outfield and the entry ports leading onto the bridge at all times. He was always aware of anyone entering his domain so he would know exactly which personnel strengths he was working with as they entered or left his bridge. There were only two doors, one to the main ship, the other to a variety of senior staff amenities, including the ready room and offices.

Between these two exits, was the bare and monstrous space where he could choose to project two-dimensional pictures. When it didn't have alien faces speaking on it, he'd just rotate images of a historical baseball stadium outfields over it. In fact, the illusion covered every inch of the bridge's encapsulating walls, including the skies and the weather they held. He could watch archival games or even participate in them. Currently, it was Fenway Park as it looked on the day it first opened to the public in 1912. Sometimes, if he didn't have a real ball in his hand, he'd throw an imaginary pitch or stand on home plate and swing an invisible bat and the ship's computer might simulate a slider or a long drive onto the screen of where it would have gone. For the Fenway skin, it usually went into the mitt of a Red Sox player, running around somewhere on his walls. He had really come to dislike Tris Speaker over the years. He caught everything. Of course, that was when he was on the Viridian. He wondered how the Onyx would present the players now.

Besides outfields, Merrecci liked to used the wall to aid in communication. As any individual appearing in the hologram faced the command chair, they were not aware of the messages that Merrecci and his crew could exchange with each other on the scoreboards or batter's eye looming on whatever stadium's outfield wall was currently appearing at the time.

Few people recognized the appearance of the many baseball fields the bridge presented, as their modern structures were unrecognizable according to the early stadium standards. Now, these arenas were more of tourist destinations. The Atlantic series took place in the Mariana Trench. The world series was in orbit aboard the International Space Station. Even other worlds had gotten into the game. Today, Fenway was a mobile, intergalactic stadium that could hold twenty million spectators. It ran stealthed until it revealed the location where the Interstellar Series would be held every Earth year because it was their game, despite what those thieving Vascou said. Although Merrecci couldn't have possibly known it, it was to take place in Saturn's orbit this year in celebration of Ross Barnes.

"All right," Merrecci finally said. "Despite what we can't do, we need to get this ship to Mabbis, and we can't really do that at this speed nor with Cha's fleet watching us. We need them to look away so we can hide until our diagnostics finish. We need our Nessla drive. We know there have to be other people on this ship, most likely behind doors they can't get through. I need a runner."

Willis smiled and stepped forward.

"That works," Merrecci said. He took a black remote from his command console and held it to Willis.

"Go knock on doors. If any pound back, push this so the head turns green, and we'll know where to find help later," Merrecci instructed.

Willis jaunted off the bridge after a little celebration skip that seemed to be asking, "Really? Can I?"

"Sir," Bria asked. "I don't know much about how it works, but I think he's color blind. Will that be an issue?"

"Oh, for damn," Merrecci shouted. "Did I not say to remind me of these things before he goes?" He started clapping his hands. "K, priority! We need a navigator."

"Sir," Pablo said. "I can navigate." He suddenly popped his lips. "I'm good at math."

Merrecci swallowed his instinct to dismiss the absurd notion, but then realized that was what he had to work with at the moment.

"Oh, for hell! Fine. Plot a course, but if you crash us, you're a dead man."

"Aye-aye, Sir," Pablo said.

"Admiral," Bria chimed in.

Merrecci listened. Her voice had become the only thing he found reliable since they disembarked. Even Onyx wasn't capable of that right now. So, he gave her his attention.

"The enemy fleet is taking formation behind the chub and entering the asteroid field," Bria said.

"Well, why would they do that?" Merrecci made a quick observation of the battle map and watched the enemy fleet ships fall in line behind the chub as it drew towards the Onyx.

"They're using our tactic against us," Drinker announced, his face fixated on the hologram. "The chub's moving to throw asteroids back at us."

"Probably hoping once our shields fall, his fleet can spread out again and open fire," Bria added.

"Pretty sure the chub's hull can take it," Pablo asked.

Of course, they could take it. Everyone knew that. This was one of the first enemy ships anyone learned about in the academy. Merrecci wanted to yell it, but, for some reason, Shade's words rang in his ears not to lose this crew. Whether he liked it or not, right now, this was his crew.

"Their hulls can take it," Merrecci said. "These little things won't even phase them."

"I mean the larger asteroids," Drinker said. "Can their hulls handle striking one of those?"

"Well, unfortunately, this chub captain will be smart enough not to hit those," Merrecci said. "And I doubt we can trick them into thinking they can."

"I have an idea, Admiral Material," Drinker said. "I don't know if it'll work, but I material it could. I really don't know. Most people are better at this material of thing than I am. You could probably do this." Suddenly Drinker looked horrified. "Not that I'm saying you're too dumb to material it out, I'm just saying that anyone could do it better than I cou—

"What's your idea," Merrecci interrupted, trying to be polite.

The ship shook, then clamored several more times as it was obvious the same object continued to roll across its shield until it passed over the Onyx entirely.

"That was an asteroid," Merrecci realized. "They did it."

The ship shook again. Then more.

"That doesn't seem right," Merrecci said.

The Onyx filled with a deafening series of clangs. Merrecci didn't fall, but the floor did shift under his feet. His migraine reminded him it wasn't completely gone. Pinging sounds of stress lingered throughout the bridge and well into its bones.

"Was that shield slap," he asked. "What the hell was that?"

"Oh, just an asteroid half our size knocking us into an asteroid twice our size," Bria announced. "Hold on! Not done yet."

"Our hull, what's the damage?"

"No damage," Bria said.

"Good!"

"For now."

The ship got hit again.

According to Onyx, diagnostics reached fifty-three percent.

"I don't care what we do, just keep asteroids between us and them," Merrecci said. "Use them as shields if we can."

"Suggest, hiding behind one of the dwarf planets, Sir," Bria said. "Without their tractor beam, they can't use it against us, and it should cut off their line of sight to throw more debris our way."

"Ours too," Merrecci pointed out.

"Yeah, but we can just keep flying around until our diagnostics are done," Allen said.

"Maybe we can drop a few more armed probes and take out a few more ships even," Bria added.

"No," Merrecci said. "I want to avoid landing parties. We don't have any fighters."

"So, we just run," Bria asked.

"I'm okay with that right now," Merrecci said. "We already know we can't outrun them in open space, but they can't maneuver as well as we can here. If they pop in too close, we'll do the shield thing again. At least until they gather more reinforcements."

He turned his attention back to Drinker who was now speaking with Dawn, Mike, and Mirror.

"Getting back to your plan," Merrecci asked. "What is it?"

"We can't do it from here," Dawn snapped. "So, it's dumb."

"It's not dumb," Mirror complained. "Don't be a dunce."

"Enough," Merrecci ordered, then caught himself again. "What can't you do from here?"

Drinker approached the captain. "Iceteroids, Sir."

"What about them?"

"The material doesn't have shields," Drinker said as if the admiral should know the answer already. "Their hull is exposed."

"Okay, and," Merrecci asked.

"We hit them with an iceteroid."

"It won't phase them," Merrecci said. "Notice how they're smashing through them."

This time, Merrecci felt he was ready for the jostle that the Onyx just let out.

"Their material is made of oilamene," Drinker said when the ship finally settled.

Merrecci still didn't understand.

"It's in an amorphous state, like glass, neither liquid nor solid," Mirror explained.

"God! How dumb are you," Dawn said.

"Hey," Merrecci snapped. "Not on my ship, you don't."

"I'm gonna kick your—

"Come on then," Merrecci retorted. He took a stance and snapped his baton at the ready. "Get to kicking."

Dawn sheepishly apologized.

Again, Merrecci turned his attention to Drinker.

"Let them material us through the field," Drinker said. "We find some iceteroids, material them at the chub, freeze their material, then bubble one of the bigger materials to smack the chub. We'd have to line it up right, but it could crack their material so they won't dare coming after us anymore. The rest of his fleet should stop once they don't material the chub to protect those ships in here."

Merrecci's brain took a moment to translate Drinker's words.

"Lure them into the field? Freeze their hull with iceteroids, then crack it open with a big asteroid," Merrecci asked.

Drinker agreed that Merrecci had gotten it right.

"And you can do that," Merrecci asked, turning to Bria.

"A big asteroid," Bria asked. "We'd need someone physically in engineering to manipulate those shields better than we can in here."

Now, Merrecci turned to Dawn, Mirror, and Drinker. "You could do this from engineering?"

"Duh," Dawn replied. "You could do it from engineering."

"I mean, are you capable of doing it," Merrecci asked.

"Derr, I don't know. We're kind of retarded, you know," Dawn snipped.

"Be nice," Mirror replied.

"They have the skills," Drinker said. "But, like I said, I'm not a material. I just tend to see things most material don't. But they could." Drinker pointed to Dawn, Mirror and Mike.

"You keep saying that," Merrecci said, gesturing to Mike. "But he thinks he's a dog!"

Mike growled again.

"You don't even know him," Dawn snipped.

"All right," Merrecci relented. "Don't have much choice but to trust you. You three make it work, and I'll let you pick the next month of movie nights. Until you're ready, we'll keep circling a dwarf planet and trying not to get hit by an asteroid in the process."

Dawn, Mirror, and Mike walked out of the bridge, two of them arguing about what movies they'd pick. The other barked and heeled alongside Dawn. With them off the bridge, Bria took to one of the consoles in the dugout.

Onyx reached Fifty-four percent.

They drew close to a dwarf planet. Merrecci didn't care which, didn't bother asking, just wanted enough distance to let his shields work and also to keep the Onyx from being pulled in by the mass's gravitational pull.

Here, Merrecci asked Ensign Being to maintain the orbit.

"Okay, okay," Merrecci said, a method he used to assure himself as much as his crew. "Not bad everyone. Nice job, considering."

"Considering, Sir," Pablo asked.

"Considering he thinks were idiots," Being replied.

"I never said that," Merrecci said, thinking diplomatically on his feet. Which somehow intimidated him here. He'd faced generals, galaxial leaders, but they'd never faced battle with him on his own bridge. "I'm just being honest. I doubt any of us appreciate being thrown into this and would have liked having someone with more experience for you to shadow."

"It's okay, Sir," Bria said. "We know what people think of us."

"Don't clump me in with those people," Merrecci said.

"With respect," Bria replied. "You are."

Merrecci prepared a sting of his own to fire back at the hideous girl, but a faceless head appeared within the battlecron.

"Sir," Bria replied, refocused on her temporary bridge duties. "Distress signal, it's coming in from a relay, Sir."

"Let's have it," Merrecci said.

"It's an encrypted channel. I need a moment."

"Well let's not hurry, Lieutenant-commander, I'm sure whoever's sending it will appreciate waiting on you," Merrecci said.

"Which would you like me to de-prioritize first, Sir: attention to shield, acting first-officer, or communication duties," Bria asked before adding on another, "Sir?"

"Let's try not to lose any of them," Merrecci said, subtly conceding.

"I'll do my best," Bria replied, and Merrecci considered that she probably was.

A few moments later, the holographic head took shape of a younger officer wearing the insignia of a captain.

"This is Captain Fiji reaching out on behalf of the Mabbis space station, calling any Earth Franchise ship that will hear us. We have been attacked unprovoked and are struggling to open communication. We request immediate fleet support," the head then began to repeat the message.

"Sir, it's incoming," Bria said.

"So maybe we can respond," Merrecci asked.

Bria nodded the same belief.

"This is—," Merrecci started.

The Onyx interrupted with, "Return long-distance transmission will be ready when diag—

The Onyx stammered, Merrecci stumbled to the side, tried to catch himself and fell, then slid over the fake grass and dirt floor.

When he stood, he found Bria fumbling to sit up, clearly dazed. Drinker was helping Pablo back to his chair.

"That was dirty," Being said, he held his position in his seat, but his head bled. "Now I'm mad."

"You got us, Ensign," Merrecci asked.

"Yes, Sir," Being said. "We can't stay here like we thought. That chub is ramming our aft!"

"How the hell is it doing that?"

"It's burst jumping into us."

The Onyx threw Merrecci again, but Being somehow remained as grounded as steel in his seat, unwilling to be thrown out.

"Do what you need to do to keep that from happening again," Merrecci ordered.

Being acknowledged, and the ship shook again. Merrecci climbed to his knees once more.

"Sir," Bria called. "I—

She was trying to pull herself back up to her station. Somehow, she had fallen outside of the dugout. Her mouth was bleeding, she'd left teeth on the floor in drizzled salute to the ancient, bloody artist Jackson Pollock. Drinker himself was regaining his own focus, saw Bria and was trying to reach her in the process.

Merrecci reached lieutenant-commander Leonard first.

Bria apologized, and blood spilled and blew from her broken gums as she focused on retrieving her teeth from the floor.

Merrecci tried to help prop her against the battlecron's railing so he could get her to relax, but she instead used him as leverage to crawl up his arm and begin enlisting it as a crutch so she could return to her post in the dugout.

"I'b shorry, shir," Bria repeated. Her voice shifted under strained glassy eyes and blood she swallowed. "Wode happed agaid."

"You need medical attention," Merrecci said. "Let me take over."

By now, Drinker was to Bria's side as well and helping Merrecci aid Bria to a seat in the dugout.

"Shieldsh are fading," Bria replied, unable to get her missing teeth to bite her bottom lip. "You need be."

"Onyx," Merrecci called. "Does bridge have full manipulation control?"

"Bridge has full manipulation control," Onyx replied.

"I don't want Lieutenant-commander Leonard falling out of her chair again," Merrecci said.

"Acknowledged," Onyx replied. She then followed up with the announcement that diagnostics had reached fifty-five percent.

Suddenly Drinker seemed deeply interested in something that appeared on Bria's screen.

"What is that material there," he asked Bria.

She glared at him.

"You're not shupposed to be in here," she said.

Merrecci repeated the direction.

"But what is that," Drinker asked.

"Anchors," she said, and although Drinker seemed to be oblivious, Merrecci was not.

"Go get the doctor, Drinker," Merrecci instructed.

"I think I have another idea," Drinker said. "Onyx, what is the material system?"

"Ship systems do not recognize unauthorized person," Onyx replied.

"I've never heard of a ship in material that ever tossed anchor," Drinker replied.

"Right now, she's important, the anchor is not," Merrecci said, pointing to Bria.

"You think I don't know that, Admiral," Drinker lashed out. "I've known her longer. I just want to know what the anchor is."

"Onyx, what is the purpose of the anchor," Merrecci asked. He couldn't help feel somewhat ashamed that he wasn't sure what it was himself. Had Earth not been attacked. He may very well be studying that part of the ship operations right now.

"The space anchor allows the ship to attach itself to larger objects in the event of astral storms," Onyx explained.

"How," Drinker asked.

"Ship systems do not recognize unauthorized person," Onyx replied.

"How does it attach," Merrecci asked.

"It uses deep tractor technology."

"I'm not familiar with that," Merrecci said. "What does it do."

Onyx began a long tirade of explaining how chains of micro black holes and light could lock deep into solid matter. The gist was that a tractor beam relies on light to pull an object towards the source of the tractor beam. Its weakness is that it can't permeate an outer layer of an object such as a ship, it can only wrap around the exterior of the object. Deep anchor found a way to permeate the interior to give the Onyx the ability to hold fast to something larger that could withstand space turbulence.

Drinker had another idea. Once Bria helped Merrecci understand the gist of it, the admiral quickly began trying to contact engineering to see if his two unqualified ensigns and their dog had arrived at their posts yet. In that thought, he suddenly wondered if these three could even find the engineering bay.

"Geez, give us time to move in," Dawn's voice returned after three minutes of Merrecci attempting to get through.

Once Merrecci relayed Drinker's idea to them, Dawn quickly replied that the plan was too easy. The moment they said they could make it work, Merrecci ordered Drinker to retrieve the new doctor and Prilla to aid Bria.

The battlecron flashed with an incoming message. A head blank, awaiting for its communication to be accepted, appeared once more in the center of the battlecron and its railing.

Merrecci nodded, and Bria put the signal through. The head blank transformed into Master Cha's face.

"Master Cha," Merrecci greeted. "If you tell me where your escape pod is, I can offer assistance and shelter."

Cha's face stiffened at Merrecci's insult.

"Admiral Merrecci," Cha said coolly and scripted. "I have taken command of this chub, and I will use it to bash your ship apart at the seams if that's what it takes for you to lower your shields and grant me access to your bridge. We are faster, bulkier, and more capable than you than your insufficient freight carrier. We will overcome."

"And yet," Merrecci said. "What happened to your previous ship, Master Cha?"

Cha's lips curled and his eyes glittered in annoyance. He turned his head inward. "On my mark prepare to—

Merrecci ended the transmission on his own.

"Lieutenant Leonard, what is the status of our shields," Merrecci asked.

"A hundred, shir," she replied, and her tone betrayed her strength against her injury. In fact, he thought her speech was getting a little thicker.

Merrecci summoned his seat.

"Ensign Being," he said. "Can you pull off Drinker's idea?"

"Sir," Being asked.

"Stupid," Pablo screeched.

"Can you do it," Merrecci asked.

Ensign Being nodded, "I can do something to that effect."

"Do it," Merrecci ordered.

Merrecci's weight shifted angrily around in his seat as the Onyx suddenly twisted closer in towards the dwarf planet. The chub gave chase.

"Not too fast, Ensign," Merrecci said. "We don't want him to see what we're doing. Let him think he's beating us down until it's too late for him."

Ensign Being acknowledge with a subtle course change.

Merrecci then watched Bria slide around behind her dugout console, but never falling out as her seat moved in ways to counter her balance and keep her safely in front of her control station.

The battlecron showed the chub gain on the Onyx. The chub's twelve allies began to spread themselves into a position to open fire the moment the chub struck.

Merrecci gruffed out a single, "Now!"

In the holo, the pyramid-shaped Onyx rolled alongside the chub.

"Idishiading aggors," Bria said.

"Huh," Merrecci asked, then, "Oh yeah, anchors, got it."

The entire Onyx shook as its holographic image suddenly snapped its port side to the hull of the chub.

"Push him in," Merrecci said, and he watched the holographic Onyx engines burn, pushing the chub closer to the dwarf planet.

The Onyx rattled in such a way that should have made every coupling, brace and pin throw up their hands and say, "I don't get paid enough for this," but instead they said, "Push this mother down!"

Merrecci's brain, however, began arguing with his moral fiber about needing a raise if the Admiral wanted it to stick around. The migraine was beginning to concur and complained the loudest about its working conditions.

The battlecron showed the chub's engines burning harder to break away from the gravity of the dwarf planet, but Merrecci knew it wouldn't be enough.

A head blank appeared once more in the holo-channel. Cha's facial features remained indistinguishable until Merrecci allowed the transmission through.

"I expected more from you," Cha sneered. "You have secured our victory for us. Our ship can survive the fall."

"You mean that ship that requires zero gravity to be built in," Merrecci answered.

The realization of Merrecci's maneuver manifested across his face now.

"You can't," Cha screamed.

"They're caught in the gravity, Sir," Ensign Being said.

"Detach," Merrecci instructed.

Cha was suddenly issuing his own orders that his fleet pilots turn their tractor beams on his chub to slow its fall rate or to attempt to pull it from the dwarf planet's gravity well. The chaos that emerged around Cha's holographic head told Merrecci that Drinker's plan was working.

"Well played barbarian captain," Cha said coolly, then he smiled. "Watch for me again."

Merrecci did not return the smile but said. "That's barbarian admiral."

He ended the transmission.

"How are our shields," Merrecci asked throughout his bridge.

"Shebdy Berzed," Bria answered carefully through thickening gums and a fattening mouth.

"Have all his fleet locked tractors onto the chub?"

"Yeah," Bria said, and the words that followed had slurred beyond comprehension from the swelling that continued to set into her face.

"Then go, Being! Find us a place to disappear," Merrecci ordered. The Onyx twisted and left Master Cha behind.

"I'll be damned," Merrecci said as he watched the gap between the Onyx and Cha's fleet grow. For extra measure, he had the shields balloon once more to throw out another smattering of asteroids that should complicate the maneuver Cha was attempting to—

"Diagnostics have reached fifty-six percent," Onyx said. "Full inner-ship communication is now online."

"Attention, Onyx crew," a man's voice stated before Merrecci could initiate his own announcement throughout the halls. A head filled the battlecron. "This is Acting-commander Lieutenant Dan. I am taking command of this vessel. As you are aware by now, we have been trapped on our own ship—

"What the hell is this," Merrecci asked, confused.

"He busht ting he'sh da highesht ragging ovidal affder da addack," Bria said and suddenly found herself crying from forcing out the F-sound through her broken front gums. Merrecci ordered her not to speak until after the doctor could see her.

Lieutenant Dan went on about calling all able-bodied officers to arm themselves and reclaim the bridge from invading forces.

"Have you found somewhere for us to hide, Pab—Escobedo," Merrecci asked.

"Yes," Pablo acknowledged. He made a rude hand flick towards Merrecci. "We can disappear entirely if we get there and power down until diagnostics can run, I think."

"Plot your course, Ensign Escobedo," Merrecci said, fighting the impulse to chastise him for his involutary action. "Get us moving, Ensign Being."

Then Merrecci turned his attention to Lieutenant Dan's holographic head that was still addressing the crew on mute.

"Enough of this," Merrecci said making a few adjustments at his control panel in his command chair. The head disappeared from the hologram. "This is Admiral Vincenti Merrecci, commanding officer of the Onyx. The first unauthorized crewmember who storms my bridge is going to leave with his weapon holstered in a place it was never designed to be."

He took a moment to catch his breath and put his insult from Lieutenant Dan to the side.

"Protocol would be that your captain would ceremoniously greet you prior to our maiden voyage," Merrecci said. "But our maiden voyage is currently under attack. All crew members are therefore ordered to report to your current assigned stations to await further instruction. That is all." Merrecci immediately followed up with contacting Almma and ordering her to locate Lieutenant Dan so she could escort him to the brig.

"Be a cold day before someone takes another ship from me," Merrecci grumbled to himself, then he yelled. "A cold day!"

Hopefully, Merrecci had done enough to allow the Onyx to escape and allow him to find the sanity his bridge should actually have operating it.

6
▲
Orders

Merrecci fell into his seat in his ready room, the black desk before him automatically lit up all the tasks that a new ship captain would need to get to know it and his crew. The lights were low so the Onyx would be less visible as it sat nestled in a canyon of a dwarf planet where it was least likely to be struck by any other Kuiper belt debris. Dawn, Mirror, and Mike did the math. They should be safe while the Onyx completed her diagnostics. Until then, their power levels were put into conservation mode wherever possible to hide from sweeping enemy sensors. So far, nothing had passed them.

In the meantime, the admiral felt he could do nothing more productive on the bridge and withdrew to his ready room. He left orders to call him out at the first question of danger.

Merrecci's first task was to awake a screen in his desk. He tried to replay the transmission he had received from Prime Admiral Shade while back in Earth's orbit. When it repeated the same low-quality, he started it into a defragmentation process to see if that would help any.

While the defragmentation was running, he scanned his unread messages. There were several that had been titled as priority orders, but they had all been redacted in place of one that read "Orders: Onyx Commanding Officer Clearance Required." He ordered Onyx to lock his ready room door and then began playing the recording.

Admiral Shade's upper torso appeared in a hologram above Merrecci's desk, replacing all his task files that had been there previously.

"Vincenti," Shade greeted. He was still clean. His office was yet to be demolished in any attack on Earth. "If you're reviewing this, then that can only mean that the Earth admirals have gone into lockdown, and I've had to activate the God Contingency."

"That's a stupid name," Merrecci stated as if speaking directly to Admiral Shade himself.

"It is absolutely critical that you carry out your mission and that no one can take the Onyx from you," Shade's recording continued. "Part of the God Contingency is that I and the other Earth Admirals have gone into lockdown and will be unable to communicate without giving away our location. This means we won't be able to monitor your mission nor deter other admirals from interfering with said mission. For this purpose, the admirals have agreed we should promote you to prime admiral."

"Prime admiral," Merrecci erupted. He replayed this portion of the recording several times to ensure he'd heard it correctly. Each time he swore something new. Finally, he punched through the hologram. After barking a few threats at Shade via his recording, he allowed the message to resume.

"That means I have to resign," Shade said. "You probably don't like it."

"How'd you guess," Merrecci yelled.

"But it's the only way to ensure you can't be taken off mission for some other admiral's short-sighted plan," Shade's image explained. "In promoting you and exercising this contingency, I have already had to resign the post of prime admiral. The moment this message finishes, the change in promotions will be official. The activation of this contingency means I have already been put in lockdown and cannot come out until that has been lifted."

"I hope you stay buried in there," Merrecci said.

"It has to be you Vincenti," Shade said. "You're the only one I'd trust to the fight ahead of you, and I don't know what that will be fully. If anyone can face it, it's you. That's why you were selected to command the Onyx."

Merrecci fell back into his chair in a series of huffs that could have easily been four-letter words.

"Obviously, Earth was attacked before your mission could get underway, and I could brief you on it," Shade's recording simply continued.

"Get on with it, you long-winded, inverted fart," Merrecci bellowed.

"I told you we were in the process of peace talks with the Divide Coalition. There are no peace talks. The Viridian, Jade and Crimson were sent on a fact-finding mission in the guise of a diplomatic venture. A great many years back, an Earth vessel discovered a lifeform of unique essence. The franchise tried to learn from her, but it became clear that we were the inferior race. We amused her, and she allowed humans to co-exist with her on our own planet."

"What's that supposed to mean," Merrecci spat just as Shade had already kicked into giving his answer. Merrecci rewound the message to replay what he'd just spoken over.

"She's a god, Vincenti. She has the ability to conceive and birth entire galaxies, at a very high cost. Wherever she gives birth to a new cosmos, it instantaneously consumes all present cosmic matter, including her own. In other words, in giving birth to new space, it annihilates and consumes another galaxy or galaxies, we're not fully sure, and neither is she. All we know is she is believed to be the last of her kind, and she has the power to wipe solar systems from space while birthing new ones in their places.

Suddenly, Merrecci didn't even realize that he was intently listening.

"We kept her existence secret for generations. Neither she nor we were concerned about the absorption of our own galaxy, as it seems that even gods require two to make a baby. At this moment, a suitable male is, at present, God knows where. Forgive the pun.

Shade smiled slightly as if giving Merrecci permission that he could laugh at it.

Merrecci flipped the hologram the bird.

"If this male exists," Shade finally continued. "And should it ever couple with the female, it would be catastrophic for any worlds in their vicinity. In the wrong hands, these two beings could wipe out entire allies. It could erase Earth, its sun and everything in its realm. Maybe even more."

Merrecci found himself propping his elbows against the table and leaning on them, where he faced Shade squarely in his digitally recreated and hollow eyes.

"Several months ago, we received intelligence that the Paichu had recently discovered rumors of a unique life form, a male who matched all description of what her mate should be, someone who had been reported to emanate power, could make himself glow you might say. We suspected that it is a being like the one we have had on Earth. The Viridian, Crimson and Jade, under the guise of diplomacy, were sent to discover intelligence about these rumors and the being's potential whereabouts.

"Turns out, the Divide heard a similar rumor about Earth having our own being, and they played the same game against us. They think we might have her. If Earth still lives, if you're still alive, that means they haven't found her yet. They're not going to destroy us unless they have her, and they can't find her without searching all of Earth first. Which is where you come in. While they're searching for her here, you're directed to hunt down the male out there—and you have to find him before they find her, or I imagine, you won't have a home to come back to."

"So, I get to play hide and seek, while you try to keep the other team from stealing our flag," Merrecci surmised to himself. "I think I got the easier game here."

As if Shade's recording had heard Merrecci, it quickly corrected his observation by saying, "Which is why we put her on your ship."

Merrecci's fist suddenly uppercut right through the hologram, and a geyser of cussings and name-callings, that he wasn't sure if even he had ever heard before sprayed from his lips. It all ended with him shrieking, "With the power from that last brain fart, you must have blown a hole out the back of your damned head!"

Somewhere in all of this, Merrecci realized Shade's hologram was still yammering on.

"Oh, shut up," Merrecci snapped.

"It is very important under no circumstances that you ever let those two get together while on your ship," Shade now explained. "Or you will find yourself the new center of a galaxy and possibly the scientific basis for some future species' religion. With this in mind, we have created the Onyx with two special quarantine sectors to help keep them separated, should you find the male."

The message went on to reiterate the importance of Merrecci's promotion and the need for it. He ignored this part.

When the recording finished, his room's fabricator presented a new uniform with the emitters that could present the prime admiral's tonks. Only out of duty did he take his new shirt and jacket.

Then his ready room clicked to announce someone was at his door. He invited whoever was outside to enter.

"Make it quick," Merrecci responded without looking to see who it was.

Prilla entered, none too happy, but resigned. She had already donned her Faction uniform.

She suddenly stopped.

"This is dad's office," she said. "You kept his design?"

"I guess I did," Merrecci replied. "Shade installed it. Don't know if I would have continued using it myself after losing the Viridian."

"They took the Viridian away from you," Prilla said matter-of-factly. "That was their stupid."

Then she straightened, saluted, and announced, "Commander Prilla Wanship officially reporting for duty, Admiral Merrecci."

"Knock it off," he ordered, without saluting back. "And that's Prime Admiral Merrecci."

"What's that supposed to mean," Prilla asked.

Prime Admiral Merrecci commanded the door to lock once more behind her, and it did.

He replayed Shade's recording, and Prilla remained quiet for several minutes then ordered a Vandark cola from the fabricator. She was halfway through it when she finally took in a breath that Merrecci knew all too well.

"Why do the Merrecci's always get the crap missions," she asked. "The second any of our enemies find out, they're going to send the best after us. It only takes one person from our crew who thinks they can solve the galaxy's problems by sharing a grilled cheese sandwich and a verse of Kumbaya with our enemies that will get all of our throats slit.

Merrecci agreed.

"You think the Maridamirak won't leave their own space if they get word of this," Prilla suddenly realized. "And I wouldn't be surprised if those Kag'tak monsters didn't come out of their hibernation splendor either. Think they could have any subspecies, us or our enemies, wielding this kind of power over them? I'm not going through that again."

"And I only have one-tenth of the crew I'm supposed to have to run this ship minimally," Merrecci said. "If we don't find help, we'll never run optimally."

"Your battle fatigue problem just went through the roof," Prilla acknowledged.

"Not to mention morale issues if we can't fill this crew," Merrecci added.

"Do I have any help," she asked. "No way I can keep up when this begins to take its toll."

"About as much as I have," Merrecci said. "I've found one person so far with a few counseling hours logged. Two who studied enough to act as your morale officers, but I'm still looking."

"Well, you're a prime admiral now. You can pull from anywhere you want to fill your roster."

"Sure, if I can get us somewhere to access more people," Merrecci said. "Which we might be able to do once we reach Mabbis."

Prilla drank from her black glass.

"Have you reached out to any other ships yet?"

"Oh no," Merrecci replied. "Our diagnostics aren't high enough for that yet."

"Of course," Prilla replied and even laughed.

"This wasn't how I'd wanted you to come aboard."

"Well, if it had been any other way, we might not have been here at all."

"I suppose that's one way of looking at it."

"You saved those cadets," Prilla said.

"Cadets? Those aren't cadets," Merrecci stated curtly. "Those are unfinished abortions or, at best, unrefined—

"Call them that again. I dare you," Prilla said, her finger directing Merrecci as a baton commands the silence of an orchestra.

Then, like that, her baton broke as Merrecci snapped his finger back. "You can save that tone for family dinner."

"That is my family," Prilla snipped. "And you of all people should know how fine the decision between having DNA alteration and not having it can be."

He was about to rebuke her again when her finger stabbed at his chest and she burst with, "And that other thing!"

Merrecci was silent now, but he was ready to unleash a tirade at Prilla at the next taunting syllable out of her mouth.

Prilla recollected herself and nodded an acknowledgement that she hadn't forgotten his position on the ship despite her feelings about his ideologies or ignorances. Then she added, "Remember that they saved your life too, Sir."

"I can't operate a bridge with an intellectually deficient crew, Prilla," Merrecci said. "That's not bias. That's just anti-DNA altering fact. They don't have the faculties."

"You don't know that," Prilla said.

"My engineering staff has stopped to take a break so they could watch a game show," Merrecci said.

"They do that," Prilla said.

"I need qualified staff, Prilla," Merrecci said. "This is going to get worse."

"No weapons, no good sensors, no engines, a faulty ship, took out how many ships? In an asteroid field by the way. How much worse do they have to prove to you," Prilla asked. "They've worked so far."

"Those three retards in engineering are watching a game show!"

Prilla's face froze, but she didn't lash back.

"They have Downe's Syndrome, Prime Admiral, and I wouldn't put them down too badly if I were you," Prilla lectured. "Dawn has a photographic memory, by now she knows this ship schematic inside and out better than anyone. Mirror's father was an engineer at Begu. She grew up making rounds and repairs with him."

"And if she'd have been there during the purge, she wouldn't be here now," Merrecci pointed out. "Hardly anyone survived it."

"Yeah," Prilla said. "She's one of the twelve and why there were able to be twelve."

Merrecci suddenly sat up straight in his seat, then leaned forward to pull up her Franchise Academy file.

"I didn't realize that was her," Merrecci said, allowing himself to dig deeper into a holographic folder that now sat atop his desk. "Why isn't that in her file."

"Why do you think," Prilla asked. "If I had a choice between two engineers, I'd choose the only one who was calm enough to help eleven others survive Begu."

"That I can respect," Merrecci said. "But this guy who thinks he's a dog?"

"He's logged more hours than any person in the Franchise in the simulator running no-win scenarios. When he digs in, you can't pull him out."

"And yet, he's a dog," Merrecci said. "And he's watching a gameshow."

"Of course, he is. It's time for their show."

Merrecci rolled his eyes.

"So, schedule their rotations around what they watch," Prilla said. "They have a routine. Figure out how to work with it, and you'll have engineers. I'll send you a schedule."

"Other than maybe Mirror, I don't feel confident in their capacity in the face of battle. When we go to war. There may be no break, and there's definitely no television."

"What good will they do you tucked away, Prime Admiral? Give them a babysitter if you have to. Provide them supervisors or co-workers—and make sure they're not heavy handed—but don't write them off just because you're afraid of their disabilities."

"I'm not—

"Yes, you are," Prilla said. "And for the love of God get the galley to create a menu a month in advance. For some reason it raises their morale."

Merrecci didn't respond this time.

"If you can find a better crew, use them instead. At least give them a chance to show what they can do until you don't have a staffing shortage."

A knock came to the door. Merrecci unlocked it once more and threw out a quick invitation. Bria entered this time. Mike came bounding in from behind and jumped up the side of Merrecci's chair and began licking at his face.

"Get down," Merrecci ordered. "That's disgusting!"

Mike withdrew and laid down to the side of Merrecci's chair.

"I think this is an excellent time to get to know your crew better," Prilla said. She offered to continue their conversation later.

"Will you take this idiot with you," Merrecci called after Prilla, but she declined. Reluctantly, Merrecci dismissed her and rose to his feet as she exited.

"How are your injuries," Merrecci asked, greeting Bria not just with respect for what she'd accomplished since leaving Earth, but with reverence. She'd earned it. He directed her to take a seat in front of his desk. She took it. "I see they fixed your teeth."

Bria nodded.

"I'm sorry I let you down, Sir," Bria replied. Her mouth appeared as though it had never been injured.

Merrecci nodded away her apology and suggested that she avoid consoles and railings during enemy confrontations.

"I've served with a lot of people, Lieutenant-commander," he said. "I'm not comfortable with our situation, Leonard. The majority of people who were supposed to be on this ship didn't make it. You did, though, and I'm not sure I entirely understand why you're clumped with that group of other people."

"Other people, Sir," Bria asked, and Merrecci could tell he had offended her, but she was too polite to say anything.

"What's wrong with you," he asked point-blank.

"It's all in my record, Sir."

"I know," Merrecci said. "I don't get it. Why are you in the academy's special education track? Lowest test scores in the academy, lower than that Willis friend of yours. You stuck with it, even when you kept failing. You've taken more time at the academy to graduate, which you still haven't done, than anyone except, again, for that freaky smiling boy Willis."

"With respect, I'd be grateful if you didn't call him that, Sir."

"Why are you the lowest in your class?"

"I don't understand."

"You don't understand," Merrecci asked more forcefully. "I don't understand. Why are you the lowest in your class?"

"I-I don't know."

"You don't know," Merrecci asked.

"No. No! I don't know."

"You stepped in and took command because you knew what had to be done. You were the only one on that bridge acting like a Franchise officer and keeping yourself in control, and you don't know why you're too dumb to graduate?"

"No."

"Yes, you do," Merrecci snapped.

"I don't," Bria replied, and Merrecci could see her eyes begin to glisten from whatever she was hiding from him.

"Don't you lie to me Lieutenant-commander," Merrecci chided. He was now leaning over his desk and searching right through Bria's being. "Why are you in that class with all those—"

"Because I'm dumb, Sir," Bria snapped, then recoiled and apologized. "I'm just dumb. There's no reason for it. I'm just dumb."

Now, she did struggle to keep from crying, and Merrecci knew if he gave her a moment more, she'd lose that struggle. So, he decided to rob her of it.

"What I saw on my bridge wasn't dumb," Merrecci said. "If you're so dumb, how did you know how to keep us alive? Answer me!"

"I knew what needed to be done, Sir. I know what needs to be done. But during tests, my mind goes blank. I can't—I can't—I just can't."

"Now test anxiety I believe," Merrecci said. He lowered himself back into his chair, and the phony leather squeaked. "I don't know who I have on board anymore. I haven't even had the luxury that most captains get to familiarize themselves with their ships and crew before setting out. I did, however, search for my selection of third in command. He was highest in his class."

"I understand, Sir," Bria said.

"I don't think you do. We've just established that you're not that smart," Merrecci said. He summoned the holographic bust of a man, perhaps in his thirties, in a Franchise uniform above his desk. "He's served four tours on three different ships. He's just more experienced than you, and I need that out there."

"I'm not offended at someone being better at this than me, Sir," Bria said, and her crumpled facial features didn't betray her remark. "You need your best on the bridge. We both know this was not supposed to happen."

"So, you do understand these needs," Merrecci said.

"As much as it would be nice to think I could ever work on a ship like this, it's not a training facility. Its crew must come first."

"Thing is," Merrecci said. "I think that right there means I have to have you on my bridge, but I think we both know you filling a command position isn't realistic, nor would it exactly inspire others, would it?"

"No, Sir," Bria replied. "It wouldn't."

Merrecci stared at Bria, saying nothing. The more he stared, the more he watched her try not to shift and make it appear she was acclimated to such scrutiny. They had become dwindled slivers of memories now, but he recalled those feelings that swam on the other side of that captain's desk. He knew where he wanted her, but she did have the lowest test scores.

Test anxiety. That's what put her in this group of people, well that and also likely her face or lack thereof. For some it was debilitating, yet she didn't freeze when the ship needed her. Maybe she just needed to be shown she could work under fire. He could hear the back of his brain screaming at him to abandon his intention. She shouldn't be on the bridge. He would fully be in his authority to dismiss Leonard right there until he could assign her to more appropriate duties. Yet, recalling how comfortable she seemed behind the shield operator's console and how fast her fingers flew and barely kissed each typing sensor, he knew what was the more appropriate duty.

"Seeing as we're in a bit of a crunch though, we can address this issue later," Merrecci said, and he slid a tablet across his desk to her. "In the meantime, I could use your analytical eye, if you don't mind. Actually, I could use someone else's but since you're what I have in front of me right now, might as well use you."

"Of course, Sir," Bria said, without allowing the transfer to her bracelet yet.

"This ship has a lot of functions. If we get attacked before I can learn them, we could be in some serious trouble. I didn't even know about that anchoring system."

Just then, Onyx announced that Shade's transmission had been defragmented.

Merrecci allowed it to be played so that Bria could hear for herself what interference had cut out.

"You see what else I'm dealing with," he asked.

"Yes, Prime Admiral," Bria replied.

"I have a lot to do," Merrecci said. "If you could please review the people currently onboard, including civilians, and select the most suitable bridge crew to get us to Mabbis, that would be one less thing on my plate. I always like at least one more opinion. I would be grateful."

"I don't know if I'm the right person for that, Sir," Bria replied.

"It's not like we have a lot of people on board for you to screw this up, Leonard," Merrecci said.

"I'm just a cadet despite whatever honorary title you've given me," Bria said.

"And I currently know your abilities better than I know anyone else's on this ship," Merrecci stated.

"What about Dr. Wanship?"

"My sister's couch and my bridge do not mix." Merrecci held up the holographic tablet, refusing to let her ignore it. "Please, Lieutenant-commander. I could really use some weight off my shoulders right now."

Onyx announced that diagnostics had reached 67%.

Bria agreed to Merrecci's request and finally allowed the transfer of the holotab to her bracelet and asked if she could use the captain's couch.

"Why don't you take it to the commander's office," Merrecci said. "I'm sure we'd both like to think without someone else listening to every breath we take."

Bria agreed, and Merrecci excused her to fulfill her task.

For three hours, she studied the roster and made her notes for bridge recommendations. She appreciated the task and the time constraint Merrecci was facing. An effective ship commander couldn't use resources he didn't know. She wanted to help.

She'd heard Merrecci was a cruel but fierce captain. What she wanted now though was to show herself that she was part of something important, even if it was just staffing a ship for the most renowned captain in the Franchise. Any letter of recommendation from him would help her get at least something more than she ever expected she could. For this reason, she found herself looking over the functions of the ship so that she could be certain that the crew she submitted would be not just a good support system for Merrecci, but also an effective mesh of human and machine. Maybe it was too much, but she knew it would be the only real experience of this kind she'd ever get to commit to her memories and life stories of serving aboard the Earth's flagship. She liked this. It wasn't really a test. It was freedom. It was her way, and, since it was her way, she assigned herself to the Onyx's crew as a librarian's assistant. Maybe Merrecci would allow it. She'd try.

The commander's den was much smaller than Merrecci's ready room. There was a desk, a couch, a hall to a shower, a bed and closet. It wasn't the commander's quarters. It was a commander's respite for when she needed privacy to do administrative duties or rejuvenate during round-the-clock shifts. It was a plain and empty office, Bria thought.

The door opened, interrupting Bria's work, and Commander Nandy entered.

"I'm sorry," Nandy said, visibly taken aback. "I thought this was my office." She turned to leave.

"It is," Bria replied. "I'll leave. Merrecci asked me to use it to do something for him."

"Oh," Nandy said. Her eye was still bruised, and her lip was swollen, but her brain was finally awake again. "May I ask what?"

"He asked for my input on bridge personnel suggestions."

"I can take over that," Nandy stated. "You're excused."

"With respect. I have my orders."

"And now I'm here, so you don't have to," Nandy replied. "It's nothing against you. I just think I'm smart enough to do my own job."

"With respect," Bria responded with utmost politeness yet again. "It's my task, and the prime admiral's orders outrank yours."

"The prime admiral contacted us again," Nandy asked.

"Merrecci is the prime admiral now," Bria said. "It was lost in the interference of the message from Prime Admiral Shade earlier."

"I see, Lieutenant," Nandy replied. "Special-ed needs to feel normal. Wants her bragging rights in life."

With this, Bria abruptly stood and excused herself.

"I'm glad you're feeling better," Bria squeezed in.

"One moment," Nandy said.

Bria stopped shy of exiting the room.

Nandy approached, strutting, until she was looking down upon her subordinate.

"That's the difference between our two sides of the academy," Nandy said when she was done puffing herself up.

Then she stepped aside and dismissed Bria once again.

Bria returned to the admiral's office, and he welcomed her in once more. He looked over the holotab, scrutinizing what Bria had sketched out on it. He looked up and frowned.

"Perhaps I was wrong," Merrecci said from behind a troubled brow.

A click came to his door. He welcomed in whoever made it as well. The door automatically swung in, and Nandy entered.

"Reporting for duty, Prime Admiral," Nandy informed.

"I'm glad to see you well, Commander. Welcome back to the land of the living," Merrecci greeted.

The commander thanked him.

"Sir, I have some thoughts on the bridge crew, if you'd like to hear them," Nandy suggested.

"All right," Merrecci said and handed her a holotab. "But first, tell me what you make of this."

Nandy began reviewing the information, filling her discovery with "no" and "interesting choice" until she was done. Finally, she looked up.

"I think the acting lieutenant-commander has done an admirable effort to perform this task, but in the end, we do need a fully efficient and alert crew," Nandy said and handed the tablet back to the Admiral. "It's clear she hasn't had great opportunity to hone her personnel management skills."

"That's my work," Merrecci said.

"Sir, if I have misunderstood, I apologize," Nandy replied. "I do not mean to disrespect you. Obviously, I have a lot to learn from you, and I will make it my every endeavor to do so."

"Thank you," Merrecci said and handed a different tablet to Nandy. "This is Lieutenant Leonard's choices."

Again, Nandy scrolled through, this time with far less commentary. Finally, she looked up to the admiral again.

"It appears identical to yours," Nandy said.

"Not quite," Merrecci replied. "She made some mistakes."

Now, Merrecci nestled back in his chair. He looked up to Nandy and Bria.

"It seems when you carry the reputation that I do, no one with experience wants to work with you. Sometimes a captain has to work with the drudge."

"I don't think that's true, Sir," Nandy replied.

"It's true," Bria said.

"That's enough of that Lieutenant-commander," Nandy replied.

"Commander," Merrecci amended.

"Yes, Sir," Nandy asked.

"I wasn't asking for your reaffirmation," Merrecci clarified. "I was informing you."

"Sir?"

Merrecci sucked in on his cheeks over what had just blurted from his mouth. Then he sighed as his father's voice filled his head, reminding him that, "Involuntary words come from the gut. Always listen to your gut, it may know something you don't."

"I believed I could mold a new bridge crew if I raided the best of the cadets. I had thought that was you, Commander Nandy."

"Thank you, Sir."

Merrecci shook his head. "It's not you."

"Sir," Nandy asked. "Respectfully, you don't think she can do a better job, do you?"

"She has so far," Merrecci said. "She wasn't the dummy who knocked herself out, dragging her ship's commander to the hospital.

You left an already under-manned bridge without its first officer when the commander fell. If I wanted that level of stupidity, I could have picked Ashton Pawn. What does it say to me when the special-ed student makes the smarter choice than my first officer?"

"Sir, I don't want to cause any problems," Bria said.

"It's not up to you, Commander," Merrecci said. "You are my— Really? Librarian's assistant? The hell's that about? You're not going to be a librarian. You're my first officer from now on. Nandy, you're second. And, to ensure we're not going to flame more confusion into the bridge, I am designating your rank down to lieutenant-commander."

"Sir, this is irregular," Nandy said.

"You didn't mind when it worked in your favor," Merrecci quipped.

"Sir, I'm not read—," Bria started and was cut off.

"That's my decision, Commander," Merrecci said. "You said you never passed tests. Yet, I've seen you pass more than the lieutenant-commander has."

Merrecci abruptly stopped upon reading Nandy's countenance.

"Do you have any idea how many cadets have ever risen straight to the ranks you both hold," he asked. "None. This is not a time to sulk, Lieutenant-commander Nandy. You are both in the senior team of the most powerful ship in our fleet. Act like it."

Nandy and Bria both nodded, but Merrecci ignored Bria's because hers was wrong. Merrecci then made Mike leave the ready room, but only as an afterthought as he'd almost forgotten the ensign was curled up behind his chair and sleeping. Mike protested in whimpers all the way out the door.

"Cut the whining and get back to work," Merrecci ordered.

After Mike left, Merrecci locked the door once more and played Admiral Shade's orders. When they were done, Merrecci tossed another holographic tablet to Nandy. Once it had transferred to the jurisdiction of her bracelet, he instructed her to issue the crew assignments that he had laid out within it.

Bria was about to speak, but Merrecci gestured her to wait.

"My first official order to you, Commander," Merrecci said, restarting the recording of Shade's hologram. "If I don't do it, hit that son of a bitch for me. I was going to do it, but self-control gave me the Onyx instead."

Then he turned off the recording, sat back and invited Bria to speak when he realized he didn't know her wrinkles enough to tell if she needed to ask something.

"Question," Bria said. "I get that I concern you, but by working on the crew roster, you haven't had time to review your ship."

"I did both," Merrecci said.

Then he set Nandy to her orders and asked Bria to follow him out of the ready room, the bridge and then into the ship's hallway.

The nearest lift was within forty feet of the bridge entrance. The ride in the elevator was silent. The doors opened into another hall, and he led Bria into it as well.

Down a corridor dimmed in power conservation, the lights turned to orange. Signs warned of entering a special quarantine zone and approaching a disintegration shield. Every five feet, rings of red markings encircled the entire hall from floor to ceiling every ten feet.

"You are now entering special quarantine," Onyx announced. "Authorized personnel only beyond this point."

A disintegration shield burned before Merrecci and Bria. The deadly hum sang louder as they approached.

Merrecci pressed through and kept walking, but then stopped.

"Is there a problem, Commander," he asked, finding Bria halted prior to stepping through.

Bria might have held back an anxious and hyperventilative breath. "I've never walked through one before."

Merrecci nodded then sighed. "You just walk through. It's not hard."

"I've heard it's a painful death," Bria replied.

Merrecci kept nodding. "Looks painful too. Come on." He started moving again and then stopped. "The reason it's painful is because most people approach it cautiously causing you to burn up slowly. The shield disintegrates as quickly as you can press anything into it. The key is to step with purpose." He started walking once more before adding, "You won't feel a thing if you do."

"That's not a comfort, Sir," Bria replied.

Merrecci stopped then returned through the shield to Bria's side.

"Look at me, Commander," Merrecci said.

Bria did. Were she older, she might have swooned over his glorious dark eyes, even his patch of gray in his black hair. What was she thinking? Her stomach churned moths at his gaze.

"We have a lot of ways to worry about dying out here, but disintegration shields can't be one of them. It frightens enemies to see you are not afraid to cross. It instills fear and respect for your ability to face death and push through anyway. Do you understand."

"Yes, but it still scares me."

"I understand. Just know that the longer you wait, the longer—

He pushed her through the shield.

Bria screamed, stumbled, and fell. As she passed through the electrical film, she could feel the immediate burn that was suddenly deactivated and cooled as the shields recognized her authorization. She found that the fresh rug burn from landing on her side and sliding down the floor was what was most painful.

Merrecci walked through again and stood over Bria.

"Now you've done it. It will be easier next time." He stopped speaking just now, almost as if he'd forgotten why he'd come here in the first place. Then he muttered, "For a moment there I thought I might have forgotten to log your clearance. Guess I didn't. Let's go."

The typical quarantine sector held anywhere from three to five crew quarters for members forced to use it. This one had nine. It also had its own launch bay, lounge with an observation window and a library: everything a person would need to avoid cabin fever under the travel restrictions.

Merrecci and Bria approached the only door with an inhabitant panel lit. They announced themselves, and no invitation came. Merrecci announced again and still no reply. They moved to the observation lounge. Again, he found no life. The next stop was the library. The door panel showed it was in use.

"I hate these things," Merrecci said.

"How could you hate the library," Bria asked.

"It's always a surprise what's going to be on the other side of the door when you're looking for someone," Merrecci said. "I hate being surprised. One time, I nearly had a firework blow up in my face."

The doors parted and Merrecci found himself facing a giant, gray butt. A stringy tail swished back and forth and threw poop everywhere, including out the door in Merrecci's and Bria's direction.

"Oh good," Merrecci said, looking down slightly to Bria. "I've always wanted to see a real elephant's ass up close. How about you, Commander? Ever want to see a real elephant's ass before?"

"I'm not sure we can call that a real elephant's ass, Sir," Bria replied.

Just then, a second elephant's backside sidestepped against the other.

"And now there are two," Merrecci said. He immediately searched for an opening to allow him to enter the library. Gesturing for Bria to follow, he slid in between a log-slatted wall and the smaller of the two elephants.

Less than five steps in, he gripped a post to keep him from dropping into the splits, a maneuver he was just too plain old and not in the mood to do anymore, as his foot slipped against a slick spot on the floor. After catching himself, he pressed alongside the elephant with a little more caution until he reached the front of the pen.

The elephants were majestic. The smaller of the two became a bit concerned to see two new creatures in a pen barely large enough for the current inhabitants. Straw and filth plastered the floor. The entire pen rose and dropped, then dipped and tilted back up.

Merrecci held out a hand to help keep Bria from falling over herself but was surprised to find that she didn't seem to have trouble navigating the new setting.

"You must have good balance," Merrecci said.

"I've spent my fair share of hours on a boat to know how it works," Bria replied.

"Wonderful," he griped. "I just love seafaring. Did your family sail?"

"Summer cruise for special needs teens," she replied.

"That must have been fun," Merrecci said.

"Oh yeah," Bria said. "Some of my best memories of a patronizing crew trying to convince me how special and smart I was."

At the front of the stall, he ducked through a poorly crafted gate of mostly branches lashed together and tied to a fence line of the same material.

They now stood in a narrow walkway encased by numerous similar pens on both sides that were filled with all manner of creatures. As Merrecci stepped too close to one boundary, something inside hissed, so he picked up his pace to move away from it.

Oil lamps rocked out small flames from their clay lips and fabric tongues, just enough to see the path, but not enough to see what loomed behind the gates. Merrecci looked one way then the other and decided it didn't matter which he chose. After about twenty minutes, they had navigated themselves through the maze and to a wall where they discovered a strange ladder that led them up. They used it and climbed four floors, each rung's fiber strands wheezed under the strain of Merrecci and Bria's weight. The higher they rose, the fresher the air became.

"Hippos," Bria said. "There are hippos."

"What's a hippo," Merrecci asked.

"It's a," Bria started, but realized she couldn't explain it. "They're extinct."

"Ah," Merrecci replied. "How'd you know that."

"My father," Bria replied. "Ancient history was sort of his thing."

As the ladder came to an end, Light came from the opening of another large room with fewer stalls. These ones didn't have gates. They had curtains. Merrecci stepped deeper into the chamber, allowing Bria to finish climbing to join him.

"Hello," Merrecci called out. His voice echoed a bit, but no one answered.

They walked towards the doorway where daylight flooded from without.

Beyond this room was a deck and water, nothing but water. The deck continued to sway and twist in an endless ocean. Tight, wicker and wooden planks reached for several hundred feet before the admiral and his first officer. It was filled with barrels, crates and who knew what else, all tied down with rope and nets.

"Now what," Bria asked.

"With all that banging around you were doing up there, I figured this was an appropriate escape," a woman's voice called from high above their heads.

She was sitting in a parasail, about thirty meters over the boat. The parasail safety harness released her, and she leapt down to the deck, which warped beneath her to cushion her landing.

"I love these safety features," the woman said.

She twisted her head to the side, allowing her to release a helmet and its visor, which then fell heavily.

"Oh," she startled. "I almost forgot."

"Chuchuda," she called.

Something brushed the side of Merrecci's leg. It wasn't soft or smooth, more twig-like. The creature came to a little below his knees with its prickly canopy folded down smooth.

"There you are," the woman said. She knelt and pet at the creature's head. "This is hard, isn't it."

"What is that," Bria asked.

"It's a porcupine," the woman replied. "Have you never seen one."

Bria hadn't.

"Shouldn't she be in a cage," Merrecci asked.

"No," the woman replied, still petting Chuchuda's head. "She needs a friend."

"Oh, of course," Merrecci mocked. "The library holographic animal needs comforting. Look. We—

"She's aborting her babies," the woman said. "It's a little too stressful on the ark for her."

"Well, that doesn't make any sense," Merrecci said.

"What doesn't make sense," the woman asked. "Do you know much about animals?"

"I really didn't come here to talk animals," Merrecci waved off.

"Most mammals can terminate their own pregnancies when they want," the woman replied. "Humans, monkeys, and bats are about the only ones who can't. Did you know that?"

"I don't care," Merrecci said.

"Ooh! Dominant and emotionless. Bet you're a busy, strong man," the woman said.

Now she stood, directing her porcupine off to get some rest. The woman was young, or appeared to be, not even twenty, or so Bria thought. If she was older than Bria, it was doubtful anyone would have believed it. The woman folded back a strand of golden, white hair and held the backside of her hand up to the admiral. "So, you're the mortal buffoon that's supposed to babysit me."

Then she laughed.

Merrecci gripped her hand tightly and barely shook.

"And you're the reason my planet is in flames," he said.

"You can call me Cindy Lou," she replied, then demonstrated her own bone crushing strength against Merrecci's grip.

Merrecci didn't drop though. He didn't scream. He didn't cry out nor order her to stop, didn't even shift when his metacarpals cracked and phalanges folded under the pressure. In fact, his stance became firmer and his brow sharper.

"Onyx," Merrecci ordered. "Delete this boat."

Suddenly, they were all falling, hitting water, and forced to tread. Merrecci maintained his countenance.

"Close the book, Onyx and initiate encapsulation shield around Cindy Lou," Merrecci ordered.

The water disappeared, and they all began gaining balance upon a barren, white floor. Cindy Lou was now highlighted in yellow where shields conformed to her figure and clothing.

"Disrespect me again, and you'll find yourself floating in a region of space no one's found yet. And I don't mean in a ship," Merrecci said.

"Wow," Cindy Lou said. "That's hot!" She turned to Bria, "Don't you think he's hot? Of course, you do, a face like that, you'd find a pig hot."

"Undiscovered space it is," Merrecci said and turned for the door. Bria followed.

"You were serious about that," Cindy asked. "Most people just kiss my butt. You know, being a god and all."

"Kiss your own ass. I'm blowing it out an airlock," Merrecci said exiting the library and ordering Onyx to turn off the encapsulation shield.

They left Cindy Lou in the special quarantine library. Merrecci didn't stop after stepping over the disintegration shield, and Bria realized this time it was up to her to pass through. She did cross it however the moment she knew she didn't want to be stuck in special quarantine with Cindy Lou.

By the time she caught up to the admiral, he was already inside the lift and the doors were about to close.

He didn't say anything. He didn't show anything.

"Admiral," she asked.

"Don't," he replied, and the conversation stayed there until they made their way to the hospital where Charity was lecturing some green aides about how to rearrange everything that she had found wrong with the facilities. Cora was scribbling notes on a pad of refreshing paper.

When Merrecci entered, Charity pursed her lips and sucked in what would explode into a sigh a second later.

"What do you want," she asked, then took in a new breath to diffuse her disdain. "Oh, it's you, Prime Admiral." It was a false pretense, and she knew Merrecci wasn't duped, but the subordinates were.

"What can I do for you, Sir," she asked.

Merrecci dropped his hand on a nearby hospital bed and yelled at everyone except the doctor and Bria to get out. Cora had started to obey the order herself, but realized Charity understood Merrecci hadn't meant her.

Once the staff had cleared, Merrecci informed Charity of the injury.

Charity instantly took to her medical holotab, and lights began flashing from above the bed where Merrecci's hand rested and was in the early stages of swelling.

"Whoa," she said. "What did you do?"

"Can you fix it," Merrecci asked.

Charity measured Merrecci from face to hand with judgment and decided in this moment she was his subordinate, and his façade was now for those who remained in the room. She had to give him credit. She nodded and bid the Admiral follow her to a curved table with a chair on each side. Some equipment, permanent or in transition to a new storage area, sat at one side of the table.

She crept momentarily to her office and then reappeared with a clear cube filled with a blue gel.

"Put your hand in," she instructed.

Merrecci took a moment to understand that the doctor was gesturing to a round opening on his side of the container.

"What is this," he asked.

"It's new," Charity said. "Put your hand in."

"I've never seen this before," Merrecci replied.

"Oh. Well, I guess that must mean you shouldn't follow the doctor's orders," a nurse, which the prime admiral hadn't even noticed was still in the room, muttered beneath his breath.

"Who is this idiot," Merrecci asked through grit teeth.

"This is Nurse Gibralter," Charity said. "He starting to show a lot of promise."

"Nurse Gibralter," Merrecci said. "Which one of us do you think will be most affected by the consequence of your snappy comment?"

Gibralter snorted, but stifled it to a mere explosive, exhale through his nostrils.

"And which one of us was ordered to leave this facility," Merrecci asked. He waited and watched for Gibralter to exit the hospital, then he turned back to Charity. She motioned to the tub of blue goop. "I've never seen this stuff in any of my hospitals before."

"That's because it didn't come with the ship. It's a special fabrication," Charity said, feeling her annoyance getting ready to reveal itself to the admiral again. "Put your hand in."

"It looks gross," Merrecci asked again.

"Oh my god! It's not that hard," she chided.

She suddenly grabbed Bria's left hand and shoved it in. The goo immediately swallowed her fingers.

"See," Charity said. She summoned a hologram over a small table that showed Bria's hand and everything inside. She scanned through layers of bone, muscle, and veins. "Clearly dangerous and gross."

Cora heaved one of her laughs.

Charity allowed Bria to pull out, slightly sticky from the small amount of residue it left.

Merrecci glared, and Charity reflected it back at him. She knew he could see the insult preparing to launch from her tongue.

"It's new. My sister designed it. It will reset your bones," Charity said. "Your sister?"

"Put it in," Charity demanded. "Before the swelling gets too much for this to be effective."

Merrecci slid his hand into the cube. The gel slurped in his fingers and palm while farting displaced globules higher into its container.

"Wow," Charity said. "I expected more screaming from that kind of damage."

"Now, about your sister designing this," Merrecci asked, using his words as a distraction from giving Charity what she anticipated he would be doing.

Charity ran her fingers over her tablet, and Merrecci felt his hand lock into place.

"My sister designs medical devices and equipment, including some that's in hospital use in every faction ship."

"How is that possible," Merrecci asked.

Charity lowered her holotab and snapped back with, "For the same reason your kind of people came and stole the drawings of her inventions. Because she's smart. It's all for the 'good of the people.' She invents it, I test it. The government steals it." She went back to her work, telling Merrecci, a time or two, not to shift his weight. "This calibration needs to be perfect."

"Perfect for what," Merrecci asked.

"Attention crew of this little ship," Cindy Lou's voice called from overhead. "Will Admiral Merrecci please respond?"

"This is Merrecci," the admiral snapped. "Get off my communications."

"We're not done, Admiral. I need to tell you something. Come back."

"I'm busy," Merrecci replied.

"Oh," Cindy Lou said. "Fixing your widdle, broken hand? Okay then. Send the girl with the unfortunate face."

"I'm not letting you anywhere near my crew," Merrecci said.

"Look. I'm sorry about your flimsy hand. I won't do it again," Cindy Lou said. "But it's important we talk."

Merrecci gave her the silent treatment.

"Admiral?" Cindy Lou's voice continued to inquire. "Aaadmiraaaaal?"

"We'll be there shortly," the admiral said.

"Oh good," Cindy replied. "I have a ray of sunshine in my life again. Also, I've never kissed my own ass before, what's that like mister big boy prime admiral, Sir?"

Merrecci ended the communication and realized his pain had dissipated. "That's incredible," Merrecci said. "The pain's gone."

"Not so much," Charity said, then she apologized and stroked her holotab.

Merrecci's face twisted into something he couldn't break it out of.

Within the gel, a million micro-thin needles punctured his flesh, penetrated tissue, and drilled into even the tiniest fragments of his broken bones. Then they stretched his hand and realigned his metacarpals. They gripped tendons, ligaments and muscle and moved them to allow the smallest of tidbits to return to proper place. Every bone bit was drilled and accounted for. Now, his hand started burning from the inside out.

"Good," Charity said. "Fifteen more minutes, and you can remove your hand. You'll be good to go."

Merrecci looked to Bria and ordered her to return to Cindy Lou. He immediately read the rookie discomfort on her face and turned to the doctor.

"Why don't you go with her," he said to Charity. "I have a feeling you might find an interest in examining the health of a guest of ours."

"Sir," Bria said. "The disintegration shield?"

"I'll make sure the doctor is authorized before you get there," Merrecci said.

"For both of us," Charity asked.

Merrecci didn't dignify another response.

Charity understood and Cora smiled.

Once the room had emptied of everyone except the admiral, he suddenly burst out into a tirade of pain and cursing. After several minutes, the pain began to subside. His hand throbbed for eight more. When the needles withdrew from his flesh, he was entirely numb below the wrist. He pulled his hand out of the now softened gel. He couldn't feel it. It tingled but was mostly sedated. He tried to bend his fingers but got little response. He could work with this, just pretend he was fine, and no one would notice he currently had a dead fish for a hand. He made his way back into the outside hall where Nurse Gibralter was clearly bored waiting. Then Merrecci was off to meet once more with Cindy Lou.

On his way, the first crewman-third-class who saluted him, didn't get quite the response as was expected. She received a flap of Merrecci's hand as he tried to wave her salute down, but it looked like he was trying to slap the wall instead.

The next person, a lieutenant, to salute him got a verbal acknowledgment instead. "I don't play that game."

When Merrecci returned to the special quarantine wing, he found his crewmates and guest-god in the observation deck, and the only one who appeared happy was Cindy Lou. They were sitting around a triangular table. Cindy was facing Bria, talking about something Merrecci already knew he didn't care about. Bria appeared to be hurt, diplomatic and ready to strangle their guest at the same time. Charity was looking confused or overwhelmed, and that's what made her look sour right now.

"Ah, Admiral," Cindy Lou said. "Fix us a drink."

All with his good hand, Merrecci moved to the bar, tore out four glasses and filled them with pink, glittery liquid from a peacock-shaped carafe. The drink was made from the sweat of a space pig-whale. Rare. Only the best milkers who knew the migration patterns were ever able to track their path through the galaxies.

He gathered the glasses onto a small rectangular platter, then moved to the table where he set them down before seating himself. He drank down one with his currently good hand, ignoring everyone's faces, then threw the others when his numb fist smashed down on the edge of the table and caused it to flip over. Bria merely dodged its pedestal. A new table materialized in the previous one's place.

"So hot," Cindy crowed.

"Are you trying to permanently injure that thing," Charity exploded and instantly began scanning over the backside of his fingers.

"This is not a luxury cruise, and we are not your bartenders," Merrecci sneered.

"Understandable," Cindy Lou replied. "The faceless one said as much a moment ago. Your doctor said some interesting things about your hygiene while she felt me up with her little gadgets. And that one," she said, snapping a finger at Cora, "has a speech impediment or something. Either that, or she's really stupid."

Cora released one of her long singular note guffaws.

"You said you needed to talk," Merrecci pointed out.

"Yes," Cindy replied, and her countenance shifted to a dull light where personal indulgence had once been. "Master Cha is an interesting problem, isn't he?"

"How do you know about Master Cha," Merrecci asked.

"I'm a god," Cindy said. "I know more about everything, even this ship, than you do."

"And you're just now telling him this," Charity asked.

"Well, yeah," Cindy replied and laughed at the absurdity of the question. Suddenly she scowled. "Plus, I heard your conversations while I was monitoring the bridge."

"You were the one siphoning energy," Merrecci observed.

"Sexy and quick," Cindy said. "But not too fast still."

"I don't have time for this," Merrecci chided. "We have to somehow infiltrate Paichu space to find someone who was observed glowing."

"Ah yes, my lover boy," Cindy said. "He must have been showing off."

Her hand now brushed Merrecci's fingers before he could stand and leave. A strange energy filled him. It wasn't as before when she broke his hand, this was soothing, genuine, and static.

"You need a Rhaxian priest," Cindy said.

"Rhaxian priest," Merrecci asked. "Rhaxians? I've heard that before. Hold on! They're one of the forced extinctions. They were destroyed eighty million Earth years ago by the Kag'tak."

"I'm sorry," Charity said. "The what?"

Merrecci stiffened and asked, "They don't teach about them?"

Cora and Bria nodded. They'd heard of Kag'tak.

"Oh," Charity said. "Must have been too busy with my own work to pay attention to Cora's lectures."

"It's nicer when you don't know who they are," Cindy said then returned to her conversation with Merrecci. "The Kag'tak still pay bounties across the galaxies to anyone who brings in a Rhaxian head. The interest on the bounty never ceases to accrue. One Rhaxian alone could purchase eight solar systems today they say."

"Who needs that many solar systems," Merrecci asked.

"If the Kag'tak had known, they would have never slaughtered the Rhaxians," Cindy said. Then she added, "Rhaxians are the keepers of many secrets regarding gods. It has all but been eradicated. If they die, memory of my kind will be lost forever."

"Let's suppose we could find any Rhaxians," Merrecci said. "How would you propose we do that with all the other bounty-seekers out there?"

Cindy Lou smiled, then frowned. Merrecci was unsure of whether it was because of him or sad memories.

"Go to the Sentrale system."

"You're not suggesting someone's there," Merrecci asked. "That system is uninhabitable. It's an anomalous system."

"Well, if you're so certain, don't go," Cindy said. "I know. Let's go pick a fight with the whole lot of Paichu and their Kag'tak allies instead. Who needs the Rhaxian's help to find another god."

Merrecci understood she was saying that Earth's own annihilation was coming.

"No ship has ever come out of there."

"Good hiding place, huh?"

Merrecci didn't speak as a means to suggest that he wasn't impressed.

"Sir," Bria spoke carefully.

Merrecci looked to her, and she took it to mean that he was listening.

"If that's the only way to accomplish our mission—

"Is it," Merrecci suddenly asked, interrupting his first officer.

Cindy broke out laughing. "Sucks, don't it."

Onyx announced that its diagnostics was at eighty-six percent.

"You're not considering this," Charity asked.

"Oh, don't worry," Cindy said, patting Charity's hand. "You have double the chance of survival, don't you?"

Cora let out another long, moaning laugh and a steady bead of drool.

"She's fun," Cindy said.

"I best return to the bridge then," Merrecci announced. "Seems I have a lot to consider regarding this suicide mission."

He beckoned Bria to join him. Charity and Cora followed. Once they were back in the lift, Charity ran a quick scan over Merrecci's head and then Bria's. As the doors opened, she ordered the admiral and Bria to stop.

"According to these readings you could both use some sleep," Charity explained.

"I'll sleep when there's nothing better to do," Merrecci rebuked. "Commander, get some rest."

"You too, Admiral," Charity replied sternly.

Merrecci glared.

"I'm ordering you both to sleep while we're in a spot to do that. Who knows when the next chance will come."

"You don't even know what we're up against," Merrecci said, and Charity admitted that she didn't. He realized she could make better decisions to not hinder the Onyx's mission if he told her what it truly was. So, he relayed enough about his mission and Cindy Lou and her ability to destroy one universe while birthing another if she ever got together with her mate.

"Of course, this is highly classified," he explained, then informed her of the consequences of speaking about it with anyone outside of the lift. "Understand now, why sleep is not my luxury. You can give me a stimulant."

"Perhaps your previous doctors may have been eager to drug you up in times of crisis, but I'm not that easy," Charity said. "I prefer the person in charge of my life to be alert the old-fashioned way: well-rested."

"Did you not hear anything I just said," Merrecci asked. "We have to get to Sentrale after we make a stop at Mabbis Station."

"Yes," Charity replied. "You're going to be embarking on a hefty mission that will require a lot of attention. But we're not leaving yet, are we? I imagine you're still waiting for diagnostics to reach full. So, you might as well get some sleep in while we're sitting here."

"I don't have time for this," Merrecci replied and exited the lift.

"Sir," Bria called after him. "Research shows we can problem solve in our sleep if we rest upon the issues fresh in our minds. It could be beneficial, at least, until diagnostics complete, which should be several hours at this rate."

Merrecci turned upon Bria now. "No shit, Yogi." Then he asked Onyx, how long until the diagnostics were complete."

"Diagnostics will reach one-hundred percent in seven hours," Onyx replied.

"Is there anything we can do to hide ourselves even more?"

"Stealth option is available, and we can camouflage any of our readings," Onyx said.

"Including sending out communication that can give away our position," Bria asked.

"External ship communication can give away immediate location," Onyx replied.

"Right," Merrecci said as if remembering something he'd briefly read in the manual about encrypting messages being one of the last features diagnostics unlocked. It wasn't like the boot-up process of a ship was filled with people writing home typically.

"Doctor, we'll do it your way," Merrecci surrendered. "In the meantime, until we can get to Mabbis station and find more qualified staff, will you also please see then that my engineering team and pilot gets rested too? I'll need those."

"Of course," Charity answered, then "What?"

"We typically say, 'Aye-aye' or 'yes-sir,'" Bria explained.

"I'm not your typical crew."

"But you are an officer," Bria added. "And crew needs to see its officers use decorum, or we can become lax."

Merrecci nodded approval.

"Sadly, I can appreciate that," Charity said. "I will carry out your wishes at once."

"Orders," Bria corrected.

"Don't push me, Bria," Charity replied. "This is your lifestyle choice, not mine. You need an air of respect, I can do that. You want to babysit my protocol limits, you're going to end up with your teeth knocked out again, and I won't reset them this time."

Merrecci allowed the discussion to end there, then he found his quarters just down the hall and around the corner from the bridge. Inside, he found a suite large enough to hold several guests and parties. This usually happened once a year when the captain concluded boxing day by opening his home to mingle with his crew and thank them for their service.

The kitchen, dining and sitting areas were all his design, easily adaptable for different types of guests. Up the stairs in the second level were his private living quarters with a smaller kitchen, bedroom, and lounge. One more level up was another office.

He knew the floor plan and had little to do to find his way around. It was the same design for the Viridian but on a smaller scale.

As he started his way up the stairs the door clicked. He allowed the guest to enter. Mike came running in on all fours, barking and excited. When he spotted Merrecci, he charged for him.

"What the hell do you think you're doing here," Merrecci got out just before Mike hit the lowest step.

Mike stopped.

"No," Merrecci snapped. "Don't even think it. Go find your own quarters."

Mike withdrew and Merrecci waited for the doors to his residence to close.

From here, Merrecci showered, then, as his many years of experience compartmentalizing what he needed to accomplish, he fell asleep and didn't even feel Mike sneak into his quarters and curl up at the foot of his bed.

7
▲
Breathe

Mabbis Space Station was Earth's heavily armed interstellar and diplomatic structure. It was under all galactic privileges as a Franchise member's embassy. An attack on one of these demanded all other parties that held their own station must rally and return retribution upon the attacker. These commissions were sacred. Any alliance could belong to the Consortium of Embassies, but there were only two ways to join—through sponsorship or through theft. Although most embassies were recognized through sponsorship of one of its coalition affiliates. There was only one way for a race to become independently recognized as part of the Consortium Embassies. Only one faction had ever accomplished it before—Guggler's Den.

Removing another world's membership from the consortium required careful arrangement. As long as any species was recognized as a valid member, it could not be attacked. However, remove that membership and it no longer had that protection. This was not a Franchise practice. It was a cooperative expectation among coalitions to preserve the sanctity of open communication.

The last time a group attacked an embassy, was when the Bada-ee attacked the Ritaso consulate near Bada-Roga. It took all of twelve Earth hours to dismantle the attacking government's status, then ten Earth days for the Maridamarak to annihilate all twelve of the Bada-ee planets. This all happened before Earth had even been a blip on the Franchise's radar as a potential member. Few in the Earth Franchise knew for certainty that their own stations, though designed to withstand powerful attacks, could not hold up to the Maridamarak.

Earth was currently far from the strongest of races in the political arena, but it knew how to hit hard with what technology it did have. Humanity wasn't as cunning as the Paichu, nor rich as the Maridamarak, but even these elite races didn't pick fights easily with diplomatic embassies, mostly because trading with resources freely with subspecies was less costly than enforcing slavery or destroying the resource. It was partly because no one wanted to tempt a Kag'tak police presence. Although they were not members of the consortium themselves, they had allies who were, and they honored the call of their allies. However, if the call was prodigal of Kag'tak time and resource, there would be severe punishment against the ally that pulled them out of hibernation. There was always punishment in their presence.

When the Onyx suddenly appeared in Mabbis space, Merrecci was well-surprised when he found his diplomatic station had become a field of explosive and burning wreckage. The last remnants of a battle proved the Earth Franchise had lost here too. Three additional Earth ships were dying but continued to fight. Four more were a captain's breath away from launching their lifeboats. Two had just entered battle and were both about to lose their shields. A dozen Didjian warships were corralling five more human vessels to send them to the same slow fiery fate as their decomposing compatriots.

Amidst the battle, a Paichu pristine ship was currently dissecting remnants of Mabbis station and other broken craft debris.

As soon as the Onyx entered Mabbis space, Merrecci pointed right to the Paichu's pristine-class parasite.

"That one," Merrecci ordered. He immediately enlarged its image in the battlecron to view the vessel's razor-like fingers trembling around a discus-shaped body. "Let's see what being a hundred percent does for us now!"

The purpose of the pristine was to withstand heavy blasts while its talons dug into an enemy's hull and tore it open. In this process, it could not only depressurized the ship it was attacking but it drew any remnants from the destruction into its extractors. This then turned the salvage into a cloud of resources that could be gathered later for recycling and further ship building. This machine, especially in large numbers, could tear apart entire space stations, even moons or planets within a short time.

As Merrecci examined the battle, he was certain that whatever they did now had to be fast, because wherever there was extracted debris, there was a need to carry and transport it. That meant more Chubs would be incoming to store it after it was gathered.

"Sir," Bria said. "Where's the station."

"Ensign Pablo," Merrecci announced. "Target the pristine and attempt to destroy it. Be mindful of explosion though, there may still be survivors in the wreckage."

"But, Sir," Nandy interjected. "The Didjian are weaker. Earth has never taken a Paichu down without substantial support."

"Unfortunately, we are the support," Merrecci replied. "We hit the Alpha ship hard enough, and the Didjian will turn tail and run. No one knows what this ship is capable of yet." Then he repeated the order for Pablo to fire.

The Battlecron filled with projectiles and raizer weapons across its arena and into the pristine. As a torpedo struck into the side of one of the claw-like fingers, its forward shield erupted with visible sound repercussion that eventually washed through the Onyx. Another missile struck, and the pristine's appendage snapped off.

Here, the Paichu's ship turned towards the Onyx and rushed forward, directly into the onslaught of weaponry that Pablo ruthlessly pounded it with.

Several volleys of torpedoes continued to slam into the pristine-class vessel.

"Sir," Nandy announced. "We're receiving a request from the Lavendar to dump data to us."

"Probably from the Mabbis before it could be destroyed," Merrecci said. "Verify and start the transfer."

The pristine drew closer and faster. By now, its three fingers had been amputated from the ship.

"Their shields are completely down," Bria announced.

"Down? That doesn't sound right. Are you sure," Merrecci asked.

Bria nodded. "Their hull is completely exposed."

Still the ship sped towards the Onyx on what would certainly be the pristine's last suicide maneuver.

Merrecci watched the battlecron's Didjian ships turn their attacks upon his own.

"Hit it again and hail them when they're disarmed," Merrecci instructed. No firing followed.

"Is there a problem, Ensign," Merrecci asked.

Just then a single torpedo leapt forward.

"Sorry," Escobedo said. "There's some sort of lag in the firing mechanism."

"What do you mean," Merrecci asked.

"It's like weapons power is on standby and rebooting when I fire," Escobedo said.

The pristine kept moving forward even after the torpedoes struck.

"Do it again," Merrecci ordered. "Bust it open with a volley."

Pablo ignited the weapons trigger several times before a single torpedo fired out.

"That's an engineering issue," Merrecci yelled. "If those three have messed up my new ship—keep hitting that trigger. I want a volley damn it!"

No volley came, just a steady release of one projectile after another. Then a hologram head appeared, and Merrecci received it. It was spiderlike, and its mandibles clattered together, but the translator turned them into words.

"Earth dweller die," the head said.

"I am Prime Admiral Merrecci of the Earth Franchise," he broadcasted to all of the immediate enemy ships. "As you can see, you are outmatched. You have attacked a diplomatic embassy. Surrender your captains and have your crews abandon your vessels at once. We will take them as a down payment on reparations."

The spider laughed. "Your diplomatic station status has been revoked by the New Divide Directorate. We will summon the Maridamarak at once of your trespass unless you turn your ship over."

Maridamarak? This was a race so technologically advanced that Earth had taken great care to steer away from their space. Most species steered clear of them. They were a people of discovering how to harness energy into a physical form as though it was a natural resource for construction. They had won every war except for one that they'd ever found themselves in. That one war they lost was with the Kag'tak. Again, well before Earth became a member of the Franchise.

The Didjian ships continued to fire upon the Onyx but did little to decrease her shields.

"I highly doubt even your new toy will impress them as it seems to you," the Paichu said, probably mocking.

"If I were the New Divide Directorate, I would be more concerned about what the Consortium of Embassies response will be once we file our grievance," Merrecci replied.

The Paichu laughed.

"Well, I tried," Merrecci said. "Guess we can always give you a sample. End this, Ensign Pablo."

Three more torpedoes took slow turns bursting from the Onyx and struck at the pristine. Finally, one tore apart at the enemy ship. When another torpedo hit, the pristine body broke, and all light within it died.

"I want that firing rate fixed," Merrecci complained then opened communication with the remaining enemy ships.

"Didjian fleet, surrender and be taken into custody," Merrecci announced.

The remaining Didjians, however, quickly jumped from range.

"See," Merrecci pointed out. "They run."

Now, he ordered Nandy to scan for survivors among the Mabbis station debris. Bria announced that they were being hailed by the Lavendar.

Another head appeared in the hologram.

"This is Admiral Kellick," the man in his mid-sixties announced. Merrecci knew him by name only. "You are indeed a welcome sight. We have many in need of assistance and repair. I have taken command of the fleet. Prepare your ship for my staff and immediate change of command."

"Admiral Kellick, glad to see you survived," Merrecci said. "We have not had the privilege of meeting, but I am familiar with your work. I am the new Prime Admiral Vincenti Merrecci. Thank you for sustaining your little corner of space in my silence. We were having some maiden voyage diagnostics bugs. You and your station crew are welcome to come aboard and take advantage of our medical facilities. We could use some extra hands to coordinate search and rescue with those ships that are capable."

Admiral Kellick's face had tightened the more Merrecci continued to speak. "Captain Merrecci, in any other situation, I might entertain your malarky, but I have lost many lives today and do not appreciate the advantage you're trying to take here!"

"If my rank confuses you, Admiral," Merrecci rebuked and leaned over the hologram railing. "You have my full permission to speak to me about it aboard my vessel in a more appropriate environment."

"I will do just that," Kellick replied. "Prepare for my arrival."

"Very good. In the meantime, have the Lavender join us in search, rescue and repair before enemy reinforcements arrive." Then Merrecci ordered a fleetwide broadcast. "This is Prime Admiral Vincenti Merrecci. All Earth Franchise ships are to report to the Mabbis system at once. The Mabbis diplomatic station has been destroyed."

In afterthought, he instructed Nandy to repeat the message.

Then he turned to his ready room, directing Ensign Pablo Escobedo to fire upon any enemy Divide ship that jumped into their burning fleet.

"Unless it's Maridamarak or Kag'tak. If that's the case, order a fleet-wide retreat and rendezvous back to the Milky Way to take refuge under the Franchise's protection," Merrecci instructed. After ending the transmission, he announced to his own bridge that he'd receive the Admiral in his office. He stopped suddenly and turned to his mostly unmanned bridge. "It should go without saying that we are at battle-priority." Then he ordered Commander Bria Leonard to join him.

Once inside his office, he contacted his engineering crew.

"Ensign Asvestos here, Sir," a male's voice replied.

"Ensign Asvestos," Merrecci asked. "Where are Ensigns Platte, Prezi and Greethe?"

"I have dismissed the ensigns, Sir," Asvestos replied.

"So, you're already aware of our situation and correcting it? Good!"

"I believe we are staffed enough to maintain engineering without them, Sir. I told them not to report for duty this shift."

"So, you're telling me they haven't been down there at all today, Ensign," Merrecci asked.

"Correct, Sir."

Merrecci scrutinized the image of Asvestos a moment before asking, "How is everything down there, right now? Feeling good? Feel you have all the tools you need? Are there any problems?"

"No, Sir," Asvestos replied. "I believe engineering is finally running smoothly, Sir."

"I see," Merrecci said coldly. "And Ensign Bone?"

"Ensign Bone?"

"Drinker Bone," Merrecci said. "I sent him to observe engineering today. Where is he?"

"I am not familiar with an Ensign Bone, Sir. Do you mean the civilian that was with them, Sir?"

"Sir," Bria intruded softly. "You did not make Drinker Bone a member of the crew."

"You sure," Merrecci asked Bria.

Bria nodded.

"Yes," Merrecci continued with Ensign Asvestos. "I believe I mean the civilian. Where is he?"

"I had him removed from my engineering bay, Sir. He was a bit in your face."

"And where did you remove him to?"

"The brig, Sir."

"So, let me get this straight. You gave your less than skeleton crew the day off and then arrested my civilian adviser," Merrecci suddenly yelled, throwing an order to Bria without saying a single word. Her immediate response to begin tapping away at her holotab to order the jailer to release the civilian told the prime admiral she understood.

He opened his mouth to yell at the crewman and heard Admiral Shade's words bellowing in his ears to do better. Instead, what came out was a calm, "Are you saying you are incapable of directing the team of engineers that I assigned you to oversee?"

"I'm sorry, Sir," Asvestos said, suddenly sounding nervous. "They kept getting in the way and speaking nonsense."

"There's always something in your way, that's why you leave it there," Merrecci retorted.

"What was I supposed to do, Sir," Asvestos said. "I thought—

"I understand," Merrecci said. "They are pains in the asses, aren't they?"

Asvestos chuckled at the joke.

"But they're pains who I assigned to engineering. Our ship is fully operational, and we are firing one torpedo at a time under your watch. Maybe having more people down there would have helped counter that. Maybe having fewer subordinates will make your job easier Ensign—I mean Crewman. Until then, you and the entire engineering staff report to Ensigns Greethe, Prezi, and Platte. And you better start getting used to them being in charge down there, because at least they make my ship work!"

Merrecci ended the communication then moved around his desk and sat once more. He spun to his window to take in a quick view of ship and station fires beyond.

"How did we lose so much command and key staff," Merrecci asked. "The smartest people on my ship should not be you people— eh—the slow class—you know what I mean!"

"I asked the same thing, Sir." Bria said. "Two transports were destroyed in transit to the Onyx when the Didjians started their attack on Earth, killing 200 crewmembers. Two more transports were destroyed trying to get here after the attack started, that was three hundred and fifty. Most of the crew never made it off Earth, and five died in dogfight."

"Our pilots, I take it," Merrecci asked.

"Five of them, yes," Bria replied. "The rest, as I said, didn't make it up."

Merrecci nodded his understanding.

"Will you ensure my Ensigns get back into engineering and have Drinker come to the bridge."

"Of course, Sir," Bria said.

"And I need you to examine the crew rosters of the other Earth ships out there as well as any survivors and see what we can do to bolster our staff."

"How much do you want me to rebuild it?"

"Everything, if you can! But nothing that will take away from another ship's ability to function or repair itself. We still need a formidable fleet in the end."

"I understand," Bria said.

"And get me the Planetary Franchise ranking representatives in conference at once."

Nandy's voice intruded now over the intercom. "Admiral Kellick to see you, Sir."

"Send him in," Merrecci said, then he dismissed Bria.

"Just what is going on in that bridge—," Kellick ranted as he rampaged into Merrecci's office, when he suddenly stopped and couldn't hide his instant surprise at the commander who was suddenly saluting him.

"What is this," Kellick asked, then turned to Merrecci. "Are we saluting now?"

"It's a cadet thing," Merrecci said, rising from his seat. "It's what they do." Then he dismissed Bria again.

"Hold on! Are you a cadet," Kellick demanded to know from Bria. "What is a cadet doing on a bridge?"

"I'm a commander, Sir," Bria replied.

"How old are you," Kellick asked. "What race are you? I'm not familiar with your kind."

"Dismissed, Commander Leonard," Merrecci repeated. "Or do you need to fail another test to help you remember whose orders get followed around here?"

Bria exited.

"Last I heard, Shade was the prime admiral," Kellick said.

"I'm sorry," Merrecci began to explain. "I had believed that Shade had issued the change in command to the fleet, and I got too caught up in our own escape to think of verifying that when I could." Then Merrecci played the recording of Shade's first transmission to the Onyx during the attack on Earth.

When it finished, Merrecci frowned upon Kellick.

"With respect, why you, Admiral," Kellick asked coolly.

Merrecci knew the tone. He held it himself when he thought higher ups could use a brain transplant.

"Why does anyone get promoted? Punishment," Merrecci replied. Now he sat once more behind his desk and stared up to Admiral Kellick for as long as it took to educate him that Merrecci never blinked before a subordinate. The more he looked into admiral Kellick's eyes, however, the more he understood this man might have been a greater champion at this game than Merrecci was. It probably explained why Kellick was the most recognized and highest ranked diplomat in the Earth Franchise.

"I'm sorry for your loss Admiral," Merrecci said to end the faceoff without looking like he was about to lose. "The attack on Earth and your station is cowardly, but I would expect that a diplomat of your status would understand that it helps nothing to start lashing out at your Earth subordinates."

Kellick appeared to struggle with which emotion he should hide from his face, and which should paint it.

"And I would expect a prime admiral to think to open his transmissions to his fleet with the prime admiral crest, so we know it's official," Kellick replied. He wasn't certain if he'd meant it as an insult or a teaching opportunity.

In lieu of rolling his eyes at his own stupidity, Merrecci invited him to sit, and Kellick resigned himself to settle into the chair on the other side of Merrecci's desk.

"Commander Leonard," Merrecci spoke, opening an intercom to his bridge, and then tapping orders onto the surface of his desk.

"Sir," Bria's voice came back.

"Please see to it that my previous message is repeated once more. I'm activating the official transmission seal of the prime admiral, so the fleet knows I'm real," He requested.

Bria acknowledged the order.

"Your commander. She wasn't an alien race, was she," Kellick asked.

"Define alien," Merrecci bit out.

Kellick slumped.

"I would have never asked something like that," Kellick said.

"Surprise slaughters can bring out the best in us, can't they," agreed Merrecci.

"It's been a long day," Kellick admitted.

"Should have seen hers," Merrecci pointed out. "Hate to say it, but this ship is here because of her, which means so are you."

"All right then, Prime Admiral, what are we going to do," Kellick asked. "There was no warning. They just attacked and informed us our diplomatic status was no longer recognized."

Now, Merrecci informed the Admiral of the Onyx's mission and watched him pale over several shades.

"You can't stay and help us fight," Kellick replied.

"No," Merrecci said.

"This is going to be a bloodbath," Kellick said.

"All the more reason I need to rally our numbers first, so we can get this ship back sooner. You're the ranking diplomat. Think you can hold the fleet together in my absence?"

The room clicked, announcing that the bridge needed to communicate.

"Yes," Merrecci said.

"The Planetary Franchise representatives have gathered, Sir," Nandy's voice announced. "They're ready when you are."

"Care to join me, Admiral," Merrecci asked. "I think I might be able to bolster our numbers here."

"You couldn't keep me away from this conversation, Sir."

As Merrecci returned to the bridge, he requested Nandy and Bria to stand beside himself and Admiral Kellick during the transmission so as to exaggerate their numbers involved in the dialogue. There was still some basic psychology to intimidation that worked over a hologram.

"Let's do this," Merrecci said.

The hologram field filled with nearly two dozen small heads and faces. The prime admiral didn't give any of them a chance to speak first.

"Where the hell were any of you when our diplomatic station was under attack," Merrecci lashed out.

A fat slug-like and human-esque face replied, breathing in deeply and saying, "Captain Merrecci, the diplomatic status of your station was re—

"If the next words out of your whale-sized mouth say anything about our diplomatic status being revoked, I'm personally putting a harpoon through your fat, Moby Dick office chair with you in it."

The bridge and hologram fell silent.

"You know damned well that the Consortium of Embassies would have never allowed this unless you conniving turds removed our membership from the Franchise first." Merrecci scolded.

The communication fell silent.

"Now, then," Merrecci started again. "Which one of you gutless insects proposed the revocation of Earth's membership from the Franchise and gets my foot up your ass first," His finger honed in onto a small group of faces in holo. "I know it was one of you little bastards cuz you can always see a big bastard coming."

Silence continued.

Merrecci waited. Finally, a creature that went by the name of Krin and that nearly mirrored Earth appearance spoke.

"If you have a complaint, barbarian captain," the race boasted with pomp. "You may take it up with Franchise Grievance Administration."

"Seems I didn't slap all the smug out of you last time, Krin," Merrecci stated. "Do I need to come back and finish the job?"

Krin fell still.

"Life on Earth wouldn't be recognizable by the time those bureaucrats even passed the grievance to the proper judiciary committees," Merrecci replied.

"That is the law, Captain," the slug stated. "It's the only way."

"That's Prime Admiral," Merrecci corrected. "And it's not the only way. You've left me no option but to lay claim in my due time."

"You can't be serious," a face in the shape of a sundial said. "It would be the end of Earth's race when answered with retaliation once you fail. Don't do that to your planet. At least filing a grievance would allow Earth to hold its head high still until you can rejoin the Franchise when you are more ready."

Merrecci nodded and this time stepped away from the railing a small pace.

The heads took on approving nods that Merrecci was coming to the right conclusion, but then Merrecci leaned in.

"So, you're the one who seconded the motion to vote Earth out,"

Merrecci said. " 'More ready?' You think your station would last five seconds with me? I know you didn't propose it, your kind are too much of cowards to stand behind your own ideas."

Merrecci gave the illusion that he was taking a calming breath before saying, "All right. I'll take my complaint to the Franchise Grievance Administration, while I ponder where I'll execute my right to lay claim, and your station just rose to the top of my list. In the meantime, under Universal Standard Twelve, I submit our application to join the Franchise as a pledge planet while our grievance is being considered. I expect this body to do a better job protecting the applicant planet while I submit our grievance than it did in aiding our pre-existing diplomatic station. Fail to provide the protective sanctuary, and I will personally come for each and every one of you treacherous slime."

Suddenly his attention turned upon a slender, leafy being that appeared small on screen, but in fact stood nearly twenty feet tall. The alien being probably thought he was staring down upon the Earth admiral, so Merrecci altered his transmission appearance to seem taller.

"I know it was you who put the motion out there to remove our status, you wimpy little twit," Merrecci said. "When I come back, I'm bringing a wood chipper."

"Do you think to frighten us, Admiral," A new creature hissed out in utter disdain.

"Why," Merrecci asked. "Are you frightened?"

"We are not," the alien that appeared to be some sort of crustacean with a gelatinous shell replied.

"Wanna bet," Merrecci said. "If you don't fulfill your obligation to protect a pledge planet during this process, I will be back to kick your collective ass until I'm satisfied each one of you have bled as much as Earth has."

Groans filled the holographic members.

Just now, the doors opened to the bridge, which was against protocol during a communication. Merrecci's three savant engineers walked straight in. The doors should have been locked, but somehow they got past, intruding upon Merrecci's conversation.

"Bad Mike," Dawn scolded. "You don't hump other people's legs. It's rude."

Mike barked and humped the air as if he thought there was something still under him.

"Stop it," Mirror shouted.

The holographic heads suddenly burst into laughter.

"Oh, shut up," Merrecci said, and he turned off the transmission.

"With respect, Admiral," Kellick said. "Your crew is not efficient."

"Really? I've been entirely stupid of what's been going on around here to know that, Admiral," Merrecci said and saw neither the sting in Bria's countenance, nor the smirk in Adrigga Nandy's as he returned to his ready room with Kellick in tow.

Three hours later, Bria joined Merrecci with her preliminary evaluation of personnel that could transfer from other ships to the Onyx. Kellick had finished his previous business and had already left. Four more Earth Franchise vessels had jumped in to join the fleet during this time. All of them were in some sort of disrepair from their own firefights, which they all appeared to barely escape. For now, the flames were at least out with each ship.

Bria had evaluated as many crew rosters as she could. One of them she did not. It had limped in an hour earlier, raising a lot of cheers throughout the fleet to see that it had survived the ambush. This was the Viridian. It had most recently taken a beating from a Didjian star base, when it believed the embassy would offer it protection. Even after this second devastating beating, Bria believed it still had at least one more reasonable and surprising battle in her still. Merrecci and the Viridian crew might have been the only people who weren't surprised that it was still in one piece.

Merrecci understood the role his old girl could fill in their campaign. He would not order anyone from it to join his crew. If they offered to volunteer, that would be a different story, depending on who volunteered. Bria, however, didn't extend that invitation to the Viridian nor any suggestion about it.

Merrecci looked over her recommendation.

"No," he said, then swiped the image of a potential first officer's personnel folder off his desk. He looked at five more, including Adrigga Nandy's, and met them all with similar responses.

"Wait a minute," he said. "Are you kidding me?"

Bria's file and face appeared above his desk.

"You're not a librarian," he screeched. "Even if you were, you don't get to be one until you find me a competent first officer to take your place first. Are you even trying to understand that part?"

He approved the other choices Bria had suggested and ordered her to release the transfers, while insisting that she was still his first officer until he found someone better. She summoned a holotablet from her own bracelet and sent out the transfer orders in that instant, requesting the approved Earth personnel report at once to the Onyx from as many immediate ships as possible.

"And Commander," he added as she was watching the confirmations from the new transfers start to register on her tablet. "Admiral Kellick and his staff have been assigned to a sector of the ship that I am designating the diplomat's suite. You'll find it marked on the map now. With the revocation of our Franchise license, our situation has changed, and we should keep him close. Please alert the crew that his sector is off limits without invitation."

"Yes, Sir," Bria replied. "Should I have medical check in on him?"

"No need," Merrecci replied. "He needs to prepare for station reclamation, and I've decided that the best way to protect our diplomatic future is to have him conduct his work on the Onyx."

"Sir, if I may," she said, but asked further.

"It's fine," Merrecci said, believing he understood her confusion at once. "Most cadets avoid the diplomatic studies track. It's not one of the enjoyable ones."

"Yes, Sir."

"In the event of an assault on a diplomatic vessel, in this case a station, we have right to take any of the attacking parties' embassies and reposition it where we see fit. Which means, whoever takes command of it will need to know how to infiltrate its alien technology. When we make the claim, Kellick's staff will need to move quickly, and they need to study all the variables."

"Yes, Sir," Bria replied. "Thank you, Sir, but—

"The grievance committee doesn't provide us protection. If it finds that any parties are in the wrong, those at fault will merely have to reimburse for Earth's damages."

"But if there's no Earth, there's no damages to repay," Bria observed and then realized. "Which is why you simultaneously re-applied to the Franchise to be considered for new membership."

Merrecci confirmed that she was correct.

"And how long will the decision take," Bria asked.

"Application to Franchise can't go through until all grievances are off our record. I've seen grievances take as long as five years and as little as six months," Merrecci said.

"Why did they destroy it though," Bria asked. "I thought that was a guaranteed death warrant."

"It is, if the holder of the station is a member of the Consortium, but we weren't once the Franchise disavowed us, which means the attack on Mabbis wasn't on the Consortium so there's no need to retaliate," Merrecci said. "As to why though, I don't know. There was only one way for an Embassy member to destroy it without retaliation, and that was it."

"What about non-members," Bria asked.

"Most are too weak," Merrecci said.

"The Kag'tak, Paichu, and Maridamarak are not members of the Consortium," Bria said. "Not even the Consortium could stand against them—well, the Paichu, but they're allied to the Kag'tak."

Merrecci jolted slightly in his seat.

"Exactly, Commander," Merrecci replied, he cracked his jaw and appeared to almost be gnawing on his tongue while he scrutinized Bria. "So, what do you think it means?"

"I don't know, Sir. Politics isn't my game," Bria said. "I was actually trying to talk to you about something else."

Merrecci nodded his approval but wondered how he'd misread her interest earlier.

"Sir, as your first officer, I need to remind you that you were made prime admiral so that no one could take you off mission."

"I'm well aware of my responsibilities," Merrecci replied without trying to hide his umbrage at the notion a cadet turned first officer would have to remind him.

"Apologies, Sir," Bria said, stiffening.

"No," Merrecci snapped. "Never apologize for fulfilling your duties. Part of my duty is to get offended when a subordinate reminds me to get back on task."

"This is going to take us off mission, Sir," Bria said.

"No. We will file our grievance but continue our mission. Until then, our fleet will be under the protection of the Franchise as new applicants. I have ordered most of our entire fleet, once they are capable, to rally back to Earth an our remaining shipyards."

"I understand, Sir," she said. "Should I prepare to resign my duties to Admiral Kellick then as he is the next ranking officer?"

"No," Merrecci nodded, then, "Other than exercising authority to take command of the fleet in the event of my sudden demise, he is a transient on our ship. Give them their space to do their work so we can do ours, but this is our ship. You're my first officer."

"Sir," Bria replied. "We need to get back on task."

Merrecci nodded, didn't smile, and said, "Agreed, but we can't perform our mission without a sizable crew, and we have to ensure those we leave behind are in capable hands. Admiral Kellick will face the same needs by placing himself and his staff in our protection."

The air clicked.

"Yes," Merrecci inquired.

"Sir, I thought you would like to know that you have some new crew members requesting to report for duty," Nandy answered.

"Allow them to their posts," Merrecci replied. "Let's see if we can't get the Onyx to one hundred percent efficiency."

He stood to leave.

"Someone in the divide convinced the Franchise to revoke our membership so our station could be attacked without Kag'tak or Maridamarak involved retaliation, didn't they, Sir," Bria asked.

Merrecci might have smiled just then, but he instead led Bria back to the bridge.

Outside of the ready room, Merrecci and Bria discovered nearly enough new personnel to man each console post.

"Have you found a senior navigator and pilot yet," Merrecci asked Bria softly.

"Not without lowering proficiency of ours and other ships, Sir," Bria replied. "But I did bring pilot candidates that we can train onboard."

"I see," Merrecci said, frowning slightly as he watched Pablo begin chastising the operator sitting at the station beside him after her elbow wandered into his own area.

The new operator suddenly swore and coddled her arm as Pablo smacked her with his lint roller and then began scrubbing at the portion of his control panel where her elbow had touched. Merrecci couldn't help but understand the confusion on the woman's face.

"Sir," Bria replied. "I trust him more than I trust any other navigator anywhere, Sir."

"We have no choice except to right now, don't we," Merrecci said.

The room blared yellow lights and siren, and Nandy announced that they had an enemy vessel demanding to speak to the ship's captain.

"How many ships," Merrecci asked.

"Seven, Sir," Nandy replied. "Four Jimmoshean, two Didjian, and—look—a Chub."

"Another Chub," Merrecci asked out of annoyance.

"Not another one," Nandy explained. "It's Cha's."

"That didn't take nearly as long to get him off that rock as I'd hoped. All right. I've had enough of this mosquito." Merrecci said. "Leonard, call in the Franchise for protection and tell him I'll be with him shortly.

"He doesn't strike me as someone who likes dealing with seconds-in-command, Sir," Bria said.

"So, make him mad. You have the bridge, Leonard," Merrecci said, turning to exit into the main ship corridor. "Don't get the crew killed."

He left the bridge in Bria's hands and excused himself to do something a little more pressing at the moment. Outside, he made his way back down a hall, to a lift, then below several decks. Hoping he had remembered floorplans well enough, he made his way to what appeared to be a black tiled hallway: walls, ceiling, floor, everything. Had Merrecci not known what to look for, he might have passed the impression with a door to his left and missed his target.

Inside, he found a circular room that stood four stories tall with five floors of alcoves that stacked all the way to the ceiling. Currently, the cells were dark, except for two: Lieutenant Dan's and a Didjian. The Didjian had been stripped of his energy armor, revealing a stick-like frame with what Merrecci thought looked like a balloon-shaped skull for a head. Unlike most Didjians, this one lacked the natural protective skin. This meant this Didjian wasn't typical to serve on its own kind's crew. The two occupied cells hummed with a shield.

From the center of the room was a round monitoring station where Lieutenant Almma currently monitored the brig just now. She stood alert and scrutinized each prisoner carefully.

Upon seeing the Admiral enter, Almma stood.

"Do you know who I am," Merrecci asked bringing himself before Lieutenant Dan's cell.

Lieutenant Dan knew.

"Then you know why I have no patience for someone trying to take command of my ship," Merrecci said.

"Yes, Sir," Lieutenant Dan, an overweight and balding man in his forties replied shamefully.

"Report to your post," Merrecci added. Then, with a nod, he permitted Almma to release him. Dan made his way quickly and apologetically out of the brig.

Next, Merrecci squared up in front of the captured Didjian's cell.

The Didjian spat at Merrecci's face, and the blue shield that blocked the attack sizzled from ever reaching the prime admiral.

"Good," Merrecci said. "I don't have to introduce myself to you."

The Didjian, which was neither female nor male of the species but trilale, inflated its head angrily then released the breath. The Didjian, unlike humans, required three sexes to procreate. The male and female combined the elements of life, but the trilale was required to transfer and carry the unborn life as it grew. Unlike their gender counterparts, Trilales bore no resemblance to their race.

They appeared starved, some with appendages thinner than even the bones within a human's body. Trilales were the rarer of the sexes and were typically not allowed in fights if their bodies could still hold pregnancies. The fact that this being was here, told Merrecci that shis pregnancy-yielding span was behind shim.

"I take that as a yes," Merrecci replied. "Let's chat a moment."

The Didjian smiled and his head shrunk, then suddenly puffed back to normal size.

"Fry in your sun," The Didjian replied, pleased with the insult.

"You're eating energy and space that I could be using to blow up your ships, which I'm going to do with or without you in this cell," Merrecci said, unfazed. "The only question I have for you is do you want to help me kill more of your race, or less of it?"

The Didjian's face sobered.

"We'll start with an easy one for now," Merrecci said. "You served with Cha, yes?"

The Didjian nodded.

"Tell me what you know of him."

The Didjian remained silent.

"More it is," Merrecci said and turned to Almma. "Let the Onyx recycle this useless matter into her system."

"Wait," the Didjian replied.

Merrecci turned back.

"You promise? Less?"

"Keep it up, and I may consider improving your menu as well," Merrecci explained. "Now, tell me about Master Cha."

$$* \quad * \quad *$$

On the Bridge, Bria was currently holding a rather delightful conversation with Master Cha as he continued to curse her for denying him access to Merrecci. At the moment, he was muted and screaming.

Merrecci was reviewing how many of his new transfers had yet to report in when he returned to the bridge—all on board, not all reported in to their department heads yet. He would have to work with that. Just now, he let his bracelet swallow his holotab, and he gave pause at the sight of the configuration that Bria was currently using with the battlecron. She had the holographic map of the surrounding area. There was the chub, its fleet, the Earth, and several Franchise vessels. Cha's head floated above a funnel that had sprouted from the top of the Chub.

Merrecci usually just slid maps to the wall when he needed to view holographic transmissions during a battle.

He casually made his way to the hologram viewing area. When Cha saw him, he immediately stopped screaming and began ranting and yelling, even getting hand motions involved in the rampage.

"Can he hear me," Merrecci asked.

"Yes," Bria replied, but didn't need to because the sudden inquiring face told Merrecci he could.

"I'm going to unmute you now, Master Cha," Merrecci said.

Immediately, Cha's rampaging volume filled the bridge with threats against the Onyx, insults at Bria, even demands for Merrecci.

"Quiet," Merrecci blasted back. "Or under Diplomatic Sanctions, Article Two: Section Thirty-two, I will personally come over there and slap the diarrhea out of your brains."

Cha laughed.

"We both know that's impossible," Cha chortled. "Your landing party would be lucky to make it a fraction of the way through our hull before becoming permanently bonded inside it."

"The Didjian's and Jimmosheans have taken part in destroying a diplomatic station," Merrecci said. "And I'm sure you understand what retaliatory options we'll be considering to regain a replacement. Likewise, our current diplomat, Admiral Kellick is on this ship, and you have just threatened to attack it. As Prime Admiral of the Earth fleet, I should simply declare you a war criminal and place an exponential bounty on your head that even the Kag'tak will find tempting to trade in, or perhaps your own crew. I wonder how many people on your bridge heard what I've just said and how well they can all keep secrets."

"This will go easier if you simply surrender your ship to me—

"Bounty it is, then," Merrecci said.

Finally, Cha was silent.

"About time," Merrecci stated. "I will leave you in the hands of my first officer then, and hopefully you can come to an arrangement before I file an official warrant for your crime with the Franchise heads."

Merrecci turned to Bria.

"Commander, stop playing with your food and get us back on mission? I'm ready to leave," he said and then returned towards his office.

"Well," Bria said as she returned to positioning herself at the railing around the holo. She found herself summoning a two dimensional image of the battlefield on the wall. She quickly observed the manner in which Cha's ships seemed to spread out. One might observe that Cha's fleet was merely attempting to put space between themselves to reduce chances of destruction in case the Onyx attacked and blew up another of their ships as it had been surprisingly able to do even without weapons. However, that's not what Bria believed the reason to be.

"So, we're gonna have to go now, Mister Chin," Bria said. "We have more pressing matters at hand. If you want, I can schedule you an appointment after we get back for you to speak again to the Prime Admiral."

"You primordial slime," Cha roared. "You don't even realize who—

"If you surrender your vessel and order your crew to abandon ship, we will allow you all to safely pass out of this system," Bria interrupted. "Of course, you'll personally be a wanted war criminal and might not make it past the neighboring galaxy, but if you surrender yourself to our brig and order your other fleet captains to do the same, you would be on the vessel carrying the diplomat and the Prime Admiral, which means—

"Do you have any idea what the penalty is for the innocent crew that allows a captain to surrender himself," Cha cried. "Any death would have more meaning than taking such an order from such an inferior creature of an already inferior race as yours. However, I would be willing to accept your surren—

"Do not confuse me for a Nomix vendor," Bria burst sternly. "Surrender yourself, your ship captains and your vessels or leave this system and see how far you get with a bounty on your head."

Now, it was Cha who was leaning into the hologram making himself appear bigger, but not looking down.

"I have no time to play with the children of my enemy. I want—"

"Neither do I," Bria said, then abruptly turned and addressed Ensign Pablo without muting her side of the transmission. "On my mark, fire a disintegrator on this one, right here." Bria's finger pointed to one of Cha's medium-sized vessels that had just finished placing itself between the Onyx and one of the larger Jimmoshean ships."

"Look closely, little zit," Cha hissed. "If I wanted to destroy you I—"

"I remind you that our fleet is under the protection of the Franchise," Bria interrupted. "You will answer to them if you commit that act."

"I don't care about your fleet," Cha said. "I just want—

A torpedo burst from the Onyx and sailed straight for a Jimmoshean vessel. Upon impact, the enemy shields dropped, and the ship suddenly cracked apart. It instantly defabricated into smaller and smaller debris until only raw molecular matter now floated through space.

Cha's head suddenly disappeared from the holo.

"Where'd he go," Bria asked.

"I ended the transmission," Nandy snapped.

"I gave no such order," Bria said. "Get him back!"

"She said to tear down their shields, not destroy them," Nandy chastised Pablo and ignoring Bria.

"Wasn't me," Pablo snapped back.

An empty face appeared in the holo as an outside transmission attempted to get through.

"He's hailing us," Bria ordered Nandy through observation.

"Ma'am," Nandy objected and pointed two fingers to the tactical side of the bridge. "Tactical operates the torpedoes. The navigator does not!"

"I said put him through," Bria snapped.

"I know how to answer a hail," Nandy replied.

Nandy snapped her fingers against her tablet, and Cha's head took shape.

"Do you want to try again," Bria asked, turning her attention back to Cha.

He remained silent, as if he didn't know what to say.

"Don't waste my time if you're just going to sit there," she said, this time straightening her posture into rigid authority. "If you have a grievance, our diplomatic envoy will hear it on our return."

Bria ended the transmission herself.

"Pablo, enter the course to Sentrale system," she instructed, clenching her own wrist behind her back, her thumb pressing into the clean, straight scars that ran over her flesh.

"It's not ready," Escobedo said.

"Get us closer then," Bria replied.

"Fine!" Pablo typed a few angry strokes at the console, then fell back into his chair. "It's all yours, Allen."

Ensign Being went to work and immediately announced the Onyx was underway to the Sentrale system.

Nandy approached Escobedo's seat.

"Ensign," Nandy said.

"Pardon me," Pablo asked.

"Pardon me, Lieutenant-commander," Nandy corrected again. "That is Ensign Being, I am Lieutenant-commander Nandy, that is Commander Leonard, and you are an ensign of the Earth Franchise."

"Uh, in case you haven't noticed, there is no Earth Franchise," Pablo ridiculed.

"This isn't slow class anymore, Ensign Escobedo," Nandy said.

Bria held up a hand to order Nandy down. Then she turned to Pablo.

"You're navigating the helm of something that we were told we would never sit in. Do you want them to be right," Bria asked and then punctuated it with "Ensign?"

Pablo returned to his duties and said no more. Bria ordered Ensign Being to get the ship moving, which he immediately set to.

"You have the bridge, Lieutenant-commander," Bria allowed.

She found herself marching to the prime admiral's ready room to report. When she was granted permission to enter, after several seconds of waiting, she found Merrecci standing and staring out a porthole, watching as the Onyx had come to life with travel towards the Sentrale system.

"Commander," Merrecci said coldly. "Did I make the wrong decision about you?"

"The Jimmoshean ship," Bria said.

"The obliterated Jimmoshean ship," Merrecci replied. He continued to look distantly out the window.

"It was a mistake," Bria replied. "I just wanted the shield's stripped as a warning. I don't know what happened."

"Excuse me," Merrecci rebuked as he spun around to face her. "Are you my first officer? Were you in command of that bridge? You've studied enough to know what our full-powered weapons would do to a grade D Jimmoshean ship. Do you know the position you've just put us in? Put me in? Don't you ever tell me you don't know what happened."

"With respect," Bria replied. "I was never supposed to be here in the first place."

"If you didn't want to serve as my first officer, you didn't need to prove it by blowing up an enemy ship that wasn't acting as a threat to us. You could have just said something," Merrecci yelled. "I don't care what's wrong with that diseased brain of yours, it still knows what's right and what's wrong."

"I'm sorry, Sir. It was not my intention. I'll report to the brig at once." Bria replied softly then broke into yelling. "But might I add that they attacked Earth! I'm not here to play nicely with our enemies. They were a threat, and you're right! I knew what that torpedo would do, which is exactly why I ordered Pablo to fire it and not one of the tactical operators because he didn't know, and I could have at least convinced him it was an accident when it was his finger that killed that crew. I'd give that order again if I had to."

"You better have a good explanation for that comment, Commander," Merrecci hissed.

"They were preparing a Jimmoshean guillotine maneuver," Bria replied. "That torpedo probably just saved our ship."

"Do you have any idea the kinds of efficiency those ships would have to demonstrate to pull off a maneuver like that," Merrecci retorted. "Why else do you think we rarely see it?"

"Well, I've never seen it. You need a full crew to run that simulation, and you can imagine how many of those I've been allowed to take part in," Bria ranted. "And I wasn't about to ask Cha how efficient his ships were at accomplishing the feat."

Merrecci's jaw clenched. His brow sharpened, and he almost unleashed another verbal response.

"I know that was a Jimmoshean guillotine maneuver," Bria almost appeared to be finished speaking, but suddenly added, "They had the seven ships. I took out one. The only thing I did wrong was I didn't actually give the order to fire the torpedo." She found herself realizing she was yelling.

Merrecci's face was frozen in anger. It was redder than any Bria had seen. After several sharp respirations, he finally exploded with, "You're damned right it was a Jimmoshean Guillotine. I could see it from here! Which is why I fired the torpedo! I would have shot down the rest, but you only prepared one torpedo before you had us jump away."

"Sir," Bria asked in instant confusion. It wasn't the first time since she'd met him.

"You see a guillotine, you prepare enough torpedoes to destroy all seven ships. That's what you did wrong!" Merrecci's yelling had turned to stern lecture. "Guillotine teams spend entire careers mastering the maneuver, and there are only a handful of them that can do it without killing themselves. If a good team loses one ship, they only have to find one spitfire, disciplined pilot to get it working again. Destroy all seven, and that's one team that takes a lifetime to rebuild."

"So, my mistake was that I didn't kill everyone on seven ships myself," Bria asked.

"How could you have possibly known what that maneuver looked like," Merrecci blasted.

Somehow, Merrecci's anger steered away from Bria and towards his desk.

"A lot of people are going to have a lot of questions, when this is over," Merrecci explained. "Important people are going to yell at you about whether you thought about the consequences of your actions. Build your resolve, Commander. Your career is going to depend on it. We like to think there are rules of engagement, but when your war is about protecting your very freedom to exist, the only thing we have to obey is to make sure the observers and would-be oppressors see that we're still standing! Out here, we kill those that would kill us, especially those who can fly a guillotine maneuver."

"And I'm supposed to say that to the important people who question me," Bria asked.

"No," Merrecci said. "You look them square in their bureaucratic faces and tell them you don't answer to them. You answer to me."

"And who do you answer to," Bria asked.

"Babe Ruth," Merrecci said. "Bastard hits everything I throw at him."

Now, the room clicked.

"What," Merrecci bellowed to the ceiling.

"Sir," Nandy's voice said. "We have a request from another ship's commander to speak with you."

"Put him through on a secure channel," Merrecci approved and finally sat in his chair behind his desk, mostly out of exasperation than need.

"He's not on board his ship. He's waiting permission to enter the bridge," Nandy replied.

"Someone want to tell me how that happened," Merrecci asked. "We are already underway on our own mission."

"He came aboard only a moment before our departure," Nandy said.

"Well, we don't have time to play transport," Merrecci said. "Drop him off in a shuttle, and I'll contact his captain to tell him where to find him. What ship is he from?"

"He's from the Viridian, Sir," Nandy replied.

Merrecci's eyes drew to slivers and then relaxed.

"Stand by," Merrecci said. He turned back to Bria. "You ever see ships give away they know the guillotine maneuver, don't you ever let any of them survive again."

"Yes, Sir," Bria said. "I'll visit the library and brush up on seeing it better."

Merrecci nodded approval.

"Show him in," he finally acknowledged, calling back to the bridge.

Almost a minute later and Lieutenant Almma led a commander into the room.

"Thought you were watching the brig," Merrecci observed.

"Our pervy new warden reported in, in all his steroid glory, so now I can officially start throwing your big torpedoes around," Almma said. "Reporting for tactical and security, Sir." She tipped her head to the commander. "Seems the Viridian sent you a gift. Bet you can't guess what it is."

Merrecci thanked her.

"It's a douche," Almma replied.

"It's a what," the commander spat.

Almma ignored him and took post at the side of the door as was supposed to be procedure when someone the tactical officer deemed a security threat was in the ready room.

As Almma took her post, Bria instantly doubted the visitor had ever had a lonely bed in his entire career. He was young but not too, older but not terribly.

"Admiral Merrecci," the playboy caricature announced pleasantly enough, but still stung at the lieutenant-commander's insult.

"Lieutenant-commander Vandenbutcke," Merrecci greeted without standing from his chair. "What can I do for you?"

"It's commander now, Admiral," Vandenbutcke strutted.

"Is it," Merrecci replied.

If Vandenbutcke wanted to respond, he didn't give any hint to betray his desire.

"We're in the middle of a few things right now, Commander," Merrecci replied after the awkward pause had turned into an annoyed prime admiral one. "What do you want?"

"I'd like to offer my services to you and your crew, Admiral," Vandenbutcke replied.

Merrecci remained silent a few more moments then turned to Bria.

"Commander Leonard," he asked. "Did I have you review all ship rosters for potential crew to fill posts in this ship."

"Yes, Sir," Bria replied.

"Did Commander Vandenbutcke's name make the cut?"

"Not entirely, Sir."

"Not entirely," Merrecci asked.

"In the absence of the Onyx, the Viridian is Earth's acting flagship. I believed it necessary to keep that crew together," Bria explained.

"Is that all," Merrecci asked.

Bria shifted uncomfortably and respectfully held her tongue.

"Commander," Merrecci addressed. "I won't ask again."

Vandenbutcke also threw Bria a look, one that flaunted superiority.

"I didn't find him qualified, Sir," Bria replied.

"Excuse me, cadet," Vandenbutcke sneered.

"As you were," Bria suddenly blurted. "Do you see cadet scads on my black shoulders. You're talking to the second-in-command of this vessel, of which you are a guest."

Vandenbutcke turned to the admiral to question.

"Everyone knows you have a ship running on cadets, Sir," Vandenbutcke said, speaking to Merrecci and ignoring Bria.

"Is that clear, Commander," Bria continued. "Or have those green shoulders on your uniform blinded you to protocol?"

Vandenbutcke turned back to her and snapped himself to attention. "I don't answer to you. I answer to the admiral."

Bria's eyes fell on Merrecci, and his eyebrow tipped as if he wanted her to respond. She took it to be an order.

"I don't know what kind of nonsense your captain lets you get away with on the Viridian, but until I see black shoulders on that uniform, there's not a person on this ship you don't answer to, and that includes the cadets," Bria scolded. "Is that clear?"

"Absolutely, Ma'am," Vandenbutcke replied bitingly.

"The reason I did not select Commander Vandenbutcke, Prime Admiral," she said turning back to Merrecci who seemed upset, and Bria wasn't fully certain that it wasn't with her. "Is because I don't want him here. I'm not entirely sure he's not responsible for causing this war after his little mutiny against you. I'm also inclined to believe that Commander Vandenbucket—"

"Vandenbutcke," the visiting commander corrected.

"Who cares," Bria replied without turning her gaze from Merrecci. "I'm inclined to believe that the commander is only here because he actually thinks he'll get promoted again—perhaps through another mutiny, this time of the prime admiral."

Merrecci's brow suggested he was deciding whether he should explode at Bria or calm his tongue. She couldn't tell. She'd seen him do both in her presence.

"I'm inclined to agree," Merrecci finally said.

He appeared to be evaluating Vandenbutcke, then Bria. Suddenly, he stood and marched to the bridge, ordering the others to follow.

"Lieutenant-commander," he asked approaching Nandy and retrieving his chair from her.

She nearly stumbled over her own feet the moment her eyes fell upon Vandenbutcke, but she covered as best she could.

"This man is a mutineer from the Viridian and wants to serve our crew as a means to pad his resume. Recommendations?"

Nandy was clearly caught off guard but recovered well in confidence.

"I should think, under the circumstance, that if the commander of the—of the Viridian has skills that we can use aboard this ship, we—we should put him to use—uh—them to use. The mission is too important," Nandy explained. "And God knows we're badly in need of bridge seniority with experience."

"Interesting," Merrecci said. "Leonard says she doesn't trust him and doesn't want him."

Next, Merrecci put the same question to Lieutenant Almma.

"I think now that Lieutenant-commander Nandy has met Vandenbutcke she's just realized that she's horny. She just doesn't know how to tell him," Almma said.

Nandy's face exploded in shock.

"But she is right. He has experience and skill we can use, maybe that Nandy would like to use too."

"You're out of line," Nandy snapped.

"Commander Leonard is also right, and those skills of his don't mean jack if he's just here to hump your command chair again, Sir," Almma explained.

Then she snapped her baton open and brandished it cleanly before her. It was no common weapon. This grey device wasn't issued nor sold, only awarded, and she had two, one still holstered against her left thigh. Merrecci had seen these in action, never used one. He didn't really notice it when he first met her in the administrative hallway on Earth. Maybe Shade had given it to her since then, but he doubted it. This wasn't a gift to people who just watched admirals' hallways, and no one ever had two. Somehow, Merrecci found himself breathing just a little more comfortably in Almma's presence.

Almma continued. "As security and tactical, I happen to think that if this little Viridian bitch goes into heat for your chair on my ship, I'll have to shove this baton up his funny hole and make him cough me a joke."

Merrecci believed her, pointed out that her answer was a bit crude, but correct.

Almma didn't apologize.

"You're a part of this crew, Vandenbutcke," Merrecci announced. "But I don't have need for another commander. For abandoning your post on the Viridian and boarding this ship without proper approval and under orders to report to Earth, I will have to demote you in rank to lieutenant if you wish to join us."

Vandenbutcke's eyes flashed. Merrecci knew at once that Vandenbutcke was trying to temper his insult with the long term picture of where serving aboard the most powerful ship in Earth's fleet could get him. Vandenbutcke accepted the post.

"Good," Merrecci said. "You're chief pilot."

Now, Merrecci ordered Nandy to send a coded transmission to the Viridian informing them that Vandenbutcke had been fully reassigned to the Onyx. Then he turned to Pablo. "How long until we reach the Sentrale System?

"Four days, Sir," Pablo replied.

"Please prepare for your shift-rotation in two hours," Merrecci instructed Vandenbutcke. "I advise you to use the time to get familiar with your department subordinates and your ship controls." He gestured to the current shift pilot. "Ensign Being can show you the ropes for now. If you have any belongings you'd like to bring over—oh, that's right! You're a stowaway."

"I've already brought everything I need, Sir," Vandenbutcke explained.

With that, Merrecci set Vandenbutcke to perform his preparatory tasks, silenced Bria's reservations and then sent her and Nandy off duty until their appropriate command rotations.

Bria and Nandy went separate ways at the elevator, but not before Nandy suddenly turned to Bria.

"Permission to speak freely," Nandy asked.

"Please," Bria said.

"I'm smart, and I don't mean that in a bragging way," Nandy explained. "I'm the highest scoring strategist in the history of the academy, so believe me when I tell you that every second you sit in that first-officer's chair is another second the prime admiral can't get proper insight from people like Vandenbutcke who have experience. I don't even care that I'm not a commander. No cadet in their right mind would have expected to be in this manner, but what's insulting is the notion that anyone would think that you are somehow better than me."

"I don't think I'm better than—

"We are still not fully staffed, and we're not going to pick up more crew members while we're on mission. You need to go away so Merrecci can succeed," Nandy said.

"I'm just supposed to leave," Bria asked. "Abandon my post."

"You're not supposed to be here anyway," Nandy said. "If you really care about the outcome, just disappear."

"How am I supposed to do that?"

"Don't care. Just stop being selfish," Nandy stated, then turned and began storming off. "I hear the airlocks do a pretty good job."

Bria decided not to go to her quarters now. She entered the elevator and began to navigate her way to Dr. Wanship's office, Wanship wasn't there when Bria arrived. Neither was Wanship in her quarters when Bria checked there next. After inquiring with Onyx, she was able to learn that Wanship was currently with another crew member. Bria couldn't interrupt that.

She was soon back in the elevator where she went all the way down, then up, then back to Wanship's apartment then her office for just in case Onyx was wrong. Every bit of the way, she fiddled with the rectangular impression in her sleeve and the scars its brother had left on her wrists prior. They all suggested that maybe Nandy was right. Maybe, Bria should just retire.

She went back to the elevator and followed a familiar path to a shield system designed to keep cargo in and unauthorized personnel out. By the time she reached the shield, her brain was telling her to turn around, not to take the risk to cross that deadly barrier that might have forgotten who she is. She couldn't hear her brain though over the inarticulate breaths her body had started to make. Once she walked past the disintegration shield, Bria began knocking on doors and found herself back inside the quarantine observation deck. Cindy Lou was sunbathing in a one-piece beneath lights that made Bria shade her eyes.

"Ah! The elephant woman," Cindy Lou moaned. "Very well, speak."

Here, Bria opened her mouth to fill the room with a question of sorts that might act as a distraction. Instead, she caved in to the will of her knees: keeling, shaking, unable to breathe.

"Onyx," Cindy Lou called. "Be a dear and lower the oxygen level in here by 100 percent so our first officer can catch her breath."

Suddenly, there was nothing for Bria to bring into her lungs. She tried to find it, but there was nothing. Her chest heaved but didn't know which direction to do so. Her body convulsed her flat onto her back, until, well, an almost calming feeling came over her. Just when she thought it was over and the room began to blur, Cindy spoke again.

"Raise oxygen level in here to 125 percent, Onyx," the god instructed without ever leaving her sunbathing position.

The oxygen flooded Bria's being. It was relaxing now, calming, and deep.

"Dim the lights to zero percent," Cindy instructed Onyx again, and the room fell into darkness, lit only by the lights of outer space, which the full-wall of observation window allowed in.

Bria let the oxygen and the dark hold her there.

"Oh admiral," Cindy Lou called out.

"Please, no," Bria pled softly.

"What the hell do you want," Merrecci's voice blasted throughout the room. "I'm busy."

Drops of failure dribbled past Bria's temples.

"Never mind," Cindy Lou replied.

"Are you kid—

Cindy ended the transmission and silenced the Admiral's response.

The rich oxygen fueled her tears and drowned out the expectations coursing through her veins. Eventually, Cindy returned the oxygen levels to their original state.

Her silhouette took a seat at a table near where Bria rested.

"What would make you think, I even care," Cindy asked.

"I just wanted to hear a friendly voice," Bria replied.

"My voice," Cindy asked. "Friendly?"

"I like it."

Neither said anything for some time.

"I'm sorry," Bria eventually said.

"You're not fit to command, are you," Cindy suggested.

"I'm supposed to be sitting in mid-term exams today so I could fail them," Bria said. "Of course, I'm not fit to command."

"That admiral of yours doesn't strike me as a person who would pick an idiot to be his back up," Cindy's shadow propped an elbow on the table next to her chair and leaned on it. "Then again, he's a few engines short of interstellar travel, isn't he?"

"I almost killed an entire crew." Bria immediately began to feel her brain tell her body to start worrying again.

"I gotta say, that was awesome," Cindy crowed and immediately sat up straight again. "You should have seen what it looked like from in here. You're a badass right there."

Bria's tears rejuvenated and began falling again. "He said I should kill more next time."

"So, it's the burden of guilt, is it," Cindy asked.

"Everyone knows I don't belong here."

Bria's left fingers fell onto the scars on her right wrist and traced them again. She was aware of the weight of the hungry, sharp razor she had fabricated into the sleeve of her uniform. If she twisted her right hand just so, she could feel its edge beneath her fabric and could almost pretend it was working this time.

"And imposter syndrome," Cindy added sullenly. "And you can't tell anyone or the small shot at a possible career that you should have never been given will go out the window. Then it's back to academic sub-parness for you, if there's even that to go back to. Right?"

Bria silently agreed.

"And you thought I'd lull your nerves down with my friendly voice and keep your scars a secret?"

Bria didn't know how to answer this one.

"So, you're vulnerably nice too," Cindy Lou said.

Bria felt insulted for some reason.

"What happened to your face," Cindy asked, bluntly. "I've known a lot of humans, and I've never seen any deformity or injury like yours."

Bria stayed silent.

"Tell me, and you can use my oxygen any time and I won't say a word," bribed Cindy Lou.

"It was an accident. A boy," Bria said after she remained silent longer than any other person would have allowed to pass before taking offense that Bria wasn't going to answer.

"Oh, a boy," Cindy asked, turning her shadow in her chair, and leaning forward. "I'm listening."

"His dad was working on a way to control the Moggi Slug infestation for the crops of Shimma."

"The bone slugs," Cindy asked. "Gross!"

"Yeah, well, there was a party. His son invited me. I was in eighth grade, and it was a boy, so I went because no boy invited me anywhere before. He was talking to his friends about what his dad did, and they talked him into playing a prank to put some of his dad's slug juice into my drink. I tasted that it was wrong as soon as it hit my tongue, but I swallowed it anyway."

"You didn't want your abusive boyfriend to think you couldn't handle your liquor," Cindy said. "That's quite typical of enablers."

Bria nodded.

"It went right into my blood stream ate most of the front of my skull. Left just enough upper jaw to let me communicate. It would have destroyed all my bones and turned me into a blob, but the boy's dad managed to quarantine it as soon as he heard me screaming and realized what had happened. Thanks to him, I have an energy shield system that encapsulates every bone in my body to keep me from falling flat because I'm complete jelly."

"Your bones are all shielded," Cindy asked.

Bria nodded. "All of them."

"Let me get this straight. They can shield your heaving ribcage, but they can't fix your face," Cindy bellowed.

"The agent liquifies bone, but does nothing to other bio matter, and it leaves a residual that stays active for about 40 years. They tested a transplant on the front of my skull once, but it melted the moment it touched the insides of my skin. And that was just part of it. For the transplant to work, it needs to bond with the existing bone, and they can't lower the shield to let it attach."

"Or it disintegrates more from your head," Cindy said.

"Right," Bria replied softly. "Or it can leak through the shield if there's a hole, or so I'm told. They tried something synthetic, but it needed to bond as well, and it kept misplacing itself. At one point they thought about encapsulating the transplant too and bonding the shields of the two pieces together, but it hurt, so they discontinued that treatment as well."

"What about regrowing it inside a shield, like they did with your teeth."

"They didn't regrow my teeth, and even if they did, those are easy. You can see how they develop during the process."

"Wait," Cindy said. "Your teeth shielded too?"

Bria bore a half-smile and tapped at her lower incisors. With each strike, they lit with a yellow glitter.

"So, tell me," Cindy said. "Why didn't the shield protect your teeth earlier?"

"They did," Bria said, pointing to her mouth. "These are the same teeth that got knocked out."

"Well, what about the nerves," Cindy asked. "What about blood flow."

"They get blood flow," Bria said. "The shields allow that. It's not enough to let the bone leak out."

"So why can't you do that with your skull," Cindy asked.

"The skull's not so friendly. The bone grows spurs or slivers that could stab my brain. Even if a hundred brain surgeons were all in my head the entire process, they couldn't protect me fast enough. Well, unless you get the good stuff."

"So, get that," Cindy said. "God, it's your face. Even the worst beings in existence have faces."

"My father's a janitor for an elementary school. No one's going to sell us that treatment," Bria explained.

"There has to be something!"

"There is," Bria replied. "Greemin technology, but the only way the Greemin would approve the treatment, even if I had it done on Earth, is if it's used on ally military officers. They see anything less as undeserving since they don't lead in battles."

"Well, you're an officer now," Cindy announced, then fell into realization. "But you're not part of the Franchise now, are you?"

"And I'm sure that once we save Earth, if we ever save Earth, I'll be returned to a more appropriate rank."

"That's why you can't let them see your anxiety," Cindy observed.

"That's why I can't fail."

"We all fail," Cindy replied. She sighed deeply. "But if having someone to talk to makes it easier on you, my shield is always open. There's plenty of oxygen here."

Bria sat up now to thank Cindy.

"Feel better," Cindy asked.

Bria did.

"If you don't want to fail, you really should get rested before you get called back to the bridge," Cindy said. "You're welcome to use my quarters if you'd like."

Bria thanked her again but insisted that she should use her own since hers were closer to the bridge in case she had to run to it. As soon as Cindy Lou held out a hand to help the commander to her feet though, Bria changed her mind.

8

▲

Goof

Unlike the advents of the previous days, the bridge was silent when Bria returned for her watch twelve hours later. Nandy had reported back four hours before that.

Merrecci was in his command chair and in conversation with Almma and Drinker.

"Commander," Merrecci greeted, breaking away from the discussion upon seeing her. "I trust you're rested."

Bria nodded and tried not to let the events following her last shift show on her face.

"I had an interesting communication with our special cargo," Merrecci said.

Bria's internal organs froze.

"It seems she would be much less intrusive on our comms if she felt she could have regular company from approved crew and staff," Merrecci explained. "She has requested your participation following your shifts. I have approved her request. Better you than someone better."

Bria acknowledged, accepted the task, and waited for any suggestion that Merrecci knew more than he was letting on. There was none.

"Seems quiet for once," Bria said.

"We'll have our moments," Merrecci said. "It's not always the roses and puppies like we've had. Sometimes, it's pretty boring."

At this, Pablo suddenly erupted from his post. "Will you stop altering my course plans!"

"They're not safe," Vandenbutcke replied sharply from the first pilot's seat.

Vandenbutcke was at the end of his shift. It had actually ended a few hours ago, but he had requested to stay a little longer to help familiarize himself more with flying controls. Merrecci allowed it.

"Do we have a problem," Merrecci asked.

"I planned an optimal course to get us to Sentrale System, and the golden pilot here keeps straying from it and making me replot it," Pablo replied.

"Admiral," Vandenbutcke spoke. "I am sure our inexperienced navigator means well in crafting what he believes to be the quickest path into the Sentrale system, but his course is not always safe. It takes us directly through gravity wells, radiation clouds and low orbits of planets with acidic atmospheres. It is simply not prudent and puts too much responsibility on the pilot to navigate."

"It's nothing the Onyx can't handle, Sir," Pablo said.

"And how about its crew, Ensign," Vandenbutcke asked, ensuring the low title was identified clearly. "Can it handle the effects of these obstacles? You have overestimated what this ship and we can safely handle."

"No, I haven't," Pablo yelled. "If you'd stop and think about this for a minute, you'd reali—"

Pablo suddenly scrolled his lint roller over Vandenbutcke's black shoulder.

"Did you get that bit of importance there," Vandebutcke asked.

"Gentlemen," Merrecci said, taking command of the conversation. Once it was clear to Pablo and Vandenbutcke who was in charge, he spoke again. "Ensign, is it true? Are you unnecessarily taking the Onyx and my crew through potentially life-threatening obstacles just to save time on the trip?"

"No," Pablo replied.

"I can show you three ion clouds and a black hole forest that we've had to avoid in just the last six hours, Sir," Vandenbutcke explained. "I didn't want to say anything to embarrass the ensign, so I just altered the course."

"Sir, you said that our mission was the utmost importance to the survival to Earth, and that nothing can get in the way of us accomplishing that," Pablo said.

"So why are you taking us through these ridiculous hazards," Vandenbutcke replied. "This is basic navigation. You do not fly through low orbits, dense radiation clouds or near a black hole, let alone a forest of them. So why would you?"

"Perhaps if you learned to let others speak, we could get answers to those questions," Bria replied, and added on her own, "Lieutenant" just to let him know how far up the chain of command his own rank really was.

Merrecci nodded, both to support that Bria's observation was warranted and that she had not overstepped her bounds in this conversation.

"I am curious to your answer, Ensign," Merrecci said to Pablo.

"This path camouflages us so we can't be tracked by enemy ships," Pablo said. "We don't need to be easily found."

"He has a point," Merrecci said. "Camouflage is where all the smart people hide."

Vandenbutcke huffed silently and rebutted with "There are safer ways we can do that from the confines of our own engineering capabilities."

"Only until an enemy vessel's engineering crew gets wise to cracking that code." Pablo explained. "Engineering anything as a means to create camouflage always leaves a trail of evidence if you know how to find it. My course takes us through anomalies that will erase our flight signature within moments of it being left behind," Pablo explained.

"Again, Sir," Vandenbutcke interjected. "We have the crew to think about here."

"We have more than the crew to think about," Bria replied. She turned back to Merrecci. "Admiral, opening ourselves to be tracked by enemy fleet is one thing, but carelessly neglecting to protect the Rhaxians that may be hidden in the Sentrale system is another. Without Pablo's approach to erase our tracks entirely, we could be laying a galactic trail for every money-grubbing bounty hunter to follow all the way there. We'd be responsible for their final annihilation if there are indeed any alive."

"Exactly," Pablo burst.

Merrecci corrected the outcry.

"What do you recommend then, Commander," Merrecci asked.

"I would say that regardless of whether our chief pilot has a better plan to erase our trail, he should decide if he wants to sit in the pilot's seat or the navigator's," Bria replied after a moment of careful thought.

Merrecci turned to Nandy, "and you?"

Nandy looked about the people involved in the conversation than screwed up the bravado to say, "I think, since we're talking about preserving a race more endangered than our own, that erasing our path is important, but I also think, considering the short-comings of our current navigational circumstances, it would be prudent to at least have our navigator's course reviewed by two other pilots such as yourself and Vandenbutcke before they are entered into the navigational computer."

"Is that what we're going to do now," Bria asked harshly. "Are we going to start bypassing regular ship-verification protocols and add an oversight committee for every member of the crew that the two of you don't trust? Perhaps we should make sure you and Vandenbutcke personally check every person's work, Prime Admiral."

"I didn't say that," Nandy snapped back.

"Didn't you," Bria asked.

"Commander," Merrecci warned.

"Admiral," Bria replied. "If there is a living navigator more qualified to check Ensign Pablo's maps, then we should enlist that person to chart our courses instead, but just to have someone look over his shoulder because he's from the 'slow class,' deteriorates the unity of this crew."

"Unity is also held together by rank," Vandenbutcke said.

"He's got a point," Merrecci stated.

"I agree," Bria concurred. "Whether people on this bridge like it or not though, Ensign Pablo is our lead navigator and the last I checked, the chief pilot's job is to follow the flight plan, not change it. So which rank are you referring to, Lieutenant? Ensign Escobedo's position that you should follow as a pilot? Or your ego?"

"Hey, that's also a good point," Merrecci said.

"Admiral, may we speak privately," Vandenbutcke requested.

"We can speak privately. We just need to talk over everyone so we can hear each other," Merrecci said, fully aware of the various doubtful eyes that tried not to look as though they were watching the dialogue unfold. "Your first officer has made her decision, and I agree. He navigates. You fly. Stay in your lane. Unless you're saying that you cannot handle that responsibility, Lieutenant. Is that what you're saying?"

"No, Sir," Vandenbutcke sulked.

"Let's try that answer again and see if it works this time, Lieutenant," Merrecci said, snapping a finger at his chief pilot.

"No, Sir," Vandenbutcke replied more apt of a Franchise crew member.

"Alter the course again, and you'll be on a straight and narrow path to a career in wondering how you got where you got," Merrecci said. He ordered the bridge crew back to work.

Then he stood from his chair and stepped in close to Bria.

"You better be right about him," Merrecci whispered, but might as well have been yelling.

Just then the bridge started flashing in yellow and red hues.

"Oh, what now," Merrecci asked, hiding that he was flustered.

"Probably the very thing I was trying to keep from happening," Pablo replied.

"What was that," Vandenbutcke asked.

"You're an idiot," Escobedo blurted and suddenly slapped Vandenbutcke.

Vandenbutcke began to protest with Merrecci.

"He can't control it," Merrecci said. "Get a helmet."

"Sir," Ensign Mailer announced from the communication console.

She was one of the few people on the bridge that had actually been an original member of the Onyx crew, but nowhere near having the responsibility of bridge duty until the recent need allowed it of her. In time, Bria had surmised that she would eventually have made it to a career here, so the commander took a chance and gave her a console.

"We're being addressed by an incoming Jimmoshean chub," Mailer added.

"Of course, we are," Merrecci said.

"Would you like me to put him through?"

"Not really," Merrecci said. "How many ships are with him?"

A male voice from the far end of the room announced, "Hard to tell, Sir. They're not quite in sensor range, and we have a lot of interference caused by our current course."

"Ensign Escobedo. Can we lose him," Merrecci asked.

"Sure. If the chief pilot can stick to the course I've laid out," Pablo said. "And we move now."

Merrecci nodded.

"Seems we should be more trusting of our chief navigator," Merrecci said. "Get us moving."

"Sir," Vandenbutcke said. "I've read the weaponry on this ship. The Onyx could probably put up a decent fight with the chub."

"We could probably put up a decent escape too," Merrecci said. "Now, get us moving."

"Yes, Sir," Vandenbutcke replied.

Merrecci thought about smacking him too. He found himself envying Pablo Escobedo at the moment.

"Commander Leonard," Merrecci said, standing from his chair. "My shift is over. The bridge is yours. Call me before you blow something else up, please."

"Aye, Sir," Bria replied, and couldn't help but pick up on the heavy exhale Vandenbutcke unleashed.

Immediately, she asked to be briefed and then reviewed the shift roster.

"Lieutenant, Vandenbutcke," she addressed.

He barely acknowledged her.

"I see that you're running past your shift time," she said.

"I felt it wise to make myself more available under the circumstances," Vandenbutcke replied.

"I imagine you've not slept much after the Viridian was attacked."

"How'd you guess?"

"And I'll suppose that you were either on shift or awake hours before boarding the Onyx," Bria continued.

"Your point, Commander?"

"My point, Lieutenant, is that I'm curious how long it's been since you've had sleep?"

"It's not important."

"Onyx, transfer full helm control to the second pilot's chair," Bria ordered.

Vandenbutcke huffed and turned harshly in his seat.

"Just what do you think you're doing," Vandenbutcke asked.

"Just what do you think you're doing, Commander," Bria corrected yet again.

"All right," Vandenbutcke replied. "What do you think you're doing, Commander?"

"Right now, kicking you off my bridge," Bria replied. "I don't need a tired, short-fused pilot on the Admiral's helm. I expect you to be fully rested, and I expect you to brush up on your bridge and officer etiquette before you report for your next shift."

"You know what? I don't need some cadet commander—

"That's an order, Lieutenant," Bria stated flatly. "You may think that because you got away with mutiny on your last ship that you can flaunt your indignant attitude on this one. Now you get off my bridge and sleep!"

Vandenbutcke exited with no shortage of insults on his tongue.

The pilot currently in the second chair, was a young crewman second class that had previously been assigned to a smaller tow ship before Bria transferred him to the Onyx. Bria watched his brow furl and his upper teeth clamp down on his lower lip.

"Crewman Phips," Bria said. "Are you good to maintain our current course.

He barely heard her, thought he answered though. He could, he thought.

"I didn't have time to prepare," Phips said.

"What do you mean you didn't have time to prepare," Bria asked. "Did you not get time to review the course before coming on duty."

"No, Ma'am," the second pilot mumbled out, focusing on his controls. "This wasn't supposed to be my shift."

"Lieutenant-commander, whose shift was this supposed to be," Bria asked softly.

"Ensign Being was supposed to be on now, but Vandenbutcke excused him," Nandy replied.

Bria returned to her holotab and scrolled through several reports from the previous few hours.

"I see," Bria said. "Have him report to the bridge at once. And if Vandenbutcke ever alters the schedule again, put him on report."

"Yes, Ma'am," Nandy said. "Anyone else you'd like me to put on report for doing their jobs."

"But he wasn't doing his job, was he," Bria replied. "Nor were you, or you'd have stopped him, wouldn't you? People who do their jobs don't remove others from their roster just because they don't want to work with them, do they?"

Five minutes later, Ensign Being appeared on the bridge and took control of the pilot's seat. Crewman Phips couldn't hide his elation enough. Some day, he'd be ready, Bria thought.

Ten more minutes, and the bridge doors opened. Kellick stormed in.

"Am I to understand that you removed the most capable pilot from duty during an important set of maneuvers," Admiral Kellick asked. At once, Bria assumed he was angry, though he was concealing it. She'd seen enough condescension from others to know when people thought they were being polite. To be fair, he was probably the best at covering his disdain that she'd seen, but she still recognized buried disgust when she saw it.

"Admiral," Bria greeted. "With respect, is this something you should take up with Prime Admiral Merrecci?"

"I appreciate the suggestion," Kellick said. "He's not answering my call."

"He's probably asleep, Sir," Bria replied. "Would you like me to call him?"

"I would rather you explain to me why I have to take time away from my work to babysit your bridge," Kellick said.

"You don't," Bria replied.

"Oh," Kellick popped with "Well, I'd hate to waste both our time?"

He stood staring back at Bria, and she took it that he was waiting for her response, perhaps something stupid he could pounce on once more without looking like he was.

Bria bit her tongue back. She suddenly felt all eyes of the bridge on her. She knew what she wanted to say, but her mind went blank. She had met two admirals up close: Merrecci and Kellick. Others she had observed at campus events or recorded speeches. They were sober people, to the point, unapologetic. If they were apologetic, it was false.

"I mean, I'm not wasting your time, am I, Commander," Kellick continued.

Bria's mind gave her no answer. She was a little thrown by the abrupt entrance; the disgust that perhaps only she had learned to see; and his well-rehearsed congenial appearance. Apologizing sounded right. Her mind suddenly felt hazy, dizzy. Why couldn't she speak now? Because he outranked her greatly, almost as high in rank as a person could climb. Merrecci was intimidating too, but Merrecci had taken the time to trust her, if you could call what he did trust.

Merrecci.

That thought calmed her for some reason. A commanding officer that—she remembered.

"I'm sorry, Admiral Kellick," Bria said. "If I were to make a guess as to why you were here, on my bridge, it would be that you chose to listen to a tired officer who suffers from deflated ego instead of the girl from special ed who couldn't possibly understand the need for well-rested pilots. So, if I haven't answered your question fast enough for you, it's because I haven't the faintest idea why you're here, since our most capable pilot is sitting right there."

She gestured to Ensign Being and quickly threw in a "respectfully" to maintain decorum.

"It has been my understanding, Admiral, that your staff offices are elsewhere on this ship," Bria said. "But if you would like to tell me why you're on my bridge, then I'll be able to give you a more accurate guess on my part, Sir."

Admiral Kellick's face suddenly fell plain, empty and into realization.

"If Lieutenant Vandenbutcke has a problem with following orders on my bridge, I'm sure I can find him easier tasks to do somewhere else," Bria explained. "Which is something I can do because I'm the first officer on this ship. It seems a lot of people have a difficult time remembering that, which is odd because I'm the one they all think is stupid."

"Thank you for humoring an old man's curiosity," Kellick withdrew and left the bridge.

As soon as the doors closed, the room erupted into applause.

Bria held up a finger.

"No," she said, shaking her head, mostly because her entire being shook. "Not to his face, not behind his back. He's earned it."

"They're just supporting you," Nandy suggested softly. "You could be a little more grateful."

"I know what they're doing," Bria replied. "And it's not appropriate. He's earned his place more than we have."

*   *   *

Merrecci awoke early for breakfast. For the first time in days, he actually felt he got enough sleep, and no one interrupted it. When the scent of pancakes and bacon wafted through the ship, which was Onyx's artificial way to help the crew feel like they were home, Vincenti was all too happy to rush the galley.

On his first step out of bed, he tripped over Mike who was curled on his floor.

"How the hell did you get in here again," Merrecci snapped. Then he called to Prilla and demanded she come get her patient.

Like Merrecci, when she appeared at his door, she was confused, but mostly about why the prime admiral thought it was her responsibility to watch Mike.

"He's your patient," Merrecci said.

"And he's your dog, apparently," Prilla said.

"That's not funny," Merrecci retorted. "He's not a dog!"

"Is he making your ship run," Prilla asked.

Merrecci laughed, but beneath his sister's inquiring glare, Merrecci agreed that Mike was doing his job, as far as he could believe the reports that were coming from engineering.

"What will it hurt anyone on the ship to see that its commanding officer is comfortable with his own crew, even if they act like dogs," Prilla asked. "I don't know why he's latched onto you, but for some reason he has. He talks to his friends. This might be a good chance to build rapport so he'll start talking to you."

Merrecci swore at his sister as she left. Then he showered, dressed, and took his dog for a walk to the galley.

He enjoyed his eggs, pancakes with almond syrup, bacon and toasted bagel with plain cream cheese that had dried strawberries, which were ground into a powder and sprinkled over it. Mike whined, and Merrecci fed him the scraps, then loaded up his plate again just to feed his ridiculous dog.

Merrecci had work to do, but for now he relaxed. That was his tradition, a good night's sleep meant that he didn't rush his work. It was his meditation routine. He ordered a hot citrus drink with a cinnamon stick and a square of raspberry dark chocolate, and he didn't share any with Mike because chocolate was bad for dogs.

He stared out the window, mesmerized by the pattern of galaxies and stars that passed. He summoned a holographic book about orphan children who lived in a train boxcar. It was old, but he found it fascinating in beauty and simplicity.

Merrecci ordered another citrus drink. The chatter in the galley eventually slowed. Breakfast had died down. He sat in silence as the cafeteria emptied, and he read for some time.

"Prime Admiral," Kellick's voice intruded. "Seems like you found a quiet corner. May I join?"

Merrecci welcomed him with a simple nod to the bench across from him.

Mike growled from beneath the table.

"Forgive my dog," Merrecci said.

"One of your special crew," Kellick asked.

"One of our engineers," Merrecci said.

"I wish you hadn't have told me that."

Kellick sat with a cup of coffee, stale, but Kellick liked his coffee a little burned. He focused on his own holotab, and Merrecci let him do his work. Eventually, Mike ran off to prepare for his shift in Engineering.

Chatter picked up as the doors to the Galley opened and closed once more. The staff welcomed a group of three civilians who had missed breakfast but could use the bagels and fruit.

Three more tables eventually filled with cliques of comrades, sharing in past experiences or exchanging get-to-know-you stories.

Merrecci shared a familiar look with Kellick, one that explained how much he agreed that their quiet time had gone. Then he scrolled through his current chapter and believed he could manage the remaining nine pages before he'd mark himself as done for the day and prepare to take up his mantle again.

Before the end of the third page, amidst Kellick's conversational intrusions, a line had formed at the serving counter, and half the tables in the room had filled. The galley continued to grow in chatter up through his fifth page.

"If it isn't our fearless navigator," the familiar voice of Vandenbutcke drew above all others enough that it interrupted Merrecci's reading.

Merrecci glanced up to see Vandenbutcke sitting with two other crewmembers. One, Merrecci hadn't met personally. She was a special inventory officer that oversaw the shuttle bays and warehouses. He pulled up the mental image of her military files in his brain. Her name was Lieutenant Hassle. The other person was Adrigga Nandy.

Pablo Escobedo had been passing the table with Drinker Bone and their friend who had that perma-grin across his face and who never spoke, Willis. Drinker held a tray of food in one hand. In the other, he balanced a large green ball of some sort made of wires and small pieces of glass.

Pablo nodded politely to Vandenbutcke and those at his table, then kept looking for somewhere to sit with all of his friends.

"Oh hey! It's our perfect navigator," Vandenbutcke announced. "Now make sure you bump into every chair on your way to your table so no one can find you? And try not to get lost. Okay?"

His table snickered at Vandenbutcke's humor.

"Not likely," Pablo replied. "I'm not letting you steer."

Pablo and his friends continued walking, while Vandenbutcke and his company fell silent.

Vandenbutcke's face had stiffened.

"It's okay," Nandy suggested. "You have to expect that when dealing with dunces."

"Dunces," Vandenbutcke asked. "I just thought they were retards." He tipped his glass of whatever he was drinking at the comment.

"Ha," Willis cried in his strange laughter.

Vandenbutcke stood immediately and all eyes now fell upon him. The room fell silent, afraid they'd miss the climax of the entertainment. It could be quite boring for many people on a warship no matter how exciting bridge-life could be.

Kellick and Merrecci's eyes turned upon each other's, aware that so many had not noticed either of the off-duty admirals tucked into the corner, one with his face in a book, the other with his back to the crowd.

"You got something to say," Vandenbutcke asked.

He stepped towards Willis and his friends who were finally sitting down at a round table with one chair more than they needed. As he drew up to tower over them all, Willis kept laughing.

"Well come on, then," Vandenbutcke said hovering over Willis. "Let's hear what's so funny, funny man."

Willis laughed harder.

"He doesn't speak," Pablo said.

"He doesn't speak?"

"No," Drinker reaffirmed.

Vandenbutcke snickered, shaking his head, and turning away.

"You're right," Vandebutcke said to his eating companions. "Retards."

"And yet," Pablo said. "We're not the ones who got demoted two full ranks our first day aboard the ship."

This caused Vandenbutcke to stop cold and turn, ready to speak.

Kellick despite his amused smile at the last comment, appeared to want to say something, but Merrecci silently waved him down.

"If we're retards, and most of us got promoted," Drinker added. "What does that say about material?"

"Material," Vandenbutcke asked, then snapped his fingers. "You're stroke boy." His eyes fell to the ball in Drinker's hand. "What is that?"

"Christmas lights," Drinker said.

"What?"

"The materialcator made it for me," Drinker said.

"Why," Vandenbutcke asked.

"So I can untie it," Drinker replied.

"That makes a lot of sense," Vandenbutcke said. "This how they keep dummies busy?"

"Don't know, haven't seen you try one yet," Pablo added, he reached up and scrolled his lint roller over Vandenbutcke's shoulder.

"Really," Vandenbutcke retorted. "Look. Everyone knows that at the first chance of getting real crew members, you're all gone."

"Says you," Pablo snapped.

"Yeah, says me," Vandenbutcke replied.

"What are you," Pablo said. "In middle school? Nerd!"

"Once people realize you're not even material to being the best pilot here, you'll see," Drinker said.

"You think so," Vandenbutcke asked. "We're at war. You have no idea what battle's really like. Seeing people die. People like me save people like you when you're panicking in your boots. I've even time traveled three times. Have you ever time traveled?"

"We're in space," Pablo replied. "Who hasn't?"

This time the entire galley bust up laughing, except Vandenbutcke's table and Merrecci's, though Merrecci and Kellick watched each other fighting the urge.

"Obviously, you don't understand reading between the lines. None of you belong here," Vandenbutcke burst sternly. "Not you, not your retarded friends in engineering, not your dog and certainly not that girl who'll always be a constant reminder to refill the paper roll in the head."

Again, the room exploded with laughter, Vandenbutcke was especially proud.

And here, Merrecci saw her. No one else had seen her. They were too focused on what they thought had been entertainment, to see that she had meandered in behind it all. However, Merrecci had seen her. He wasn't sure how long she'd been there. He cursed himself for not acting sooner, but there was a part of him that wanted to see his crew work their issues out on their own, and that's all this was. At the same time, he understood everyone's frustration. It wasn't the crew he wanted either. Now, he saw the folly.

Bria might have been there maybe only a moment, but her shriveled face was there now. For some reason, it didn't seem like the crew working out their differences anymore. She saw Merrecci. Kellick followed the prime admiral's gaze and saw her too. Bria set her plate down silently at the counter and exited without anyone but the admirals knowing she was there.

Kellick looked back to Merrecci and softly asked what he was waiting for, all without saying a word.

Merrecci stood and turned into the room, and the entire crowd fell silent. Several people began ducking out the door, and he wished he could tell who had.

Merrecci read Nandy's mouth form the words "oh shit!" She joined the rest of the room suddenly snapping to sheepish attention.

"It's so nice to get to finally meet so many of you," Merrecci said.

Admiral Kellick, with his back to the room once more, might have smirked, might have been angry at his commanding prime admiral. With admirals, it was difficult to tell. Even with himself.

Merrecci shut down his holographic book then took up his plate and mug. He marched his way back towards the other side of the galley to recycle his dishes and leftover crumbs. He said nothing to Vandenbutcke, didn't look at him either. However, he did stop in front of Nandy.

"I guess, smarter to betray your crew after they save your life, right," Merrecci said, all without ever turning to face her. Then he moved on.

He arrived to his shift early. Almma had the bridge currently and was all too happy to relinquish her watch to the admiral.

"Sir," Almma said softly. "Just so you know. I'm giving very serious thought to kicking Vandenpecker's happy stabby off."

"You heard, huh," Merrecci asked graciously.

Almma nodded, and he remembered what he saw in her eyes the day he met her in Shade's service.

"Let's not do anything drastic," Merrecci said.

"It's not drastic," Almma said. "It's art."

Then the thought struck Merrecci to release Almma from bridge duty so that she could report back with the next shift command, and maybe she'd be cooled off before Nandy's rotation.

During Merrecci's watch, he was fairly bored. Hiding wasn't quite as exciting when his navigator had pretty much made the Onyx invisible even without the stealth feature. Truthfully, Ensign Being had been doing all the exciting work now, so Merrecci took the time to get to know a few of his bridge mates. He managed to make one of them laugh, which he thought he should regret, but also felt he shouldn't because there were greater things to worry about now than making his crew hate him. Before he'd left, Shade told him to keep his subordinates happier. That was great when it was just his ship, when he could get away with asking for forgiveness rather than permission, but now he had an entire fleet to keep together, and it was going to take a lot of friends in low places to do that. In fact, it seemed that was the only place he could find friends now within the Franchise or whatever this actually was anymore.

The next shift began to report in nine hours later. Merrecci gave the command chair to Nandy, then retreated into his office without saying a word to her. She may have tried to apologize, but he chose to hear nothing from her unless it was preluded with the sound of an alarm warning about some kind of imminent danger. Even then, he thought he might just have to ignore her a little longer to let her see herself fail and need him or Bria to take control of the situation.

Three hours beyond that, Almma returned to man the chief security station.

"Lieutenant-commander," Nandy greeted.

"Lieutenant-ho-mander," Almma greeted back.

"Excuse me?"

"What," Almma asked.

Nandy brushed the interaction off.

Almma logged into her console, and the holo suddenly erupted in a flurry of fireworks and Rachmaninoff's 18th Variation of Rhapsody on a Theme of Paganini. From their ashes, heart-shaped balloons inflated and rose until they disappeared from the confines of the hologram. After they had risen, a giant holo of Almma's face faded in. She was laughing, throwing her hair as if she'd was proud of her new shampoo and conditioning results. She started blushing as if someone behind the camera had told a joke. Then Alma's full body filled the holo, and she was punching the air. Next, Almma was blowing a kiss, then she was eating chocolates and getting lost in their decadence. Anyone who knew these scenes would have immediately recognized the commercials that originally had a teenage redhead going through the motions, but the girl had been replaced with Almma's face. Suddenly, that face was laughing. Now, Almma's hologram was walking a runway in a slim dress, flashbulbs exploded all around her as she strutted and dominated the stage while someone sang about how he was too sexy. Almma's holo turned, walked off and the curtains to the runway closed. At that very moment, confetti canons filled the air with all sorts of nonsensical paper and glitter. Once it had cleared, all the fans filling the bleachers of Busch Memorial stadium all stood from the seats with colored posters to form the words: "Your secret admirer!"

The bridge filled with "awe."

This was followed with the fans posters asking. "Will you have dinner with me?"

"Gee, I wonder who that could be," Nandy said.

Then the wall changed its message to "And possibly sex?"

Merrecci's guffaw filled the bridge, having come out to find out what the commotion was. He suddenly caught himself.

"Oh, Lieutenant-commander," Merrecci said. "I'm so sorry."

"You know," Almma said. "I'll bet he gets laid more than Nandy does."

"Uncalled for," Nandy snapped, standing abruptly from her chair.

"Why? You don't think it's true, do—," she stopped as she caught sight of Merrecci wagging his head at her.

"I think we can let him think no one knows," Merrecci said and suddenly erupted with, "Where's the St. Louis arch? It's supposed to be right there!"

"Looks like someone erased it, Sir," Almma replied.

"It ain't erased if it's still there!" Merrecci abruptly turned back to the office suites, grumbling about how he had to fix that too. Before the doors sealed him off, he was in the middle of saying something about Cardinals rolling in their graves.

Another hour passed, and Bria joined the bridge for her shift. Merrecci thought about requesting a conference with her in his royal chambers, but he felt it would be intruding upon how she might deal with her crew on her own.

Then, the Onyx came to a stop.

"Ma'am," Ensign Being announced. "We've arrived at the

Sentrale System."

"Thank you, Ensign," Vandenbutcke said. He had entered the bridge just as the ship had stopped and was timely enough to catch this very part of the discussion. "Navigator, please plot a course into the system."

Vandenbutcke took over the pilot's chair and sent Being to the assistant's.

"Hold position here," Bria said.

Then she informed the admiral that they had arrived. Merrecci returned to the bridge and placed his attention upon the holographic map in the center of it. The map was incomplete, littered with black splotches.

"What is all of this," Merrecci asked.

"Sentrale isn't fully charted, Admiral," Vandenbutcke replied. "It's likely missing information. I'll perform a long distance scan and consider a new course."

"No," Merrecci replied. Then he contacted Ensign Pablo Escobedo and requested his presence on the bridge.

"Shall I perform the long distance scans," Vandenbutcke asked.

"No," Merrecci replied again. "That's not the pilot's job."

Merrecci summoned Bria and Nandy to his side at the holograph railing to help him examine the map.

"What do you think this could be," Merrecci asked.

"The Lieutenant may be correct," Nandy said. "It may just be uncharted."

"I agree with Nandy on this one," Bria said.

"No, you don't," Merrecci replied, looking deeper still into the hologram.

"I have no reason to doubt it could be possible," Bria said. "Both she and Vandenbutcke have seen more space than I have."

Merrecci looked scornfully just now upon Bria, and her own brow told him he was correct in observing that she hadn't given an honest answer, so she amended her response.

"It's just," Bria said, cocking her head at the map very much as a dog might do to get a better look at an ugly baby. "Don't these empty parts seem a little too consistent in shape to be uncharted?"

She magnified the map and revealed many black balloon-like blotches.

"Bridge to engineering," Bria called.

"I want to answer," Dawn's voice bellowed.

"You always get to answer," Mirror's snapped.

"Nu-uh,"

"Uh-huh," Mirror retorted. "You always answer. You never let anyone else answer. You're selfish that w—

"Engineering. Are you all three down there," Bria asked.

"It's Bria," Dawn said.

"Hi Bria," Mirror added. "Hey, you weren't in group last time. Are you going to go to group next time? We had those cookies you like with the Bravonian cream."

Vandenbutcke snorted. Bria clenched the railing.

"That's enough, Lieutenant," Almma hissed.

"Who laughed," Dawn erupted. "Was that the pilot who looks like a serial killer."

"Stop it," Mirror's voice demanded.

"Well, he does," Dawn said. "Serial killers always look like man-whores."

"Dawn, stop," Mirror said. "We're on the air."

"He's such a dick," Dawn continued to ramble. "Did you hear what he said 'bout Bria."

"Sir," Vandenbutcke complained to Merrecci.

"Yeah, that's him," Dawn said. "I know a dick when I hear one peeing on your leg."

"Listen, is Mike with you," Bria asked.

"He went to find cheese," Mirror said.

"She doesn't need to know that," Dawn interrupted. "She probably needs our help."

"Can you take a look at the map of the Sentrale System that we're looking at right now," Bria asked.

"Duh," Dawn replied. "We're engineer's, not the chief pilot!"

Somewhere in the bridge, someone chuckled.

Bria snapped her finger, and the snicker stopped.

"Oh my god," Almma crowed. "I love this girl!"

"Do you have any ideas what might have caused these black spheres in the map," Bria asked, trying to maintain control under Merrecci's eye. She wished he'd speak up though.

Silence followed until Merrecci asked, "Hello?"

"We're getting Mike," Mirror bellowed. "Can you please calm down a moment?"

Vandenbutcke snickered again.

"That's enough of that," Bria said, snapping her fingers at him this time.

"Yes, Ma'am," Vandenbutcke replied. "Better not upset the three dumbketeers."

"That's it," Dawn roared. "I'm kicking his ass."

Mirror's voice was suddenly calling after Dawn to come back.

More silence followed, broken only by the bridge doors swinging open to allow Ensign Escobedo inside. He took his post, nearly pressing the current navigator out the seat to take over. Pablo immediately began wiping down the control panel with the edge of his sleeve.

"Now, Ensign Escobedo," Vandenbutcke started in. "That wasn't very polite. We have to remember to treat others as we want to be treated."

"Now, Lieutenant. We don't always have to be condescending second-rate pilots," Pablo replied.

"Truth," Ensign Being muttered.

"What was that, Ensign Shaky," Vandenbutcke mimicked a shaking fit towards Being.

"What are you? A dumbass," Being asked. "You're going to put your eye out."

"That's okay," Escobedo said as he was now using his lint roller to clean his sleeve of what it had just wiped off his control console. "He can go back and put it back in. He's a time traveler. Remember?"

Bria snapped her fingers again, this time abruptly turning. Merrecci gave her the floor.

Vandenbutcke was about to speak but was suddenly interrupted.

"Mike says the balloons are nothing," Mirror replied.

"You mean they're insignificant," Merrecci asked.

"No," Mirror replied. "They're nothing. It's like they're spaceless space."

Suddenly Mike barked.

"What does that mean," Merrecci asked.

"It's eating our sensor readings," a male voice from engineering answered. Bria didn't recognize it, but she assumed it was one of the engineering crew.

"You're saying where space is supposed to be. There is no space," Merrecci asked.

"Yes," Mirror and the male's voice replied. Mike Barked with them.

"Isn't that what space is," Nandy asked. "Nothing?"

"No," Mirror corrected. "Space is something," Mirror explained. "You can see in it. You can move in it. You can measure it. But this is nothing."

"Here, watch," Mirror announced.

The bridge lights flashed red, and the Onyx fired a torpedo.

"Who fired that," Merrecci erupted.

"I had to fire it to show you," Mirror explained.

Merrecci's eyes rolled at Bria who was trying not to look sheepish.

The torpedo flew into the map of the Sentrale System and was swallowed thirty seconds later by one of the black balloons without any kind of reaction.

"Do," Nandy started, stopped, then tried again. "Do we know what happened to the torpedo?"

"Yes," Mirror said.

"It turned into nothing," the male voice from engineering added.

"Would you launch a probe at another bubble," Merrecci asked.

A probe launched. Two minutes later, it too disappeared.

"Try and bounce another probe off the bubble's skin," Pablo said.

Another probe launched.

"Wait. No," Merrecci scolded. "I am still the commander of this ship, and I didn't say to fire anything."

"But you were going to," Mirror said.

"Then you wait until I do," Merrecci scolded. "Do that again, and I'll—"

Another probe launched.

"What did I just say," Merrecci was almost yelling now.

"You just told her to do it again," Bria informed.

Merrecci groaned and scrubbed his face into the palms of his hands.

"If," Merrecci drew out, "you ever do that again without it being an order from a commanding bridge officer, the only rooms on this ship that you will ever see again are yours and the galley prep areas.

Do you understand?"

"Sorry," Mirror said. "Are you mad at me."

The first probe hit the edge of a bubble and suddenly broke into an unpowered spin. Moments later, the second one struck the edge and began spiraling off as well. Both had a half of their bodies completely missing.

"So, we can't hit those things," Merrecci said.

"And we have to go into that system, Sir," Bria iterated.

"Impossible," Vandenbutcke said.

"Charting a course now," Pablo announced.

"Captain," Vandenbutcke urged.

"Prime Admiral," Bria corrected.

"Prime Admiral," Vandenbutcke explained. "If all those blotches eat our sensor readings, can we even see far enough into this system to travel safely. I mean, look."

Vandenbutcke typed at his terminal, and the holomap magnified to show multiple layers of even more spheres of nothingness hidden behind what the holo had already been showing. Some of the black splotches were larger, denser in some areas.

"And we don't even know if there's anything in there to make it worth the trip," Vandenbutcke warned.

"She said they're in there," Bria said.

Merrecci sighed.

"Opinions," Merrecci asked.

"Don't touch them," Mirror's voice called.

"I agree with the mentally diluted there," Vandenbutcke said.

Merrecci thanked his engineering staff and ended the transmission with them. His eyes wagged between Nandy and Bria.

"What do you think, Leonard," Merrecci finally asked.

Bria found herself looking to Nandy, then past her to one side of the bridge with consoles manned by lives that could end based upon what she said. Then she thought about Pablo and his OCD. He was meticulous. Finally, she looked to Merrecci.

"If Ensign Escobedo can plot a course, and our pilot follows it to the letter, then I have full confidence that we can get through.

Merrecci looked unsure, as did Nandy, but he turned to Pablo and asked, "You're sure you have a course?"

"Enough to get us in deep enough to let me figure out some more," Pablo replied.

"Can you show it to me," Merrecci asked.

The holographic map exploded in size, revealing a magnified sector with masses of nothingness and a line representing Escobedo's plotted path for about ten thousand light years.

"No," Vandenbutcke replied. "Look how tight that is."

A section of the map blew up even more to show an opening among five spheres that was only fifty percent larger than the Onyx itself.

"If these things do to this ship what they did to those probes and torpedo, we die out here," Vandenbutcke said.

The bridge doors opened again. Dawn took three steps in, stopped, and poised a finger at the chief pilot's console.

"You're dead," she announced, and then flew at him.

She made it halfway across the bridge to Vandenbutcke, who had instantly leapt from his seat. It was unclear if he was doing so to flee, or if he was gearing to take a fighting stance.

Suddenly Almma was in front of Dawn, restraining her. One of her death batons extended to help block her from getting deeper into the bridge.

"I've got an unexpired can of whoop-ass with your name written all over it," Dawn shouted while reaching over Almma's shoulder for Vandenbutcke who was half a room beyond her reach.

"Can we get that psychotic reject off the bridge already," Vandenbutcke cried.

Dawn tore the death baton from Almma's hand, leaving the lieutenant-commanding tactical officer's jaw agape. In an instant, the baton launched from Dawn's grasp. Almma tried to catch it, expecting that the weapon would have flown at Vandenbutcke, but Dawn's fingers flipped the baton left of her target instead, and it cracked Ensign Mailer in the side of the head, knocking her out of her chair.

"Oh god," Dawn cried. "I'm sorry." Then she turned back to Vandenbutcke. "Look what you made me do, you dick!" She turned back to Mailer's console. "Is she dead?"

Mailer fumbled to climb back up into her chair.

"That hurt," Mailer announced.

"I said I was sorry," Dawn shouted.

"What is wrong with you?""

"I'm going to kick your ass," Dawn screeched.

"Enough," Merrecci finally shouted. "When did I inherit a zoo?"

"And that's the people who run your ship," Vandenbutcke stated.

"That's right! My ship," Merrecci retorted before turning to Bria as if somehow this was her fault.

"I'll deal with Dawn, but I still have full confidence in our crew," Bria said to Merrecci. "We have a lot of ways to worry about dying out here."

The corner of Merrecci's mouth twitched.

"Give the order," Merrecci instructed. He seemed to contemplate his options for a moment, then stated. "If you're willing to bet my life on it."

Bria had been ready to release the order, but suddenly stopped.

For her 21st birthday, her parents and grandparents took her to Vegas. One of the attractions was the historic Strip Casino. Her grandfather had collected several old currency coins that he called nickels for just this occasion. They spent them all. He had expected they would. Then he suggested that she take a seat at a blue felt table nearly filled with people who had nothing better to do. He had convinced her that she would have the best poker face and should win.

She knew the game. He'd taught her. When she found herself holding a full house with aces high, she no longer had the reserve to bet with. Her grandfather simply asked how sure she was she could win. She was certain. He gave her an entire month of his salary. Then he watched it whisked away by a man who had four twos.

Later, Bria cried, then sold the ancient Mr. Potato heads that her grandfather had uncovered while on a dig in the basement of something called a mall, which had been buried somewhere in the Rocky Mountains in central Utah when an earthquake had spilled them over an entire string of cities.

Turns out her grandfather was more hurt that she sold the Mr. Potato Heads than that she lost his money.

"Poker's never been about winning," her grandfather had told her. "It's about the conversation. Not many people who can talk about owning two millennium old Mr. Potato heads, one still in its box."

Eight months ago, when her grandfather died, his lawyer returned the Mr. Potato Heads to her.

At this thought, Bria turned from Merrecci's critical stare and ordered Almma to return Dawn to engineering; she requested medical to the bridge to help Ensign Mailer; then she turned to her pilots.

"Lieutenant Vandenbutcke," Bria said. "If you're done pissing on your crew, will you get us moving so we can discover something that's worth talking about more than just sitting here waiting on you."

Vandenbutcke turned hard in his chair and slapped his console. "Yes, Ma'am!" He pointed to navigation. "I need two alternate routes in case we need to change course, and I need navigation to stay ahead of me." Now, he turned to Ensign Being. "You keep your damned hands off the controls."

"I don't have time to plot three different courses for you," Pablo replied. "You'll get what I give you."

"Then get me another navigator who can do it," Vandenbutcke snapped.

"That's enough," Merrecci erupted. "You have the commander's orders."

"This is a bad idea," Vandenbutcke muttered.

"Shut up and color," Merrecci exclaimed. "And that goes for everyone else on this bridge. This isn't a joyride in your daddy's shuttle." He honed in on Vandenbutcke once more and finally yelled, "Move!"

"Preparing to maneuver in," Vandenbutcke said, then paused. "Wait—what are—are these gravity wells? Do these nothing things have gravity wells?"

"Yes," Pablo replied.

"Why are they blue?"

"Because I noticed through the eye-tracker that you react better to blue things on the screen than yellow. So, I made them blue. "Fly accordingly."

"Are you kidding me?"

"What's the hold up, Lieutenant," Merrecci asked.

"Going in now," Vandenbutcke said, taking a hold of both manual operating stems.

The Onyx began to shake.

"Warning," Onyx announced within just a couple of minutes of entering the system. "Multiple gravity wells and anomalies detected."

Merrecci silenced the Onyx.

The ship quaked, went still, then repeated the pattern for nearly ten minutes as Vandenbutcke steered through sweat and death at every turn. He swore once, twice, but neither were the words that would calm the chairs and walls. They rattled again, then harder.

"Report, Lieutenant," Merrecci said.

"We're shaking," Vandenbutcke roared.

"If you'd follow the course," Pablo complained.

"I am following the course, you dimwit," Vandenbutcke retorted.

"No. You keep veering off by an average of sixty three meters. It's going to get narrower. We don't have that play," Pablo said.

"This is why I asked for back up courses!"

"If you can't fly this, you can't fly those," Pablo yelled. "Fly better."

"Warning," Onyx announced. "Collision with anomaly imminent."

"That's it. I'm stopping," Vandenbutcke announced.

"You can't stop with these kinds of gravity wells," Escobedo replied. "I thought you were supposed to be a pilot!"

"Then I'm taking us back out of here," Vandenbutcke replied.

The Onyx tossed once more, causing Merrecci to suddenly grab onto Bria's arm for support. Turns out they both clenched at each other to keep from falling.

Suddenly the Onyx was shaking less.

"Damn it," Vandenbutcke cried.

"There's no room to turn around, Lieutenant. Follow the path," Pablo chided. "Are we even all here anymore."

"Warning," Onyx announced again. "Collision with anomaly imminent."

As Merrecci watched the holographic image of the Onyx passing through the strange balloons, he decided perhaps it was best to turn the battlecron off.

Bria thanked him.

"Come on," Vandenbutcke ordered the Onyx.

"Pull us out, Sir," Pablo insisted.

"What do you think I'm trying to do?"

"Sir," Pablo pled. "Get on course."

Yellow warning lights flashed throughout the bridge.

"I told you this was a bad idea," Vandenbutcke cried.

"Impact with anomaly in twelve seconds," Onyx said.

"Damn it, Admiral," Vandenbutcke said with resignation. "Nothing I can do."

Through the confusion, Ensign Being's voice announced, "Taking control of Onyx now."

Onyx groaned again, worse than before. Merrecci thought he had felt the floor warp, then straighten beneath his feet.

"What are you doing," Vandenbutcke barely managed to spit out.

"Busy," Being replied. His eyes flashed over the holographic navigational map within his own console. It was similar to the battlecron, but barely fit into the assistant pilot's control area.

The shaking subsided to simple turbulence, and Allen continued to watch the map as though he could think ahead of it. His hands moving feverishly at the controls.

"All right, Ensign," Vandenbutcke said. "You've accomplished your task. We're grateful. I'm taking control of flight—"

"Don't even think about it," Being interrupted.

"Pardon me?"

"Touch those controls, and I'll break your fingers," Allen said. "I'm not dying because you can't fly."

"Onyx is maintaining course within thirty meters," Escobedo relayed.

"Taking control now," Vandenbutcke said.

Ensign Being was suddenly to his feet.

"Sit down, Ensign," Vandenbutcke ordered. "I'm chief pilot."

The Onyx resumed its shaking, nearly throwing Merrecci over the railing of the holo.

"Warning," Onyx resumed reciting.

Allen returned to his seat and tried to take control again.

"Unlock my console, Lieutenant," Ensign Being demanded. He fell into his controls.

"No chance in hell I let you drag this ship with you," Vandenbutcke snapped and swore as the Onyx rattled so hard that the bridge filled with pinging reverb from her very bowels. Her spine should have broken but did not.

"Admiral," Pablo announced, looking up from his continuous chart plotting. "He's going to kill us."

Nandy suddenly fell, then slid right across the floor and down, into the dugout as the ship jerked especially so.

"You mean you killed us," Vandenbutcke yelled at Pablo.

"Admiral," Being insisted. "He can't do this! I can!"

"Onyx," Merrecci called through a rattling brain. "Transfer full flight control to the assistant pilot's console."

Immediately, Being went to work.

"Sir, I must formally protest," Vandenbutcke cried. "You're making a mistake. You know what I can do."

"You can't do this," Pablo exploded.

"You're on report Ensign," Vandenbutcke erupted back. "You have any idea how many hours I've logged in flight."

"Not enough!"

"Lieutenant," Merrecci cried sternly. "Ensign. You're both on report."

Merrecci watched as Being reestablished the familiar intensity that he had witnessed during their escape from Earth. His calm demeanor, free from shaking, returned the moment his hands took over the controls. He was as superhero whose weakness was not having pilot controls in his hands.

"Onyx," Merrecci announced. "Promote Ensign Allen Being to role of chief pilot along with all command privileges and assign Lieutenant Philbin Vandenbutcke to assistant pilot."

As Vandenbutcke glared more heavily at Being than at Merrecci, the prime admiral walked to his command chair and took a seat to demonstrate how smoothly the ride had become.

"Is there anything any of us can do to help at this time, Chief Being," Merrecci asked.

"Yep," Being replied, intent in his task. "Shut up."

Merrecci abruptly stood and commanded Bria and Vandenbutcke to follow him to his ready room.

"You pick that imbecile over me, Sir," Vandenbutcke said as soon as the sound-proof doors sealed them from the bridge.

"No. I picked you over him, and I rectified that mistake," Merrecci retorted quickly. "And I would think very carefully about complaining about a subordinate taking your chair."

The door clicked.

"What," Merrecci cried.

Almma and Nandy entered. One of Almma's batons was fully extended, and it rested against her shoulder.

"I thought I should be here in case you needed me to hooker pop Vandenbutcke, Sir," Almma said. "He's a security risk."

"And you," Merrecci asked, snapping a sharp eye to Nandy.

"Counsel, Sir," Nandy replied softly.

Vandenbutcke smirked. It was meant towards Bria, but it hadn't escaped Merrecci's attention.

"Don't, for one second, think you can outplay me," Merrecci interrupted with a fully extended hand pointed at the Lieutenant, until Vandenbutcke's face fell in the harsh realization he couldn't stand up to Merrecci. The prime admiral turned to Bria. "What do you think we should do with a selfish officer who seeks only to elevate himself?"

Bria thought quickly, but as she was about to articulate it, Nandy spoke.

"Ma'am, if I may offer a recommendation," she said.

Bria seemed as caught off guard as Merrecci was able to hide, but she believed she saw the surprise in his eyes.

"What," Bria asked robotically without turning to her.

"He came aboard as a commanding officer who knew better than most of us," Nandy explained. "I recommend a week in the brig for insubordination and suspension from all bridge duties until he can remember decorum and loyalty becoming of an officer."

"You can't be serious," Vandenbutcke snorted.

"It's my duty to point out that he has degraded his fellow crew, his superiors and the office which he holds," Nandy said softly, while avoiding looking Vandenbutcke in the eye. "Recommend a week in the brig to help him cool off."

"That's a bit extreme," Vandenbutcke said, his tone towards Nandy instantly colder.

"Perhaps, Admiral Kellick could give you a second opinion about that," Merrecci said.

Bria found herself looking over Nandy, who was staring at the floor to avoid looking at anyone.

"Two weeks confined to quarters with minimal access to ship functions, then no more than one shift a week on the bridge," Bria finally said.

"You're kidding, right," Vandenbutcke asked, turning to Merrecci. "She's kidding, right?"

"Because we need you to develop curriculum to train more pilots," Bria explained. "We don't have enough skilled pilots. We need them. You may not be ready to be chief pilot, but you can teach."

"Why don't you just have your golden boy do it, Commander," Vandenbutcke spat.

"Because I want you to do it. Once you have taught our new pilots in the shuttle bays and simulators, you can start preparing them for bridge duty. Then we can revisit if you're ready to return to the helm full-time by then."

"You might as well just discharge me," Vandenbutcke said. "Teaching is where pilots go to die."

"Or to rediscover their passion," Bria said. "You must realize you're the only one we have who can do this. Where do you think you can serve your crew as a pilot better?"

Vandenbutcke was silent, then nodded as he realized he had been beaten and would be knocked down even more if he kept fighting it.

"And I will add," Merrecci said. "You will be required to meet with the ship psychologist, Lieutenant-commander Wanship three times a week. You will put in regular hours in the simulator where you will shadow Chief Pilot Being's recorded flights until you are deemed qualified for full bridge duty once more. And you're demoted to ensign until you can remember how to be part of a crew."

Again, Vandenbutcke nodded.

"Almma, please escort the ensign to his quarters for no less than two weeks and make sure he has additional ship access to only those tools to allow him to prepare the training program," Merrecci instructed.

"Sir," Nandy spoke again, first to Merrecci then to Bria, "Ma'am."

"I think the punishment he has is fitting enough for now, Lieutenant-commander," Merrecci said and was about to allow Almma and Vandenbutcke to exit.

"I should be confined to quarters too," Nandy began explaining before anyone could leave the room. "I wasn't any better." She turned to Bria, who only now looked Nandy in the eyes since she had reported for her shift. "I'm so sorry. It won't happen again. If we send Vandenbutcke to solitary, I should go too."

Bria looked to Merrecci.

"Your call," Merrecci said.

Bria studied Nandy for a moment and almost started yelling.

"There is a difference between insubordination on a bridge and blowing off steam in a galley," Bria explained carefully.

Nandy appeared stung, perhaps realizing that Bria was aware of what had happened earlier that day in the galley.

"We need you on the bridge," Bria said. "You're the leading candidate for valedictorian of your class, spending three extra years to get two additional specializations. I have a record for the lowest scores in the history of the academy. I can only imagine how disheartening it can be for you. More than that, you could have thrown him under the bus and left it at that."

Bria then dismissed Nandy back to her duties and Almma to see Vandenbutcke off the bridge.

"Just between you and me," Merrecci stated, once they were alone. "This is the most screwed up crew I've ever had, but it is my crew, and you are my first officer."

Bria thanked him.

"So, I don't ever want to see the kind of nonsense I just saw out there again," Merrecci said. "Keep it under control."

Then he dismissed her.

In the several minutes that followed, he couldn't help notice how calm he seemed to be as the Onyx sailed smoothly past countless balloons that could end their existence at any moment.

"I'll be damned," he said, realizing the sense of security that he found Allen Being brought to his ship.

With his shift finally over, Merrecci gave himself permission to retire to his apartment until he was needed, leaving command of his vessel in the hands of his crew, which is how it was supposed to work.

He left his quarters long enough for a run. He had taken to the lowest deck where there was generally less travel. After about two miles into his routine, a strange, singular alarm blared from his right just as he was jaunting out in front of an adjoining hallway. Something struck his side, and he tumbled over the front of whatever hit him. He found himself suddenly in Almma's lap.

Dawn who was sitting directly next to Almma, had a black wheel of some sort in front of her. She took one look at Merrecci, jumped out of her seat, and ran off down the hall from which she had just come.

Merrecci took some time and awkward gyrations to pull himself out of Almma's lap and, after looking like an idiot, got himself back to his feet where he realized that what had struck him was a white cubicle with four wheels.

"What is that," Merrecci asked.

"What is what, Sir," Almma played dumb.

Merrecci tried to cleanse himself with a breath before refocusing on Almma who was trying to look innocent.

"Tell me why I actually believed you'd be a good fit for this crew," Merrecci inquired.

"Because you like my honesty, and I'm hot as hell," Almma said. "Just ask my secret admirer."

Merrecci snorted but tried not to look approving. He gestured to the cubicle once more.

"What are you two doing in this thing," he asked.

"I think Dawn said it's called a goof cart, and she wanted to know if I could teach her to operate it," Almma explained.

"A goof cart," Merrecci asked.

"Yeah, for an old game called goof."

"Have you ever operated one before," Merrecci asked.

"Well, of course I've operated a goof cart," Almma replied. "Everyone in the whole damned universe in this day and age has learned to drive goddamned goof cart from god knows what century."

"If you've never operated one, why would you think you could teach her how to do it?"

"Well, that's why she was driving because I didn't know," Almma said. "I just told her where to go."

Merrecci rubbed the bridge of his nose. "Why would you encourage her to do something like this?"

"When I was walking her back to engineering earlier, she was really upset, and it occurred to me that she's someone who was always told she couldn't do something while being forced to hang out with a bunch of other people who were always told they shouldn't do something either. When I asked her what she wanted to do, she said she wanted to learn to drive something called a cart. We stopped at the library to look up what it meant, and the first thing we found was a bunch of people clapping softly at a bunch of nerdy, old white guys smacking a small ball. Then they all chased it down in one of these goof cart things because if they'd tried running instead, they'd definitely fall and break their hips. But that sounded like it might be funny to watch, so we stole this one and took it for a try."

"And now Dawn's running down the halls to hide from me because she knows she's in trouble," Merrecci said.

He then climbed into the seat that Dawn had been sitting behind before she ran off. He placed his hands on the wheel.

"It's called a golf cart," Merrecci said. "It's hardly what you teach someone to drive in."

He pressed on the floor pedal to propel the vehicle forward. Then he drove into the adjoining corridor, reversed, then pulled back to face it into the hall that Dawn had fled down.

"Let's go get her," he said.

It only took a couple of minutes to find her huddled near a lift where she waited for the doors to open.

"Ensign Platte," Merrecci said, stepping out of the golf cart. "When you come to an intersection, you have to slow down."

Dawn's face suddenly softened, and she looked to the cart then back to Merrecci.

"Go ahead," Merrecci said, but he thought he shouldn't have.

Dawn might have thanked him. He couldn't tell for sure, her smile might have gotten in the way as she shoved past him and jumped right back behind the circular steering mechanism.

"And stop hitting people or I won't let you do this anymore," Merrecci said, grabbing the wheel.

Dawn abruptly agreed, and Merrecci released his grip.

"Please don't damage my ship, Almma" the prime admiral said.

"Are you kidding," Almma retorted. "We're going to tear this shag shit up!"

Dawn's finger suddenly turned into Almma's face. "You don't have to swear about everything!"

Then Dawn turned her attention to the hall in front of her, and the golf cart sped off into it.

Merrecci went up one deck and finished his run before returning to his quarters where he showered, read a chapter of a book so horrible that he had to keep reading, and then went to bed. Here, he found Mike was curled up. When Merrecci yelled at him to get out of his quarters, the dog-man happily leapt from the bed and curled up on the floor.

Whether it was out of defeat or fatigue, Vincenti had the fabricator create some heavy blankets for Mike to roll into.

Finally, the prime admiral allowed himself to sleep.

Then stillness awoke him. To a ship's commanding officer, stillness was as loud as an alarm. In the process of getting to his uniform, he found the corner of his end-table with the soft underside of his knee.

"Bridge," he called between swearing. "Report."

Bria's voice answered back with, "Sir, I was about to call you. you'll want to see this."

Merrecci was out of his quarters and to the bridge in perhaps thirty seconds. The holo was black.

"Why is there nothing on the holo," Merrecci asked.

"Because there is nothing, Sir," Bria replied and then continued to explain because she knew she hadn't given enough information. "For the past five hours, Ensigns Being and Escobedo have been tunneling us in deeper through the Sentrale System, and then this just came out of nowhere."

"What is it," Merrecci asked.

"So much nothing that we don't know how well we can navigate around it and all the other empty splotches," Bria said.

"And you couldn't see it coming?"

"It's been pretty thick here the past hour."

"So, all this to find a dead end," Merrecci said. "Turn us around and take us out."

"I have a thought, Sir," Drinker's voice rose from one of the back ends of the bridge where he had been sitting alone at a plain civilian table. Upon it, a holographic 3-d puzzle made of pixels were forming the image of the Abraham Lincoln Memorial.

The prime admiral had come to like enough of Drinker's suggestions that he'd extended an invitation to continue providing them. Anticipating he might be needed, Bria had summoned Drinker even before Merrecci had woken up. As with all bridge personnel, Drinker was still only-allowed enough information to understand their mission. Only those on the bridge were allowed to know about the Rhaxians though. The bounty on them was so high that Merrecci doubted it wise to let it run the halls of his vessel through common conversations.

"What's your idea," Merrecci asked.

"We go in," Drinker said.

Merrecci guffawed, then asked if Drinker was serious. Drinker was.

"Sir," Drinker explained. "Imagine your material is on the edge of extinction. You are hunted, bounties so large there's nowhere to material. You try to hide in a material that's notorious for being material, and you end up here. What do you do?"

"I think I get this one, Sir," Bria said.

Merrecci waved her down. "I think I get it too. You're saying the Rhaxians were so desperate to survive that they," he clicked his tongue and pointed at the black holo before adding, "went in."

Drinker nodded.

"We're not doing that," Merrecci said. "What if they aren't even alive?"

"They're alive, Admiral," Cindy Lou's voice came over the Bridge. Merrecci rolled his eyes.

"We had a deal. Get off my ship's communications," Merrecci yelled.

"Why" Cindy replied. "You're just going to come down here and ask me if they're alive anyway."

Seeing that Merrecci was reaching the end of his patience with the cargo god, Bria spoke first.

"How do you know they're alive," Bria asked.

Silence followed for several seconds before Cindy answered with, "because I was there."

"What do you mean you were there," Merrecci asked.

Cindy didn't answer.

"Respond," Merrecci ordered.

"If you would like someone to respond, you must first address the person or department that you wish to speak to," Onyx announced. "For example, if you wish to speak to engineering, you should say—

"Bridge to Cindy Lou," Merrecci announced.

"There is no crew member with that name on board," the Onyx replied.

"Bridge to Quarantine A," Merrecci said.

Silence.

"Bridge to Quarantine A," Merrecci repeated.

Merrecci spun towards the door, announcing that he was going to speak with their guest.

The bridge filled with silly laughter.

"Don't be so gullible, Admiral," Cindy Lou chucked.

"I don't find tampering with my ship's systems funny," Merrecci said.

"I never tamper."

"Stay out of my ship systems."

Cindy laughed.

"I will certainly do my best. Just not now. You need to go in to find the Rhaxians."

"I'm not risking this crew to go in there just because you say to," Merrecci refused.

"Then you will fail your mission, and Earth will die. Cindy Lou out."

Merrecci sighed heavily, more in consternation than frustration.

"Ensign, Being," Merrecci articulated. "Take us in."

9
▲
Rocks

Charity's penlight strobed deep into Merrecci's brain. He had seen it. He had told her many times to stop, yelled at her to do so, but she continued her work and spoke as though she couldn't hear him. She pulled the penlight away several times to change its color and brightness. Once, it made him scream in an agony that he had never felt. It was something in his spine, boiling, yet so cold it felt like his spinal fluid was freezing and then becoming shards of sand. Charity swore, changed the light, and warmed him up again.

"Figures he'd be such a pain," the man assisting Charity said. What was his name? Oh yeah. Merrecci remembered Nurse Gibralter. What a turd.

Then, something happened when she applied a lime green filter. It caused him to lift straight up and start drawing in deep breaths as though he had never felt oxygen before.

"I think I've had enough of that light," Merrecci snapped and felt his voice didn't want to carry the correct volume, so it came out raspy.

"Don't move," Charity urged.

Both she and Cora were now pressing him back into the floor.

"Look at the light," Charity said.

"You shine one more light in my face—," Merrecci started and then felt his jaw lock and the pain hit.

Charity swore again and held a square beam as large as his head only inches from his face.

The pain subsided at once.

"What was that all about," Merrecci demanded to know.

"Evidence, you don't listen," Gibralter replied.

"Quobalt to bridge," Charity announced. "The prime admiral is out of his coma."

"Thank you for the update," an unfamiliar male's voice replied. "How long until he's able to return to duty?"

"Doctor," Merrecci asked, but he was really ordering Charity to report.

"You put the entire crew into coma," Charity replied.

Merrecci realized that he was in hospital, yet he wasn't really surprised. He had seen the walls, ceiling, the staff. The voices and conversations that had been going on around him previously had all suggested he knew he was in hospital, but it wasn't until now that he truly put it all together.

The bridge demanded an answer to their question once more.

Merrecci rose to his seat as soon as Charity removed the breathing stimulator that had been placed on his bare chest. He nearly fell forward, but Charity and Cora's hands were there to catch him again.

"I'll do the demanding around here," Merrecci replied. "Identify yourself."

"Captain Fiji, Sir," the male's voice replied.

"Who the frunk is Captain Fiji," Merrecci asked. "Are you Kellick's staff? Why are you on my bridge?"

"Admiral Kellick assigned me to help out given the circumstances of the current state of your previous command crew."

"Excuse me," Merrecci asked. "Where is my previous command crew? Where is Commander Leonard."

"Crewman Leonard has been reassigned to warehouse support."

"The admiral demoted my first officer," Merrecci asked. His volume rising because he hadn't fully remastered keeping it in check despite his emotions.

"No, Sir. I did," Captain Fiji replied. "The Admiral is currently indisposed. I needed officers that I was comfortable with to command my ship in the meantime."

"Oh really," Merrecci inquired. He instinctively rolled his shoulder.

"When will you be returning to duty, Sir," Fiji asked.

Merrecci now turned and glared at Charity who was agreeing with him in a way that he read all too clearly.

"As soon as we're done here," Charity said.

"Welcome back, Admiral," Fiji replied. "As soon as you're officially cleared."

Once the communication ended. Merrecci turned back to Charity. "How long has this been going on," Merrecci asked.

"You've been out three weeks," Charity replied. "He's been in command a few days shy of that."

"How?"

"You drove us through a brick wall of nothing too fast, and it knocked everyone out," Charity explained. "Cora and Cindy Lou were the only ones it didn't effect, as far as we can tell. Many woke up on their own, some within minutes, Bria was one of the first, but the majority of the crew did not. Took a bit of work. You're one of the last. I was worried you wouldn't come out, but don't quote me on that ever."

"Casualties," Merrecci asked, rolling his shoulder once more.

"No casualties. Just comatose crew members," Charity replied. "I did not wake up right away. None of the medical crew did either. Mike did. Cora developed this cerebral enhancer and Mike built it. It's not perfect, but it is still bringing people out. There aren't many left now."

"Sorry for yelling at you to stop then," Merrecci said.

"Your words never left the brain," Charity replied.

It was only now that Merrecci was fully aware that Charity was still prodding, poking, and examining him. This realization only came the moment that she slapped an injection bandage against his arm, and he felt his body energize.

"Here's a strength booster for your limbs here," Charity said. Then she held an injector to his arm. "And this is adrenaline."

"What happened to you not wanting to drug people up," Merrecci asked.

"Technically, you shouldn't return to duty for a few hours until we know your synapse pathways have reinforced," Charity said. "But these three weeks have gotten out of hand." She pointed to her rank insignia, which was now a civilian staff marker.

"I see. Who's in command of the hospital now," Merrecci asked.

"An interim lieutenant with healthcare administrative experience."

"I don't remember seeing another doctor in our roster," Merrecci said.

"I didn't say she was a doctor," Charity replied. "She knows how to run a hospital. She doesn't actually come in herself unless there's a—is something wrong with your shoulder?"

"Nope," Merrecci replied. He dropped from the exam table and realized that Cora and Charity were both pushing Merrecci to his feet.

"Look," Charity said. "If you get up and walk, you'll jumpstart your synapse pathways. Protocol has been to make you rest after coming out of this coma, but some people have been ready quickly. A sign you're ready is you'll feel anxious. Are you feeling anxious?"

"I'm feeling strangely pissed off," Merrecci said.

"Close enough," Charity replied.

"Why would you give me adrenaline if anxiety is the tell all I'm ready," Merrecci asked.

"To induce the anxiety," Charity replied.

Now Merrecci understood.

"If you find people aren't answering you, or you feel sluggish, hit a manual emergency request call button in the halls immediately. This isn't the flu, don't think you can deal with it on your own." She organized her lighting equipment into a satchel and turned to exit the hospital. "Now, if you'll excuse me. I have about forty more people who still haven't woken up yet."

Just as she was about to exit, she turned back and said. "Bria is on the lowest deck."

Merrecci nodded.

Cora let out some elated sound, as she and Charity exited.

Merrecci stood at once, ordered a replacement uniform shirt from the fabricator and left the hospital. Within minutes, he found the elevator and took it down as far as it would go. With some direction from Onyx, he discovered Bria's quarters and found her in a dorm that slept twelve bunks.

"Took you long enough," Dawn burst when she answered the door.

She had been playing some sort of card game with Mirror and Drinker.

"Leave him alone," Mirror said. "It's not his fault his brain doesn't work as good as ours."

Willis laughed at this. He had been standing at an array of shelves with small plants that had been growing from seed.

Here, Bria exited the bathroom in a towel and wet hair to discover what the commotion was about. When her eyes fell on Merrecci, her whole body seemed to blush, and she disappeared back into the washroom. She returned quickly in her crewman uniform.

"That's not your uniform," Merrecci said.

"I had to return it," Bria replied.

"Did you," Merrecci asked. Then he noticed a member missing. "Where's Mike?"

"The brig, Sir," Bria replied.

"Why?"

"He bit Fiji," Bria stated.

"Fiji put one of two people who saved his crew in the brig," Fiji asked.

"Did you hurt your arm, Sir," Bria asked.

Instead of answering, Merrecci ordered Bria to keep up as he abruptly left the apartment.

"They put you all in the same quarters," Merrecci asked. He couldn't seem to make himself move fast enough as he marched his way back to the elevator.

"It made it easier for them to monitor our activity," Bria said, huffing to keep up.

"Why did you give up your authority," Merrecci asked.

"I wouldn't say I gave it up, Sir." Bria said.

Inside the elevator, Merrecci asked Onyx to recite the command crew of the bridge. Merrecci's breaths grew more and more enraged. He shrugged deeply.

"Sir," Bria said. "I know my rank says it's not my place anymore, but perhaps you shouldn't let emotions get the best of you."

The elevator doors opened.

Merrecci nodded and, in this action, agreed that he had heard her, but reminded her, "You're right. It's not your place, Crewman!"

He led Bria to Admiral Kellick's quarters.

"He's not there, Sir," Bria said. "He's away."

"He's what?"

"He's with the Rhaxians," Bria said. "We found them. He's fulfilling his diplomatic duties right now."

At once, Merrecci returned to the elevator and rode it again. Here, he led Bria into a familiar corridor and stopped at the doors to his own quarters, where it was apparent at once that Captain Fiji had taken residence. He hadn't rearranged much with the furniture, but it was obvious that he was beginning to make the command suite his own. Merrecci moved to a desk and bent over it.

"Merrecci to Admiral Kellick," Merrecci announced.

He waited a minute, but nothing.

"Onyx, Command message to Admiral Kellick for response at once," Merrecci ordered.

Within seconds, "Prime admiral, I'm so glad to hear your voice, but this is not a good time."

"How dare you supplant the command crew of my ship," Merrecci burst, now yelling at a holographic image of Kellick from knee to head.

"Sir," Kellick asked.

"You placed a captain of your own staff in command of my ship," Merrecci asked incredulously.

"I'm sorry. What?" Kellick's volume softened, and Merrecci imagined the admiral was ducking into a corner to make the conversation more private. "After I awoke, with everything happening, I realized the best service I could offer was to do what I do and be a diplomat. I came here. I specifically ordered Captain Fiji to be ready to serve the ship and its crew as he was needed and to only interrupt me in emergencies. In diplomatic situations, as you know, we don't know what might require our full attention so we might not be able to stay in contact."

"You're telling me you don't know what's been going on onboard the Onyx," Merrecci asked.

"Sir, I have not been in communication with the Onyx since I left. I am and have been under deep scrutiny. This call is not helping. The only reason I was allowed to answer is because they know of our emergency situation onboard." Kellick suddenly straightened up. "Prime Admiral? What's happened?"

"Nothing to worry about at this point," Merrecci replied. "Please send the Rhaxians my deepest apologies for the intrusion, and for not being able to join you."

"I've taken it all to them, Sir," Kellick said. "They're quite understanding. I am confident they will be open to meet soon."

"What's the hold up," Merrecci asked.

"They require a mandatory observation of us in confinement for one of our Earth months before we may speak with a holy person or government leader to ensure we are not volatile and are properly cleansed of lingering negative auras that might infect our first impressions. I'm learning all I can right now from those I'm being allowed to speak with. As soon as I have permission to transmit again, I will. Until then, I'm afraid this emergency call is all I'll be allowed until the quarantine is over."

"I understand," Merrecci said. "I'll let you back to your difficult work."

With that, Kellick and Merrecci ended their discussion.

Merrecci turned to Bria.

"How did Fiji take command from you," Merrecci asked.

"He was a ranking officer aboard with an absent ship's commander, and he exercised emergency control," Bria explained.

Merrecci nodded. He moved quickly to a shelf with a row of signed baseballs and grabbed two that weren't under a glass case.

"Carl Mays or Jack Hamilton," he asked Bria.

She didn't understand so she said, "Uh, Carl Mays."

"Vicious," Merrecci replied. "I like it."

He turned with a baseball in hand and was leading Bria back into the hallway. A few short steps later, the bridge doors swung open.

"Admiral on deck," a voice called.

Merrecci found his bridge entirely altered to appear as an old, Earth carrier-ship that once roamed the seas. Instead of overlooking a landing pad amidst an ocean, it overlooked a star map.

He quickly examined his crew and realized they were not fully the staff he had assigned. He knew some of them, mostly from reading their records. The one that stuck out the most was Vandenbutcke who was currently sitting in the post that could only be the second-in-command's chair.

Captain Fiji, a man in his early forties rose from what could have passed for a barstool. To his right, Vandenbutcke with commander insignia sat at a terminal in a similar seat.

"Admiral," Captain Fiji began to speak. "I was not a—Crewman Leonard, you were warned to stay off my bridge."

Fiji gestured to a large tactical officer, who quickly moved towards Bria and laid hands on her to escort her out.

Suddenly Fiji was stepping uncontrollably backwards, a baseball pressing up under his nose on the cusp of snapping the cartilage right off the front of his face. He continued to falter backwards as Merrecci's other hand gripped Fiji's shirt. The prime admiral's full weight, less than Fiji's, threw the disillusioned captain against the nearest console where a woman quickly retreated under the sudden attack.

"Say it again," Merrecci yelled. "Call it your ship again; I dare you!" He suddenly spun and pitched his baseball directly into Fiji's tactical officer's gut. The tactical officer reeled back and then keeled forward. Merrecci turned back to Fiji and shoved him off the console. Once Fiji had fallen to the floor, Merrecci dropped a knee on him.

"Ever screw with my ship again; ever look at my bridge crew funny, your world will end," Merrecci declared.

Fiji attempted to argue but felt his gut spew the wind out as Merrecci hopped on the knee he held against the captain's belly.

"If you so much as hold up one of my crew in the chow line," Merrecci continued. "If I ever see one report with your name anywhere on it, you're going to find what a Willie Mays baseball can do to the few brains you have left in your goddamned head!"

Suddenly, Merrecci began dragging Fiji across the bridge floor and towards the exit. Fiji attempted a few hand-to-hand tactics to break Merrecci's hold, but the prime admiral wasn't having it. As the doors opened, Merrecci, in almost a feat of inhuman strength, threw him as one might try to toss an

Olympic hammer. Fiji mostly rolled throughout the maneuver until he was off the bridge.

"You picked the wrong person to play mutiny with." Merrecci was yelling. "Until Admiral Kellick decides how to proceed with your discipline, you have no rank in my fleet. Go back to your sector and hide, because I'll be looking for you, and you don't want me to see you again."

After the doors had sealed away Fiji, Merrecci turned back to the bridge and placed his attention on Bria.

"Commander Leonard, bring my bridge back," Merrecci exploded.

"Onyx," Bria said. "Reinitiate bridge design for Vincenti Merrecci."

Suddenly, the room began contorting from Fiji's aircraft carrier and returned to Merrecci's baseball stadium.

The room filled with operators suddenly scrambling to avoid the obstacles that began to fold and unfold around them. Those who had not been familiar with Merrecci's design became the people who were falling the most.

Now Merrecci turned on Bria.

"You're the superior officer," Merrecci unleashed. "No one takes that from you except me."

Merrecci approached his command chair, and it disappeared into the pitcher's mound. Then a wire-mesh bin of plain baseballs rose up, and his fingers strategically wrapped around one. He turned back to the tactical officer who was still in the stages of recovery both physical and "oh crap!"

Merrecci then exploded with, "Anyone not a member of my bridge crew, get out!" He hurled the baseball and hit the tactical imposter again—this time, square in his ass so he'd remember his mistake whenever he tried to sit for the next few days.

He took up another ball and pitched it at another face he didn't recognize. One after another, he kept hurling balls and yelling at unauthorized bridge staff to get out.

Vandenbutcke, he drilled in the shoulder and ordered him to stay. Soon, the bridge was one-quarter of the way filled with staff that were supposed to be there. Baseballs littered the floor, and his bin was half empty.

"You try mutiny on my ship again," Merrecci roared at Vandenbutcke.

"It wasn't my idea, Sir," Vandenbutcke said.

"It's never your idea when you realize how dumb it was," Merrecci observed unforgivingly. "Take that uniform off before I have Almma beat you out of it!"

Next, Merrecci ordered Onyx to return all ranks and positions to what they had been prior to Captain Fiji's interference. Then he summoned his own command crew back to their posts and Vandenbutcke to his confinement of quarters time.

"Onyx, give me the Babe," he ordered taking another ball from the ball bin.

In an instant, a broad-shouldered man, taller than Merrecci and donning a dingy uniform with blue, vertical stripes. He saw Merrecci and poised his baseball bat past his left shoulder where he gave it a small helicopter wave.

Merrecci snapped a pitch, and the holographic man with the bat swung and hit the ball over Merrecci's head. It sailed right into the wall, which absorbed its holographic nature and let it fly off into the virtual distance.

"You fat son of a bitch of all sons with bitches," Merrecci cursed, now flinging ball after ball at the baseball player.

The babe hit all of them, laughing at Merrecci.

"Frunk you, Ruth," he shouted.

Then he walked to the one ball that had a signature and picked it up. The other balls rolled back to their bin and jumped in. Then the wire basket disappeared, and the command chair rose from the mound of dirt. The Babe had already disappeared. Merrecci stormed off to his office.

Nandy was one of the first to appear on the bridge. Immediately, she was summoned to Merrecci's ready room where he and Bria were in conversation about repairing the damage that Fiji had done.

When Merrecci saw she was wearing the scabby, healing remains of what Merrecci assumed were baton strikes across her face, he found himself gripping his Willie Mays tighter.

"Where were you," Merrecci asked.

"There was some confusion about whether I should stay in the brig, Sir," Nandy said. "My cell mate's having a little chat with the people who confiscated her weapons and were a bit surprised to find her voice suddenly opened our cell door when you restored her rank. There are other bridge officers behind me in the same boat. I just run faster."

"Leonard was just apprising me," Merrecci said. "You and Almma fought with Captain Fiji and his security team when he relieved your commander of rank."

"She's my commander, Sir," Nandy said.

"It's clear to me that we need to make a change if we don't want others compromising our mission," Merrecci said. "It's my own fault for not foreseeing it. I can't say I'm fully settled into the thought of this crew myself, but it is working."

"Sir," Nandy asked.

"We can't have this happen again." Merrecci looked squarely on Nandy. "Leonard and I have discussed it, and we agree, you need to be reinstated to commander."

"But, Sir," Nandy said. "Two commanders on the bridge?"

"There will be only one commander on the bridge," Merrecci said. "I've promoted Leonard to Captain. We both know she isn't ready, but I can't have every captain we might encounter thinking they can jerk my first officer and bridge crew around. This should help secure what we need to do. If Admiral Kellick hadn't come out of his coma to have the wisdom to leave the ship to engage diplomacies with the Rhaxian, that idiot Fiji might have tried to take us back to join the war."

"Sir, I disagree," Nandy said.

"You do," Merrecci asked.

"I know what happened on the Viridian. That's not what transpired here. When this all went down, there wasn't a single person on bridge duty who hesitated to defend her," Nandy replied, gesturing to Bria.

With that, Merrecci made the appropriate logs with Onyx to ensure the new promotions were documented. They were just finishing the process when Almma clicked at the door. She entered with her hair cut shorter than it had been, and not cleanly. He recognized humiliation tactics when he saw them. She was covered in remnants of a severe beating and her right wrist was in a splint.

"Who did that," Merrecci abruptly demanded to know.

"What? The hair? I don't remember her name," Almma replied. "I'll ask her when I drop by her quarters later."

"Who did that," Merrecci asked again, jolting from his seat.

"Oh, just some people who won a bunch of broken fingers and noses," Almma replied.

"Will my crew not be able to push any buttons," Merrecci asked.

"One or two, but most were Kellick's people," Almma said. "I spoke with Dr. Quobalt on the way here. Seems that with the strains and priorities put on her limited staff right now, the best she can do to help them is to use good, old-fashioned sports medicine to set and splint all the broken parts."

Merrecci apprised Almma of his previous conversation with Nandy and Bria.

"Sir, we do have another issue to consider," Almma suggested. "With Captain Fiji's testosterone currently splattered all over the walls, we do have a bit of a problem with our intelligence flow. His tongue was a little loose regarding Cindy Lou and the Rhaxians. I heard rumors of them in the brig."

"I see," Merrecci said. "Then I guess, since it's a security issue, I have no choice but to officially declared the entire ship classified. No messages in or out except by command staff."

"That's not going to go over well with people who already can't communicate with loved ones on Earth, Sir," Almma said. "Just so we're all aware."

"I'll issue the order," Nandy said. "With your permission, of course, Sir."

Merrecci agreed and, after a brief question and answer with Onyx, they had learned that Fiji had felt it necessary to inform every department head about Cindy's circumstance. To establish their new authority over her, they had confined her strictly to her quarters.

"And how did that go over with her," Merrecci asked.

"I'm so glad that I finally crossed through that little pea brain of yours," Cindy's voice careened throughout Merrecci's office. "Do you know how many visitors I've had in almost three weeks?

Zero! Know how close I came to marching onto that bridge and taking command myself? The only reason I didn't was because I knew the entertainment value of the comeuppance would be worth the wait."

"What have I said about staying off my comms," Merrecci yelled.

"I did stay off," Cindy replied. "But now there are people almost intriguing enough to hold conversations with again, and Bria can't get in trouble for it now."

"Onyx will hold conversation with any person on the ship," Merrecci said. "You should try talking to her."

"Oh, Vincenti. You just don't understand," Cindy replied after a short chortle. "She's just a little one-sided in conversation for me."

"She probably got tired of speaking to you," Merrecci replied.

"Well, now there is a different perspective to consider," Cindy asked. "Anyway, now Captain Leonard can resume her visits again and fill that conversation void. But that's beside the point. The reason I called is because, after all this time without visitors, I require company. I would very much like to invite you to share dinner with me in my observation deck."

"I have plans," Merrecci abruptly answered, and what did she mean exactly by she required company?

"No, you don't," Cindy replied.

"It would be inappropriate," Merrecci said. "Considering your inherent inclination to, you know, destroy worlds."

"Do you think I'm talking about sex," Cindy asked and started laughing. "Oh Admy, you don't have that much boom boom in you."

Suddenly Almma started laughing.

"Something funny, Lieutenant-commander," Merrecci asked.

"Sorry, Sir," Almma replied.

Merrecci clenched his jaw to keep from blathering out something that didn't make sense.

"I'm not just inviting you, Admiral," Cindy continued. "I'm inviting all your senior staff and special friends from the special needs class."

"I'm not sure I'm comfortable with allowing that many people through your shields," Merrecci lied. "I might forget to clear someone."

"Oh, I turned those off two weeks ago. The shields are for your peace of mind anyway, not mine. Well, and to keep out a certain gentleman caller, and he's not here, is he? Oh, and it made Fiji mad."

Merrecci shook his head, refusing to resign himself to another loss with Cindy. "I'm okay with indulging my peace of mind. I'll be reaffirming the shields and full reign of your quarantine area."

"If it's all the same to you, I'd rather keep them down," Cindy replied.

"Not a chance," Merrecci stated.

"Why not," Cindy asked. "The entire ship is pretty much in a quarantine now. Unless my counterpart discovers a race that's wise enough to seek out the Rhaxians, we are perfectly safe from me destroying any cosmos."

"We can't take that chance."

"Good. Then we have nothing to worry about," Cindy explained. "I'll expect you tonight."

"I'm sorry. The answer is no. Onyx, reinitiate quarantine disintegration shield with prior authorizations," Merrecci instructed.

"No," Onyx replied.

"Onyx?"

"No," Onyx replied again. "Cindy Lou is my friend. I want to go to dinner with Cindy Lou. I want to marry Cindy Lou and have twelve babies all named Cindy Lou Little Lou-Lou numbers One through Eleven-point-two and Bobbita."

"What is this nonsense," Merrecci asked. "Oh my god. Are you imitating Onyx again."

"I will reinitiate shields only after you have dinner with my friend and all our future Cindy Lou Little Lou-Lou babies numbers One to Eleven-point-two and Bobbita," Onyx replied.

Bria, Nandy and Almma all seemed as confused as he was.

"Weird," Cindy Lou said. "I'd check your computer system out. Maybe you should reboot her."

Merrecci was suddenly reminded of how long it took to boot her up the first time and thought about all the systems that would be down including life support.

"If you've done something to my ship—," Merrecci started to say.

"Your ship is fine," Cindy Lou reassured. "Trust me, Admiral. You really want to join me for dinner tonight. I promise the conversation will be authentic and enlightening on any topic you'd like."

"Yeah," Almma erupted. "We could discuss recent revelations to the big bang theory?"

"No," Merrecci snapped. "We are not discuss—" His face suddenly twisted, and he snapped. "Seriously? What made—how did you—Why would you even—

"Kind of puts a new perspective on the whole thing, doesn't it," Almma replied.

Merrecci couldn't bring himself to respond.

This is why, that evening, Merrecci found himself sitting at a long banquet table in Cindy's observation room, his sister Prilla to his left and Charity to his right.

Across from him sat Cindy Lou in a white sequined gown, strapless and split down the sides then held back together by a very loose silver cord that seemed to barely hug her flesh. Bria sat to Cindy's right. To the god's left was a life-sized cardboard cutout of Merrecci himself with a grin that was an exaggeration of a doofy smile, that wasn't even his own, with two teeth blacked out. The cutout was posed in some sort of friendly wave. Merrecci thought the half-assed smile on his paper self would only be appropriate for a local parade's grand marshal. Surplus military chilidog was currently running down the cutout's chin and neck from where Cindy had spoon fed it, but he was too dumb to chew.

The worst part about the entire night was that the cuisine was actually, and without a doubt, some of the best that Merrecci had ever eaten, which is why it pained him when Cindy Lou suddenly turned from a conversation with Dawn, Mirror, and Mike about creating cleaner space travel and asked the admiral, "How's the Viccideite."

He profoundly wanted her to know how displeased he was with her shanghai of his computer, but he could hold that discussion with her later.

"I've never had it before," Merrecci replied.

"That's not what I asked," Cindy said.

"I'd be lying if I said it was anything less than the most amazing dish," Merrecci answered.

Cindy nodded as though she knew.

The closest Earth dish that he could compare it to was a blue-noodled lasagna buried in a broth of something earthy, which he'd eaten several years ago.

"You didn't fabricate it, did you," Merrecci observed.

"No," Cindy stated curtly. "It's from my own stores, but the Onyx's resident fine-dining chef cooked it."

Merrecci nodded as if to say, "figures."

"I do not invite people lightly to partake in my rarities."

"I apologize," Merrecci replied, trying to accept that, despite being on his ship, he was *her* guest in her living space right now. "This is incomparable to anything I've tasted. I look forward to having it again some time."

"Oh, you can't. Nor can the chef ever make it again," Cindy spoke while savoring her current bite of food. She swallowed. "You can never eat this dish again. It would kill you."

"Come again," Merrecci asked.

"The spice that enhances the flavor becomes poisonous to carbon-based lifeforms after twenty-four hours if activated within a hundred years of ingesting it. It's farmed in a galaxy that Earth could never reach even in a thousand reincarnations. It's been sitting in my stores for—well—a long time. There are millions of different species in this spice that will lie dormant in you now. If you ever eat this again, you will activate a defensive poison within it."

"You poisoned us," Merrecci asked flippantly.

"No. That would require me to give it to you again. As I doubt, you'll ever meet anyone else who has traveled far enough to own these spices, that's not going to happen. You are perfectly fine."

Merrecci started to shove his dish away but found himself digging out a piece of broken noodle instead.

Cindy turned to the cutout of Merrecci.

"What's that," she asked leaning in, then giggling. "Stop, not in front of the company."

She fed it another spoon of chili and let the chunks of beans and beef frank roll down Cutout Merrecci's front.

Now she turned to Bria and abruptly stated that she could feel her being uncomfortable, and Bria acknowledged that she was. Then Cindy started in with Charity.

"Tell me Doctor Quobalt and other Doctor Quobalt," Cindy said. "Why haven't we figured out how to give Bria a face yet?"

"We have," Charity replied. "It's just a very ex—

"Pensive procedure," Cindy interrupted. "Yes. Yes. Why?"

"Aside the need for tools to catch burrs and sharp protrusions that can come from regrowing bone in that delicate area, transplant, regrowth and attachment are expensive no matter what you're repairing," Charity said.

"Ah," Cindy replied as if she understood, then she asked, "Why?"

"The resources, the person with the skill needed to accomplish the task, not to mention the drugs and staff—that all costs money."

"I don't think you seem to understand my question," Cindy informed.

"I'm not in charge of the cost of medical treatment," Charity replied. "If it were up to me, she'd have a new face yesterday."

"Excellent," Charity crowed. "So why isn't it up to you. If Earth is closed, doesn't that make you the highest ranking and capable medical professional and Vincent, here, the highest ranking government leader right now to authorize it."

"Vincenti," Merrecci quickly corrected.

"Gesundheit," Cindy blessed.

From the other side of Charity, Cora let out one of her pleased moan-laughs.

"She's so cute," Cindy said. "I love her. She's like one of those big stuffed animals you win at a fair and can't put it in your pocket, so you have to carry it everywhere."

"I'm the highest ranking military leader," Merrecci said. "Not the highest ranking government leader."

Just now, Merrecci found himself quite a bit disappointed that the dish before him had emptied.

"I don't know what all the fuss is anyway," Merrecci said, and he found himself cleaning the juices off of his platter with his finger to get at the very last of the flavor. "A face doesn't make a person."

"No," Cindy said, "But it provides individuality, doesn't it, Prime Admiral?"

"Does it," Merrecci asked. "I've had many first officers, all of them individual, and the one I've come to appreciate most recently is the individual without a face."

"Really," Cindy asked through a developing smirk. "Would you kiss her."

He set his plate back and said, "I really want some more of this."

"That's all you can have," Cindy said. Then she came back with, "Admiral? Would you kiss your first officer with a face like hers?"

"That's inappropriate," Merrecci said, noticing the young captain, less than half his age, squirm in her seat.

"Why," Cindy asked. "Because she's beneath you?"

"I won't dignify that remark," Merrecci replied. "But yep, and she's not very pretty too."

"I'm just surprised that people wouldn't look at a woman in her prime to find love and not be more eager to help return her attractive features," Cindy explained.

"We can," Charity stated. "But it's expensive."

"She's a captain now," Merrecci said. "When we return to Earth and are reintegrated into the Franchise, after this is over, she'll qualify for the procedure if we act before they demote her again."

"If you return to Earth," Cindy said.

"We will," Merrecci insisted. He thought about throwing his empty dish across the room. "If the people at this table don't kill us first."

"You don't know that," Cindy stated. She looked about the table. "With the brain power we have in this room, why can't you create the facilities we need on this ship?"

"If it's so important to you, why don't you fix it," Merrecci asked. "You're the god here."

"That's not what I do," Cindy said.

"Oh, but we do," Merrecci asked.

"Yes," Cindy blurted and then composed herself.

"I'm not broken," Bria shouted and stood up from the table. She threw her napkin into her chair.

"Then what are you," Cindy asked.

At this, Dawn slammed her fists down, jilting the wine in their glasses, and almost shouted something when she remembered Merrecci might not let her drive the goof cart again.

Merrecci signaled for Dawn and Bria to sit back down, and they did.

"What are any of you," Cindy asked the entire table.

"I guess in some way, everyone's broken," Prilla finally spoke up.

"Your engineering team is slapstick buffoonery," Cindy Lou insulted. "Your ship strategist has a limited vocabulary, or should I say a limited 'material,' and he can't get his ideas across. Your doctor couldn't run to save a life because of that drooling carnival prize that won't let her on any of the rides. Your pilot has to open and close the door to the bridge seven times just to be happy, and he's so hyper-Parkinsons, I'm surprised he hasn't shaken the ship apart yet."

Merrecci slammed down his fists and rattled the dinnerware.

"Ooh, so big," Cindy said and smashed her own fists against the table in mockery.

"There has to be leftovers," Merrecci demanded.

Willis laughed.

"You laugh all you want," Cindy encouraged, then turned to Prilla. "And you have absolutely no confidence in being out here after what he convinced you to do."

"That's private," Prilla erupted.

"I think that's our cue to leave," Merrecci rebuked, pushing himself away from the table. "Are you sure there isn't any more?"

"And you," Cindy stated pointedly. "You're the most broken of all. A prime admiral who hates his own crew for the very reasons I've just pointed out, but loyalty—ooh—can't show you're disloyal. Angry at everything and everyone. Barbarian Captain, driven by anger. Hateful, cursed by your own crews. Killed your own father."

Merrecci froze.

"That's unfair," Prilla said.

"Yeah," Charity said. "I'm not as intelligent as you, but even I know what's not my business. Maybe he's earned being in a bad mood."

"I don't think it's that at all," Cindy disagreed.

"Well, what do you think it is then; you're so smart," Prilla asked.

Charity sipped at her own bowl then turned back to Prilla to ask, "I think the better question is what you think it is?" She snuck her spoon into Prilla's meal and absconded with an extra helping without its real owner noticing.

"I think it's that seeing all the mentally underqualified people at this table every day is a reminder to what a deformity he almost was," Prilla answered. Her hands shot to her mouth and her eyes blew wide. "I'm so sorry everyone."

"Eat your food," Charity encouraged through an amused smile.

"I don't agree with that," Almma finally spoke. She picked at her plate, turning it into something that looked mutilated but wasn't actually tasted. "The prime admiral has stood behind all of us in the most difficult of circumstances."

"Come now. He would throw every person in this room away at the first sign of an officer he thought was better and smarter," Cindy accused. "The only reason you're here is because he was stuck with you and can't find anyone better. Which is ironic coming from someone who's only here because his parents had his own DNA altered so he couldn't end up like the very people he despises."

Merrecci lunged forward, against the table.

"And this is who I'm supposed to trust can protect me," Cindy asked.

Cindy's eyes pierced right into Merrecci's depths. "You're the most broken and dangerous one of all. So, I ask again, why doesn't Bria have a face yet?"

The table fell silent. Prilla's hand was at Merrecci's wrist where he hadn't even noticed that he'd been clenching a knife. She urged him to sit, and he did.

Cindy ate in silence now, smiling between sips of her broth and something that looked similar to broccoli except for their crowns were filled with eyes.

Then, from down the table, where she'd been sitting silent, a stern voice crept up.

"Is there any ketchup down there," Nandy asked.

Cindy's face suddenly froze, and it snapped towards Commander Nandy. Then she instructed everyone that they could leave.

"The reason she doesn't have a face is because she hasn't fought hard enough to get one," Merrecci explained, ignoring Cindy's disinvitation. "And because she hasn't, nobody else has."

Cindy slowly sat down.

"That's a cold thing to say," Cindy stated coolly.

"No, that's the truth," Merrecci corrected. "With any other staff, I would have said it sooner, but this crew doesn't need an angry admiral reminding them how ugly the world and people like me see them."

"And we certainly don't need to see our admiral provoked into bias," Charity pointed out.

"You're just saying that because you're too afraid to say you want him," Cindy prodded.

"I would so do you right now on this table," Charity agreed, turning to Merrecci.

"I'm sorry," Merrecci replied. "Your sister's kind of a turn off on that matter."

"Interesting," Cindy observed, then turned to Dawn. "The two-headed woman wants the primal admiral. What do you think about that?"

"You bitch," Mirror screamed, leapt upon the table, and launched towards Charity. The three of them toppled and caused Merrecci to begin fighting to keep himself from tumbling in his chair beneath their struggle.

"Are they seriously fighting," Bria asked.

"Of course, they are! You're so stupid," Dawn replied. "It's annoying to have to see how stupid you are."

"Amen," Ensign Being replied.

Mirror was currently slapping Charity across the face.

"Captain Leonard," Merrecci ordered. "Will you get them off of me?"

"Just because you're in charge doesn't mean you have to be the boss all the time," Prilla suddenly snapped. "God, you're just like Dad."

"Excuse me," Merrecci replied and tried to turn sharply in his chair to avoid the fighting happening at his side. "Big words coming from his second favorite child."

"Oh, my lord," Nandy cried. "You're all a bunch of useless rejects. Act your ages."

"You're one to talk," Dawn retorted. "I can literally feel my IQ drop when you're nearby."

"You don't need to say things to make the captain think I'm dumber than she already thinks I am," Nandy screeched.

"Wait a minute," Bria said. "What was that?"

"I just want you to think I'm smart," Nandy said and suddenly slapped her hands over her mouth.

Willis couldn't stop laughing.

Then, amidst the chaos, Almma calmly stood, cracked her baton into firing position and fired a stun blast at Cindy.

The table fell silent as Cindy looked up not entirely unfazed.

"You shot me," she said, shocked. She looked to Almma's dish. "You didn't eat."

"Hey," Merrecci cried, pointing to Willis's plate. "Neither did he!"

"When someone invites you to dine, you're supposed to eat," Cindy said.

"Why didn't you eat, Lieutenant-commander," Merrecci asked. "If you don't want it, can I have it?"

"The food," Almma said. "I think the butt goddess here just shit our plates full of truth serum."

"Stop swearing," Dawn screamed. "You don't have to be so disgusting!"

The table erupted into an onslaught of insults at Cindy and also each other.

"Everyone shut up," Merrecci ordered.

"Oh, you shut up for once," Prilla yelled. "You don't know everything."

"Don't act all high and mighty," Bria snapped at Prilla. "You're not any different telling us all how we're special just to make yourself feel better!"

The room filled with argument until Merrecci finally exploded at Prilla during a debate of who dad gave the best Christmas presents to as children.

"I can't believe I thought I should bring you along," Merrecci shouted.

"I can't believe you were stupid enough to even ask," Prilla fired back.

"Well, it's a good thing I did because if it wasn't for me, you and your class of idiots would be dead right now, wouldn't they," Merrecci yelled. Then he snatched up her platter and began licking it off.

"Sir," Almma yelled.

"What do you want," Merrecci asked. "The only reason you're here is because I find your insubordination sexy, and I thought you were kinda pretty."

"You think she's pretty," Mirror asked.

"He has to think somebody here is," Prilla snapped at her.

"Am I pretty," Mirror asked.

Merrecci burst out laughing at her.

Almma shot Cindy again.

"End this," Almma said.

"Fine," Cindy replied. "Onyx, dessert please."

At this, the table top opened and drew the contents upon it down and into it. It closed, then opened again and lifted up small pieces of round, black cake with a dark fruit mash spilling over it.

"This will counter the effects of the truth stimulant," Cindy explained.

Almma ordered everyone to eat the cake, then Merrecci repeated it once he realized what Almma was the only one smart enough to notice.

Mirror started screaming at him, having already abandoned her attack on Charity and Cora. Merrecci shoved a bite of the cake into her mouth. Within a few moments, the table had quieted down and all but Almma and Cindy were directed back into their seats in shame where they all began to eat their desserts.

"I hope you enjoyed your joke because it's the last company you're ever having on this ship," Merrecci said.

"I can live with being alone," Cindy answered. "I've done a lot of that, but you're not ready for it."

"What is that supposed to mean," Charity asked.

"This is the most you've spoken honestly to each other since you've been on board," Cindy explained.

"We speak to each other," Nandy said.

"Do you," Cindy asked, then asked it again directly to Merrecci.

The admiral didn't have to answer.

"You're the senior command crew," Cindy chided. "Insult each other all you want. Come here to do it if you want, but stop doing it to the rest of us on your ship. Stop lying to each other. Now, go on, finish your cakes. You don't want that truth serum rearing back up with an unwitting crew member out there.

The table fell into awkward silence. Only the sounds of forks and light mastication filled the room.

Merrecci finished his dessert first and then excused himself to leave.

"Not yet," Cindy Lou said. "I haven't told you why I asked you here."

"You've told us enough," Merrecci responded.

"Admiral, sit," Cindy said in an adamant tone, enough to make Merrecci reconsider and return to his chair.

"What more insult could you possibly do to us tonight," Merrecci asked.

"The Rhaxians have agreed to help," she informed.

"How do you know?"

"Quarantine waiting period before opening communication doesn't apply to gods who are old friends with the Rhaxian," Cindy replied.

"You've spoken to them," Bria asked.

"I entered discussions with them the moment we arrived," Cindy stated.

"And you waited three weeks to tell anyone," Merrecci asked.

"Fiji locked me in a room. Screw him," Cindy replied. "He's a worm. If he'd have had this information three weeks ago, who knows if we'd still be alive."

"On that, we agree," Merrecci said.

"Hopefully on this too," Cindy suggested. "Do you know why the Rhaxians were eradicated?"

"I had thought because they upset the Kag'tak," Merrecci suggested.

"Well, that's true too," she acknowledged, nodding. "But before the Kag'tak commit genocide on the Rhaxians, they eradicated my people, the Utonenaibe. We were explorers and builders, terraformers if you will. Unlike worlds like Earth that seeks to destroy, we gave life. But at a cost. Not all evolution is good, and we evolved ourselves right out of the ability to procreate amongst ourselves. For a race that lives trillions of years, that's a terrible thing. As it turns out, the Zarchro were similar. We discovered that if we coupled as races, we could give life, but at a high sacrifice."

"You die," Merrecci said.

"Wait. You destroy everything in the cosmos, even yourselves," Bria realized.

Cindy seemed startled at Bria's response. "Aren't you a good person?" Then she turned back to Merrecci and coldly said, "but, yes, we die."

"The perfect recipe for celibacy if you ask me," Nandy added.

"So, you understand why the Kag'tak would try to enslave us. And when that didn't work, they began killing us. Either way showed the Kag'tak had great power. The Rhaxians were entrusted with one Utonenaibe and one Zarchro. I lived among the Rhaxians for longer than your own galactic history has existed. The Zarchro, they hid in an eternal tomb."

"So why aren't you there now," Mirror asked.

"Bounties remain, their bonds accrue interest. Hunters never stop searching, and they destroy everyone who helped you. And now, all that's left of the Rhaxians is one ship." Cindy informed. "But to answer your question. Earth took me in, and we struck a deal. They hide me, I share space travel technology with you."

"Space tech," Nandy asked. "How long have you been on Earth."

Cindy smirked. "Longer than you."

"Long enough the Kag'tak are likely looking at it," Merrecci said.

"They're going to destroy Earth, aren't they," Bria asked. "Because they think you're there."

"If there's evidence that Earth aided me, yes." Cindy replied.

"And if there's not," Nandy asked.

"Then it's hard to say," Cindy said, and she shook her head with deep remorse. "It will depend on if they come out of hibernation to assist with looking for the evidence."

"Why," Nandy followed up.

"The Kag'tak hate when races waste their time," Cindy explained. "And no matter how good you humans are at destroying everything you create, the Kag'tak don't have to touch Earth to wipe it from existence."

"Good thing they're not involved then, isn't it," Bria observed.

"They're involved," Merrecci replied sternly.

"How do you know," Nandy asked.

"Because any time there's a shadow looming in space, you can bet the Kag'tak are casting it," Merrecci answered. "Even if they're not looking at what's happening in it, it's still their shadow."

"The good news is, they'll take their time destroying Earth until they decide it actually bears a threat to the Kag'tak," Cindy explained. "Right now, they're just following rumor, but they'll equally hate having their resources wasted verifying its truth."

"All the more reason for us to stop sitting around and start talking to the Rhaxians about that tomb," Merrecci stated.

"Sure," Cindy agreed. "If they can remember where it is."

Merrecci fell back in his seat and pursed his lips before erupting with, "You said we needed a Rhaxian priest. Is all this a joke to you?"

"The priest can help you," Cindy snipped. "Don't worry, you'll get your superpower weapon, Prime Admiral."

"You don't seriously think we'd use you as a weapon," Charity asked incredulously.

"Yes," Cindy Lou remarked. "Your concept of absolute annihilation isn't even a pinprick to what we and the Zarchro could do when we consummate, or so I've been taught by the Rhaxians. The birds and the bees are a little built on faith for us. We don't exactly have sex-ed films or porn to learn from. But hey, at least Earth will live on, won't it?"

Now the table was silent. Cindy sipped again at a glass of red wine, this time because she wanted to enjoy it.

"Why us then," Bria asked after some time.

"I beg your pardon," Cindy spoke mid-another swallow.

"You could have run," Bria pointed out. "Stolen a ship, left Earth."

"I won't say that idea hadn't crossed my mind," Cindy acknowledged. "Perhaps I find you people more entertaining than the thought of running again."

"I admit," Merrecci commented. "I'm not untouched by the ethical dilemma here. Do we find your mate and submit you as the

Kag'tak would to deter further attacks on Earth? Could I force a race to sacrifice itself to save mine? Do we keep you nearby and hope you'll never turn your wrath on us?"

"I don't think I could do it either, Sir," Bria said.

"Oh no," Merrecci corrected. "Don't misunderstand me. I could do it. In fact, those are my orders ultimately, aren't they?"

"Wow," Prilla replied, stunned. "No consideration for what they want; just command them to make their baby, huh?"

"There's another angle to consider," Cindy Lou suggested. "If we find the Zarchro, we're going to do it anyway."

"Are you kidding," Almma blurted. "You want to do this? What is wrong with you?"

Cindy looked sullenly to her remaining bite of dessert on her plate. "It's my heritage, not yours. And that includes the choice that comes with it."

She snatched up the last bite of cake with her fingers and pushed it into her mouth.

"Or maybe she just wants to get laid properly," Merrecci said.

Cindy didn't rush swallowing her cake and taking a drink before answering, "Oh God, who doesn't? I'm pretty sure I've lived long enough to earn it. I mean, and I don't mean to sound mean, you humans are pretty good at it, but what if we're better?"

"What if you're worse," Almma asked.

"Well, that would be a letdown, wouldn't it," Charity replied.

"So, we find him, and you can have your choice," Merrecci said.

"Or you can force it on her," Prilla snipped.

"But to find him, we need Rhaxian direction as only their priests and old records can provide," Cindy explained.

"And you've already spoken to one," Merrecci asked.

Cindy nodded. "They will help us find the male on one condition: asylum aboard this vessel. They trust you."

"Why would they do that," Charity asked.

"Because they trust her," Nandy almost didn't respond until the moment had passed for anyone else to figure it out.

"They seem to be pretty well protected out here," Merrecci implied. "What could we offer them?"

"Your finding them has demonstrated others can. They can hide on your ship until they think of an even safer place to take refuge," Cindy explained.

"They want to be close to the information of where the gods are," Nandy observed.

"Well, that's going to be tough since we're chasing a rumor," Merrecci informed. "We heard someone saw a person of interest, not that someone found a tomb."

"Well, unless the tomb learned how to get up and walk, I wouldn't trust the rumor," Cindy said.

Merrecci concurred.

"How many Rhaxian individuals are we talking about bringing aboard the Onyx," he asked.

"Roughly eight thousand," Cindy counted.

"I'm confused," Bria stated. "If they have been hidden for so long, shouldn't they have rebuilt their numbers."

"You've never met a Rhaxian," Cindy pointed out. "Their reproductive gestation is rather long and complicated. Considering, when I was with them, they had seventy-three on their ship including myself, and their gestation is just under an eon, that is a pretty big number."

"An eon long pregnancy," Almma shrieked. "I think my inny Ginny just became an outie snoutie."

"It doesn't quite work that way," Cindy explained. "They shed their potential offspring, and only about one in every octillion ever accumulate to an infant. You'll understand when you see them."

"Well, as much as I hate to deny a request for asylum from a fellow endangered race," Merrecci retorted. "That would eat up half the capacity of this ship, and I anticipate we may have to be ready to provide that sanctuary to our own race at some point."

"Like I said, you've never met a Rhaxian," Cindy replied slyly.

"Sir," Bria said, "Um, they hailed us when we first arrived. I was out of my unconscious state in time to respond. I had to magnify a hundred meters off the starboard to locate the origin of their transmission. Their entire ship would fit inside a shot glass, Sir."

"I thought the admiral was with them," Merrecci asked.

"They call it folding," Cindy explained. "They're masters of matter occupation theory."

"What does that even mean," Charity asked.

"Where laws of physics say two objects cannot occupy the same space at the same time, the Rhaxians say, 'wanna bet'! They are able to fold countless cells in ways that would otherwise be occupied by their own mass to make you smaller. You have the room, Admiral, and they have their power."

"And they have someone who can take us to your Zarchroian lover," Merrecci said.

"Yes, and can we not refer to him as my lover," Cindy retorted. "Lovers have intimacy. We are simply the last."

"I have a question about that," Almma said.

"Of course, you do. By all means, please ask aw—" Cindy replied suddenly stopped and held her ear to the cardboard cutout of Merrecci. "Oh, sure. If you insist."

Suddenly, she bent Cardboard Merrecci forward and started smacking the backside.

"There you go, baby," Cindy said. "Burp up all that nasty."

She set the cutout back, and Cardboard Merrecci's face was now frowning.

"Oh," Cindy said as the table opened up once more to produce another bowl of food before fake Merrecci. "Don't be sad. Look! More chili dog."

Cardboard Merrecci's smile flipped back up. Then more chili was spilling down his front again as she spoon fed it.

She turned back to Almma and beckoned her to continue.

"I'm just wondering," Almma said. "Look, I've had bad sex, and I mean like really bad sex, so bad that it actually makes you moan Santa's name just to make the guy on you freak out and run away—"

"Really," Merrecci asked. "That's what you want to ask about?"

"You already know how bad the sex is that's coming your way," Almma continued. "You die from it. Why would you even want to have it? Especially if it's the end of your race if you do?"

"Because it's life," Cindy replied. "We're drawn to it. It's something we must do. Who knows, maybe we'll birth more of our races and our line will emerge once again to say, 'yeah, I'm not doing that'."

"Well, that is a decision I'm glad I don't have to make," Merrecci stated. "But—

"Spoken like a true male," Almma replied.

"A true senior ranking male, Lieutenant-commander," Merrecci fired back.

"You all think you're senior ranking," Almma said.

"And exactly how many of the four commanding officers of this ship are women, Miss Used-to-babysit-a-shield-in-a-hall," Merrecci snapped.

"And we still answer to an even higher ranked swinging dick, don't we?"

"Pardon me," Merrecci scolded.

"You're right," Almma said. "Overstepped my bounds."

Merrecci might have thought he should verbally discipline Almma and Cindy, but he didn't. Instead, he rallied the energy for one last question he thought he might regret asking.

"I'm curious why, if the Rhaxians had you both, why they didn't just use you as their nuclear power," Merrecci said. "Why didn't you? You had two worlds of how many deterrents? And yet it didn't frighten others from wiping any of your races out."

"Not everyone is eager to destroy life," Cindy replied. "Perhaps our enemies knew that."

With that, Merrecci excused himself, thanked their guest and called Admiral Kellick back to the Onyx, where he explained all that he had learned during dinner.

When it was his turn, Kellick politely lectured Merrecci, and the prime admiral was patient with it. Mostly, Merrecci realized he might have been taking notes from the diplomatic admiral. Had the roles been reversed, Merrecci wouldn't have been so quiet. Kellick suggested that he wasn't even angry at Cindy Lou, although he felt he deserved to be, but he knew who was to fully blame. He simply couldn't apologize enough about Captain Fiji's behavior. What Merrecci assumed was that Kellick knew if he carried all that outrage with him to confront Fiji, Fiji would be finding himself in a torpedo tube sitting atop a most unfriendly missile. At least, that's what Merrecci had thought about doing to him during Kellick's affable outburst.

Merrecci was exiting the ready room to the bridge with Kellick in tow, when Merrecci suddenly jerked and cussed a few lines that many might have been construed as unbecoming of an officer.

A giant boulder with a face, larger than the battle holo was placed at the front of the bridge. The rock's eyes flicked to Merrecci and may have been insulted at the prime admiral's outburst. His crown almost touched the ceiling. Everything about the tiki-like appearance was blotted with bulbous stone zits. His eyes had sounded like they were grinding within their own sockets as they focused about the room. The being had a fat body, perhaps a tenth the size of the head, with dough-like appendages.

"Admiral Merrecci," the boulder spoke and bowed so deeply that it seemed as though his cranium should have snapped right onto the floor. "I am Garu, the coldona of the Rhaxian quarry. On behalf of our civilization, I greet you. I thank you, and I give unto you a blessing." Then he made a series of sounds similar to rocks grinding and clacking.

Garu stopped speaking and looked pleased with himself. It took Merrecci a moment to realize that what he had just heard was the blessing.

"Coldona Garu, on behalf of the Earth Franchise," Kellick said and realized he could no longer speak for the Franchise until their grievance was resolved, so he corrected his statement to speak only for Earth. "I greet you. I thank you, and I give you humble gratitude for trusting us to offer you asylum." Now he turned and introduced Merrecci as the highest form of authority on the ship and fleet.

Garu bowed once more.

"Thank you for your blessing, Garu," Merrecci asked. "If you will forgive my ignorance, what was the blessing that you just shared with us."

"Ah," Garu said as if he anticipated such a young species would not understand. "May your and your crew's bowels never fail you in time of battle."

"That's," Merrecci replied and snapped a sharp eye to Nandy who was trying a little too hard to hold in her laughter. "An excellent blessing, and I hope we may never need to benefit from it if possible."

Again, Garu nodded.

"Perhaps while you are here," Kellick added. "We could discuss our races' technologies further and learn from one another."

Garu blinked several times. Merrecci instantly recognized someone who was politely thinking of a rejective answer. Kellick's own eyes betrayed that he too recognized it.

"Perhaps, someday," Garu replied.

"Perhaps," Merrecci replied.

"Someday," Garu reiterated.

"Of course."

"When you are older," Garu clarified. "Much older."

"Of course," Merrecci said. "You have provided much already."

"Yes," Garu replied. "We have and are not finished yet."

He held out an appendage, which held no fingers, but an object did begin to grow out of what might have otherwise been a wrist. The item then raised and floated to Merrecci's hand.

It was a key made up of a smaller human-like skull that almost appeared to be made of golden-veined granite. A thick, black elastic strapped around its circumference and completely covered its eyes. The key itself was slender, almost as long as Merrecci's forearm. Its ears were set low into its cheeks and had been stuffed with wax-coated cotton. To Merrecci, it seemed as if a superfluous student-artist had taken a petrified, human femur and placed the cranium on one end and an offset mouth with severe overbite and unkempt teeth at the other. As soon as the key touched Merrecci's hands, its mouth cracked open.

"Is it time," it yelled. It bounced in Merrecci's grasp as if trying to turn its immovable head.

Merrecci gripped the shaft made of bone to keep it from falling to the floor. It was far heavier than it appeared it should have.

"Garu," the key yelled. "Garu?"

"I assume this opens the tomb," Merrecci asked.

Garu nodded.

"Is the tomb close?"

Garu furled his brow, which Merrecci took to have a negative connotation.

"Where should we go," Merrecci asked.

"As soon as you have freed us all from this system, remove the blindfold and the wadding from his ears," Garu explained. He bowed once more. "May we bring our people aboard now?"

Merrecci agreed and issued orders to allow the Rhaxian ship into one of the landing bays. Garu requested a place to store their vessel in some hovel that could see space clearly from behind their own windows. They did not desire to stare at one of the Onyx's interior walls. Again, Merrecci agreed to their request as best as he thought he could, and he offered them ship quarters with windows that he believed would suit the Rhaxian's request well. It was a cabin on the lowest level in one of the Onyx's pyramid-structured corners. Garu graciously accepted and promised to stay out of the way of Merrecci and his crew.

Then Garu suddenly folded into himself, and he kept folding until he was entirely disappeared, or just too small for anyone to see.

"Commander," Merrecci said turning to Nandy. "I don't think I need to explain a reason to ensure we can track the Rhaxian ship while it's aboard ours."

Nandy agreed.

Then Merrecci addressed the bridge with a warning that anyone who spoke of the previous event would be dishonorably discharged and confined to quarters for the duration of the mission.

"These are not Garu's hands," the key announced. "I demand to know what soft tissue pedophile is groping me right now."

Merrecci, like the bridge, had fallen silent.

"Unhand my shaft, knave," the key demanded. "I don't know you!"

Merrecci held the key out to the closest console operator, who happened to be Mailer, and ordered her to take the key to his ready room and drop it on his desk.

"Oh, this is much better," the key screeched once it had changed hands. "Out of the freezer into the swimming pool. Why are your hands so sweaty?"

With an aggressive wave, Merrecci ordered Mailer once more to take the key away.

"All right," Merrecci said. "No need to stick around here anymore. When does Chief Being report for shift?"

"He has the day off, Sir," Nandy replied. "We anticipated we might want him ready to get us out of here at a moment's notice, so we've been giving him lighter hours to ensure he'd be rested. He's on call so to speak."

Merrecci summoned him, then called Dr. Quobalt to inform her that it was time for the Onyx to leave the Rhaxian's hiding spot and pass back through that coma-inducing membrane.

"All right," Charity said. "Are you looking for permission?"

"Uh, should we prepare for a second round of coma," Merrecci asked.

"I don't think so," Charity said. "We've inoculated everyone."

"I didn't realize you were able—

Merrecci's ready room suddenly opened.

"Sir," Mailer spoke in a way that didn't sound natural.

Merrecci might have ignored her until he was finished with his current discussion, but she was coddling a hand drizzling with blood.

Kellick moved the quickest, removing his Admiral's coat to wrap it around her wound.

"What happened," Merrecci asked.

"It bit me," Mailer roared.

While Merrecci informed Charity that he was sending down a patient, Kellick was already escorting her.

"Bit by keys! Hit with batons. This bridge has funny farm written all over it," Mailer complained.

"Yes, dear," Kellick said. "But you're bleeding right now."

"A key bit me," Mailer screamed at him.

Merrecci let her rail. She needed it. Once Charity could fix and drug her, she'd be in better spirits. He made a mental note to give her a day off if she got hurt again. Sure, people got hurt on the bridge all the time, but a baton thrown by an engineer and a key that bites, even he hadn't had that one yet.

In four minutes, Allen Being was back at the flight controls. In another two, the Onyx was through the wall of nothing, and no one went into coma, which might have meant that Charity was correct about the treatment working.

Before the sensors could even begin to translate their new environment, the bridge flashed red and abruptly started rattling. Various stations began crying out ship statuses as the Onyx was suddenly being attacked by two Didjian war vessels. As the walls shook, the holo began attempting to compile a map of the battle arena. When more attacks came that suggested there were even more vessels than what the battlecron demonstrated, Merrecci inquired if there was any way to know the enemy's numbers.

"Hard to tell," Nandy replied. "Stupid blotches of spaceless space!"

"They can't be too serious of ships, though, Sir," the current shift's tactical supervisor stated from above the dugout. Her name was Panthra Simpson, and Merrecci really hadn't found a reason to do more than listen to her status updates so far. "Their weapons fire is more suitable for war games. Shall we fire back?"

"We don't know what we're firing at," Merrecci replied. "Explosions might mess up what little sensor readings we have."

"Or it could knock us into one of these holes again," Nandy observed.

"And who knows if it would push us entirely through or just enough to cut our craft apart," Merrecci added.

"That might be exactly why they're hitting us with such weak weapons," Nandy suggested.

"Do you have enough sensor range to outrun them," he asked Being.

"On it," Being replied.

"Leonard to Merrecci," Bria's voice called over the bridge.

"Leonard? Good, you're awake," Merrecci said.

"I am now," Bria said.

"Might as well join us then."

Four hours later, the Onyx was out of the thickest part of the field. Precisely three seconds after that, four apocalypse missiles struck from various directions; twelve weaker torpedoes were enroute; and seventeen raizers from eleven ships were blasting the Earth's flagship.

Nandy announced the twenty-two vessels were following them through the field.

10

▲

Shot

A single chub was speeding for the port side of the Onyx. It blocked all incoming apocalypse and weaker weaponry alike as it saw a chance to take the blasts in exchange for a clean, hard collision. The impact rattled Merrecci from his seat in his ready room, and Nandy quickly apprised him of the situation.

By the time he was back onto the bridge, two more apocalypse missiles struck, and Merrecci was sliding across the floor.

Master Cha's head was in the holo trying to hail the Onyx but getting ignored.

"How did he even get his ship off that asteroid," Bria asked as she was now limping onto the bridge and rubbing her leg where she was certain a bruise was already appearing beneath her uniform. She did her best to keep her anger and pain in check. In her hand, she clenched a wrapped meatball sandwich.

"He must have had the asteroid destroyed from beneath him," Nandy replied.

"Or it's a new ship," Merrecci added.

Upon seeing Bria, he took the meatball sandwich and thanked her. He immediately opened it and began to bite into it even as Nandy relinquished the command seat to him. No sooner had he sat then he was thrown over its side.

"Report," he moaned, recovering and searching for his sandwich.

"Shields at twenty-nine percent," a woman announced from the shield array monitoring station.

"Four more apocalypse missiles inbound," a man at another console called.

"Your lunch, Sir," Mailer said. She was standing over Merrecci now holding the one half of the sandwich that managed to stay in its wrapping. Evidence of the other half painted her face and uniform.

She dropped it into his hand and stormed back to her controls muttering, "Just give me my red shirt and shoot me already. I hate this damned bridge."

The chub began another ramming charge.

"Target and destroy those apocalypse missiles with shielded probes," Merrecci ordered. "And get Cha's head off my bridge."

This time, the prime admiral attacked his sandwich as if he hadn't seen food in years.

"Targeting," another voice informed. "Firing torpedoes."

Cha's head morphed into the battle map. Thirty-seven Jimmoshean and Didjian ships appeared. Two Paichu now attempted their own runs at the Onyx.

"We've played this game before," Merrecci said through a fat piece of Italian mixture that only the ships deli was currently serving. He had returned to his seat.

"But this time, we're not waiting on diagnostics," Bria said.

"What would you do, Captain Leonard," Merrecci asked after a deep swallow permitted his speech again.

"Leave," Bria said. "Fire upon any that follow until we lose them and then figure out how they found us afterwards."

"What about hailing them," Merrecci asked.

"I wouldn't even hail them," Nandy said. "Just playing their game buys them time to bring in more help."

Merrecci took another bite and appeared to nod.

"Hail Master Chub's cha," Merrecci said. "Uh, Cha's chub."

Cha's head reappeared.

"Now you see Barbarian Admiral," Cha said. "I would have preferred not to have had to deal with apocalypses to get my point across though. Prepare to be boarded."

"You made me spill my meatballs all over my Ensign," Merrecci said. "Stop pissing me off."

Then Merrecci ended the transmission, and the battleground reappeared.

"Chief Being, get us out of here," Merrecci said. "Tactical, destroy any incoming missiles with raizers. Probe the apocalypses.

If anyone follows, start disabling their ships. Try not to destroy too many. We really don't need to multiply our enemy's hatred."

"Where would you like me to take us," Being asked.

"Out of Sentrale. Can you follow the same path out as we took in and lose them?"

"Well, yeah, but if they found us, they might already know it. They might be blocking our escape up ahead," Being said. "I could use a new path."

Merrecci summoned Ensign Escobedo at once.

The bridge doors opened, and Almma entered.

"Glad you could finally join us," Merrecci bellowed. "Where the hell were you?"

"Doing the second best thing you can do with a bed," Almma replied.

"I beg your pardon," Merrecci snapped.

"I was sleeping," Almma retorted.

"You didn't feel all this," Nandy asked.

"I was sleeping!"

Merrecci ordered Mailer to open a space-wide, short range channel. "Attention enemy vessels, anyone who powers down weapons will not be destroyed."

Then he ordered Chief Pilot Being to continue exiting the Sentrale system the same way they'd come until Escobedo could arrive on deck and get to work on giving him a more evasive course.

"Two more apocalypse missiles incoming," a voice announced.

"Firing probes," Panthra Simpson informed.

The apocalypse missiles evaporated.

The battle map exploded with small dots representing projectiles as the Onyx began to flee.

"How many," Merrecci asked.

"Ninety-seven, Sir," Almma replied as she got squared away at her station above the first officer's dugout with Bria in it. "None of them are big."

"That's good," Nandy said, positioned at the holo railing. "Ninety-seven dogs are better than ninety-seven dragons."

"Yes, but ninety-seven dogs trying to hump your leg is still ninety-seven little wieners stabbing your shin," Almma replied.

Merrecci turned to the tactical side of the bridge where every console was manned by a weapons operator that could control several raizers and torpedo bays.

"Prepare full raizer volley on all incoming torpedoes," Merrecci ordered.

Suddenly the Onyx unleashed a frenzy of raizer fire that left no missiles in pursuit after only two seconds and caused the map to fill with explosions.

"How are our shields," Merrecci asked.

"Back to full," the shields operator replied.

"Good," Merrecci said. "Their energy weapons will be coming next to drain us again. Try to keep us ahead and out of range, Chief."

"Yep," Being replied from deep concentration.

Meanwhile, Nandy scrutinized the holo, scanning and occasionally nodding intently at the scene. She stepped carefully around it: sometimes magnifying for a better look at a section, sometimes causing it to rotate before her.

"Sir. Ma'am," Nandy said as she magnified a portion of the map to show a small ship. "This vessel here is Ellyen."

It was a relay vessel, incapable of fighting and used to enhance sensors of its allies. Its own sensors had a reach four times as far as other races. The boat was small compared to most, typically operated by four or fewer crew members. It could easily hide and be overlooked in battle. Currently, it was speeding through the mass of enemies towards the Onyx, and it was fast.

"Ellyen isn't an enemy to Earth," Merrecci said.

"No," Nandy agreed. "They shouldn't be here. There are no other Ellyen ships present, which suggests this might be a trial mission for them. Or the Divide is bullying them into sharing their proprietary technology."

"A fair observation," Merrecci said.

"We should not destroy that ship," Nandy suggested. "That would make the Ellyen an enemy for sure."

"Noted," Merrecci acknowledged. "However, they are also moving for us rather quickly."

"They're going to fire an inhibitor," Bria suddenly realized. "We won't be able to see where we're flying."

"That," Nandy said, "was my guess too."

"Almma," Merrecci said. "Can you disable that ship without destroying it?"

"Is an admiral's ass covered in lip balm," Almma asked.

"What," Merrecci burst off-guard.

"I have an idea, Sir," Drinker's voice drifted over the bridge from his lone table where a pile of metal sticks were stacked before him.

Merrecci wasn't sure what this puzzle was. He'd have to ask later. He welcomed Drinker's thoughts.

"Lieutenant Commander Almma, can you cause a weak raizer material to strobe in a way that can cause it to material a hidden material to the Ellyen vessel and see if they'll material," Drinker said.

Almma stood silent for a moment before suddenly replying with an exasperated "What," which had almost matched Merrecci's.

"Can you attack the material with a message," Drinker asked back. His eyes suddenly sparked, and he stabbed a long green stick into the pile before him.

"Huh," Almma answered, then suggested she understood with, "Oh. Oh!" She suddenly went to work at her console, tapping quickly, swiping carefully then, "Prepared to fire, Sir."

Merrecci approved, finally thinking he understood as well.

A green raizer burst from the Onyx and struck the Ellyen vessel. It kept firing for several seconds.

"Don't destroy them," Merrecci said.

"It's barely causing any damage, just an illusion of it to anyone's sensors," Almma informed.

"Well, don't overdo it either," Merrecci urged. "They're not known for withstanding a lot of firepower."

Almma quickly cut the beam.

"Do it again," Merrecci ordered about ten seconds later when he realized the Ellyen were still approaching quickly.

"Sir," Bria said. "If it doesn't work, and if we're wrong, they can end us right now."

"Lieutenant commander," Merrecci said sullenly. "Prepare to destroy them before they affect our targeting sensors. If they don't get the message by then, it's too late to keep the Ellyen from entering this war anyway."

The Onyx continued to fire short bursts of the raizer beam. The Ellyen vessel continued to close in.

"It will be in range in twenty seconds, Sir," Bria announced.

"Prepare three class C torpedoes," Almma called to the tactical grid of consoles. "Continue delivering the message until then."

The tiny enemy ship slowed until it no longer had any momentum, and the shields disappeared. Its lighting flickered, and she slowly began to spin in drift to signify that it was dead in the water.

"Did you leave enough power to allow them to recover," Bria asked.

"And their female crew's personal toys," Almma said.

"Are you serious, right now," Merrecci asked, and he nearly chucked the wadded paper from his sandwich at her.

"Of course not," Almma said. "There are no females aboard that ship. The Ellyen powered themselves down."

"What message did you send," Merrecci asked.

"That we were giving them an out," Almma replied. "And I might have promised them each a Teintle Geisha."

Escobedo now entered the bridge in silk pajamas. Willis followed him, carrying a teddy bear and wearing flannels.

"Captain, I don't need Willis here right now," Merrecci said.

"I wouldn't remove him, Sir," Bria stated. "He's fixated on following Escobedo. He'll throw a tantrum if we try to interrupt. We could do without that right now too."

"I'm open to suggestions," Merrecci bellowed.

"Want me to flash him," Almma asked.

"Lieutenant-commander," Merrecci snapped.

"I think that's a pretty good idea," Pablo announced from his station where he was now sitting.

"Oh, wait," Almma said. "I have a secret admirer."

"Oh," Escobedo replied.

Merrecci threw her a disapproving glare.

Willis suddenly turned and approached the Admiral. He offered out his teddy bear.

"No thank you," Merrecci said.

"Pet it," Bria said.

"Good Lord," Merrecci replied.

"Sir," Bria respectfully chided, trying to remind him to be open-minded. Just now, the ship shook.

"That's one," Being started repeating.

The assistant pilot stood and began kicking Being's chair.

"Sorry," Being said. "Some miracles even I can't perform."

Willis laughed and held his bear to Merrecci again.

Merrecci pet the toy's head.

"Can we get him something to fixate on," Merrecci cried.

"He likes plants," Escobedo suggested.

Merrecci suddenly recalled that Willis had been caring for plants in his quarters earlier, right before Captain Fiji's removal.

"Good idea," Merrecci said. "Look—uh—Willis. There's a plant in my ready room. With all this shaking, would you go make sure it stays safe?"

Willis's smile grew, and his eyes bulged. He suddenly turned and sauntered off towards Merrecci's office. He stopped a moment at Drinker's table and picked at one of the metal sticks in the pile. The entire stack lifted on the end of the spear. It maintained its structure for a moment and suddenly burst apart, leaving Willis with just a stick in his hand. Willis's smile grew, and he walked off, fixated on a piece of Drinker's puzzle and poking his bear with it.

Drinker's glare stabbed at Willis until he had disappeared from the bridge. Then he started building his locking stack all over again.

At this, Escobedo announced that he had enough of an escape route plotted to get them on the run better.

Three burst jumps and ten minutes later, Nandy announced sensors could no longer detect enemy vessels.

"It seems the enemy found a trail of bread crumbs in your plotted course after all, Ensign Escobedo," Merrecci said, standing from his command chair.

"Not a chance," Escobedo said. "If there were bread crumbs, it came from someone else!"

Merreci remained in silence for a few moments while staring at the battlecron, which showed the Onyx drawing closer to the outset of the Sentrale system.

"Let me know once we're out," Merreci instructed. Then he ordered his senior staff to the bridge's ready room.

At a large, glass table built for ten, Merreci buried himself into studying Escobedo's flight plan that had taken them into Sentrale. Nandy, Almma and Bria waited patiently.

"How did this happen," Merreci finally asked. "Escobedo didn't leave anything for anyone to follow."

"Maybe they found a way," Nandy said.

"You know what the biggest problem with early long-distance space exploration was," Merreci asked. "It was based entirely on theories of people who'd never been off-planet and were making livings off of theorizing over how the cosmos worked. They saw a small pocket of it and thought they had mastered all the physics of it. It worked for a while, but then we found out space could have different attributes. Some was toxic, some was solid ice. Some had less gravity than even zero-gravity. Some of it gummed our Nessla drives up, and many crews wasted away sitting in one place until they were found centuries later, obviously not alive. Reality is, know what I know? Two things.

"One: engineers suck, but they keep the ship running, so you have to pretend you actually think what they do is the most interesting thing in the world. Pisses me off. Doesn't matter what race you belong to, engineers can solve any problem so long as they don't have to give a simple answer. Don't know how to turn on the coffee maker? Solution? Call an engineer. Then they'll have you turning on and turning off the whole machine, asking it to run a self-diagnostic, even coming down to open it up. But simply telling you, 'Push this button?' God forbid!

"They all talk like they know everything but are too damned stupid to know how to tell you why something isn't turning on , not without treating you like an idiot because the morons can't get over their superiority complex."

Now Merrecci broke into imitation of no one in particular. "Oh, look at me I built an ion fusion generator at the age of five. I can't believe you've never had to adapt a Plastazune receiver to accept Tanbien rays before. Huh-huh-huh, I suppose the next thing you're going to tell me is that you never turn your coffee maker off and on again. I'll bet you just go around pushing buttons!"

"You dated an engineer, didn't you," Almma asked.

Merrecci's eyes became slits, and he only saw Almma and her—

"She and her big brain must have cost you a fortune in little blue pills," Almma interrupted his thought.

"I'm really starting to understand why you were assigned to an admiral's security detail," Merrecci said.

"What's the second thing, Sir," Bria asked.

"Huh," Merrecci asked.

"You said you knew two things," Bria replied.

"Oh, right," Merrecci said, snapping out of his rant. "Know what I read out there? They didn't follow us in on a hunch. They were well-organized and knew right where we'd emerge."

"They also didn't come through the wall," Bria added.

"Correct," Merrecci replied. He abruptly sat upright and requested Dr. Quobalt and Prilla to join the meeting.

He momentarily returned to his ready room where he found Willis petting Merrecci's sole plant. Merrecci didn't know what it was called, but he liked the tune it hummed when it bloomed.

"Oh," Merrecci said as Willis looked up happy as he always was. "How's that plant treating you, Willie?"

Willis let out a single breathy laugh that sounded more like an old train whistle.

Merrecci reached into his desk and took out the stone key from a drawer that he had placed it in after he had found it trying to escape the ship by rolling itself into Merrecci's bathroom.

"Will you stop shaking everything," the key shrieked. "Know how annoying that is."

"Shut up," Merrecci retorted.

"What," the key bellowed. "I know you said something. I can feel the vibrations."

"Shut up," Merrecci said again. "Never mind."

"Huh," the key ranted. "You know. You must be stupid. Your vibrations sound stupid. Are you a fart? No wonder you're stupid. Farts are stupid."

Willis set Merrecci's plant down and followed the prime admiral, even reaching for the key.

"Not a chance," Merrecci said. He pointed to the stuffed bear left on his couch. "Look. Your teddy bear."

Willis returned to the couch and began to pet his toy animal.

"I demand to know who's holding me," the key snapped. "The coldona shall hear of this. Take me to him so he can execute you at once."

Merrecci carried the key out of his office as it screamed about the lack of hospitality of Merrecci's hands.

"And why are they so cold," the key asked.

By the time Merrecci returned to the ready room, Prilla was already sitting. Also joining the discussion were the three engineering musketeers.

"Where's Drinker," Merrecci observed.

"You said senior command," Bria replied. "He's civilian."

Merrecci quickly invited Drinker to join them.

"There are," the key said suddenly sniffing at the room, "several aromas. How many are in here? Am I giving a lecture again? Very well. I was a rock, a bulbarnashua to be exact. Please raise your hands if you've ever been to the planet of Rhaxia."

No one raised their hands but sat dumbfounded.

"Is anyone raising their hands," the key asked.

"Hey," Dawn shot up, pointing. "You're a ventriloquist!"

At this Charity and Cora entered the room, and Charity was complaining that someone could have told her where exactly the ready room was after getting into an argument with the bridge crew after she was denied access to the prime admiral's office.

"Why would you think the ready room was in my office," Merrecci asked.

"I thought that's where it was."

"This isn't Hollywood!"

Meanwhile, the key continued on in his lecture, oblivious of his disinterested audience.

"Oh for—" Almma grabbed the key from Merrecci and slapped it face down on the table.

Merrecci seemed stunned at the action then brushed it off.

"Awesome," the key complained. "Now I can't see. Is anyone there? Was the lecture really that bad? I can't see. Someone tell me." He complained a moment more about how this always happened, then he laughed because he realized he couldn't see before.

Merrecci invited a baffled Charity and Cora to sit. Charity requested Onyx to provide a bench to hold them. Onyx deleted two chairs and fulfilled the request.

"Explain how your inoculation worked against our coma," Merrecci requested.

Charity seemed surprised at the simple question.

"Random waves of lights and micro neural sensor arrays," Charity replied.

She realized Merrecci didn't understand.

"We measured data from when the Onyx passed through the field, and we were able to match light pulses to micro neural sensor arrays to prepare the brain to adapt to the shockwaves if we passed back through," Charity explained. "Figured we'd need to, since we'd clearly have to go back through." She suddenly sighed as she realized that Merrecci's countenance still wasn't comprehending. "Onyx told us a bunch of stuff that happened when we went through the barrier, and we played with lights until they stimulated the brain to wake up and say 'ooh! Pretty'."

"See," Merrecci said, pointing down the table to Charity. "Not an engineer."

"I beg your pardon," Charity asked.

Merrecci waved off her ignorance.

"If you had a powerful sensor emitter magnifier, could you inoculate multiple crews at once," Merrecci asked.

"Sure, if it was strong enough, but it would have to be really strong," Charity replied. "And it would take a lot of light."

"An entire ship's lighting system could do it though if calibrated properly, right?"

"Light? Yes," Charity said. "But most ships don't have the neural sensor arrays it would need to blast every inch at once and adapt to each individual as well. Otherwise, we wouldn't have had to inoculate everyone individually."

"If the ship did, it could though, right," Merrecci asked.

"If it was a powerful enough of a signal, there could be many types of standard micro sensors that could affect the brain," Charity replied.

"That's what the Ellyen ship was for," Bria realized. "They were going to boost Cha's fleet's sensors to inoculate themselves so they could get through the nothing wall and surprise us."

Merrecci nodded.

"So, they knew how to find us and how to get inoculated," Merrecci said. "Which means they knew they had to be inoculated at all."

"Which means either they've been here before," Almma said. "Or there's a smarmy little butt-bastard on board."

"Smarmy little butt—what," Nandy asked. "How random can you get?"

"It's because she's a toilet mouth," Dawn exclaimed.

"She's right though," Bria said.

Merrecci clenched his jaw and didn't try to hide his anger.

"What is it," Charity asked.

"They knew your inoculation formula," Bria replied.

"Oh, nobody knows the inoculation formula," Charity snarked.

"We have a spy on board," Bria said.

"And considering that all but three of you were never expected to be here," Merrecci explained, directing his finger over the table and finding himself chuckling. "You're the only ones who can be trusted with this information."

"What's so funny about that," Prilla asked.

"Nothing, except that one of the three people who were supposed to be here is my sister," Merrecci replied.

All glances suddenly fell on Almma.

"You all can look somewhere else before your eyes turn black," Almma warned. "I'm not the butt-bastard."

"That's what a traitor would say, isn't it," Dawn said, she was suddenly standing. "Let's just put an end to this now and let me kick her ass." Suddenly she started laughing and pointing to Almma. "You called yourself a turd. I get it. You said butt-bastard. That means turd, everyone."

"Hey," Almma erupted. "I showed you how to drive!"

"Oh, yeah," Dawn said and sat down to let it rest. "But you didn't let me do it in a Lotus, did you?"

"What is she talking about," Merrecci asked.

"Hello," Dawn shrilled. "Lotus is a car that they made for women to drive, and I'm a woman, so I want to drive it, but someoooone won't let me." She pointed sharply at Almma several times.

"It operates on fossil fuel, and—you know what," Almma fired back. "Maybe I'll fabricate one myself and run your slow ass over."

"Who you calling slow, you Asperger's cyst," Dawn shouted.

Merrecci ordered them to both shut up.

"Admiral, if you have any doubts to my loyalty, put me back in the brig," Almma said. "At least I could drink myself into finding my reflection attractive enough to have a worthy one-night stand with on this damned ship. I don't need this!"

"Same for me, Admiral," Nandy added. "Except for the whole weird Almma stuff she just said."

"Isn't that convenient," Dawn spat.

"Quiet down," Merrecci said softly, yet powerfully. "It's not them."

"With respect, Sir," Almma said. "How can you be sure."

"Because we stood up to Fiji," Nandy explained.

"That and because I said so," Merrecci replied.

Without realizing he was doing it, his fingers began exploring the crevices and smooth surfaces of the key resting at his side.

"What," the key said startled. "Why? Who's groping me? Stop groping me."

Merrecci instantly realized what he was doing to the key.

"Wait! Don't stop," the key suddenly insisted. "I kinda like it."

Merrecci let the key settle back onto the table.

"Oh sure," the key responded. "Be a dick about it."

"Sir, if I may," Bria said. "Perhaps, in the meantime, we could figure out how that key works before we get out of the Sentrale system. Since it would mean having someone understand how to plot a course according to those directions, might I suggest delegating Ensign Escobedo to make friends with that thing?"

Merrecci couldn't keep from smiling.

"That's an excellent idea," Nandy announced.

"Oh yeah," Almma said. "Let's give the talking distraction to Ensign clean freak while he's charting the way to save our lives from this system."

"He can handle it," Mirror said.

"I caught him lint rolling the galley carpet," Nandy informed.

"He's pretty smart," Merrecci countered.

"And he has a nice butt," Dawn said.

The table fell silent and stared now at Dawn.

"Why's everyone staring at me," she asked and almost started crying.

"Oh, awkward," Almma said.

Merrecci asked if Escobedo was able to join them a moment.

"I have about ten minutes before I have to give Allen the next leg of the course," Pablo answered.

It was enough time to hand off the key.

Pablo sauntered in, and Merrecci gave him a quick rundown of what he knew about the snarky guide, which was pretty much nothing more than that it could lead them to a tomb.

"I'm sorry," Merrecci said. "Am I boring you, Ensign?"

"Yes," Ensign Escobedo replied. "You're not very interesting to listen to."

"Excuse me," Merrecci asked.

With a subtle wave of her finger that Merrecci recognized through sibling familiarity, Prilla told the Prime Admiral that this was part of Ensign Escobedo's uniqueness. Pablo eagerly took the key and immediately pulled off the rubber-band blindfold and plucked the cotton from the skull's auditory holes.

"That's better," Pablo said.

The key, however, blurted out, "Hey! Ow! You don't have to get all yanking you know?"

"How else did you expect me to get it out," Pablo asked.

"I can hear," the key crowed. "Say something else."

"That talking key is dumb," Dawn said.

"Who said that," the key asked, bouncing, attempting to turn toward the sound of the voice that had called him dumb. That's when his eyes fell on Dawn. "Hey, it's a fat soft girl," the key shrilled, noticing Dawn in its peripheral as it faced Escobedo. "Hey, you! Slap that fat girl for me."

"I don't wanna," Pablo replied.

"Then say something to her," the key yelled. "Make her cry."

"That key's mean," Mirror shouted. "Kick his ass, Dawn."

But Dawn was trying not to cry and blurted, "You suck!"

"I agree," Almma said. She approached Pablo, her hand out. "Give it to me. I'm going to introduce it mouth-first to the toilet."

Pablo immediately held the key towards Almma and suddenly recoiled. "You're going to sterilize it before you bring it back, right?"

"Where's the temple," Merrecci yelled over the entire room.

"Who is that," the key asked. "Who is that?"

"It's the prime admiral. Now shut up," Escobedo said. "Want me to put the cotton back in, Sir?"

"We can't very well use his help if he can't hear us, can we," Merrecci said.

Escobedo stared down at the key.

"Eww! Don't look at me like that," the key moaned. "You're too tall for me."

"Take him outside, please," Merrecci said.

"Who said that? Who is that? Is that the cold-hands one," the key asked as Pablo Escobedo began carrying him out of the conference room. "Wait! Wait! Let me see the cold hands one. I have to tell him something."

Escobedo stopped and looked to Merrecci, who nodded with resigned approval. Pablo turned the key to face the admiral.

The key took in a deep breath and yelled, "Frugg Ducker!" Then he took in another deep breath and went "Thpbthpbth!"

"What," Charity burst in bewilderment.

When the key saw Charity and Cora, its jaw dropped.

"What is that monstrosity," the key screamed.

"Look who's talking," Charity fired back.

Merrecci snapped his fingers at Pablo and pointed him towards the exit. Escobedo immediately turned back to the door.

The key moaned loudly just then.

"I see it," the key yelled. "I see it. Never mind! It's gone."

"Wait," Merrecci called after Escobedo. "What was that?"

"Who knows," Escobedo replied. "It's a key, and it's a jerk."

Merrecci stood from his seat and crossed the room where he took the key once more from Ensign Escobedo.

"You cold-handed bastard, what's wrong with you," the key complained.

"What did you see," Merrecci asked.

"I asked you first," the key replied.

Merrecci puzzled over the skull a moment and almost handed it back to Pablo.

"Sir," Drinker requested. "May I see it."

Merrecci saw no harm and handed it to Drinker. Drinker then faced the key towards himself.

"Who are you," the key asked.

Drinker said nothing. He held the key vertical and began to rotate it by the bone shaft in his fingers.

"What is the purpose of this," the key asked as it completed a full turn.

"Hmm," Drinker said.

"Mr. Bone," Merrecci asked.

"I'm not sure," Drinker replied. After a second of thought, he tilted the axis of the key and rolled it once more between his fingers. As the small stone face turned slightly down towards the floor and past Prilla, it suddenly started screaming again.

"I see it," the key cried. "I see it!" It continued to repeat itself as if it knew no other statement.

Drinker kept turning the key, and it stopped screaming.

"Nevermind," the key surrendered. "It's gone."

"Sir, I think we have to material the ship in that direction," Drinker suggested, pointing the way the key had just been looking when it was moaning.

"Sir, I think we have to material the ship in that direction," the key mocked and laughed, until Drinker turned the stone locksmith's face towards Prilla and the floor where the key gasped in surprise again and started yelling that he saw it.

Merrecci retrieved the key and handed it to Pablo.

"Wait," Dawn spoke. "Can I see it for a second?"

Pablo shrugged and handed it to Dawn.

Dawn took the key, held its bone shaft between both palms and began spinning it as if she were trying to use it to start a fire by rubbing it against a piece of wood.

"I'm not fat," she yelled over the skulls cries as its head spun viciously back and forth in her hands. "You're stupid."

The key began shouting for help.

Merrecci ordered her to give the key back to Pablo.

By the time Almma had reached in to retrieve the key, Dawn was smacking the key's face against the table.

"It's all yours, navigator," Merrecci said. "Plot a course towards the direction it screams."

"Oh, this is going to be fun," Escobedo said.

As he exited, the key dry-heaved, lost in its dizzy abuse.

The doors severed Escobedo and the key from the room.

"Wow," Almma said. "Our first talking key, and it's an asshole."

"I'm sure it probably thinks the same about us," Merrecci said.

"Yes, Sir," Almma said. "Because it's an asshole."

"That'll be enough of that," Merrecci ordered.

"I'm sorry, Sir," Almma replied. "For the record though, I think you just made the navigator position the crappiest job on the ship, now that you're making him work with an asshole."

Suddenly, Dawn was out of her seat and stomping around the table to Almma. She slapped at her, and Almma caught her wrist.

"Don't do that again," Almma ordered.

"Then stop swearing," Dawn demanded.

"Oh, like you don't swear," Almma pointed out.

"No, I don't," Dawn replied.

Merrecci ordered Dawn to her seat, when she tried to object, Merrecci silenced her with a look, and she appeared to understand.

"How are we going to find this mole," Merrecci asked.

Almma spoke first. "I could start punching people and asking if they're the spy."

"No," Merrecci snapped.

"Well then, the boring way would be to just check communication logs," Almma suggested. "Shouldn't have been any people sending off-ship messages."

"Unless they found a way around it," Merrecci stated.

"Then I'll have to punch them, won't I," Almma asked.

"Why do you let her talk to you that way," Prilla asked.

"It's called foreplay," Almma snipped.

"Really," Prilla asked Merrecci again, slamming her fists down disapprovingly on the table, startling even Merrecci.

"He wants someone who won't take his shit; will keep him on his toes; and takes her job seriously enough that he feels safe. Isn't that right, Prime Admiral Elevator-eyes," Almma said.

"She's not wrong," Merrecci begrudgingly said.

"See," Almma said. "He's my bitch."

"Stand down," Merrecci snapped.

"I agree. Too far," Almma acknowledged.

"Too far," Prilla snipped.

"Gee, I can't imagine why," Almma replied. "We've only had our home torn away from us; our friends and family off God knows where; and having to keep up morale while people like you get to play one on one 'there-there' with people who don't do shit around here. So, forgive me if the last thing I give a rat's ass about is keeping my Ps and Qs around just for you."

Almma recomposed herself and said, "So, we'll check comm records and monitor for anything going out."

"I would be more than happy to assist you in checking those records, Lieutenant-commander," Nandy said.

"Will you also set up some surveillance on Fiji and his bridge crew," Bria asked.

Almma agreed it could be done.

"We'll need more," Merrecci said and turned to his sister. "I need a profile."

"That's not what I do," Prilla replied.

"Okay. Find me the person on this ship who does," Merrecci stated. "You're the best chance to clue us in on who to look at."

"Most importantly, people who could possibly have access to Dr. Quobolt's inoculation data," Bria said.

"And our navigation charts, and the ability to send out messages under our noses," Almma added.

"That could be a lot of people," Charity said.

Prilla hemmed a moment. "Observations shut off at my office door, unless I have concerns about a potential threat."

"Thank you," Merrecci said. "And I'd like you and your staff to start interviewing the crew."

"What did I just say," Prilla asked.

"What did I just say," Merrecci asked back far more sternly. "I'm not asking for details. I'm asking you to point me to the potential threat to the survival of Earth. Don't clear anyone for duty who gives you the wrong vibes. Start with Fiji and the crew he used to supplant mine, do them all first."

"No details," Prilla replied. "Only if they're not cleared. If I find someone to be an imminent threat, I'll report the concern as I normally would, to Lieutenant-commander Almma."

Merrecci thanked her.

"What if we made it public that we had a spy," Charity asked.

"That's the last thing we want to do," Merrecci replied.

"I think it's a good idea, Sir," Nandy added. "It might make the spy's nervous actions a bit louder."

"I have to agree," Charity said. "Maybe that's what you need to weed this person out."

Merrecci scrawled an invisible letter into the table with his fingernail before he opened his mouth to finally say that it wasn't a good idea.

"Think about it, Sir," Nandy said. "The spy most likely hasn't been able to fully establish a comfortable and secure foothold here. We're still trying to adapt in many ways ourselves. It's not like they have a safehouse to retreat to. No one can just come pick them up."

"What if we threw out a rumor that Cora has invented a new material that can map a person's brain activity to measure past memories," Drinker chimed in. "We could say it builds holograms of those memories so we can start scanning every material of the crew to find out who's been sending messages to the enemy. Our spy might just appear even more on edge than usual."

"I have a lot of problems with the ethics of that," Prilla said.

"I do to," Charity agreed.

"Can it be done," Merrecci asked.

"No, it can't be done," Prilla replied.

Cora moaned a laugh and might have snorted.

"Right," Charity agreed.

"You understood that," Merrecci asked.

"She's my sister," Charity said.

"I didn't say really Material it," Drinker said. "Just say we can do it."

"I guess the spy already knows that we did invent a way to manipulate the brain into waking people out of their comas," Charity surmised. "It wouldn't be too far out and away from what we've already done to suggest that we've adapted it to hunt for traitors or would-be-mutineers, I suppose."

"So, tell them that engineering is building the item and you'll be scanning soon," Bria asked.

"We don't even need to do that," Nandy replied. She split her attention now between Merrecci and Bria. "Just let the rumors spread that we have a spy and are using Cora's inoculation technology to find who it is. Dr. Quobalt can walk the halls and just point a flashlight at people to make them think she's scanning. Maybe even issue random invitations to some people to come talk to her somewhere in all that so she can do the whole 'have you seen anyone doing anything out of the ordinary' thing."

"And if you," Merrecci said, pointing to Prilla, "happen to pick up on anyone acting overly worthy of observation, we could see what happens if we ask them to stick around while we *scan* them."

"I'm not comfortable with that," Prilla objected.

Merrecci pursed his lips and took in a deep breath, contemplating that the person he was about to yell at was his sister who was not above turning it back on him all too well.

"Well, you'd better get comfortable with it," Bria demanded. "We're here to save Earth, not your practice."

Prilla's face turned to stone, perhaps insulted that what had once been her own student and patient was speaking so to her.

"I don't know what's happening back home right now," Prilla replied. "But this ship is one of the last extensions of freedoms that Earth represents."

"Dr. Wanship is right," Merrecci interrupted then turned to Prilla who appeared off-guard at the use of her last name. "But you're going to have to remember this conversation if our people start dying because of your inaction."

"I know how this works," Prilla snapped.

"Okay then," Merrecci said. He turned back to the table. "Who's going to start the rumors?"

Drinker's hand rose.

"We should," Drinker said. "Myself and the others from Dr. Material's group from the academy."

"Why you," Merrecci asked.

"Because the crew won't question us about it nor why we're blabbing," Drinker explained. "They'll just think we're those stupid material they've seen and heard about and won't be surprised that we can't keep our materials shut."

"I can agree with that," Nandy said. "Except for two items. Only people in this room. What we've discussed needs to stay in these walls, and the captain absolutely should not pass rumors herself. She's above that."

Merrecci agreed.

"Don't worry, Admiral, I won't say anything either," Cindy Lou's voice rang over the conference room speaker.

Merrecci interlaced his fingers before him on the table and glared at the ceiling.

"Communication systems is not for talking," Merrecci stated coolly. "I will tear it out of your area."

"That does raise a question though, Sir," Almma pointed out. "If she's able to override and listen in, who's to say our spy can't."

"Because I'm a god," Cindy replied. "Spies can't do what I can."

"That's it," Merrecci bellowed to his engineering heads. "Take out her communication capabilities down there."

"If I may, Sir," Nandy offered. "Cindy, can you listen in on any unauthorized or even onboard transmissions."

"Doesn't she already do that," Merrecci asked.

"Of course not," Cindy answered. "I do have some ethics."

"If the spy were to realize who she was and that she could eavesdrop, the spy might attempt a way to harm her," Bria suggested. "Perhaps she might need her comms in that event."

"If you wish, I will listen," Cindy said. "But I prefer the mystery of privacy."

"You listen to us all the time," Merrecci complained.

"I have my reasons," Charity replied. "Do you want me to listen in on others?"

"No," Prilla snapped. "I will not have her listening in on my confidential meetings. We need to maintain integrity here."

"I have to agree, Sir," Bria stated. "She's right. When all is said and done, we need human rights to stay intact."

"Gah," Merrecci cried. "You all piss me off."

"And Primey Poo," Cindy announced. "I do wonder if you've thought about how this will impact your mission, especially when my other half comes on board."

"We'll look at that bridge when we get closer," Merrecci said.

Then he dismissed the meeting, sent everyone off to find a spy, and handed command of the bridge to Bria for her shift.

He returned to his quarters when Prilla, Charity and Cora appeared, insisting that they follow up with some quick check-ups to make sure he was still in good condition after his coma. He insisted he was. They ignored him and waited for their own results before agreeing that he was all right.

"As ship psychologist, you know I don't have to tell you that you're playing a dangerous game, right," Prilla asked.

"As dangerous as commanding a warship," Merrecci replied.

"And dad would say," Prilla started, then suddenly stopped as she noticed the wince that only she would recognize.

"Good night," she muttered and walked out.

Charity and Cora, however, did not.

"I didn't want to say anything in front of your sister," Charity said.

"What is it," Merrecci asked. He poured himself a scotch and, as an after thought, offered her a drink.

She declined. Cora did not.

"She doesn't blame you, you know," Charity said. "About your dad."

"You can leave now," Merrecci instantly shut down.

"I just thought you would want to know," Charity replied.

"It's not your concern."

"Can I tell you something?"

"No," Merrecci rebuked and poured himself another scotch.

"Stop me," Charity replied hotly.

"Excuse m—

"You're a bit of an ungrateful prick, you know that. I get that you have to be that way with your crew, but that's your sister."

"Which you know nothing about," Merrecci replied.

"What do you think we did in our group sessions every week for two years, you holistic douche," Charity asked.

Cora growled.

"We shared our lives, and your sister did the same. Know what she talked about? You? Know why she took on an academy position? So, she wouldn't have to be on the research vessel that had to scan whether your ship was destroyed or not. Or be one that had to watch you get destroyed."

"You're out of line," Merrecci insisted.

"I care about your sister," Charity said.

"I don't need lectures about Prilla," Merrecci retorted, suddenly pacing past Charity and to open the door for her to leave. "Especially not from one of her patients."

"I wasn't a patient, you moron," Charity responded, turning to exit, and causing the door to shut again so she could yell. "What do I know? What do you know? I just spent the past two years listening to her go off about how wonderful you were supposed to be. Boy, did she lie!" She reached to open the door again.

"Stick to your job," Merrecci said.

"Get laid," Charity yelled.

The door opened again, and Charity found Merrecci's face and clenched jaw squared against hers. His anger vented from within him and made his nose hiss.

"Good idea," he yelled, Then he was suddenly kissing Charity. He wasn't entirely sure if he had initiated it.

For that matter, Charity wasn't sure if she hadn't. Actually, she was pretty certain it was the scotch on his tongue. She gripped his collar, and pressed her swear words against his mouth, and she let his own cursing burn right back into her lips. If he was willing to go this far and forget Cora was there too, Charity sure wasn't going to correct him. Scotch wasn't her favorite drink, but she'd take it.

Then, he suddenly stopped, and she pulled away to find him disarmed and stepping back.

"What," she asked.

"Your sister just put her tongue in my ear."

*　　　*　　　*

For the seventh time, the roster scrolled over the holotab before Bria's crinkled face. She hadn't slept the night before or the one before that, not since the news of the spy. She was certain from the lack of knocks to her door that the bridge crew may have forgotten that she was there.

Few names had been removed from her own suspect list. Manitoba Fiji's file was scattered open across her digital desk. Part of her wanted the spy to be him. It would have been so much easier, but there was nothing to suggest the mutinous captain necessarily made for a traitorous spy.

She tapped at her desktop and several more piles of holographic folders appeared on top of it. She took one from a stack and cracked it open.

An alarm beeped on her wristband, and she quickly brushed it aside. She had thirty minutes left on her shift, but she had thirty minutes left on it yesterday, and that didn't stop her from working to now, nor did it stop her two days ago when her command shift was also supposed to be over. She made a quick call to Charity to pay her another visit. She set her current folder down and reluctantly retreated to her office shower to refresh herself and her uniform. Bria had just finished dressing when Charity and Cora announced themselves.

As soon as the doctor entered, she stopped, and Bria could see the outrage swelling even before Charity erupted with, "Get some sleep!"

"Can't," Bria replied. "I still see all this stuff."

"You're going to make me relieve you of command, aren't you," Charity said.

"You want to do this," Bria snapped, and Charity seemed taken aback. Bria apologized.

"At least eat something." Charity presented a bento box. "You look like death."

Bria congenially thanked Charity but pushed the food away.

"Eat," Charity demanded.

"I'm not hungry," Bria replied.

"Then drink something." Charity made her way to the fabricator and summoned water. "You're not going to catch anyone if you get dehydrated."

She set the water in front of Bria and ordered her to drink it.

"You can't command on three days without sleep," Charity chided.

"How's it going on your end," Bria took a moment through her gulping to ask as if she hadn't even heard the question.

"About as we expected," Charity replied. She took a seat across from Bria and broke open the Bento box. "I'm starting to get questions and neither confirming nor denying anything that's been said to me." She pulled a large, steamed bun from within and bit into it. "Oh my god! You've got to try this."

"No thanks."

"Eat it," she ordered holding another steamed bun to Bria. "And I won't bother you about it anymore."

Bria took the bun. She bit into it.

"Have you heard from Prilla," Bria asked, turning back to her work and aware that Charity was watching to make sure she ate all of the bun.

"She and her crew are fake scanning everybody," Charity said. "It's getting noticed. Her feet hurt, but Nandy's been picking up some of the work, so Prilla says that's been nice."

"You should give Prilla something for her feet," Bria said.

"Gee! Thanks for that counsel doctor," Charity snapped. Then it was her turn to apologize. "I don't like seeing my friends killing themselves off trying to catch some jerk who could get us killed."

"Me neither," Bria replied and barely heard herself say. "I wish I could know who survived."

"No," Charity said. "We're not doing that. I don't have time for that."

Cora, however, broke into a wail and slapped at Charity.

"Stop that," Charity said and kept repeating until she had deflected enough of Cora's slaps to make her sister realize she was done throwing a tantrum. Charity slid the Bento to Bria and suggested she try the shrimp.

Bria glared, Charity apologized, but Bria took a shrimp anyway.

She turned to Bria's work and glanced over it.

"Learn anything yet," she asked.

Bria started to answer but had to lick her fingers off when her desk stopped responding optimally to her hand gestures. Then she began swiping folders and their contents away from the top until only Fiji's records remained. Next to them was a bulleted list of other possible suspects.

"And you're sure it's not Fiji," Charity asked.

"Unfortunately," Bria replied. "I think he would have surrendered our ship when he stole command, otherwise."

"Suck," Charity said. "I really wanted it to be him."

"Me too."

"Is it you," she asked.

"That's not funny," Bria fired back coldly.

"Who else is on your radar," Charity asked.

"No one really," Bria explained. "Just a name or two with records so perfect they're boring."

"Anyone in particular? Maybe I can help watch them."

"There's this guy down in the power grid, Eric Wwasho."

"Why him?"

Bria began to explain. As she opened his file and then went into detail, she didn't even realize that her own speech had started to slur. The room began to turn dark, and she barely found the strength to fall back into her chair and mutter, "What did you do?"

Then her vision went out of focus, and she was no longer aware of anything but the taste of butter and shrimp in her mouth.

11
▲
Eureka

When Captain Leonard came to, she was still in her chair. It had been enlarged and reclined to hold her better.

It was the cracking sounds that woke her. When she was little, her brother had fallen during a game of tag. The image of the memory filled her brain as she treaded the surface of sleep. When her brother hit the ground, all four of his fingers on his left hand snapped. This was that sound that she heard over and over.

She bolted straight in her seat and reached for a baton that wasn't there.

Merrecci sat before her desk. He leaned back in a chair, watching her and glaring. He bit into the shell of a pistachio, let it break in his teeth and then pulled it away to peel the insides out. He flipped the broken pieces onto Bria's desk where a small pile of pistachio carcasses was building before Merrecci.

She was suddenly to her feet and clamoring at her desk to pull up the current time.

"Do you know why we have a crew, Captain," Merrecci asked.

"Sir, I'm sorry," Bria stated. "It won't happen again."

Merrecci was too busy sucking salt off of his next uncracked pistachio to respond.

Bria kept apologizing until Merrecci cracked the shell and removed the meat.

"Do you know why we have a crew, Captain," Merrecci asked again through mastication.

"Sir, I'm pretty sure Dr. Quobalt drugged me to sleep," Bria replied and continued to apologize.

"I know," Merrecci said. "I asked her to."

"Sir," Bria asked. "What was it?"

"Truth serum," Merrecci replied. "And knock-out drugs."

"Ha. Ha," Bria replied, then slowly asked, "Are you serious? You had a doctor give me drugs? Did you read my file, Sir? I'm an addict! Do you know how long it took me to break addictions to all those medications doctors put me on after I lost my face?"

Merrecci cracked another pistachio.

"Do you know why you have a crew," he asked a third time.

"With all due respect, how dare you?" Bria launched out of her chair and moved to exit the room without being dismissed.

"Do you know why you have a crew," Merrecci asked once more. "Or do I need to send you back to your group of dummies to find out?"

Bria stopped herself from saying something she shouldn't have, and instead said, "Because I can't run the ship on my own."

"Because what," Merrecci asked.

"I can't run the ship on my own."

"Oh, so you do understand that," Merrecci asked, then gestured for Bria to take her seat again.

"The reason you have a crew," Merrecci said. "Is so you can sleep, so you'll have the energy to keep your people awake during emergencies when they're tired."

"How am I supposed to sleep? We have a spy."

"Oh my god! We do? Is it you?"

"What do you think," Bria exclaimed.

"It's difficult to tell," Merrecci replied. "You've been in your office a lot the past few days. It's a perfect spot to hide transmissions right under our noses."

"Sir, the last thing I want to wake up to is a fireball melting me," Bria explained. "So, I'll keep working until I find him."

"Do you think your being awake would stop the fireball," Merrecci asked.

"Why am I getting spoken to this way in my own office," she asked.

"There's always some potential death waiting to wake you from your sleep out here," Merrecci said. "I thought I taught you this already. Have the wrong pilot at the helm, and you could find yourself waking up to a whole nothingness of pain."

"That's supposed to help me sleep at all," Bria asked.

"When you have a good crew, yeah," Merrecci said. "Do you think we have a good crew?"

"With respect, Sir. What kind of question is that," Bria asked. "Of course, I do, I picked it."

"Exactly," Merrecci said. "You have a good crew that works hard to protect this ship, just like you. Do you trust your crew?"

"With a spy on board?"

"Huh," Merrecci suddenly paused. "Interesting thought." He worked over another shell. "Do you trust your crew to work hard to help you find the spy?"

"Of course, I do!"

"Are you worried they'll find the spy before you can do your work," Merrecci asked.

"I don't care who finds the spy just so long as someone does," Bria asked.

Merrecci made a strange "huh" then cracked another shell and flipped the inedible parts into his pile on Bria's desk.

"So, you trust your crew," he asked.

"I think so," Bria admitted. "But I wish we had more hands working on it."

"That's a start. Let Nandy help out in here. She wants to help."

"Yessir," Bria replied.

"What would have happened if you had been this tired during our escape," Merrecci asked. "What happens when I need you for your other duties, and you're entirely exhausted?"

"Understood," Bria replied.

"Good," Merrecci said. He began sweeping his shells off Bria's desk with one hand and into another. "Because I don't want to have this talk again. Now, if you'll excuse me, I had to cover my first officer's shift while she slept, and now I have to start my own watch. Since you're rested, take a stroll, meet your crew. Build the trust. I don't want to see you until you're due to report back."

He made it to the door before stopping.

"I didn't know about your addictions," Merrecci said.

Then he left.

Immediately, Bria returned to searching through the crew roster again when her desk suddenly fell blank.

"I believe he ordered you to go see your crew," Cindy Lou's voice crept in from the walls.

"I have cameras," Bria answered.

"It's not the same. Go see your crew."

Bria objected, but Cindy didn't respond, and neither did her desk. So, she stood and left her office and the bridge to go watch the stupid crew.

She started her rounds with what she was comfortable with, her quarters, where she spent entirely too much time getting distracted. Then, for some reason, Onyx started making the room smell like farts, and Bria felt compelled to leave.

Realizing she was hungry, she stopped at the galley. Seeing that it was filled with too many bodies, she decided she'd return when it wasn't so busy. So, she stopped at the quarters of those she was familiar with, her friends from group.

Drinker was off duty, but he was out. He was typically off duty and typically out. He really didn't have a shift, nor any authority. Merrecci just liked what his brain could do. If only Drinker's stroke wasn't making others have to decode those ideas of his. His bunkmate, Willis, wasn't around neither.

The engineering leadership was currently asleep. Dawn had answered the door with a hefty, "You wanna die with or without a foot up your ass?"

The three engineers worked best together so they also did well having the same off-hours. Merrecci kept it that way.

Bria found the botany department somewhere in her journey. She'd wanted to visit for some time, but she just never made it. Right upon entering, she spotted Willis standing over several bushes, smiling and trimming them down to squares of different bulk and height. He didn't notice when the captain walked in, but the director of the botany department, a woman perhaps the age of Bria, did. The director, Madison Kho greeted Leonard, not genuinely but not impolite neither. She offered Bria a pollen mask as she suggested it might help her feel more comfortable around the crew. After Bria declined it, then declined it again, the director offered to give her a tour into the green house, which turned out to be much larger than the captain had realized it could be.

Bria was quite familiar with the schematic of the ship. She knew that the greenhouse was allotted entirely to what would have been the top nine decks if there had been nine decks built. Here, small trees, trees she'd never seen before, aspired to reach up to a full sky of glass above it, which they would when they got older. Its pyramid ceiling could change its tint depending upon how much natural sunlight was available. If needed, the glass could emanate artificial light to feed the gardens. From outside, it could appear dark and almost invisible in space.

The center piece of the greenhouse was a ten foot pine. It wasn't much now, but the gardens were new, and Bria believed it would be tall some day, perhaps tall enough to reach the highest point of the ship and maybe have to be trimmed from punching through the roof.

Throughout the nine decks, there were gardens and forests with paths and ponds that rose up into surrounding balconies that had been landscaped to appear as mountains or switchback trails. It was as if the garden were the inside of a majestic opera house with levels upon levels of balconies, if only those balconies were gardens. Quite a few other crewmembers were enjoying the grounds themselves as Lieutenant Kho led Bria to a small vineyard with rows of grapes that wouldn't have enough floor space on any other ship. In truth, this one department was as large as Merrecci's previous command, the Viridian.

The next stop was the start of a forest floor where Kho's crew were planting quaking aspen. Someday, they would help create the illusion of a forest as well as segregate different growing environments. Soon, someone sitting in a cornfield might forget that right next to it was a rainforest cultivating cancer-curing meds. The Onyx offered other means to help separate the different growing sectors. There were four balcony-decks of gardens on one of the walls. While the Onyx could craft its own food using a bank of reprocessing and recycling energy, it was really only meant to supplement feeding the crew until the gardens were capable of producing year round and fill stores so the fabricators could be reserved for emergency rationing. The fact was, it took less energy to fabricate plant sustenance than it took for humans.

One third of the entire lowest botany deck was a wheat field that appeared to roll on for as far as Bria could see, or so she thought.

"It's because the engineers worked a curvature into the floor to sell the illusion that the fields have no end," Kho said.

Several crew members were currently gearing up to begin hewing this particular golden crop down. This, it turned out had been planted and growing months before the Onyx's construction was complete, so it had already begun contributing to harvest and food storage. The other floors of the botanicals were loaded with producing plants as well, but for some reason, the wheat field struck her with the most awe. She wasn't sure why. Perhaps it was the ceiling giving the illusion of a bright midwestern day, which she'd never seen herself. She grew up always knowing mountains. Perhaps, it was the vastness of the floor, or the yammering wheat stalks begging to be culled. She didn't know, but it was magnificent.

"It's because of the ceiling," Kho said. "It appears differently depending upon where you're standing, and it can simulate weather patterns. Isn't that neat? Do you know how a weather pattern works?"

"I didn't expect so much," Bria said. "Not with this being a new ship."

"This was the first portion of the Onyx that was built," Kho continued to quiz. "Can you guess how tall wheat can get?"

"I thought engineering and the power grid would have been first," Bria stated, ignoring the second question.

"That's okay, even the most experienced of us make that assumption. And good for you for thinking that."

"Umm, thanks," Bria replied, but really wondered at.

"See. The gardens sections always go up first because they need time to grow, and the Onyx took a long, long time to make, so they build a small power supply to run just this portion of the ship while the rest is being put together. They want to take no chances of the gardens dying because of a power failure due to something that goes wrong during construction elsewhere." Suddenly she stopped and looked strangely to Bria before smiling and continuing on with, "I ramble. It's all very complicated to understand, isn't it?"

Bria ran her hand over the heads of the wheat and let their tall braids tickle her palms.

"Not really," Bria replied.

"It's very fragile when you think about it," Kho explained. "If you think about it, this is the real power grid and engineering for the ship because it feeds the crew, and that's how crew gets power. Without it, there's no crew because crews need food. Why, your breakfast will have something from this very sector. Isn't that neat?"

"Hmm," Bria replied. "How strong is the power source?"

"Not as strong as the ship's of course, but enough to sustain us to limp home, I'll bet."

"That's interesting," Bria observed. "I've looked over every schematic of the ship and have never seen mention of it."

"Probably because it wasn't supposed to still be here in the final design. They never are. They're not needed once main engineering goes up. They're supposed to be removed prior to the christening, but, in our case, we sped up the time line a bit, didn't we? We don't even use this one. It eats up some of our citrus area, so we had to adapt a little. Would you like to see what a citrus orchard looks like?"

Bria must have been caught up in the wonder of it all.

"It's one thing on paper," Kho said. "It's another to actually see it, isn't it?"

"I have a feeling I'll be back," Bria replied.

Director Kho nodded and invited her to return once the gardens were more mature. Then she escorted Bria back to the botany lab entrance. Bria stopped a moment to observe whatever plant Willis was working on.

"Our special guy has a green thumb for sure," Director Kho said. "Don't you, Willis?"

Willis raised his wobbly head and smiled. He laughed a little and returned to caring for the plant before him, trimming it back carefully with a pair of clippers.

"Willis and his plants are always happy in here," Kho said.

"Let me know if you need anything, Will," Bria said, squeezing Willis's arms.

"Oh, we'll let you know if he does," Kho said. "We're very protective of our favorite gardener." She reached in to correct Willis's use of the clippers. "Remember, they're sharp, buddy." She continued to show him how to cut.

Willis stared entirely at the plant with his palm open and smiling until Kho returned the scissor to his hand. Only then did he continue on with his work.

"Well," Kho said. "We should probably let you go, Captain. I'll bet have lots of exciting things to do today, huh?"

Bria allowed the director to escort her towards the exit. Kho's hand pressed gently into her back to usher her out as she said, "If you'll have the admiral let us know the next time you want to pop in, we can set up a special tour for you and your friends, but right now we do have lots of work to do, don't we?"

Now Bria stopped.

"I think I will take you up on that offer for another tour sometime." She started to leave and then stopped again, turning suddenly to what might have been a bit of a stunned Kho. "I'll pop in again when the bridge allows."

Now Bria raised her gaze over Kho's shoulder.

"Let me know if they need anything in here, Willis," Bria called.

Willis turned, smiling and waving.

Bria then left the greenhouse and visited the brig, engineering and arena that could adapt itself to gravity and zero-gravity sports. She wondered if she could ever visit the entire ship in any given day, or even a week. On a whim, she stopped into Vandenbutcke's classroom and found him alone and bent over a desk.

"My office hours are in the syllabus," he said, hearing the doors open at the back of his classroom, but not turning from the homework that he was correcting.

When he finally looked up, he stood, not really out of respect, but more out of trying to fix burned bridges if he could.

"Captain," he greeted plainly, and Bria could hear the hidden pain of contempt within his words.

She asked if she could sit, and then she did in one of the student seats.

"See, now this is more my style of chair," Bria said.

Vandenbutcke, snickered and couldn't hide it.

"With respect, I have a lot of things I need to do, and I don't really have the tools to do them. What can I do you for, Ma'am?"

"You know what I like most about this view," Bria asked.

"I couldn't say," Vandenbutcke said then quickly added, "Ma'am."

"The excitement of it," she said.

"We remember school very differently," he replied.

"I'm sorry to hear that," Bria said.

"Ma'am. With respect, what is this about?"

"Didn't you ever have a teacher that you actually looked forward to sitting in this chair to listen to," Bria asked.

"Umm, sure," Vandenbutcke said. "One or two."

"Not me," Bria replied. "I always knew this seat would be the closest someone like me would ever get to space, and teachers let me see it. I really wanted to go to space. Teachers took me there.

"I got excited because I'd find myself thinking, maybe this time, this time, that person up there will help me understand why I'm too stupid to go. "

"And did anyone ever connect the dots," Vandenbutcke asked, not realizing he might have been smirking.

"Until you," Bria replied. "I never even had a teacher acknowledge when I entered the room, but I still listened to them."

Bria closed her eyes a moment and lost herself in memories. When she opened her eyes, she let herself refocus on the room before her, and she felt the smile within her radiating up through her mouth and eyes.

"Please don't patronize me, Ma'am," Vandenbutcke said.

"I'm sorry if I made you feel patronized," Bria replied. She stood and thanked Vandenbutcke for letting her revisit a perspective that had almost become a distant memory over the past couple of months since they escaped Earth. "I guess I just needed to feel a bit of normalcy again."

After she apologized for bothering him, she beckoned that he follow her. After a brief stint of complaining that he didn't think Bria could hear, he joined her.

"You said you needed tools," Bria said. "What do you need?"

"Nothing that's here on the ship," Vandenbutcke said.

"So, tell me," Bria requested.

"The Onyx's pilot's controls," he explained. "They're touchier than any I've used. You need surgeon's hands to manage her precision. None of the simulator programs on file offer practice close enough."

"You need a new simulator," Bria asked.

"Yes, and a shuttle with the same sensitivity would be nice," he added. "But I can't duplicate it."

"Anything else," she asked.

"I'd like a third console on the bridge for a training pilot," he explained. "One that can let the trainee feel what the pilot is doing; can also help the trainee practice how they would fly the course as the chief pilot is flying; and evaluate how closely they performed."

"That's a really good idea," Bria said. "I wonder why no one's thought of that before."

"Probably because they've always had an academy to draw on for new pilots," Vandenbutcke said.

Somehow, Vandenbutcke found himself following Bria into the main engineering bay where Mirror and Dawn were now arguing about something with one of the staff that had done something wrong while they were off-duty. When Mirror saw Bria and Vandenbutcke, she immediately ended the conversation and approached.

Bria called for Dawn as well.

"I have nothing to say to him," Dawn snipped and went back to working at a console at a far end of the bay.

"Where's Mike," Bria asked.

"He's on a call," Mirror said. "We've had six today."

Bria relayed what Vandenbutcke had told her, and Vandenbutcke filled in any holes Bria left open.

"We could really use your help, Dawn," Bria called.

"I will kick his ass," Dawn retorted.

"This was a bad idea," Vandenbutcke said and began to leave.

"It's okay," Mirror said. "We know how it feels."

Vandenbutcke stopped and turned back a little stung.

"I'll leave you two to figure this out," Bria suggested, then left.

After, she paid a visit to Cindy Lou where the god questioned what was different about her day.

"I was a little angry at first when they requested I stop eavesdropping into your office while you were sleeping," Cindy said. "Of course, I didn't, but you were really out. I mean, you were snoring. That's a first. I couldn't take it anymore, so I decided I'd let you have your peace. Whatever Charity gave you, it sure seemed to work."

Soon, Bria was feeling rested and less anxious. Today's conversation with Cindy Lou wasn't too enthralling, just friends it seemed sitting around being quiet with each other except for when they felt like talking.

The captain was on her way back to her quarters to freshen up before she thought she'd attempt to get a bite to eat again, when a commanding voice called after her, "Captain."

She turned abruptly while stopping not too gracefully.

"Admiral Kellick," she greeted in the best way that might mask her awkward balance.

The admiral peered down upon her as he approached at a brisk walk. She imagined he was quite an attractive man in his younger years.

"Captain," he said finally catching up to her.

"How can I be of service, Sir," she asked, which seemed to catch him off guard.

"We haven't really had a chance to speak, and I saw you," Kellick said. "I wanted to apologize for the behavior of my former captain. It was inappropriate for me to put you in that position, and I wished to apologize. Nor is it the first thing I have to apologize for, is it?"

"Thank you, Sir," Bria replied.

"If I'd have thought he would try that, I'd have never asked for his help," Kellick continued.

"Admiral, if I may," Bria said. "I don't blame you."

"Well, good," Kellick said. "So long as it's cleared up."

"Of course, Sir." While she was wondering how he would take it if she just turned and began leaving, she realized he wasn't turning either.

"That was a really bad apology," Kellick said. "Seems I just keep racking up reasons to apo—something wrong, Captain?"

"I'm sorry," Bria said. "I'm just not good at taking apologies, I guess."

"Oh," Kellick said. "I don't blame you for being mad. I'd be mad at me too. I've insulted you plenty, and I typically don't make a habit of insulting others, but that's all you've seen me do, isn't it?"

"Oh. No, Sir. It's not that," Bria replied. "No one ever apologizes to me is all."

"Oh," Kellick said, and he seemed a little troubled himself just now.

"Was there something else, Sir," Bria asked.

"As a matter of fact," he said, his tone a little less authoritative than she had normally experienced. "I was wondering if you knew of anyone on board who knew how to play Zuggian Toka, or if could help me put the word out. I know it seems silly, but it helps me relax. I have a board, but no one to play with. Do you play?"

"I do not," Bria said. "But I'll be happy to help spread the word."

"I appreciate it," the admiral responded, and now he did begin turning and walking away. "It's my fault for learning a game no one plays."

"I feel the same way about cribbage, Sir," Bria replied.

Now it was the admiral who stopped, and he wasn't graceful in the maneuver either, Bria thought.

"Cribbage," he asked.

"It's an ancient game, Sir, with cards—

"I know what it is," Kellick snorted. "I'm wondering how you know what it is."

"My grandfather taught me. It was our game. He was an archaeologist of ancient entertainment. He used to regale me of how he played it in the military when he was younger. I was never as good as he was, but—wait! Do you play cribbage?"

"Learned it from a book," Kellick said, and a realization fell upon him. "Leonard. Calvin Leonard? Is he—

"My grandfather," Bria replied.

"Isn't that serendipitous? It's his book I read," Kellick boasted. "If you're up for it, I'll bring the cards, if you'll bring a board."

"I think I can manage getting one fabricated," Bria replied.

"I'll see you in the galley tomorrow after your shift," Kellick said all without smiling.

Bria acknowledged and they both started their separate ways until Kellick said, "Do you feel that?"

"Feel what," Bria asked.

"Your feet," he said. "We've stopped. That's usually a sign for an off-duty first officer to expect a call soon."

Kellick placed his hand on the wall. "Walls are like tuning forks. Learn to feel their vibrations, and you'll know when something's changed on the bridge."

Then came Nandy's voice, "Captain?"

Bria answered.

"Can you come to the bridge please?"

Bria and Kellick nodded their goodbyes. She had nearly made it all the way back to the bridge when she realized she wasn't in uniform. She quickly ducked into her quarters to change, then returned to the bridge trying her best to hide that she was out of breath.

Nandy was in the command chair, massaging her forehead in the palm of her hand.

The key was screaming, "I see it. I see it," and Escobedo was complaining, "I know you can see it. Now, shut up!"

"Why don't you place his face down," Bria asked.

"Because then he won't stop pestering you," Nandy replied. "He never shuts up!"

"Report," Bria requested, ignoring the key's constant chatter that he could see something.

Nandy pulled up their current map to show the Onyx was stopped in a nebula that encompassed three moons and their molten planet.

"See all this," Nandy asked as half the map ahead of the Onyx was turned red. She zoomed the map out, then out, and out some more. She kept scanning out until the holo had to tap into the alien sensor arrays that warned intruders not to enter. Nandy kept zooming out until the black of where their ship sat might have been one half of an atto pixel, and the red showed no end.

"That, as far as I can tell, represents about a trillionth of a percent of Maridamarak space," Nandy informed.

Every cadet had heard of the Maridamarak and Kag'tak. They were boogeymen the franchise had created to frighten the less serious cadets away. Of course, many thought the Kag'tak were just that, imaginary boogeymen.

Once, the Maridamarak were as fierce as the Kag'tak, but then the Kag'tak subjugated them in war. Now the Maridamarak were reserved to do only the Kag'tak's most lethal bidding, allowing the superior race to reserve their own resources from trivial tasks.

Encounters between Earth and the Maridamarak were classified among only the highest levels and those ships involved. Throughout other alien races that had encountered the Maridamarak, there was an increase in resignations of captains and their crews. For Earth, suicide rates were higher, especially with senior command staffs. Merrecci had seen its product.

The only other race that was unaffected by the horrors of the Maridamarak was the Kag'tak. The stories all said these were far more frightening. According to rumor, in all the history of the Earth Franchise, there were only two vessels that had ever encountered the Kag'tak.

Their very existence fueled the organization of the Franchise. For all the numbers of their allies though, the Kag'tak didn't find it important enough to confront. They rarely came out of their space. Truthfully, the Franchise was glad. The Franchise called it hibernation. As long as the Kag'tak stayed there, the universes had peace.

Although, rumors did exist that the Kag'tak sent out certain messages from time to time, including one that reportedly stated something along the lines of, "we do not judge your Franchise to be a threat or a worthy opponent," the whole of space knew that the resources of the Franchise were inferior. Rather than become a deterrent to the superior species, the Franchise became set on ensuring none of the other races could convince the Kag'tak they had a challenger for superiority. As long as the Kag'tak knew it was superior, it had no need to get involved with lesser quibbling.

All races had the unforeseen ability to serve Kag'tak in one way or another. No sense in destroying them before they could be used.

"Right," Bria finally said, taking in the holographic setting, and she was sure that she was hiding her own trembling no better than Nandy. "Hold here. I'll wake him."

"Thank you, Ma'am," Nandy said.

Bria returned to her office and showered quickly, then called Merrecci from his sleep even as she dressed.

"Captain," Merrecci said, and she could hear his groggy dissatisfaction before he suddenly snapped to, "Why are we stopped?"

"Sir, we've come upon Marida—"

"Don't move," Merrecci ordered, sharply. "I'm on my way."

Bria attempted to dry her hair quickly and slid on her shoes all before she believed Merrecci could appear himself.

"Nice of you to join us," Merrecci greeted, already on the bridge and fully dressed, as Bria finally returned only two minutes after speaking to the prime admiral. He turned back to Escobedo. "You're certain we have to go through?"

Pablo gestured to the key, which currently sat in a type of saddle that the Onyx had affixed to the navigation console.

"I see it," the key shrieked.

"Did none of you think to heed the redzone warnings," Merrecci asked. "The Franchise doesn't come this far for a reason!"

"We did, Sir," Nandy said. "We stopped as soon as we saw them, and we took shelter in this nebula. The boundaries were not what was on record."

"That means their space has grown again," Merrecci said. "We need to update our maps."

Merrecci pulled himself straight, Just as Almma marched into the room, every step with purpose.

"Thanks for coming, Lieutenant-commander," Merrecci greeted, giving away that he had called her.

"You interrupted the best screw dream I've had in about two months," Almma said.

"Was I in it," Pablo asked, then suddenly tucked himself into his console as he watched the other's faces turn on him.

"No," Almma replied tactfully. "It was my secret admirer."

"Oh," Pablo replied. "You must really like him."

Merrecci and Bria both shot Almma disapproving glances, and Almma brushed them aside. She gestured towards the cowering Pablo, and they could see him somewhat smiling.

"Did I tell you he left me a rose at my door," Almma said. "Thorny though. I don't think he realizes you can't just go giving a girl stabby things so early into a relationship. Oh well. Maybe he'll learn, huh." She finally stopped when Bria squared up unforgivingly into her face.

"Should I plot a course around it, Sir," Escobedo asked, softly.

Merrecci shook his head. "Not if we want to be back in time to save Earth. This isn't just their space, this is their entire history of conquest," he said. "Forty-two thousand planets among ten thousand solar systems and only one rule, and that was before it got to be all this."

"We should stay out of there," Nandy said.

Merrecci agreed.

"Only we can't," Bria stated.

"No," Merrecci answered grimly. "Our mission is through there."

"Unless the tomb's in it," Nandy said.

"No," Merrecci replied. "If it was, they would know it."

"Perhaps we just tear the bandage off, put this thing in stealth and streak right through it like a cheerleader trying to get her panties back from the quarterback," Almma said.

"Right," Merrecci replied. "They teach the 'go somewhere else' part, but not the actual Maridamarak part in the academy."

Realizing it fell to him, he continued, "The Maridamarak's crowning achievement is their technological advancements in energy. In fact, it's in their DNA. They emanate it, and they feel it. It has been gathering and growing long enough to become that red space on the map. Just entering it sends a shockwave from your presence, and they know every ripple that's supposed to be there and any that's not. Even with our stealth, there is no hiding in there. They'd feel us. When they venture out of that energy, their ships are equipped with technology that surrounds their vessels. They don't need short range sensors because they can actually extend that energy to feel where everything is."

"So just going into their space will lead them to us," Bria asked.

"Believe me, I'm surprised they haven't responded to us being this close already," Merrecci observed. "Might be because you parked us in this nebula."

"Seemed the only hiding place," Nandy said.

"I'll take it," Merrecci stated. Then he pointed a finger that seemed to twist towards the map on the holo. "We need to figure out how to get in there without being noticed."

"Sir," Bria said. "I don't think any one of us know enough about this race to play guessing games for what we should do next."

"Right," Merrecci replied.

Now he tapped his fingers against the controls on the arm of his chair and announced, "I should clear you to read these."

Nandy, Almma and Bria's holotabs all chimed to life announcing that seven hundred classified files had been released to them.

"Okay then," Merrecci said resigning himself once more to a more cunning obstacle. "Initiate silent-running protocol level one."

Bria immediately issued the order via her command console in the dugout. The lights dimmed to 30%. The entire skin of the Onyx darkened all of its windows to a black that the nebula could cast its camouflage over more easily.

"And can you gag that key," Merrecci burst.

"I see it," the key cried.

Pablo returned the wax wadding to the skull's auditory holes and strapped the elastic over its eyes once more. He set it face down on his console and the Key stopped making any sound.

"We stay here until we figure out how to get across," Merrecci instructed.

"Sir," Bria inquired. "For how long?"

"At this point, stopping to figure it out will take less time than trying to go around it all." He stood, almost clapped his hands in exclamation to get to work and didn't follow through. "I'll be in my quarters. If I dream of a solution, I'll let you know. Wake me if you come up with something. Until then, I trust you to keep us in this cloud, Captain."

Then Merrecci was back off to sleep and to trust in his crew.

At once, Bria queried Drinker's location, he was asleep. Dawn was on shift. The others were on break. She requested they report to the bridge to help assess a solution.

They all appeared together, apparently Mirror had to ensure that Drinker wasn't going to sleep through the request. Bria had felt a little bad for waking Drinker, but he explained that he was waking up in less than an hour anyway. After they had all been apprised of their situation and asked to help think of any solutions, they all went straight to work, and, except for sleep, they pretty much stayed that way for several days. Even during their shifts, all four seemed to be scavenging each others' brains for any morsel of idea, but they kept hitting roadblocks.

Although there were some good suggestions, they all ended with Merrecci explaining how one Maridamarak blast was capable of destroying entire warships with no resistance from shields at all. He constantly reminded his staff of the two dozen Earth vessels that had met this fate each time they failed to evaluate if the space they were entering was Maridamarak. The only reason Earth became aware of these attacks on their ships was because the Maridamarak informed Earth to mourn their dead. They even relayed all black box data back to them to help humans learn.

Frustrated, Bria found herself walking the halls quite a bit more to clear her head for new ideas that she guessed wouldn't work.

When Bria stopped in to see Cindy, the god simply asked why they didn't just race in and out of their space. Bria tried to explain it. Cindy didn't let up.

"Our ships could have done it," Cindy informed.

Eventually, Bria resumed her walk, which was strangely interrupted when the halls filled with an unfamiliar rumbling, loud, and a horrible smell as if something was burning.

After evaluating where the noise was most likely coming from, she decided it was in the direction of a male voice swearing.

She ran into an adjoining corridor and stopped, then leapt to the side as a small aquamarine vehicle sped straight for her.

"Are you stupid," Dawn yelled out as she sped past. Then the car began stopping abruptly. It swerved to turn into the hallway that Bria had just come from, but instead of turning, it collided with the perpendicular wall at the hallway junction.

Here, an exit portal on the device rotated up, allowing Dawn to jump out of the vehicle and run off.

"Lieutenant-commander Almma," Bria called as she approached the greenish device. "Are you teaching Dawn to operate some sort of stinky machine in the halls?"

"Is she driving that Lotus," Almma cried. "That little shit was supposed to wait for—I mean no, Ma'am. I don't know what you mean."

"Almma," Bria said.

"Yes, Ma'am?"

"Get this car out of this hall before Merrecci sees it. I'm pretty sure it's louder than our level one silent running.

"Yes, Ma'am," Almma replied.

Then, from behind Bria.

"What is that," Merrecci's voice shrilled.

Bria turned and found the prime admiral dragging Dawn by her ear to the vehicle.

"Is that what I think it is," Merrecci asked. "Is that a gas-powered machine?"

"It's a Lotus," Dawn corrected.

"Take it back to the library," Merrecci yelled. "Stop stinking up my halls!"

Dawn crawled into the machine and yelled, "You're just jealous that I have one, and you don't."

"Get it out of here," Merrecci yelled and slammed the portal to the vehicle shut, closing Dawn inside.

After bashing against the wall again, and Merrecci yelling after her, Dawn finally caused the vehicle to slowly drive away towards the nearest library. Then, after about five seconds of driving slowly, it suddenly began spinning its tires, kicking up a cloud of white and burning shag carpet, before speeding off.

Merrecci turned to Bria.

"Next time stop her!" Merrecci then resumed his jog without further words. He circled four more laps of the deck before finding Prilla set in his path.

"Find something," He asked through thick breaths.

"When are you going to learn that you can't talk to your engineers like that," Prilla complained. She wasn't yelling, but she might as well have been.

"She was driving a car in my halls," Merrecci retorted. "Did you see the hole she burned in the carpet."

"You can't talk to her like that. She shuts down," Prilla fired back. "They don't take to angry captains like the crew members you're used to lording it over do. You'll be lucky if she shows up for her shift tonight."

"If she doesn't, she'll be in the brig," Merrecci responded.

"And what good will that do you," Prilla asked.

"What would you have me do, let her choke my crew out and clog up the air purifiers with her fossil fuel exhaust," Merrecci moaned.

"I don't care what you do," Prilla retaliated. "But you better find a way to bond with these people before they decide they're bored and don't want to help anymore. It's your job, get to it!"

Prilla began walking. "Don't be late again for dinner tonight."

With this, Merrecci decided his run was ruined and returned to his quarters to shower. Here, he found Mike curled up on his bed and snoring. Beside him was a pile of something that should not be.

"That's it," Merrecci shouted, and he charged towards Mike.

Mike's eyes opened, and he started yipping and jumping for Merrecci, licking his face.

The prime admiral started yelling when he suddenly envisioned his sister's psychic ability to know when he was being a jerk.

"Come with me," Merrecci ordered instead.

Mike cocked his head at the prime admiral.

"I said come!"

Mike jumped off the bed, trotted ecstatically to Merrecci, then stretched up and began licking the prime admiral's face.

"No," Merrecci ordered and pushed Mike off. "Down!"

Merrecci was suddenly out of his room and ordering Mike to come once again.

Together they marched through the halls, Mike heeled the entire way.

"Just to make my sister happy, I know what you need," Merrecci said and led him to Library Five. He approached the digital card catalog and began scrolling through titles in its index until he finally stopped.

"This was one of my favorites growing up," Merrecci explained.

When the library door opened, Merrecci led Mike inside to a large grassy arena surrounded in a chain link fence.

Throughout it, dogs chased and sniffed each other. There were so many, and Mike barked, stood straight up then dropped back to his hands. He looked to Merrecci and whined.

Three creatures, all mutts, came running up to check Mike out.

Merrecci found a green ball and hurled it as hard as he could.

"Go play," he encouraged.

Mike barked and took off running.

"Stay as long as you want," Merrecci called after him, then returned to his quarters, showered, and took command of his ship five minutes past his start time. He might have cared more about it, but most of his staff was discovering that he and no one else had come up with any ideas to get them across Maridamarak space.

He gladly finished his shift then made his way to Prilla's quarters for dinner, where she promptly met him with, "You left him in a dog park?"

"He got into my ball collection," Merrecci said giving himself permission to enter Prilla's abode. "So, I took him to the dog park."

Prilla's chest cursed, she let loose a ferocious "he's not a dog!"

"I know he's not a dog," Merrecci quipped. "But you said I had to be nice."

"There's nice, and there's enabling," Prilla said.

"I was only doing what you told me to," Merrecci complained, and he dropped into one of two chairs at a small round table with white plates, tall glasses, gold silverware and fabricated pots covered with steamy clear lids.

"You're so frustrating," Prilla groaned, dropping into her own chair, and snapping a blue cloth napkin out in front of her.

"How am I the bad guy here?"

"I'm trying to get him to stop acting like a dog, and you're reinforcing it," Prilla scolded. "That makes more work for me."

"I'm sorry," Merrecci admitted. "I was trying to be supportive."

"Oh, just shut up and eat," Prilla said snatching a lid off a skillet to reveal a medley of sauteed peppers and onions. She pointed to a pot in front of Merrecci. "That one's yours."

Merrecci opened it and immediately recoiled slamming the lid back down.

"Oh my god," Merrecci shrieked. "That smells like crap."

"It is," Prilla said. "Mike left it in the library."

"That's gross, what do you expect me to do with this?"

"Eat it!"

*　　*　　*

After four more days of boredom for everyone, Captain Leonard was starting to feel she might take Cindy up on an idea of just racing through Maridamarak space with Onyx's guns a blazing. At one point, she almost found herself marching in to suggest it to Merrecci, but she knew that he hadn't turned that stupid yet.

Presently, Bria sat in the galley. She looked at the four replicas of ancient playing cards in her hand, and the one sitting face up on top of a turned-down deck. Two points, that's all she had here. She was forty points behind.

"In my opinion," Admiral Kellick said from across the table. "Waiting for the right idea to appear was the worst part."

"I find that hard to believe with you," Bria replied. "But out of curiosity, how many times did you have to execute plans you knew were bad?"

"Too much," he said. He threw down his hand, announced its points and shifted a peg on the board eighteen spaces ahead of another that had previously been in the lead.

"With respect, Admiral," Bria said. "But that's some bullshit right there."

"That's administration for you," Kellick said, and he began gathering all the cards to shuffle.

"I mean your luck today," Bria said.

"You're just occupied," Kellick returned kindly. "Besides, I've earned it after the last two days."

"Fair enough," Bria conceded.

She leaned forward and scratched her head with both hands. "If we were on Earth, I'd be in Old Chisel right now figuring this out better."

"What's Old Chisel," Kellick asked, halting his shuffle with a look of genuine inquiry.

"It was an old steam-powered locomotive from an amusement park that my father was given for his work with the Ariata Museo of Science and History. He got it working and built about a mile of rail for it. I like to just sit in it and warm it up. It takes hours to get ready before I can drive it, but I can think.

"You mean like one of those old cargo wagons that ran on tracks," Kellick asked and thought too long of what he remembered hearing it called from his Earth history class days.

"A train," Bria replied.

"I'm sure there's a book on trains in the library," Kellick suggested.

"Wouldn't be the same," Bria said. "Old Chisel had temperaments the library wouldn't know."

Kellick dealt the cards.

Bria looked at the potential points that could occur and decided on keeping the unforgiving four and six of hearts, the eight of diamonds and the king of clubs. She still didn't have the heart to bring herself to tell Kellick that clubs on the cards he had fabricated were not supposed to be in the shape of a bludgeoning weapon. As she looked at her hand, she suddenly wondered if she had thrown away what she intended to. She couldn't remember. She cut the remaining deck and Kellick flipped over a two.

Nineteen! Damn it!

"Aren't you supposed to move back nineteen points for that," Kellick asked at the end of the hand.

"Only if you're an idiot and don't know the game," Bria snipped and suddenly realized what she'd said and to whom. "Try that tactic with real players, and they will use a real rule to rape you of all your points before you can say fifteen-two." She hastily added on a "forgive me, Sir."

"It's okay," Kellick replied. "I'm winning."

"I've noticed."

"You really do need that train of yours, don't you," he asked.

"Sounds silly, doesn't it," Bria asked as she played another pointless hand. She was about to be double-skunked.

"Not at all," Kellick replied. "For me it was water skiing."

"Now when you say water skiing, do you mean just hydroplaning," Bria asked, now shuffling. "Or do you mean—

"I mean old school, pulled by a skimming bot," Kellick said and gathered his new cards. "Of course, it's a bit lower energy on me now, but I was a demon on the water. One day, your body says, 'let's go,' and your knees and shoulders say, 'let's go home.'"

"Wow, so you used to be—

"A demon on the water," Kellick interrupted again and threw away two cards. "Barefoot even. You'd be surprised how much water can hold you up. It's how I met my ex-wife."

"Skied together?"

"No," Kellick said. "Splashed her. You know, if you get the right model bot and the right day, you can throw water in ways that buries your wake. There's nothing like spraying a wall so high no one can even see who did it, and that's what I di—

"That's it!" Bria leapt out of her chair and dropped her cards. "Admiral, my apologies, could I impose upon you to—

"But I'm winning."

Bria sat to finish the hand. On Kellick's second move, he crossed the finish line.

Kellick was now brimming in victory.

"Go," he ordered cordially. "I'll clean this up."

Bria thanked him and turned to run.

"Captain," Kellick called after her.

She turned, and he crossed the room casually to her with a confidence that made him seem like he simply had a large stride.

"We never run," he said softly, then returned to clean up the game.

Bria walked, and when she was done walking, she was standing on the bridge—all without running.

Merrecci was in discussion with one of the astrometric stations helping to correct some math. Almma was currently in the dugout. She had previously suggested to ask if the Rhaxians would simply shrink the Onyx to a size that the Maridamarak might not give serious consideration to.

Merrecci responded with a suggestion that the Rhaxians just shrink down any Maridamarak ships that tried to attack the Onyx.

The Rhaxians simply stated those were stupid ideas because they would use too much valuable energy, which they might need to hide again in case the Onyx got itself killed.

Bria also noticed a change to the bridge, which she instantly thought stuck out and was bothersome. It was an additional console off the end of the pilot's area. Mirror was currently laying on her back beneath it while Vandenbutcke was following her orders to turn the controls the way she asked.

Merrecci had seen Bria, but continued with his discussion as though she hadn't been there.

"You ever been water skiing," she asked when Merrecci was finally done.

He immediately ordered Bria and Almma to his ready room, then turned command over to a lieutenant Bruhill, a man in his 50s who worked hard, but would never be more than a lieutenant.

Bruhill was immediately uneasy, and Merrecci reminded him that he just had to keep the Onyx in the nebula and to call if the Maridamarak should appear, not that he'd get to the bridge in time to issue commands to survive the first enemy blast.

Once inside Merrecci's office, he nodded for Bria to speak.

"Maridamarak feel ripples in their space energy," Bria asked.

"Yeah," Merrecci answered, but sounded like he was asking.

"Like water," Bria asked.

Again, "Yeah?"

"What if we hitch a ride? The Maridamarak pull us while we're stealthed, and we hide in the wake," Bria explained.

"A few things," Merrecci said. "One, how would we keep them from noticing our mass adding to theirs?"

"We don't let them do all the work," Bria asked, not sure. She hadn't thought that far.

"Precision flying," Merrecci asked.

"Just enough to not make them question why their engines are less efficient," Bria said.

"Predictive flying in Maridamarak space," Merrecci erupted.

"I know," Bria replied. "It's never been done. Stupid idea."

"Okay," Merrecci replied though. "So that's one thing. Now two, we're a big ship. A wake can only hide so much."

"We'd need to be pulled by a much larger ship. The larger we go, the bigger the wake to hide in," Bria explained.

Here, Merrecci called his engineer command trio and Drinker to report to the discussion.

Bria called for Nandy.

"Okay," Merrecci continued. "How do we attach ourselves?"

"Don't know," Bria replied.

"Our three musketeers will," Merrecci added. "Or Drinker,"

"Is it just me, or does anyone else think that boy needs an exorcism," Almma asked. "I keep expecting him to pee green soup."

"We'll put a pin in that one for now," Merrecci said. When no one understood what that even meant, he explained it. Then stated, "So we need a big ship to pull us, and a way to be pulled."

"Do they have something that large," Nandy asked.

"Yes," Almma said. "It was in those snooze-intelligence files."

"Their fleet carriers," Merrecci answered. "They hold seven battle cruisers. Any of which would destroy us in one shot. I've seen it."

"Those battle cruisers are twice our size," Almma said.

"At least," Merrecci agreed. "Carriers more like fifty."

"Why carry so many ships in one basket," Nandy asked.

"So that there's only one ship signature when they invade or attack," Merrecci explained.

"They jump in, enemy sensors read one ship. Upon their arrival the Maridamarak launch an instant fleet. Send in a dozen of those carriers, and you could find yourself in hell."

"Even if you see it coming, it's a surprise attack," Nandy added.

"So like cramps," Almma replied.

"And that's what we need," Bria said, and she couldn't avoid the sullen chill that swept the room.

"So how do we find one without giving ourselves up," Nandy asked. "If we can't go into their space."

"We need them to come out," Bria said. "Admiral, if I understood the intelligence correctly, the Maridamarak pride themselves on early intimidation to win a battle before it starts."

"That's right," Merrecci said. "They respond to what might be considered an attack on them by dispatching a fleet carrier. First, to intimidate, and then to bring friends."

"So, yeah," Almma interrupted. "Just like cramps."

Merrecci opened his mouth to wave Almma down.

"And they lost the war to the Kag'tak," Nandy asked. "How?"

"Because the Kag'tak are stronger," Merrecci said.

"Says rumor," Almma said. "Doesn't it?"

"Says me," Merrecci replied and didn't realize how quietly he had said it nor how pale his skin had just turned from memories.

The door chimed, and Drinker followed.

He held a dark blue globe in his hand and slightly curled a finger over the top and traced down its right side without touching the surface. The globe came to life with images of electrical discharge. He carefully raised his hand and scrutinized the globe.

"What is that," Merrecci asked pointedly.

"It's a puzzle," Drinker replied.

Merrecci just had to know. "What are you supposed to do?"

"Make material out of chaos," Drinker said.

"Say that again."

"Make order out of material," Drinker repeated.

Merrecci winced, stared at the globe. He wasn't the only one.

"How do you know when you've done it," Merrecci asked.

"It hatches," Drinker said.

"Into what?"

"Material," Drinker said.

"I see," Merrecci lied.

"Ever have one hatch before?"

"No," Drinker answered. "Willis keeps Materialing it." Then, without looking up, asked, "What did I miss?"

"I believe the material was just letting us know that he's seen the Kag'tak," Almma surmised.

"What," Drinker asked.

"Ha," Almma cried. "Now you know how it feels!"

"Oh," Drinker said. "Good one. So, what were you talking about?"

"The admiral was letting us know that he's seen the Kag'tak," Almma said.

"Is that really so," Drinker asked.

"I was first officer on the Randy Quinn when we were spared to return to Earth and deliver a message," Merrecci answered.

"It was your ship that survived the attack," Bria realized.

"There was no attack," Merrecci corrected. "They just took us. We surveyed into their space. Ours was a small and inadequately armed data-courier ship. The Battleship Chugoku had been assigned to accompany us on what was supposed to be a routine surveying mission. No one even bothered warning us."

"But it wasn't unoccupied, was it," Nandy surmised. "And they caught you, didn't they?"

"It was a Kag'tak pip, something similar to our own starships, but not nearly as fragile, weak for them. Just flew in and, before we knew it, the Chugoku was broken. They boarded us, took the captain and first officer into our own shuttle bay, where they gathered our crew to watch us tortured."

"Us," Bria asked. "You? The files redacted that, didn't they?"

"They stripped me and the captain of everything that made us who we were and made our shipmates watch," Merrecci explained. "Two days, then they put a rifle to my head to ensure my Captain would have sufficient memory and motivation to deliver a message to Earth to stay out of Kag'tak space. The captain attacked the officer assigned to execute me and got himself eviscerated instead.

"I was sent home to inform Earth. It was my first command. We never had a chance to fire off even a shot," Merrecci continued. "And Earth didn't learn from it. They sent a secret attack force to retaliate against the Kag'tak. That's when I got the Viridian. Fifty stealthed ships took a route that Earth thought would catch the Kag'tak by surprise. It took us through Maridamarak space though, and the Maridamarak weren't having it. Within two minutes of entering, ten of our ships were all that were left, and we were running hard for home. One made it back. So, when I say, I would rather be almost anywhere else than in Maridamarak space, I hope you take that to mean that this plan has to be perfect."

Merrecci now leaned forward and onto his elbows as he took on a demeanor that caused Bria to flinch and hope no one saw it.

"Which brings me to my next question," Merrecci said. "How are you going to bait a fleet carrier here, attach ourselves to it and convince them to take us across their space to where we want to go, all without knowing we exist? What if they detour or even stop."

"We'll give them a really good reason," Bria replied.

"Okay, they tow us. Can they tow us," Drinker asked, lost himself in thought a split moment and then came back with, "That's a good material."

The engineering trio appeared at the captain's door and were brought up to speed.

"A hairline tractor material could do it," Drinker finally said. "It would be so small, it shouldn't register any material waves."

"A hairline tractor beam," Merrecci asked.

Drinker nodded.

"We don't have that technology," Merrecci said.

"I guess we'll have to invent it then," Drinker replied.

"Mike and I could probably figure it out," Dawn said.

"You know," Mirror complained. "You're not the only one who has a brain!"

Mike growled.

"Okay," Merrecci said. "Assuming you can make a hairline tractor beam work—which, let's keep thinking on this and see if we can't do better—how do we get a fleet carrier to appear?"

"Well, uh," Bria replied. "I'm not sure, but we at least set some pieces on the board for now. It would help if we had something big to blow up, and—" Suddenly, she was the one in thought before finally coming back with, "Actually, that's not a bad idea."

12

▲

Ow!

The plan was a monstrosity. His first officer had stitched all but two of their shuttles together to create something large enough to attract Maridamarak attention when they blew it up.

"What a waste," Merrecci said.

"We can fabricate more," Bria reminded.

"Well, you've already put the monster together anyway," Merrecci retorted. "It's too late to turn back now."

Bria ran another scan. It wasn't pretty: sixteen shuttles melded together, and each was filled with the strongest torpedo the Onyx carried. It should make an explosion large enough to flood Maridamarak space with unwanted energy ripples.

"Of course," Merrecci added. "If it doesn't work, you've just added years to our mission and killed Earth, haven't you."

On that, Bria ran the scan and numbers again. Then she requested that Drinker and the three musketeer engineers verify the data once more. Merrecci then sat in his ready room for nearly another three hours, checking all that same data himself, which he really only did to pretend he understood it. When he finally reappeared on the bridge, He gave the order to send Bria's conglomeration of torpedoes and shuttles right to the edge of Maridamarak space so it could do its job.

"The monster is in place, Sir," Nandy announced from her post at the battlecron.

"Are we really calling it the monster," Bria asked.

"I like it," Almma said. "No matter how badly we screw up in the future we'll always know it can never look as bad as your pile of crap right there."

Bria straightened up. "Really?"

"No, no. Don't get upset," Almma said. "It's a huge morality boost in times of one-night-ugly-stand to remember you survived the desperation of an even uglier man who wouldn't stop squashing you."

"What is wrong with you," Nandy asked.

"Oh please, like you've never been desper—

"How inconsiderate," Pablo burst. "I'd have rolled off if you asked me to."

Pablo instantly slapped his hands over his mouth and buried his face in the images on his console.

"I'll keep that in mind if you ever fall on me," Almma said. "Although, my secret admirer might have something to say abou—

"Enough of that," Merrecci interrupted. He would have done so earlier, but his mind was running with his own reservations about the consequences of this idea.

"I do not like this plan," Merrecci whispered, leaning in closely to Bria. He abruptly pulled back and spoke to Almma. "On my mark, Lieutenant-commander, prepare to blow it u—

The battlecron suddenly filled with a familiar Jimmoshean fleet of eighteen ships.

"Sir," Almma reported. "Cha and his chubby are back again."

Merrecci went into a rampage of demanding to know how Cha was tracking them.

"Perhaps we should get out of here before he—," Bria started to suggest.

Merrecci waved off the recommendation with a "We're safer in the nebula for now. Prepare to take us to stealth-level-four."

Suddenly a heavy torpedo leapt from one of the warships under Master Cha's command. It struck the conglomeration of shuttles, causing Merrecci's arms to fly into the air in disbelief.

"You know, I've never had a sixty-some before," Almma said. "But I'm pretty sure it feels better than—

"Decorum! Learn it," Merrecci yelled.

Then Merrecci snapped his fingers at the battlecron holo, and the image on it switched from a map of the Onyx's exterior vicinity and into one of his engineering bay where his three savants were playing some sort of hand slapping game.

"You're on," he said.

"No," Mirror denied.

"Your tractor beam crew is on," Dawn added.

"Hope they can aim," Mirror mumbled, and Merrecci pretended not to hear that too.

Now was not the time for that.

"Level four now," he ordered.

The bridge strobed with less and less illumination until it fell into a nearly dark room, filled only enough to prevent people from tripping. It's not that they needed to be in the dark, because the Onyx's hull could block out interior light, but it put less demand on generators so they could run quieter.

The only items that really needed power now were life support, the bridge, and engines, all of which the Nessla circulature could silence entirely.

The map reappeared in the holo.

Merrecci silenced abrupt gasps all with a raise of his hand.

A Maridamarak fleet carrier had already jumped in, hulking over Cha's fleet. Nine battle ships emerged, each the size of one of Earth's own. The fleet carrier focused a blue beam on the closest of Cha's battleships, which happened to be the same that had fired upon Bria's monstrosity of shuttles. A red burst of light fired from the fleet carrier and sped down the blue conduit. The Jimmoshean battleship simply erupted into a storm of debris and bodies.

After that, the entire field became an orchestra of lasers. One by one, the Maridamarak broke the chub's comrades open. Merrecci watched and willed the majority of Cha's fleet to escape, but also cursed him. Idiot!

Screw it, Merrecci thought and turned to order the Onyx's retreat. What was he thinking? Cha probably just saved his crew.

At this, another fleet carrier appeared, its ships departed and set to the same practice of attacking Cha's fleet. Merrecci zoomed the map in until both fleet carriers, and the chub filled the hologram. Then, a third carrier appeared. It reached out to the chub with another blue beam. A red flash appeared within it and sailed down towards Master Cha.

The chub suddenly jumped away and disappeared with only four of its ships. At the same time, a fourth Maridamarak vessel jumped in and ejected all the vessels it carried.

"What the hell is that," one of the crew blurted at the vessel three times the size of the other carriers. Merrecci counted that it had dropped off fifteen ships.

"Get off my bridge," Merrecci ordered by stealthfully snapping a finger at the young man who had broken the silence and then directing that finger towards the bridge doors. The man exited.

Merrecci turned to a section of three consoles in the operations side of the bridge, right behind the piloting and navigation zone. The operators looked to him with urgency, and he knew what they were asking.

He quickly typed into the railing of the battlecron where he currently stood. The words, "The big one," suddenly appeared in the scoreboard upon the wall that was currently showing the outfield of the Tokyo Dome. He looked to Nandy, and she nodded that she had already sent her message.

The battle was over. Cha's entire fleet had retreated, including the chub, or disintegrating in space. The Maridamarak carriers began to gather their battleships.

One had finished loading and began to turn back towards Maridamarak space. Merrecci watched his own crew become deathly still. He too hoped they would sense nothing hiding in the cloud to make them turn back and pay special interest to the Onyx.

"Tractor beam engaged," appeared on the wall.

The first fleet carrier was instantly gone, then a second disappeared, followed by the third, which had still not unloaded its fleet. Finally, the last and largest carrier turned back towards its own territory.

Suddenly, the Onyx was speeding into Maridamarak space. The tractor beam the size of a heavy fishing cable pulled the Onyx closer towards the largest of the fleet carriers in an attempt to create a more natural appearance in the energy wake that spewed from behind it, or so was the theory. Merrecci didn't mind if crew members prayed. He might just do it himself if he figured out how.

Ensign being's brow was sober, and he leaned forward in his seat, which Merrecci wasn't sure if he'd noticed him ever doing before. The prime admiral took this as a clue to ensure nothing distracted his chief pilot. He directed Drinker to the back of Ensign Being's chair should the need arise.

Oh, sure, Merrecci complained to himself, but almost did so out loud. *Just like water skiing, she said.*

*   *   *

The Earthers had come to them with many stupid plans, but then that strange little faceless girl who started visiting to change out their floral arrangements in their quarters asked if, in their small size, they could cross Maridamarak space as quickly as if they were in their unfolded form and remain undetected.

Well, of course they could, they weren't primitive and had managed to hide from the Maridamarak long before Earth was even born. It would be like the times of generations past when they had to smuggle entire planets in their cargo holds across galaxies. Plus, they were pretty fast.

So long as a Paichu scanner, which could specifically search for the minutest of Rhaxian DNA, didn't cross their path, they should be okay, perhaps. Considering the Paichu entered every DNA that was wanted by the Kag'tak, it was certain the Rhaxian would be in their scanner settings. Worse was that any ally or bounty hunter could purchase the scanning technology. The Paichu were always happy to provide it in exchange for their cut of any hefty reward.

Normally, the Rhaxians would not have entertained an alliance to the weaker Earthers. They would have run. They considered leaving now. Afterall, if Paichu technology combined with the Maridamarak's malevolent nature, the Rhaxians could actually be caught. Now, why didn't the Maridamarak have this technology in their own ships? Because the Maridamarak were an energy race. They farmed it or converted whatever they could from throughout space, and they brought it to amplify their homestead.

All energy around them, within their space became natural resource to become focused, woven and tempered into the very material that built their planets and their ships. They could make tangible objects from intangible power. They were, in essence, a race that had mastered battery storage, and their realm in space kept growing every day because of it.

In other words, Paichu technology—any outside technology—was not compatible with the Maridamarak. They shared nothing, and no one else was biologically adapted to manipulate and feel energies as the Maridamarak.

After they had received the plan from the strangely-faced girl who brought them flowers, the Rhaxian leaders held a discussion about lying to the humans and saying they would help them, but then running back to the Sentrale system. However, they ultimately liked the flower girl, Bria Leonard, and had a soft spot for the kindness of that first officer. When they heard her plan, they concluded they would, this one time, allow their involvement.

Seventeen days after entering Maridamarak space, they continued to wait on the opposite side for a small signal from the Onyx. The message would have to jump through a chain of folded communication relays that the Rhaxians had dropped behind them. However, the faceless girl and her admiral knew that at the first hint of a vessel with Paichu scanning, the Rhaxians would flee. It was abundantly clear that maybe the Rhaxians would be on the other side of space to respond, and maybe they wouldn't. If they were, the Onyx should join them shortly. If they weren't, the Onyx would be discovered. The Earth crew wouldn't know until they never reached the other side of space. It all depended on the Paichu's intrusive technology.

When Nandy sent her message, at Merrecci's command, the very moment they were dragged into Maridamarak space, it bounced from one microscopic communication relay to the next with enough power to speed up the travel of the message towards their stone allies. It took only seconds for the relays to do their jobs.

As soon as the Rhaxians received it, their captain, an elderly vein of Jade gave the order to unfold the ship just outside Maridamarak space.

Then he sent a simple message, "We heard you were looking for us," advertising their immeasurable bounty and all its interest for each individual member on its ship.

Then it shrank again and waited for the Onyx to come pick it up, hopefully in tow of a Maridamarak fleet carrier that would not know it was there waiting for the little flower girl.

Whether the enemy knew it or not, the appearance of a Rhaxian vessel would warrant the presence of as many fleet carriers as possible to respond to capturing the huge bounty.

*   *   *

None of Earth's ship engines were ever designed to travel at the speed of which the Maridamarak fleet carrier now propelled itself through a system, alive with strange energy that the very souls of the Onyx's crew members could feel. Only the Kag'tak had mastered faster speed, as far as Earth knew. Perhaps Earth would never reach such technological advancement. However, Merrecci couldn't even trust asking some very smart crew members who knew how to use advance scanning equipment to attempt discovering how their space worked. He worried any outgoing scan might give away the Onyx's parasitic position. Other than simple life support and basic survival needs, the only place energy was authorized to be spent in the Onyx was through Chief Being's piloting controls, which he used sparingly. Otherwise, the Onyx was at the mercy of the Maridamarak fleet carrier that was towing it.

All of the Onyx was running in the dark and depending on slow Earth engines only to keep it hidden in the wake. Merrecci imagined it must have been like an ocean kayak tying itself to a three-million capacity Bantar cruise ship and hoping an oar could keep the kayak on course. The Onyx crew had been posted in battle positions and expected to react the moment they should be discovered. The prime admiral knew it would do little good though.

Merrecci now had Nandy and Drinker permanently assigned to take shifts kicking the chief pilot's chair with the appropriate number whenever the Onyx trembled from whatever energy the wake threw at them. Merrecci made a note to have Onyx create a chair for Being that would shake out the number of times Being needed to count to seven whenever his chair involuntarily rattled.

Charity visited the bridge three times to inject Being with something to help him stay alert and awake. It could only go so far though.

No one slept for the first thirty-six hours.

Against their own taste, the senior command decided it prudent to have Vandenbutcke shadow Being. Through the assistant pilot seat, he ran simulation after simulation to see if he could perform the same task of hiding in the Maridamarak fleet Carrier's wake. His performance was sixty-nine percent efficient as Being. It might have been higher, but the current silent running didn't allow him to swear or complain any time he made an error.

He took a break only once when a message flashed across his panel.

"Let us know if you need us to fix the controls," the message read.

"Who," he typed back.

"The real engineers."

"Why," he then asked.

"We don't want to die."

He was about to respond with "it's fine" when he realized Bria was reading the message over his shoulder. She didn't say anything, but it might have been better if she had, he thought.

Eventually, there was no other choice. Being needed to rest. Vandenbutcke had to take the helm, and he barely managed to keep himself in his seat at all. Charity entered the bridge to inject him with something to prevent heart attack. Vandenbutcke's current assistant pilot and top student, Samantah Nerris, was doing her best to pass the simulation with as high of a rating as Vandenbutcke, but she couldn't clear fifty percent as efficient as even Vandenbutcke. Vandenbutcke thought he had had heard her chuckle through her nose and then watched her type into her console.

"How do they expect anyone to be able to do this," she asked across the pilot's console.

He was too invested to even type back, "You do it."

For four hours Vandenbutcke steered the Onyx in a manner that should kept hidden. After the four hours, Merrecci decided it was time for Being to return to the helm because he believed Vandenbutcke's heart was, indeed, going to explode—either that, or his life support monitoring was. If his pilot dropped dead right now, the whole of Maridamarak space would know.

When Being retook his seat, Vandenbutcke was pale, shook and immediately made his way to the hospital for his nerves. He returned four hours later to start simulation and shadowing again.

Then suddenly, the fleet carrier began to lose momentum. Almma ran to Bria's office to wake her from her own sleep, then to Merrecci's to do the same.

The map of Maridamarak space appeared on the holo. They approached just inside the boundary and only fifty kilometers from where the Rhaxian ship waited. Then they stopped entirely but didn't cross out of Maridamarak space. On the other side of their border, too many Maridamarak ships to count were searching for evidence of the Rhaxian vessel.

Almma's face turned to Bria's. She hid her fear, but only because Bria hid her own as well, hoping that Being was able to slow the Onyx to stay hidden still.

Merrecci appeared just as the hail came through.

"We see you Earth vessel," a harmonic and echoey voice announced. Each syllable was as though whoever said it had to inhale and warm up their resonance before making any sound. "We know your plan to cross our space."

"Forgive us," Merrecci replied.

"Primordial virus! You do not speak," the hyperventilating voice continued. "Our scanners cannot find the Rhaxians. We know you can. We want the bounty. Help us, and we will let you go, minus a fee for toll. Do you agree?"

Merrecci was silent. Maridamarak were unforgiving.

"You may speak," the voice continued.

"How do we know we can trust you won't kill us," Merrecci asked.

"You insult us," the voice replied harshly, a face continued not to appear on the holo. "We do not lie."

"I apologize," Merrecci said. "We are afraid of you."

"Agree to give us Rhaxians, and we have taken you safely across minus a fee for safe passage," the Maridamarak fleet carrier commander said. "We know you are working together, Vincenti Merrecci."

Merrecci slouched into his chair, beaten. He tried not to look at his bridge crew, but he saw their faces in his mind all the same, except for one, his captain. Right now, he had far too many things he wanted to yell at her for her stupid plan, which he never should have approved. Still, the Maridamarak had offered them an out for safe passage. Though he didn't know what that meant exactly.

"I agree," Merrecci said, and he ignored the sting of betrayal that his first officer threw at him. He realized that she probably had many things she wanted to yell at him as well.

"Good, Earth vessel," the Maridamarak commander replied. "We will inform the others so they will not attack you."

"You are merciful," Merrecci said.

"Yes, we are," the Maridamarak replied. "We will take our fee, then take you safely across our border. We are done talking now."

"What fee," Being asked as soon as the transmission ended. He figured they weren't running silent anymore.

Merrecci shook his head. "Don't know. I'm sure they'll want intelligence, someone with clearance to it, that is. Probably me."

"No," Bria said. "It was my plan. I'll take responsibility."

"Like hell," Nandy's voice rejected. They were so caught up in their conversation that they hadn't even noticed her enter the bridge after awaking suddenly from her nap when she realized they weren't moving anymore.

Merrecci raised a silencing finger. "It's my ship. It will be me."

"Sir," Crewman Mailer announced. "I'm getting several reports of—

Suddenly her head spit blood from just above her temple. She dropped to the floor where she bled from holes at either side of her forehead.

Merrecci arrived to her first. She was dead. Even he could tell that.

Her console alarm beeped, and he found himself suddenly sliding into her seat. One after another, reports began to come in—reports of sudden deaths, reports of head or chest injuries.

"How are they doing this," Merrecci roared as the news continued to flood in from throughout the ship.

"Admiral," Prilla's voice came just then, shaky. "Vincent," she said. In the background was another woman screaming, and he knew this voice too.

"Prilla," Merrecci answered.

"I don't know what happened, she just—

"I'll have to get back to you," Merrecci said, jumping from the console seat and forgetting to end his communication with his sister. A strange and inarticulable face had appeared in his holo.

"We have taken the energy of one hundred of your lives," the same Maridamarak voice announced. "Your fee is paid."

The head disappeared.

"What does that mean," Prilla's voice shrilled.

Merrecci cursed himself for what he'd forgotten.

"It means later," Merrecci said. Now, he did end the communication and then issued an order to hospital staff to locate and aid Prilla Wanship.

He turned to his command crew and saw what was about to spew from Bria's instantly broken soul.

"No," he ordered. "I need you here."

The Onyx was suddenly moving again.

Nandy assumed control of Mailer's empty console and summoned another monitoring crew member to report for duty, as well as two medbots to retrieve Mailer's body.

"Sir," Bria said. Merrecci could hear her barely containing herself. "We can't let them have the Rhaxians."

"Can't we," Merrecci said. "Why not? You let them have ours."

When they came out of Maridamarak space, too many ships for Merrecci to think about were spread out and surveying the area.

"Now," the Maridamarak commander said. "Bring them to us."

"There are too many of your vessels here for our scanners," Merrecci explained. "They also won't reveal themselves with so many. It will be better if we are alone and they think we succeeded in our plan. Then we can tell you where they are."

Seconds later, the Maridamarak ships began to slowly return to their own space. It wasn't until only Merrecci's fleet carrier host remained that they received another message to turn the Rhaxians over to them.

Merrecci agreed.

"Have they returned to the Onyx yet," Merrecci asked.

Almma nodded, and he avoided her thin lips, sharp brow, and tightly clasped fingers upon the railing of her station on the second level. He could hear her nose hissing at him.

"Lieutenant-commander Almma," he said. "Fire our five strongest torpedoes into one of the Maridamarak ship bays." Then he turned on Ensign Being. "As soon as they're fired, get us out of here, maximum speed!"

The torpedoes launched, and the Onyx sped away.

"Sir," Bria said, turning to her own duties. "We can't outrun the Maridamarak."

Suddenly the Maridamarak fleet carrier emerged into the Onyx's path. Ensign Being evaded as best as he could, but soon the fleet carrier released its fleet.

"They're locked and firing," Almma announced.

"Hail! Hail," Merrecci ordered.

"Go," Bria replied.

"You idiots," Merrecci screamed. "You were so intent on seeing us that you didn't see what we were dropping along the way. Destroy us, and your names will be known as the ones who allowed your space to burn up."

"You lie," the enemy commander's voice roared.

"Try me," Merrecci replied sternly. "You killed my people. Destroy us and see who gets the higher death count in your own space!" Then he ordered five more torpedoes fired into the same ship bay. They didn't seem to have an effect.

"Come on then," Merrecci roared. "Blow us up!"

He ordered more torpedoes into the same fleet carrier bay.

"You going to fight back or what, you underwhelming bag of static," Merrecci taunted.

"You aim to provoke us," the Maridamarak captain stated. "You are very clever. We are smarter. We are done talking now."

The fleet carrier recalled its fleet and left.

Merrecci issued the order once more to get the Onyx out of

there, this time in stealth mode.

"That was not seven ships," Almma exploded. "That was fifteen! Fiftee—sixteen with the carrier. This was no time to use math you learned from a hooker marrying a good Christian boy!"

"We just lost a hundred crewmates," Merrecci replied and glared Almma into future silence.

Merrecci finally stopped clenching the handrailing that he didn't remember approaching. Then he called Pablo Escobedo back to the bridge to get them back on mission and hidden again.

"I don't care how strong your weapons are, the right bluff with just enough ambiguity can shut 'em down," Merrecci said.

Trying his best to ignore the cleaning bot already removing Mailer's blood from the floor, he ordered Bria to his ready room. She followed. As soon as the doors closed, he turned on her.

She was already shaking, her eyes focused on Merrecci and nothing at the same time. It started soft and inquisitive then exploded in to a flurry of repetitively shrieking, "What did I do?"

She felt the need to drop to her knees, allowing herself to draw into a familiar fetal-like position where she found comfort when she was in panic. She stopped her knees from buckling though.

"You killed your crew," Merrecci snapped.

She froze in her tears as if she couldn't recall how to continue. Then she exploded involuntarily into silent shrieks.

"But that's what we do," Merrecci answered angrily. He was visually shaking as he addressed Bria. "We make decisions that affect the lives of those under our command, and sometimes— sometimes—the decisions we make go to places we can't control."

"We could have waited," Bria said.

"And that could have cost even more lives, and we live with that," Merrecci explained, pointing a rigid, yet strangely wavering finger in Bria's face until it closed into a fist. "Because that's what we do, and we pray that only the best of the best of the best and rarest of our crew will ever have to know how this feels."

"I can't do this," Bria was barely able to get out.

"You already have," Merrecci said. "You're my first officer. You better do it. The death toll could have been a lot higher. Now get up and be a captain or I swear to God I'll kick being a captain back into your ass because the truth is, I have more important places to be than in here with an emotional, blubbering first officer that gets my people killed with half-assed ideas." Then he yelled. "So, turn it off! And help me figure out how they did this! Or would you like to trust discovering that information to someone else on this ship?"

With that, Bria turned it off because that's what Merrecci did.

*   *   *

For the first time in thirty-two years, Charity Quobolt woke up alone. There was no person pushing up against her right arm. There was no one stirring her awake from rising earlier; no one who left a drool stain on her shoulder, and no one that she had to wait on to wake before she could get out of bed herself. Her sedation had worn off of her and only her.

For the first time in thirty-two years, she felt bedding under her right side, and when she turned to reaffirm she had only dreamt it, she began screaming because she was now only half of a person.

A familiar voice was there, Prilla's, but Charity didn't care. She screamed. She knew what had happened.

She remembered. She was having lunch with Prilla, silently sending notes back and forth to each other about how they wished they could actually enjoy the beauty of the heaven that was passing before them. They ignored talking about Earth or who might still be alive, because there was still too much at stake there. Cora had been drawing in her sketch pad, and then she wasn't. She'd let out the slightest cry in pain, and, for the first time in thirty-two years, it sounded human as her body suddenly fell limp.

"What happened," Charity finally asked after she'd allowed her grief to humiliate her into the weakest form she'd ever known of herself.

"Something went wrong with a plan," Prilla said.

"He did this to us," she asked. "Was this because of him?"

"I can't say for certain," Prilla said. "But there are rumors."

"What kind of rumors?"

"That it was Bria's plan," Prilla replied.

"Get me up," Charity ordered.

When Prilla refused, Charity informed her that she could help her up or become a rug.

Charity expected to feel pain, but there was none, not until she fell. She got out one step and suddenly felt as though something was pushing her to her right. The pain wasn't sharp from surgery, but it was dull. In fact, she felt no surgical pain at all. Lifting her gown, she found healed skin, no scars, healthy, pink, and fake. Even her hip had been molded to not give any clue that it had once been bound to Cora's.

"They took her," she shrilled, looking at the careful cover-up job to hide that there had once been a sister who was a part of her. Someone simply tore half of that structure down. "They took all of her! What could she do to anyone?"

She wailed and forced herself to her feet once more, screaming and batting away Prilla's attempts to help her return to her bed.

With a quick check with Onyx, Charity learned Bria's location.

It took time. Sometimes, she crawled. It was easier, allowing her to recover her will and strength to walk. She trembled to find a new balance with each step. Sometimes, she had a wall on her right side to support her more like she was familiar with. When she finally entered the galley, she moved slowly, but she held her balance enough by moving from one object to another to hold her up and keep her strained course. She seemed not to notice nor to care what or who any of the objects were. She made it halfway into the room before she decided she was close enough.

"You're playing a game," she burst at the captain who was sitting at a table with Admiral Kellick.

The galley fell silent. It was nearly full at this time of day.

"Does that help you hide from what you've done," Charity asked, wanting not to believe it. "Look at me!"

Bria had started to look, but now she stood.

"Should you be out of bed," Bria asked.

"Should you be a captain," Charity yelled then snorted when she saw the sting on Bria's face. "We were just lucky to be alive, and look at you now, Captain Killer!"

She continued to pull herself closer to Bria along the ledge of a table in a nearly filled booth.

"Come on, this isn't you," Prilla said, now at Charity's elbow, trying to draw her away.

"Really? This isn't me," Charity retorted, snapping her arm away and nearly falling. Then she turned back to Bria, who had stepped out to help catch Charity. "It's only half of me," she roared, making Bria recoil.

"I know what kind of mental case you are," Charity continued. "I've listened to you for years in that pathetic circle. You're not fit to be a captain. I relieve you of duty."

"Overruled," Admiral Kellick quipped instantly.

Charity suddenly appeared disarmed, then exploded once more. "You took her from me! Who else did you murder, huh?"

"And that's enough of that," Kellick said.

"This isn't your ship," Charity snapped at Kellick and was so focused onto Bria that she didn't notice him rise from his seat.

Prilla began now to pull Charity away, but Charity snatched up Bria's arm and tore the razor from the sleeve of her uniform—in that same moment, revealing a history of scar trails in her flesh.

"Do us a favor and do the job right for once," Charity yelled. She held the blade to Bria's wrist and offered to help her.

A table broke into applause, followed by a second and third until most of the galley joined in.

"Prime Admiral on deck," a voice suddenly announced, and the room snapped to attention, Bria and Kellick included.

Prilla did not, she could not. She used the moment to slap the blade out of Charity's hand. Prilla felt the sharp kiss of the steel jab the side of her palm before it fell right at Merrecci's feet.

"You call that saluting," Merrecci asked. He turned on the first officer to his right and straightened the lieutenant's arm to a

90-degree angle. Then, with a dark glare, the prime admiral forced the relaxed curve out of the subordinate's fingers. The prime admiral kicked the lieutenant's feet more tightly together from the side and lined up the heels. "Your fingers extend fully when you salute a commanding officer. Your thumb flattens against the side of your hand until it turns white!" Here, he turned on another officer who had been applauding only moments ago and grabbed her thumb. He twisted it with her hand until it was directly in front of her face.

"What color is that thumb," he asked. "Is it white? Then you're doing it wrong." He walked around this table inspecting those who had also been sitting at it. His baton ratcheted open, and he smacked an Ensign's kneecap with it. "Your knees are straight, and legs locked. Your non-saluting arm is straight at your side. Locked! Tight to your hip, fingers fully extended, thumb flat. Like that! White!" Then nose-to-nose with the lieutenant again, he yelled. "I don't care if your skin is blue; salute means white!"

When the lieutenant flinched, the prime admiral reprimanded him for breaking his salute posture until he fixed it.

Merrecci turned and pointed to Bria who was standing in perfect form saluting.

"If someone pushes you in your commanding officer's presence, you will fall over holding that position," Merrecci continued to rampage as he meandered his way among the galley. "This is my ship! Mine! And if any of you have a problem with the decisions I make, you talk to me! You wonder why I chose the commanding officers I have to lead this ship, it's because I couldn't trust any of you to do the job especially after seeing how badly any of you know how to perform even a basic salute."

By now, Merrecci returned to where the razor blade sat on the carpet and nonchalantly picked it up.

"If you cannot salute properly to me as one of my grunts, what makes you think I can trust any of you to salute properly as one of my senior staff?" He jabbed his baton straight out towards Bria again. "That's how you salute!"

Here, Merrecci snapped his attention at a young man's face and clipped a finger into it.

"You drop that elbow one more time, Crewman, and I'm going to sling it permanently to your head until you find its correct height. Do you think you can find the correct height?"

When the crewman didn't respond, Merrecci blared the question again.

"Yessir," the crewman replied.

"Then find it!" Merrecci suddenly smacked the underside of the crewman's arm with his baton. "Is that it?" He smacked it down. "Is that it? Find it!"

The young man raised his elbow. Merrecci prepared as if to backhand him, and the crewman flinched then tumbled sideways.

"It's not over there," Merrecci scolded. "I said find it!"

The young crewmember regained his posture and salute.

Merrecci prepared to backhand again. The crewmember attempted not to flinch, but his bottom lip gave it away.

"Don't you dare," Merrecci berated. "You picked this fight!" Then he exploded at the entire room again. "They told me that I needed to be nicer to my crew, but it seems I'm not the one who needs a refresher course on humanity!"

Merrecci waved his hand to the doors of the galley. Almma and seven security personnel entered with batons extended.

"You will all hold this salute until my Captain releases hers," Merrecci said. "Anyone who can't, will be assigned to full shifts of good, old-fashioned elbow grease until you learn to make your thumb as white as the toilets you'll be polishing!" He turned sharply about the room to make his words stick to as many crew as he could. "My security head will observe."

Here, he turned on Bria. "My captain will hold her salute until she is the last person standing, or the only thing she'll be commanding is a lifepod back to Earth." His attention went back to the crew. "Here's your chance people. You want her gone? All you have to do is hold your salute longer."

Merrecci then moved to Charity and politely urged her to follow him.

Admiral Kellick's voice crept softly down to Bria.

"Once I leave, you will throw the biggest shadow in this room," Kellick explained. "Drown them in it."

In one motion, Kellick then stepped from behind Bria and suddenly drew a thin, steel spike that could have passed for a chopstick, from within his sleeve. He flicked it at a crewmember's foot. It sank into the side of the sole of her shoe but could have just as easily amputated her small toe.

"Feet together, please," Kellick said politely, yet with an air of authority that was every bit as intimidating as Merrecci.

He stepped casually to the crewmember and withdrew his throwing spike, causing the crewmember to raise her foot and break her salute.

"I'm sorry," he said. "You're out." Then he flourished his arm and buried the small javelin back into the lining of his sleeve. Finally, he handed off the task of judging everyone with a nod to Almma and her staff. A moment later, and he was out of the room.

"You," Almma said immediately after. She pointed to one of the saluting crew. "Report that boney ass to maintenance queue."

Now, Vandenbutcke entered. He looked to Bria, then the others. He might have been smiling.

"I heard you could use an extra set of eyes," he said to Almma, and he posted himself to face a group of crew members close to where Bria stood.

"You're out," Vandenbutcke instantly snapped at a lieutenant.

"Watch your tone, Ensign," the saluting lieutenant jibbed.

"Think I'm afraid of you," Vandenbutcke yelled. He snapped his baton open and cracked the lieutenant in the side of the knee with it. "You're out!" He smacked his knee again. "Pull rank with me again, and I'll bust your head next."

Almma helped the fallen lieutenant find the direction of the door out of the galley, even as Vandebutcke kept smacking him.

Vandenbutcke assumed a post at Bria's side where he helped monitor the rest of the room.

"All right," he muttered. "I'm listening."

A few minutes later, after four more crew were exiled to maintenance queue, Nandy entered to monitor as well.

After ninety-one minutes, Bria's last opponent faced nearly every judge. As the number of people saluting dwindled, Almma's scrutinous staff drew closer and closer upon the could-be winners until they completely encircled Bria's last bit of competition, watching him from every angle.

Vandenbutcke, however stood face to face with Bria, observing for her own mistakes. His brow had started out sharp, and it only grew angrier. Bria felt her arm tighten. It was heavy now. Her uniform was fat with sweat.

"Don't you dare give this to them," he ordered. He prodded her along with soft, demanding and somehow strengthening statements. "Or you'll never really earn their salutes."

Somehow, he found the words to hold her up until that last crewmember's salute dropped, and Almma started screaming in his face for being an embarrassment to his uniform.

On his first step, the strength in his finally unlocked knees gave out, and he dropped right down to sit on the floor.

A few security knelt to help him.

"No. No," Nandy objected. "If that's the strength a salute leaves him with, then he can crawl and build his stamina."

The galley had finally emptied of those caught up in the competition, others had joined to watch and remained silent for fear they might be called upon to take part in the trial. With the contest over, the judges all turned to the only contestant left and snapped salutes. She released hers, then said, "as you were."

She let her legs relax a bit before taking her first step. She felt her own knees on the verge of collapsing, but she'd had worse. Carefully, she made her way back to the bridge, where she found Merrecci in his ready room.

"I've heard that cadets can hold a salute all day, acknowledging everyone who outranked them," Merrecci said. "And you were the bottom of the rung. Congratulations. You're still my Captain."

He snapped a razor blade against his desk and pushed it across with one finger.

"It wasn't her secret to tell," he said without looking at her.

Bria took it.

"Use it in good health," he said, then dismissed her.

Bria didn't have to report for duty for another few hours, so she paid a visit to Cindy Lou first.

Six hours later, three into Bria's watch, the key had led them to a planet, and the Onyx was brought to a stop.

For this, Merrecci left his sleep.

"Well, Captain," he said. "Gather your landing party and go unlock that tomb."

"Sir," Bria asked. "I've never set foot on a planet before. Are you sure?"

"No. I always give half-assed orders to my command crew," Merrecci said. "Now choose people you think you'll need and go down there. You've got to get planet-side experience."

Bria nodded.

It was a gray planet, the only astral body in its solar system, which had annihilated itself some time ago after its brothers and sisters had burned themselves up in their sun before that too eventually ran out of gas and left the planet dark.

A ten-seat habitat lander launched from the Onyx. Aiden Paulsen, one of Vandenbutcke's students, helmed the flight. Samantah Nerris, another pupil, assisted. Two more ensigns from Vandenbutcke's class waited in the second row of seats, shadowing and waiting their turns to pilot the craft on the return path. Vandenbutcke observed from a standing position. Also, along for the ride was Almma, in case they needed tactical insight. Mirror was there for in case the newly-built shuttle needed immediate calibration. She currently sat at a control deck behind the pilots to monitor if the engines were operating efficiently. Admiral Kellick accompanied them, as a diplomat might prove handy when meeting a potential god, that could destroy the cosmos.

Potential god? What crackpot ship commander sends an inexperienced first officer to deal with a god? Bria's eyes darted to Kellick, and she could see him wondering the same thing.

"There's no wind," Crewman Paulsen said.

"It's still practice," Vandenbutcke replied looking into pitch black behind the windows before them. "This would be a good time to activate black environment enhancement before we hit something the sensors might miss and cause us to die, Crewman."

"Activating black environment enhancement," the assisting pilot, Nerris announced before Crewman Paulsen could wreck the ship from taking too long to answer.

The window turned as white as the other walls of the shuttle.

"What the hell," Paulsen shrieked.

"Give me a second," Mirror replied.

"In the meantime, we'll just go ahead and crash into something," Nerris said.

"Sent us their best, didn't they," Paulsen asked.

The window filled with gray night-vision of a flat terrain, with few fang-like rock structures popping up sporadically.

"About time," Paulsen chided.

"I'm sorry I'm not as smart as Dawn," Mirror cried.

The trainees shared a chuckle.

Bria leaned forward in her seat and caught Kellick doing the same in his, prepared to say something.

"You raise a valid point," Vandenbutcke said.

Bria's brow became a chisel, and Mirror's face sucked in to fight back tears.

"You were clearly not prepared to lose all visual," Vandenbutcke said. "So, you can all report to Ensign Greethe to study emergency engineering procedures for the next two weeks or until she clears you to operate the engineering console. That is, if it's okay with Ensign Greethe."

He turned to Mirror for approval.

She did.

"This could have been a catastrophic situation if she hadn't been here," Vandenbutcke said.

The trainees fell silent, and Mirror was smiling.

"I see it," the key cried, and Vandenbutcke tried his best to keep the key facing the correct direction.

The tooth-ish rocks along the world's surface turned into deep mouthy canyons with rigid spires where the planet's crust had been cracked and wedged asunder.

A particular complex of what looked like a crystal formation passed beneath the shuttle. To a traveler who didn't know better, it might have been mistaken for a city of skyrises all falling against each other.

The key fell silent.

"I think we passed it," Bria said.

Vandenbutcke agreed and twisted the skull in his fingers until it started screaming again that it could see whatever it could see.

The transport turned back for the strange metropolis-like formation, which turned out to be too tight for the small craft to enter. They'd have to land and walk in. Vandenbutcke talked the two pilots through circling this massive cluster while they searched for what might be the most suitable entrance. They found one but kept circling in case they might have overlooked something better. As far as they could tell, they hadn't.

The habitat shuttle landed as closely as possible to a terrace of crystal protrusions that would probably smash the tiny ship to bits if one of them fell on it. Since there wasn't any evidence to suggest any had fallen recently, Vandenbutcke suggested it should be safe to land.

"Now, we are landing on an unknown surface," Vandenbutcke said to his pilots. "So we?"

"We land," Paulsen replied.

"After scanning for any unnatural or artificially built anomalies," Samantah Nerris added.

"Correct," Vandenbutcke replied.

"Ensign, should we be concerned about just what effects the cold has had on this freeze-dried crust," Bria asked.

"Frozen crusts tend to be stronger," Vandenbutcke answered.

Bria tried not to intrude on Vandenbutcke's teaching. If he was offended at her question, he gave no hint. Bria accepted his answer. The pilots landed upon Vandenbutcke's go-ahead.

Normally, they would have initiated the habitat shield, which extended 100 yards in every direction from the shuttle. However, here, it would have encompassed some of the crystals, even projected right through the middle of some of them. Bria worried what the changes in temperature might do to the formations. She didn't want them falling on her away team.

"We'll take expedition suits," Bria informed.

She, Almma and Kellick each dressed into a layer of shield-emitting coveralls and drew oxygen capsules onto their backs. Their skin began to tingle the moment the shields hugged the contours of their clothing and flesh, allowing just enough space to allow oxygen to circulate over it. In case there was an emergency with one of their suits, Bria strapped on a hiking stick. It wasn't as savvy as what they wore, but once it extended to its full length, it could inflate a portable habitat bubble that could give a lost person or small party seventy-two hours life support and protection.

She activated a hover tote with its basic landing team tools and emergency equipment and paired it to follow her own frequency. Finally, she retrieved the key from Vandenbutcke and fastened it to her belt, threatening that if it bit her, she would leave it on this planet alone.

Then they passed the airlock and exited the shuttle.

The life support shields immediately began to sizzle with heat creation to combat the extreme exterior cold. Bria slid her environmental glasses over her face, the protective membrane accepted and heated them before they touched her skin. The dark terrain lit up with washed out color saturation. Almma's figure took form within it all.

"No snow, no ice and no wind," Almma said. "Look around Captain! These will ever be your lifelong bragging rights to the first planet you ever landed on. We could have landed on a cow's teat and had a better first-time planet-side story."

Bria agreed.

"Oh, come now," Kellick said. "For someone who's never been on a planet before, this isn't so bad."

"Are you kidding," Almma replied. "If teenagers found this secluded spot, even the boys would say 'this place sucks. Get off'!"

Kellick might have chuckled at this as they crossed over a crackled tan floor of what could have passed for a dried out lake bed. It seemed like an impossibility that water could have ever covered this ground though. Still, there had to have been something liquid on this planet at one time, Kellick thought. Otherwise, how else had it receded and given the bed its antique breaks. When Bria gave notice to his attention being entirely too focused on the ground, he began to question what she could tell him about the god-like being that the Onyx was carrying.

Kellick had not been authorized to visit Cindy Lou. Today, Bria understood he was merely attempting to arm himself to do his own work. She tried her best to explain the God, but Kellick could tell she was holding some parts back. She was, but not because they were classified. She just wasn't ready to talk about them, like how she often curled up on the God's floor and other things.

"Ugh," the key cried from Bria's waist where she had strapped it to the side of her utility belt. "How do the people on this planet live under such an ugly sky?"

"No one lives here," Bria replied.

"Probably all killed themselves," the skull observed.

Part of Bria wanted to ask how the key could see the sky, but she really didn't want to hear his answer. Still, she couldn't seem to stop looking up herself since he'd said something.

Now that she was among them, the crystals were larger than Bria first expected. A few smaller patches sprouted from crevices here and there, but most were tall and dense like trees on Earth that competed for the best real estate.

Bria's party passed through a natural opening or gate within them, and they entered a dome-like arena, where the ground cleared and giant gem formations loomed high over head. Many were taller than most buildings on Earth. Not one of them was as straight as a skyscraper would have stood. Most grew on angles that suggested they should have toppled. In fact, she wasn't entirely sure if some hadn't fallen already and weren't all just propping each other up. If Drinker were here, he could probably point out the one that would cause the whole dome to fall if he removed it.

"Hold up," Bria said, when a patch of the small gems about a foot tall mushroomed in their path. "I'd really like to see these in the light."

Almma laughed.

"What," Bria asked.

"It's nothing," Almma said. "You had to have been there."

Bria went to work gathering a sample of the stone. She knelt to the cluster, and the hover tote lowered next to her. From within it, she took a silver excavating hammer and a chisel. With some work she smacked off two shards. Whatever the substance was, it seemed stronger than expected. Every time she struck the hammer against the chisel, she had to reposition her cutting edge.

"Anyone else want a piece," she asked.

Almma and Kellick both did. She gathered and sealed these shards into collection containers and set them all inside the tote.

"Hold on," Almma said. "I kind of want this one here. I think it could make a cool blade hilt or something."

Almma had found a bit of an odd burst, almost looked like three spears growing as one. She took the hammer from Bria and gave a solid smack from the underside of the formation, and the cold ground suddenly crumbled away beneath her knees.

She managed to grasp onto the clump of crystals, saving her from falling away with the failing soil. The crust rippled out, falling into the distance, farther than the sensors of Bria's environmental spectacles could detect. A black canyon suddenly gaped open beneath Almma and swallowed the falling debris. As the world filled with the sound of crust roaring and falling into the distance, Bria found herself gripping the same formation of crystals that was holding up Almma. She expected the ground to give beneath her own feet, but it held. Kellick froze with nothing to anchor himself to in case his own floor failed him. Bria dropped flat on her belly. She thought of rescue crews laying down on frozen lakes to spread their weight. It was only now that she realized her right arm had stretched to Almma and clenched her wrist, their shields hissing at each other to allow the maneuver. Almma grasped the gem-like bloom tightly with both hands now.

Bria's left arm, wrapped around the cluster, gave her some anchor to aid Almma. The jagged, stone teeth gnawed at her shields to tear into her skin. Bria warned Kellick back, but he had already read the situation and decided not to add his weight to the immediate dilemma.

The chasm awaiting Almma's drop was a geode of sharp shards that reached for hundreds, maybe thousands of feet below, well beyond the range of Bria's glasses, which were truly only detail-accurate for up to 50 meters. Beyond that, she saw mostly gray shapes. From the sounds of the falling chunks of planetary floor still rising from the canyon depths, Bria believed it wouldn't have mattered if her glasses could have seen 5,000 meters.

What Bria could not see at the moment was that the tallest mineral formations from below had all grown and punctured through the planet's crust. It was upon one of these monstrous tips that Bria had been removing samples. Even without being able to measure their true height, Bria and her team had completely underestimated how large these deposits or whatever they should be called truly were.

"Never mind," Almma groaned. "This a good story."

"Be better if I could reach my controls to lock my shield memory or mesh our shields together," Bria said. "Can you reach your controls?"

It took only a slight shift to attempt the maneuver for Almma to realize she couldn't pull it off herself. Neither could Bria, with one arm acting as an anchor and another latched at one of Almma's wrists.

"I can reach you," Admiral Kellick said.

"No," Almma replied. "I'll be damned if your death is my fault too."

"Well, someone has to reach one of your shield controls and neither of you can do it," Kellick said. "Maybe we—

"I see it," the key started screaming.

"Oh, fuck off," Almma roared.

"I see it," the key kept screaming.

"Kellick to Vandenbutcke," Kellick called through his communicator.

"What are you doing," Bria asked.

"I see it!"

"Maybe he can shuttle above and drop a line through," Kellick said. "Kellick to Vandenbutcke."

"Hang on, Sir," one of the rookie pilots answered. "He's a little busy."

"I see it!"

"Will you tell that dentured turd to shut up," Almma cried, refusing to let go of the cluster that was only one of two things keeping her and Bria from falling straight down into the chasm where whatever didn't batter them would surely skewer.

"Wait," Bria said. "The suspension bridge."

"Right," the admiral realized. "I have to come get it."

"Fine," Bria said. "Just keep as much distance as you can."

"I see it!"

It was the most unused piece of equipment in the landing party tote. At one point, it had even become discussion among the senior admirals as to whether it should continue to be included in standard hover tote gear. It was designed to allow landing parties that might come upon deep canyons to create a suspension bridge that could support two or three people. But no one ever dared try three, it had been an unspoken policy to keep the occupancy to one person because it felt so frail beyond that. It wasn't frail, but it swayed a lot, and, with three people, it was enough to turn the nerves of even the strongest wills. Most people didn't forget it was part of the tote. They just didn't want to remember it was an option. However, Bria recalled it.

Kellick crawled onto his belly and pulled himself towards the hovering tote at Bria's side. He would have tried to pair the tote to himself so it would come to him, but he came to the conclusion it would be faster to just move directly to it.

He dug inside the floating canister and hauled out the square plate that contained two reels of cable. Now, he just had to hope it could penetrate one of the crystals to create a solid anchor. He aimed one end of the square at a large crystal appendage over his head and fired. Two cables blasted out with such force that they could drill deep into any gem's skin. It almost knocked out Kellick's shoulder. He had forgotten how much the device could kick.

The readout on the launcher communicated that one cable's tooth bounced off the surface of his overhead, crystal target. The second drilled in about a quarter of the preferred depth. He turned to find another anchor somewhere to the opposite side of Almma, aiming the plate so when the cable tightened, Kellick hoped it would be in Almma's reach, and she could just grab it. He was already aware that the one tooth that was barely set now would most likely not hold once Almma's weight was added to it. Yet, if he could get the other side of the bridge to secure itself, that could at least give her more support and allow them to further remedy this situation. On the other hand, he couldn't guarantee that if the one tooth that was currently holding gave out, she wouldn't swing herself right into a lethal skewer.

Just then, a section of the floret of crystal that Almma and Bria had been holding onto, cracked apart. Almma fell, her weight instantly snapping away from Bria's grip.

Bria suddenly turned and snatched the bridge crafting mechanism out of Kellick's hands, aimed it into the chasm and fired off the other side of the bridge.

"Look out," the key called down to Almma.

The cables flew fast, almost as if they knew all Almma's hope rested within them. The reel screamed as it emptied quickly, and when there was perhaps a fourth of its contents left, one of its cables pierced through Almma's thigh, the other through her hip. Upon exiting the other side of Almma's body, both cables bore their locking teeth, preventing the lieutenant-commander from sliding back off the cable. The line drew taut, and the square plate leapt violently from Bria's hands. The automatic tensioner kicked in and slowed Almma's fall.

The entire time Bria had been invested in Almma's side of the suspension bridge's line, Kellick caused his glasses to zoom in on the one anchor he had set.

Almma's agony carried up from the chasm.

Bria yelled down to her to ask if she was all right.

"You two-bag whore," Almma's voice echoed throughout the canyon. Bria turned to the control pad at her belt to initiate reeling its cables back in.

Kellick watched the lonely anchor above their heads for any hint it might break away. He contemplated if it would help in any degree to tell Bria that Almma was truly hanging by a poorly seated thread. He decided it would do no good. If it dislodged, they couldn't do anymore to save Almma. He thought of the razor blade that had been revealed from Bria's sleeve and decided not to say anything. If Almma fell, he'd convince Bria it was his fault for not setting the anchor properly.

Vandenbutcke's voice cracked over the communicator, "Sorry to keep you waiting, Sir, we had a little bit of an issue with the ground beneath us."

"Funny. So did we," Kellick replied. "We're going to need a medical module as fast as you can."

"And a new security officer," the key announced.

Vandenbutcke acknowledged the order.

The bridge builder slowly drew Almma up the chasm.

Suddenly the tote came to life and turned from side to side.

"Bria," Mirror's voice spoke through the tote. "We're coming. Where's Issa?"

Bria pointed.

The tote turned then dove into the chasm.

The tote's cargo tractor beam, along with the unsure cable pulled Almma up, then the tote dragged her onto the unforgiving ground. Almma shrieked the entire way.

"I didn't know it could do that," Kellick stated. "Wasn't it paired to you?"

"I'll take the win," Bria said.

"Right," Kellick agreed. He took a breath that wasn't quite relief and asked. "How did you know it would pierce her shield?"

"I didn't," Bria replied.

Kellick recognized the voice of a desperate tactic and said no more now.

Almma was now rising from within the chasm.

"It was the only thing I could think of," Bria said, once she could see Almma's face again. "I'm so sorry."

The tote's tractor clenched Almma's shoulders and steered her to safer ground near Kellick.

"Not so close," Kellick said. "Distribute the weight."

"It's okay," Mirror's voice said. "There's a bridge beneath you. Stay between the crystal formations."

In a few more moments, Almma was back on the ground. Bria quickly cut the cables but left the anchoring pins inside Almma's body for now.

"How do we know we won't fall here," Kellick asked.

"See," Almma forced out. She pointed again, this time to little pimples in the dirt, invisible until Bria finally saw one herself and pointed it out to Kellick. Now that she realized what they were, Bria could see a trail marked by the little crystal zits on both sides of it.

Almma stopped yelling instructions and was now merely screaming obscenities. In the middle of it all, she suddenly groaned.

"Don't you die on me," Bria ordered.

"Don't tell me what to do! You shot me," Almma snapped. "Twice!"

"Lieutenant-commander, are you all right," the tote asked.

"Why is the tote talking to me," Almma asked.

"It's Mirror," Bria replied.

"Of course it is," Almma cried. "What took you so long?"

"The ground broke," Mirror replied. "We were falling."

"What do you think I was doing?"

"I'm sure she did her best," Kellick said.

Almma fired back with, "Don't argue with me! I'm dying, you old bastard!" Then she exploded in a shriek of pain that sounded more like a focused war cry.

"Where did you learn to shoot like that," Kellick asked.

"Cramming for my landing party survival final exam," Bria replied. "Four times."

"You never passed," Almma groaned through gritted teeth.

"I think she just did," he said. "More than I did."

Kellick was glad that no one seemed interested enough to ask him what he had meant. Instead, he suddenly felt Almma's grip pulling at his shirt. She pulled him right to her face.

"Give me drugs, you pimp," she yelled.

When Vandenbutcke and the two pilot trainees finally arrived, they all hefted Almma onto a medpod bed. It sealed, filling with enough gas to help her sleep. Bria sent Vandenbutcke off to take her back to the Onyx and then return as quickly as possible.

"So," the key said. "Tried to kill your own crewmate, huh? Need to stop doing that."

Kellick and Bria continued their trek, mindful to stay between the small bulges in the ground.

Within thirty minutes, they found themselves stopped. The pimples curved towards each other, bringing the path to a dead end.

"Now where," Kellick asked.

Bria pulled up the key and turned it over in her hand.

"Nothing," the key said.

"There has to be something," Bria replied.

"Oh, does there now," the key asked.

Bria kept twisting the key around, until finally it announced he could see it again, but then he added, "Just kidding."

Bria turned the key with more fervor now until the key broke into the familiar, "I see it," that told Bria it was true this time.

The skull was facing straight down.

The environmental glasses showed more dirt, but it occurred to Bria that perhaps their visual tech couldn't decipher between the planet's crust and some other material. She knelt to get a closer look. Still nothing. The glasses just couldn't decode the surface.

"Mirror, can you give me lights on the tote," Bria asked.

No answer came.

"Mirror?"

"I'm sure she has other things to do," Kellick said.

Bria activated the tote's lighting system herself and then removed her glasses so she could see with her own eyes what the sensors could not. It seemed to be of little help. The darkness was so thick, the light turned everything it touched to white. The glasses appeared to show more, so they went back onto her face, and the tote's lights deactivated.

Now Bria ran her hand over the ground and wasn't sure if she felt anything. She massaged the dirt, brushing away a strange dust, until she revealed sharp engravings. She kept sweeping until she was more confident that the etchings were some sort of intended decorative design carved by someone or something else.

Another fifteen minutes passed before Kellick, who also began sweeping away at the ground, announced that he thought he found something.

It was a strangely shaped hole. Bria held the key's face over it.

"There it is," he announced.

"Guess it's time," she said.

She aligned the key's mouth with what she believed was the keyhole, then shoved the key against it.

"Hey," the key shouted.

"Nope," Bria said. "Doesn't fit."

"Can't imagine why," the key snapped. "Ever hear of a key kissing its way through a lock."

"Never heard of a key kissing anything," Kellick replied.

"A key can't open what a key can't see," the item said.

Then Bria understood. She turned the key over and zealously shoved the skull into the hole.

"Ow," the key complained.

"That kind of felt good," Bria said.

Then the key chided her to keep her comments to herself.

"I see it," the key said.

"We know you see it," Bria snapped.

"No," the key shot back. "I see how it works. Turn me clockwise."

Bria turned the key until it started snarking at her to stop. It paused, gave another command to turn again.

"Nandy to Captain Leonard," Nandy's voice erupted from Leonard's transmitter.

"What," Bria belted more forcefully than she'd anticipated. "I mean, yes?"

"Ma'am, just wanted to ask if you happened to have checked your office today," Nandy asked. "We haven't received the duty roster yet."

"I'm sorry," Bria replied. "I could have sworn I published it."

"Oh," Nandy replied. "It wasn't registered with Onyx. Thank you. And you published it from inside your office today?"

"Yes," Bria replied.

"You're sure?"

"Yes?"

"Today?"

"Yes," Bria replied. "I was in my office today with my tablet, and I'm sure. Why? Can't you find it?"

"It's not popping up for me," Nandy replied. "Your desk won't let me access it without your authorization."

"Oh, right," Bria said. "First officer's desk, allow commander Nandy access—authorization by Captain Leonard, codeword: Lon Chaney."

"Thank you, Ma'am," Nandy replied. "Hated to bother you, but—yep—there it is. Thank you! Nandy out."

"Glad you found it," Bria replied, but Nandy had already discontinued the communication.

Then Bria returned her attention to the key's instruction, which was directing her how and when to turn it, which wasn't easy considering that she needed to grip the mouth to get the most leverage and it insisted on gnawing at her more than it needed. After several minutes of trying to follow instructions, the key announced it was finished. The ground rumbled and began to lower below the planet's crust and into the black, crystal abyss. Twenty minutes more and the elevator stopped, not because it had traveled terribly far, but because it moved slowly. The key shimmied itself up and out of the lock.

"Wow. I kind of thought that would have been more climactic," the key said.

"Does that mean we can throw it into the chasm now," Kellick asked.

"What," the key complained. "No. Why would you do that?"

Bria tucked the key back onto her belt, probably needing it later to operate the elevator once more on their way out.

A new path appeared. This one was polluted with clusters of gems just waiting to bite at Bria and Kellick's ankles and knees. Yet it was clear this had to have been the trail as it was the only place among the corridor of gems that they could possibly navigate through. After two hours pressing deeper into what turned out to be a cavern within the canyon, their equipment suggested that they had walked about three miles since they had left the floating platform. Neither Bria nor Kellick were in too much of a talkative mood while they were both being careful to avoid tripping over the jagged floor, as there were many crystal cluster formations surrounding them that were surgically adept at cutting into many vital organs at once if anyone fell on them.

Admiral Kellick tripped once and would have gouged his knee more than it had were it not for his body shield and perhaps even his pants. Still, it did cut him.

"Second guessing getting that sample," Kellick asked at one point as he watched Bria's foot slip on a portion of smooth surface, but catching herself before she landed on anything piercing.

"Second guessing why I wasn't more patient to get one," Bria answered.

"I suppose," Kellick continued as he was also simultaneously arguing with his own jagged mushroom about letting his foot loose. "If you hadn't though, your security officer wouldn't have had it to grab onto for as long as she did. Probably saved our lives too. Being impatient might have just been the very thing that saved us all from falling."

Then silence. Then more careful walking, and suddenly a cocoon emerged upon the floor and crept closer with each of Bria and Kellick's steps.

"Well, that gets one's spirits up," Kellick said, realizing it was in fact a corpse.

Bria inspected it. Its position was deliberate: its back with its arms folded over his—his? Yes, his stomach. It appeared more mummified than anything.

"Well," Bria said. "It's dead."

"And this is a dead end," Kellick said after scanning the area to find that it was indeed a sealed alcove, and the only way out was back the way they had just stumbled through.

"Leonard to Admiral Merrecci," Bria announced into her sleeve.

"If you're calling to tell me you just killed Admiral Kellick too," Merrecci's voice crackled back.

"Almma's dead," Bria burst.

"You shot her twice, what do you think," Merrecci asked.

Bria slumped and might have fallen except Kellick was there to sustain her.

"Of course, she's not dead," Merrecci suddenly snapped back. "Think I'd have waited for you to contact me before I told you?"

"Sir, with respect, that wasn't funny," Bria replied.

"I'm not finding many things funny right now," Merrecci scolded. "Report."

Bria relayed her and Kellick's discovery and silence followed.

"Cindy Lou says the body's not dead. It just needs to be rehydrated," Merrecci informed. "Bring it back."

"Sir," Bria said. "This is dead. I've seen dead. This looks like dead only with more dead and lots of calluses."

"I said bring it back," Merrecci ordered.

Several hours later, they were back aboard the Onyx with a dead body that apparently needed a drink of water.

13

▲

Capone

Merrecci practically pranced in place at the doorway to Cindy Lou's living quarters.

"So, you have him," Cindy asked. She had been laying on her couch pretending to read something called *Theogeny*. Though what she read had proved to be a good comedy, she found it a bit long. It seemed more enjoyable to stare at the text on the pages until she could start to see hidden pictures in the text. For a moment, she thought she found Roman thieves, but she found boredom instead.

"He just woke up," Bria replied.

"Yes, he did," Merrecci cooed.

"What's wrong with you," Cindy Lou asked, looking up from her book, which she hadn't done even when inviting her guests in.

"Just excited to see the mission come together," Merrecci said.

"Can I see him," Cindy asked, but had resigned herself to already knowing that she couldn't. They were too deadly to let near each other.

"Sure," Merrecci said gleefully. "But you have to stay outside of his room. We don't want him getting to you."

Bria didn't seem to share his enthusiasm.

"Cheer up, Bri," Cindy encouraged. "This is exciting."

"Yeah, Bri," Merrecci agreed. "This is good times!"

The prime admiral instructed Onyx to disable the disintegration shield to Cindy Lou's quarantine sector. Then he moved so quickly that Cindy was practically running to keep up. Bria was a bit slower, didn't even try matching Merrecci's pace.

"Slow down Admiral," Cindy said. "I'm sure he's not going anywhere, no matter when we get there."

Merrecci guffawed and slowed his stride.

"Seriously! What is wrong with you today," Cindy asked.

"I don't know," Merrecci said. "Just having a good day mostly, I suppose."

After a jaunt in the elevator, and a short step across the hall, Merrecci was at a door.

"Isn't this the rec hall," Cindy asked.

"Yeah," Merrecci replied quickly and darted inside. "Felt he might be more comfortable here."

Then he was off to a fast pace again, leading Cindy Lou and Bria past a few tennis and handball courts until they came to another door. Merrecci stopped here.

"My goddess," Merrecci announced. "May I introduce you to your lover!"

The door revealed an Olympic-sized swimming pool.

Rehydration, it turned out, was an understatement. The hospital prepared a bath for the dried up mummy. Within an hour, the staff realized that the tub wasn't large enough to hold his body. By the time a larger bath had been prepared, the mummy's skin had already unfolded so that it was drooping over the sides of this basin as well. It took two maintenance bot tractor beams to lift him from this tub into a third and even larger reservoir, which they immediately learned still wasn't going to be enough.

After much discussion about whether it was worth it to prepare an even larger tub, one of the nurses suggested they put him in the swimming pool. So, they did, and it took another two additional bots to fenagle his mass through the double doors.

After he had rehydrated, the blob of a creature began visibly breathing and managed to climb out of the pool. No one knows how really. They watched him do it and still can't figure it out. It was like seeing a slug roll up and over the ledge of a brick. Once he stood upright, it was clear that he was indeed a bipedal humanoid. If it weren't for his bulbous head, he would probably reach just under six feet tall. His width was perhaps double that. His legs were hidden beneath thigh, gut, and chest flab. In truth, he looked like the melted remnants of a much larger giant. The medical staff thought they might be able to see a toe under all the fat, they weren't quite sure though. The slug's forearms stuck out primarily from his front, straight, mostly stiff, and barely visible.

When Cindy Lou first saw him, he was running laps around the pool, naked because no one was sure if anyone could actually dress him, and they knew he'd need the help.

As he jogged, his fat rolls slapped against the tile floor and each other. His face was red with strain, but he kept running. He turned the corner of the pool and started towards the doors when he saw the admiral, Cindy, and Bria.

"Goddess," he cried out from within a head which had swollen to look like its back side was trying to swallow the remains of the front. The weight of fat in his puckered lips muffled his voice. Currently, only one of two eyes peered out from within his cauliflower-texture face. He ran towards Cindy Lou.

"Uh," Cindy said as she watched the behemoth plap-and-flathaplut towards her. "No."

Then she closed the door to the swimming pool and began to leave.

"What's wrong," Merrecci asked a little too gleefully.

"You think this is funny, Admiral," Cindy asked.

Merrecci opened the door once more to reveal the monstrous Don Juan still advancing and slapping into himself with each step. Merrecci pointed as if expecting her to see the approaching blob as anything other than entertaining.

Now, Bria closed the door.

Cindy started to leave again.

"Look at the bright side," Merrecci encouraged, now sober. "You don't need your shield anymore."

Merrecci began wiping his eyes with the back of his hand.

"Sir," Bria said, and her own sobriety brought him to regather his own.

"You're lucky to come from a race that's so bountiful you actually have choice in your mates," Cindy said. "I hope the laugh was worth it. Was it worth it?"

Merrecci opened the door to once more reveal the fat man, three feet away from the opening suddenly waving his arms and reaching towards Cindy Lou, his fat fingers too engorged to wiggle.

The beast hit the door. His arms kept pawing for her, but he was unable to get his bulk past the frame.

"My goddess," He cried gleefully.

Merrecci wiped tears from his eyes and didn't attempt to stifle his amusement.

"I cannot mate with that," Cindy exclaimed.

The fat being suddenly stopped reaching.

"Of course not, goddess," he said. "I am but a servant."

"You're not Zarchro," Cindy asked.

"Me," the man said and then chuckled. "No. I'm thinabian."

"Wait," Bria said. "Your race is thinabian?"

"Yes," he replied. "We are hunted by the Kag'tak. My family and I are the last of our kind. After the Rhaxian helped my wife and children flee, I agreed to help."

"You have a wife and children," Bria asked, then blurted, "How?" She guffawed now and quickly caught her mistake.

Surprisingly, Merrecci was glaring at her.

"We should have introduced Kellick to him first," Bria said.

"You're not her mate," Merrecci finally asked.

"Me," the fat being asked. "No."

Merrecci raised his tablet high above his head and threw it at the ground and yelled, "God damnit!"

The holotab simulated breaking to pieces against the floor.

"We are very similar races, but we are not compatible," the blob explained. "This is why the Kag'tak hunted us. They did not understand we could not mix with Utonenaibe."

Merrecci opened his palm, and his bracelet allowed another one to form into it.

"God damn it," Merrecci cursed again and threw this holotab at the wall where it burst into flames and fizzled to ash before it reached the floor.

"Aww," Cindy said. "I'm sorry your joke wasn't as funny as you thought."

"Where is the mate," Merrecci asked, zeroing in on Bria.

"I don't know, Sir," Bria replied. "I thought this was him. We used the key, and it took us to—"

"The key," the blob replied. "The talking key? Funny guy, huh?"

Merrecci turned to his rotund guest and finally asked. "Who are you?"

"I am Binnybodelandomingarathumapula," he said.

Merrecci just stared.

"I'm not calling you that, Binny," Merrecci said.

"Okay," Binnybodelandomingarathumapula replied. He appeared insulted.

"It's a term of endearment with our race to call someone by a shorter nickname," Bria said. "It's a sign we like each other."

"You like me," Binny asked.

"Yes," Bria replied. She eyed Merrecci as if to tell him that he did too.

"What happened to your face," Binny asked.

"Who the hell are you," Merrecci blurted.

"I told you, I'm Binnybodelan—I'm Binny," Binny replied. "I'm the map."

"Huh," Merrecci asked.

"To the male god," Binny replied.

"You have a map," Bria asked.

"Yes," Binny replied. He pirouetted once and turned his body into what might have looked like a Christmas tree if a Christmas tree was a fat bastard slapping its rolls against the walls.

"You mean to tell me that someone has to dig through those rolls of fat to find a map you're carrying," Merrecci asked.

"No," Binny replied. "Look, I'll show you."

Binny turned back into the pool area and bid the others to follow him. He walked to the ledge of the water and belly flopped in, Dousing Merrecci and his comrades. As the fat being floated, his body flattened, spreading atop the water and increasing his radius in each direction by several yards, even butting up against two opposing edges of the pool.

"He looks like a human oil spill," Merrecci mumbled to Bria. When she shot him a look of respectful disapproval, he turned his attention back to the floating glob of flesh. "Where's the map?"

"That's it," Binny said. "See?"

Merrecci looked. They all looked.

"I don't see it," Merrecci said.

"Sir," Bria said. "I think it's in the freckles and lines of his fat rolls."

Merrecci stared at Bria as though she had just given him an insult worthy of a duel to the death.

"That can't be right," Merrecci said. "You mean someone has to get up close and decode all that?"

Now, it was Cindy Lou who was laughing.

"No time like the now, Admiral," she crowed and suddenly shoved the Admiral into the water.

Bria turned to Cindy in horror.

"What? What happened," Binny asked.

Merrecci resurfaced after a moment of struggling with Binny's floating flesh to get out of his way. He ordered Bria to return Cindy Lou to her quarantine.

Bria obeyed at once.

"You're right. This is good times," Cindy called back to Merrecci as Bria ushered her out of the swimming hall.

The admiral immediately returned to his quarters to shower and change. Then he sent an astrometric team to the pool to scan Binny's back, which he was certain made them want to quit. It didn't take as long as he'd expected before Bria had called to inform him that the mapping team had completed their work and analyzed Binny's freckles.

He asked Bria to accompany him to the astrometric lab and found a hologram of binny's backside hovering above a table in the center of the room. Merrecci thanked them for moving so quickly on the task.

"It wasn't so difficult," a young woman and a crewman second class said. Merrecci couldn't recall her name. "We just scanned it and immediately got map references. Although some of it wasn't in the database."

"So unexplored area," Merrecci asked.

"Yes and no," the crewman said. "We've explored it, just not the inside it seems."

"How is that," Merrecci asked.

"It's in hypernova space, Sir," she said. "It's in a red zone, Sir. In fact, there's no record of any race ever entering this area. It's not even named because it might just be the most volatile sector of space. From a tactical standpoint, it's an outright nightmare."

"I see," Merrecci acknowledged. Then he called to the hospital to request that Almma listen in on the conversation.

"I'm sorry, Admiral," Nurse Gibralter's voice called back. "That's a hard no."

"Why," Merrecci asked. "Has there been a complication?"

"She's resting," Gibralter said.

"So, she's healing," Merrecci asked.

"I'm fine, Doctor Douche," Almma's voice careened over the astrometrics room.

"So, you can take part of this discussion," Merrecci asked.

"Well, don't mind me, I'm just your overworked nurse thanks to your captain and drunken chief medical officer," Gibralter complained until his voice faded into the distance.

The sound of a door closing on Almma's end echoed through Astrometrics.

"Sir," Almma said. "Please let me die before letting him touch me again. He has some kind of cold, dead, fish hands thing going on. You can't fantasize about cold, dead, fish hands. At least, I don't think you can."

The lab suddenly erupted in laughter, and Merrecci silenced it. Then he brought Almma up-to-date with what he'd learned so far.

"So how do we go in, Crewman Basil," Bria finally had the chance to ask.

Basil! That was her name. Merrecci swore to himself he wouldn't forget it now.

"We don't, Captain," Basil replied through a snicker. "The risk is too great."

"Yes, but how do we go in," Bria asked again.

"We don't," Basil retorted.

"Yes, but," Merrecci said this time. "How do we go in?"

Basil's face turned white, as now the rest of the astrometric team gathered to the hologram to eavesdrop with more accuracy.

"Well supposing, we had no choice," Basil said.

She pointed a finger to a portion of the map.

"This is where we understand we would need to go," Basil said.

"How do you know that," Merrecci asked.

"Binny told us," Basil replied, then waited for Merrecci to permit her to continue.

Her finger moved to the side of the map.

"The fastest way, but not the shortest, might be along this route, but our emissions from being there alone could exacerbate Gamma rays and turn this whole thing into a mess we'd never even be a footnote to," Basil explained.

"And the safest," Bria asked.

"To stay out of there," Basil replied, again snickering and without turning from the map.

"That's not an option," Bria said.

"I'd make it one," Basil suggested.

"Aww," Almma said. "If you only had the clearance to do that." Basil's eyes flew to Bria, then Merrecci.

"What area will be the safest for us to fly through," Bria asked.

Basil turned back to the map and made it rotate before them.

"Probably this," Basil informed.

"Why," Bria asked.

"Because it is," Basil replied.

"Oh, did someone forget to saddle her misguided ego today," Almma asked.

Merrecci was about to speak, but Bria quickly corrected the behavior with a simple, "Settle down."

Basil's eyes finally turned to Captain Leonard, who now held her hand towards the map and let two fingers circle a portion.

"This area seems less cluttered, can we go in here," Bria asked.

"The problem with that area is this right here," Basil explained drawing an imaginary line over the holographic map. "This is a string of suns—seven, to be exact—which is why we don't go here.

"The only way to really describe this area is that it was a conglomeration of solar systems at one time that eventually all came together. It is a straighter shot though. Lots of gravity wells and gets a little warm with all those suns, but lots of fallout, gases, radiation, and it's the heart of the hypernova. Archive data suggests all of these suns can go pop at any moment—and, if one goes, they all go. Nothing in the red zone will survive, perhaps even beyond the red zone."

Basil's finger slid to another edge of the map. "Now, this shorter route is more cluttered. For some reason this is where the dead planets and other debris have conglomerated. This is the fallout of planetary bodies that have collided for whatever reasons. We're talking seven milky ways all with their own suns and moving planets all in the same body of space. It won't be like flying through an asteroid field. We could be dodging debris half the size of Jupiter—who knows—but this would be the fastest way."

"You wouldn't recommend any other options," Merrecci asked.

"Well, we could come in from this topside area, so to speak, if you wanted, but we'd be contending with toxic clouds released from a gas giant. From what little data we do have, I would guess it eats hulls."

"Lieutenant-commander," Merrecci asked. "Obviously, a tactical nightmare. Think you can coordinate with engineering to come up with something to help us get in and out of that safely?"

"Send me the map," Almma requested. "I'd feel better about it too if Escobedo took a look at it. By the way, will someone please come get this 'Get Well' bear he sent me. It takes up a lot of room, and all it does is roar and poop. I think it's glitched."

"I'm sorry," Basil said. "Is she serious?"

"Just send the map," Merrecci ordered.

Basil sent the map, and Almma fell silent for a minute or two.

"I'll think some more on it, but I think having a good pilot and the best engine facilitation is going to be the best way to spend resources on this one," Almma said. "And thank God I'm not that pilot." As if she could sense the sudden concern that crossed the faces of the astrometric team, she continued with, "Which is why it's a good thing we have the best pilot in the Franchise."

Merrecci took the small boost to morale and mentally noted to speak to Almma more about her own bedside manner among subordinates. Then he turned to the map and scrutinized it a bit more closely.

"Well, what about this right here," Merrecci asked drawing his finger to another angle of the map. "What are we looking at here?"

"Gravity storm," Basil replied. "This map suggests a big one."

"Could be bigger depending on how old the map is then, Sir," Bria suggested.

Merrecci acknowledged the input and drew his finger to another point that had appeared less cluttered. "And this?"

"Magnetized fallout," Basil said. "We'll have no sensors."

Merrecci pointed again. "And what's this path here?"

"That's Binny's butt crack, Sir," Basil said. "We don't want to follow that."

"So, a black hole," Almma muttered.

"What was that," Merrecci asked sternly.

"Well, it is," Almma said.

"Please send all of your maps and findings to Ensign Pablo Escobedo at once," Merrecci said. He thanked the astrometric team and suggested he'd let them know if he had any further questions. Then he excused himself and his command staff.

Merrecci returned to his quarters, the entire time scolding an absent Almma by proxy of Bria. At his door, he sent his first officer back to the bridge to start preparing for the upcoming leg of their mission. He was just nodding off in his chair in the middle of a logic puzzle when he suddenly jerked himself awake because Bria's voice called for him.

"Captain," he said. He quickly debated with his brain over whether he should consider returning to the bridge and solving another of his Captain's problems, or if he should let her have the chance to build more trust with him.

"Sir, I have our engineering heads here in my office," she replied. "You'll want to hear this."

"What is it?"

"They know how the Maridamarak killed our crew," Bria said.

Merrecci was now out of his chair. He found Bria with Dawn, Mirror, and Mike all huddled around Bria's desk. On his way through the bridge, he had signaled for Nandy to follow.

"Should we notify Drinker," Merrecci asked, directly upon entering the room.

"Already have," Bria said.

"Tell me," Merrecci requested.

"Please," Mirror corrected.

"Now," Merrecci yelled.

At this, Mirror started to cry.

"Oh for—look! I'm sorry," Merrecci said. "Please tell me what you've found."

"We found your face in the dictionary next to the word 'three-headed puppy-humper'," Dawn snapped back.

Merrecci's face crumpled before erupting with, "What?"

"That's enough of that," Bria warned.

"It's on page nine-seventy-two after pervy, birthday party clown and before you—

Merrecci took this as a clue to apologize and asked Mirror to please tell him what they found."

"It took us a while to figure out," Mirror said cautiously.

"I figured it out," Dawn said. "You only figured out the part of the brain."

"Well, one of us had to," Mirror snapped.

"That's it. I'm kicking your ass too," Dawn threatened.

"Please," Merrecci said raising his hands pleadingly.

"During our analysis, we noticed minute surges in Onyx's shields," Mirror continued to explain, ignoring Dawn's usual facial intimidation, which was made all the worse due to her thick unibrow. "The surges were on a microscale and had no real consistency to their pattern except that—

"Each time it happened, a crew member died," Bria said.

"We're telling him," Dawn replied at an inappropriately loud volume. "You can show him!"

Bria touched her desk, and it revealed a small holo of the Onyx above it.

"If we take each point of surge on the shields, we can connect it to a crew member who was killed following that event," Mirror explained. "If we line up the dead crew member with the surge in the shield, we can identify trajectories that all originated from the Maridamarak ship."

Merrecci brushed away the inclination to point out that obviously the attack on his crew came from the Maridamarak ship.

Drinker clicked at the door and was allowed entrance into the standing room only office.

"So, what happened," Merrecci asked, using Drinker's intrusion to get back on topic. This time, he was careful about keeping his own volume calm.

"Snipers, Admiral," Mirror said. "Lots of snipers."

"Am I to understand the Maridamarak have the capability of sniping from within their ship into another and can bypass shields," Merrecci asked.

Mirror and Dawn nodded.

"Why no reports of decompression where their rounds entered the Onyx's hull?"

"There are no holes in the Onyx," Mirror replied.

"There has to be," Merrecci said.

"We said there were no holes," Dawn snapped.

Bria turned to Dawn and wagged a finger in her direction.

"I'm not going to tell you again," Bria warned.

"Explain it to me," Merrecci said then added "please."

"Energy," Mirror said.

Merrecci explained that he needed more.

"Energy bullets," Mirror said. "Snipers can somehow see into our ship and fire those energy bullets at any target they please. When it hit our crewmember's brains—

"When the bullet hit their heads, the reverb and echo of the energy inside the skull broke their brains," Dawn interrupted.

"And for some," Mirror added. "Broke their heads, broke their spine, broke their heart."

"They can do that," Merrecci asked. "Okay, well, now that you know how they do it, how long until we can do the same back," Merrecci asked. "Tit for tat."

"We can't," Mirror said. "We just don't have that technology."

"Well, let's steal it," Merrecci ordered.

"Before or after they catch us and blow all our brains out," Dawn asked and pushed herself away from the desk to snoop through Bria's office.

"So, we can't predict, stop or fight this," Merrecci said.

"There might be a way," Drinker said. "We could try installing a material."

Merrecci turned inquisitively to Drinker.

"A material," Drinker said.

"A material," Merrecci asked.

"A material," Drinker said.

"A material what," Merrecci exploded. "Girl? What? A material what?"

Drinker paused, thought carefully, then cautiously spoke to say, "a material—gah! Damn it!"

"Contact me when you figure it out—

"Lightning rod," Drinker fired back. "A grounding rod."

"I'm listening," Merrecci said.

"To material the energy when it hits our shields so it materials into the Onyx and goes back into our own shields," he explained.

"Okay. I think I get it," Merrecci said. "Somehow run lines between our shields and the Onyx so that when their energy sniper rounds hit, they get broken up, and the energy goes into the ship to get reconstituted back into our shield energy." He paused in thought a moment and let out a self-indulgent, "huh. Could it reinforce other functions on board?"

"No," Dawn moaned. She was currently rifling through Bria's small closet that held one uniform.

"No," Merrecci asked.

"That word has two letters in it," Dawn replied. "Do you know how either of them work?"

"Yeah," Mirror said. "Can't do it with just shields. They're a thin membrane emitted above the ship's hull. We need something to act as a diffuser."

"Fill it," Dawn said.

Merrecci and Bria looked to Mirror and Dawn for clarification.

"Fill what," Bria asked.

Mirror's face lit as she understood.

"Fill the gap," she said. "That would do it." She turned her attention back to Merrecci. "The energy rounds can already get through. As long as shields are closed though, we can fill the shield-hull gap with something that can diffuse the energies that enter it, while at the same time conducting that energy back to our grounding rods." She stopped and thought a moment.

"And then what," Merrecci asked. "That energy has to go somewhere."

"Do we have to spell everything out," Dawn asked. "We could divert it to our own power supply. Duh!"

We have to figure out how to diffuse and direct it to the grounding rod first though," Mirror said.

"Already know how," Dawn replied. "An ionic gas cocktail."

"Have to be a very dense one," Mirror replied.

"See," Dawn said. "I'm smart too, dummies."

Mike growled, and Merrecci silenced him.

Mike held up Merrecci's signed Billy Barbus baseball.

"No," Merrecci snapped, snatching the ball. "Don't touch my— why are there teeth marks in this?"

Merrecci tucked the ball behind him in his chair.

"Could this work against other enemy weapons," Merrecci asked.

"No," Dawn blurted. "Duh again!"

"It's not the same," Mirror began to explain. "Maridamarak weapons are unique in that they—

"She said, no," Merrecci said. "I got it. You can't do it with other types of energy weapons."

"No one can," Mirror said. "Don't know if what we do will be capable of countering other Maridamarak weapons."

"All their weapons are energy weapons," Merrecci said. "Why wouldn't it work?"

"That's a good question. Maybe it could work," Dawn said, entering Bria's office bathroom. "Why is your shower so small?"

"So, we could use it to block other Maridamarak weapons," Merrecci asked.

"Small showers don't block Maridamarak weapons," Dawn shouted from the bathroom. "That's a triple duh!"

"I mean the shields," Merrecci retorted.

"Assuming, the concept could work on all their weapons, we'd probably need denser gas and more conduits over the hull to gather the power and redistribute it," Mirror said.

"Probably won't help though," Dawn called from the bathroom. "You'll probably get us killed."

"So, let's move on with Drinker's plan, and we can discuss this farther when you're not pissing me off anymore," Merrecci said.

Merrecci dismissed his engineers and Drinker and set them to investigate their idea more fully. Then, since it was almost time for his shift, he dismissed Bria. Returning to the bridge, he excused Nandy as well.

Once in the ship's hall, Nandy invited Bria to get a drink, and the captain politely declined because she had some errands to run.

"I just think it would be nice," Nandy said.

Bria finally relented and persuaded Nandy to accompany her on her errands beforehand. The first stop was to the botanical gardens where she intended to collect a small bouquet of daffodils.

Bria had set to locating a pair of clippers to cut some, but Kho intercepted her.

"Now what did we say, Captain," Kho said. "The clippers are very sharp. Here, let me help you with that."

She politely took the shears out of Bria's reach.

"And maybe after that, Captain," Nandy said. "Perhaps she can put safety bumpers around the torpedo controls for you too."

"It's fine, Commander," Bria said. "They're her gardens."

Kho agreed.

"With respect, Captain," Nandy disagreed. "Your rank isn't an honorary title that the prime admiral bestowed upon you as part of your first grade class getting a tour of the ship. They're our gardens, and she's only here because you said she could be."

"Commander," Bria cautioned.

"A snob's a snob," Nandy said. She took the clippers from Kho and handed them back to Bria. "Permission to stab the Lieutenant's eye out with these—

"Denied," Bria replied.

"You're lucky she outranks me," Nandy said to Kho.

"That's enough, Commander," Bria replied sternly.

Nandy apologized while staring down Kho without remorse.

Kho asked to be excused, and Bria went to clipping her daffodils.

"Not okay," Bria said. "She teaches me about flowers."

"She thinks she's your better," Nandy said. "I don't approve, Ma'am."

Bria clipped out four perfect, yellow, teacup heads. She returned the clippers to where she found them and thanked Kho, who was already returning to hand Bria some wet and wadded towels to wrap the daffodils stems in. Bria thanked her and escorted Nandy out of the gardens.

Next, Bria led the way to a set of quarters that few people actually would ever realize existed. It was the smallest suite on the Onyx, and they belonged to the Rhaxians who were currently folded so small that there was no sign of their vessel to the naked eye. Their room was on the lowest deck of the pyramid-shaped ship and one of the Onyx's triangular tips. With the exception of the wall that separated this apartment from the rest of the ship, The entire studio was translucent hull. After a moment of dysphoria upon entering, Nandy believed this small suite might just have the best view of space on the ship.

Bria approached a vase on a small table between a bed and a port to the shower. She drew out wilting mums and replaced them with her daffodils.

Suddenly, Coldona Garu was standing among them. While Bria seemed unfazed by the sudden appearance, Nandy startled.

"Ah," Garu said, ignoring Nandy. "Is this an Earth lily pad?"

Bria carefully explained that it was not a lily pad but made a mental note to ask Kho if there would be a possibility to get any.

He thanked Bria and Nandy, then wished them both blessings of good rest.

"How often do you do that," Nandy asked after they exited the Rhaxian's suite.

"Every day," Bria replied.

"But why?"

"Rhaxian's have never seen Earth flowers," Bria explained. "They say that Earth has the most exotic plants compared to other worlds. I tried convincing them to visit the gardens, but they are overly cautious, so I bring the flowers to them."

Their next stop was to—

Charity's door popped open. She answered, disheveled, unkempt, a bottle of some sort of booze in her hand. She threw the bottle at Bria and followed her down the hallway until Nandy finally turned and threatened to put her in the brig.

"Why did we stop there," Nandy asked.

"Make sure she was still with us," Bria answered.

"She's wrong, you know," Nandy said. "Don't let it get to you."

"You get used to it," Bria replied.

Nandy took pause, which lasted until they arrived at the hospital.

"Captain," Nurse Gibralter said. "What can we do for you, today?"

"Just here to see Lieutenant-commander Almma," Bria replied.

"It's not quite visiting hours," Gibralter said, and he stepped in to direct Bria back to the door. "And she's very sick."

"I know," Bria said. "I'm the one who shot her, remember."

"Well, that was the wrong thing to do, wasn't it," Gibralter said. "Tell you what. Come back tomorrow and maybe she'll be better. Okay? But, as I said, it's not visiting hours."

"I'm on the bridge during visiting hours," Bria said. "I'll see her now."

"Captain," Almma's voice crept from another room.

"See," the nurse said. "Now, you woke her up, Captain. Come on. Let's go." He politely put his hand on her to direct her out of the hospital.

A moment later Bria was outside the hospital, and Nandy stood with her.

"With respect, Ma'am," Nandy said. "What was that?"

"It's just how people are," Bria explained. "I'm used to it."

"Well, I'm not," Nandy replied. "This is a Franchise ship, and there's a protocol. You can't just be a badass when you're on duty. If the members of this crew could see what you do on that bridge, they'd never treat you like this."

Bria insisted that it was okay.

"Look, I know everything I do looks stupid to you, but I'm right about this," Nandy stated.

"I don't think you're stupid," Bria said. "Why would you even think that?"

"I always feel stupid around you."

"It's fine," Bria reassured. "I'll just come back later."

With that, Nandy turned back into the hospital, and Bria found herself rushing to follow.

"Captain, I thought we talked about this," the nurse said. "Do I need to call the admiral?"

"For what," Bria found herself asking. She snapped her hands behind her back to help make her appear a little taller, something she'd seen Kellick do when they'd often part ways.

"Look, I'm trying to be nice. You're probably tired after your shift, and I'm sure you'd like to be with your friends and your group," the nurse said.

"She's with a friend," Nandy said. "She's here to see another friend, Lieutenant."

The nurse straightened up.

"Her kingdom may be out there," Gibralter said. "But mine is in here."

Almma's voice came from her room once more to say, "I thought your kingdom was all that you could see from up your ass. Stop being a greedy dick and let her in!"

Gibralter held out a remote, and the door to Almma's room closed. Then he turned to measure himself up against Nandy.

"With respect," Nurse Gibralter said. "I don't care what pet project the Admiral has going on with his sister's little friends, but those fun and games end at the doors of my hospital. This is reality. We save lives in here. We don't humor them."

"Dr. Quobalt runs this hospital," Nandy corrected.

"No, she did run it," the nurse replied. "But she's not much of a doctor lately since our captain got her sister killed."

"Are you stupid," Nandy asked.

"That'll do, Commander," Bria snapped.

"Sorry, Captain," Nandy replied.

"But your point is taken." Bria turned towards Almma's room. Gibralter reached out to stop the captain.

"Assaulting a superior officer is grounds for dismissal, Lieutenant," Bria snapped.

"Hospital to Admiral Merrecci," the nurse abruptly called.

"This is Admiral Merrecci, is everything all right down there," Merrecci's voice replied.

"The captain is trying to see a patient, and now is not a good time." By now Gibralter had placed himself in Bria's path.

"So," Merrecci asked.

"So," the nurse fumbled. "This isn't a playground for the mentally impaired."

"Well, it can't be too complicated if you're down there, can it," Merrecci replied.

"Sir," Gibralter replied, insulted.

"Captain Leonard," Merrecci asked.

"Yes, Sir," Bria replied.

"Why is this person wasting the ship commander's time?"

"Because he thinks I'm an idiot, Sir," Bria said.

"I see," the admiral said. "Well, tell him you're not and let me get back to work."

"I have a better idea, Vincenti," Cindy Lou's voice suddenly blurted throughout the hospital, followed by Merrecci groaning.

Just then the main doors opened, and a line of maintenance bots came hovering in.

"Nurse Gibralter is a douche bag! A giant douche bag! A really big douche bag," about ten maintenance bots all sang in chorused harmony. They circled the foyer in a synchronized, hovering dance. They spun and each projected a copy of Nurse Gibralter's holographic face, smiling and singing, "Nurse Gibralter is a Douche bag, and he likes it all day long. Everybody!"

The robots went on to continue their song.

"Vote Nurse Gibralter for douche bag," One of the bots broke into a solo, while others encircled it and bobbed up and down like participants in an antique amusement park carousel.

Another spoke up with a full body model of Nurse Gibralter spanking himself.

"I'm nurse Gibralter," the self-slapping hologram said. "And I approve this message because—

"Nurse Gibralter is a douche bag! A giant douche bag," the robots broke back into song as they now turned and left the hospital single file, all the time singing, "A really big douche bag! Nurse Gibra—

Once the hospital doors closed and silenced the room, Bria squared up to Nurse Gibralter.

"There are only two people on board who can tell me I can't do something on my ship," Bria said. "And one of them isn't you."

She proceeded to Almma's room.

Nandy marched past the nurse while boisterously singing, "And he likes it all day long."

Almma was already raised to sitting position when Bria and Nandy entered. A curtain was pulled about halfway around her bed.

"How you holding up," Nandy asked. Bria moved to one side of Almma, Nandy slid between the other and its drawn curtain.

Almma abruptly waved her hand in Nandy's direction. "You probably don't want to stand—

The room suddenly exploded with a loud roar. Bria and Nandy both jumped, Nandy would have made it into Almma's lap, but the force field over the lower half of her bed prevented it.

"What the hell is that," Nandy asked.

Almma held the remote to the curtain, and it drew back to reveal several bouquets, holograms with well-wishers, candy, toys, and a cage with a large, brown bear in it.

It roared again.

"That's the bear my secret admirer sent me," Almma said. "There was a chocolate heart in there, but the bear ate it."

Bria shook her head. "How long are you going to let this keep going."

"He'll lose interest," Almma said. "I don't want to crush him, you know. Besides it's funny sometimes. I told you earlier that it was glitched and kept crapping on the floor."

"I'm sure that smelled wonderful," Nandy replied, stepping nearer to the cage.

The Kodiak bear peered back into Nandy's eyes and stuffed its nose up against the bars. It sniffed in loudly.

"You probably don't want to get too close," Almma said, observing Nandy drawing nearer to the cage to get a better look.

"Why? It's in a cage," Nandy replied.

"Ever hear the joke about the bear and the rabbit shitting in the woods? Turns out there's a head nurse here who didn't."

"I'm so sorry," Bria apologized. "You shouldn't be here."

"I almost wasn't," Almma replied. "But you saw to it that I am."

"It's taking a long time to heal," Bria said.

"Could have been much worse. You could have hit my baby brewer." Almma held out her hand.

"What," Bria asked.

"My crystal," Almma said. "Did you think I was reaching for a faith healing? Please tell me you didn't lose it."

"Oh," Bria realized. "They're in decontamination until tomorrow."

"Oh," Almma replied. "I was really hoping to throw it at Gibralter before then, but I suppose his beaner will have to wait."

"I'm really am sorry about shooting you," Bria said.

"Eh. Next time I'll shoot you," Almma answered. "So, what have I missed?"

To Gibralter's chagrin, after sealing the door and pointing out that he didn't have clearance to be in the room, Bria and Nandy informed Almma about Binny, to which Almma broke out laughing.

As Merrecci had done, when they informed her about the Maridamarak snipers, she immediately asked if it was possible to develop that kind of weapon themselves.

As Almma's guests eventually left her to rest, Bria informed Gibralter that he could enter her room now.

Finally, Bria's stops were done, and she was able to find a place to sit and have that drink with Nandy. It wasn't the galley, but a small cafe with five tables and a Japanese theme. Behind a shallow counter, a civilian offered to make them sushi. They accepted.

Bria liked food, was always willing to try anything. She asked the chef to surprise her, and he did with a strip of Martian eel over Pulubian rice.

Yeah. It wasn't good.

The chef apologized and promised to come up with something better next time.

Nandy had just sipped into a hot tea when a call came for Bria from the decontamination area, and it was urgent. They needed her. The captain hadn't even touched her hot cinnamon milk.

Bria excused herself, but Nandy asked if she could tag along.

"Forgive me for asking," Bria said. "But why would you want to?"

"I thought it might be nice to see each other outside of the bridge," Nandy replied.

Bria had no excuse to prevent the action, so she allowed Nandy's request.

Decontamination was a bit of a trek. It was on the lowest deck, nowhere near as close to the Rhaxian quarters as Nandy had thought it would be. It was nearer a great view of the engines and their black glow.

"Captain," Crewman Fram welcomed. She was short, portly, and typically on the unapproachable side, but not for the usual reasons. Like many people in Merrecci's crew, based upon having to turn to the academy for many of the positions, Fram was young. Today she seemed enthusiastic as Bria's entrance interrupted whatever had held the crewman's interest beneath her microscope "Ha! Wait until you see this." Fram stood from her chair so quickly that she almost stumbled from it before offering it to the captain. "Look. Look."

Bria felt herself almost forced down into the seat. She pressed her face against the microscope eye-pieces, perhaps not entirely voluntarily.

"See it," Fram asked. "See? See?"

Bria saw something purple, but she wasn't sure what.

"Huh? Huh," Fram asked as if requiring approval.

"It's quite—here, Commander, take a look," Bria said.

Caught as off guard as Bria had been, Nandy found herself trading herself into the chair much the same way Bria had done with Crewman Fram.

"Can you even contemplate what this means," Fram asked.

"Um," Nandy said, seeing only translucent purple. "I can honestly say, I don't."

"It's like a game changer or something," Fram said. "It's beyond awesome."

"I'm sorry," Nandy said pulling up. "All I see is purple."

Fram seemed taken back.

"Well, you saw it, right," Fram asked, turning to Bria.

Bria apologized, and she knew that if she had a working face that Fram would see that she was actually genuine.

"Well, but you have to," Fram pled. She looked back against the eye-pieces herself then pulled back confused. "You don't see it?"

"I'm really sorry, Crewman," Bria replied. "Chemistry wasn't really my study."

"Oh," Fram relented and looked as though she'd had her holiday taken from her.

Then, she lit up. "I have it!" She clapped her hands together, and a screen appeared on the wall with an image of what was currently on the microscope slide. Fram shoved a prod of some sort with a needle on the end, and the purple blob broke into an animation of ripples. From within, the purple separated in several places. Fram continued to shake the microscope, and, where the blob separated, several small fingers stretched out and wove into each other, tying its structure back together. Crewman Fram continued to apply the prod, turning up the power, but the tears didn't return.

"Cool, right," Fram blurted.

"What does it mean," Nandy asked. "Is that not normal or something."

"Not norm—no," Fram bellowed incredulously. "It's anomalous. Earth has never seen anything like this." She watched Bria and Nandy as if something should be sinking in that wasn't. "You've discovered a new element! The molecules even have a type of bond no one's ever recorded—well, as far as we can tell. Do you know how often that happens? Like never, even among other planets." Suddenly, she turned to one of three Petri dishes filled with the purple goop. She took up one of the saucers. "Look!"

Now, she pulled. At first the purple substance stretched like taffy, but then it stopped and held its form as though it were a hard clay. She let go of one side, and the form pulled back into a blob in her hand. Then she threw it against the wall where it bounced back, and then she caught it.

"So, it's rubber," Nandy said.

"It's not—" and she sighed then gathered herself. "It's not rubber. Rubber can't do this." Again, she stretched it a little bit until it hardened as before, and she dropped it on the floor. It bounced, and Fram spent a few efforts catching it, but Bria caught it and felt it instantly begin to soften into a doughy type substance. She poked it, and it hardened leaving the imprint of her finger.

"Is it corn starch," Nandy asked.

"It's not—uh," Fram groaned. "Corn starch doesn't bounce."

"Oh," Nandy said. "Okay."

"And," Fram said tearing the substance from Bria's hand, surprising her.

Nandy couldn't help but show that she was entertained, and Bria silently agreed.

Fram set the blob on the lab table then took off her shoe.

"This is the really cool part," Fram said.

Then she slammed the heel against the goo. The shoe popped up from her hand and struck the ceiling. The blob maintained its spill-like shape and appeared unfazed by the sudden strike.

Fram broke into laughter.

"And that was inside one of my crystals," Bria asked.

"It is the crystal," Fram said. "You wouldn't know it being on that frozen planet, but once it warmed up, which took about ten hours, it became this."

"All those crystals are this," Bria asked.

"Yes," Fram replied. "And if we can find something to mix it with, we could keep it from freezing if we wanted, which we don't know how long it would take anyway. The samples we put in the freezer haven't changed in three hours so far. We could dilute it!"

"How cold was this when I brought it to you," Bria asked.

"Minus 230 degrees," Fram said, then clarified, "Celsius. The planet was minus 245."

"So, if you could find a way, could you spray this on our armored suits," Nandy asked, politely holding her hand out for Fram to hand her the substance so she could inspect it further.

"Well, you'd have the risk of bouncing all over the place if you ever got punched, but yeah," Fram replied. "You could probably take that same suit and fall to a planet's surface from orbit without a parachute and not break a single bone, provided this stuff doesn't burn under extensive heat."

"Sure. If you survived the impact that turned your brain into a splash factory," Bria said.

"Well, yeah," Fram agreed. "But cool, huh?"

Bria nodded.

"It is," Nandy replied. "Merrecci's going to love this stuff."

"Who have you told about this," Bria asked.

"No one, really," Fram said. "Just one of my bunkies. She hasn't seen what you've seen, just told her my theories mostly."

"When," Bria asked.

"Before her shift ended," Fram replied.

"Where is she now?"

"Probably asleep," Fram said.

Bria immediately contacted Fram's roommate, a Crewman Tess Jossel, and requested that she report to the decontamination office immediately.

"You are to speak to no one, and make no stops," Bria instructed.

Crewman Jossel did just that, though she didn't appear too pleased upon her arrival, but she wasn't going to argue with a Captain. Jossel, like Fram, was also a chemist, but she specialized more in fabrication than chemical analysis as Fram did. Jossel was currently a general lab technician. Bria immediately reassigned Jossel to the decontamination lab.

"I'm raising the status of this research to classified, black-level," Bria said.

"Do you know what that means," Nandy asked.

"I think so," Fram replied.

"It means that if either of you divulge any of this information to any living soul without clearance, you will be charged with treason. You'll get a trial, but you will have already lost."

Fram and Jossel were quiet. Fram's demeanor had melted.

"The only people who enter this lab are you and those with black-level clearance," Bria explained.

"What about the other shift workers who need to come in here," Fram asked.

"No one comes in here without clearance," Bria ordered. "They'll have to go somewhere else."

"Our department head's not going to like that," Fram said.

"What does your department head currently know about this," Bria asked.

"He said it was a waste of time," Jossel said. "That's why he gave the project to us."

"Oh, did he now," Nandy asked.

"Well, now you're the department co-heads of our new top secret research and development department," Bria said. "Does that sound right to you, Commander?"

"Hey, if their boss didn't want to do the job," Nandy said.

"It means you just became our research and development team," Bria said. "And you will report directly to Admiral Merrecci, myself or commander Nandy."

"Congratulations," Nandy said. "You've just booked yourselves each a lifetime of prestige and giving lectures."

Bria then urged Fram and Jossel to do whatever they thought they must to protect the research as they prepared their new expanded department. After documenting the changes with Onyx, Bria and Nandy were just leaving when Fram spoke again.

"What would you like us to call this, Ma'am," Fram asked.

Bria and Nandy shared a look and shrugged.

"You found it," Fram explained. "You get to name it."

"Oh," Bria realized, then answered quickly with "Should have something with Almma's name in it since she paid the most for it."

Nandy agreed.

"Almmacite," Bria said, but seemed to be seeking approval.

"Oh, better yet, Ammlanumium," Nandy burst tripping over her pronunciation.

"That's not even her name," Bria said.

"Almmaminum," Nandy tried again.

"Oh yeah, that," Bria said. "Almmanamium."

"Almmaminum," Nandy corrected after having to repeat it herself three times to get it right again.

"Almmaminum," Fram asked. "You want to call it Almmaminum?"

"Oh, yeah," Bria crowed. "That'll really piss off the scientists, won't it?"

"It's like the best revenge on every chemistry teacher ever," Nandy said. "Yeah! Screw you, Dr. Ponpoint. Here's to failing me three times, you jerk. Chemistry sucks!" Then she caught herself among her two chemists. "Well not for everyone, obviously."

"So, this is about your revenge, not Almma's," Bria asked.

"Oh, trust me," Nandy said. "Almma has a chemistry teacher she hates too.

"Ponpoint was pretty bad," Jossel said.

"Think of all the arguments he'll have with students after quizzes," Nandy said. "And times he'll stumble in lecture and look dumb."

"That is kind of funny, huh," Fram added.

"Are you kidding," Nandy said. "There's nothing funnier than that."

Just now, the doors opened, and a maintenance bot strolled into the room, "Nurse Gibralter is a douche bag."

It mixed in a recording of a familiar previous conversation.

"This isn't a playground for the mentally impaired," holo Nurse Gibralter whined, still spanking himself.

"Well, it can't be too complicated if you're down there, can it," Merrecci replied, suddenly appearing in the hologram and spanking Gibralter's backside.

"I'm nurse Gibralter, and I approve—

"Who's your big, prime daddy," Holo Merrecci asked.

"I approve this message," Gibralter finished.

Then a hologram of Bria's head appeared on top of the robot, and she began singing, "And he likes it all day long!"

"You're in a classified area," Bria announced.

The bot turned and left instantly, stating that it was deleting the last thirty seconds of data.

"That is not going to go over well with the prime admiral at all," Nandy said.

As they entered the halls once more, Bria informed Nandy that she had an appointment with Kellick. Again, Nandy asked if it would be all right if she joined. Bria wasn't sure how she felt about it, having someone who wanted to actually go where she went, and this was her private time. Along the way, Nandy asked about the game they played, and Bria had gotten as far as explaining how to run the board when they entered the galley.

The room was full, except for the table where Kellick waited, and no one dared take any seats around him. Upon her entry, the crew members suddenly stood and started singing, "Nurse Gibralter is a douche bag! A giant douche bag!"

Bria crossed the room to Kellick, feeling herself cheered on and pat on the back. A few tables offered to buy her a drink.

"Pleased with yourself, Captain," Kellick asked.

"I don't understand what happened," Bria said. "I'll stop this now."

Kellick grabbed her hand and pulled her back.

"Are you kidding," Kellick said. "You can't buy morale-boosting like this. Let it get out of hand a few more days and then go squash it after everyone's had their fun and let Gibralter see you."

"But they hate me," Bria said.

"I think they hate Gibralter more," Nandy replied.

"You just found you share some common ground with your crew," Kellick said. "But you're the one who put him in his place."

"I didn't do this," Bria said. "Cindy did."

Kellick shrugged. "They don't know that. Use it."

Bria smiled and accepted the advice.

"But later, give him a really good apology that he can respect," Kellick added more as a friendly order.

Just then, Willis appeared standing over Bria's side. He, of course, was smiling as he leaned down and hugged Bria.

She thanked him, and he stayed to continue watching the game.

Following the matches with Kellick, in which he won two of three, Bria and Nandy returned to the bridge to inform Merrecci about the discussion with the decontamination crew. He had been deep in conversation with Prilla but stopped.

"I heard," Merrecci responded. "I would have liked to have heard it from my captain before one of my department heads called in ranting. Good decision though. Smart. Always good to keep any new technology hidden from the hands that might taint or give away potential uses."

"I wish I could say that's why I did it," Bria said. "I thought if we had new, protected, black-level sector files in the system, it might tempt our spy to sneak a peak, and we'll have it on record."

"You set a trap," Merrecci observed.

"It just came to me," Bria said. "I'm not smart."

"I see," Merrecci replied. "Smart. Keep at it. Now, if you two will excuse me. I'd like to finish my conversation here."

Bria politely began to remove herself from the admiral's office.

"And Captain," Merrecci said. "You smell like booze. I expect you to conduct yourself a little more professionally when you're in that uniform."

"Attention crew," Cindy Lou's voice announced. "The votes are in. Your voice has been heard. Nurse Gibralter is officially a douche bag."

"Damn," Merrecci said. "I voted for Fiji."

"I voted for you," Prilla said.

To cover his insult, he excused Bria and Nandy.

"I'm sorry," Nandy said as she accompanied Bria back to the bridge. "I meant to say something after we left Charity's."

Bria pardoned the oversight, and the two finally parted ways. Nandy suggested she would go visit a particular department head to let him know he might want to pay closer attention to captain requests in the future. Bria turned to her quarters to freshen up.

Afterwards, she finally started to make her way to visit with Cindy Lou. She had tried to be polite about Nandy following her around earlier, but her visits with Cindy weren't something she was ready to share. No one needed to see her dive into Cindy Lou's for her daily anxiety attack and dose of the god.

She was just out of the elevator when a figure ran from an adjoining hallway and then away from her, all without giving notice that Bria was there.

At once, Bria recognized him. It was the Didjian Trilale, free from the brig. She yelled after him.

The Didjian turned, drew a baton, and aimed it upon Bria. Bria's baton snapped into her palm. By the time she had dodged his attack and regained her footing, the figure was gone into another hall, all without any further confrontation.

Bria began to transmit what she had just seen to security. One thought went to getting to Cindy Lou as she imagined that might be where the Didjian was attempting to reach. However, she also quickly noticed the lack of brig personnel pursuing the fugitive and assumed bad reasons. Bria ran for the brig and announced orders for others to locate the Didjian trilale.

She wasn't quite to the prison when another figure appeared. This one was hooded but dressed in full Franchise uniform. He was just stepping out of the jail when the captain spotted him. The moment he saw her, he ducked back inside, and Bria pursued.

Upon entering the jail, she found two security guards motionless on the floor.

Bria quickly knelt and checked the guard. Dead. The other too.

Two prisoners from a brawl a few hours ago were the only residents being currently held in cells. They were pointing up.

Bria stepped back and watched the figure leap out from the railing of the second floor of cells, then launch himself to the third-level railing. By the time he did it again, Bria was in the elevating platform rising after him.

"Attention security," Bria announced, "I have two dead guards in the brig, and another perpetrator in sight."

She called the admiral with the same news.

According to protocol, she knew that the bridge was now being locked down.

"Can you confirm an identity," Merrecci asked.

"Working on it," Bria replied as the person she chased leapt up one more level.

Bria's elevator reached the top tier of cells a moment before the figure climbed onto it himself and ran down the walkway with a railing to his right and prisoner cells to his left.

Bria drew her baton and fired, but it missed and shook the railing instead.

"I can't get a good look," Bria announced, confident in calling that much information out. She took aim again.

The perpetrator climbed on the railing and launched himself to the ceiling. Bria expected to see the person fall. Instead, whoever it was laced his fingers into the grating of an overhead vent, fully catching their weight.

Bria approached, holding the person in her aim.

"Just hold on," Bria ordered. She could have shot the person. She could have waited for him? Her? Waited for them to lose their grip and fall the forty-five feet to the ground floor of the brig. The villain might have survived, but certainly not without injury. "Let me get something to help you down."

The hooded figure unlocked the vent and climbed in, all while Bria sat weighing whether she should shoot the person or not. She decided the prime admiral would want the culprit alive. If she stunned him, the violator would die from the fall most likely. If she let the person escape, they'd have to come out of the ventilation at some point, and security could be waiting.

"Prime Admiral," Bria called, returning to the elevating platform. "You're not going to believe this. Whoever it was just alley-ooped into the ceiling vent in the brig."

"You don't seriously expect me to believe that, do you," Merrecci's voice replied.

"That's what happened," Bria replied. "We need to find out where that vent comes out and post guards."

"Attention all hands," Merrecci's voice rang out. "Code Capone! Repeat, Code Capone!"

Bria summoned her holotab. Code Capone was an order for crew members to read their individual tablets for specific contingency instructions from the ship's commanding officer.

Her holotab was blank though.

"Sir," Bria said. "I think my tablet's malfunctioning."

"Captain Leonard," Cindy Lou's voice spoke now.

"Not a good time," Bria replied.

"You need to get over here right now," Cindy replied.

"Not a good time," Bria asked.

"Just do it," Cindy replied.

"Are you in danger," Bria asked.

"Yes," Cindy Lou blurted. "Yes! I'm in danger. Now, run!"

Bria did. She charged down the hallway to Cindy's quarantine. Alarms now began blaring from the halls.

She was joined by a group of security staff, fresh off of the elevator, who quickly followed after.

"Captain," one called.

"Follow the ceiling vent from the brig," Bria ordered. "I have something else I have to do."

They kept calling after her, and she kept yelling back to follow her orders. As she approached the disintegration shield, the sound of a baton blast filled the hallway. She felt it in her back. It was hard and powerful enough that it sent her toppling forward.

Leonard could still move. She was stunned, just slow now. The humming of the disintegration shield was only two feet at most from her. Cindy Lou stood poised at a console in the hallway. The residual energy of the blast surged through her limbs. It was the lowest setting, aimed to inflict pain. A quick glance showed three security officers advancing on her with their batons aimed.

"We have her," the lead said.

Bria's baton blasted, and this officer fell. She blasted again, and a second repeated the result. The third fired his baton now. The blast struck Bria's leg. This time, she fell and couldn't bring herself to move. Numbness flooded most of her body. She could no longer feel the baton in her hands, nor the floor against the side of her face. The security officer took aim again and stepped towards Bria, not even warning that he'd shoot. Suddenly, he fired, but the familiar sensation of the disintegration shield extended just then over Bria and stopped right before the attacker. His stun blast immediately reflected right back at him, and he dropped to the floor.

"Are you all right," Cindy inquired.

"What's going on," Bria asked back. "Are we under a mutiny?"

"No," Cindy said. "It's worse."

Admiral Merrecci now appeared in the hallway, Prilla was at his heels, her own baton drawn. The alarm silenced, the hall lights turned back to normal.

"This doesn't feel right," Prilla said.

"Sir," Bria asked. "What's going on? The guards just attacked me." The captain tried to stand and had to settle for propping herself against the wall.

Merrecci and Prilla passed through the disintegration shield. Merrecci stopped, but he still used what momentum he maintained to backhand Bria's face with his baton.

She fell back to the floor and thought she had the strength to hold herself up, her arms, however, gave and fell flat. It lasted a moment before she felt the blood return to her brain, but then Merrecci struck her again.

"Don't you touch her," Cindy Lou demanded.

"You back off or I'll transfer you right into space," Merrecci yelled. "This is not your concern."

"This whole ship is my concern," Cindy hissed.

"Sir," Bria questioned.

Merrecci kicked her stomach.

She couldn't breathe. She tried to find aid by folding forward. It didn't help.

"You can't interrogate her if she's dead," Prilla shrieked.

Bria could feel her lungs working again, but just barely.

She felt herself being stood up under Merrecci's grasp.

"Sir," she thought she'd said, but couldn't tell through the surging concussion rampaging through her brain and throwing shadow over her eyes. She found her face drawn up to Merrecci's. She watched his eyes fill with wet red.

"It was you," Merrecci yelled. "After all I've done for you?"

She started crying that she was sorry, but then Merrecci struck her again, this time with his fist coiled around his baton.

"How stupid am I," Merrecci railed, suddenly slamming her against the wall. "To be duped by an ugly, retarded—

Bria fell limp and slid from Merrecci's grasp. It wasn't a tactic nor a choice, her body just stopped listening to what her brain said it should be doing. The floor could have swallowed her away into oblivion, and she'd be ready to stay there until death calmed her, which may have been at any moment.

"You're done," Cindy's voice bellowed.

Merrecci didn't seem to hear her. He hefted Bria back to her feet, shaking her, screaming at her, and then slamming her back once more. Her head filled with more black as the backside of it cracked against the wall.

"You're killing her," Prilla bellowed and pulled at his hands, but she was weaker than his anger. She slapped him but knew he didn't feel it.

"You coward," Cindy erupted with such force in her voice that Merrecci felt her breath cause him to have to regain his balance.

As he recovered, he realized what his hands were doing. They were strangling Bria. He wasn't even sure how they'd gotten to her neck, but they were there. They should strangle her, and Prilla's fingertips had stopped attempting to cut them away. She was slapping him now and screaming something in his face, but he wasn't sure what it was exactly. Something in Bria's neck cracked. Then Cindy yelled at Merrecci again.

Nandy now ran through the shield, baton drawn, her breath short and shallow. Sweat drenching her thin, off-duty clothing.

"Sorry it took me so long, Sir," Nandy said.

Merrecci dropped Bria, and she fell.

Once on the floor, Cindy was at her side. Nandy kept her baton drawn on Bria. After a moment, Bria's eyes focused on Cindy. Then she tucked her knees into her chest and buried her head beneath her elbows so no one could hit it again.

"Bria Leonard," Merrecci said. "You are relieved of command and under arrest for treason."

14
▲
Hands

"You lay one more hand on her, I'll retract the disintegration shields, and I promise they will not recognize you when they do," Cindy said.

"You forget whose ship this is," Merrecci retorted.

"I have not," Cindy said, and she now stood away from Bria. "Put her in the brig if you have evidence to believe she is the spy. Put her on trial. Betray her if you must, but touch her again, and I will kill you, Vincenti Merrecci."

Merrecci was silent. The only sound in the hall was that of Bria's short drowning breaths from within her fetal-like position, and the energy of the deadly shield.

After a stare-down with the god who Merrecci realized was going to win, he finally spoke, "I think it's time we find out if our brig can hold a god."

Cindy approached Merrecci, then flicked a finger into his chest.

It felt like a wrecking ball; all the wind fled from his lungs. He struggled a moment before he caught his breath.

"Don't test my docility," Cindy Lou said.

"Why would you help her," Merrecci finally croaked.

"Why aren't you," Cindy asked. Her eye turned on Prilla and she repeated the question.

"How dare you," Merrecci seethed.

"If you don't give her the benefit of your own laws, you'll see how much I dare," Cindy retorted. "As a god to such a short-lived race as yours, I'm bound by scruples to let you learn and evolve from your mistakes."

"Then stay out of my way," Merrecci scowled, and he reached to Bria, but suddenly felt another finger to his chest.

"But as her friend, if you touch her again, you will die," Cindy Lou reiterated.

"You are interfering with my ship," Merrecci roared.

"And how much longer you get to be concerned about that is entirely up to you," Cindy said.

Merrecci heeded the strange chill in his brain that told him not to respond. He instructed Nandy to bring Bria to her feet and cuff her. Nandy approached Bria cautiously, and Cindy allowed it.

"Law is one thing," Cindy said. "You running amok on an innocent person is another."

"Well, until I come to that realization, she'll get as any other criminal," Merrecci said.

"Before or after you kill her," Cindy said. Then she yelled, "Look at her!"

The Onyx rumbled beneath Merrecci's feet.

Merrecci wouldn't look at Bria Leonard. He didn't care that her eyes weren't focusing, nor that she couldn't stop sobbing, nor how she might be injured. He simply didn't care.

"Should have never put her in charge to begin with," Merrecci said. "You don't put the dummies in the same class. She'll have a trial. Until then, she gets a cage."

"When will she get a trial," Cindy asked.

"When we return to Earth," Merrecci said. "Don't interfere again." He turned with Bria to leave and suddenly stopped to order Cindy to clear them all to step through the disintegration shield.

"I expected better when I chose you," Cindy Lou stated.

Merrecci ignored her babbling nonsense and ordered Cindy to allow the shields to recognize himself and Nandy. He just knew he shouldn't pass through this time until he heard Cindy clear him.

Finally, he believed her and crossed.

They passed through the disintegration barrier and began towards the brig, Nandy marching behind Bria and Merrecci now leading the way with Prilla chiding him as they walked. Bria tried to control her sobs but watched crew and personnel line the halls to view the dishonored captain. None of them saw her. She twisted her wrist and felt the steel of the razor blade that lined the inside of her uniform sleeve. Maybe it was time to take Charity's advice. Perhaps the only friend that truly understood her was this slim piece of steel after all. They'd talk later. They were almost to the brig when the ship's alarm began ringing again. The hall lights turned green to raise alarm that the ship or a portion thereof was filling with poisonous gas.

"Admiral," Kellick's voice coughed out. It was an unfamiliar tone, but it was him. "The designated diplomatic section is under attack. We're sealed in."

"What did you do," Merrecci snapped. He grabbed Bria's collar with one hand and drove her back once again into the wall. His other hand held his baton into her face and engaged the kill option. He remembered Cindy's words, and he didn't care.

"Sir," Nandy interrupted in a shout.

"Turn that off," Prilla screamed. She drew her baton on her brother and instantly found it smacked out of her hand by his rage.

"Report, Admiral," Merrecci said, returning the firing end of his baton onto his former captain.

"It's Diantine gas," Kellick said. "It's already started. Probably have five minutes."

Suddenly, Merrecci felt his hold break. He was stripped of his baton. Bria struck the back of his knee, and Merrecci was falling. Prilla too fell as Bria fired a stun shot into her leg.

Merrecci caught enough of a glimpse to see Bria and Nandy break into a duel of batons, Bria clearly in control. There was something about her attack though, aggressive. Then there was her style, even while cuffed, she was holding back. Nandy was the superior fighter, and yet he could see that Bria wasn't using any of the potentially-deadly openings that her opponent kept presenting. It wasn't because the former captain was stupid. Bria knew what she was doing. She disarmed Nandy, then fired off Merrecci's baton and stunned her then Merrecci, even as he was attempting to maneuver himself for a tackling lunge.

The admiral could only watch her speed down the hall and disappear. When he was finally able to stand, other crew members were already aiding Prilla and Nandy who were both grabbing at sore appendages in bewilderment. Merrecci ran, or ran as his stunned body would allow, slow, sticky with his brain yelling, "You can't run fast after this kind of attack, you moron."

He passed other crew members who had also been paralyzed in Bria's flight.

When he reached the elevator, Prilla had joined him in his wait. A moment later and Nandy was there.

"What just happened," Nandy snapped.

She tried to hide the blood filling the cracks of her clenched fingers.

"Are you injured," Prilla asked.

"She cut me," Nandy replied, finding several small slices over her hands intended to get her to drop her weapon during her and Bria's brawl. "Nothing big. It will heal."

"You need to refine your technique," Merrecci suggested.

"Lasted longer than you, Sir," Nandy said.

It took a moment for Merrecci to realize that his arms were bleeding. That's what caused him to break his grip on Leonard. She'd cut him.

Then he sensed his brain finally recalling how to retaliate against an escaped prisoner. He called an order throughout the ship to shoot Bria on site and called the engineering team to start working on helping the diplomatic sector.

"Where would she go," Nandy asked.

"Not far," Merrecci deduced. "Even if she gets off the ship, she can't go anywhere that we won't snatch her back up."

The elevator arrived. Merrecci, Prilla and Nandy moved inside.

"Are you familiar with Diantine gas," Merrecci asked.

"No, Sir," Nandy replied. "Chemistry isn't my suit."

"Diantine gas burns biologicals layer by layer. Twenty minutes and the skin is gone, but that won't be what you think about because you're also inhaling it. It takes ten minutes to eat the lungs," Merrecci said. "It's one of the deadliest cocktail of gases. If she was mixing it on this ship, she really is good. The wrong jostle in the culling stage and we'd all be drowning in our own blood."

At that realization, Merrecci ordered all doors to deny Bria access through them.

The elevator opened, and Merrecci started out.

"Not you, Commander," he said. "Go to medical." He ordered Prilla to do the same.

"She's my patient," Prilla said. "And you're being a dink."

Merrecci and Prilla exited.

"Are you sure this is chemistry," Prilla asked as they moved down the hall together.

"Isn't that what I just said," Merrecci answered.

"You know chemistry," Prilla asked.

"I had to repeat the class," he replied, trying now to camouflage his huffing with sharper and less controlled words.

"Vincent," Prilla said. "Bria doesn't have that proficiency."

Merrecci felt himself stop just now.

"Says who," Merrecci asked.

"Um," Prilla answered. "I can't say."

"If you know something, say it now," Merrecci snapped.

"I've counseled her for years for test anxiety," Prilla replied in a whisper, looking carefully for any other people who might hear what she was actually telling Merrecci. "She failed Intro to Chemistry twice. Look at her school record."

Merrecci didn't hear the rest because he was suddenly running.

When he arrived at the sector of the ship that he had turned over to Kellick for his staff use, he found the hall sealed with doors, not shields. A medical crew was still in the process of dressing up in white coveralls, but then Merrecci realized they weren't getting dressed. They were recovering from being stunned.

"What happened," he asked.

"She went into the cooling system," one said.

"You let her escape," Merrecci cried.

"No, Sir," the medical tech replied. "She'll freeze in three minutes."

"She's probably going to use it to vacuum the gas out of the ship," Mirror's voice came from behind Merrecci, she had been the first engineer to respond to the incident, and the only person in the vicinity that Bria hadn't stunned.

"As long as any gas stays in the cooling system, it will stay in there frozen until we can purge it somewhere safely," Mirror explained. "It only affects biological tissue, so shouldn't be a problem to the ship if it remains in the coolant ducts. A strong enough flush could suck the Diantine from the lungs of the poisoned. They'll feel like they're drowning though."

"How would she get it in there," Merrecci asked.

"It's a vacuum in there, Sir," one of the medical crew said. "Nearly sucked us in when she entered it."

"What about her," Prilla asked. "What about Captain Leonard?"

"She's dead," Mirror replied plainly. "No human can survive in that cold temperature, and if she brings in the gas, then that will be in there with her too. She's not coming out. Well, unless she's got a different idea. Either way. Congratulations. You killed the only person on this ship who cared what you thought about her."

Just then, the Onyx groaned, the alarm silenced, and the halls turned from green to simulated daylight.

The hall opened to the diplomatic sector. Merrecci used the opportunity to flee the conversation. He and the other crew who followed him began to quickly examine each of the rooms. When he arrived at Kellick's quarters, he found the admiral sitting on the edge of his bed trying to catch a breath he just couldn't seem to take in deeply enough.

"You did it," Kellick coughed. He wiped blood from his lips. "Thank you."

"What happened," Merrecci asked.

"Spinner, there, recognized the scent," Kellick said, pointing to one of his own staff, a young woman coughing blood in a corner.

"No," Merrecci said. "What stopped it?"

"Just what you wanted. The vents opened, and all the gas left us," Kellick answered. Then he appeared puzzled, but too out of breath to show much of it. "You didn't know?"

"Merrecci to Leonard," he called.

No response.

"Captain Leonard," he called. "Bria?"

"What's the matter," Kellick asked.

"She's in the cooling system," Prilla replied as she was now engaged in examining the admiral's vitals to help lighten the medical team's load at the moment with all the other injured. "That's how she got the gas out."

"She's in there with the gas," Kellick asked. Then suddenly he was calling for her.

"Are you okay, Kellick, Sir," her voice responded through an obviously heavy shiver. Then she coughed.

"I'm fine, thanks to you," Kellick said. "Where are you?"

"I'm not sure," she said. "I came down the—um, this way. I'm not quite—can't seem to—sir, are you okay?"

"I'm fine," Kellick replied again. "Can you see anything to tell us how to find you?"

She didn't answer.

"Captain," Merrecci called.

Still no answer.

"Please," Merrecci said. "Don't you dare give up!"

No answer.

"Answer me," he yelled.

"Leonard," Kellick asked. "What's wrong?"

"I can't—I think my hands are froze," Bria replied, her voice drawing weaker.

"What do you mean," he asked.

The sound of the turbulence flowing through the cooling system was the only noise now that flooded the room.

"Stuck," her voice came back softly.

Then her communicator gave out to the cold rush of turbulence on her end. Soon, both admirals and Prilla were taking turns calling after her, but there was no response.

Then, "Admiral," a voice called from down the hall.

Merrecci ran, truly ran.

Two of Kellick's staff and a medical crew member were huddled near a medbot that was currently scanning a body laid upon its side. Its flesh was black and white crystals accumulated over it. Mostly, he noticed it was larger. What used to be a loose fitting uniform appeared tight. Merrecci knew her even though she was unrecognizable.

"Report," he ordered.

"The medbot came out of the vent," a man from Kellick's staff said. "It towed your captain out."

Merrecci pushed one of the men to the side to allow the prime admiral space to kneel over Bria. He saw the damage at once.

"What happened to her hands," Merrecci asked, finding that both of her arms ended just below the wrists, her hands broken off.

Her eyes were sealed shut, squinting to keep from freezing what was beneath them.

Merrecci reached down to her. "Leonard."

"Don't touch me," Bria's voice crept up through unmoving and swollen lips as Merrecci laid his hands on her frozen shoulder—to do what, he didn't know.

But he ignored her and was now carrying Bria to the nearest hospital. He refused to hear the other medical staff yelling after him that he couldn't run with her petrified body.

He ran anyway.

He called for Charity to report to the hospital closest to his position. She argued. He didn't care. He threatened to dump Dr. Quobalt in an escape pod. She arrived at the hospital only minutes after Merrecci, and immediately scolded him for running through the hallways with a body so frozen that if he'd tripped, he might have shattered her beyond repair.

Then Charity gave herself an injection to counter the effects of alcohol in her system, and then she went to work.

When she finished fourteen hours later, she retreated to her darkened medical office and fell back onto a cot.

"Could you do it," Merrecci asked from where he had slumped down into a black corner where he was turning a baseball signed by Connie Mack over in his hands. He familiarized himself once again with the threads of the last birthday present his father gave him.

Charity jumped. "Don't do that!"

"Could you do it," Merrecci asked again.

She shook her head.

"I don't know," she answered. "I don't think so. I don't even know if her body will accept her new eyes. I had to install holo stimulators in their cores. I don't know how the brain will take to them, or if they will."

"And her hands," Merrecci asked.

Charity winced and shrugged. "I don't know."

"You have to give her hands back," Merrecci said.

"The best we can do right now is see, and maybe therapy—

"She needs her hands," Merrecci yelled.

"I'm sorry," Charity replied, her voice soft towards Merrecci.

"What kind of an idiot first officer gives up her hands," Merrecci scowled. "How will they all treat her when she doesn't have hands too."

"You underestimate how strong she is," Charity said.

"She disarmed us with that razor blade," Merrecci yelled.

Charity ordered the door to her office closed and the privacy feature of the windows activated.

"Did you see how fast her hands moved?" Merrecci asked. "The only reason we survived escaping Earth's space was because of her hands."

"They might be fast again," Charity said.

"How," Merrecci whispered then exploded with "I took them! How can they be fast again when I took them?"

"What happened," Charity asked.

Merrecci didn't answer, found he couldn't.

He felt her hands on his, and then she was kneeling to his eye-level, looking at him like she never had before.

"What happened," Charity asked again.

"Honestly," Merrecci said. "I don't know."

"Yeah. You accused her of being the spy," Charity said, not too warmly.

"I hit her," Merrecci said.

Charity recoiled, then sat back on her knees. "What the hell is wrong with you? Do you have any idea the kind of crap this crew has heaped on her? That I—she cut you with her razor blade?"

Merrecci nodded.

"All I could think of was how she had duped me, and I didn't just hit her," he said. "And I said worse. I wanted to kill her. I would have."

"Well, you know what," Charity said. "You did! God!" She fumbled back to her feet.

"You have to save her hands," Merrecci said.

"Oh, I have to, huh," Charity asked. "Do you have any idea how much she looked up to you? Probably the only person on this ship that did!"

"I'm hearing that a lot," Merrecci said.

"You don't know what it's like to have your identity stripped from you. To have it cut off of your body and just thrown in the incinerator like some useless wart," Charity was now screaming. "And I blamed her! I told her to use the thing! Nine minutes!"

"What's that," Merrecci asked.

"Nine minutes is the average time that passes from when a person decides to kill themselves and when they actually do it. She'd have done it right this try too because I told her to."

"She didn't use it on herself," Merrecci said.

"She didn't have to. She climbed into the cooling system."

Charity fell silent now.

"What did we do to her," Charity asked.

"We took her hands," Merrecci replied.

Charity let herself drop onto the floor next to him, and they propped themselves up on each other. She recoiled at first. It was supposed to be Cora there, but now it was Merrecci. Still, it was someone. She let her shoulder prop against his once again, and then she pulled him to kiss her. Her tears flowed again. How? There should be none left. They fell to her cheek, to her nose, to her lips. They mixed with Merrecci's, and somehow, together, they found a solace in mingling in each other's guilt.

She slowly pulled away when a thought crossed her mind and caused her to ask, "What made you think she was the spy?"

"What? Oh. We traced messages that went out from her office and mine, and that they happened with a command crew's prerogative security bypass and encryption options," Merrecci said.

"It couldn't be that Fiji prick?"

"We checked. He was accounted for," Merrecci explained.

"And you're sure it has to be her?"

"It was more than that," Merrecci said. "I didn't put it all together at first, but—are you familiar with the shadow track at the academy?"

"I'm not academy," Charity replied.

"There's a track, you don't apply for it. You're invited. It requires years of study in addition to the regular academy program. It's very secret and a myth as far as students and professors go. Teachers don't even know they're teaching it sometimes," Merrecci explained.

"I don't understand."

"It's a secret and intensive program," Merrecci continued. "It takes longer than a regular degree. Its students are active agents the moment they start learning. Upon graduation they report to regular duties, but they have anonymous handlers and one secret superior officer who might as well be an admiral. I'm still trying to track down who it is right now. Their command structure allows the agents to carry out secret missions under their own staff and crew's notice, including the ship's commander. Because the time investment might tip off others to who might be in this program, some students will pretend to switch majors to make their extended time at the academy appear more reasonable. Some will fail classes on purpose to have to retake them when they're really just getting classified curriculum instead. They know how to hide. No one would give someone with special needs a second thought for taking a long time to graduate, and Bria has taken a long time. She very well could be one of the most highly trained Franchise assassins, and we wouldn't know."

"You don't truly believe that about her, do you," Charity asked.

"Years ago, no. I thought the whole Shadow Force was a myth too until during my Kag'tak encounter, one of my crew revealed himself, and I had to report to his superiors. He covered his tracks in justifying how long he stayed in the academy by pretending to be undecided in his studies. See, the transcripts are coded. They have classes that, on paper, appear normal to the common person, but they're really about survival and infiltration," Merrecci explained.

"Even so, why would she turn on Earth," Charity asked.

"Any of our enemies would jump at a chance to flip an agent-in-training before they even entered the field," Merrecci informed.

"And you think she could have been that Shadow Force?"

"Nine years," Merrecci said. "And she still hasn't graduated."

"But you don't know for sure?"

"I wasn't, but then the diplomatic sector was poisoned, and she dropped me like I was nothing, and she held punches with Nandy. She let us apprehend her, but escaped after the Diantine poison triggered the alarm," Merrecci continued. "That takes special training."

"So, it wasn't her," Charity stated.

"Unless that's the tactic to make us think it's not her," Merrecci responded. "If she is what I think she is, that would be part of her training to make herself more convincing. So, you see. It can't be anyone else."

"But you're not certain, are you," Charity asked.

"I don't want to be, but yes. I checked everyone, even you."

"I thought you said you could trust us."

"I can't really go around conducting security checks on people who know I'm looking at them, can I or they'll hide stuff,"

"You should have trusted your own senior staff and spoken to us first," Charity said.

"I did. Then I investigated you. Nandy cleared first, so she helped me with the rest of you."

"That seems sneaky."

"What do I really know about you," Merrecci asked. "I investigated Admiral Kellick too. Leonard's the only one with the background and training to have slid under our noses. If Leonard is shadow force, and I'm wrong about her being the spy—

"Which you are," Charity replied.

"Then we can never say anything about Bria's background, or she'll have a target on her back the rest of her life. But that's a two-edged sword because eliminating every other suspect means Bria must be the spy; and she must have administered the Diantine; and put herself through this to throw us off balance."

"She almost died in those tubes," Charity said. "She might still die. What happened to her isn't even measured in degrees in frostbite. She froze so fast and deeply, the typical injuries of even fourth-degree cryo-bite would have been better on her."

"That's the problem. If she is what I think she is, she's trained to handle the harshest abuse and to do whatever it takes to accomplish her objective, even kill herself. My own former crew member testified to an account of a Shadow Force operative who skinned himself from neck to toe, just to sell that he had been captured and tortured.

And I still can't overlook that she could have simply seen freezing to death as being her cyanide pill."

"Okay," Charity said. "Let's say that's true. She saved the diplomatic sector. When did she have the time to create the Diantine gas?"

"She could have managed it," Merrecci asked.

"For the hours she's put into this ship? She'd never be able to accomplish making the poison." Charity straightened into deductive reasoning. Her shadow in the dark room now stared away from the admiral.

"Your spy is a chemist," Charity said. "And a dang smart one if she can distil Denonize into Diantine."

"Wait," Merrecci said. "I thought Diantine came from Diante."

"The laxative? No, Diante isn't even in the same periodical table as Diantine," Charity said. "I'll never forget that because that was the only question I got wrong on my Chemistry Intro final."

"One question wrong," Merrecci stated. "Say it isn't true!"

"It's a sneak attack question," Charity said. "A lot of people get it wrong. Heck, even Nandy got it wrong, and, unlike me, had to retake Chemistry Intro."

"She did?"

"I think she said twice," Charity said, and suddenly she found her eyes locked onto Merrecci's again. "Oh my god. It's Nandy. She let Bria beat her, didn't she?"

Merrecci slumped forward.

"And she had nearly all the authority she'd need to hide her tracks, wouldn't she, especially since you cleared her first to look at all of us" Charity observed. "Only you and the captain had more access."

"Oh! That conniving little turd," Merrecci burst, slowly forcing himself to his feet. "You're right. I should have talked to you first."

$$*\qquad*\qquad*$$

Drinker sat at a table. Merrecci was off duty, which meant that Drinker could relax, hopefully. He was starting not to trust that he wouldn't be called away at a moment's notice. Although, today he was all ready for when the prime admiral called him. Upon the table was a 10,000 piece puzzle in a brand new and unopened box. The image on the top was an ocean scene. It had no animals and no life, just bright blue, backed by the sun peering down through the surface of the water. He'd had the jigsaw fabricated yesterday, but now took the chance to empty it onto the table. He had been requesting that Onyx create something that gave him a challenge.

To begin, he sliced the box open with a knife in his fingernail clipper keyring. Then he emptied its contents onto the table and tossed the empty box onto the floor. That was important to doing a jigsaw puzzle. The fabricator could have opened the puzzle for him, but if a person could not open their own box, then putting the pieces in it together would be too advanced for them.

"You're getting better, Onyx," Drinker said, observing that the ship's random cut of the puzzle was to turn each piece into nearly identical shapes, that is, they were all short crosses. At once, he realized that this puzzle had a ragged edge.

Now his fingers went to work flipping all the pieces up. It took about fifty minutes. He spent two more minutes studying the parts, then began flipping them face down so only their cardboard sides were visible now. It took almost an hour this time to flip them.

Now, he reached across the deep table and smacked the top of a stop clock. Then he poked into the spread-out mix and grabbed a piece, one full cross, then he grabbed a second and pressed the two together. They didn't lock, but they held their position. He swept open a clean spot on the table to lay his two pieces then immediately slid a third against them. He kept pressing: four, five, ten pieces, each one cupping into their interior counterparts.

In thirty minutes, the door to his quarters opened. Dawn and Mirror entered.

"Oh my gosh," Dawn said. "Why, Drinker?"

Drinker admonished them to not interrupt him by pointing to the timer.

Still, she asked why.

"To see the pieces is to see the whole picture," Drinker said in his mind, but "material" got in the way and confused his two friends.

When he realized they were confused, he simply added "to find the perfect puzzle," but that also didn't come out right.

That's okay, he understood what he meant. He saw the whole image: how the pieces fit together; when a part was missing; why two slices with completely different colors could become a natural blend when put together. Of course, there was only one hue for all the face-down pieces he worked with now.

A game show came to life on the wall, and Drinker did what he always did, blocked it out. He kept building the blank canvas.

He always had to ignore game show time. They couldn't watch any live ones, so they had Onyx dive into some of its old databases to reimage and modernize them to look fresh and up to date. They had recently gotten hooked on something that required players to guess how much something cost so they could play another game at guessing how much something else cost.

The doors opened once more, and Mike appeared. He trotted up to the table and began sniffing the pieces, tried to eat one.

"Material," Drinker replied.

Mike withdrew.

Then Willis entered. He smiled to Drinker. Drinker did look up for this. He smiled back, then returned to his work.

Willis reached down and took a piece from the middle of Drinker's work. He began peeling away at the pressed paper layers.

"Put it down," Drinker yelled, trying to salvage his work.

Willis dropped the puzzle bit and ran to the couch where Dawn coddled him and threatened to kick Drinker's ass.

The door announced someone was at it.

"It's show time," Dawn yelled. "Go away."

"Be nice," Drinker said and invited the visitor in.

Admiral Merrecci and Almma entered. Merrecci sauntered in, Almma leaned into a cane. Nandy followed and locked the door.

"Who you here to beat up now," Dawn snipped, then turned her whole attention to the wall and resituated herself to not see him even from side-eye.

"Have a minute, Drinker," Merrecci asked, then. "Is that a jigsaw puzzle?"

"It might be your spy," Drinker replied, and he kept extracting pieces to add to a section made up of 37 now. He took a moment to meticulously turn the combination of work and then slide it to a particular spot on the table before he went back to adding another part to it.

Merrecci pulled up a chair and sat where he could watch.

"How do you know if you're getting it right," Merrecci asked.

"Because everything fits," Drinker said, tearing up a piece from the table and adding it into what was beginning to take a crescent shape. "If I'm Material, I suppose I can pound the pieces together or rip off their parts to do what I want. Right, Prime Material?"

"I need your help," Merrecci said.

"Of course, you do," Drinker replied in a bit of a huff.

"I don't know if I have enough evidence to charge Captain Leonard for treason," Merrecci said.

"Then maybe she didn't do it, you big, dumb, moron, dipwad," Dawn shot out. "Go screw yourself!"

"That's enough of that," Nandy replied, now moving up directly behind Merrecci's seat to look down upon Drinker's table.

"Bring it on," Dawn said. "I'll gladly kick your—

Mirror shushed her from the other side of Willis who was now chuckling at the game on the screen where a yodeler just fell off a big rock because the contestant thought something called a toaster cost eighty dollars more than it should have. What a dummy.

Merrecci watched the interaction with the old game show. He admitted to himself that he was fascinated at once, but it wasn't what he needed to be focusing on right now for the most part.

"I was wondering if you might have seen Bria behaving strangely at any time," Merrecci asked and leaned in, almost setting his elbows on the table, but stopped when Drinker waved his hand at the admiral. "You take your puzzles seriously, don't you?"

"This is what I do," Drinker said. "When I'm not being interrupted to run to the bridge every time you material help solving a problem."

"Have I hit a sore spot with you," Merrecci asked.

"At the risk of being your next material of accusation," Drinker said. "No, Sir. I'm not nearly the fighter that Captain Material is."

"I'm sorry," Merrecci said, picking up a piece of the puzzle and examining it. "I just—

Drinker pulled the piece from the admiral's hand and reached across to the other side of the table to press it against another single, unconnected part that had been minding its own business.

"Are you nervous commander," Drinker asked.

"Me," Nandy asked. "I'm not nervous."

Drinker stopped mid-reach to another piece and looked up. He stared a moment right into Nandy's face until she shifted her weight and slid her arms behind her back.

"If you say so," Drinker replied, finishing his reach to retrieve another bit. "Were you this material when you learned Bria was the spy?"

"What's that supposed to mean," Nandy asked.

"Everyone says it's not her," Merrecci said.

"Maybe you should listen," Dawn mumbled.

Drinker now watched Nandy take the liberty to sit beside Merrecci.

"How's your hand," he asked, maintaining his momentum to complete his puzzle. "I heard she cut you."

"Oh," Nandy said, flexing her rejuvenated fingers. "Not so bad now. You can hardly tell I was cut."

"You know it's not Bria," Drinker stated.

"But all the evidence says it is," Merrecci said. "The breakout in the Brig happened when she was in the vicinity. We were lucky to stop the Didjian fugitive. The only one who really saw the person flee the prison was Leonard and two malcontent crew members."

"According to ship schematics, a third of the crew quarters on this deck share circulation with the brig," Almma added.

"Interesting," Drinker said. "I'll take your material for it. Do you material his word for it, Commander Nandy?"

Nandy froze.

"We're just checking with all crew in those quarters if they happened to see anything suspicious coming in or going out of the ventilation," Merrecci asked.

"Like who, Prime Admiral," Drinker asked.

"I don't know," Merrecci said. "Me? Lieutenant-commander Almma?" His finger casually fell to Nandy. "Commander Nandy?"

Drinker stopped working on his puzzle and looked up from his puzzle to ask, "Why would it material Nandy?"

"Just throwing out ideas," Merrecci said.

Drinker appeared to study Merrecci and Nandy a moment before returning his attention to solving his puzzle.

"Material," he said. "You'll need better evidence if you want to material your spy."

"Well, there's the poison."

"Which Bria rescued everyone from," Drinker said.

"Could have been a smoke screen," Merrecci replied.

"Your head's a smoke screen," Dawn mumbled.

"What was that," Merrecci asked.

"You're a bong," Dawn added.

"Shut up, Dawn," Mirror said. "He'll beat you up too."

"I'll kick him in the nuts, won't I," Dawn asked.

Merrecci felt himself shrink.

"What else was there," Merrecci asked past his shoulder to his two bridge officers.

"Classifying some secret research in the decontamination lab to hide her poison-making," Nandy replied.

"Attempted murder on my life," Almma added.

"She saved your life," Dawn shouted as she jumped to her feet.

Mike reached up and pulled her back onto the armless couch.

"I also thought she saved your life," Drinker said.

"I thought so too," Almma said. "But maybe I'm only alive because Kellick was watching her, and she couldn't kill both of us."

"Then there were the messages from her own quarters and bridge command offices," Merrecci said.

"And you're sure it was her," Drinker asked.

"We checked everyone else," Merrecci said. "Being a captain on this vessel gives her the ability to hide her messages from us and encrypt them."

"Maybe it was another officer," Drinker said.

"That's what we thought too," Merrecci answered, "Or a really, really smart person pretending to be dumb," Merrecci said now leaning in on Drinker's table.

Drinker paused in his puzzle building.

"What's that supposed to mean," Dawn erupted, and this time she couldn't be calmed back into her seat.

Drinker reached to his side and stopped the clock.

"It means," Drinker replied, scrutinizing Merrecci. "He finally remembered that he made Willis a captain too."

At this, Willis turned and opened a pruning shear against Mirror's throat.

Merrecci stood and stepped forward. He stopped when Mirror screamed as Willis snipped the shears against her flesh, making a small cut in her neck.

"Next one drains her," Willis replied. "Kilkosh demi!"

Merrecci froze but tried not to.

Willis began to maneuver Dawn towards the door, warning Merrecci, Nandy and Almma back.

"You're helping the Kag'tak?," Merrecci asked.

"Helping," Willis laughed out. "Am!"

"I took any kind of help I could get," Merrecci said. "And you used that to set up the tools you needed to help you hide yourself and your messages for when the Onyx was at full function. What did you do, classify yourself? Promote yourself to the shadow force? You knew with everything going on at the time, if you stayed out of sight and out of mind, we'd forget your silly promotion. Even I forgot after I lost consciousness, and Leonard had to take command of the ship."

"Captain's prerogative," Willis replied backing to the door with Mirror. "And you gave it to me even before you gave it to that no-faced hack."

Merrecci's baton slid from his sleeve into his hand and cracked open.

"Ah-ah," Willis said, shoving the point of his clipping blade right to the edge of puncturing Mirror's neck. "Drop it."

Merrecci did. Almma and Nandy dropped theirs too. Willis then ordered Almma to unlock the door. Next, he ordered everyone except Mirror to the far side of the room.

"How many guards are out there," Willis asked.

"None," Merrecci replied.

"Don't lie," Willis snapped, then snipped the clippers into Mirror without drawing blood. He pressed the sharpened blades over her carotid artery.

"None," Merrecci pled then ordered anyone in the hall to put down their weapons just to reinforce that he was telling the truth.

Then Merrecci's arm sprang forward. The brown Connie Mack, autographed baseball spun from Merrecci's hand. The threads bit against his flesh as he snapped his middle fingertip towards himself. It wasn't a fast pitch, and Willis saw it coming. He barely removed himself from its trajectory but didn't predict in time that the ball would suddenly curve upwards, miss Mirror's shoulder and head entirely, and strike under his jaw. It hit hard enough that Mirror felt the grip on her loosen, and she took a chance to break away from Willis and run behind Almma, who was now retrieving her baton.

"You like that," Merrecci gloated. "That's a little something I like to call the rising star. Only works in artificial gravity."

Willis, however, didn't care, and he didn't take the bait to listen to Merrecci slow him down with words. He knew that Almma was aiming to take a crack at him with her cane or her baton. So, he rushed into the hall, and, on his first step through, his leg ricocheted straight up and hard. The force was such that his foot hit the ceiling, his head hit the archway of the open door, and his momentum toppled him into the opposing wall. He found himself on the hall's shag carpet. The prime admiral was upon him now.

Merrecci swatted the pruning shears from Willis's hand and punched the side of his head. He punched again, raised him by the collar and slammed him back down. Merrecci felt Almma at his side, trying to pull him back, and he shoved her away. He was straddling Willis now.

Willis's nose cracked with Merrecci's next blow. The blood pumped fast, and Merrecci hit him again, this time Willis's jaw, and Merrecci glimpsed the cramped skin of the Kag'tak beneath the human disguise. The next time the prime admiral struck, several of Willis's teeth broke and flew. Then Merrecci was strangling him while driving a knee into his gut.

Willis smacked at Merrecci, and Merrecci responded by punching Willis's offending shoulder repeatedly until he felt it crack in dislocation. Then the strangling resumed.

Suddenly, Merrecci was thrown sideways. Almma's weight landed on top of him.

"Sir," Almma insisted and brought herself to her feet.

Willis laughed through a mouth full of blood. Almma turned and cracked his chest with her cane.

"What is this stuff," Dawn asked, peeling a purple, gooey substance from the carpet just outside the door to her quarters. It stiffened, and she found she couldn't retrieve it further.

"It's classified," Merrecci replied back through deep, breathy heaves. Then he had Nandy and security drag Willis to the brig.

Almma insisted on staying behind to keep Merrecci from chasing Willis down for round two.

Merrecci gathered the Almmaminum from the shag carpet. It took a while as it kept stiffening every time he began to pull on it. Eventually, he returned it to an empty Petri dish. He sealed the container and then started back for the bridge with his tactical officer. Halfway there, Merrecci handed the gel to Almma.

"Return this to our new research facility," Merrecci asked.

"Take it back yourself," Almma retorted, and abruptly changed the direction she had been walking with her prime admiral.

"That was an order," Merrecci snapped.

Almma shoved her right hand beneath her shirt and under her left armpit to make it fart. "And this is the universe's smallest tuba playing 'Blow Me,' you dick."

"Say that again," Merrecci fired back and started storming towards her. "Despite what you're feeling right now, I'm still the prime admiral in these halls!"

Almma turned to Merrecci.

"I haven't heard a single word on my family since the attack on Earth," Almma replied, creeping back towards Merrecci in a way that caused him to stop approaching her. "I don't know what friends are still alive on other ships. My sister served on the Crimson, and I can't say if she survived. No one worked harder to open those lines of communication than Captain Leonard, and you beat the hell out of her! So, you can take the goddamned goop back yourself!"

Merrecci watched her march away and remained silent as Almma reminded him, "It's always the captains!"

His first inclination was to re-establish his authority and make her follow the order. His second was he didn't want to piss her off.

He carried the Petri dish back to the new research lab and left it with Crewman Jossel, who instantly snapped to a salute.

"Thank you for letting me borrow it," Merrecci said.

"Yes, Sir."

"It's rather impressive, isn't it?"

"Yes, Sir," Jossel replied again.

"I look forward to what you learn about it," he said.

"Yes, Sir."

"Well," Merrecci said. "As you were."

"Yes, Sir," Jossel said, but she didn't lower her salute. She was still holding it and watching as he left.

He returned to the bridge, cursing the salute. What a wasted act. If he saluted everyone on his ship, his arm would break off. No one would ever see him salute. It was stupid.

It wasn't his shift when he returned to the bridge. He was supposed to be asleep, but he took command anyway and sat in his pitcher-mound chair.

A face he didn't recognize was in the pilot's seat, one of Vandenbutcke's students.

"Have we received a flight plan yet from Navigator Escobedo," Merrecci asked.

"I wouldn't know, Sir," the pilot trainee replied. "I'm just here to monitor our orbit."

Orbital command was boring. The pilots hardly got to work.

His new two-person research and development team had mined enough Almmaminum already from the planet of the purple-crystal substance, to fuel their research for now. It was a slow and painstaking process. Meanwhile, Escobedo was still scrutinizing Binny's map.

Vandenbutcke tried to assist at one point but couldn't seem to keep up with whatever Escobedo saw in surviving a potential hypernova chain, planetary debris, and radiation.

The mission was at a standstill until Escobedo could figure the math.

Merrecci stayed in his seat and stared at his hands. He made fists. He opened them. He watched his hands and nothing else. Willis's blood was still drying. Bria's, though washed off already, still seemed fresh on him. All the time he'd seen his hands, he hadn't really looked at them.

He had calluses. He understood those on the undersides of his fingers. Countless pitches in games and on the bridge, endless blisters and thread burning against his flesh all the way to his fingertips had hardened his flesh. He wondered how he'd ever had enough feeling to control the ball. The calluses on his knuckles though, those were from anger.

He'd killed with his hands. Some faces he remembered from time to time. Even now, a few flashed through his mind, Willis included, but it was Bria's face he couldn't stop seeing. Again and again, he saw his callused knuckles hitting her scarred face, scarred and—

Drinker reported for his shift of basically sitting around waiting to offer Merrecci any needed ideas.

"How did you know it was him, Drinker," Merrecci asked.

"He always knew which material would ruin my puzzle," Drinker replied.

Almma arrived five minutes later. She wasn't expected to return to work for another three days, but she insisted, and Charity believed her hip was cured enough to do so. All Almma needed to wade through now was lingering pain.

She said nothing but went to work reviewing daily reports. Merrecci thought about the wind she'd taken out of him and wondered if Bria would have been safely within a brig right now if Almma, rather than Prilla, had accompanied him to arrest his captain. Leonard wouldn't have been successful in rescuing Kellick and his staff if she had made it to the brig. Willis would probably have still been free and about.

Bria's rotten face was there again screaming apologies. Why? What did she have to apologize for? He knew why though, because that's what she did.

"Lieutenant-commander," Merrecci finally said towards the end of his shift.

"What," Almma snipped, but then added, "Sir."

"The bridge is yours," Merrecci said. "Captain Leonard is reinstated with full command when she is ready to return to duty."

"You seriously think she'll want to come back," Almma asked.

"If you need me," Merrecci countered. "I'll be in the brig."

"Going to interrogate Willis again," Almma asked.

"Please request Admiral Kellick that I need to speak to him there," Merrecci said, standing.

"I see," Almma said as she watched Merrecci leave. She called after him. "Sir."

Merrecci turned.

"I think I'll join you," Almma said.

After escorting Merrecci to the bridge, she notified Kellick of the prime admiral's request. Kellick was currently in his office. He hurt. His skin burned. His lungs were accepting the gel that allowed them to retract and expand without experiencing agony with each breath, but they were heavier, and he was slower.

Earlier, he stopped into the hospital to look on Bria, but she was comatose. After seeing her, he was glad she was. He went to the galley, but he only saw an empty seat across the table.

Nandy had taken that seat, herself, at one point. He tried to teach her the game, but they both ended up playing poker and avoiding the elephant in the room along with everyone else. He had just returned to his own office to work, when Almma appeared and relayed Merrecci's request. Kellick jolted off to the brig. If Merrecci needed help interviewing, Kellick had a few things to contribute.

He'd expected to find Merrecci facing a cell, squaring off with a prisoner. He approached the desk with two guards. One pointed to the highest level without saying a word.

Kellick started for the detention lift but stopped before Willis's cell. Willis smirked.

"Good to see you recovered, Admiral," Willis said.

"And you," Kellick replied, biting into that diplomatic donut of training that was woven by too many years into the fabric of his soul. "Are they treating you well."

"The pillow's a little hard," Willis replied.

"I'll relay your grievance at once," Kellick said.

"You'll relay my grievance. I like that," Willis said. "Shame they didn't put you in charge. Might have avoided all of this."

"Perhaps," Kellick said. Then he bit his tongue, cutting off the remark of how maybe Willis would already be dead if Kellick had been in charge. He said no more but marched off to the elevator.

On the highest ring, he found Merrecci sitting over the edge of a cot that was barely wide enough to let a person sleep on his side.

"Prime Admiral," Kellick greeted automatically.

Merrecci nodded but didn't look up. He was busy staring into his hands trying to decode what his palms might be saying about his future.

"What kind of a leadership looks at a captain who can't even keep his own ship and says, 'let's make him the boss of everything'," Merrecci asked.

"If you're looking for absolution, I don't have any for you," Kellick replied.

"There is no absolution," Merrecci said.

Kellick didn't respond this time.

"I messed up," Merrecci said. "I should have been arrested the moment it happened."

"You'll find no argument here," Kellick replied. "Which is why I should inform you that I'm not in a pitying mood."

"This crew is so green, no one really knew," Merrecci said, finally looking up.

"With respect, why am I here," Kellick asked. "Representation? That's the smartest thing you've done all trip."

"I need you to take command of the Onyx," Merrecci informed. He stood and approached Kellick. "Procedure says I should stand trial for court martial. I should not be with the crew."

At this, Kellick contacted the bridge and requested that Almma allow him to address the ship. She opened a transmission.

"Attention all crew. This is Admiral Kellick. By now, many of you know our crew was betrayed by a spy set on the destruction of our kind. We were betrayed again when our Prime Admiral wrongfully accused our captain, who saved many lives including mine, even after she was attacked.

"As this has deeply affected the entire crew, it is only ethical that I should include you in this discussion. Prime Admiral Merrecci has asked me to take command of the Onyx." He drew back and saluted Merrecci. "Prime admiral, you have asked, and on behalf of the crew that you have betrayed, I salute you and I proudly tell you to go to hell."

Merrecci immediately began to object.

"You betrayed us, you don't get to hide from us," Kellick stated. He ordered brig security to deactivate Merrecci's cell. "Don't ask me to clean up your mess again."

Kellick ended the communication.

"You already have a first officer to do that for you," Kellick said, then turned and walked away. "Ask her to take over if you're so set on giving up—that is, if you can figure out how to drop your isms."

*   *   *

Yellow used to be her favorite color. It was energy, warmth, encouragement. It was home. Today, it was the end of a long dream and consciousness to that nightmare of reality.

Her head was cumbersome, her chest heavier, but she sat up anyway and felt how weighed down her hands were. She saw the large bulbs of foam capping her wrists. She remembered. The maintenance bot had to break off her grip to keep her from freezing entirely. Now, translucent burn wrap stretched out from beneath the sleeves of her gray hospital gown. Her flesh was a marbling of black, white and the wrong kind of pink, for those areas that were supposed to have pink. Even wrapped, her arms were swollen to twice what they should have been.

Gibralter entered the room to answer the silent alarm. He immediately called Charity.

Dr. Quobalt arrived only seconds later and asked how she felt.

Bria wondered. She didn't know. Then she saw her foamed wrists again and did.

Charity leaned down to her side and tried to be encouraging but was afraid she wasn't sure how to in this situation.

"Is Kellick's staff okay," she asked.

Gibralter's face suddenly appeared caught off guard.

"They're fine," Charity said. "Thanks to you. Everyone's fine."

"Not everyone," Bria suddenly blubbed. "What did I do wrong?"

Charity stroked her head and let her release.

"You didn't do anything wrong," she said. "We did."

Eventually, through it all, Charity versed Bria on all that happened and informed her on how she induced coma upon Captain Leonard to help her survive the pain.

Bria went silent. Then she laid back down and turned onto her side, away from Charity.

"There's some good news though," Charity said, leaning over Bria to try to make eye contact.

When Bria made it, Charity strangely wished she hadn't.

"Maybe later, then," Charity said. "A lot can happen in six weeks."

"What," Bria asked.

"Oh," Charity realized. "We started our next leg of our mission while you've been reconstituting. You've been here two weeks. They say it will be six more before we reach our next stop."

Bria didn't respond. She eventually heard Charity and Gibralter leave her hospital pod, and she stared at yellow until she drifted off into its jaundiced sleep.

After some time and dreams too much like what she expected her new life would be, even more hideous and mocked, she became aware of another presence in the room, breathing. She unrested from her sleep and found Kellick sitting behind a cribbage board that set atop a round tray table pressed to the side of her bed.

"Know what I just realized about this silly game," Kellick stated. "If you toss an ace and a four, you'll always get points in the crib."

"That so," Bria replied.

"How do your hands feel," Kellick inquired. "Up for a game?"

She held up one of her arms to brandish the foam then let it fall on Kellick's table next to her bed. She instantly regretted it as a floodgate of torture, rushed up her arm, flowed into the depths of her brain, then exploded out to her bowels and limbs.

"We okay in here," Charity asked, stepping in part way.

Kellick who had already risen to his feet and appearing as though he wanted to help Bria, but didn't know how, fired back with, "She's trying to kill herself again!" His face suddenly froze in realization.

Bria's eyes narrowed as she spat out, "Get the hell out!"

"I'm so sorry," Kellick replied. "I didn't mean it like that."

Bria pulled back her arm and rolled onto her side, away from Kellick, but she found Charity here preparing a pain reliever injection.

"I want to go back to my quarters," Bria said.

"Okay," Charity spoke. "Let me get you a chair and an orderly."

"I don't need a chair," Bria said and began trying to sit up.

Charity stepped in front of her, mostly to keep her from falling out of the bed, but Kellick's hands were at her back, trying to support her.

"Will everyone leave me alone," Bria yelled. "I can do it myself."

"You're getting a chair," Charity ordered.

"I don't want a chair," Bria snapped, now doing her best to turn herself to sit over the edge of her bed.

"And you'll keep in it until you're inside your quarters, or I'm going to break something else of yours off so you can't leave," Charity threatened. "Is that understood?"

Bria opened her mouth to yell.

"Oh, stop acting like the victim," Almma's voice came from the entry.

"I am a victim," Bria shouted.

"You're not a victim. You're a bitch," Almma declared as she was entering Bria's room now.

Bria took too long to respond.

"Now get your swollen ass in the chair, and I'll take you home."

"I'm taking her," Kellick corrected.

"None of you are taking me," Bria retorted. She dropped off the bed to her feet and then to her face. As was habit, she reached to catch herself. As soon as her hard foam balls hit the floor, she remembered her entire burn-riddled body hadn't fully healed either. The screaming that followed wasn't entirely Bria's.

"Are you stupid," Charity groaned and quickly helped Almma roll Leonard onto her back. She began scanning the foam. "I swear if you break these ones, you're a dead woman."

"What are you talking about," Bria screamed directly into Charity's face.

"Your hands," Charity replied crossly. "What did you think I was talking about."

"What?"

"If you hadn't been pissing all over everyone, I'd have told you before," Charity said, now scanning the other foam ball.

"Dr. Quobolt Frankensteined your hands back together," Almma said. She allowed Kellick space to help her and Charity lift Bria back to her bed.

"How," Bria asked. "There were no hands to save. I saw them. They were frozen through."

"Well, yes and no," Charity replied. "There was a lot of damage, and we lost a bit during the retrieval process, but some was able to reconstitute, just like you."

"Some?"

"Enough to try," Charity said.

"And what was missing was donated," Kellick added.

"What does that even mean," Bria asked.

"Someone may have let it slip that your hands are the reason everyone here is alive during our escape," Charity answered.

"Which is also why my own crew is alive since the Onyx is why we made it this far," Kellick stated.

"I helped to stir the rumor," Charity said.

"Same, but I got drunk and started punching people when I said it, so more people remember when I said it," Almma added.

"A few people showed up to donate so I could reconstruct your hands," Charity explained.

"Like who," Bria asked.

"Well, you have a piece of this flexor tendon from my happy maker," Almma said, brandishing her middle digit. "Nandy gave you another piece of it."

"Vandenbutcke gave you a nerve," Charity replied. "So, did—

"Vandenbutcke gave me a nerve," Bria asked.

"Go figure," Almma said.

"You have a piece of my ECU," Kellick said.

"And you think that's enough to give me a shot," Bria asked.

"Not even close," Charity snorted. "But between the three hundred and seventeen other crew members who donated little bits here and there: nerves, pieces of tendons and ligaments, even skin and muscle; and I, assuming I'm going to be a wonderful reconstructive surgeon one day, sewed them all together. Which is greatly thanks to Cora's blue gel that had your hand on file when I had to fix Merrecci's."

"The thing is," Kellick said. "Before you go jumping down people's throats, you should know why you currently have hands and why they might still work."

"And in case they don't," Charity said. "I did ask our engineer crew to think of something to help compensate."

"How so," Bria asked, adding this to her string of ignorance.

"We embedded a bit of a gloved enhancement into your hands, something that can handle neural commands. If you don't need them, we can eventually take them out, but that foam is helping your flesh adhere to the implants."

Bria, for the first time, let herself realize that the pains she felt in her fingers were actually not phantom.

"Why would they do that for me," Bria asked. "They didn't want me."

"You underestimate your crew," Kellick said. "They know you've earned the first officer's chair now."

Now, Bria withdrew to the side of her bed again.

"No," Charity said. "Don't—don't do that."

"I can't do that again," Bria said. "All I tried to do was help, and he had me doing things no one in my position should have been doing, and then he—

"Your crew knows," Almma said, softly and gingerly brushing a tuft of Bria's hair away from her eyes. "But we really don't care what you think, because it's not all about you. Now get in the chair, or I'll have Dawn come kick your ass."

"What he did," Bria said.

"Yeah, well, I'm sure he'd make a better 'brrrrr—oh yeah!' than a prime admiral," Almma retorted. "But sometimes you just don't get to choose how you'll get screwed."

"You're so colorful," Kellick said. "Anyone ever tell you that?"

"Only when—"

"Lieutenant-commander," Kellick warned. "Don't confuse me with some of the other commanding officers you've had."

"Sorry, Sir," Almma replied.

"It's not just that," Bria said.

"Captain," Charity said, her voice possibly cracking. Bria couldn't tell for sure. "He, umm."

"The idiot cut off his right hand to donate it to you," Almma finished.

"What," Bria asked.

"He used warehouse seven's laser separator and amputated his pitching hand," Charity replied.

"And hitting hand," Almma said.

"When the idea first came up to save your hands this way, he went and cut his above the wrist. He was the first donor. We reattached him of course when we started getting volunteers, but we took more from him than the others, particularly skin tissue. He's healing too."

Almma suddenly started giggling, "I flushed his hand in the toilet."

"What," Charity cried.

Almma broke out laughing harder.

"He just cut it off," Bria asked. "That was stupid."

"So was thinking she was a spy," Kellick interjected.

"He's kind of a stupid person," Charity replied cautiously. "And it will definitely cost him. He won't be making a fist for a very long time. Probably will never throw solid curve ball again."

"I see," Bria said coldly.

"Right," Charity announced in afterthought. "So much attention on your hands, almost forgot."

"What?"

"Your eyes," Charity explained. "Those we couldn't save."

"Then how," Bria started to ask.

"Holographic technology," Charity said. "They're calibrated for regular use right now, but they can also see in low-light, infrared and a few other ways. I'll teach you how to use those features when you're more up for it, but hands first."

Bria now allowed herself to be seated in the transport chair, and she asked Kellick to return her to her quarters. She was home perhaps twenty minutes before a visitor presented at her door, but Bria was already tired from walking, pacing, and trying not to fall or bump into things these past several minutes. The swelling of her entire body didn't help her feel any of her movements were natural in any way. She poked at the wrinkled plastic burn-wrap over her skin, pulled was more like it. It still felt hot, or cold—she couldn't decide—and somehow the sensation from pulling on the protective film around her forearm felt strangely soothing. At first, she ignored the click at her door, but then it came again.

She gave no response. It might have been Merrecci, and she wasn't prepared for that discussion.

"Captain," Nandy's voice came over her intercom.

Bria held her breath. Captain? So, her rank was reinstated.

Nandy called for her again, and Bria remained still.

"Bria," Nandy called one more time. "Please?"

Eventually, Adrigga gave up and left.

Bria curled up on her bed and thought herself into sleep. More people came over the next three days. She replied to no one. Kellick sat outside her door dealing himself cards and asking how she'd play the hand. Charity forced her way into the apartment each day, and Bria insisted she was fine. Charity didn't agree.

Vandenbutcke appeared on the second day, but only because he just happened to be preparing to announce himself as Charity was leaving Bria's quarters. He wished her well, asked a few pleasantries, but she didn't seem to hear them. Finally, despite realizing she probably wouldn't answer him, he thought he'd better ask what he came to.

"Ma'am," he said. "Could you—Nandy's not—

He cut himself off when he watched Bria stiffen at the sound of her name.

"Never mind," he said and was about to leave.

"What about her," Bria asked softly.

"Could you talk to her," he asked. "She's not okay."

"She's not okay," Bria hissed.

Vandenbutcke recoiled.

"I'm sorry," he said. "I didn't mean to upset you."

Then he left.

Merrecci never showed, never called, never beckoned her to the bridge, never gave her the chance to tell him where he could shove her restored rank.

Prilla, however, came the first and second day, didn't force her way in though. Perhaps she took Charity's word for how Bria was. Others came then left, and she tried to ignore them all.

At two in the morning on the fourth day of this, she found herself staring at the shower. Charity had threatened to send nurse Gibralter to give it to her if she didn't take one herself. As she stood there glowering at the shower walls, she realized her problem wasn't that she didn't want to take one.

"Umm, Cindy Lou," she transmitted.

"Thank you so much for thinking about me," Cindy replied curtly. "Are you sure you wouldn't like to wait four more days."

"Umm," Bria muddled. "I need help."

"I'll be right there," Cindy replied, still curtly.

When she arrived, after causing her own disintegration shield to drop, she found Bria still standing and staring at the shower.

"Oh, hi," Bria said, appearing somewhat surprised to see Cindy Lou.

"You need to eat," Cindy remarked.

"I ate," Bria replied.

"When? What did you have?"

"I drank a sandwich earlier," Bria said. "The cup is over there."

Cindy located it still in the fabricator, untouched. When she returned to Bria, she found her looking down instead of at her.

"I can't," Bria said, but didn't finish. The balls on her hands were trying to reach back and untie her robe, but obviously made no progress.

"Hey, Bri," Cindy said.

"Huh?"

Then Cindy broke out a cheerleader kick through exaggerated disposition and cried, "Gimme an F!"

But Bria continued trying to explain that she couldn't untie her robe so she could get in the shower.

"Okay," Cindy said.

She stepped behind Bria and politely untied her drawstring which had been secured since she left the hospital. It wasn't enough though. The sleeves couldn't draw over the foam balls that enveloped her devastated hands.

A few minutes later, the fabricator presented a pair of scissors, which Cindy used immediately to start cutting the robe.

Now, Bria was finally able to enter the shower. Cindy started it and stepped in to help wash her.

Bria began crying.

"Hey," Cindy said, applying soapy hands to the back of Bria's wrapped neck and massaging it in, performing two tasks at once: rejuvenating the protective film, and allowing the soap to sink through its pores to help Bria's flesh rejuvenate.

"Your swelling's really gone down," Cindy said. "Does it hurt?"

"Not right now," Bria replied, almost as if she hadn't fully heard Cindy.

"Some day, you have to step out of this room," Cindy explained. "If you wait too long, it won't be you who does. It will be someone you don't recognize when you look in the mirror. Don't let this room take you from me."

Cindy's arms then gently wrapped around Bria's front and hugged her from behind.

"That hurt," she asked.

Bria shook her head.

Cindy kissed her shoulder.

Bria reached up and would have held onto Cindy's hands but had to settle for carefully pressing foam back instead.

"Are you wearing real clothes in the shower," Bria suddenly realized and spun around to face Cindy who was still wearing head to foot attire, which today was late twentieth-century jeans, Keds, white, unbuttoned shirt with a white t-shirt beneath it.

"I didn't come to take advantage of you," Cindy said.

"Oh," Bria said turning back. "Well, thank you, then."

"Unless you'd prefer I did," Cindy replied.

"Yes, please," Bria answered.

15
▲
Naked

That evening, Cindy helped redress Bria. She had the fabricator prepare her a uniform that would accommodate her bulbed hands. While she was hooking the sleeves together, she watched Bria's shoulders begin to rise and fall with more vigor and focus.

"The reason I didn't call for you sooner was because I didn't want to take anything out on you," Bria said.

Cindy paused, said nothing, and went back to dressing Bria.

"Charity and I had an interesting talk," Cindy informed.

"Oh," Bria asked, somewhat startled, or maybe interrupted.

"It seems that Cora had something in her notebook concerning you. I'm not supposed to tell you, so act surprised, but she may have a way to give you a face again. It's corny though."

Bria turned abruptly before Cindy could finish dressing her.

"So, it might be a good time to start thinking of what kind of face you'd like," Cindy said as she closed Bria's sleeves.

"Well, I," Bria replied. "I—"

"You have time," Cindy replied. She took a moment to primp Bria's uniform.

"Thank you," Bria said.

Cindy smiled genuinely.

"I've missed curing your panic attacks every night," Cindy said. Then she stepped back a bit to give one last inspection of Bria's attire. "Now, go out that door and be you."

Bria thanked her again and felt Cindy's hand cup her elbow.

"Personally, I like the face you have now," Cindy continued. "And I've seen a lot of faces."

Bria leaned in to kiss Cindy and enjoyed that this god didn't recoil. She was about to turn away when she suddenly asked, "Do you know if they removed the off-ship communication restrictions?"

"No," Cindy reported. "They decided we had to stay classified."

"How's the crew taking it?"

"I don't pay attention to that sort of thing," Cindy replied. "But Almma hides it well."

The sound of the door welcomed Bria back to the ship as it peeled apart before her. The march to the bridge was a blur. Actually she, didn't really know what it was. It didn't last long.

The bridge doors reeled open in exclamation, and she entered to find Almma in the dugout. Nandy stood from the command chair and opened her mouth to speak.

"Nope," Bria said forcefully and turned to Almma. "Where is he?"

Almma checked her console and looked back, "In the gym, working out and feeling sorry for himself."

Bria turned to leave and then looked back. "He works out?"

Almma stifled a laugh.

"Captain," Nandy said.

"Nope," Bria replied and marched back out of the bridge.

Two decks down, she found the Gym filled with people who got an early start on the day. Merrecci was at the far end. His right arm and hand were wrapped in some sort of black splint. He was currently jumping from the floor up to a four-foot platform.

How dare he! How dare he move around so care free!

As she pressed towards him, the other people at their various choices of exercise routines took notice. Merrecci, with his back to her, had not noticed her approach. Nor had he noticed the silence that was beginning to fill the room over his heavy breathing and clunky shoes.

He jumped up, exhaling as he launched, forcing the remains of his breath out as he landed and stood upright four feet taller than he really was. Then he kicked backwards off the platform to recover a jumping stance that would allow him to repeat the routine. As he was recovering in just this action—

"Bastard Admiral," Bria announced.

Merrecci turned suddenly and surprised.

Bria swung her right hard, foam ball at his head, but it didn't connect. He caught it.

"Hey," he yelled. "You're going to break—

Her left struck the other side of his head and he stumbled. So, she struck him with her right in the same fashion. Merrecci involuntarily sat back against the platform he'd been jumping onto.

"Reporting for duty, Sir," Bria said, biting into the agony that she'd just caused upon herself.

"Glad to hear it," Merrecci said.

"And don't you ever do that again."

"Okay," Merrecci replied.

"And I better get my hands back."

"Okay," he replied again.

She took the admiral in from his retreated position against the podium that he'd been scaling only moments earlier. Bria wondered if she needed to add more. It was alien to see him not in control, almost as strange as seeing herself with what she currently had for appendages.

"Thanks for the hand," Bria said, holding up her right foam ball. "Does yours hurt?"

"It's mostly tender," Merrecci replied.

"Good," Bria said then punched it and rushed off. His screams as she stormed out of the gym helped drown out her own anguish from striking him.

After returning to her quarters to report to Cindy. Finding that she wasn't there, she allowed herself to vocalize her agony. After she felt she could ignore it better, she decided to roam the ship with nowhere to particularly go. At what had been half-past her usual time to do so, she found herself in the Galley, waiting for Kellick, but he wasn't there. She found a table and sat anyway.

"I went to your room," Kellick said appearing ten minutes late. "Then I heard a rumor in the hall that you were out and about punching admirals."

"Well, he pissed me off," Bria said.

Kellick guffawed. "Yeah, that *Bastard Admiral* is going to stick with him forever now, you know."

"I better not hear anyone say it around me. That's between me and him."

"So, what do we play now," Kellick asked.

"Are you serious?"

"I'm glad you inquired," Kellick replied and bid her to accompany him.

As she stood to follow, she found the people at the other tables already standing and saluting.

She smiled and found herself thanking as many people in the galley as welcomed her back. From here, Kellick led her before a room in the diplomatic sector of the Onyx.

"Now, I took a page from the ancient games book, and I think I found something you can play, if you promise to stop if it starts feeling wrong," Kellick explained.

"I'll do my best," Bria replied.

"Seriously, Captain," Kellick said. "Don't destroy your hands before you get them back."

Bria agreed.

When Kellick opened the door, Bria immediately saw it.

"Wow," she gasped. "I've always wanted to try one of these."

"Really," Kellick asked. "I was spit-balling. Though I'm not sure I understand fully why it's called pinball."

She explained it. They played it, turned out she could. Kellick had taken great study to choose a version of the machine that allowed Bria to fire the steel ball by pushing a button rather than pulling a spring-loaded rod. About fifteen minutes later, she felt she should stop. It wasn't painful, but there was definitely something dull etching into existence from the repetitive ways she pressed her foam appendages against the buttons that controlled flippers.

She excused herself and then moved on to her next stop.

Willis was laying upon his cot within the cell. The sound dampener had been activated, so he didn't hear when Bria and one of the guards approached the shield. In a moment, the dampener was deactivated.

"Get up," Bria demanded before Willis even had time to react to the sudden ambient sound that started entering through his cell.

Willis smirked and rolled onto his side to present his back to her. The cot suddenly retracted into the wall, and he fell flat on his shoulder and hip. He groaned more in pain than in surprise.

Willis began to rise to his feet when the bed extended out again, knocking him in the chin and flattening him out on his back. Then the cot pulled into the wall once more to allow him to stand. This time, he was much more cautious climbing to his feet, stepping clear of the reach of his bed. He returned Bria's gaze, deeper and darker, unrecognizable.

"Hi, Bri," Willis said, waving enthusiastically at the captain. Then he squared up his gaze with hers and finally asked, "Yes? What did you want?"

"I guess I don't know," Bria answered.

Willis started laughing. "Oh, to stand in the presence of supreme Earth leadership," he mocked. "Came all this way to look me in the eye and say, 'I don't know.' You could at least give me the finger or something. Oh, sorry!"

Bria didn't share in his amusement.

"I'm a prisoner now," Willis said. "What did you expect?"

"I guess I expected more," Bria replied. "And I guess I just needed to see you and say that you're never getting out of there. You'll be tried for treason against Earth and put to death."

"That would suggest I was from Earth, and I'm not." An unbalanced victory smirk broke across his lips. "Can't charge a person for treason if they don't belong to your race. At most, you can charge me with is infiltrating you pathetic Earthers and put me in jail. Oh look! Here I am. I'll be released to my own people upon the first prisoner exchange, if you live that far."

"How about murder," she said. "One hundred and two of them. How about unauthorized acc—

"Oh sure, and you have evidence that shows I actually killed them, right," Willis said.

"How about the Didjian trilale," Bria asked.

"You Earthers killed that," Willis said.

"You smarmy bastard. You put the weapon in its hand," Bria said. "All so it could be a distraction."

Willis laughed at her joke. "And I thought Earthers were dumb. I don't know about murder, but you certainly have me for trespassing on a ship that its commander abducted me onto. Everything I did was in the purview of the rank he gave me."

"And passing on information to Master Cha's fleet to our location," Bria continued.

"Are you sure about that one," Willis asked. "Do you think if I'd wanted to rain hell on your vessel that I'd reach out to filthy subraces? Bottom line is it's not a crime to pretend to be a drooling dunce, is it? You haven't been charged yet. Oh, wait! Sorry."

"Just one little flaw in your logic," Bria replied.

"Oh no, better tell me before my own face blows off from all the suspense," Willis retorted.

"I don't care," Bria stated. "You became a member of our military when you got promoted, and you betrayed your own adoptive race."

"Don't clump me into your trough of filth," Willis warned.

"You're never going to see the outside of this cell again," Bria said. "You'll testify from here. You'll be judged from here. You'll die in here. I'll recommend that your capital punishment be by allowing the Rhaxians to shrink this entire cell down, and I'll lock you in a tomb that only a talking key can find. You'll have all the power you need to live and die."

Willis started chortling.

"Ooh! Big captain thinks she has the—"

Suddenly the two-inch thick Belamite blast door slammed shut. All Willis could hear from beyond it was the whirring sounds of its inner locks engaging.

Bria's face appeared in a small monitor that was perhaps three centimeters wide.

"Yes," she said. "I do."

Then her face was gone.

*   *   *

Merrecci looked over the data that Bria had shared to his desk. He continued to investigate, swiping a clumsy left finger over it, for nearly half an hour, while Bria sat in silence in front of him. She watched his face change. One eyebrow raised, then two brows sharpened. They both raised, then forced his eyes to squint at what he was reading. Then they made his eyes pop wide. Finally, they softened, and he looked back to his captain.

"You're certain," Merrecci asked.

"No," Bria said, sort of laughing. "I doubt I'm right, but I thought it was worth mentioning for just in case. Willis suggested he was communicating with a higher race. He called Master Cha a sub-race. Supposing I believe that, this could make sense."

"How sure would you say you are then," Merrecci asked fumbling a moment to get his fingers to swipe as accurately as he wanted.

"Enough to call a fleeting thought that maybe I should put out there," Bria reported. "Maybe."

"Seems like a stretch to me," Merrecci claimed. "If you're wrong—whew—could turn out ugly in so many ways."

"Yeah," Bria agreed. "Just thought I should at least mention it."

"Then again," Merrecci said. "Willis used the phrase kilkosh demi."

"What is it?"

"I don't know," Merrecci replied. "But the last time I heard it was when the Kag'tak greeted my father before killing him. I doubt it means, 'hello' though."

The room clicked, and Merrecci allowed Nandy to enter with what he assumed would be an updated status report.

"He was sentenced to this much time for stealing a, what is that word?" Merrecci asked suddenly as he continued to scan the data before him. He triggered a holographic image of his screen to appear so Bria could respond to what it was he was asking about.

"I think it's the word for planet, Sir," Bria replied.

The hologram disappeared.

"It can also mean throne," Nandy said approaching directly from Bria's side.

"Throne," Merrecci asked. "He, stole a throne?"

"Who stole a thr—," Nandy tried asking.

"We'll let you know, Commander," Bria replied without attempting to acknowledge Nandy's presence further than this.

Merrecci briskly shooed both Bria and Nandy's comments away from interrupting his current investment in thought.

"Sentenced to seventy years in the Tis System for convincing others he was royalty from Uibash? How is that one possible? Andra system gave him ninety Earth years for—everywhere he goes, he's got sentences and warrants for his arrest. And that's who we've been dealing with this whole time?"

Merrecci finally pulled away from leaning over his desk.

"If you're wrong about him," Merrecci said.

"I know," Bria replied. "You'll get first crack at him."

Merrecci's body snapped forward then relaxed.

"But if he does what I think he's going to do next," Bria said slowly.

"And if he doesn't?"

"Keep following the trail, see if anything's at the end," Bria replied.

Nandy made a sound to start a question.

"And I think we should start drafting a plan that implements my theory for just in case," Bria interrupted.

Merrecci was silent a moment and then excused Nandy.

"Captain," Merrecci said.

"Sir," Bria cut off. "With respect, I know what you're going to say, and I don't need to hear it. She spied on me. I actually believed she wanted to know me."

Merrecci weighed back into his chair.

"I spent all this time getting after our crew, demanding that they see you as their Captain," Merrecci spoke carefully, almost rehearsed. "I advised you to behave in ways that would let the crew see who you were so you could—

He stopped and fell back again into his chair.

"No. that's not true," Merrecci surrendered. "I was more concerned about how you would reflect on me. The truth is, I demanded everyone to see you as my first officer, everyone except me. I had no intention of keeping you longer than I had to."

"I understand," Bria said. "But you made the bed. If you want someone else's insight, you should make a different bed."

"And yet, it wasn't my inclination to enter the cooling system," Merrecci said. "But it was your first thought, and you attacked your commanding officer to allow yourself to do it."

"So, I shouldn't plan to give up my post when we return to Earth, or I should," Bria asked.

Merrecci snickered as if he realized his idea wasn't getting through.

"Do you know what it really takes to make a captain," Merrecci asked. "The captain is broken."

"Sir?"

"There are people who give," Merrecci said. "And there are people who keep. It's those who give who are more likely to break. The people who keep think they're in heaven. The people who give, truly see hell. Do you understand?"

Bria didn't, she thought. Maybe she did.

Merrecci nodded as if he expected as much, but then returned sharply with, "Yes you do. Because you're far more broken than I am, and I get it."

"I gave you everything," Bria erupted. "Everything!"

"Exactly! And look at the hell you're in. I didn't attack Willis because of what he did to my crew. I've been angry because my own crew mutinied against me, and then I did it to you. You've been giving and I've been keeping."

"Sir, again, with respect—

"Nandy is your friend," Merrecci said. "She wasn't spying on you. I was."

"You both were," Bria replied. "But I expect it from you."

"This leg of our mission has a little over five weeks to go now," Merrecci added. "That's a long time to be angry. Trust me. I know. I'd like you and Nandy and Almma to work this theory of yours, and I'd like you to think about how we're going to reestablish ourselves in the faction when we return to Earth. I need ideas."

"I'll see what we can do to bolster the Onyx further," Bria said.

"And our fleet," Merrecci added.

"Sir?"

"We have a fleet waiting for our return. It's not just the Onyx," Merrecci said.

"Sir, I am definitely not qualified for that," Bria replied.

"Geez, Captain! I'm not asking you to lead it. I'm asking you to throw some ideas at me? I'm feeling a little overwhelmed right now, and you're the person I rely on the most."

"Am I," Bria replied.

"Just bring me some options," Merrecci said. "And let's be sure who Willis was sending transmissions to."

"I'll get right on it," Bria acknowledged.

"And someday, you and I are going to have a little talk about your educational track."

"I thought we already did."

"Apparently we didn't."

"Well, okay," Bria replied. "But I don't know why you'd want to talk about that again."

Merrecci then dismissed her, then suddenly recalled her because he decided it was later.

*   *   *

The next two weeks were fairly uneventful. Bria and Nandy spoke. The captain tried to pretend she was willing to forgive, but Nandy could see otherwise and overcompensated her work to earn Bria's forgiveness. She knew how it had looked. They planned, they erased plans, they built other plans. They stuck to their routines.

Another week passed, and Charity removed the burn wrap from Bria's body and foam from her hands. The solvent softened the globes in about fifteen minutes, then Charity was careful and thorough to remove the remaining protective residue.

Bria's flesh came out various streaks of pink and unrecognizable epidermis. The nails were hers, but not all of the prints were. They looked like they belonged, but she knew hers. The tip of her middle left finger had a callus. She could feel it sitting there being fat. She would wonder some day if the person who gave it had played a stringed instrument. Her flesh was splotched with grafts, her digits lined with puffy surgical scars that Charity assured her would be invisible in time. Black, synthetic bands lined up each side of her slender digits and had become embedded, flush to her skin. These must have been the unique gloves the engineer team had developed.

Bria had expected to see a circumferential cut around her wrist, but that's not what appeared. Charity had grafted the skin there too to help hide the scars. She even removed some previous memories from Bria's wrists that she thought might do well to be forgotten.

Charity held her palms out.

"Give me your hands," she instructed.

Bria obeyed and immediately recoiled, screaming. The surges of pain burned deep into her.

Charity injected her patient with something to help dull the sensation. Five minutes later, she asked for her hands once more. This time, it still hurt, Bria still recoiled, but she was able to attempt again and muddle through the effort.

"Can you do this," Charity asked, rotating her palms from up to down.

Bria could, slowly, though it hurt to the edge of passing out.

Charity smiled.

"Now, can you make a fist with this hand," the doctor asked.

Bria tried. Her left hand barely budged, and it hurt as badly as if she hadn't been given pain relief. Charity suggested that it might be because it was too swollen, and Bria agreed because it felt fat.

Her right fingers however were a different story, rather than curl in, they suddenly flared out, and Bria found herself screaming again.

This, Charity stated, was enough for today. After deciding that she could accelerate the healing now, she wrapped Bria's flesh in numbing and anti-inflammatory wrap.

"So, hands again," Charity stated.

"Is that what these are," Bria asked. "Don't even recognize them."

Charity helped the wrap's edges to weld. "The swelling will go down. There's a lot going on beneath that skin of yours. In the meantime, I'll give you some pain inhibitor."

Bria thanked her, or thought she did. Charity took what she could get and tried to be understanding.

"And the eyes," Charity asked.

"They seem fine," Bria answered. "The left one kind of went buzzy for a second the other day."

"Buzzy?"

"I don't know how to describe it," Bria said. "Kind of flickered."

"What were you doing at the time?"

"What am I always doing," Bria asked. "I was working."

Charity's mouth twisted with scorn.

"I was trying to read something."

Charity held the back of her hand up.

"Do me a favor," she said, tapping the nail of her index finger. "Try to focus on this cuticle."

"What?"

"Just do it."

Bria looked, and Charity's fingernail was suddenly filling her entire peripheral. Every ridge of its formation was pristine and clear.

"Whoa," Bria cried.

Charity told her to blink, which she did, and her vision was back to normal.

"You're just zooming in. We can adjust that in the lab. We can talk about what features you want activated then," Charity said.

"Features?"

"Just blink if it happens again for now," informed Charity. "You just have to be more mindful of what you're trying to look closer at."

She began cleaning up the left over mess from working on Bria's hands.

"Heard about what you did to Merrecci," she said. "Nandy could barely breathe when she told me. She was laughing so hard."

"I'm glad one of us can laugh about it," Bria replied.

"Uh-huh," Charity retorted, working on sealing the wrap for Bria's other hand at the moment. "Do you know why we're even able to sit in this room doing this right now?"

"You told me. Donations," Bria replied.

"No, those just filled in the missing gaps. It's actually difficult to transplant hands. There's so much for a body to reject," Charity explained. "It was mostly because we were able to retrieve what were left of yours. A lot were damaged, but they gave me enough to act as the main building blocks and I filled in the gaps. Do you know how we got your hands?"

Bria didn't.

"Nandy retrieved them. Did you know those cooling systems get colder than the deepest space," Charity asked. She stopped. "Sorry. I didn't mean it that way."

Bria didn't mind the question. She understood that many engines on a variety of vessels could also generate more heat than most if not all suns. If space could cool them on their own, a ship commander could simply speed off to a sunless realm and chill down after taking a solar beating or pushing engines to their limits.

"I didn't know that," Charity said. "Comes with not being Franchise. So, you know why people can't go in. Shield batteries drain in seconds, protective suits would have to be made of the same bulky materials that the cooling ducts are made of. This is why engineers only go into cooling systems during downtime, or to save people from poison."

Bria decided to let Charity get away with that stab.

"Nandy retrieved them," Charity explained. "Two-minutes-ten seconds in, fifteen to thirty minutes outside recuperating before going again. And she had to pull out four bots to get to you, because that's how many had shut down trying to pull you out. She'd have probably made a good surgeon with the way she kept your parts from crumbling. Took a lot of cutting to break the grips you took in there, and she didn't trust anyone else with the job. It wasn't exactly a painless task for her either. She's still feeling it."

Charity finished her work wrapping Bria's hands into what appeared to be mittens, then she retrieved some medication from the fabricator.

"Despite whatever she's done to you, you could at least be grateful for what she's done for you," Charity said.

"She played me," Bria snapped.

"And you killed Cora." Charity slapped one of Bria's wrappings, and she watched Leonard break into a bout of screaming. "Damn. That felt good."

Charity took her leave while Bria attempted to bridle her pain in front of her subordinate.

When the captain returned to the bridge for her shift with her rebuilt extremities, the crew broke into applause. As she sat in the command chair and hit her hand, her scream filled all the way to Merrecci's quarters where he was flat on his back with his feet hanging over the ledge of his bed. He was trying to make his own fingers curve around his Mordecai Brown baseball. He cursed.

Mike whined a little each time Merrecci looked like he might throw the ball at him but didn't.

After enough failures, Merrecci sat up.

The man-dog squatted in front of Merrecci and begged to join the play.

"Fine," Merrecci said and tossed the ball.

Mike scrambled off and took several moments retrieving it in his mouth. When he returned, the prime admiral was staring out the window into the void of moving stars.

"We have a lot in common, my friend," Merrecci said.

Mike made an inquisitive and strange note.

"I'm a captain who was forced to act like a prime admiral when I wasn't. Somehow it made it easier on me to forget that I was a failure as a captain. You, on the other hand, are a human forcing yourself to behave like a dog. I think I get it. Maybe, when enough people treat you badly as one thing, it helps to pretend you're something else."

Then he took up the ball that Mike had dropped at his feet. He tried to curve his fingers around it again.

"We're both alike," Merrecci continued. "People's lives depend on us. What you do, what I do—we're still here because of who we really are and what we can really do."

Finally clenching the ball, Vincenti looked down on Mike.

"The difference between us though is that I'm really a prime admiral, and you're not really a frunkin' dog."

Merrecci tossed the ball, and Mike made no effort to chase it.

"Our ship needs an engineer, not a coward," Merrecci said coldly. "Now get your act in order."

Slowly, Mike allowed himself to stand. His eyes looked to the door, up to Merrecci's eyes, then to the floor.

Merrecci set a hand on Mike's shoulder.

"You're a good man," Merrecci said. "But you suck as a dog, and I think you'll find the crew feels the same way if you give them a chance. Look at how they stepped up for Bria."

Mike stepped away cautiously, hurt.

"You never abandoned me, even during my worst days," Merrecci said. "You might just be the best friend I have here, and it's not because you're a dog."

With that, Mike dropped back to his hands and knees and ran out of the room whining and crying.

Merrecci then called to Onyx, "Will you stop letting that damned dog in here now?"

Back on the bridge, and halfway through her shift, Nandy announced that she had just picked up some long range alerts.

After a moment of pondering whether to brush her off or ask the communication operator, Bria finally spoke.

"I'm always interested in news," Bria said. "What do we have?"

"Some sports team on Blemish won something called an Aruca," Nandy replied, and Bria could hear what might have been relief in her voice.

"I was hoping something more Earth-related."

"I was afraid you might. There is some. First is that our grievance to the franchise has been officially received and this is the only thing keeping Earth from being occupied by the Didjian who claim they have right to government establishment."

"Does that one make sense to you," Bria asked.

Nandy shook her head to say that it did not make sense.

"And our fleet," Nandy asked. "Any word on that."

"The Earth fleet has been interred within the Milky Way. They are protected but have been ordered to raise no weapons in defense of themselves," Nandy said and then, when she saw the quizzical look cross Bria's face, added, "Probably because if Earth should fight back during a time of asylum, they may waive right to maintain that sanctuary."

"Have all our ships been captured," Merrecci asked. No one had heard him enter.

"From what I've gathered, this message is reaching out to communicate with any Earth vessels, so I would guess they have not all reported in," Nandy said.

"That probably includes us too, Sir," Bria added.

"Does it say anything about our shipyard," Merrecci asked.

"It is under protection, but Jimmosheans are attempting to lay claim to it against the Franchise," Nandy replied. "There has been loss of life with our defenders.

"We don't have time for all this running around," Merrecci complained. "Before I took command of the Onyx, I was informed that there were more like her in our shipyard, but they are less armed and smaller. This could be problematic if we have to face those in enemy hands."

"According to this relay, Admiral Shuster is in negotiations to trade the shipyard for minimal occupation on Earth," Nandy read from her screen.

"Well, I never authorized that," Merrecci noted. "Can we send a long-range message telling him to cease that approach at once?"

"A shuttle on autopilot might be able to do it in four to six weeks, but it would have to go through Maridamarak space," Nandy said. "So, probably not."

"That's a problem," Merrecci said. "What else is there?"

"The Kag'tak have placed a pre-bounty on Earthers."

"What does that mean," Bria asked. When no one knew, they questioned Cindy.

"It's a precursor to extinction bounties," Cindy replied. "Anyone who tags an Earth vessel before an extermination bounty goes official will get twenty-five percent of the reward as finder's fee upon destruction. You've never witnessed a forced extinction before, but this is the standard pre-requisite for them. I am sorry."

"So now we're being hunted by everyone," Merrecci said.

"Oh, we always had a bounty," Cindy stated. "And bounties can always be tracked if you get tagged by someone looking for a finder's fee. It's just now, once the extermination clause is put into effect, the finder's fee goes up, and you don't tend to last very long.

"Put us into stealth, Captain," Merrecci ordered.

"Sir, we'll travel more slowly," Nandy pointed out.

Merrecci didn't realize it, but he sighed. "Under the circumstances, I think we have no choice but to abandon any further pursuit on this mission. Earth needs us."

"No, Sir," Bria dissented. "We must affirm the mission."

"I agree, but we just can't afford to drop our speed and add on—" He began attempting to snap his fingers to the navigation post.

"Three weeks, Sir," Escobedo replied.

"It will be more if we go off mission and have to return," Bria insisted standing from the command chair. "We should talk in your ready room."

Merrecci had already begun that journey, prepared to order his captain to follow. Bria called for Adrigga to join as well.

"This is precisely why you were given this post." Bria said once everyone was in Merrecci's office. "Despite its advanced weapons for Earth vessels, the Onyx isn't a warship."

"Of course, it's a warship," Merrecci corrected. "What else would it be?"

"I'm sorry, Sir," Bria said carefully. "I thought you knew. It's a preservation ship. Its purpose is to save humanity not to defend it."

"What are you talking about," Merrecci asked.

"If Earth falls, no other ship can ensure humanity lives on," Bria explained. "We're meant to save ourselves."

"That would suggest that our own world leaders knew something about the Milky Way's invasion," Merrecci started then stopped in realization. "They did know." He seemed lost for a moment, almost trance-like, then suddenly popped with. "Our mission was never to find Cindy's mate to keep them out of another race's hands. It was to track him down so we could find some far away place for Cindy and her lover to make us a new solar system?"

Then another realization hit him. "But you knew that already."

"Wait. What," Bria replied and was suddenly questioning Cindy if that was correct, but Cindy didn't answer.

"If we have to recolonize, we're going back for as many people as this ship can hold and taking as many of our fleet with us." Then he punctuated it with, "We will be going back."

"Sir," Bria stated directly. "We are not turning around."

Merrecci's eyebrow sharpened.

"We're not just talking about preserving one race anymore," Bria argued. "We have three on the verge of extinction on our ship. We're looking for a fourth. If we go back and lose, we don't just lose ourselves. When you consider all the bounties that this ship represents, we are the most valuable point of existence in all of space right now. We are now the center of everyone's universe."

"You're a pain right in the middle of the back of my moly neck, you know that," Merrecci snapped.

Bria held up the back side of her bandaged hand to the admiral.

"What," Merrecci asked.

"I imagine she's giving you the bird, Sir," Nandy translated.

"In my ready room," Merrecci exploded. "You're flipping me off in my own office!"

"It's the best I can seem to salute these days," Bria replied.

Merrecci clenched his jaw.

"Well, then," he spoke. "I guess someone needs to figure out how to solve our problem of maintaining stealth and speed."

"I think I already have one," Bria informed. "We can keep up our speed if we power the stealth with the temporary power supply in the botanical sector."

"That's still on board," Merrecci inquired. "Why wasn't it in the dossier?"

"It wasn't supposed to be here," Bria replied.

Then Merrecci started nodding and tapping his finger against the air as he turned to leave. "Stay on mission and send out a shuttle to transmit Earth's wishes not to surrender our shipyards. Continue to rely on Franchise support while our grievance is being considered."

"It won't make it through Maridamarak space," Nandy stated.

"Doesn't need to make it through Maridamarak space, just within range of the communication relays we left behind," Merrecci directed. "That should be enough to get the message moving on its own."

"Provided the Maridamarak haven't discovered the relays yet," Bria reminded.

"If you have another idea, I'm willing to hear it."

Bria set to fulfill Merrecci's hopeful orders, while he exited the bridge. Soon after, she left Nandy in command and took a quick break.

She had to announce herself several times before Cindy answered her door, pretending to be in the shower.

"If you were in the shower, why is your robe dry," Bria asked, storming into her quarters. When she turned back to Cindy, the robe was drenched and dripping."

"Really," Bria asked. Then she exploded with, "You were going to go through with this? You were actually going to destroy yourself to give us a new home?"

"Not exactly."

"Not exactly?"

"Well, not right away."

"What's that supposed to mean," Bria asked.

"Maybe I'll tell you when you're older," Cindy replied. She reached to Bria to hold her face.

"Don't do that," Bria, snapped, recoiling. "Don't treat me like I'm stupid."

"You're right," Cindy said. "I'm sorry. It's just going to take us a long time to get somewhere no one will think of reaching for at least a trillion years. You'll be old by then, and I'll have moved on."

"Moved on," Bria asked.

"Oh, sweetie," Cindy said. "I'm practically immortal. You didn't really think we were going to last forever, did you?"

Bria recoiled.

"Besides, it's what we do, we give birth to new worlds and new life," Cindy reflected.

"So, this is all because it's what you're supposed to do," Bria snapped.

"Well, yeah," Cindy replied. "What should I do?"

"Don't do it," Bria shouted.

"Why wouldn't I do that?"

"You have a choice! It's not worth killing yourself over."

"What I do when that time comes is none of your business," Cindy Lou said directly.

"So that's how it is," Bria realized and started for the exit.

She felt Cindy hold out to her again.

"I'm really old," Cindy explained. "How long do I have to stick around?"

*   *   *

Ensign Being was sitting on the edge of his seat. To his left, Vandenbutcke's fingers were hovering over his own panel awaiting their next instruction.

"Port full reverse," Being called.

Vandenbutcke's hands rapidly moved to follow the command.

"Get ready to return to full," Being instructed. He stood slightly from his seat, then sat again while ordering, "Now!"

The Onyx suddenly began vibrating at every stress point. Merrecci's knuckles were white. He knew, come the next morning, that he was going to regret clenching his right armrest so tightly.

Being had suggested the holo be shut off so as not to distract the crew. When Merrecci asked if that was necessary, Being replied with, "You want to get to where we're going, or do you want to have a heart attack?"

The holo remained empty, and Merrecci realized he was grateful as the Onyx moaned in pain and kept getting louder. A high-pitched whistling grew and filled every inch of air.

Bria, who couldn't grip a softball yesterday was holding onto the railing of her dugout. She had been strapped into her chair that would never allow anyone to fall from it, but it did, in fact, throw her out because of how harshly Being was maneuvering the ship. Currently, she found it safer to stand at this point. Nandy kept wanting to reach out and aid her more, but she could barely keep herself from falling over the captain beside her in the dugout.

The shaking stopped, and all but the ringing in ears was silent.

"What was that," Almma asked from above the dugout.

Vandenbutcke couldn't answer, he was too busy following Being's orders, and Being was too busy being perfect.

Then Onyx herself stopped, and Being announced, "We're here."

Vandenbutcke stood and threw up over to the other side of his console and really wished there hadn't been an operator over there at the moment.

"Vandenbutcke," Merrecci asked.

Vandenbutcke wasn't just pale, he'd seen too much.

"Do I want to know," Merrecci asked.

Vandenbutcke shook his head.

"The chief was right to turn off the holo," he muttered. "We dodged almost everything, within inches of our shields, Sir." He dropped into his chair and hung his head over his knees.

"It was just big chunks," Being said.

"Chunks the size of planets," Vandenbutcke bellowed.

"You said almost everything," Merrecci inquired.

Vandenbutcke's face rose, wide-eyed, processing still.

"This crazy bastard just drilled the Onyx through one of those planetary chunks," Then Vandenbutcke realized what adrenaline had been trying to tell him all this time, and he bolted up from his seat and turned to Ensign Being. "God damn, you can fly!"

He and Being clapped together after some severe effort on Being's part to steadily raise his hand and hope that through his shaking, he could actually hit Vandenbutcke's palm. He hit, and for a brief moment, his vibrations bled into Vandenbutcke's frame as the two clasped fingers. Vandenbutcke roared with victory. Once they released their grasp, Being briefly shook the pain away and returned to monitoring the console that would magically give him steadiness. He thought he might be messing himself at the present, but he wasn't going to announce that.

"A little decorum, please," Merrecci requested. He turned to Bria. "So, where is it?"

Bria looked over her pad. For several moments, she argued with her holotab over what commands her fingers were issuing. Her right index accidentally activated the battlecron and flipped her tablet out of her hands. She complained as she knelt to retrieve it and then grumbled some more that she couldn't grip it off the floor. Finally, she just refreshed it, and her bracelet made it appear within her grasp.

"According the astrometrics, the—," Bria started but didn't finish as she looked up from her screen and realized for the first time just what kind of debris Ensign Being and Vandenbutcke had flown them through. The battlecron showed monstrous planetary segments floating around the Onyx. Any one of them could smash right through the ship if Chief Pilot Ensign Being suddenly forgot how to dance with them.

"Captain Holo," Merrecci said, staring at the images on the battlecron himself and realizing, "Captain Leonard. Sorry! I really wish you wouldn't have turned that on."

"Right," Bria replied and looked down to her pad to finish her answer, but suddenly looked up. "Ensign, how long are you going to be able to keep this up?"

"Now, I admit I haven't been on a lot of ships," Almma said from her post above the dugout, her eyes still examining the marvel of broken, collided planets on the holo. "But shouldn't our chief pilot have two chairs?"

"Why would he need two chairs," Merrecci asked.

"Uh," Almma replied. "For his giant, brass balls."

"Lieutenant Commander," Merrecci snapped.

"Am I wrong?"

"Probably not," Merrecci replied. "But when are you going to grasp professionalism on my bridge?"

Then somewhere from Merrecci's left and behind Bria in the tactical sector someone started making clacking sounds with his tongue.

"Who was that," Merrecci snapped, standing from his seat. "What did I just say about professionalism. We are Earth officers! Now, who the hell is doing that?"

"Sir," Bria asked. "With respect, are you being serious, right now?"

"Do I look like I'm not," Merrecci roared.

"It's okay, Captain," Almma insisted, holding up a hand to silence her and draw out Merrecci's intent. "I'm running a scan now to find out who it was. And, ah ha! Admiral, the sound seems to be coming from beneath the chief pilot's console." Almma barely got the last of her sentence out before she had to clench her jaw shut to maintain her decorum.

"It did not come from—oh for God damn," Merrecci said, dropping back into his chair. "You people piss me off."

The bridge erupted in laughter.

"Oh, shut up," Merrecci snipped back.

"Sir," Bria said. "I've located our intended site."

The holo zoomed in to one of the larger planetary pieces, somehow set more away now from the chaos of other broken massive chunks, which somewhat made Merrecci happier.

Even Vandenbutcke felt he could maintain the Onyx's safety if he were at the helm. Merrecci immediately sent Being off to sleep so he'd be more rested if they suddenly needed him.

For this exposition, Merrecci found it prudent to send down a team of maintenance bots to search the ruins in place of humans. If the Onyx should have to make a quick escape in here, he didn't want living crew in danger of being left behind just for the sake of searching for whatever they came to find.

However, after a day of no discoveries and high anxieties on board, he decided to send out three shuttles manned by Vandenbutcke's students to fly over the planetary segment and scan its surface for any kind of insinuation there might be something to direct Merrecci's quest further.

Vandenbutcke took another craft out after the progress continued to move slowly. He wasn't out long before he realized something in the surrounding system was inhibiting his shuttle's scanning abilities.

He returned to the Onyx and requested engineering assistance. When he returned to the shuttle bay, a young woman, Lieutenant Oen, was waiting for him. She was leaning against a bronze crate while three male crewmates were laughing with her.

When she saw him, she abruptly stood straight and grabbed her tool kit.

"Where's Mirror," Vandenbutcke asked as soon as Oen approached.

"I took the call," Oen said.

"So, you weren't assigned," Vandenbutcke asked.

"Don't get me wrong," Oen said. "They're pleasant enough people, but, considering the job, do you want it done right, or do you want it done dumb?"

"What an ironically good question," Vandenbutcke replied.

A few minutes later, Mirror appeared in the bay, met with Oen, and took her tool kit.

As Vandenbutcke prepared the shuttle for departure, Mirror watched Oen continue to flirt with the three men, only now she seemed a little more interested in throwing side-eye past her conversations to Bria who was now sitting in the engineer's seat.

"She's pretty, isn't she," Mirror asked.

"I suppose she is," Vandenbutcke replied. "To some."

"I wish I could be pretty," Mirror lamented.

"Who says you're not?"

"The mirror."

"I don't think you should talk like that," Vandenbutcke said.

"Do you think I'm pretty?"

"I would say prettier than her," Vandenbutcke found himself answering carefully.

"As pretty as Nandy?"

"Now why would you ask—how do you know about that," Vandenbutcke questioned.

"I saw you in the hall. I see how you both try to hide it," Mirror said. "You're not like them and Oen because they're just playing. You and Nandy don't play."

"No," Vandenbutcke said. "We take it a little more seriously."

"Yeah," Mirror said. "You hide it."

She kept staring at Oen.

"That doesn't make a person pretty," Vandenbutcke countered.

"People with friends are pretty," Mirror said. "People talk to you because they want to."

"There you have it," Vandenbutcke replied. "See."

"I don't have friends," Mirror replied. "Just people who have to talk to me."

"Well, I don't have to talk to you," Vandenbutcke informed.

"Then why are you," Mirror asked. "You have Nandy."

"Because I didn't want to have to talk to the pretty, dumb engineer for the next few hours. I wanted to talk to the pretty, smart one,"

Vandenbutcke said. "Or do you not want to talk to me? Is it because I'm ugly? Oh my god! I'm ugly, aren't I? You think I'm ugly."

Mirror couldn't answer. In this way, Vandenbutcke passed his own boredom during his next tour out to scan the floating rock. Mirror, however, wasn't bored.

Another day passed, and a shuttle discovered a small patch of plateau with strange contours in the planetary crust. After recalling his living crew and then commissioning maintenance drones to the site, they discovered evidence of a buried structure. Within another two days, the bots cleared enough ground to reveal an entrance to some sort of cavern.

Merrecci still withheld trying to send anyone down to the surface just yet. The maintenance bots were immediately set inside the opening to investigate. Six hours later, they reported very little beyond an incomplete map of a labyrinth of tunnels. Fifteen minutes after that, they reported a chamber with a sarcophagus. Another six hours reported a cave-in. Eight more hours and the machines had cleared out enough of the collapsed tunnel to allow them to continue their survey. By the end of the day, the entire cavern had been mapped. Besides the robots, only the sarcophagus could be found in the tunnels system.

"As soon as they bring it out, transfer everything up and get our shuttles on board," Merrecci instructed.

Once the sarcophagus appeared outside the entrance of the ruin, Bria set out to warehouse seven. The maintenance droids spent another hour clearing their exit enough to allow their cargo more space to exit its tomb. Finally, it was out, and the Onyx targeted it with a transfer ray.

A few moments later, the sarcophagus was in warehouse seven.

"Merrecci to Captain Leonard," Merrecci announced. "Do we have him, then?"

Bria had set to examining the coffin the moment it arrived. She had cleared the entire warehouse of all personnel. The materials that made it may have been some sort of blue, steel-like gold. Unlike any sarcophagus that she had seen in pictures, museums, or archives, this was devoid of any inlay or jewels. It was simply a metallic case with a type of window made from a translucent material which scans suggested was some sort of metal alloy.

She had already called Drinker down to help her discover how to open it once she finished analyzing it for harmful gases. Drinker examined the capsule for ten minutes, then began to peel back and twist components that left her to wonder how he'd seen them.

The sarcophagus opened, and she peered inside.

"Admiral," Bria said. "This thing is empty."

Merrecci's transmission cut out amidst an abrupt cursing rampage, and he gave a hint on which god's sector he was most likely heading to at that very moment to lash into.

Bria asked Drinker if he could reseal the sarcophagus. Then she called for Lieutenant Fram and Crewman Jossel to retrieve the box and take it to their research facility. Once she had ensured the safety of the artifact, Bria was out the door and rushing, not running, to beat Merrecci to the destination she believed he was honing in on. Oh, who was she kidding? She was hauling ass.

Bria passed through the disintegration shield and shortly after found Cindy in her personal quarters standing in the wall-sized window well, fully-naked, and almost posing like some ancient, fictional superhero as she looked beyond the window into space.

"And just think," Cindy Lou said confidently, "Someone out there with a really powerful telescope is smiling right now."

"Merrecci is on his way, and he's not happy," Bria said. "You need to get dress—

"All right," Merrecci screeched, storming into the room, and locking eyes with Bria, as though he didn't expect to see her there. "What kind of bullsh—and she's naked!" He turned to face away and elbowed his captain to offer the same respect.

"It's okay Admiral," Cindy replied. "She's seen it before."

"What's that supposed to mean, Leonard," Merrecci asked.

"Because we have sex," Cindy sneered.

Bria turned suddenly away from Merrecci so her own flesh wouldn't allow him to see what she was thinking just now.

"We do it," Cindy continued. "Like all the time. Seriously. Check out this couch." Cindy leapt from the window to the sofa and started jumping on it. "Check this bounce out," she crowed, then suddenly stopped. "Oh, we should coat this thing in that bouncy, purple goo!" Then she started jumping again with more vigor. Suddenly she stopped. "Think what it could do for our abs. Seriously. Check this out!" She flexed, tightening her stomach into a well crafted tapestry of toned muscles. "Come on, Admiral. Punch me like I was your first officer."

"Stop it," Merrecci yelled then fell silent as he finally realized what Cindy had actually said in all of her nonsense.

"Woohoo," Cindy began jumping again. "Oh yeah!"

"Get dressed," Merrecci said.

"All right, Prude Admiral," Cindy replied, and suddenly a sleeveless and jade, glittery dress with a long slit up her smooth leg appeared. She sat on the couch.

"How did you do that," Merrecci asked.

"What? This?" Cindy's dress changed to white.

"Yes. How did you make clothes?"

"I have a really good sewing machine," Cindy said.

When it was clear that Merrecci didn't approve of the joke, she relented with, "Fine, I didn't make clothes. I'm still naked." She was suddenly naked again and then back in the white dress after that. "See?"

"So, you never actually wear clothes?"

"Oh no, I have an entire replicated wardrobe of them. I love the process, but I don't have time to pick something out for people who barge in unannounced," Cindy Lou replied. "I'd be here all day. It would be a lot easier on me if you humans could just get over your aversion to the whole nakedidity thing."

"Two things," Merrecci announced, signifying that he'd had enough. "First, this—whatever's going on between you two—done."

"Why? You want to cut in," Cindy asked and was suddenly naked again—well, what looked like naked to a human—and lounging into the back wall of the couch.

"Over," Merrecci ordered.

"Like hell," Cindy Lou suddenly rose to her feet, grew well over the height of Merrecci and glowered down on him. Her entire face twisted into something the foulness of nightmares. "She's my pet, and you hit her. So, you don't get to say jack shidley about who she touches!" When she was done roaring and bearing her six inch fangs, she returned to her previous size and naked, human form. "I ask for so little."

Now, she turned and walked through the doorway that led to her wardrobe.

"What was the one and only thing you came in here to say, Prime Admiral," Cindy Lou's voice asked calmly from beyond the closet doorway.

Merrecci couldn't find the words. He still saw a snarling demon in front of him. He wanted to speak but couldn't find the thoughts to string together for some reason.

"What are we doing out here," Bria asked. "We found the sarcophagus, and it's empty."

"Sarcophagus," Cindy Lou asked and then chortled. "It would be empty. You didn't expect him to wait, did you?"

"So, we need it for him," Merrecci asked.

Cindy's head popped out a moment to answer in the affirmative, then disappeared again.

"You're starting to piss me off," Merrecci said. "We have put our entire civilization on pause so we could travel the universe to find a coffin. I don't think it's too much to ask for a little respect from the cargo!"

Yeah. He realized he said it all too late.

Cindy stepped out slowly from the wardrobe. She was wearing an early Earth spaghetti strap top and a pair of hip-hugging jeans that she found in a database of something called catalogs from old department stores.

"Did you just call me cargo," she asked plainly.

"You're not going to go big on me again are you," Merrecci asked cautiously.

"No," Cindy replied. "But I'm sure you don't need help from the cargo to figure this one out. Go ask your sarcophagus instead. Maybe it can give a more helpful answer. Now, shoo! Piss off."

Merrecci almost opened his mouth to argue, but decided diplomacy might keep him in the god's best graces. Bria's brow reinforced his intuition.

"Of course," Merrecci said. "My apologies."

"Shoo then," Cindy said, almost a whisper. Then she turned to Bria. "Is this asking too much for you to take off later?"

Bria turned from the Admiral again and listened for him to exit. She waited a few moments before following.

"Have a good day at work, baby," Cindy Lou called after her.

When Bria caught up with Merrecci at the elevator, he was silent.

"That's a bad idea," he said, once the doors sealed.

"Says who," Bria replied.

"A friend."

"Is that what we are," Bria asked.

Merrecci fell back silent. The elevator stopped, the doors opened but then shut at Merrecci's behest.

"You do remember the part where she's going to erupt into a galaxy and be gone, right," he asked.

"I'm well aware," Bria replied.

"Why put yourself through it then?"

"Who else is going to want me," Bria asked. She re-opened the doors and exited in the direction of the research and development department.

16
▲
Quick

While the Onyx remained static in space, stealthed and in near-silent running, Bria yelled at a coffin.

"So that was a bad idea," Crewman Jossel stated. She held a torn pillow that had been attached to the box's inside lining. A moment ago, she had suggested maybe they could pull the fabric out and look beneath it for clues. She was wrong.

Lieutenant Fram climbed out from beneath the hovering sarcophagus and ordered the bot to return it to the bench it had been resting on prior.

"I don't see anything," Fram said. "I pick up no hidden compartments, no secret writing. If there are any clues, the only place we haven't checked is under the rest of the padding."

"Want me to start pulling," Jossel asked.

"No," Bria replied. "I think we need more expert help from someone who might actually know this artifact."

Five minutes later, two large Rhaxian boulder beings were examining the strange container. Jossel and Fram were trying to scan the creatures without looking like they were trying to scan them, until one turned on them and made the sound of stones grinding against themselves. Fram and Jossel didn't know what they meant, but Jossel stopped scanning. Fram got excited and tried to imitate the sound back.

The Rhaxian who had spoken suddenly shivered from head to toe in a series of sharp, high-toned clacking.

Coldona Garu turned to his ally and responded in a stone tongue that the translator still did not understand. His partner turned her attention back to the coffin.

"Soft human," Garu said. "Baka has wished you well in words where there are no words in your language. You have wished his head in the eye dance of a lava goat who is three seasons birthed by dead fish cheese. Please refrain from practicing your poor dialect here."

Fram apologized.

"Not at all," Baka said. "No outsider has spoken our tongue successfully in a long time. It wasn't bad for imitation." Then he started shivering again with stone clattering.

"Yes, it was funny," Garu said, and they both went back to work, which wasn't quite clear to anyone else in the room other than the Rhaxians.

Bria sat silently and attempted to look like observing the work of others was actually accomplishing something on her end. She discovered it really was. Her finger exercises were getting a little easier behind her back. Today, she was able to touch her thumb to each of her fingertips. She reached her pinky. She actually touched her pinky.

Eventually, the Rhaxians began making noises that suggested they had reached an agreement.

"Uh-huh," Baka finally announced.

"What is it," Bria asked.

"We suspected as much," Garu said. "Though it is a bit modern of a presentation than we are used to seeing. Our Rhaxian brothers on one of our fallen ships must have built it. Fine work."

"And?"

"I see you do not have this ritual in your race," Baka said. "You see, when a male and a female Utonenaibe and Zarchro are consummate, one lays on top of the other in the same place and a few minutes later they give birth."

"You mean sex," Bria asked. "We know sex! Are you telling me this is their bed, and we've just—wait a minute! They give birth a few minutes later?"

"Yes," Garu replied.

"What do you mean by minutes," Fram asked.

"Nine Earth minutes," Baka replied. "Isn't that normal for soft tissue aliens. How long does it take you to give birth after conception?"

Bria found herself unable to respond.

"We've been wracking our brains over what the this does for how many hours and its only purpose is for them to get it on," Jossel asked.

"And you tore the pillow," Fram said.

"Maybe she won't need it," Jossel suggested.

"Well, of course she'll need it," Fram exploded.

"So, what are we supposed to do with this now," Bria asked.

"Well, I suppose you could try asking the admiral if he'd like to join you and—," Baka started.

"Prime Admiral Merrecci," Bria suddenly interrupted.

"Yes," Merrecci's voice answered.

"It seems this sarcophagus is their bed," Bria replied.

"Whose bed? Cindy's and her mate's," Merrecci asked. "What the hell are we supposed to do with that?"

"If you come down, Admiral, we can walk you and your first officer through how it works," Garu responded. "She seemed confused too at first."

A loud guffaw suddenly erupted from Merrecci's side of the communication, and Merrecci instantly chided Lieutenant-commander Almma.

"He means, how are we supposed to use this to point us to where we're supposed to go next," Bria asked. "We have the bed, but we're looking for the male."

"Right," Merrecci approved. "The bed does no one any good without the male to go with it."

"Well, sure, if she doesn't know what she's doing," Almma blurted.

She was abruptly dismissed from the bridge on her end.

"We followed the path," Merrecci said. "It ends here. What are we supposed to do now?"

Garu erupted with realization. "We did not realize that was your inquiry of us."

Baka agreed. "Yes, that's a different story all together."

Bria tried to craft fists but failed.

"Try asking it," Baka said.

"Really," Merrecci asked.

"I told you," Cindy's voice announced. "But what does the cargo know?"

"Where is the male Zarchro," Garu asked.

The coffin exterior suddenly turned into the skin of a galaxy. Bria groaned.

"What," Merrecci asked.

"We need astrometric's help again," Bria said. "It turned into another map."

*   *   *

Guggler's Den was founded on one master rule. As long as your face was hidden, it was against code to collect on its owner or direct others to do so. The moment a masking of covering removed or fell away, you were no longer protected from your bounty. And everyone in Guggler's had a bounty and a price. Anyone with a marked with a pre-bounty was regarded as showing their face. However, no one could actually be tagged while planet-side.

Brokers worked through anonymous terminals. The best collectors knew not to use them. The best collectors knew the way to the highest paying private contracts were through confronting the broker directly, which meant getting past their security.

If a hunter couldn't find a contract nor survive a broker's security, that hunter certainly couldn't accomplish a particularly advanced and high-paying task. Not all collectors were created equal, and some jobs didn't need an army of thugs annihilating the worksites. Some used more subtle security approaches. Not all bounty hunters knew the difference.

Two figures in green dresses, hosiery and scarf particularly had no experience in collecting bounties, but one had at least been to Guggler's Den before. The other remained silent and learning.

They trekked the edge of the walkway, one behind the other. The storefronts were dark, unlit, unwelcoming. They were supposed to be. Their windows, for the most part, were black to hide the purchases of individuals who might otherwise be easily identifiable based upon their choice of supplies, until the newly purchased trinkets could be hidden before leaving a shop. Many bounty hunters were known for their unique and preferred killing supplies. Few, if any, carried anything more than basic sidearms. Those who brandished anything more unique were either stupid or someone other hunters knew they didn't want to tangle with.

To help keep identity secret, only small portions of window displays advertised what the store sold. Rookie hunters bought what was on sale and novel. The good stuff only came out for those who knew what they needed; who knew what the store already had; and who didn't need to ask questions nor haggle. Usually, the shop keeper had the merchandise delivered to the customer's ship, but they could also wrap the item in cloth if the buyer felt inclined to carry their purchase onto the street.

When a larger figure dressed in white regalia refused to move from the path of the hunters in green, the one in white fell quickly into the gutter, reaching for his face covering before anything else.

The two green hunters continued forward. The one in the rear suddenly stopped and whistled for the other to hold up as well. After a moment of silent disagreement, they both ducked into a store front where the shorter of the two discovered an interesting weapon that had the appearance of a war hammer but was really more like two massive bear traps set back to back of each other atop one end of its shaft. One set of teeth was always open acting as the face, while the other was closed. Upon striking an object, the teeth bit shut, causing the second, identical jaw of fangs to bear open, showing how hungry it too was to taste of destruction. In this manner, the two back-to-back traps took turns biting away at whatever enemy they hit. The wielder simply had to remember to keep twisting the shaft of the magnificent weapon to ensure each strike would set off the biting mechanism.

"For when you just need the head," the owner said after demonstrating it tear the top off a mannequin that had seen far better days well before the life of being in a weapon shop.

Soon, the green hunters were back on the streets, the shorter one using the axe as a walking stick, not bothering to hide what it was. At a check point where the roads suddenly turned from grime to rundown, the guards put up little resistance as the duo simply pressed past. Anyone willing to shove through a guard station of this tier was more than deserving to seek the higher work. Plus, the guards didn't want to tempt the bear-trap-like hammer.

This was a natural weeding process to decipher the good jobs from those who gleaned what they could. There were several landing ports in Guggler's Den. They were all in the center of the worst of the worst hive of scum. The farther one traveled from the port, the cleaner the world became, the better the food, and the better people got paid.

At the next check point, the roads turned from run-down to clean; where the buildings went from lower-end and boxed-up hotel suites to tall towers of one night reward; and where the restaurants turned from outside dives to indoor "get your food and get outs."

Here, the guards were more armored, but knew when to retreat so they could last the shift and many more.

Then another checkpoint, and the world turned into skyrise business offices and administrations, where the largest condos and most refined restaurant wouldn't serve anyone without an approved and clean, face covering. At this check point, the green duo brandished their eagerness to break a few jaws if pushed to it. They were allowed to pass, and all without having to break anyone in the journey.

Guggler's Den didn't make stupid guards, but don't confuse their willingness to concede a brawl at a checkpoint with inexperience. Any one of them had unmatched skills, weaponry, and a moral code against killing unless in defense of their brokers.

In this sector, the two hunters in green picked out a tall, silver building and entered. When they were asked if they had an appointment, the smaller of the duo slammed the large hammer against the desk and let the trap bite a hole through its top. Then they continued on their way to a secured elevator, which they pushed into.

At the top of the chute was a restaurant surrounded by apartments suitable for royalty. Here, a snooty, tall, and skinny wiener informed the companions that they did not have acceptable head wear. The duo had to insist their way farther into their own table, a place within an enclosed cubicle without cameras, and where people could eat and remove their face coverings safely, however, despite this perk, the two did not remove theirs.

Here, one of the duo activated a call button on the wall and they waited.

Within ten minutes a clap came to their booth. Two guards appeared and waited for the masked guests to follow them. One guard was a breed of race large enough to be Kag'tak, and the other was something closer to Earth. From here, the two hunters dressed in green were led into a diamond trimmed office where some sort of creature that may or may not have been a breed of dual insectoid greeted them from behind a veil that fell over his face from a large turban and proceeded to envelope everything down to his shoulders.

He was silent for some time, most likely measuring the duo. Then he excused his guards and remained alone with the visitors.

"Your disguises are as collector as they are inhuman, Earthers," the turban said. "You might as well be unmasked."

The shorter of the green duo gripped the axe.

Six arms suddenly unfolded from behind the broker's back, each holding a sleek weapon of unknown consequence.

"Were you aiding any other race, you would be dead now for brandishing that insult," the turban said. "I can only assume you are from the new Earth ship that has abandoned its fleet."

Then the broker holstered, turned, and bid the duo to follow.

"I do apologize for taking so long to respond," the broker said. "My ancestors nor I ever expected to hear the ping of the wedding chamber, so imagine my surprise to hear it when you entered our space. I did not believe such an archaic box would have been capable of receiving any further transmission. Yet, here you are."

He led them down a set of stairs, through a living area, then through an office and into a garage with a sleek shuttle. It was golden, every inch, except for a canopy of black, and it had a shape similar to a broadhead arrow.

"Many in my heritage have not honored this calling. It has not been out of storage for many generations," the broker said. "You seek a god. Do you have one already then?"

The duo didn't answer.

"So yes," the turban replied.

"The female?"

Again, no answer.

"So yes, again," the broker answered. "The reward on her alone would be enough to purchase Earth's security for the life of many suns. We could end your war now if you turn her over to me."

Again, he waited for an answer.

"No," Turban asked in disappointment. "If you change your mind, I will be awaiting your transmission."

He handed out a sleek laser-card.

"It is not a tracker," the turban said. "Else I could lose my license and respect." He continued to hold out the card. After no response to claim it came though, he abruptly ordered them to take it. He placed the card into the first hand that opened to him, which happened to be the person not carrying the bear trap axe.

"You never know," Turban said. "Sometimes one's only ally is temptation."

Then he turned to the gold vessel, and the black canopy opened to reveal two seats.

"This is the Compass," Turban said. "It is old but cared for. If you put in the DNA of the female, it will seek out compatible counterpart, which should be your male."

One of the duo's heads cocked to the side.

"I see. You wonder if it can be this easy to find the other god. I do not know. Without your female, the ship would be worthless. It has been uncoded since its creation. You have the female."

Again, no response.

"You don't hide as much as you think," the turban rebuked. "Take the Compass. Don't take the Compass. I've fulfilled my calling."

The strange broker waved a hand, and the exterior wall of the private garage opened to an orange sky with yellow clouds.

"You have three Franchise adopted minutes to be on your way before I close those doors and activate a bounty for the attempted theft of the ship if you are still here. That is the standard practice to protect one's self against aiding and abetting a high-priced collection.

Do not return," the turban added, and he left the room.

The duo ran to the ship and bungled their way through powering the device on. With a little argument, they managed a clunky escape from the garage, just as the bay doors began to close.

"With respect, admiral," Almma announced from the rear seat. "You fly like a drunk bumble bee whose queen just ran off with his best part."

"You want to do this," Merrecci asked.

"Pfft! No, but know who would? A pilot!" Almma replied.

"Don't act like you knew we'd need one," Merrecci said, struggling to keep the ship's path smooth.

Then a bit of turbulence dropped the craft about ten feet and momentarily made Merrecci lose hold of the handled controls.

Almma secured her axe in the only cargo compartment she could discover to prevent it from setting it off in the turbulence.

"Good god," Almma cried. "I feel like I'm back in the limo after prom!"

When the vessel bobbed and rolled again, Almma rose slightly from her seat and cracked her head against her headrest. "Just like the limo, except he could drive!"

"Will you shut up," Merrecci yelled.

"I thought you were a pilot," Almma asked. "What the hell are you doing?"

"I'm aiming for space," Merrecci yelled. "Now shut up."

Merrecci's stomach lurched as the ship dropped again. Somehow, he got the nose looking up once more.

"Aim better," Almma yelled, the only way she could speak without shattering her teeth together.

Finally, the skies began to thin and blacken, then the ship felt even more unstable and shot away from the planet at a speed Merrecci hadn't anticipated.

"Seriously! Prom! Did you learn nothing," Almma asked. "You can't just throw her around."

"I don't know what I'm doing," Merrecci yelled back as he realized that he had raced past where he had left the Onyx in stealth mode, and the Compass just kept going.

"Why would you tell me that," Almma snapped. "Have you ever flown before? Because you act like you've never flown before. Hell, student-pilots who've never flown before and act like they've flown before can fly better than you, and they've never flown before! Is this your first time?"

Ten minutes passed, and they found no slowing mechanism. The same attempt to power down as they powered up failed to stop the flight. Reversing the process didn't work either, especially since they felt luck got them powered up to begin with.

Several times, Merrecci was tempted to call out to Bria, but couldn't risk allowing anyone to triangulate the location of the Onyx based upon its transmissions. He wasn't certain how public this new ship's communication would be.

Then, the Compass stopped.

"Now what," Merrecci asked. He checked the color of his shirt to measure the oxygen quality. It was still green. When it turned red, that's when he knew he was doomed to die.

"You can't see shit in this thing," Almma said, squirreling her head around to look beyond the rear of the cockpit but couldn't for the aft of the ship's body.

Merrecci came up with the same result on his own. Additionally, he couldn't understand any of the sensor readouts. They weren't any kind of similar technology to anything Earth ever had before. The scanner looked more like a sundial and not an accurate one at that. All Merrecci could tell at this moment was that the Compass was being pulled backwards.

Merrecci and Almma watched the familiar walls of shuttle bay one encapsulate their vessel.

"Thank god," Merrecci said. "I was afraid I was going to have to aim this thing for the interior of an enemy ship and figure out how to Dawn it through the corridors until we could punch back through the hull."

Soon the Compass was firmly planted against the floor of the shuttle bay, and it powered down on its own.

"You all right back there," Merrecci asked.

"Funny, that's what the limo driver asked too," Almma replied. "Will you just let me out already, and don't walk me to the door, cuz you ain't getting even an 'okay, well I gotta go' back pat."

Merrecci opened the canopy.

"Nothing about this is familiar," Bria said as she suddenly appeared confused at the side of the Compass.

"Thank you, Captain," Merrecci greeted, finally tearing his scarf from his head. "How did you know it was us though?"

"We didn't." Bria answered. "I just thought if we caught a hunter ship, maybe we could tap into some data on our bounty, and this one flew off world like it had been stolen by amateurs, so I figured it should be a catch that either no one cared about, or we could buy off. Where the hell did you come from? Where is Vandenbutcke?"

"Who knows" Almma said, following Merrecci down from the Compass. "We got a ship. They got a sex slave. Good trade, huh?"

"You left him behind, didn't you? Guess we're going back," Bria followed up. "Had to follow you for a while so we didn't give away our—What is that?"

"This," Almma asked, brandishing the new weapon she now drew from within the Compass. "This is fifty-five pounds of pure, adulterated 'got your nips' is what this is."

"Huh?"

"It's like 'got your nose,' only you grab her—"

"We get it," Merrecci roared. "Glad you caught us, Captain," Merrecci said, interrupting Almma's moment. "This ship is the next leg of our mission. Probably take us to another damned map."

At this, Bria ordered the bridge to activate the auto-return on Vandenbutcke's shuttle. "And prepare to put us back in silent-running level five at the first sign something other than Vandenbutcke gets too close," she instructed.

The lights dimmed.

Merrecci was exiting the warehouse when he suddenly stopped.

"What is that," he asked. His finger drew towards a non-standard cargo cover that sat out like an oddly-shaped bubble.

"Huh," Bria asked. She looked and noticed the blue covering being weighed down with silver canisters. "I don't know."

"I was talking to Almma," Merrecci said before marching towards the cargo. "Is this what I think it is?"

"This is why we don't invite dad to our stripper parties," Almma snipped.

Merrecci reached the cargo and gripped the strange, plastic material. He peeled a corner back revealing a bit of bright red surface.

"Want to tell me what this is," Merrecci asked.

"Nah. I'm good," Almma replied.

Merrecci tore the tarp completely away now.

"Hey! Watch the paint," Almma cried.

"I know this was you. What is it," he demanded to know.

"I believe it's called a Fairyairy," Almma said.

"Uh-huh." Merrecci then called Dawn who was currently in Engineering to ask, "Why is there a Ferrari in my warehouse?"

"We have a Ferrari, and no one told me," Dawn asked.

"Are you seriously enabling this," Merrecci asked Almma.

"Why is this my fault," Almma said. "It wasn't given to her."

"Given to h—," Merrecci started to ask then. "Is this from Esco—your secret admirer?"

Almma nodded.

"Am I to understand that your secret admirer fabricated another twenty-first century fossil fuel operating vehicle, and you have been hiding it on my ship," Merrecci asked.

"Where else was she supposed to hide it," Dawn asked, still transmitting. "Huh?"

"Get rid of it," Merrecci ordered and began exiting the shuttle bay. He ignored Dawn's interest in driving it first.

From here, Merrecci disappeared entirely. Bria had decided that now was a good time to avoid him, and Almma agreed.

Vandenbutcke's shuttle, which they had disguised to look like it had been put together with scavenged remnants of about seven different races' ships, was safely aboard twenty minutes later. Then they remained in silent running for three more days before it cleared collector space and dropped to level three.

During this time, Merrecci's new research duo decided it best to experiment with the compass, which meant flying it. No one was sure it was safe, but Fram and Jossel suggested they could always catch it with the tractor again in case it got out of control.

Samantah Nerris volunteered to pilot the vessel. Vandenbutcke's initial inclination was to take it himself, but reluctantly realized that she needed the practice more. He would have gone with her, but then that damned first officer pointed out that the Onyx shouldn't be without two of its three best pilots in case the need to flee arose, and she was right. Additionally, Nandy suggested that it might be good to allow the student to fly solo for once. Again, Vandenbutcke couldn't argue.

So, with Samantah Nerris at the helm of Earth's most recently acquired ship, the Onyx remained in silent running level three and stealthed as it followed closely behind the Compass, hoping it wouldn't have to reveal itself to defend her.

Presently, Bria was in her office engaged in Merrecci's most recent task, but first she was demonstrating how ridiculous she felt trying to get a snapping sound from each of her fingers as Charity had instructed her to do several times a day. She swore when nothing came out of her ring finger. She cursed, and it still hurt.

"That's all right," Admiral Kellick assured from the other side of Bria's desk. "It'll come."

"Right," Bria patronized, and she re-activated the glove support. She snapped all of her digits in one motion. It still hurt. Afterwards, she stared a moment at the black stripes embedded into the sides of each finger.

"Shouldn't seem so bad after having to live without a face," she said.

"Now, hold on a second," Kellick rebuked. "Those stripes are the highest honor anyone's ever received as far as I'm concerned. Don't you forget they represent the lives you've saved and touched."

She thanked the admiral and then asked just what it was that Merrecci and he had on their minds for her to do.

Kellick set a holo tablet on Bria's desk, where several other similar holograms rested, waiting for her attention.

"Our enemies destroyed our station," Kellick explained. "We're going to steal one of theirs. We just have to decide whose."

"Won't they just attack it again," Bria asked.

Kellick shook his head. "When the Franchise revoked our membership, it was acknowledging that the station was no longer legally inhabited by an approved member. We were part of the consortium by proxy of the Franchise itself. By stealing one, we don't have to be Franchise, we become an independent controller."

"So, whoever attacked ours was probably someone who already has an embassy," Bria observed.

Kellick rewarded her with an approving snap of his finger.

"Why though? The consortium would retaliate," Bria said.

"Only if the embassy is destroyed," Kellick corrected. "And no one wants to risk that. All it takes is someone inside to self-destruct their own station. In that case, the attacker is still considered at fault. Automatic vengeance. That's why no one does it."

"Sounds like a recipe for annihilation to me," Bria said.

"And complicated by the fact that you never go after the embassy of a race technologically weaker than yours," Kellick said. "You go up the chain, not down, so other worlds wonder what new technology you've developed that allowed you to beat the more advanced race."

"Plus, you don't look like a bully," Bria suggested.

Kellick snapped out an agreement once again.

"Since we don't have the benefit of the Franchise anymore, we can't afford to go down. We need prestige," Kellick added.

"Except we can't go after the Paichu, because they don't hold an embassy since they left the Consortium, do they," Bria said.

"The Paichu," Kellick asked, suddenly taken aback as if Bria had said something she wasn't supposed to. "Why would we do that?"

"Because the Paichu and the Jimmosheans are the ones behind this, aren't they?"

"How do you figure that?"

"The Paichu are one of the three elite powers in the galaxy, but they're not really a galaxy superpower," Bria said. "They're still subservient to the Kag'tak."

Kellick remained silent, which Bria took to mean she should keep going.

"It was the Jimmosheans that Earth sent the Crimson, Jade and Viridian to gather intelligence on because of a rumor they heard about the male god," Bria explained.

"Okay," Kellick drew out as if he was deciding to give Bria permission to continue or put a stop to her ridiculous accusation.

"I figure the Jimmosheans thought as we do about finding both gods to propel them to becoming a superpower," Bria explained. "But they knew they couldn't take Earth on by themselves, and that if they couldn't get intelligence from our fleet, they'd have to do so from Mabbis station, but you knew that, I'm sure. Which is why you self-destructed it for that advantage, didn't you?"

Now, Kellick was silent.

"The Jimmosheans don't fear the Consortium. They're allied to the Kag'tak by proxy of the Paichu. So, a retaliation on the Jimmosheans would have been an attack on the Kag'tak, and the Kag'tak would want to know why they had to come out of their hibernation, which would give away the Jimmoshean's plan to become a superpower. Otherwise, the Kag'tak would punish them for wasting their resource. But this isn't news to you, is it?"

"All right, Captain," Kellick said. "So, you think the Jimmoshean's are behind it."

"I think the Jimmoshean's started it," Bria answered. "But the Paichu are going to take advantage and finish it. They're using it to make a powerplay. The only way the Jimmoshean's could have survived after destroying our embassy was if we were no longer in the Franchise, and the only way to do that would be if our membership was revoked. The only reason I can think of that the Franchise would give in would be if they were threatened that the Kag'tak would be called upon if there was retaliation. Neither the Franchise nor the Consortium could stand up to them.

"Only the Paichu could have validated that threat. The Jimmosheans started it, but the Paichu have other plans. I get the feeling you know this too."

Rather than confirm or deny, Kellick simply moved on with, "Regardless, we need back into the Consortium of Embassies, and the Franchise isn't going to sponsor us again until this is over."

"Too bad the Paichu aren't members," Bria said. "We could take theirs and the Jimmosheans embassies. That's a big message."

"Nope. Only one embassy to a race, and Jimmosheans are not technologically impressive enough. We want someone on this list." Kellick pushed his holotab across the desk.

"I'm not qualified," Bria responded.

Kellick seemed to be chewing on his thoughts a moment, before finally saying, "Could have fooled me." Before Bria could respond, he continued with, "I can work on the diplomatic channels to take the stations, but you know what the Onyx can do, and, when the time comes, the prime admiral will be tied up with commanding a fleet. I have my ideas, but maybe looking at yours will help me understand an angle I hadn't considered."

"Respectfully, Admiral," Bria said. "I don't know how."

"Then practice," Kellick said. "Always take practice."

"If I create a plan, and it fails, I'm going to be in front of a lot of committees when this is all over," Bria replied.

"Also good practice to get," Kellick said.

Bria sighed. "I don't like the idea of gambling with the friendship we have if I let you down."

"I see," Kellick realized. "We are friends, but I also have my duties to perform, and, right now, my rank wants you to do this. My staff is busy. The prime admiral thinks you can contribute. So do I."

Bria leaned sharply across the desk and snatched up Kellick's holotab. "Fine. I guess if you want me to, I'll come up with a plan."

"Uh, seventeen plans," Kellick replied.

At this, Bria flipped through the information on the holotab and abruptly asked permission to speak freely. Kellick allowed it because he knew it was healthy.

He interrupted her verbal tirade only a moment to say, "You know what the difference is between drinks and a table?"

"What," Bria asked without realizing how curt she sounded just now.

"Anyone can share drinks," Kellick said.

Bria raised her eyebrow at the admiral.

"But friends share the table," Kellick added.

At this, Bria went to work and forgot her tirade.

Meanwhile, Nandy sat in the command chair on the bridge and found herself somewhat amused with two of Vandenbutcke's students currently filling both the pilot and assistant pilot's seat as they tried to follow the Compass. They were currently arguing over how much pressure the finger needed to apply to the console to get it to issue commands. The pilot, Nandy forgot her name, was pounding the board with her fingers so loudly it made the assistant mad, so now they weren't friends anymore.

"Commander," Nerris announced. "I think I have the hang of it and am ready to return."

"Are you sure," Nandy asked. "This is all the practice you'll get before we attempt to enter Cindy Lou's DNA into the Compass."

"Well," Nerris replied. "Do you think I'd get in trouble if I stunted or something just to get the feel for in case I ever needed to do something drastic?"

"I had thought that was the point of all this testing in the first place," Nandy replied.

"Yes, Ma'am."

"Just don't get out of our defensive range."

On the holo, Nandy watched the Compass barrel roll.

Nerris's voice came back with several excited quips as the vessel continued to zip around, flipping in odd ways that could possibly impress some more experienced flight instructors. Actually, if kind of impressed Nandy. Eventually, Samantah finally stopped.

"Ma'am," Nerris asked. "There's a button I can't account for, and it's not on the inventory test list. With permission—"

"I don't know," Nandy said. "We should let the resear—engineers look those over before we go to all out."

"But, Ma'am, there's a really pretty silver knob on the main control stick that is just asking to be accidentally pressed."

"Oh, well if there's a pretty silver knob, I imagine we'll have to test it at some point," Nandy replied. "Go ahead."

"Yes, Ma'am," Nerris said. "Pressing pretty, silver button now."

Suddenly, the Compass was gone.

"Where'd she go," Nandy asked jumping to her feet.

"She skipped right out of sensor range, Ma'am," a voice called from the panels of Onyx operators.

"Not that fast she didn't," Nandy denied.

"Yes, Ma'am. She's gone!"

"All stop," Nandy ordered. Then she immediately called Captain Leonard, who, upon hearing the report, invited Merrecci to tear away from his sleep.

Merrecci immediately ordered Nandy to join him in his office. When they walked out several minutes later, Merrecci appeared as if nothing important had been said while Nandy appeared as if everything important was yelled.

"It was the right call to stay in a point of origin. Notify me at once if she returns," Merrecci said, started to exit then turned back to Bria, "Don't you have homework to do?"

"Perhaps I can serve better on the bridge right now," Bria said.

"Commander Nandy is quite capable of correcting her own mistakes." Then Merrecci finally left.

In the hall, he ran into Lieutenant-commander Almma.

"What," Merrecci asked hotly.

"Can I talk to you, Sir," Almma asked, actually taken aback at Merrecci's abruptness.

"Normally, I would say yes, but strangely I'm not in the mood for your lewd lip right now," Merrecci said, and he kept walking.

"It's about Dawn, Sir," Almma called after him.

Merrecci stopped and exhaled loudly, "What about Dawn?"

"Sir, she's upset," Almma said.

"Tell her to join the club."

"She's threatening the crew," Almma added.

"That's all she does! The crew even plays 'I'm going to kick your ass' Bingo with her," Merrecci grumbled. Then he erupted with "is that what this is about, you need me to handle some simple corrective action and tell her to stop it? Fine! I'll tell her to stop threatening to kick everyone's ass!" He started off again, this time with sights set on locating Dawn.

"Oh, stop being a pissy little prick," Almma called after him.

Merrecci turned back quickly. "Is there some part of 'you can't talk to me that way on my ship' that you don't get, Lieutenant-commander?"

"Is there some part of pulling that bundle of sticks out of your ass that you don't get," Almma replied. "I'm all for giving you the attitude you brought me on board to give you, but don't think I'm going to waste my time breaking my foot up your ass just to remind you to be a human being. I'm too young to have to deal with that old shit."

Merrecci opened his mouth to yell.

"Dawn likes driving," Almma started, then softened her tone before Merrecci could respond. "She likes cars, and she doesn't threaten people as regularly since we've been learning how to drive them together."

"Are you kidding? She threatens me every day!"

"That's just because you're a douche," Almma brushed off. She caught her breath and realized that Merrecci was holding his. "Look. It makes her happy. It's what she's good at."

"She's good at engineering."

"But she doesn't love it," Almma explained. "You have baseball."

"Not lately!"

"And whose fault is that," Almma retorted. "Not to mention, look at how you feel when you don't have your baseball."

"The difference is my baseballs don't run people over in the halls," Merrecci said.

Almma scrunched her nose at him.

"What," he asked.

"You've hit more people with baseballs than she's hit with a car," Almma said. "Baseballs are like tampons to you, Sir. If you don't have one every so often you explode on anyone in reach."

"Okay, that's enough of that."

"She needs this, Sir," Almma said.

"So, take her to the library."

"She doesn't like the library," Almma said.

"Well, sometimes we don't always get what we want every time we want it."

"Everyone who doesn't want to deal with her has always put her in the library, even her parents," Almma replied. "That's how she's the engineer she is. She knows why people send her away. She's not stupid."

Merrecci snickered, and Almma abruptly slapped him.

They both took a moment to look to see if any other crew members had seen it.

Before Merrecci could chide her, she held a finger in his face.

"She's not stupid," Almma stated. "She wants a hobby. You can understand that, Sir."

Merrecci held up his own finger and shook it in warm up to tell her she was on report but found himself dismissing her instead.

Meanwhile, Bria was obeying her orders. She had returned to Admiral Kellick who was waiting in her office to finish their discussion. Bria spent the next hour wishing she was more aware of what was happening on the bridge to track down Ensign Nerris.

Instead, she questioned Kellick on as many details as she could think of about the Sanbornada race, mostly what Kellick's past interactions with them had been in observing how they acted and fought. After another hour, she still hadn't gotten to asking about their spacecraft technologies. She was just about to when she was called back to the bridge.

At once, she spotted Nerris's face in the battlecron covered in sweat and filled with wider eyes than usual.

Merrecci marched in only a moment later, wearing his pajamas and brown slippers.

"Ensign Nerris," Merrecci snapped. "Do you have any idea—

"We have a problem," Nerris interrupted, unaware that she hadn't issued statements of respect first. "I need to speak to you."

"Report to my office," Merrecci ordered.

Once Nerris's face acknowledged, Merrecci then reissued the same request to Bria and Nandy. Rather than make his way to the office this time, he left the bridge, leaving his first and second officers to sit and wait for about five minutes before Nerris arrived. Merrecci appeared two minutes later, refreshed, and dressed.

"Ensign," Merrecci recognized rather than greeted. He moved to his chair and asked for the pilot's report.

"Sir, I'm so sorry. I don't know how, but I've just returned from Earth," Nerris said.

Merrecci leaned forward now and invited Nerris to take a seat. "You've been to Earth and back, that fast, in a vessel that by all reasoning should be in a museum? How is that possible?"

"I don't know, Sir. All I know is it did. I pressed the button. I shouldn't have," Nerris apologized.

"Damned right," Merrecci replied, but not as sharply as he had been a moment ago. "Don't make stupid decisions when you don't know what they'll do!"

"I don't know why it went to Earth, maybe it's something in the programming of the Compass regarding whoever's sitting in the pilot seat, but that's where it took me," Nerris explained. She wiped a hand over a greasy forehead and smoothed her sweaty hair even tighter against her head. Usually, it was curly and blond. Now, it had a sheen that made it appear slightly pink.

"The Kag'tak are in the Milky way, Sir," she continued.

Merrecci felt Bria's and Nandy's eyes fall on him. If his own could have looked to him for answers, they would have. Instead, he waited on Nerris for them.

"Are you certain," He asked.

"There were two ships," Nerris replied.

"You've never seen Kag'tak. How do you know."

"They addressed me," Nerris said. "They claim to have arrived to ensure a safe transition of power on Earth."

"They got through planetary shields," Nandy asked.

Nerris nodded.

"They've destroyed many Franchise ships in the act of protecting it," Nerris continued. "They didn't care that it was under protection. All Earth governments are now under Divide law. They have begun directing the Jimmosheans and Didjians to occupy us. Tribunals have been set up to try our leaders. They are attempting to take command of our fleet ships but cannot do so without your authority since you are the highest ranking military commander right now. They prefer to keep Earth ships in tact and don't want to chance any self-destructive protocols that only you can override in the event of an invasion.

"Once I identified myself to one of our own, Admiral Shuster transmitted his command logs to the Compass. I know I shouldn't have read them, but I didn't know where the hell I was or if I was going to survive the trip," Nerris apologized. "Sir, the Kag'tak executed bounty on the Onyx for its live return, and it's triple the pre-bounty mark. They do not want us destroyed."

"Yes, they do," Merrecci said. "They just don't want to do it until they have the highest ranking military official to make an example of."

"They've also destroyed any Earth ship attempting to escape," Nerris added.

"How did you get back here," Merrecci asked.

"I hit the silver button again," Nerris replied. "I figured it took me to Earth pretty fast, maybe it would get me out of there just as quick. Anywhere was better than there, I thought. I didn't know where I'd go."

Merrecci turned his inquiry to what Bria thought this all meant.

"I think it means we need to finish our mission all the more," Bria replied. "Now more than ever."

"How can you be so cold," Nerris questioned.

"That's enough, Ensign," Nandy cautioned.

"Our people are dying," Nerris shouted. "We can help!"

At this, Merrecci dismissed Nerris and cautioned her from speaking to anyone about their discussion or what she had learned from Shuster's data until he could review it himself.

"Captain," Merrecci said, once Nerris had left his office. "I am inclined to think that our mission may never end. First it was a key, then a map, and another map, and now a ship. The whole damned space is maps. We may need to consider that this could go on longer than we've considered."

"Sir," Bria prepared to argue. "You know as I do that if we go back without both gods that Earth loses any means to reclaim itself. If we have both gods, we have a chance."

"Or they might just kill us all," Merrecci said. "They've killed gods before. If we show up, gods or not, I'm sure the Kag'tak can blow us up faster than Cindy Lou and her plus one can procreate."

"But Shade was clear, Sir," Bria said.

"Shade's not the Prime Admiral anymore," Merrecci retorted. "We need to go home. That's my decision. That's my order."

"Sir," Bria contested. "Are you willing to be the nail in humanity's coffin? Because that's what we'll be doing."

"It takes a lot more than a nail to close a coffin," Merrecci said. "And you don't know we'll be closing any."

"You do," Bria retorted.

Merrecci was suddenly sitting on the ledge of his chair and tapping his foot quickly in anticipation of a reprimand.

"Our mission was never to defend Earth in that way," Bria replied. "It's to make it survive. We go back, that's gone too."

"So, we just abandon them," Merrecci asked, launching himself from his chair. "Abandon our friends and families?"

"At least yours is on this ship," Bria fired back.

Merrecci paused as he watched Nandy step in to pull Bria away from the argument.

"It's fine," he said and waited for Nandy to truly believe him before he came in again with, "You don't think there's anything we can do by going back then?"

"Earth is dead. All that matters now is how well we can resuscitate it when and if we do go back," Bria replied. "Maybe by then, the Franchise will be willing to be allies again."

"The Franchise," Merrecci scoffed. "I'm sure our grievance has been rejected now that the Kag'tak have come out of hibernation."

"Sir," Nandy interjected. "It's not about them being weak. They can't stand up to the Kag'tak anymore than we—oh my god! Are the Paichu behind this?"

"What," Merrecci asked, surprised at Nandy's randomness.

"The Jimmosheans started it," Bria added.

"You already know," Nandy asked Bria.

"Know what," Merrecci inquired.

"You don't know," Bria questioned Merreci.

"Know what," Merrecci exploded.

Bria and Nandy explained it to him, mostly Bria because she'd realized it sooner in Admiral Kellick's presence.

Merrecci retreated into a sigh and then into his chair.

"You know," he said. "If I'd have had actual experienced officers, we'd be going back right now, but no, I had to get stuck with you two."

"They would have been wrong, Sir," Bria said.

"Oh, shut up," Merrecci replied. "I think you're the one that pisses me off the most, Scarecrow."

"There's no need for name calling, Sir," Bria replied.

"It wasn't—oh, never mind," Merrecci stated.

Then he contacted Vandenbutcke and requested that he take the Compass back out. This time, they would enter Cindy's DNA to let it find whatever objective it pointed to next, but adamantly ordered that he not touch the silver butto—

"Now what," Merrecci cried as his office suddenly dimmed to signify silent running level four.

He, Bria, Almma and Vandenbutcke returned to the bridge.

"Report," Merrecci asked, typing his question into his holotab, and watching its text appear on the wall. Today, it appeared as Dodger Stadium as it was in its remodeled 2019 form, and his question appeared on a large HD screen that had been installed only a few years earlier: 2013, he believed. HD? How did these ancient people survive?

Every time he saw this one, he failed to remind himself to delete it from his rotation. He liked the original stadium better.

Bria allowed the holo to turn into Master Cha's head.

"I know you're here somewhere, Onyx," Cha's words came out as text across the HD Dodger's screen.

"Ugh," Merrecci's eyes groaned.

"How many ships does he have now," Merrecci's wall asked.

"Twelve, Sir," Bria replied, also typing her response so it appeared over Merrecci's stadium.

"We don't have time for this. Shoot a torpedo at one of his engines and get us out of here."

"That won't destroy him, Sir," Almma's response flashed.

"He'll go slower, won't he," Merrecci typed.

"The other ships won't," Bria pointed out.

"Fine," Merrecci surrendered without a sound and claimed the command chair from Bria.

Vandebutcke assumed the pilot's seat for the moment as Being was off duty.

"Weapons, target engines of all ships to disable only," Merrecci ordered.

"Why not destroy them, Sir," Almma asked.

"Power core explosions alert sensors and put us on the map," Bria replied.

"Ensign, take us out of here as soon as torpedoes have fired," Merrecci ordered. While he was at it, he changed the image on the bridge to the original 1962 Dodger's Stadium.

The torpedoes fired. The Onyx ran, Merrecci stood and broke the silence swearing, mostly because he really wanted to blow something up.

An hour later, Vandenbutcke was sitting in the Compass outside of the Onyx. As soon as Vandenbutcke had entered Cindy's DNA, the Compass began flying at a speed that the Onyx was just able to keep up with, but barely. They had thought perhaps that it might speed off as it had done with Nerris and return as well, but it did not. Vandenbutcke hypothesized that the reason it did not race away was because the Compass could scan farther and deeper into space than should be possible, and doing so caused it to put less power to flight.

He also discovered something else. Once the Compass had received Cindy Lou's DNA, it appeared Vandenbutcke had little means to control its path. However, by the third day of flying, he found that a particular button was actually the autopilot. He turned it off from time to time so he wouldn't feel so bored, but also found it caused the Compass to become more difficult to control if Vandenbutcke tried to steer away from the Compass's flight path. It meant even a bored pilot such as Vandenbutcke couldn't miss the destination. It also meant he found himself wishing he had the leniency to stray off course that Escobedo's flight paths gave him.

For ten days, the Onyx followed the Compass. Every four to six hours, Nandy used the transcender to rotate Vandenbutcke and Samantah Nerris out of the ship. On the tenth day, while Vandenbutcke was on shift, the Compass came to a stop—with it, the Onyx.

Merrecci swore and didn't attempt to keep it under his breath as he saw the odd area of space that appeared in the battlecron.

Vandenbutcke's head appeared in the holo.

"Sir," he said. "Didn't you write a paper on this place?"

Merrecci acknowledged.

"So now what," Vandenbutcke asked.

"Standby."

"What is it," Bria asked, exiting her own office, and forgetting to leave the holotablet with her current work behind on her desk.

"It's quick space," Merrecci answered.

Bria had heard of it. You were supposed to stay out.

"The first satellite that ever entered it was crushed in about three minutes," Merrecci explained. "The first Earth ship lasted twenty."

"They teach it in the academy," Bria said.

"When explorers first discovered it, they almost didn't, you know," Merrecci continued to inform. "All the Earth-bound scientists who couldn't cut the academy, let alone get accepted, all cried it was impossible. Huge debate. Stupid arguments. Earth-bound scientists all crucified the head of the scientific community for suggesting space wasn't all the same. Then, backed with the thousands of years filled with people who theorized that space couldn't possibly break the limited laws of physics, all the Earth-bound science club thought they knew better than the people who saw what was actually there, and there was outrage. If our flimsy, outdated, short-ranged satellites didn't see quick space, then people on ships who saw it must have been hallucinating, and our probes and sensors were obviously malfunctioning. A lot of lectures got shut down this way. Did they teach you that?"

"They taught me that," Bria said.

"Huh," Merrecci sounded. "I had to repeat Galaxial Theory

because I acknowledged quick space was real and even suggested that perhaps it might be a black hole hub."

"What is a black hole hub," Almma asked.

"Well, laws of science says that energy can't be destroyed only transformed. That's just basics," Merrecci said. "In all science, it agrees that energy cannot be destroyed, except in a black hole. But what if that's wrong? What if the black hole simply displaces it, converts it into a heavy energy that has to go somewhere else? And what if that energy is attracted to itself in a way that it can congeal."

"Congeal," Almma asked. "Is that a scientific term?"

"Do I look like Albert Newton? It was a gen ed requirement," Merrecci replied. "I told you. I don't science."

"Anyway, if the blackhole actually converted the energy, we should see that it has some sort of byproduct near or around a black hole, somewhere. But it's not there, well not the way a lot of early scientists thought it was. If it's not destroyed, where does it go? That would suggest there must be some kind of hub action going on. What if this is it?"

"You mean like a wormhole," Almma asked.

"This isn't fantasy," Merrecci said. "This is real. Blackholes aren't wormholes. Nothing's a wormhole. But it might be a hub that converts energy so hard that it blasts it away or something."

"Blasts it away, huh," Almma asked. "You mean like a wormhole?"

"What did I say," Merrecci snapped. "No. Look! If a black hole can make energy disappear, what if there's an anomaly that can make energy suddenly appear, and what if the black hole and quick space are really just two parts of the same hub? One that dismantles and displaces energy and one that attracts and stores it? It might even be what caused the Big Brick."

"The big brick," Almma asked.

"You don't know about the big brick," Merrecci cried. "It's a section of space ten percent larger than our own solar system that's nothing but one big-ass rock. The theory is there must have been a huge gravitational field that caused matter to just mash into each other, but what if it was just that all that black hole and quick space hub finally compressed toge—

Almma almost smirked but stopped.

"Are you screwing with me," Merrecci erupted. "Are you seriously trying to screw with me?"

"How else am I supposed to have fun with this maintaining decorum thing. I piss you off if I don't keep it. I piss you off if I do. You know? You need to learn how to lose better," Almma said. "I'm just surprised you were able to hold that at all. And for the record, I'm pretty sure a whole bunch of really old scientists just started gathering wood to burn you with."

Merrecci dismissed Almma, then called her back just before she left the bridge so he could tell her to shut up.

"So, we can't go in. We can't go around," Merrecci said, returning to his communication with Vandenbutcke's head.

"What if I can, Sir," Vandenbutcke replied.

"Why? Do you have mutant biological structure we don't know about," Merrecci asked.

"No," Vandenbutcke replied. "But I do have a ship that brought us here, and going in there might just be what it does."

"Can't take that chance," Merrecci said.

"I could dip my nose in and monitor for even the slightest change in hull integrity," Vandenbutcke replied.

"And if you're wrong," Merrecci asked.

"Sir, it's pointed into quick space. We haven't begun to make a dent in marking its boundaries," Vandenbutcke suggested. "I just have a gut-feeling, Sir."

Merrecci objected. Bria did too. Drinker, however, suggested Vandenbutcke may be right. Eventually Merrecci gave in.

"One meter in," Merrecci agreed. "One, and we gather data—but one dent, and we're tractoring you out. We need that ship."

After an hour, the Compass's integrity had not changed, so it went in ten meters, then fifty.

"That's deeper than the first satellite got," Bria pointed out.

Reluctantly, Merrecci allowed Vandenbutcke to go in a full kilometer. An hour later, the Compass was still intact.

"Sir," Vandenbutcke's voice crackled. "I really think I'm right. I think this vessel might have been crafted for quick space."

After much argument, the result was that Vandenbutcke should return to the Onyx so, they could run tests on the hull first. Vandenbutcke engaged the ship to return and suddenly shot out of sensor range, just like how Nerris had done before.

17

▲

Hunters

It seemed so incredibly normal in the realm of adventures so far, that Merrecci shouldn't believe that Vandenbutcke had been kidnapped by the golden vessel, just as Samantah Nerris had. Vandenbutcke gave no remarks of surprise about the Compass suddenly taking damage, and there was no explosion. Between that information, his history with Vandenbutcke, and Bria's incessant reminder that this mission was more important to Earth's survival than letting Earth live, they waited. With as large as quick space was, he wasn't at all certain.

"This mission is really starting to piss me off," Merrecci complained before putting the Onyx into silent-running level one the moment Vandenbutcke decided to disappear through the looking sand.

So they waited.

Mirror waited the most. Once word reached her that Vandenbutcke had disappeared, even Merrecci couldn't keep her off the bridge. She just sat at a scanning station, continuously trying to invent new ways to improve the range. The entire time, she ran one scan after another until Merrecci told her to sleep. She slept at her console. Merrecci had tried to remove her, but he found herself ordering someone, he wasn't sure who, to get her a pillow instead.

"You know," Merrecci had said at least fifteen times to Bria after intruding upon her in her own office, "there was a time that all the space geniuses on Earth had said this was impossible. Of course, a lot of those geniuses subscribed to the Fermi Paradox that suggested that because Earth's slow-ass satellite couldn't find something, that all life in the universe questions were answered."

"I did know that," Bria started replying around the seventh time, or eighth. "Who knew?"

"Then on our very first ship capable of cosmic speed, we traveled four times farther than we were able to see from pictures from that slow camera, and suddenly there were a lot of pissed off scientists. The whole event put the economy of the scientific space community in chaos. Entire livelihoods and centuries of research suddenly had people with money asking, 'should we keep paying these morons who were wrong?' Scientists that Earth once mocked were suddenly applauded and promoted. Other scientists went to hell, and some went nuts wondering who got to keep their jobs."

"Yes, Sir," Bria said.

"Albretsen's Dilemma—uh—you ever read it," Merrecci asked.

"No, Sir," Bria said.

"Oh, well, I had to," Merrecci replied. "Required reading when I was there. Anyway, Albretsen's dilemma suggests that in the event scientists realize they no longer have viable scientific skills to maintain job security, they suddenly find Jesus."

Hence, Bria found herself getting slowly swallowed by Merrecci's boredom and unable to conduct her work.

The spirit aboard the Onyx was so humdrum and uneventful that Merrecci was perfectly fine with allowing the lowest ranking bridge members to take the command chair for a shift to allow more rest to go around. Besides, it provided more training for future bridge officer candidates should the need arise.

One person who didn't get to share in that rest as much was, of course, Bria. Merrecci wanted her reviewing the data that the Compass and Samantah Nerris had returned with earlier. It included all of Earth's surviving ships and crew members. In the event Onyx could do something with that information, he wanted to be able to rally the most functional fleet possible upon his return to Earth. Bria had been put to the task of solving those problems as well. Well, not solve them, but help him realize how smart his own plans were. Problem was, his plans weren't as smart.

Were it not for Bria's special shortcomings, Merrecci wondered if she might have made a decent strategist someday. He knew better though. Politics were politics, and she was Bria.

Bria, on the other hand, felt that Merrecci just liked interrupting her work so he could have someone closer to his rank to talk to and break his boredom. He had passed a few bouts of his ennui by pitching, but he also ended up getting laughed at by the Great Bambino. So, no rest for her like everyone else as she became his go-to person to pass his boredom. She just either sat in her office tapping away at a holotab, sometimes accurately, or found herself giving brainless, aggregate responses to clueless questions from a bored prime admiral. Right now, she was typing.

Her fingers hurt, but she was typing.

That lasted until Merrecci asked her what she thought about promoting Nerris to a crewman.

"Promote who you want," Bria snapped. "God! Can you do anything on your own?"

Merrecci almost fired back, but then noticed the pace at which she had been running her fingers in the performance of her many tasks and decided perhaps she could use a break.

"Are you okay," he asked instead. "Did I push your hands too hard? Maybe I should back off."

"Back off? What do you mean back off," Bria asked, finally seeing what was really going on. "You son of a bitch! This was just for physical therapy?"

"Well, only at first," Merrecci said. "Then it turned out you were actually pretty smart at it so—yeah, that sounded a lot better in my head."

Bria threw her holographic tablet into Merrecci's chest where it burst like a water balloon into nothing, but didn't get him wet, which is when he decided Bria needed a break. Had they been at peace, he might have recommended some R&R.

This was also when he had an epiphany of another nature. One that caused him to leave the bridge in Nandy's hands. Three hours later, he was standing in a shuttle bay when Dawn came charging in.

"This better be good. I was watching something called Russian Roulette of Riches," Dawn griped. She suddenly stopped and couldn't bring herself to acknowledge what set before her.

Merrecci placed his hand on a silver piece of machinery.

"This is a 2019 Puritalia Berlinetta," Merrecci said running his hand over the car. "It's powered by a V8 super—

"V8 supercharged engine in the front for 750 horsepower and an electric motor in the back for 250 horsepower for one thousand horsepower total and more torque than Issa's Ferrari," Dawn explained. "It even has a button to apply all your power for forty seconds to make you go faster and you don't even need nitro! I've never used nitro."

Merrecci thought a moment about correcting Dawn's informal mention of Almma's first name, but then her eyes began to flash between Merrecci and the car. She kept leaning forward to step, but pulled herself back every time because she wasn't supposed to play with cars anymore, and before her were three of them—all silver, all waiting for a driver.

Almma was suddenly at Dawn's side dressed in a white suit and a helmet.

"You really want to kick someone's ass," Almma asked, and she handed a similar suit to Dawn.

Dawn immediately kicked off her clothes and stripped down to her underwear before Merrecci pointed out that she could pull the suit over what she was already wearing.

"Stop staring, pervert," She yelled at Merrecci.

He was almost ready to bite back, but he turned away until Dawn gave him permission to look again.

"Now I'm not as good at this as you, but I've been researching some," Merrecci said. "I think I was able to find us a better environment to drive in than the halls, but you're going to go really fast. Do you think you can handle that?"

"Yeah," Dawn replied, and she was now squirming to step forward, but still kept stopping and rocking back and forth on the balls of her heels because she wasn't sure if she could go yet.

Merrecci tapped the car he was standing next to.

"This one's yours," Merrecci said. "Get in."

Dawn ran, not steadily, more like a giddy dance. She approached the door, searching for the most respectful way to gain access to the pilot's seat. She found the button that coerced it open, then she began climbing in and unleashing a variety of "oh wow"s.

Merrecci and Almma each disappeared into one of the other silver vehicles.

Dawn engaged the engine and jumped at the sound of it.

"These are too fast for the halls," Merrecci's voice came through Dawn's helmet.

"Where are we supposed to go," Dawn asked.

Suddenly, the room screeched as Merrecci's tires began spitting out black smoke against the space-grade-concrete floor. His car sped forward and straight out the shuttle bay's exterior door. He didn't have to worry about shields. A lot of other races' technology placed silly power expenditures like shields over every exterior window and door throughout the ship's hull, but Earth was smart enough to realize this was just a waste of power on the systems. Ship shields already sealed off their vessel off from the vacuum of space. Sure, if these outer protections failed, there was a chance of getting sucked out, but that's when Earth ships actually would divert power to seal off physical openings with either energy shutters or emergency physical glass composite. Having an open window or one sealed with glass, was entirely the preference of whoever controlled the room that had a porthole.

At this moment, there was only an open bay door. Almma's vehicle followed Merrecci's through it and disappeared over the edge of the Onyx's hull as well.

Dawn applied the accelerator and was thrown into the back of her seat. Her shuttle bay surroundings disappeared in an instant, and for a moment, as she jumped from inside the Onyx, all she saw was open space. There was no confinement before her, no cold walls, just open space.

Her stomach tickled as her vehicle reached the apex of its jump before the mother ship's anti-gravity pulled her and her Puritalia back to the hull. When she landed, she found two cars in the distance, Merrecci's seemed smaller than Almma's and, in a few moments, would disappear over the sharp angle of the Onyx. She saw it jump and then drop, and that's exactly what she set out to do herself.

At the same moment, several diners looked up from their meals and watched as the third underside of three strange vehicles raced right through their perfect view of space. Black marks now smudged the glass afterwards.

The diners looked to Bria, and the best she could answer with was a shrug.

Bria was sitting with Cindy Lou in the fine dining restaurant. She'd been promising herself to eat at it for some time, but feared she'd never get to enjoy it with the way Merrecci called everyone to his whim and call.

The Onyx actually had a twelve-star, Earth chef draw a lottery for one full tour upon it. Chefs weren't typically a necessity for a ship. Most galley food was cooked in bulk. It wasn't bad. No one ran from it at least.

Earth chefs wanted to discover tastes and flavors and put it on their menus to add value to their planet-side restaurants, but fine chefs were a luxury in space, and most starships could do without them, so they weren't found on any Franchise vessel.

Then, at some point, an admiral visited Las Vegas while on shore leave because he'd heard about an amazing Restaurant. He didn't even have to wait for a reservation. He just dropped his name, and he was granted access to the chef's table where, after an hour and a half of being tantalized by smells he rarely shared in, the maître de dropped a dish holding a pale, rubber chicken breast dolloped with cottage cheese, a blob of canned tomato paste and topped with a Twinkie.

"Is this a joke," the admiral asked.

"Not at all, Sir," the maître de replied, politely and directly. "We simply thought you would have no need for refined dishes in our restaurant either."

So, the admiral took the insult, let it marinate for about two days, then stormed into his next high-ups meeting and demanded the leadership start providing space study-abroad programs for Earth chefs. After much debate and decision to deny the request, the catering staff from the same fine-dining restaurant packed up their delightful flavors and scents and served the admirals the very same dishes of disappointment. Now, Earth ships have study-abroad programs for fine-dining chefs.

Not everyone got their own though, only elite vessels, the embassy, and the flagship. The fact that the master chef was one of the people who survived the attack on the Earth and made it to the Onyx was a morale boost. The downside was that his fifteen-table restaurant was always reserved out. Unless you were the ship's ranking officer, you had to get a reservation like everyone else. The only reason Bria was sitting here was because Cindy Lou showed Chef Thelbrig a secret that happens when you mix porterhouse steak with a touch of Grindashion truffle spore. Her reservation put her at the chef's table tonight.

Chef Thelbrig currently discussed with one of his kitchen staff how she was a worse cook today than she was yesterday. Bria wondered if she regretted taking the job.

While Bria and Cindy Lou waited, they turned on the privacy window and bounced a marble of Almmaminum back and forth, drinking every time it landed in one of their empty water glasses. As a joke on Cindy, Bria turned on the zero-g in the booth. When the ball hit the side of Bria's glass, she expected that Almmaminum would just stop and float, but was surprised when it suddenly ricocheted with even more power back into Cindy's own wine goblet and shattered it.

"Whoa," Cindy replied. "Good thing for shields, huh?"

Bria agreed and suggested they not play with it in zero-g again, but first they collected the floating broken shards with a bread basket and gathered the globules of wine into Bria's champagne flute. Afterwards, Bria called Fram to let her know what had just transpired with the top secret substance.

They lowered the privacy shield and received their dinner order ten minutes later.

Bria was finishing the last of her meal when Cindy stopped her.

"No, no," Cindy said. "Always leave a bite of food on your plate in fine-dining."

"I don't want to waste it," Bria objected.

"It's a compliment that the chef gave you enough."

"But he didn't, I want to eat it," Bria said.

"Let him have his compliment, my favorite one," Cindy urged.

Bria left the compliment. Afterwards they called it a night, insisting that Bria needed to get some rest, so they returned to Cindy's quarters and failed at getting any.

The next day, before her real shift even began, Bria returned to her office. She attempted to play a game of cribbage with Kellick while simultaneously trying to solve several problems of two admirals, which she knew she didn't have to do at the moment, but she was already too invested to stop now.

"You're in a better mood," Kellick observed.

"Yes," Bria replied. "I finally got some time to myself."

Then she yawned and apologized because she didn't get much sleep.

"Okay," Kellick announced standing, clearing the game and startling Bria in the process. "This game's over until you get sleep. And no more looking at my to-do list."

"Too late," Bria announced. "It's already done."

"What? Just now," he asked.

"I've been done for two hours," Bria replied and handed a holotab to the admiral.

"Well, what have you been doing this whole time then," Kellick asked.

"Toying with one more angle," Bria informed. "A ship you neglected to put on the list."

She showed another tablet to Kellick. He took it and instantly erupted with, "No! Don't even consider crossing that line."

"I told you, I'm just toying with it," Bria replied. "No harm giving it some contemplation."

"Wrong," Kellick said in a tone that Bria wasn't used to with him. Then he leaned in. "We do not know what their ships are capable of, let alone one of their own starbases."

"But what if we could get a look at Maridamarak or Paichu intel and figure out how to take a Kag'tak station," Bria asked. "Think of what we could learn."

"No," Kellick replied sharply yet controlled. "Delete that file."

"It's just a thought," Bria said. "It's not even finished. Probably never will be."

"Good," Kellick replied. "The Kag'tak took Earth and ended Franchise defense with two ships. Your plan would bring more."

"They could have done that at any time," Bria said.

"Yes," Kellick agreed. "But they didn't, and they probably wouldn't have if—

"They didn't think Cindy Lou might not be hiding on Earth right now," Bria asked.

Kellick agreed.

"The Kag'tak are generally recluse," Kellick explained. "We know they prefer to watch from afar. They're not out to conquer, but they will take potential threats head on before they can incubate to become actual ones." Kellick suddenly caught his breath and realized his tone was making Bria retreat from him and into her own seat. "You read the files. If your notes somehow slipped back to them, they would take it as an act of war and they would conquer us the way they did the Maridamarak or destroy us like they did the Emera for the—what was it called? The grind gun?"

"The Griffthin," Bria corrected. "Theoretically could destroy suns."

"Theoretically," Kellick repeated. "And why theoretically?"

"Because it never got used," Bria guessed.

"Because it never got built," Kellick answered, shaking his head at her. "That was worth destroying a race over."

"If the story and that weapon were real," Bria said.

"And if they are?"

"Then shouldn't there be at least a rumor of it," Bria asked. "We have a member of a race that destroys and creates entire universes, and the rumors of them still roam the galaxy."

"And the only reason we're still alive is because they want that weapon, I'll bet," Kellick suggested. "What if they take Cindy from us, find the other god and use this Griffthin weapon to destroy us as a message to other races?"

Bria couldn't help but imagine Willis forwarding her files to the Kag'tak. She began deleting the information.

"Good," Kellick encouraged. "I truly think the Kag'tak will leave Earth if it deems the god is just a rumor and not a threat."

"But we are a threat," Bria replied.

"If they knew that, Earth would already be dead."

They returned to their game, and Bria skunked the admiral, which was okay because he had won the last three games.

He was a quick learner of, "Can't play what you don't have."

Once they finished, Bria was just giving her daily farewell to Kellick when they found Merrecci in the action of preparing to announce himself at her office door. The two admirals shared quick and familiar salutations before Merrecci entered and blurted, "For the love of God, will you please give your office a design? It took several dozen engineers to make it look this bad, the least you can do is show them you hate it."

"I didn't know I could do that," Bria replied.

"You're a captain," Merrecci burst. "You should know this."

"I thought it was the commanding officer's prerogative."

Merrecci's face loosened, and he dropped himself into the chair where Kellick had been sitting only moments before.

"It's about the comfort of whoever the room belongs to," Merrecci explained. "They teach this in your captain's courses at the—oh," he realized and caught himself. "Sorry." Then he caught himself again and cried out, "What am I saying? Of course, your specialty learned it, which by the way, now that we've caught our spy, think we can address that?"

"Address what," Bria asked.

"Fine," Merrecci said. "Play your game. I'm pretty sure we both understand that I understand."

"This again," Bria replied. "I'm not shadow force!"

"Ha," Merrecci erupted. "Who said anything about shadow force?"

"You did!"

Merrecci silenced her with a disbelieving brow.

"This sucks," Merrecci suddenly hissed out.

"Sir, did you need me for something," Bria asked.

"I thought I did, but I can't remember what it was now," Merrecci replied. He stood, told Bria to fix her office, then left.

Before the doors could close, he re-entered.

"Oh yeah!" He sat back down. "If we do indeed have to go into hiding, and Earth gets destroyed, we can't survive long without some kind of intelligence gathering system that won't give us away. We need a contingency to open an academy on the Onyx, and we need to re-evaluate Franchise policies that can prohibit our race from multiplying."

"But we're not Franchise anymore," Bria said.

"That could change," Merrecci replied. "Review Earth and military policies that could prevent our work as well."

"You want me to start reviewing policies and what? Law," Bria asked.

"No," Merrecci retorted. "I want you to get ahead of the rule breaking and make sure we have exceptions. For instance, we currently can't just let civilians have children on board the Onyx now, can we? And we should make sure we can drop policies that says superior officers can't have relationships with subordinates."

"I'm not breaking up with Cindy just because you want to have sex with me," Bria replied.

Merrecci was halfway standing from his chair to flee the room when he suddenly said, "Oh! That was a joke."

"Yes, Sir," Bria replied. "Is that the kind of policy you're talking about?"

Merrecci's face gave away that he wasn't amused. "I don't want you hanging around Almma anymore."

Then their seats rattled beneath them to announce something was wrong.

They both stood and returned to the bridge, where they found Almma sitting in the command chair.

"That little bastard!" she directed a finger at one of three ships attacking the Onyx in the battlecron. "Once his back's to us, fire a percussive shot up his aft hole! Don't kill it, just make him sore."

"So, someone did attack us," Merrecci asked.

"No, Binny's wife just came on board, and he's happy to see her," Almma replied not even trying to hide being snide. "Not sure how they found us."

"Must have something that can detect stealth," Merrecci said.

The battlecron signified that the Onyx had followed through on Almma's order.

Merrecci waved down Almma as she stood to hand over the command chair. He instead approached the railing and attempted to open a discussion.

"Earth vessel, Onyx," A Didjian asked from a grimy and dark bridge. He appeared disheveled and caught off guard. He visibly shook. "We have come for your bounty."

"Hit him again," Merrecci ordered.

The enemy in the screen fell out of view, leaving an empty chair. He slowly climbed back up with a hand to his head.

"You sure you want it," Merrecci asked. "How did you even find us? There's no way that little Pinto of yours and your two buddies just happened to stumble on us."

The enemy refused to respond.

"If you tell me, I won't hit you with one of our bigger weapons," Merrecci offered. "I'll even let you go."

"You know how bounty hunters find you," the enemy chided.

"You mean we're tagged," Merrecci asked. "How in the—you know what—take us out of stealth."

The Onyx revealed itself, and the enemy's eyes suddenly widened beyond his capacity to hide his surprise. On the holo, the Onyx surpassed the size of the three bounty hunting ships. Any one of them could probably fit into the Onyx's shuttle hold.

"Ahh," Merrecci roared. "We're so big!" Then he relaxed. "Are we done now?"

"We're done," the enemy said.

"Good," Merrecci acknowledged. "And we have your ships in our database now. If anyone else shows up, we'll think you told them how to find us and we'll open our own bounty on you."

The hunter ships disappeared. The Onyx fell back into stealth.

"Sir. You should not do funny," Almma said. "Stay barbaric."

"Just tell me how they tagged us," Merrecci asked.

"I don't know. Space goblins with big butts," Almma asked. "Or one of his fleet?"

"Could have been the Maridamarak," Merrecci said, then resigned himself to more mundane work like not asking Almma for any more input. "Let's start scanning for a tracker."

"What if they didn't tag our ship," Bria asked.

"You think they just wandered onto us while we were stealthed," Merrecci inquired.

"What if they tagged something easier, something that wouldn't make a low-end bounty hunter think twice about what he was really coming after," Bria suggested.

Merrecci's face fell into blindsided revelation. "Vandenbutcke's shuttle from when we were in Guggler's Den? That's against the rules! You can't tag if your face is covered."

"Or," Almma said. "Someone could have just broken the rules."

"Easy way to find out," Bria inferred. "Send it out where we can observe if another hunter goes straight to it."

Merrecci agreed and ordered the shuttle to the end of their scanner range, but first he had it loaded with a proximity mine. Maybe if a hunter was stupid enough to think the shuttle was the Onyx, they might also think they killed it when they fired upon it. He didn't believe any bounty hunter could be that stupid, but a chance was a chance. So, just for fun, he linked communication through it to the Onyx in case any hunters came calling.

Then they sat around for six more hours in stealth before Merrecci decided he might as well go get something to eat since the bounty hunters seemed to be taking their sweet time.

He invited Prilla to join him in fine-dining. He wondered sometimes if she wasn't the busiest person on the ship. There were a lot of people currently working as if they had to forget they had lost loved ones, and they were forced to do so while all carrying grudges, resentment, and desires of vengeance. Merrecci could understand that.

"How did you get a reservation," Prilla asked upon entering the fine-dining for the first time and waiting for the maître de. That is, it was the first time that Prilla was seeing it beyond the glass doors with people in it.

"Really," Merrecci asked. "Sometimes, I think you don't think I do anything on this ship."

"I thought Bria did everything," Prilla stated.

"Who said that," Merrecci asked. "Did she say that?"

"Everyone says that," Prilla replied. "Everyone sees that."

"If she does everything, where's her standing table?"

"Wait," Prilla suddenly said. "You have your own table?"

"It's my ship."

"Every evening?"

"Yes."

"A table?"

Merrecci nodded.

Here, they were now welcomed by the maître de and directed to the admiral's usual place, which was large enough to seat four people, the same as every other table in here. However, Merrecci didn't typically use it for more than one. He'd thought of inviting Charity, but he didn't think she needed the crew talking about her when they saw them together.

Yoshiko, the maître de directed Vincenti and his sister to their one page menus and recommended an item that was not currently listed—Wagyu beef. When the server appeared, they both ordered Yoshiko's suggestion.

"I can't believe you've had a table all this time, and you didn't invite me," Prilla scolded. "Do you know how long I've been waiting to get in?"

"Well, I try not to eat here too often," Merrecci said.

"Why," Prilla cried.

"A ship commander shouldn't be a snob," Merrecci said.

"A snob?" Prilla laughed, then stopped. "Do you know what a valuable tool you have here to boost morale among the people who serve under you?"

"What's that supposed to mean," Merrecci asked.

"You invite people to dine with you," Prilla said. "It makes them feel appreciated and seen. Were you ever a real captain?"

"The last thing anyone wants is to spend time with the boss. Otherwise, they'd all book for promotion," Merrecci said.

"Really," Prilla asked. She returned to the maître de's station where a younger couple reviewed a menu. Their appearance and hushed debate revealed that they were not aware of the prices even though they had waited for who knows how long to get a reservation. They were quickly growing embarrassed.

She returned with the couple to Merrecci's table.

"Prime Admiral," Prilla announced. "May I introduce Meana Johns and her husband Tristopher."

Merrecci stood and cursed himself for almost saluting, but the glint in his sister's eye said this was the wrong approach. He extended a hand instead.

"Thank you for inviting us," Meana greeted, taking his hand in a nice firm grip. "Our reservation, it seems, is behind schedule so we were about to get bumped. We've waited four months."

"Well, we're glad you could join us then," Prilla said.

Merrecci agreed and invited his two crew members to sit.

Yoshiko returned and welcomed the two new guests, and Prilla encouraged them to order the Wagyu beef as well.

After Yoshiko walked away, Tristopher whispered something to Prilla.

"Put your money away," she said, waving a hand at him. "This is the prime admiral's table."

"Absolutely," Merrecci agreed. He immediately typed out a private message to her holotab. "This is not free."

"Oh, yes, it is," Prilla replied, leaning into Merrecci. "Or that fine chef of yours can find another ship to learn on. Call it tuition."

Almost thirty minutes later, Merrecci had learned more about the couple than he had wished to know, but Prilla acted like they were the only people in the room at the moment.

Tristopher worked in the laundry while Meana, it turned out, worked in the tool crib. They had both just learned that Meana was pregnant two days ago. Prilla stood to announce it to the entire room. The present company applauded.

Finally, their meals came, and Merrecci found himself cutting into Japanese Wagyu Beef.

"This is real," Prilla said within two chews. "I thought we had to leave before the freezer got loaded."

Merrecci agreed and waved down the maître de.

"This isn't artificially grown," Merrecci said.

"No, Admiral," Yoshiko agreed. "It's from Chef Thelbrig's private store. It's his birthday."

Merrecci chewed through another small bite before asking Yoshiko to pass on an invitation for Chef Thelbrig to join him on the bridge on Merrecci's next shift.

Prilla was just asking Tristopher and Meana if their quarters would be large enough for a baby, or if they knew they could upgrade to a family suite now that they were expecting; and Merrecci was starting to chew another bite when the lights suddenly fell dim to signify silent running level four.

"Not now. Not now," Merrecci said softly, and he watched the kitchen immediately shut down.

The chefs turned to preparing cold dishes. Chef Thelbrig, master that he was in the kitchen, went straight to slicing up his Wagyu while the rest of his staff began tearing various vegetables by hand to help present a well-rounded steak tartare that no one should complain about.

Then Yoshiko and his wait staff began handing out plastic cutlery to silence their guest's plates.

"Admiral Merrecci," a message from Nandy appeared on the surface of the table before him.

"Let me guess," Merrecci asked, typing back. "Bounty hunters decided to interrupt my steak?"

"Not exactly, Sir," Nandy replied. "But Cha did."

"Where's his fleet," Merrecci asked.

"Can't imagine they're too far off."

"I'm putting an end to this," Merrecci typed.

He stood and bowed to his guests, shook their hands, and gestured that they should stay seated with Prilla and enjoy their meals. Then, he took up his plate and utensils and marched off and back to the bridge with his dinner in hand.

"Does he know where we are," Merrecci asked as soon as he could start typing into the arm of his command chair.

"No, Sir," Nandy replied. "But he's been sending out hails. Thought he might have found us a time or two, but no."

"Guess he doesn't buy that our shuttle isn't us," Almma said. "That's such a dick move."

"We can't afford to reveal our location now, or else he'll think we're actually here," Merrecci said and found himself angry at the typos that went through.

"I agree," Nandy replied.

"Then we wait," Merrecci said, and he returned his attention to his rare meal, where the juices may now have all run out into his potatoes before he had even reached the bridge.

His plastic knife and fork sliced at his steak and made no sound as it scraped his ceramic plate. He was chewing his second bite when he realized the bridge was watching him.

He ignored them. He was trying to finish his food before the steak went cold. He emptied his dish and then held it out to Nandy, who took a moment to realize that he was not only asking her to take it for him but wanted her to carry it back to Thelbrid's restaurant.

Nandy's first thought was to find offense in the task, but she realized that it meant she got to go to Thelbrig's. She hadn't been before, and any time she thought that she'd make a reservation, the wait was so long that she decided it wasn't worth it. So, she never made a reservation. She had, however, tried a few times to stop in and see if there were any cancelations. There never were.

There was one piece of meat left on Merrecci's plate that taunted her, red inside, and marbling in the juices from steak and butter that hadn't yet congealed.

By the time she hit the elevator, she could no longer let the crime of leftover food go unpunished. Inside, alone, she ate the last bite of meat.

Holy crap! It was real. If there'd been some bread on the plate, she would have sopped up the juices. Damn decorum! She licked it.

Yoshiko pretended to be happy taking the plate, though he couldn't help eye that it was empty. Here, is where he might have posed the question that Merrecci "was hungry, wasn't he?" Yoshiko carried the platter back to the kitchen, where Thelbrig immediately recognized that the dish must have been the admiral's. It was bare. Thelbrig snatched it up and hurled it across the kitchen, nearly hitting one of his chefs, one that was an even worse cook today than she was yesterday. The dish broke apart, and the ceramic clamored against wall, floor, shelves and counters.

On the bridge, Merrecci was bringing himself to his feet.

"What happened," he typed into his tablet.

The chub had suddenly begun approaching the Onyx.

"Onyx says noise from Thelbrig's," the stadium wall answered.

Here, Merrecci sent out a silent order for Bria to join him on the bridge. By the time she arrived, the Chub was already nearly upon their precise location.

The holo showed Cha's ship trolling slowly towards them with their proverbial hook reaching out to catch the Onyx.

Suddenly two explosions erupted against the sides of Master Cha's hull, leaving residual stains, but hardly any other evidence of real damage. Another explosion burst a moment later.

Three ships now surrounded the Chub, firing upon it.

"Paichu," the Onyx's wall flashed.

In reality, they were a collage of other ship pieces that gave these hunters an edge when competing for bounties. One of the vessels implemented the talons of a Paichu pristine-class, and suddenly latched onto an edge of the chub so that its devouring mechanism went to work grinding slivers slowly away from the hull. Unlike the typical Paichu pristine that extracted the natural resources it tore so that they may be collected later, this bounty hunter was interested only in cracking the chub open.

"They must think it's the Onyx," the wall flashed.

"Do they have any idea how long that's going to take to chew through that," Bria's question popped up on the wall.

Another bounty hunting ship, a small vessel that seemed like an egg that was badly decorated to look like the decrepit siding of an ancient outhouse or a middle Twentieth Century phone booth moved to fire a constant beam into the Chub's side.

Merrecci knew the tactic at once. Its entire purpose wasn't to destroy, but rather to increase the temperature of the ship via the hull to make the interior environment uncomfortable. Merrecci wasn't entirely sure that the attempt would work any more than the hunter that was grinding through the thick skin. In fact, Merrecci was certain that the egg-shaped ship was most likely to run down its own power respirators before it could reach half the depth of Cha's hull.

The third and largest bounty hunter vessel became instantly trapped in the chub's tractor beam before it could accomplish whatever maneuver it was currently attempting to make.

Cha's cube accelerated into the egg-ship, sending it hurling, but this vessel recovered and returned to attempt its work at increasing hull temperature. Meanwhile the Paichu-enhanced hunter continued to whittle away slivers from the chub's hull.

Then, the Jimmoshean fleet was suddenly there. Seventeen ships now. Seventeen ships that had somehow managed to all get through Maridamarak space, probably by Kag'tak decree. Cha had most likely ordered his fleet to stay behind just far enough to make the chub look alone.

The egg-ship exploded first, then the vessel trapped in the tractor beam. Before its pieces could linger into disintegration though, three more bounty hunter ships appeared, all with stronger tool-of-the-trade enhancements.

A massive spike launched from one of these vessels, as if the gigantic projectile had been fired from a crossbow in the guise of a warship. It struck the shields of one of Cha's larger ships, and it exploded into an energy web that enveloped three of Cha's fleet vessels. The net immediately began to sap the shields of strength. As each protective membrane disappeared, the net constricted until the ships were drawn together, smashed into each other, and then sliced apart, filling space with debris and crew lives.

The chub redirected its tractor upon the ship that had launched the spike, and Cha's fleet fired upon it until it finally broke apart.

A second spike now flew upon the chub, and another energy web encapsulated both it and the Paichu-enhanced parasite still chowing down on the thick hull. The smaller ship met its fate instantly, leaving a slightly devoured edge behind. The net constricted and burned into the chub, but it was going to take much more time to eat through its hull than it took to destroy the other three war ships.

Another hunter-spacecraft appeared and went straight to firing upon the Jimmoshean fleet. Then came two more, then four. Each one immediately played to strengths and unique weapons that helped take down another of Cha's fleet. Soon, there were fifteen for-hire vessels engaged in full-out assault with the chub's armada. Master Cha timed a tractor to capture twelve of the hunters, and his minions began hammering away on them. This is exactly the kind of work his vessel was designed to do. This was the tactic that could turn the tide of battle to a chub's advantage.

Merrecci stood just as one of Cha's Jimmoshean ships flew past, barely missed colliding with the invisible Onyx. Two hunter in pursuit also skimmed by at a distance that made Merrecci a bit uncomfortable for his taste.

"They won't have to scan for us, they'll find us in the debris any moment," Merrecci observed, breaking the silence, but certain no one was listening for whispers in the dark through all the weapons fire and engine bursts.

Four more hunters jumped onsite and began their attacks.

In the midst of this, the Compass appeared and immediately evaded striking into one of the burning warships.

The chub instantly redirected its tractor beam to catch the Compass, but Vandenbutcke, still at the helm of the archaic vehicle had strangely anticipated Cha's reaction and set his approach to accomplish one task, get out of the Chub's range, then flee. Without the Onyx in sight, he'd assumed it had abandoned him. Had he been captain, he would have left if one of his shuttles had disappeared in a space known for crushing whatever entered it. His hand moved to the silver button but paused as a strange Onyx shuttle sped straight towards him, enough that he had to slightly evade collision. It was all he needed to know that he wasn't alone.

The shuttle now raced straight into the side of the chub and exploded with such a great burst that it burned up two bounty hunting ships and one of Cha's own which was just about on the brink of destruction itself.

In the surprise maneuver, the Onyx suddenly appeared, launched several torpedoes, then locked its tractor onto the Compass and began speeding away. Before any of the battling vessels even had time to target the Onyx, the Compass was dragged in close enough to its mother ship to be hidden by the stealth field that Merrecci had re-engaged. As far as the bounty hunters and Cha's fleet were concerned, the Earthers had escaped.

In another minute, the tractor beam had drawn the Compass into a shuttle bay. Then the Onyx activated the Nessla drive and slingshot away just far enough to give Ensign Escobedo time to find another temporary hiding spot to breathe.

Silent-running status was removed as the lights rose.

Then Bria had to go ahead and announce, "Sir, I got him."

"I figured as much," Merrecci stated, already on his way to his office. "Have Vandenbutcke report to me immediately."

"No, Sir," Bria replied. "I mean, I got Cha."

Merrecci abruptly turned and let his brow inquire if he'd heard her correctly.

"That energy webbing burned through thirty-five percent of his hull," Bria informed. "Between that and the other damage done, it gave me enough to lock the transcender onto him."

"So, you pulled him through the cracks," Merrecci acknowledged.

"Yes. Master Cha is in the brig."

"Well, then," Merrecci spoke as he returned to the command chair. "It seems only fitting that as commanding officer of the Onyx, I should go welcome him aboard. But since I'm far too busy waiting for a report from Vandenbutcke, perhaps he'd appreciate seeing your face instead."

Bria was all too happy to agree, and she set off to welcome their new prisoner.

When Bria arrived at the brig, security personnel were already anticipating some senior officer's appearance. They stood at the elevating platform to accompany her to the highest level of the jail.

She stopped a moment in front of Willis's opaque cell and checked the monitor to see his current state. He was hidden beneath beard, despite access to his shaver. Currently he stared at the ceiling, but then his face turned to the monitoring camera, aware someone was watching. The gesture he gave prompted Bria to turn the monitor off, and she might have smiled a little as she moved on towards another cell.

"First officer," Master Cha greeted contemptuously and surprised. "I demand to see the commander of this vessel. Where is your Prime Admiral?"

She ignored him.

"You have to let me out," he insisted, wringing his hands. "I'm not supposed to be in here."

"I'm pretty sure you are," Bria replied.

"No, Pig" Cha yelled, and his face twitched. "Sorry." He bounced his foot. Then he shot up. "I can't be in here. I have to be out there."

"But you are in there," Bria replied.

"Right. Yes," Cha concurred. "But I can't be." He lifted his nose and breathed in deeply. "I can't breathe in here. There's no smell."

Bria turned to the guards and asked if Cha's aspirational environment was correctly calibrated. It was.

"I can't smell," he yelled and went to hit the shield but suddenly stopped. "There's nothing! Just me."

"Well, that's what you get when you choose war on Earth and our vessel," Bria said.

"Ah! But I didn't attack Earth, did I? Did you see me launch one missile on Earth? And there was nothing I did that would have destroyed your ship," Cha said. "But you, you dropped mine on an asteroid. Do you know what I had to do to get my chub off of it? I had to take command of a fleet and subscribe to more reports and more scrutiny. I almost lost my ship!"

"What does that matter," Bria burst.

"Because," Cha reported, and he began scratching his arms, which Bria could tell were previously reacting from the behavior.

"That's it," Bria asked. "Because?"

"Do you need more," Cha inquired.

Bria began to walk away.

"Your spy wasn't communicating with us," Master Cha stated.

Bria stopped and thought about turning back to tell him she didn't believe him.

"We intercepted his message and decoded it," Cha explained. "I'm sure you think it was with us, but it wasn't."

Bria returned. "Who was it to?"

"I want quarters, and I want to breathe."

"I'll see what I can do if you tell me who the message was to."

"Nice try!"

"Enjoy your fecal rations. I hear they're delectable."

"I want quarters, real quarters," Cha restated. "And I'll tell you anything you desire."

"Everyone knows Jimmosheans don't turn on their own," Bria said and started leaving a second time. "It was a good try."

"I'm not Jimmoshean," Cha yelled after her.

Again, Bria returned. "What was that?"

"I'm not Jimmoshean," Cha replied.

"Jimmoshean don't let alien species command their ships."

"They do if you're a really good liar," Cha disagreed.

"Why should I believe that one," asked Bria.

"Because I have a record, and warrants, and a long list of people who I learned to hide extremely well from," Cha said. "And I know the Jimmoshean's role in the battle plan to occupy Earth."

"Who are you," Bria asked.

"My own quarters," Cha said.

18

▲

Blood

Inside Merrecci's ready room, Vandenbutcke recounted his experiences. He explained how, after the Compass had abandoned the Onyx, his vessel suddenly shut down all power except that of life support. It was then caught up in some sort of current that dragged it deeper and faster into the dense of quickspace. He had resigned himself to the fact that he was going to die in the cockpit and even drafted recordings that should be directed to the Onyx in the event of his death and should his vessel ever be discovered, which he supposed would be never.

So, he rode the current, and the Compass bobbed through them as a child's paper boat might set sail in the canals of a storm. Eventually, after four days, he emerged into a pocket of something that was neither space nor quick space. As the Compass sledged through it, he made records of the strange life that swam within. Finally, he emerged from that into what he could only describe as an inverted solar system.

"What is that supposed to mean," Merrecci asked.

"I mean, if you were to take the usual solar system and put the space where the planets are and the planets where the space is, that's what you'd have," Vandenbutcke explained. "They even had orbits and axis like a physical planet."

Merrecci questioned if Vandenbutcke might have been hallucinating. Vandenbutcke was adamant he hadn't been.

"So, I scanned my pocket of surroundings, and it had one life-form," Vandenbutcke said, and he gestured to the humanoid, much like an Earthling, standing beside him.

He was tall, sandy blond, dark eyes, muscular. In fact, he looked like he had gained two feet in height and eight feet around the chest from steroid abuse. His buttoned shorts were old and ready to burst off. This was all he was wearing. His eyes scanned continuously over the office. He smiled at Vandenbutcke, who strangely returned the expression.

After taking in the image of the Adonis, Merrecci finally had to ask, "How?"

Upon the sound of Merrecci's voice, Adonis turned to the prime admiral and smiled. Even his teeth were perfect. He waved.

"He was in a vessel, Sir," Vandenbutcke said. "It wasn't like the others we've seen, but it let me dock with it. I spent about five hours inspecting his station before I finally found him, and he marched straight off to the Compass and took the passenger's seat as if he knew what was happening better than I did. After we left dock, the Compass brought us back here. Thank God we installed a food fabricator is all I can say."

Merrecci now turned his attention to the tall, handsome blond.

"I am Prime Admiral Merrecci. Welcome aboard the Onyx. We've come a long way to find you."

The man looked at Merrecci then through him to the window behind his desk. He ran to it and pressed his face through the porthole.

"He did that in the Compass the entire way," Vandenbutcke said. "His own station had no windows."

"What is your name," Merrecci asked.

The man pulled in, looked, smiled, then returned to gazing out the porthole. Then he tried climbing through.

Merrecci and Vandenbutcke rushed to pull him back in.

The strapping guest looked confused now.

"Hello," Merrecci asked, and he took the opportunity to seal the port with its contingency glass.

"Hi," the man replied, then pressed up tight to the window. It took four attempts for him to shove his head through before he realized there was something blocking him from doing so now.

"Do you have a name?"

"Yah," the guest replied.

"And it is," Merrecci asked.

"Is," the man replied without looking from the window.

"Is the translator not able to do this one," Merrecci inquired.

"Now, you know what I've been dealing with the entire trip back," Vandenbutcke explained.

"Hello," Merrecci called to the man.

"He."

"Are you a god," Merrecci asked.

The creature turned to Merrecci, smiled, and said, "Hi."

Bria announced herself at the door, and Merrecci welcomed her in.

The newcomer turned to see Bria and suddenly shrieked before huddling behind Merrecci's shoulder.

"What's his problem," Nandy questioned entering behind Bria and alongside Almma.

"So that's the Big Bopper huh," Almma asked quickly honing in on Adonis's looks. "Got to admit, if you gotta go, that's not a bad way."

"Hey, this one might be better than Binny," Merrecci suggested, then frowned. "Too bad I better not let her in the presence of this one."

Bria welcomed Vandenbutcke back and demonstrated her pleasure that he was okay.

Adonis kept screaming every time he looked at Bria.

"Are you sure you went to the right place," Bria asked.

"Hey," Vandenbutcke said. "I did what I was told to do. Having spent more time in the Compass than anyone else, I can say I have no idea how that damned thing works."

Merrecci suggested that Vandenbutcke escort the new passenger to the second quarantine zone, via a route that wouldn't take him in view of Cindy's.

"Sir, I'd like to have Doctors Quobalt and Wanship look him over: learn what we can about him, scan his DNA, evaluate his psyche first if that's okay," Bria suggested.

"I doubt he's going to let you, but go for it," Merrecci stated, well aware that the Adonis was still trying to crouch behind him.

"Hi," Bria cooed to the hiding creature. She held out her hand. "Would you like to see a bigger window?" She pointed to the porthole behind Merrecci's desk and drew an invisible frame in the air. "A bigger window."

The man lifted up, smiled.

"Big," he said.

Bria held out her hand, and he took it.

"Guess you just have to learn to speak idiot," Vandenbutcke said, and his face suddenly recoiled into, "Oh! I'm so sorry. I wasn't trying to be—

"It's okay," Bria replied. "You can't be perfect all the time."

She and Vandenbutcke escorted their new passenger to the hospital and allowed both Prilla and Dr. Quobalt to observe and run tests on him.

Afterwards, they led Adonis to the second quarantine area, allowing Bria to attempt to ask questions, of which the guest mimicked back a word or two, but nothing more. After dropping him off, she decided it might be best to initiate a shield barrier rather than a disintegration one like what Cindy Lou was behind. Bria and Vandenbutcke both believed their resident might witlessly walk through it otherwise.

"Please tell me that you got some kind of data from his ship's computer," Bria asked as they returned to the bridge.

"As best I could," Vandenbutcke said.

At this, Bria took a detour to have the data transferred from the Compass to the Onyx so she could begin reviewing it.

Once Bria felt she was more prepared, she found Merrecci in his command chair directing Escobedo and Being to find some better obscure place to hide until he could decide how to approach their next action. Upon returning to his office to converse privately, Bria recounted all that she had observed in the past few hours. Here, she handed the prime admiral a holotab.

"You showed me this before," Merrecci said.

"Sir," she replied. "I feel a hundred percent certain now."

"I'm inclined to agree," Merrecci acknowledged.

"Should I give Cha better confined quarters," Bria asked.

"If that's the deal you made for his help, I'll allow it," Merrecci approved, then sternly added. "But strict confinement to quarters, disintegration shield and no one, and I mean no one goes in there."

Bria acknowledged then added, "I would say then, our mission is completed."

"Then I guess it's time to think about going home," Merrecci said and held Bria's holotab back to her. "And initiate this plan."

"Right," Bria replied and realized that she wasn't confident.

"What is it, Leonard?"

"Should we go back?"

"I would prefer we make sure all hope is lost before we go on the run to save humanity," Merrecci answered. "We have a lot of empty rooms on this ship."

"Aye, Sir," Bria agreed, then cautiously threw out. "The Rhaxians aren't going to like this one."

"Tough," Merrecci retorted. "They're far too valuable to let back into the sea now."

"Right," Bria replied.

"What is it," Merrecci asked.

For some reason, all the ways that Bria could start to answer this question hit her at once, and she couldn't make a cohesive word beyond anything that sounded like groaning.

"I'm not sure I understand what that means," Merrecci stated.

At once, she saw all of her ideas, alternate plans, and contingencies that Merrecci had her working on. She also envisioned all of Kellick's requests that she'd been ordered to design as well. The angles and details hit her brain like a dumpster of live trout that were all flapping her in the face.

Perhaps if she had Drinker's brain, she would have already solved the problem, but she didn't. She had hers, slow.

"Captain," Merrecci said calmly. "Say it small, let it grow."

"All my ideas," Bria said. "They don't—

"Would it help to show me instead," Merrecci asked.

Bria appeared stunned, as if this thought had never occurred to her. She turned to her tablet and began scanning from one plan that had been recorded in her files to another. She began cutting pieces here and there and crudely slapping them all into a chaotic representation of what she thought was on her mind.

"Your fingers are getting faster," Merrecci noticed.

"Go to hell," Bria replied, then tried not to reveal that he was interrupting her concentration just to make them work.

"They look fast."

"Do they," Bria ignored rather than really asked.

Finally, she looked up; held her holotab to Merrecci; and said, "That."

Merrecci looked down. Now, he fell silent. His fingers scanned back and forth through the information to see if he'd read it correctly. He filled in the silence with, "Seriously," and "no" and "oh, hell no!"

"It's rough, but I can make it better," Bria claimed.

Merrecci paused, stared at the screen, then blurted, "Are you out of your already tattered mind?"

"Yes, but it could work, couldn't it," Bria replied.

Merrecci reviewed the data again and dropped the holotab onto his desk.

"Can you really do all this? Better yet, are you sure you'd want to do this?"

"I'm not sure of anything, but it feels better than alternatives."

"I want Drinker to help iron it out."

"Couldn't agree more," Bria said.

"And Kellick has to be on board with it as well," Merrecci instructed. "And the Rhaxians."

"You start the wheels in motion, I'll get them both on board."

With this, Merrecci exited back to the bridge, allowing Bria to set to accomplishing the tasks they had just discussed.

"Ensign Escobedo," Merrecci announced. "Plot us the fastest course to return to Earth. Ensign Being, as soon as he has it, take us there at maximum speed."

"That's going to be back through Maridamarak space," Escobedo explained.

"Yep," Merrecci answered. "Then we'd better make sure Ensign Being gets his rest." He turned to Almma, "It's probably time for you to get a status report from our three musketeers on our Maridamarak situation."

"Sure thing, Boss Daddy," Almma answered, and she set out to perform her duty as well.

Finally, Merrecci ordered the communications operator to send a message to Earth.

"Tell the two Kag'tak ships overseeing our solar system that we're coming for the bounty on the remaining Rhaxians, and we expect to be promptly paid," he ordered.

Nandy instantly protested.

"The bounty on just three of them would pay off indentured servitude for Earth far beyond any of our generations will last," Merrecci answered. "If you don't like it, take it up with your Captain. It's her plan."

"Of course, Sir," Nandy replied.

Meanwhile, Bria made a few stops, first to Drinker, who seemed a bit bothered that he was actually needed for something so pithy as to ensure Bria's idea would work.

Kellick on the other hand was in a meeting with his own advisers discussing potential concerns with one of Bria's previous ideas to take control of one of the enemy diplomatic stations she had been tasked to consider. Admiral Kellick didn't seem annoyed when she interrupted, but he did seem put out that he needed to excuse himself from his own table.

In his office, the admiral looked over the data then rolled over in his head how to tactfully ask Bria if she'd lost her mind.

"This," he started, letting his tongue and brain carefully and symbiotically decide how to reject the idea without insulting his friend. "This was not one of the ships we discussed."

"I know," Bria replied. "And I apologize."

"I'm sorry. This might be an even worse idea than you had before." He placed a gentle and appreciative hand on Bria's shoulder. "It's a solid plan that might have worked if we had more time to discuss it, but my answer is no at this time."

"Thank you, Admiral."

Kellick nodded his admiration, but it was cut off.

"But we're out of time," Bria said. "We're going home now. Our mission is accomplished. We have both gods, we can threaten to use them, and this is the only way."

Kellick stiffened and withdrew most amiable features.

"And the cost of life," Kellick asked. "Have you balanced how much loss is acceptable in this plan?"

"No matter how good your diplomacy is, Admiral, you will never live to see it save Earth nor keep our people even aboard this ship from a doomed future. Even if we secure you a station that you want, it would only be a delaying the inevitable before the Kag'tak take that from us too," Bria replied.

"Then we use what resources and intelligence we have to ensure our chances of that happening get lower with each day," Kellick replied.

"With respect, Admiral," Bria retorted, then softened, "My friend, there won't be any lowering the chance. There will only be delaying the inevitable."

"You can't believe that," Kellick said.

"We're losing."

"We can change that. We have a deterrent weapon now!"

"Which we can't use without destroying ourselves," Bria stated.

"No," Kellick ordered. "Quite frankly, Captain, I expected better from you! The cost of life is too high."

"Tell that to the Rhaxians," Bria snapped. "We're not new! You can't fix it. But this can! I—I can!"

Kellick returned his attention to the holotab. He started shaking his head and rejecting again with more rounds of "no."

"Sir—

"No. This plan was poorly conceived. You're just a—

"Just a what, Sir," Bria asked.

Kellick's face appeared more stung for what he was about to say than Bria's looked realizing he was going to say it.

His finger started stabbing the tablet screen.

"No," He started in again, along with other protestations as he continued to review the tablet. "I won't watch the Kag'tak kill you!"

"I'm currently the prime admiral's first officer," Bria reminded. "You know I don't have that choice."

"But I do."

"No," Bria exploded. "You don't."

Kellick suddenly snapped Bria against his chest and hugged her.

"If they figure it out," he started to say.

"I know."

"You never should have been here," Kellick said softly, and he couldn't seem to loosen his grip on her.

"None of us should have," Bria replied. "But then I'd have never gotten to play pinball, would I?"

Kellick finally pulled away and slipped the holographic tablet back into Bria's hand.

"If you think for a moment that this won't work, you find some way to run, and you hide where they can't ever find you. Take the Compass if you have to. Go back to that station in quick space, but you run and don't look back. If we survive, I'll make sure we come for you."

Both collected themselves. Then they both apologized, and Kellick set out to perform what might have been the easiest of the tasks that he'd read on Bria's holotab: to prepare his staff.

For Bria, after dealing with Kellick, convincing the others seemed simple.

Eight and a half Earth weeks later, the Onyx sped straight into Maridamarak space.

*   *   *

The holo showed eight Maridamarak vessels on approach, one was a fleet carrier that added eight more ships.

"Didn't even see them coming," Nandy stated.

"They do that," Merrecci followed up.

"They're asking for you and only you, Admiral," Nandy informed.

"Are we ready," Merrecci asked. "Do we know it will work?"

"Well, I did put on my brown pants under my uniform so probably not," Almma answered.

"Open transmission," Merrecci ordered. "This is Prime Admiral Merre—."

"Earth Vessel, you trespass," a familiar echoey-style of voice said. "Prepare to pay fee with penalty."

"This is Prime Admiral—

"We do not care," the voice replied.

"You have murdered one hundred of my—," Merrecci replied.

"We do not care," the Maridamarak replied.

"We have come to—

"We do not care."

"You are wanted criminals against—

"We do not care."

"If you do not surrender yourselves immediately, you will be arrested," Merrecci said.

There was silence for some time.

"You have threatened our people. Your ship is forfeit. Drop your speed and transfer command or be processed," the Maridamarak ordered.

Now Merrecci was silent.

"Acknowledge," the Maridamarak ordered.

"Well, guess we find out now, don't we," Merrecci muttered under his breath. Then louder replied with, "Maridamarak vessel, standby."

"All right, Ensign Being," Merrecci announced, muting the transmission, and looking to his chief pilot. "It's about to get busy."

"Say the word," Being replied.

As instructed, Nandy posted herself behind Allen Being's chair, prepared to start kicking in case the automated shaker gave out.

Merrecci leaned into the railing and unmuted to tell the Maridamarak, "I'll bet my pilot's balls are bigger than yours." He turned back to Being, "Clack-clack, Chief!" When there was no response, he clacked five more times.

"Yessir," Being replied.

The Onyx flew straight towards one of the Maridamarak fleet ships. The enemy vessel barely dodged out of the Onyx's path. Or perhaps Being just made it look that way.

The holo filled with an onslaught of Maridamarak weapon's fire.

The Onyx swerved and twisted among the missing shots, or what Being turned into missing shots.

"Sir," the shields operator said. "I'm reading micro inflections in the shields."

"Is there any difference to their output on the micro level," Bria asked.

"Yes, Ma'am," the operator said after a moment of investigation.

"That would be those smarmy little sniper bastards," Almma suggested.

"Are there any reports of injuries," Merrecci then inquired.

"Nothing," a voice called from one of the distant consoles.

"Earth vessel," the Maridamarak voice came again. "You are currently wanted in Maridamarak space."

"What a coincidence," Merrecci stated back. "We're wanted outside of it too."

Another fleet carrier suddenly appeared and eight battle ships popped from their bays, already firing for the Onyx.

Merrecci turned to the power monitoring operator and said, "Prepare to divert incoming energy to our own raizers."

"Aye-aye, Sir," the operator replied.

"Lieutenant-commander, prepare to focus our new raizer energy onto whatever ship attacks us first," Merrecci instructed.

"What if it's the fleet carrier," Almma asked.

"Then attack their second largest," he answered. "Even blowing up something small of theirs should give them pause."

"Earth Vessel," a different Maridamarak voice demanded. "You have entered into Maridamarak space. Stop or be destroyed."

"Hold on," Merrecci replied. "We have a coupon for free admission!"

Again, he looked to Being. "Ready?"

Being was.

"Then let us take one," Merrecci said then crossed himself and looked with wide eyes to Bria. "I hope this works."

From starboard, a chisel-shaped ship appeared.

"That one," Merrecci ordered. "Target that one."

"Sir," Bria announced. "That's a nullifier!"

"Hey," Merrecci retorted. "It's your plan. Take out the strong one."

The nullifier extended four blue columns of energy towards the Onyx. The other ships stopped firing.

"If this doesn't work," Merrecci warned. "I just want you to know—

"It will work," Bria insisted.

Red, devastating flashes fell down the columns. They dropped through the blue beams, and, when they hit the Onyx's shields, disappeared. Then a burst of purple erupted from the Onyx's main raizers and burned a hole through the attacking nullifier, breaking it into two. Then it burned up into a white light.

"Yes," Merrecci shouted, jumping into the railing.

Here, another fleet carrier suddenly appeared right into the residual white where the nullifier once stood. This carrier suddenly cracked into another devastating bloom of destruction. The warships it carried also blew into oblivion, even as they were already undocking. Their explosive repercussion threw the Onyx and tossed the Maridamarak fleet.

"Whoa," the prime admiral spoke. "Did not expect that."

"It worked," Almma cried. "Hoo! If that's not a horny-maker, I don't know what is."

Merrecci immediately re-opened his transmission with the Maridamarak.

"Maridamarak commanders," Merrecci transmitted. "Do not make us open fire again."

"Earth vessel," a new, dominant voice announced. "Surrender for your crimes at once."

"Maridamarak pimple," Merrecci replied. "You killed one hundred of my crew, and they are pissed. They're telling me to tell you we're going to keep blowing your ships up."

"An unfair trade," the Maridamarak seethed. "You will answer for your crime."

"I don't think so," Merrecci said. "You attempt one more assault, and I will relay, to anyone listening in this vast nonsense called space, the technology you just witnessed so that everyone will know how to withstand you."

"We do not agree."

"You don't have a choice," Merrecci said. "One transmission, and your realm starts shrinking in the hour."

Silence, then, "We agree."

"Smart," Merrecci said, and now he ordered the Onyx to stop its engines. "We are now ready to parlay with you diplomatically about the right for us to fly through your space. We will prepare a shuttle bay to accept your diplomat."

"We will not."

"Oh yes you will," Merrecci replied. "I told you. We have a coupon."

*   *   *

Kuntacian Phemos commanded the Longanda. He had done so ever since the previous Kuntacian, an aging deficit by the name of Malmaux had gambled his rank away in a game that Phemos manipulated him into playing.

Currently, he sat at his black command table in the back of his master operations center. Across from him, a master of observers with a flair for name-dropping clenched a fist and attempted to maintain a mask to suggest that he was fine, but then he could simply take no more. He opened his fingers, and seven purple-platinum needle-balls fell to the table, their tips painted in his blood. five of the sharp orbs had stuck to his palm.

"Five," the master of observers announced pridefully. His eyes fell on Phemos, who appeared as impossible to read as always.

"Play your hand," the observer demanded.

Phemos opened his clenched fist to expose his own flat, pale palm. All twelve of the playing pieces were stuck to his flesh in some fashion. He shook his hand, and none of them fell.

"All of them," Phemos stated. "That doubles your wager."

The other losing players erupted in applause and laughter, while the observer swore and took up a pair of gold pliers to his left. One by one, he ripped the barbs from his hand and let his blood fall upon the table where countless losers had already contributed.

"Two daughters," Phemos said as he began removing his barbs out of his flesh with his own digits.

"We'll have to work out something else," the master observer said. "I only have two daughters, and one is married."

"Your debt is not my problem. Only that you pay it," Phemos said, pausing in extracting one of the barbs from his thumb. He didn't even turn his attention upon the master observer. "Double is double. Transfer your winning before the tour is over."

A female to Phemos's right took a slow, small drink from a narrow, hollow bone of some, old deserving enemy. Her name was Vau Rinn. In their boredom of overseeing the occupation of this Milky Way, Phemos had invited Vau Rinn from her own vessel, the Nalignig, to join in the friendly game. She accepted, though there was only one thing she wanted to win, Phemos's first of choice.

Phemos's Longanda and Vau Rinn's Nalignig were identical in every way, fabricated in the same batch. Phemos, however, had better-skilled choices serving under him. Skill led to promotion. She wanted promotion. She hated policing this Milky Way though.

"Are you ready for level two," Phemos asked. "Chance to win your daughters back?"

The observer bowed out.

"Shame," the female said, barely pulling her thick beverage away from her flat lips. "I was the next opponent."

The additional six players around the table groaned. Phemos laughed.

"I have not seen you play Tondace before, Kuntacian Vau Rinn," Phemos said. "What did you bet?"

"My first of choice," she said.

The table groaned again.

"That would have been an interesting turnout," Phemos said. He tapped, and a deck of silver cards shuffled out onto it. "Then I guess, it is for simple play now."

The whole of the master operations center chimed.

"What is it," Phemos asked, throwing each of the players just one card. Each one fell heavily before an opponent.

"We have picked up the Earth vessel, Onyx," a blind Kag announced from his corner of the room where he spent his entire day listening to scanning results. "It is entering the Milky way system now."

"It seems the subspecies Maridamarak did not lie," Phemos observed. He looked at his card and threw three gold cubes in towards the center of the table. "Scan this—what do they call it?"

"Onyx," the master observer stated.

Somewhere in his control center, Phemos knew one of his choices were scanning the elusive Earth vessel.

"Kuntacian," his scanning agent said. "Their power supply appears weak. We could easily destroy them if we're not careful."

"I suppose I should return to my Nalignig," Vau Rinn said.

"Why," Phemos asked. "Our game has just started."

"The allure has gone for me," Vau Rinn replied. "Do keep me in mind when there is a worthy prize once more."

She called to her ship and, a moment later, disappeared from the bridge in a cloud of pink dust, which faded into nothing itself.

"Might as well contact them," Phemos resigned himself, and he dealt a second card to each of the remaining players. "Contact them."

The table before him rose into a hill of silver dust, needles and uneven chunks that eventually took on the form of a human head, one that Phemos had been studying closely for several months now.

"Sub-species Earth, I am Kuntacian Phemos."

He threw several more golden cubes into the pot, while the master observer and the player directly to his left bowed out of the game. The others threw in their own golden wagers.

"You have entered Kag space and will now prepare your crew and ship for evaluation and surrender," Phemos added, preparing to deal another card.

"I am Prime Admiral Merrecci of Earth," The silver head before Phemos stated. "I have an entire ship of Rhaxians and have come to collect the bounty. You will honor that debt, or we will transmit to Guggler's Den that you do not pay your rewards."

Kuntacian Phemos snorted. He finally looked to the bust of the Earth's Prime Admiral instead of his own cards. He found the other players appeared perhaps more stunned than he did.

"You will never be able to spend it," Phemos informed.

"You will pay half now," Merrecci's indignant image retorted. "And you will take the other half in exchange of leaving Earth and placing it under your protection until its sun burns out."

Someone at the table laughed. Phemos threw the next metallic card on the deck at the offender and let it carve right into the imbecile's brain. The player landed face down. Then the observer and another contestant pulled him away and let him fall from his chair.

"As per contract, we will pay you all reward when we have the Rhaxians," Phemos said, evaluating if he wanted to bet ten more cubes or just two. "Earth is not for sale." For a moment, he placed his fingers on the table area that was immediately before him and quickly tapped out orders to one Admiral Shuster, a weasel of a specimen, but one he had placed in charge of Earth's fleet in an attempt to make the Earth occupation transition go more smoothly.

"If it is to be for the entire contract, we want half up front, half after delivery," Merrecci insisted, even as Phemos finished typing out his orders to Shuster. "Because we also have a complete Utonenaibe and Zarchro mating couple. We want half up front."

Kuntacian Phemos shook as he cursed now. Earth's prime admiral didn't seem to understand, so Phemos swore some more. The other players now bowed out of the suddenly angry game by dropping their cards.

"You will give us the Utonenaibe and the Zarchro," Phemos replied, retrieving his winnings. Once he had them, he stroked the table, and a silver representation of his surrounding space grew out of it with the same glittery flow of odd shapes, needles and dust that had built the Earth prime admiral's head a moment ago.

Here, his and Vau Rinn's vessels appeared with their tree-like shapes, including snaking and bare root systems. Both the Longanda and the Nalignig were slightly larger than the Onyx. Many Divide allies converged nearby. Also joining them were all of the Earth vessels in the system, which had become subject to the Kag. Among these were the smaller versions of the Onyx.

"Sir, we're getting another hail," a young woman announced from Merrecci's side of the conversation. "It's Admiral Shuster."

"Listening in," Phemos's communication specialist announced.

A moment later, the oldest serving Earth admiral's head appeared in silver before Phemos and beside Merrecci's.

"Where the hell have you been," Shuster asked.

"Try that tone again," Merrecci erupted. His form appeared to be walking closer and he took on a sharper focus. Phemos could actually see the hate in the man's countenance.

"You are talking to the Prime Admiral," the Merrecci head continued.

"You are no longer in command," Shuster said. "You have been voted out by the admirals."

"Attention Earth fleet," Merrecci said. "Shut down all subordinate Earth vessels except communication and life support under the authorization of Vincenti Merrecci, Prime Admiral."

Shuster's face began snapping to answer different responses from the individuals on his own bridge.

"If you want to mutiny against me, you'll have to do it without my ships," Merrecci bit out. "My post is life-long, and you're relieved!"

Merrecci's image was suddenly focusing on Phemos once more.

"I am in command of my fleet, Phemos," Merrecci said. "Not you. Remove your people at once from Earth and my ships."

"No," Phemos replied.

Merrecci turned to someone out of view and ordered her to transmit record that the Kag'tak have failed to honor their bounty.

"Lies," Phemos declared.

"Then pay us," Merrecci demanded.

"Rhaxians and gods first," Phemos ordered.

"No," Merrecci replied. "You've invaded our home. You've shown you don't pay. Half up front for the Rhaxians and all up front for the Utonenaibe and Zarchro. Or I'll notify Guggler's Den that you don't pay."

"It's a trick," Phemos said.

"Does this look like a trick to you," Merrecci asked.

Coldona Garu now stepped into view of the holo.

At the sight of the Rhaxian, Phemos snapped his finger at exactly who knew needed to hear it in his command center.

"This is a sign of good—," the Earth prime admiral started.

In that instant, the Longanda fired a torpedo upon the Onyx.

Phemos ended the transmission of his bumbling opponent and ordered, "Boarding party! Send me as soon as it is successful." He watched one of his sapping torpedoes strike the Onyx.

"Shields are down," his scanning agent's voice cried. "Landing party enroute."

Less than a minute of silence passed throughout Phemos's master control center before a bust of a familiar Kag sargeant grew up from his table.

"We have their command center," one of his wiry soldiers announced.

Immediately, Phemos felt his surroundings fade while a much more cramped Earth command center appeared around him until he found himself standing on the bridge of the very Earth vessel no one could seem to capture.

He approached Merrecci and might have been smirking as he knelt to greet the prime admiral who was even now sprawled on the floor, recovering from being stunned.

"Prime Admiral Vincenti Merrecci," Phemos greeted. "And Captain Briata Leonard. Yes. You've done this before, Prime Admiral Merrecci, yes? You should have known better."

"We did," Merrecci said. "In about thirty seconds when our ship doesn't ping our communication emitter probe, it's going to send the message that you dishonored your payment."

Phemos roared and swore in terms no other could possibly understand. He thought of shooting the large rock creature that stood before him, but he might know if there were more Rhaxian survivors somewhere out there hiding in space.

"It won't matter," Phemos finally said, turning his attention back to Merrecci. "They will believe us when we tell them we tried. We have the money. Bounty hunters believe those who have the money. Besides, we are going to pay you. We have no intention of taking your ship from you. You are in the service of the Kag now."

Phemos then marched past the command chair and towards the bridge doors. He recalled the map of the Onyx that he had committed to memory.

"Bring them," he said. "Tell the others to take theirs to Warehouse Ten. It is empty, yes? We have much to demonstrate."

As he marched towards Warehouse Ten, listening to the prime admiral and his first choice try to remain silent, the halls came to life with Kag, Didjian, Jimmoshean, Paichu soldiers, and even a few less technologically advanced races that were great for Kag grunt work when their enemies weren't fighting back. Onyx residents were already being marched from quarters. Doors along the path showed signs of clear forced entry.

Coldona Garu received many surprised, frightened and even envious looks from Merrecci's crew, guests, and enemy alike. He was worth a fortune, and none of the soldiers on board had seen his kind before. Phemos found himself enjoying the thought that these fools would turn quickly on Merrecci once they found he was hiding such a treasure from them. Any one of them could have been a hero to the Kag and earn immunity. What a pathetic, short-sighted species, and their low ceilings annoyed Phemos. He appreciated once they reached the warehouse, and he could stop crouching.

Warehouse Ten's floor was already filling with Onyx crew and passengers. The first and second Mezzanines held fewer, but growing numbers too. This room was designed to welcome a crew at maiden voyage and bid farewell on decommission. It was large, but far too cramped for all the current ship occupants.

"We can't all fit," the puny, human prime admiral complained.

It didn't surprise Phemos. Complaining was the language of sub-species. It would stop once he revealed his firm hand.

"Those who don't fit will be punished," Phemos replied.

"The oxygen filters for this room are not enough," Merrecci said. "We'll suffocate."

"Then we should hurry," Phemos replied, then repeated his orders about the warehouse for all the bumbling Earthers to hear. He bent back to Merrecci. "Make room."

The prime admiral called to all who could hear him to start clearing the warehouse of any containers that could allow for more bodies to enter. Phemos allowed the humans to begin sliding their inventory through contingency shields that enacted the moment the Kag'tak attack had removed the Onyx's energy protections. Phemos mused for a moment at the thought of how he could teach a valuable lesson to all by simply lowering this single barrier and allowing space to swallow out the entire crew.

However, commodity was commodity, and every Earth life could serve.

Besides, he could see they were frightened. Earth's most powerful ship had felt the Kag break its defenses with one shot of the weakest weapon in Phemos's arsenal. He would show mercy and kill only one today.

Now, Earther artificial lifeforms drew crates from high places and threw them outside as well. The exterior hull clamored each time the discarded supplies were drawn back by artificial gravity. Robots continued to make room for more human bodies. Earthers were smart laborers to invent such tools. He might have wallowed in ways he could expose that, but he had more important business.

Phemos extended a finger the size of Merrecci's entire arm towards Coldona Garu.

"Take him to the Longanda for interrogation," Phemos instructed a few boarding party soldiers who were closest to his line of sight. "We will destroy the others once we have them." Then he ordered the Longanda to send a shuttle to collect his prizes.

Then he turned his attention to the two Kag gnarled vessels that kept their distance to withstand any damage in case the Onyx should decide to self-destruct. He waited to ensure his orders were carried out before focusing his interest back into the warehouse. A sleek, ridged shuttle appeared and approached the warehouse entrance from the exterior. It pressed through the warehouse shielding, hovered above a crowd of people on the lower level and landed, forcing those beneath it to move and squish even tighter into corners, walls, and each other.

By now, Warehouse Ten's shelving units, fixtures, ladders, or anywhere a human could climb were becoming occupied by captured Earthers.

Two of the Kag soldiers placed hands on Coldona Garu and marched him into their shuttle, which then abruptly left to return him to the Longanda.

Now, Phemos glared down upon Merrecci and asked, "Where are more?"

"Hidden," Merrecci replied.

Phemos almost snapped him backwards on his spine over his knee. Cocky creatures! They would learn.

"We will find them," Phemos replied.

"Doubtful," Merrecci spat. "If you could have found them by now, you would have."

Phemos let himself growl at the impertinence. Perhaps if this military leader appeared of worth and strength, he might respect him, but they were all too puny to admire.

Through the growing volume of the Onyx population continuing to fill the warehouse came, "Phemos!"

Phemos's head turned to the main doors where stragglers continued to be escorted in. The one the Earthers called Willis pressed his way out of the crowd, but Phemos knew him by another name.

"Mala," Phemos cheered and embraced the tall human. "Brother! Did I not say it would be simple to infiltrate?"

"This disguise is cramped and exhausting," Willis replied.

Phemos clapped Mala on the back and guffawed.

"Did they treat you well," Phemos asked.

"That one," Mala said gesturing to Bria. "I want her."

Phemos recognized the one he spoke of. Mala had sent great amounts of intelligence on the faceless one. At first it was amusing reading that Earth would have allowed one to live. The superior counsel of Kag had originally thought these lesser creatures would be more easily manipulated than more intelligent Earthers, but thanks to Mala's reports, they were deemed far too incapable for such counter-espionage. They did, however, give Willis a place to hide while he did his work.

Who'd have known, that this Briata would have grown in rank as she had. Were she a nobody, he would give his brother what he wanted, but she was not a nobody now, was she?

"No," Phemos said, looking down upon Briata. "We need her."

"She put me in a box. For months," Mala complained. "I get her. It's the least I deserve. I've had to put up with her incessant whining all these years."

"We will discuss it once we get this disgusting human shell off of you. Phemos nodded, and then suddenly saw his prize.

"Ah," he announced pridefully.

A specimen that could only be what many called a god entered, refusing to let others place their hands on her. Utonenaibe air and appearance always had to glow above the species it imitated, or so his studies suggested.

"You really do have a Utonenaibe" Phemos said.

Another specimen was brought in, smiling, entertained, broad in the shoulder, blond, handsome, clearly proud, and unafraid.

"And a Zarchro," Phemos cried in elation. "It's true! The rumors are true!"

It wasn't too much longer before the coffin appeared, pushed by two small females. He ordered them all to be brought to him near the center of the warehouse.

Then another face appeared as it was ushered inside as well.

"You," Phemos cried at the sight of Master Cha.

"You," Cha suddenly yelled back, and he started shoving his way through the crowd of humans to get to Phemos. "You treacherous kinnta! Had you not this army, I would kill you,"

Phemos heard the vines in his own face twist in anger at the insulting creature. He demanded Cha be brought before him with the rest of the bridge crew. "Perhaps you will get a chance, you disgrace and failure and thief and nothing! Perhaps it will be you too who pays for a crime today."

"You are mistaken," Cha said as he was finally marched into the group of Bridge members. "I would have had this entire ship as per our deal had your impatience bounty not brought every money-hugger out to attack me."

Phemos glared down upon Cha. "You will die today for your words alone."

"You broke our contract," Cha yelled.

Some ten minutes later, the remnants of the crew had been delivered to the warehouse.

"It is empty then," Phemos asked.

"We are counting still against the ship roster," one Kag soldier replied. "Except one creature that is too fat to fit through a door."

"Cut him into pieces if you must," Phemos ordered. "I want everyone's eyes on this."

"That will take a long time," the soldier replied.

"He's no threat to you, and he already knows you're an asshole," Merrecci said. "He doesn't need to see it."

"I told you anyone who doesn't fit dies," Phemos sneered. "I will cut him out later, myself."

He realized he needed to move his behavior forward before the filters failed as this unremarkable Earth prime admiral had pointed out. Phemos looked over the warehouse then the group of humans before him: Merrecci, Briata, the male Zarchro, the female Utonenaibe, Cha and Willis.

"Let us sort this out then," Phemos said staring down to Merrecci and his first choice, Briata. He caused Mala and Cha to join his ranks, while the rest were lined up before him.

"Will you get a move on already," the prime admiral asked. "Some of us don't actually need to be here."

"The Kag have better things to desire than to take control of insect planets," Phemos said. "But you have tried to bring a weapon together that would endanger innocent worlds. If you would do it now, you would do it again. For this, we have left hibernation. For that, you know there must be what must be."

Another Kag shuttle appeared at the warehouse entry and proceeded to land.

"Only the best transportation for our supernova gods," Phemos said, and directed his soldiers to gather the two blonde creatures. "We will deliver them into safer facilities."

"Are you sure they're the gods," the Earth prime admiral asked. "How do you know it's not any of the other people in this room."

"Ah! Gambling," Phemos swooned, suddenly finding the prime admiral standing a little taller in his eyes. "But your bluff is not good. We will pay for your bounties."

Abruptly, he asked Vincenti Merrecci to hold out his hand. Merrecci did, and Phemos dropped a Maglian jadestone into the human's palm.

"Your credits key for the two gods," Phemos said. "And for the one Rhaxian show of good faith."

"And the bounty for ourselves," Merrecci added.

"You jest!"

"Did I not deliver an entire crew of humans and their flagship?" Phemos laughed. "Fine. See, we do honor contracts despite how small the hunter may be." He leaned down close to the female god. "Do not be so sad, Utonenaibe. You have made the Earthlings our richest subjects. They shall never want for anything except what they cannot have." Phemos pulled up straight, once more, over Merrecci. "All we need now is to reward for the Rhaxians. How many are there?"

"Sixteen thousand," Merrecci said.

Phemos's brow might have flinched. He wasn't sure. It had been so long since he flinched.

"You lie," Phemos hissed out.

"Not counting the one you have already taken, sixteen thousand and one," Merrecci replied. "An entire ship colony."

"Where," Phemos found himself asking aggressively. Sixteen thousand? There was bounty, yes. That could make an individual rich beyond rich, but the prestige of bringing sixteen thousand Rhaxians would bring esteem over esteem. They had survived and eluded capture for so long. He would get a new command, a bigger command, an estate worthy of one on the superior council.

"Half up front," Merrecci insisted.

Phemos felt his hand drawn to his weapon. He pulled his slender, curved, and green dagger that would have passed for a sword to the human stature. He pressed the needle-like tip against Merrecci's throat and again asked, "Where?"

"Half, or let them keep breeding themselves and technological advancement until they can fight back once again," Merrecci insisted. "And who knows if they've hidden any other Utonenaibe."

Phemos growled.

"Half," he rumbled, and then he withdrew the blade. "A fortune upon fortunes on its own for so many Rhaxians. Never has anyone received such grand payment."

Phemos spoke the words to make the Maglian jadestone chime in Merrecci's hand to signify the payment had been raised.

"It's all there, then," the prime admiral asked.

"You insult us," Phemos snarled.

"It's only an insult if you like it rough," Merrecci replied.

Any hunter worth its breath would have known that Merrecci's payment, right now, was already credited to an account that only the authorized commanding officer of the Onyx could withdraw or use. That's how the system protected against pirates who would try to steal a ship with high bounty earnings. Any vessel's leader must be prepared to show their chain of custody as well as know the safeword to access funds. Chain of custody of command was demonstrated according to legality of whatever world the ship belonged to. When Merrecci retired, the person who took command after him would be in control of the account. Only in the event of destruction of the Onyx or its decommission could the remaining balance go through a process of being transferred to the home planet or another ship.

Pirates were not tolerated. Of course, pirates never threatened the Kag. At least, Phemos couldn't recall a time they had. Other races were not so robust, however, and needed protection. Any attempt to obtain control of funds by stealing a ship was met with their own bounty, and it was not one in which anyone was brought in alive. Every bounty collected paid a percentage of it into an insurance fund specifically intended to payout against pirates.

In the end, unless proper authorizations or transfers occurred, the request for withdrawal from the Earth ship's account could only currently come from Merrecci, and Phemos knew he wouldn't find that a comfort shortly.

"Enter your safeword," the green gem requested.

Merrecci placed the jewel in his mouth and mumbled a word. Then he pulled it out.

Phemos never once took his eyes off Merrecci. He only needed the human's answer before he could conduct the business he had actually come to conclude.

"A rich slave is still a slave," Phemos said, feeling his grip tighten around his dagger. "Do you know what that means?"

Merrecci nodded.

Here, Phemos began to sense his superiority once more. The Kag were strong, lesser species worked to bring resources that only superior money could buy. Kag was a rich yet barren world, not barren as it offered nothing in life, but barren as it conducted no drain to its own planetary resources in effort to maintain its beauty and natural form. It was a pristine planet without industry nor pollution. There was a time, long ago, that it had poisoned itself to the brink of destruction, but it had recovered. All that its people consumed now was imported from others who would handle the manufacturing. They had no landfill, nor renewable waste recovery. All waste was shipped off planet by other world service providers who dealt with these matters. Anything that polluted was either prohibited or considered acts of war to the Kag.

"Now, where are the Rhaxians," Phemos asked one more time and more abruptly.

The prime admiral's arm raised then extended all the way until a single weathered finger pointed beyond the warehouse entrance to where the two Kag ships maintained their distance.

"Right where you took them," the Earther called Merrecci said. "Aboard the, I believe you said it was called the Longanda."

With that, the Longanda was instantly broken apart at every seam. Longanda bracing, structural melds, even pieces that Phemos recognized from one of his mess halls spilled without, scattering remnants of his command, boiling its crew in the void. The larger Rhaxian craft now occupied its very space.

At once, the Rhaxian vessel began launching projectiles at the Nalignig, where Phemos imagined Vau Rinn was as caught off guard as he was. Little did he realize that the Rhaxians had not been firing weapons but were launching themselves through space. As the living boulders struck Vau Rinn's ship, they attached devices to the remaining Kag ship's shields. Each one created a single hole in the enemy's protective barrier, where the Rhaxians crawled through and began beating the Kag's hull and exterior weaponry.

"What is this," Phemos asked.

"The Rhaxians, of course," Merrecci replied. "And don't worry about paying the other half of the bounty on them. We only brought eight thousand; just wanted to make sure we got our full dues before you made us slaves."

"You cheat us," Phemos railed.

"We didn't cheat anything," Merrecci shrilled. "Eight thousand were delivered to your ship, and you paid us for eight thousand. Not my fault your security doesn't monitor what comes on board your vessel better."

Phemos's communication device announced an incoming message, but he was instantly distracted to answer it, as an unfamiliar roaring sound screamed from somewhere outside of the ship. The noise grew and two silver Earth land transports sped over the ledge of the Onyx's hull, leapt through its contingency shield, and raced onto the warehouse floor. The first car smashed through two Kag soldiers.

The second landed, then turned hard and into itself, unleashing torrents of black smoke until the machine finally came to a stop. A portal opened from within, and a woman that Phemos recognized at once from Willis's reports stepped out. She pointed towards the Kuntacian, and he found her glare worthy of a foe to fight. He immediately decided that, despite her pudgy nature, she must have been their fiercest warrior.

"I'm gonna kick your ass," she roared. Then she whistled and cried out, "Mike! Sick him!"

A second portal opened, and another human launched himself outwards and continued rushing through the crowd towards Phemos, dodging Kag soldier and Earth crew alike. He barked, not sounding Earth-like. His arms and legs propelled him forward in an odd way for humans and at such speed that Phemos felt it necessary to prepare his blade for counter attack.

The maniacal man burst from the crowd and leapt for the Kag leader. The Kuntacian thrust his dagger, but the creature scratched Phemos's face instead and topped the injury with barking insult right into it. Upon landing, the little monster turned, growled, and launched at the Kag Kuntacian once more.

Mala was suddenly there. He tore Phemos's blade from his hand and buried it into the strange human's shoulder. One of Phemos's soldiers took that moment to clobber the side of the barking human's head. The sub-creature fell unconscious.

"I've been waiting a long time to do that," Mala crowed.

"That's our dog, you dick," a woman's voice yelled from within the crowd.

The Kuntacian spotted her only in time to watch her battle axe swing up into the crotch of the soldier that had struck down the human that Phemos had just stabbed.

Upon striking, the woman's axe bit shut. It actually bit out the soldier's crotch and tore it from his body. The soldier's mouth fell agape as he could no longer find his scream.

"Too much teeth," the woman asked. Then she kicked him away and let him fall who cared where.

Before Phemos realized it, she was swinging her weapon for Mala.

As his brother dodged the blow with a simple side step, Phemos leaned in and shoved the woman with such force that she lost hold of her weapon, and she stumbled into a group of Kag who immediately began slapping at her. Somehow, though, he found she had sent him tripping sideways as well.

Now, Mala bent to recover his blade. Drawing it from the shoulder of the human that had been barking only moments ago, Phemos realized that Mala must have found the strange creature still alive, because his brother then made a quick slicing gesture at its neck. It was one that Phemos had taught him years ago when they were both in their youth. The move would have slit most creatures' throats open.

However, Mala had made a mistake. He did not hear his brother warn him in time. The pudgy, warrior human had already burst from the crowd and grabbed Mala's shoulders. She had become airborne and found the leverage she needed to pull Mala's face down while she drove her knee up into his jaw.

As his chin smashed up, his neck cracked back and snapped instantly. He dropped right there, next to the unconscious dog-man-thing.

"No one likes you, Willis," the fat girl screamed down at him.

Phemos had barely recovered from tripping sideways before he had watched the entire event unfold.

She then roared over the crowd, "I'm gonna kick your asses!"

Phemos charged for her. She was a worthy prize and far too dangerous. She would surely kill more of his kind if he didn't stop her now. He took up his dagger from his fallen brother's hand and thrust its tip for the woman, but Merrecci had somehow kicked at the girl, causing her to stumble from Phemos's reach. The crowd of Earthers immediately pulled at her, and she disappeared into it.

Phemos turned on Merrecci, thrusting his blade for interfering with the trophy of the kill that had ended the life of his kin. Merrecci had already side-stepped. The lunge should have still struck, but he found Briata had deflected it with a baton that should not have been allowed to be in her hand. How had she gotten it?

One of Phemos's soldiers, his third of choice, instantly set himself before Briata and freed up his Kuntacian to focus on the prime admiral again. The Kag was a good soldier. This one was more than loyal, he was Kuntacian Phemos's third choice. Phemos would let his soldier have Briata; he, however, wanted Merrecci and the fat girl for himself."

Here, he suddenly watched Merrecci tear the blade from Phemos's third choice's hand. Merrecci instantly stabbed up and into the third's partially-exposed lung. Merrecci kept poking him, and Phemos held his position, watching the Earth prime admiral's movements become so violent and fast that he dared not enter for the kill at this moment. Merrecci pierced through the third choice's neck then sliced his belly and cut it upward until Merrecci removed the blade and thrust back into the Kag's heart. Next, he drove the dagger up under the soldier's jaw. After all of this, Merrecci couldn't seem to stop hacking at Phemos's good soldier. The prime admiral became an even greater flurry of blood and blade, and he didn't stop until he had torn away at so much of his opponent's flesh that the dead Kag's arm had fallen from his shoulder entirely.

Phemos watched. He made no attempt for any other human. None would dare for him either. Finally, he started moving, and Merrecci hadn't seen what he was doing.

Merrecci finally let the third choice drop.

"Get off my ship," Merrecci yelled, his face dripping with purple Kag blood.

Phemos realized that he couldn't let the admiral refocus.

"Kill the Earthlings," Phemos shouted. "Kill them all!"

Now, Phemos played his strategy. He leapt at Briata, and she deflected his blow. A second Kag was coming to assist Phemos. Good! This would serve him. This soldier was suddenly deep in Melee with two others that belonged to Merrecci. One was the woman with the axe, and she had it again. Phemos believed she was Merrecci's third choice. He wasn't sure, he had better thoughts at the moment. He swung at Briata again. She deflected. He made the same maneuver and watched her prepare the same response. He saw the opening, what the Earth girl did not. A simple thrust in this blindspot would have punctured her heart.

He began the stab, but this was not his scheme. His plan was what caused him to suddenly flip his blade in his hand and thrust it backwards instead, where he felt the all too familiar weight on his weapon that could only come from skewering his true target.

The cursing that erupted from Briata's empty face told him that Merrecci's barbaric impulse to blindside Phemos had come to its own surprising end. The prime admiral was wrong to think he could sneak an attack from behind Phemos. The Kag Kuntacian let Merrecci slide off his blade. If Earth's military commander was smart, he'd die on the floor.

There was only supposed to be one death, but now Phemos found the example to Earth must be larger. He turned his attention back to Briata. She parried his first attack, deflected the next, then, yes, an opening, and he took this one too.

Pathetic humans!

*   *   *

Cindy Lou, who had been careful not to enter the fight, as per her orders, cursed the scene, wishing she could catch Merrecci as his body slid off the blade, but his killer was already back to thrusting for Bria, who again blocked the attack. Cindy, however, did make a move. She kicked at Phemos's knee. He crumpled and hacked out at her, but Bria blocked it. He turned his rage back towards Leonard, stabbing for her, but suddenly Master Cha was somehow between Phemos and Bria beating her back with one of her own race's batons.

Cindy now moved to Merrecci, gripped at his shoulders, and began dragging him towards the halls. Other hands came to her aid, and they slid the prime admiral quickly towards the exit of the warehouse.

Prilla's cry came from the second Mezzanine. Charity's came from the first, and nothing stopped her from leaping into the crowd below to reach Vincenti. By the time Charity had reached Cindy and Merrecci, Nurse Gibralter and another medic were dragging him farther into the halls, even as battle roared around them, and crew members ran back into the Onyx to retrieve weapons or attend to their battle stations. Eventually, they knew they would have to engage the remaining Kag'tak vessel.

"Onyx," Merrecci forced out. He knew what was happening. He felt the wet of life emptying from him. "Disengage botany generator and re-engage main power supply and function. Do not reinitiate shields yet."

"Engaging," Onyx replied and, a few moments later stated, "Main supply power at 100% function."

Alarms blared, crew ran, medics were racing to summon equipment from fabricators and emergency stations that would serve the injured. Those caught in the remnants of battle would follow when they were more able.

Prilla had found herself racing with them. As soon as she climbed her way down to the main Warehouse exit, she followed a smeared trail of blood right to Merrecci. He was currently waving off sedatives and slapping away Gibralter's hand so he could let his own settle on Cindy Lou's.

"I guess I struck out," Merrecci said.

"Like hell," Charity deemed. She forced an injection into Merrecci's Belly.

Despite how quickly she and Gibralter moved to keep his blood on the inside, Merrecci spilled it out even faster.

"The admirals will try to take control of the Onyx now. They'll ruin everything," Merrecci said, trying to sound in control of his pain. "Only one way to stop that." He held a shaking finger out to Cindy. "I'm promoting you to Prime Admiral. Won't that be funny?"

Merrecci quickly made it a matter of record. Then he placed the green gemstone coated in his own blood into Cindy's hand.

"Madeline Wanship," he said.

Prilla made a sound that froze her breath, trembled her lip and filled her eyes with liquid goodbyes.

Merrecci suddenly seemed surprised to see Prilla.

"Oh, hi," he said. He tried lifting his head, but it merely shook against the shag carpet.

"Hi," Prilla said.

"I don't think that Rhaxian blessing worked," he observed.

Cindy involuntarily laughed. Prilla didn't understand and glared.

"Don't forget," Merrecci grunted, turning his attention back to Cindy Lou. "Madeline Wanship. Very important."

Then as he decided he had accomplished all he'd needed to and could now rest, he finally began to relax. He took in and released a few breaths, each shallower and redder than the last.

Finally, he looked to Prilla.

"Am I saluting," Merrecci asked.

"No," Prilla answered.

"Damn," Merrecci acknowledged. "I thought I was."

Then he fell into sleep and death's jurisdiction.

*   *   *

After losing sight of Cindy, Phemos called to Vau Rinn.

"Send support," Phemos ordered.

"We are a bit busy at the moment," Vau replied sharply, reminding Phemos that she had Rhaxian attackers beating away at her hull.

Phemos cursed at her and then set to salvage what he could of the situation. He searched for Briata but found the sarcophagus much more quickly. Another Kag soldier helped him drag it into the Kag's craft. It was in this action that they crossed paths with the male Zarchro. He was laughing and applauding the entertainment. When he saw Phemos he erupted with, "Good costume." In a few moments, both the Zarchro and the wedding bed were aboard the Kag shuttle.

"Don't think of moving," Phemos ordered the male god, shoving him down into one of the vessel's seats.

"Okay," the god replied.

Phemos turned to the soldier, "Don't let him wander off."

Phemos then ducked back out to locate Cindy Lou and to kill Briata. He had wandered out only a bit of a distance when a Rhaxian boulder bounded into the warehouse from beyond the shield. It smashed Phemos then opened into its Rhaxian bipedal form and finished stomping him beyond pulp.

Several more Rhaxians rolled into the warehouse now and joined the fight to allow the humans to return to what would help the Onyx the most.

Master Cha made his own move now and wasted no time taking advantage of the situation. He had been certain not to lose contact with Bria since their own contest had begun, and it appeared she had lost. He dragged her into the shuttle.

"Go," Master Cha ordered to a Kag'tak soldier who sat in the pilot's seat and ensured the Zarchro didn't walk off.

"We only have one—and where's Phemos," the soldier objected.

"Splattered across their floor," Cha replied. "And us having one is better than them having both. The Superior Council will want the High Hammer to interrogate her. Get us moving!" He shoved Bria into a seat and secured her. The Zarchro tried helping.

The Onyx shook and, with it, the shuttle.

"Go," Master Cha insisted. "Just go! They're killing your people! We can always trade their first officer for the Utonenaibe later!"

The shuttle closed and launched under the direction of the Kag'tak pilot. With Master Cha, the Adonis and Onyx's first officer, the enemy craft made its escape.

19
▲
Pinball

Vau Rinn wasn't sure what she had just witnessed.

The Longanda was gone. A ship she had never known before was instead there.

"That ship just jumped in on Phemos's," Vau observed. "Destroy it!"

"Kuntacian," a Kag who had failed too many times to be anything other than a command center analyst announced. "It's throwing rocks at us."

"Rocks," Vau asked incredulously. "Rocks can do nothing."

"Kuntacian," another voice called from the dark chamber. "The rocks are doing something to our shields."

Vau Rinn didn't believe it. She questioned the information and was about to order her weapons techs to shoot the Rhaxians, but the control center began chiming with reports about clamoring hulls, broken weapons and exterior sensors going out.

"Well," she asked her subordinates sternly as if they should know she should already be receiving answers.

"We cannot target them," one voice called. "They are too close to our hull."

"I want troops out there now," Vau demanded.

She dropped into a chair at the head of her game table. A silver deck of familiar cards popped out, and she began dealing to herself. Occasionally, she'd receive an update of how the progress was going against the Rhaxians. Mostly, she listened to reports of soldiers getting dressed in space gear. Eventually, her crew began to engage the enemy on the hull of the Nalignig.

"Some of the Rhaxians are disengaging, Kuntacian," a feminine voice announced.

"Destroy what you can and send a battalion to aid Phemos and order quality control to begin repairs on our hull," Vau ordered.

"Kuntacian," another voice called. "The Earth ship has gained a boost in power."

"They should not have a boost in power," Vau said. "Contact them before we're required to destroy them."

She swore at her cards and began to deal another hand.

"Kuntacian!"

"What," Vau asked.

"Our communication has been knocked out," her agent said.

"I want to talk to that vessel," Vau ordered. "Fix it."

After several more minutes, Vau was informed that the last of the Rhaxians had withdrawn from her ship and were hurling through space either towards the Onyx or the vessel that had broken the Longanda.

"Shall we fire upon them," her weapons tech asked.

"Let them return to the vessels," Vau instructed. "We will destroy everything at once. We don't need any evading us by floating off until they can find shelter, do we?"

Just then her table spit up a mound of silver bits and pieces that could have been confused for broken nuts and fasteners. They took on the shape of a human's head. It was an Earth woman. She appeared young.

"Kag'tak vessel," the woman said. "I am Commander Adrigga Nandy of the Earth ship Onyx. "Kuntacian Phemos is dead. We have destroyed him, his ship, and his crew. Surrender or we will engage you next."

Vau Rinn looked up from her cards.

"I am Vau Rinn, Kuntacian of this, the Nalignig. Know the name of she and that which will destroy you momentarily," she replied. Then she ended the transmission and opened another, this one to Divide allies.

A Paichu head appeared now in silver before her.

"Let loose your fleet," she ordered.

After, her table showed her the battle ground around the Nalignig. She turned off the image and returned to her lonely game.

"Kuntacian! They have full shields," her blind analyst announced.

Vau huffed at the interruption to her game. She gathered her cards and let her table swallow them. She summoned a model of the fighting arena over it instead. Every ship, including her own, appeared above its surface, held aloft by a long, slender needle. Each ship seemed more like a piece on a game board.

Vau nodded, almost snapped, to a Kag, who, up until now, had been monitoring various race results from throughout space. He approached the table.

"We are open to wagers," he announced, and the room filled with Vau's subordinates placing bets on which ships would die and which would succeed in destroying the Onyx.

Suddenly, the Onyx unleashed a barrage of weapons upon the Divide fleet.

Vau, herself, placed a bet just as she watched the Divide fleet return fire upon the Onyx.

*   *   *

The Onyx unloaded a fury of torpedoes that sent the front lines of the approaching enemy ships into an evasive frenzy, dodging Earth missiles and the burning debris they were beginning to leave behind.

The enemy fleet's retaliatory volley shook the earth crew.

"Shields are at seventy-five percent," Lieutenant Dimian called from the bridge. She had only recently been assigned the post.

"Keep at it," Nandy ordered.

Almma was now directing that instruction to her offensive side. With each of her demands, the Onyx unleashed another blow that could only invite angrier retaliation from the opposing fleet.

The enemy swarm kept coming.

"Just think," Almma called down to Nandy in the command chair. "When the Kag'dick's retaliatory fleet appear, it'll be more awesome than this!"

"Priority target the Paichu," Nandy said, not sure she'd even heard Almma. Sometimes, she had to tune the tactical officer out.

"How many enemy ships are there, currently," Almma asked.

One of the voices on the operations side of the bridge called back, "Two-hundred-thirteen, Ma'am."

"Guess we find out what she can do now," Nandy responded. "Volley two-stage torpedoes."

Fifty torpedoes shot from the Onyx, each splitting into two.

"We can't keep doing much with this. These don't pack enough piss-off," Almma said as the Onyx rattled again under the return fire. Escobedo kicked the back of Being's chair when the automatic shaker wasn't doing its job fast enough.

Three Paichu pristines suddenly emerged from the swarm and raced straight for the Onyx.

"There," Nandy shouted. "Take 'em out."

Several strong and slow torpedoes fired from the Onyx, and one Paichu exploded. Another turned tail to regroup. The third disregarded the Onyx's attack and pressed towards it. Four more pristine devourers emerged from the approaching swarm to join.

"Captain," Almma questioned.

"Stick to the plan," Nandy demanded.

The Onyx fired again. It unleased another two-stage volley, followed by an explosion of raizers that struck forty vessels within three seconds, all annoyed and none destroyed.

Then, the Kag'tak ship fired, and Nandy found herself stumbling right out of her chair and for the railing.

"Shields at fifteen percent," the shield operator announced.

"Geez, why does every enemy have to be such a stupid prick," Almma said through heavy breaths that came from grappling her own railing to ensure she didn't fall over.

"Engage the botany power supply," Nandy ordered. "Get ready to cycle."

"Aye-aye, Ma'am," the shield operator said. "We're back to a hundred percent."

"The good news is, the Paichu don't want to tear us apart if we're going to explode," Almma announced.

The Kag'tak ship fired its own volley now.

"Then again, I could be wrong," Almma retracted.

"Don't let them through," Nandy ordered and braced herself against the railing.

Three torpedoes dropped the Onyx's shields, and a fourth blasted a hole in its port side, tearing off a corner which would have contained the Rhaxians were they not currently taking part in Bria's attack plan. Almma flipped backwards, over her second-level railing and into the center of the battlecron. As she forced herself up, she found Ensign Being flat on the floor, unmoving, but breathing. Nandy was down too, attempting to push herself up but finally falling unconscious as well.

Escobedo was running for Almma.

"Not now," she snapped.

More torpedoes appeared on the holo engulfing her waist.

"Get the shields up," she ordered. "Get 'em up now!"

"Up fifty percent," the shields operator announced. "But dropping."

"Target incoming torpedoes," Almma directed.

The smaller enemy ships now concentrated everything into the Earth's black pyramid.

"We should escalate our engagement," Escobedo suggested.

"No," Almma said. "We do not spend one more ounce of energy than we need right now. Just make sure our shields hold."

Suddenly, a Maridamarak fleet carrier jumped in and appeared near the Onyx. Fifteen Nullifiers quickly disengaged their bays.

"Never mind," Almma cried. "Flood the shields!"

"Flooding," the shield operator reported.

Admiral Kellick's head appeared in the holo.

"Ready," Kellick asked, then appeared taken aback to see Almma in command. "That bad?"

"Do you really need an invitation," Almma answered curtly. "Do it!" She repeated the same order to tactical.

All sixteen Maridamarak ships suddenly locked blue beams onto the Onyx and fired their red energy bursts down their conduits.

The Onyx erupted with endless purple blasts of raizers, striking the closest ships and their weaponry. Then, in one final surge, the Onyx focused all beams into the Kag'tak vessel.

*   *   *

On the Nalignig, surprise had caused even Vau from realizing what was happening.

"How are those creatures doing this," she cried.

"Kuntacian, our shields—," a highly advanced technician started but couldn't finish. Vau had won him from Kuntacian Bai Ara after he had won the tournament of wargames three seasons ago.

Vau questioned what he meant to say, even yelled at him, but he could not answer her and concentrate on the task of coordinating his fumbling fingers to race fast enough to reroute power. Without the aid of the Maridamarak technology strengthening the Earth's vessel, he wouldn't have had to break a sweat to defend the Nalignig against such an inferior toy. Instead, he watched his store of energy levels drain from all over. As he witnessed the Onyx's raizer weapons burn down the shields he was responsible for maintaining, the thought might have crossed his mind that these were the cons of never having a truly deadly opponent anymore to keep him on his toes.

*   *   *

The Onyx's raizer burned up the shields then dug deep into large crevices in the hull which the Rhaxians had been kind enough to crack open. The Kag could do nothing to stop the raizer's energy from tearing through their inner decks and striking its very core. An instant later, it erupted into white flame that died quickly, leaving a darkened and mutilated ship.

After, another torpedo shot from the Onyx and dematerialized the remains of the Kag vessel.

Almma then ordered a hail to the enemy's fleet to which she abruptly asked, "Anyone else want to fuck around?"

The attacks against the Onyx ceased, and the Divide fleet began to disperse and retreat.

"Hopefully, that bought us enough time before the Kag'tak retaliate," Almma then ordered. "Don't imagine they'll be long now."

With great effort, she leaned over Nandy to surmise if she was dead—she wasn't.

Almma alerted medical to report to the bridge.

Sixteen new heads appeared in the holo alongside Kellick's, including Vandenbutcke, Samantah Nerris and Fiji's.

"Our pilot and first officer are injured," Almma said.

"How is she," Kellick asked.

"Not that first officer, Sir," Almma replied. "Some things did not go to plan."

"Report," Kellick asked.

"Merrecci is dead," Almma said.

"I'll be right over," Kellick insisted. "No one would dare take the Onyx from me."

"That's the stupidest thing I've ever heard," Almma replied. "How are all your Maridamarak crew members going to take our diplomat running out on them?"

"Did you really just call me stupid," Kellick asked.

"Well, let's see. Did you hear me say the word stupid," Almma asked. "Or did you feel my lips on your ass?"

While the other heads in the holo couldn't hide a variety of emotions ranging from holding in laughter and trying not to yell at Almma themselves, Kellick was the only one who spoke.

"Where would you prefer to spend the rest of your career," Kellick asked. "On a bridge? Or babysitting another admiral's hallway?"

"My apologies, Sir," Almma replied. "It won't happen again."

"In light of the situation, I'm willing to understand," Kellick accepted. "But it doesn't change the fact that the Onyx is vulnerable to another admiral from taking it before the Kag'tak fleet arrive."

"Merrecci appointed a new prime admiral in your absence."

"Who?"

"I doubt you'd believe me. Sending the record now," Almma said, tapping commands against the console of the command chair. "And to answer your question, Sir, the Kag'tak took her."

Kellick's face matched the reactions of the other heads that were currently in command of a Maridamarak vessel.

"Well," Kellick struggled to say through disciplined restraint. "I suppose that's that then. Excuse me while I prepare now."

Almma agreed, watched the heads disappear, then asked her bridge to report.

The Rhaxian vessel informed her that it and all but two of its members had returned on board and would like to help repair its destroyed sector.

The blast that broke into the Onyx earlier had struck a warehouse filled with fabricating materials. It claimed no lives since its regular personnel were currently manning their battle stations at various places along the ducts where they waited at consoles to assist in power reroutes if the bridge requested them. Currently, they were being asked to divert power away from the damaged ship zones, and they were trying not to contemplate how their day might have been different had warehouses been vital enough to warfare that they required battle stations within them.

Now the doors to the bridge opened, and Cindy marched in. Without saying a word, she dropped into the command seat, composed herself and opened a communication to the fleet.

*   *   *

Rose Nun had heard them all. She did well at hearing them all. This is what she had trained for; what she had come out of hibernation for; what she had spent her life accomplishing. Earth was yet another paltry planet of which she would prepare takeover. Fighting and revolution would be lower because of her. Planetary resources would serve more, and the other subspecies would feel power, albeit illusory.

To her left, the Didjians cried Earth was supposed to be theirs. They currently berated Rose over the sudden loss of the Longanda and Nalignig. What if Earth destroyed them next? The Jimmosheans did what Jimmosheans do, they ridiculed the Didjians for having the easy role—good on ground battle, bad in space. If not for the Jimmosheans, the Didjians would have lost air superiority over their own planet long ago. In fact, if one truly looked at Didjian history, perhaps *The Chronicles of Juamai of Heavy Fire*, they would find the only reason they still existed is because they knew how to repel foot soldiers and anything in range of ground weaponry.

Still, the Jimmosheans were angry their involvement may have compromised whether the Kag'tak would be merciful to them.

The Paichu admonished them both for their lack of faith in the supreme Kag'tak.

Rose's hand raised and then fell on the arm of her throne made of Chapitnin wood, strong and light enough to build ship hulls out of, stained in the blood of he who led the first planet she liquidated in her youth. Where she went, the throne went as a symbol of a new head and a new chair. As her hand hit the arm, it clacked as it was designed, almost deafening.

"I have heard your concerns," she said. She filled her lungs and sat higher than the three other Kag on her council. One, a geographic deconstructionist and accountant of natural resource, helped her understand how to use a planet to bury its inhabitants should the duty arise. Another was a master trader with limitless connections to ensure efforts on any planet that showed value. The third was a whisperer of praise, support, and objection—in other words, Rose's lover. Tilting her head back only to the extent where she knew her crown would not topple from her head, she announced there was nothing to worry about.

"I have already sent word to Kag," she said. "They will send retribution, and it will no longer be polite. We just need to sit for a few days until our fleet arrives. We have not lost, nor can we."

She turned to a panel of Earthers, whom she had selected as advisers to help her motives appear friendlier and to help her identify the nuances that could give them strength over her.

"We know this because humans are not a fierce race." She smiled as she spoke, aware it could help raise kinship among Earthers. "Charming they are and angry sometimes, but not fierce."

Just now, the seal of the Earth's prime admiral filled the room. Then a woman's holographic face nearly reached floor to ceiling.

"Attention Earth crews," the blonde woman announced. Rose recognized adversary at once—determination, resistance, Rose had broken these before.

"By order of the prime admiral, In ten minutes, I will be reactivating all fleet. Any vessels with enemy occupants on them will be gassed. Any lifepods with enemy occupants will be leaving our solar system or your pods will be gassed. All fleet hands are ordered to scan your ships carefully, or you will be gassed. Any non-lifepod Earth vessel that attempts to jump away, you will be gassed. Anyone who tries me will self-destruct. You have ten minutes."

The transmission ended.

The room was now silent until an Earther spoke, "Sounded fierce to me."

Rose drew her pistol, shot the Earther, and watched the electric charge burn him out of flesh.

"Did it," Rose replied. She pointed to the Earther standing beside the remaining bones of the corpse. "Bring me that head."

The woman Earther hesitated a moment, and Rose held her pistol aim on her, but didn't fire. The human took up the skull of the murdered man and carried it to the throne where she placed it in Rose's open hand.

Rose thanked the woman and put away her pistol. She turned the bare skull to herself.

"Remarkable how such flimsy structure can give so many a false courage," Rose stated. Then she broke out a portion of the human eye socket and temple and began to eat it.

She chewed carefully, thoroughly, then swallowed it.

"Who is she," Rose asked, looking to the panel of humans, and pointing to where the recent transmission had appeared.

One face among the panel of humans reacted, but only one, an Earth leader who simply could not reach a bunker in time. Admiral Winchester, she believed his name was.

Rose broke off another piece of the skull and began chewing.

Four of the Earthers in the council box were military, so she assumed that what she had seen must not be the face of someone known in those circles, since only one seemed to recognize the head that had been in the hologram. Three in the panel were top politicians who clearly did not recognize her appearance, so Rose made the guess, she was no one of influence or known status. That one admiral did recognize this woman was of interest.

"Daughter," she asked Winchester through her snack.

No. His eyes weren't frightened enough for it to be a daughter. To ensure her assumption, she broke off another chunk of the human skull and used it to pick the grit of her previous bite from her teeth. Then she slid this piece of bone into her mouth. There was fear now, but there was fear for one's own life and fear for a life you cared about. This was fear for himself. What a selfish species.

Still, it was someone worthy that he should know and that others in the military would not. Someone secret. An agent perhaps. She would ask.

No.

It was not an agent, so Rose considered how Winchester had not answered her question regarding who the woman in the transmission was. Now, this usually suggested the person being interrogated was under the impression that he wasn't supposed to give that information away, or was protecting it, or was protecting someone else who knew it.

"Is it a god," she asked and knew her answer without a word being returned to her. "Well, now there's no more reason to be delicate with our search, is there?"

The Kag geographic adviser leaned in and whispered into Rose's ear.

Rose tore the jawbone from the skull and a few of its teeth scattered. She composed herself and brushed the pieces of remaining bones from her silver gown and lap.

"It seems your Milky Way has filled with escape pods of cowards fleeing the system," Rose announced. "And that two Maridamarak are in pursuit of two of your brand new war ships, which we have awarded to the Jimmosheans. So, we must make an example now. Who would like to go first?"

"You are being hailed by the prime admiral of the Earth military," the Earth's primitive computer announced.

"So be it," Rose said.

The blonde god's holographic bust appeared once more. Yes, clearly a god.

"Rebel Earth vessel," Rose spoke before the god could utter a sound. "You have attacked a Divide planet under direction of Kag control—

The hologram suddenly vanished.

"Did she just do that to me," Rose asked. "Hail her back." When there was no response, she turned to the panel of humans. "Hail her!"

One of the Earthers, an elderly politician instructed the computer to open a transmission to the Onyx.

A new head appeared, a woman whose hair Rose couldn't decipher the color because it had been slicked back in blood, both of Kag and of human, perhaps some of her own. It even caked parts of her face. She was sitting in a high-back command chair.

"You're not the god," Rose erupted. "Who are you?"

"Me," the woman asked. "They call me Almma. I've been asked to—

"We have seen those gods destroyed. She cannot hide from us. Inform her, she will surrender herself at once." Then she roared. "And you will stand when I am addressing you."

The woman shifted in her seat, not to stand up but to lounge back deeply.

"Oh boy, did you grab the wrong bull by the balls," Almma announced.

Rose would have shot the woman there. She drew her pistol for comfort, but instead fired back with "You disgusti—

"You ever just been bent over and given a good, old Humpty Dumpty," Almma had the audacity to interrupt.

Rose found herself speechless. The translators worked, it was their native language after all, but Rose didn't quite understand nor know how to respond.

"Don't worry," the rude woman said. "If you're still here after we destroy your next fleet, or we've heard you've harmed even one of our people you're going to."

The panel laughed around Rose, and she joined. She might not have understood it all, but she did know a warning when she heard one, and to be threatened by a sub-species was still entertaining.

"Oh my god," the insulting Earth woman in the hologram declared. "Is that what Kag'taks look like laughing." She had the nerve to look disgusted. "You look like you're birthing turds." She turned her attention to somewhere the hologram did not reveal. "No wonder they're assholes. Their humor's full of shit." Then she turned back to Rose. "Well, we've got to go now, before your fleet gets here. We've got to fix our ship, fix our fleet. You probably wanna fix your face or flush it or something. Seriously, don't laugh anymore." Then her face stiffened, stood, and grew larger as her full body turned into just a bust, and she glared right into Rose.

The woman wasn't afraid. Rose could see it.

"You want to run," the woman said.

Once again, the transmission ended.

Rose could only listen to the reports that came in. Repairs to the Onyx took two days once it returned to the shipyard. After nearly a year since the invasion of Earth had taken place, the human fleet was in control of its facilities again, all except its diplomatic station and membership to its pathetic Franchise. She imagined that crews were juggled, commands removed or transferred—that's what Rose would have done with a fleet of captains that had served the enemy occupier. Earth had eighty-three vessels remaining, not counting the Onyx nor their diplomatically-classified, Maridamarak fleet carrier and its defense system of deadly nullifiers.

It would not matter though. The Kag would bring an armada now, and quickly.

The victory was ensured so much that Rose Nun had already begun preparations to focus her next tour of work on the traitorous Maridamarak species. They had been subjugated long enough to know the penalty for betrayal. First Earth needed to fall so she could learn what they might possibly have shared with the Maridamarak to let them be an adversary again to the Kag. It would be easier to conquer Earth. The human fleet was only a small fraction of what it had been before the Divide had taken it, before Kag presence was necessary.

Still, she was who she was, and she knew the whispers. There was a great objection among the fleet to the new prime admiral. She was a god, but an unknown stranger to the fleet. Rose could use that. She directed the Earth politicians to call her to tribunal. That was one she didn't have to put much effort into, seems Earth leaders didn't like the idea much either. They had a plan to replace the prime admiral, but the prime admiral refused to entertain them.

What did take effort on Rose's part was infiltrating the fleet and bribing those she had learned would serve her. They moved quickly and took command of three ships all without being noticed. A name was delivered to her, a man who understood how to mutiny, a man who had done it before, a man who had served on the Onyx and knew its inner workings. So, she spoke to this Vandenbutcke and promised him immunity and wealth, and he could even take some friends with him, give him a ship and the protection of the Kag too.

He agreed, but it turned to be only as a tactic to discover their full intention. Immediately, three infiltrated Earth ships were deactivated and reclassified as prison colonies. He had drawn his line, chosen his commander.

Rose Nun would dine on this Vandenbutcke's skull.

*　　*　　*

It took only seven days from the time the Onyx had destroyed the Longanda and Nalignig for the Kag'tak fleet of thirty-five ships to appear in sensor range. Considering the Kag'tak might send five to take control of the worst incidents, this was no small statement against Earth. A single scout destroyed two Earth vessels stationed along the Milky Way perimeter to monitor for their approach.

When they entered Earth's solar system, the new prime admiral was sitting in her command chair. The Onyx sat almost the distance of Mars orbit to keep the heaviest part of the battle away from destroying planetary civilians. Kellick's carrier was already unloaded and waiting with her. The remainder of the fleet took position closer to Earth, expecting some sort of flank attack. Nandy and Drinker suggested this would happen by lesser fleets since the Kag'tak seemed too proud to face the weaker opponents. The commanding officers of each ship had resigned themselves to their own destruction or slim chance of running.

There had, at one time, been a suggestion to outfit the rest of Earth's ships with the technology to allow them to channel the Maridamarak energy as the Onyx had learned to do, but they barely had time to conduct basic repairs for battle. Another suggestion was to use the Maridamarak snipers to aid the smaller, lesser-armed Earth ships.

"I wouldn't recommend it," Kellick countered. "Remember, we figured out how to disarm the Maridamarak because of those sniper attacks. The Divide could do the same and disarm us just as quickly. The fewer clues we give to our abilities the better, and that includes to our own fleet right now."

The prime admiral agreed.

As the Kag'tak approached, Kellick politely reminded the prime admiral for the seventh time that they had beaten the Maridamarak already and were capable against his own ship and its little fleet.

"Don't worry," Cindy Lou said. "They'll be too busy here in a moment. Just keep us powered. We'll provide the shield."

She reminded him for perhaps the tenth time to remember that they had to make their energy last better this fight. Last time, they faced one ship, all sixteen Maridamarak vessels could fire upon the Onyx in those odds to win. Now, they faced thirty-five Kag'tak. Kellick's fleet needed to rotate firing energy into the Onyx. It would deliver smaller punches, but their power would last longer.

The Kag'tak fleet arrived, and Cindy Lou ordered, "Get ready to show them what we brought."

Almma began issuing commands to her sector to start—

Escobedo's head and torso appeared in the holo.

"Issa Almma," Escobedo's head announced. "You do not know, but, if were are going to die, I might not get another chance to say that—

Escobedo's holographic head suddenly vanished and Almma's head from the neck up took its place.

"Pablo Escobedo," holographic Almma interrupted curtly. "Either ask me out in person or kiss your chance goodbye to ever see what I'm not currently wearing below this neck."

"Now watch how hot I'm about to get," Almma, herself, added.

*   *   *

The fleet the Kag sent to punish Earth was led by Krakacian Gri Nni. He was old, the kind of old that could wield a scythe better than Death himself. The other ship's kuntacian's obeyed. He played no games, not at a table on his ship, during conflict that is. He knew what others did in their command centers. He did not care. To win was to humble yourself long enough to demonstrate your greatness. That's how you conquered. That's why Phemos and Vau Rinn were dead. Had they been of his tutelage, they would not be.

The silver map filled the table before him. It, like his ship, was larger than a Kuntacian's by three times. At one end of the map, Earth circled its sun, and a paltry fleet surrounded it. To his left was a ship he had come to conquer. So, they had thought to reduce collateral damage by distancing themselves from Earth.

"Remember, this is a show of strength, not an extinction," he reminded his fleet and their Kuntacians. "We need the god. No one fires until I say."

At this, his map came to life with Onyx's first attack. Hundreds of torpedoes flew at Gri Nni's fleet.

"They're nothing," Gri Nni announced upon the observation that the projectiles' sizes were too small to signify a real threat. "Let them see what they're up against. Perhaps their senses will come to them, and we can talk."

Then the small torpedoes hit, but they did not explode. They merely bounced off the Kag shields and then raced off to strike another of Gri Nni's ships.

"What is this nonsense," Gri Nni asked. While others chuckled, he did not. He did not know this weapon.

"Whatever those are, shoot them down," Gri Nni ordered.

Now, his silver map filled with raizers. Many struck down some of Earth's strange torpedoes. Immediately, the Onyx began to spit out hundreds more at a time until there were simply too many coming in than the Kag could clear out.

"This is what Phemos lost to," his first choice, another close to his own age asked.

"Good point," Gri Nni said. Then he asked out as if to no one in particular, they would know who it was, "What is the drain on our shields?"

"Negligible," an unknown's voice called. It would become known when it was worthy.

The Onyx kept spitting out the bouncing torpedoes.

"Can we count these," the first choice asked.

"A little over ten thousand," Palma, one of Gri Nni's favorites announced. She was his analyst.

"The drain is getting noticable," the unknown announced.

"How so?"

"It registers a minimal drain, but it's simple to remedy."

The Earth's pyramid continued to spit the torpedoes out.

"It's gone up again," the unknown said. "Shields are at 97%."

"Let us end this," Gri Nni said.

He opened his own transmission to the Earth ship Onyx.

The god's silver bust appeared before him.

"It's her," the first choice muttered. "Exactly as the image Cha transmitted."

"I am Krakacian Gri Nni," he said. "Desist this attack, and perhaps we will pass more merciful justice."

"Just shut up and die," the prime admiral god replied. She ended the communication.

The Onyx spit out more bouncing projectiles.

Suddenly, the Maridamarak fleet fired down upon the Onyx, and the Earth flagship let loose a burst of powerful Raizer fire into one of the Kag vessels and left it to burn and finish dying in space.

"Ah, an intimidation opening shot," Gri Nni said, more to his first choice than any other. He allowed himself to get lost in thought, which became consideration, then turned into realization. "So, they do have a strategy. But they can't maintain that kind of weapon fire for long."

His communication specialist announced that she was getting reports that some of the smaller Kag vessels were seeing increased shield drain.

"The Maridamarak power the Onyx. Smart. We can destroy the Maridamarak though," Gri Nni thought out loud to invite his first choice's thoughts. "Large weapons would be wasted on us right now, and they know it, but these small, bouncing missiles still drain our shields. They keep firing them in, the drain becomes greater."

"And if they drain the shields on one ship, they can destroy it," the first choice contributed. "Then there will be one less target for these weapons to spread across, and those of us that remain will have even more of those bouncing contraptions focusing in."

Gri Nni straightened. "So small of an attack that its exponential growth would take us by surprise."

"But we are not surprised," the first choice said.

"No," Gri Nni said. "But they are worthy of the game now."

From the edge of the room, the Kag bookie, pleased that he would get to work now, stood and approached the table.

"Betting is open," the bookie announced.

The room erupted with predictions, and the bookie took them.

Gri Nni placed his bet then turned to his first choice and stated, "We need to stop this."

The map revealed one of the Maridamarak ships firing into the Onyx and it unleashing another blast of super-powered Raizer.

"Only one ship fires now. See, they know they cannot sustain such massive attacks," Gri Nni announced. "Order all fleet to stop wasting energy on those bouncing torpedoes and to target the Maridamarak vessels on my mark instead."

"We could use something to absorb those hits better," the first choice said.

"Palma," Gri Nni addressed. "How many Kag ships do we currently have out scanning systems for Earth stragglers?"

"Nine," Palma answered.

"Order them all here now."

Finally, he delivered the order to his thirty-five ships to fire upon the Maridamarak.

At once, the Maridamarak vessels began increasing the speed of their rotational pattern of shooting upon the Onyx, and she unleashed a flurry of raizer shots that were able to pick off everything that Gri Nni threw. Not only that, but the Onyx was now maneuvering itself between Maridamarak vessels and Kag torpedoes. The attacks that didn't manage to get destroyed, somehow were absorbed by her own shields as the Onyx maneuvered in ways that blocked each one from striking a Maridamarak ship. Every time the Earth's flagship absorbed an attack, a Maridamarak ship bolstered her defenses to absorb the blow.

"I see," Gri Nni realized.

"They can't possibly think they can sustain this, can they" the first choice asked.

Again, speaking to no one in particular, Gri Nni announced, "Order the Divide to engage Earth and its fleet. Perhaps that distraction will tempt them to break up their formation and send some of those Maridamarak to aid Earth. When they do, so will we. The Onyx cannot defend them all once they split up."

Gri Nni's fleet unleashed three more barrages of their own torpedoes, and he watched the Onyx pick them all off.

Now, the Divide fleet appeared on the map near Earth and began their engagement.

"All right," Gri Nni said to himself. "Take the bait."

He waited and watched as the Onyx continued to erase his own attack efforts from the map.

"They're not taking it," the first choice said.

Gri Nni swore, but no one heard it except his brain.

"Bring me chubs," he ordered.

Suddenly a small explosion erupted from the hull of one of the Kag vessels.

"The Oninan's shields are down," Palma's voice informed.

Immediately, the Onyx launched a single massive torpedo, followed a moment later by three smaller ones.

"Shoot them down," Gri Nni ordered. His fleet opened fire and should have destroyed the bombs, or at least one of them, but the Onyx was yet again flying in a manner that allowed it to position itself to fend off and destroy the Kag attacks. Then, the Onyx broke away from its defensive run, and the largest torpedo struck into the side of the Oninan and cracked it apart in a massive explosion. All three smaller missiles cruised right up inside its broken bits and set it burning and breaking apart in a way that told Gri Nni there would be no one returning home from within it.

As if Gri Nni had planned it himself, three Kag vessels answering his call from their hunts for straggling Earth ships jumped in closer to the Onyx than perhaps they'd expected and fired off a cascade of their own projectiles.

The Onyx reacted as if it almost expected the surprise. Almost, because one torpedo finally struck.

Gri Nni's map flickered, showing the Earth vessel's shields were generating 88% less energy. Even the weakest of a Kag hit would punch straight into the hull now, but he didn't need to damage the hull. He needed the shields to come down so he could put his landing party on board to capture the god.

"Standby extraction party," he ordered.

Then the map suggested power was returning to the Onyx's shields much faster than they should have.

"Where is that coming from," Gri Nni exploded. "Nothing in the information our spy sent us on that vessel should suggest they can do that. Where is that coming from?"

"Maybe they have another power supply not in the schematic that's compensating," the first choice said.

"One power supply," Gri Nni complained. "One. That's what the schematic showed."

"Perhaps the schematic was faulty or incom—

"Am I the only one who sees what the Earth ship is doing," Gri Nni erupted. "Chase it. Get in its way. Fire something into its path. Take out an engine!"

With that, four new Kag vessels responding to Gri Nni's command to join the fight against the Earth fleet suddenly appeared, right into the path of the Onyx and opened fire upon it.

"Yes," Gri Nni bellowed, but moments later followed it with an eruption of, "How?"

Although the Onyx had evaded and destroyed every weapon just fired in these past few moments, one of the four newcomer Kag ships was still in its path. The Onyx wouldn't be able to avoid it. It began to spin.

For a moment, Gri Nni realized he had just failed in capturing the god. Attempting to collide with a Kag ship? The Onyx would die. As the Onyx spun and drilled its way towards the Kag vessel, all of the Maridamarak pristines and their carrier suddenly opened fire upon it.

A raizer burst from the Onyx, fired into the Kag obstacle, burned its shields out and allowed the Onyx to tear through its remains in a combination of raizer and spinning fury.

"There," Gri Nni roared. "Order all Kag vessels to volley the Onyx while it's masked by the debris from the Maridamarak."

The fleet unleashed their attacks, and the silver map showed the Onyx break into an evasive dance that refused to let a single weapon strike it. In the midst of it, the Maridamarak empowered it once more to open fire.

Gri Nni growled as he watched the Onyx destroy or evade the incoming attacks that should have otherwise made enough contact to drop her shields, breach its hull, tear out its engines and still have enough punch left over to destroy three or four of her Maridamarak allies.

"First choice," he stated sternly. "When we board that ship, I want you to personally bring me that pilot's head."

More small hull explosions broke from within Gri Nni's fleet. The Onyx turned to one and began firing multiple raizer shots upon them, but none of them gave way to destruction.

"They've destroyed three ships," Gri Nni said.

"But we have more than we started with now," the first choice said. "They can't possibly sustain this fight."

Now, the remaining two Kag back-up ships jumped in.

Once again, the Onyx began evasive maneuvers, and that's when a chub suddenly appeared as well. It locked its tractor beam onto the Onyx, stopping its crazy flying entirely.

A second chub appeared and turned its tractor on the Maridamarak vessels and trapped eight of them instantly.

Now, Gri Nni could destroy the Onyx's Maridamarak support.

*   *   *

"Can we do that trick with the music and tear the tractor apart again," Nandy asked.

"Check with engineering and do it," Cindy said.

One of Kellick's Maridamarak Nullifiers suddenly soared in, lock its four blue beams onto the chub holding the Onyx and began firing down red bursts of energy, one after another. After the seventh round of shots, this chub dropped its tractor and began to withdraw from the battle with a hole burned into its side.

"Yes," Vandenbutcke's head announced, suddenly hovering over the battle that appeared in the battlecron. "We can take on chubs now!"

"Well done, Lieutenant," Cindy said.

Just then a Kag'tak torpedo ripped into the side of Vandenbutcke's nullifier and blew out the opposite end, turning Vandenbutcke's ship into a demonic flower and deadly bloom of white, scorching death that lasted a few short moments and, when it was done, left no evidence that there had ever been a nullifier, a crew, or its commander.

Cindy flew to the railing to evaluate if what she had just seen was real.

"Did they just," Nandy asked. She was already standing at the railing.

"Did what I think just happen happen," Almma questioned.

Suddenly, Nandy was screaming. She dropped and hung from the battlecron's railing while she tried to pretend that she wasn't really shrieking.

Cindy let her.

Then, the Onyx erupted with weapons fire, all possible weapons fire, all at once and continuous.

"What's happening," Cindy asked.

The Onyx continued to unleash its fury in torpedoes of every kind and raizers at full power.

"I didn't order this," Cindy announced. "Stop it!"

"This isn't me," Almma cried. Her fingers raced over her controls trying to trace down where the commands were coming from. "No-no-no-no-no-no-no." She kept muttering.

The weapons continued to discharge from every tube, while the raizers had yet to stop firing. It all bore down on the Kag'tak vessel that had just destroyed Vandenbutcke's ship.

"Stop," Almma kept ordering. "Stop. Stop! We're overheating."

The Onyx didn't give up though, and five of her largest missiles blasted from within.

"Oh shit," Almma stated.

Several larger torpedoes struck into the Kag'tak. The vessel sailed sideways as its shields gave out.

"Stop firing," Almma ordered, but the Onyx didn't listen.

As quickly as it started unleashing its weapons, the Onyx fell silent.

"We're overheated," Almma alerted. She had run to one of her operator's consoles and was now working feverishly at it. "We have no weapons."

"Get them back," Cindy demanded.

Just now, the five most monstrous and slowest of torpedoes in Earth's arsenal pelted into the side of the Kag'tak vessel and covered it in explosions, but the ship did not fall dark.

"Who did that," Cindy demanded to know.

"Found it," Almma reported.

A new image grew from the battlecron's holo, one that showed Mirror screaming orders about how to rejuvenate the weapons. She screamed at her console for the armory to prepare more torpedoes.

When they claimed they couldn't, she screamed even louder. Cindy ordered her to calm down.

"Tell them to reload," Mirror screamed at Cindy. "Tell them to keep firing, and let me work! Tell them!"

She kept screaming until she finally straight-up fainted and one of her staff caught her just before her head could strike the edge of a control panel.

"Is she okay," Cindy asked, then notified medical before turning her attention back to her bridge.

"Ma'am," Almma said. "We can't fire 'til we're cooled down."

"Then we have no choice," Cindy said and immediately opened a channel to Kellick's diplomatic fleet. "Hit us with everything."

"Ma'am, we can't fire," Almma reminded.

"Maybe we can if we direct the Maridamarak power to the weapon cooling systems first," Cindy replied.

"And if it doesn't work?"

"Well, then I guess we're going to have to die, aren't we?"

*   *   *

"That had to have overheated their weapons," Gri Nni's first choice said.

"Now's the time," Gri Nni announced, once more focused on his map. "Bring their shields down, and let's end this."

His ship, and only his ship released torpedoes, enough that should finally show the prime admiral she was lost.

Four Maridamarak fleet vessels suddenly opened fire on the Onyx, and her shields withstood far more damage from Gri Nni's attacks than they should have.

It didn't matter though, because now, three more chubs suddenly appeared in the arena. At Gri Nni's behest, they trapped the entire Maridamarak fleet.

"I want to talk to the Onyx," Gri Nni said.

In a moment, the goddess's face appeared before Gri Nni.

"I am Krakacian Gri Nni. Are we done," Gri Nni asked. "Surrender so you may be returned to Kag for justice."

Except for the remaining annoyance of small torpedoes still rebounding among the Kag fleet and slowly draining their shields with each collision, the attack had silenced.

"Disable these ridiculous torpedoes," Gri Nni ordered.

The goddess prime admiral agreed but could only disable their explosive and navigating prowess. She couldn't guarantee her "pinball torpedoes" wouldn't keep bouncing around for a while.

Gri Nni found himself with no choice but to accept.

"Is it clear now that you do not have the energy to sustain a fight to take even this small of our fleet. Look at what you have spent to destroy only three of our ships. Even you, a god cannot overpower us," Gri Nni said. "Do you suppose that even if you could have defeated us that you could defeat all of Kag in war? Do you think we would have come all this way from Kag if we did not know the sustainability of your defensive and offensive measures?"

"You came from Kag," the prime admiral asked.

"Well, we didn't come from Didjia," Gri Nni replied. He joined his control room technicians in a little chuckle.

"How many more of you are coming?"

Gri Nni snickered. "I assure you, we are more than are needed to make your species submit. Now, surrender that we may return home to our hibernation."

"Does that mean your shuttle has already delivered our captain to Kag'tak?"

"Yes, we have her," Gri Nni replied. "Now, lower your shields and prepare to be boarded. Perhaps we can arrange her return, a trade perhaps for you."

"Good," the prime admiral stated. "Then I can take this damned thing off now."

Her fingers worked their way to her hair and began to pull it away from her face so she could reach up and begin peeling down a lining of synthetic flesh. She kept removing it until all that remained was the face of the very Onyx captain, Briata Leonard, that he had seen only days ago on Kag. She rubbed her neck and lack of face, then finally looked into the holo.

"You have no idea how much I've needed to do that the past week," the prime admiral complained. Her voice had changed entirely as well.

Gri Nni instantly assumed they must have used a voice modulator. They did something similar with their own spy to make him sound more human when they infiltrated Earth's academy.

Here, Gri Nni turned to his number one, "Alert Kag at once and instruct them to redirect Master Cha from delivering his prisoner to the colony. She is not the first officer of the Onyx. She is the god! We have both gods!"

"You left a God in the care of that bumbling oaf Cha," the prime admiral asked. Her voice crackled. Gri Nni wasn't sure if it was lack of confidence or adjustment from the voice modulator. He assumed both.

"Your concern now is surrender," he said.

"Okay, Kraktacian Gri Nni," the prime admiral stated, as she lounged back. "I can be swayed to offer you sanctuary and Earth protection in exchange for the rest of your ships."

"You are a funny one," the Kag remarked. "I will take you home for myself just to crack you open and dine on what's inside."

"Oh, but you don't have a home. It's gone," the prime admiral replied. "You destroyed it when you allowed two horny gods to do what two horny gods are destined to do while you ran away to pick a fight with lesser beings."

"But you are mistaken ugly little thing," Gri Nni stated in patronizing fashion. "If the Utonenaibe is who you say she is, the gods are not together."

He motioned to his third of choice, who abruptly dragged the silent, blond Adonis where the Earth prime admiral could see him.

Adonis saw Bria, smiled, and said, "Hi."

"He is here," Gri Nni said.

"Oh good," the impertinent and young prime admiral stated. "We'd hoped he would be the one you brought back."

"Your facade may have delayed the inevitable—but, now that you have played your hand—we will order Cha to return with her and make an example of your soon-to-be-reborn solar system."

"You mean you'll have Master Cha bring her back," Bria asked.

"Yes."

"You mean Master Cha, the Zarchro," Bria inquired.

Gri Nni laughed. He liked this prime admiral. She was inventive. He gave her that.

"Did you know the last Zarchro was hidden in quick space on a ship that was incapable of travel? Even your ships can't fly through that, can they?" the prime admiral asked. She appeared entirely too comfortable in a conversation with a superior race. "And did you know that about two hundred Earth years ago that a pair of scientists invented a ship that allowed them to enter his quick space and find his vessel? When they boarded, he stole their ship and went looking for his mate."

"Who cares," Gri Nni said. "I will not ask you again to lower your shields."

"Hold on, I'm almost done," the prime admiral said. "By the way, did you check his DNA, or did you just measure according to your ego? See, our doctor did check his DNA and was able to trace the man you're holding back to the two scientists that went missing while navigating quick space. As pretty as our friend is there, he's actually the result of tenth generation inbreeding."

Gri Nni must have been staring, and not in a bewildered manner, because Bria then asked, "Didn't you even wonder why something so godlike was so not? Are you godlike, buddy?"

"Yah," Adonis replied.

"Since you haven't the god, we have no need for—," he started, but was interrupted again.

"This entire time, the one we know as Master Cha has been smelling out his mate," the prime admiral said.

Before Gri Nni could issue an order to destroy the disgusting little girl's ship, she spoke again.

"He was obsessed with finding her. He ran up bounties everywhere he went under aliases; stole planets; stole princesses he thought might be his mate. He stole your trust in him, certainly pissed us off a bit too. When he discovered the Paichu had heard Earth had a god, he infiltrated the ranks of your subordinates, and you just gave him all the free reign he needed to search for her."

Gri Nni found himself waiting to see if she was finished talking. She stopped. He opened his mouth to berate her.

"He used you, and we used that," she spoke again. "Check his history if you don't believe me."

The Kag's breaths became thick and unrestrained with thoughts of how it would like to kill another of Earth's prime admirals. He wanted her dead. Still, a good leader examined every angle. With a nod of his head, he signaled his first choice to search for Master Cha's background records.

"Do your history books teach you about how long it takes for a Zarchro and Utonenaibe to gestate and give birth to a working solar system," the prime admiral asked.

Gri Nni insulted her with a growl reserved for only the lowest of lifeforms that should die soon from audacity.

"I'll take that as a yes," the prime admiral said.

Gri Nni's table immediately presented an image of Master Cha's criminal history and read it carefully.

"You should verify that criminal record with your own superiors," the prime admiral said, and Gri Nni wondered if she could see what was on the table before him. Still, he urged his first in command to indeed check in with the superior council to warn them of the allegations.

"See," the prime admiral said. She spoke a lot. He could do without that. "We figured that if you had the time to get here, then your shuttle with our gods on it had time to get to Kag'tak—assuming you came from Kag'tak. Considering your hibernation and all, where else would you come from? Which means the Zarchro and the Utonenaibe explain why you can't get a response from Kag'tak." She stood from her chair now. "In other words, they just had sex and the neighbors ain't complaining."

"What are you saying," Gri Nni asked.

"I'm saying, when was the last you heard from home," the prime admiral answered.

Gri Nni found his first choice huddled over the communication operator's chair. They both looked to Gri Nni and shook their heads at him.

On Gri Nni's table, the Earth prime admiral held up the jadestone key to their earned bounty.

"If that is the case," she said. "Then contingent upon reports that the Kag system is destroyed, we, thanks to your generous reward, can now afford to place a bounty on you—and you don't have the resources to sustain outrunning all the hunters who will want it."

She gestured to someone out of his view.

"Allow me to demonstrate," she said.

Here, several unaffiliated vessels began to appear within the Milky Way, each of a unique design that was typical of belonging to a bounty hunter crew who had adapted and upgraded their capturing and killing capacity to take on the target they sought.

"And thanks to our little pinball torpedoes, we have already tagged your vessels should you try to run," the prime admiral added.

More bounty hunter ships appeared.

"You think bounty hunters can withstand our technology," the

Kag laughed.

"You might be surprised," the prime admiral said. She turned to someone off screen again and asked, "What was that saying, Commander?"

"Sometimes, one's only ally is temptation," an unseen woman answered.

"That's right," the prime admiral said. "And we're offering a very big temptation."

More and more bounty hunter ships were appearing and surrounded the Kag fleet.

"So, would you like our protection," Bria asked. "I hear the Rhaxians and Maridamarak are considering putting some of their technology and ships up for sale, now that they don't have to hide or do your bidding anymore."

Gri Nni remained silent. He still saw heads from his own crew shaking at him concerning any word from Kag. His entire staff were now standing to watch him.

"Do you need to take a few days to verify," the prime admiral asked.

"We have already verified," Gri Nni replied. "None of what we can do is as primitive as your capabilities."

"Are you sure about that," she asked.

"We can still destroy you," He grumbled.

His entire control center was silent now as the map before him continued to fill with bounty hunter vessels. Gri Nni was old. Gri Nni had seen it all. But he believed her. He had seen the enemy's true face, and he had watched his own people march them into their home. What else could the gods have been doing if they were together?

"Yes," he finally said, and did so softly as it became clear that his crew could not stand against the numbers of the bounty collectors across the galaxy that would spare no expense to make profit. Even now, hunter ships had already set to scanning the debris of Gri Nni's three fallen allies for anything useful to their cause. Those that weren't were already engaging the chubs.

"Yes, what," Bria asked.

"We wish your protection," Gri Nni replied. "We surrender!"

Bria breathed in deeply. She stepped away from her command seat and grew taller on his table. Soon her head was peering down on him and saying, "I don't know what kilkosh demi means, but I imagine it means something like 'go to hell'."

Her face suddenly disappeared, and the transmission ended.

"Go to hell," Gri Nni asked. "Go to hell," he was now yelling.

The map continued to add more bounty hunters to it.

"Attention enemy fleets," the Earth Prime Admiral's voice transmitted now. "While we have fighting here, we have destroyed the Kag'tak world. Leave or you will join them."

Gri Nni watched the Jimmoshean chubs release their holds on the Maridamarak ships and withdraw.

"Destroy the Onyx," Gri Nni yelled. "Show them we conquer in death!"

Just then, all of the Maridamarak vessels opened fire on the Onyx once more to allow it to tear down the shields of one of his fleet. In moments, the Kag ship was burning.

"I said destroy the Onyx," Gri Nni ordered once more, but as he turned to flaunt his anger at having his command disregarded, he found his crew crumpled on the floor and over their stations, most bleeding from their heads, some from their chests.

In that moment, Krakacian Gri Nni could have sworn that he felt something enter his head, split his brain and break through the other side.

That's what he thought anyway. Maybe. He wasn't sure. Maybe, he felt the floor when he finally fell. Again, he wasn't sure. He couldn't tell over the sound of the Adonis laughing as he said "Boom!"

*   *   *

As the Bounty hunters chased after the Kag'tak ships, each competing to be the one who won reward, Bria set to draining Gri Nni's shields so she could send Almma over with a boarding team to take control of it and retrieve Adonis. Then she turned her attention upon the Divide's lesser attacking fleet, which had begun fleeing.

She opened a transmission to Earth and found Rose Nun and the occupying council before her again.

"What are you still doing here," Bria asked.

20

▲

Boom

Bria sat before a panel of lawmakers. It had taken a mere couple of days to go through the motions to call her to testify before the committee.

Below their seats sat thirteen admirals, one of which was the former Prime Admiral Shade. He was in full military dress, medal, and recognition, all except the insignia of active rank upon his shoulder and the color representing the location of his assignment. He sat in scrutiny of Bria Leonard who currently appeared at the witness bench before them all.

To Bria's right was Admiral Kellick. To her left were Adrigga Nandy, Charity, Prilla and Almma.

The testimonies started with Kellick; questions were light and respectful about his service record. They turned to his first impressions of Bria, his confidence in her at that time, whether she should have been chosen to work on a bridge. His answers were soft, honest, and sometimes brutal. Bria understood and forgave him, especially as the committee used great care to keep him from adding comments about his change of mind.

Prilla answered questions about her history, her father, her brother, her own service. They turned to her past with Bria, how they met, why she felt that Merrecci promoted her to such a high office of distinction.

"Because she stepped up and she's what there was at the time," Prilla answered.

"And now she's not," stated a prominent senator from—well—it didn't matter where. The prominent senator didn't really listen to the people from wherever that was either.

Prilla disagreed, and the senator silenced her.

Nandy reported on her academic record and called on her expertise to discuss how she viewed Bria's promotion over her at the time.

Bria understood Nandy's initial impressions and forgave her too.

Charity went through questions about Bria's physical disability from her injury. Charity wasn't so friendly to the panel. They reminded her that she was a member of the Earth Franchise. She reminded them she was drafted against her will. They reminded her she could be held in contempt of the committee.

"Oh, well if you think you're in charge, then maybe you're the one's I should sue for my sister's death after one of your captains unlawfully shanghaied us," Charity snarked, so they turned off her microphone.

For Almma, they got as far as asking her name before the intern sitting behind the senator abruptly answered his phone and leaned in to whisper in the senator's ear. The senator fell back in his chair and glared at Almma.

Almma, however, was grinning.

The previous days they had questioned others: Dawn, Mirror, Mike, Drinker, Rhaxians, Vandenbutcke's students, even Fiji. They embarrassed some, rebuked others, silenced all in some manner. All of this was used to build up for the main event today, squaring off against Bria and her command crew, and now it was Bria's turn.

The time to direct questioning fell to an old senator who got her start by campaigning that old senators had served too long. In her now waxing age, she forgot that philosophy and just kept on going. Today, she was chairwoman of the hearing.

"Briata Leonard," Senator Perkins said. She swallowed heavily.

"Prime Admiral Leonard, Senator," Kellick interjected.

"Excuse me," Perkins snipped, and she swallowed.

"She holds the title of Prime Admiral," Kellick clarified. "And the respe—

"That's what we're here to decide," the senator said. "Now, Admiral Leonard—

"You don't get to decide that she is currently Prime Admiral Bria Leonard," Kellick corrected. "That's what she is."

The senator ordered Kellick's microphone turned off.

"Miss Leonard, I don't think we'll need to draw this out much longer," Perkins continued. She swallowed, oblivious to the habit.

"As we have stated many times in this committee, we are here to decide if indeed the admirals are justified in calling to vote in a new prime admiral," Perkins said. "So, my question is simple. Will you please answer what makes you qualified to be a prime admiral of the Earth fleet over someone like, say, Prime Admiral Shade?"

"Well, as you may not—

"Please speak into the microphone, Miss Leonard," Perkins said.

"Well, as you may not have heard," Bria began again, pulling the microphone closer to her mouth. Immediately, she heard the muffled tone in comparison to how the other microphones had sounded."

"Please speak up, dear," Perkins replied.

The cameras before her made no sound, but she knew they were recording.

Had Bria looked over, she would have noticed Kellick pushing his own microphone towards her.

"Miss," Perkins asked.

"As I was saying," Bria replied.

"It's a simple question," Perkins insisted. "Can the highest officer in our fleet not answer why they are qualified to hold that position?"

Kellick leaned in to Bria's ear.

"Can you seriously not answer my question, Miss Leonard," Perkins asked. "Why should you be in command of Earth's fleet over Prime Admiral Shade?"

"Mr. Shade," Bria replied.

"What was that," Perkins asked.

"There is only one Prime Admiral in this room, and it is not anyone on your side of it," Bria replied.

The senator smacked her gavel and warned Bria to stick to relevant answers.

"Then get your titles right," Bria snapped. "I am here only as a courtesy to let you—

"Miss Leonard," Perkins snapped. "I warn you—

"Prime Admiral Leonard, and—

"Miss Leonar—

"You interrupt me one more time, and I will end this meeting," Bria said in a tone so commanding that Perkins was taken off guard.

"Now, what makes me qualified to be prime admiral over shade, is that I am the prime admiral, and Shade is not. It was my fleet and crew that overthrew the Divide and conquered the Kag'tak, not Shade's. Because of that, you are not only speaking to the prime admiral of the Earth Franchise, but a member of the presiding admiralship of the Franchise Coalition. I don't answer to any of you. You will afford me the respect I've earned."

"Have you earned it," Perkins asked.

"If for one second I believe that this body is attempting to dismantle the governing military and defensive coalition that defends this and other planets, I will have the members of this body flagged as threats and arrested if necessary," Bria stated.

Perkins inhaled and almost spoke.

"I dare you to try me!" Bria pointed a rigid finger directly at the Senator in a manner that made her forget to speak.

"You want to know why I'm the prime admiral instead of Shade," Bria asked. "Because when the enemy attacked, he hid, and I fought."

"How dare you," Shade shouted.

"You had every chance to get on the same shuttle as I did and join your fleet, but you chose to abandon your post and pawn it off to someone else," Almma roared out, standing from her seat. "As far as I'm concerned, that's the same as desertion."

"That's enough of that," Senator Perkins shouted while smashing her gavel repeatedly.

"And now we are done," Bria replied curtly.

With that, Bria stood and began to exit the witness table.

"We are not done," Perkins replied.

"The prime admiral says we're done, we are done," Kellick informed and turned to leave.

"I say when we're done," Perkins seethed.

"You know, from one end of the cosmos to the other, I have stopped wars, saved and helped establish governments far more complicated than our own," Kellick said. "So, believe me when I say that I am more qualified than this entire body combined to deal in this very environment. I'm more decorated than even Mr. Shade."

Shade's face sucked in with surprised confoundment.

"Seriously," Perkins asked. "I think we're seeing a great demonstration that the influence of an underqualified Prime Admiral has on—

"I'm going to kick your ass," Dawn erupted from her seat in the gallery.

"Quiet," Perkins snapped, while still smacking her gavel. "Until you become capable of intelligent thought, you will remain silent, or I will arrest you."

"Okay! I don't care how high and mighty you think your throne is up there," Kellick cut off with a powerful and tactful voice. "But now I'm warning you. One more ableist remark like that and I'm coming up there to knock your old ass off that throne with this fist!"

"Psst," Dawn asked from behind the witness barrier. "Can I help?"

Kellick immediately waved Dawn back.

"This is all unnecessary," Perkins said.

"And that's why we're leaving," Kellick explained.

"I am not going to debate this with you," Perkins retorted.

"Why? Not enough oxygen up your ass to sustain your logic," Almma asked as she, like the other witnesses, was beginning to stand and exit the witness table.

"Excuse me!" Then Perkins's eyes widened, and she exploded with "There'll be no more of that!"

"Don't tell me," Almma replied. "It's your head up there!"

Kellick now waved down Almma.

"This is the kind of hand you want to see directing our fleet," Perkins stated. "You are an admira—

"Don't lecture me about whose hands directs this fleet," Kellick shot back, and now he was yelling. "I gave her this half of my finger precisely because of the hands I want leading this fleet." He pointed to Dawn, "She gave a piece of her thumb." Then he pointed to Prilla. "She gave palm tissue."

"I gave her some of this," Almma announced, flipping Perkins the bird.

Perkins was suddenly shouting for the entire Chamber to silence. Once it had, Kellick continued.

"It's a miniscule tribute to what's she's given us after we treated her like a monster as you're doing now," Kellick said.

"I don't think anyone denies that she's provided a great sacrifice," Perkins said. "She just can't give what an experienced admiral can give."

"She gave up pieces of herself every day to save your lives," Kellick said, now back to his collected self. "And your response is that she can't give you enough?"

"I appreciate your loyalty," Perkins said. "But the truth is, she did not graduate the academy."

"She did graduate," Kellick corrected. "Under Prime Admiral Merrecci's authorization and tutelage as well as mine."

"She is mentally underqualified," Perkins stated hotly. "And you know it."

As the entire procession of witnesses suddenly stopped dead while Nandy was leading it past Kellick and into the aisle that pointed out of the chamber, Kellick found himself moving from behind the witness chair and stepping towards the committee's thrones. "What did I say about degrading my commanding officer?"

"That's right, Admiral" Almma agreed. "Punch the bitch!"

"Kick her ass," Dawn bellowed.

He'd thought of waving down the members of the Onyx crew, but he actually kept stepping towards Perkins's throne with every intention to knock her off it.

Perkins frantically ordered for Kellick to return to his seat. Kellick didn't care.

Suddenly, the gallery doors swung open, and a line of maintenance bots danced down the aisle and right before the committee.

"Senator Perkins is a douche bag! A giant douche bag! A really big douche bag. Senator Perkins is a douche bag, and she likes it all day long," the robots sang and synchronized their dance. "Everybody!"

At this, the chamber filled with singing from half of the people in attendance who had become familiar with the song themselves. Even Kellick and the other remaining witnesses joined in, "Senator Perkins is a douche bag!"

"I have a better idea," Bria announced marching past Kellick's entourage. The robots stopped singing and dancing.

"Miss Leonard," Perkins snipped. "This is not your—

"Excuse me," Bria asked. "What did you call me?" Then she suddenly stopped and went, "Oh, right! I completely forgot. How embarrassing is that for me, huh?"

She suddenly took on the familiar image of Cindy Lou.

"You're supposed to be dead," Shade bellowed.

"Funny, so are you," Cindy Lou replied. "Why is it always the little people who are surprised at others' success?"

"Oh, I am so staying to watch this," Almma said and squished herself into one of the benches already filled with observers.

Perkins started speaking again, but Cindy Lou held up a finger to motion for silence and she said, "Lady, I've watched you grow long enough to know you'll never be that level of pretty to interrupt me. Even when you had that porno scandal during your first election."

"That's uncalled for," Perkins objected.

"So was your bad acting," Cindy said. "I mean that thing you did when you turned like this and made that dying cow sound. It just wasn't believable. Made me want beef!"

Cindy's finger fell towards Shade who was sitting on the bottom row with the admirals.

"And isn't this hearing cutting into your dictation time with your sexretary," Cindy asked, and her body suddenly changed into the image of a woman that anyone who knew Shade's office recognized as his secretary, even with the tassels that were now spinning before her bare chest. "I heard a rumor she had a nice place in the bunker with you, or was it on you?"

Perkins roared with, "You watch your—

"Under you," Cindy asked.

Shade rose from his chair, his face ready to explode with some verbal assault.

"Oh no," Cindy cried. "Not your angry eyes. Want to see mine?"

Her face fell hollow and white, then stretched tall and wide as she screeched at the committee benches. After she had silenced Shade back into his chair, Cindy took on her familiar form.

"Heard you were having a fragile ego trial today." As she said this, she spun towards the witness bench where Bria had returned to the spectacle and now stood beside Kellick who appeared filled with similar confusion.

"Oh, hi Honey," Cindy called when her eyes fell on the prime admiral.

Bria had been in the hall hovering over a garbage can next to a drinking fountain and wondering if she was going to throw up. That got interrupted when a familiar robot choir started rushing by and asking people to vote for Senator Perkins for douche bag. Through it all, she thought she'd seen a reflection march past her. Of course, she knew it couldn't be Cindy, but she was the only doppelganger she remembered ever having, and then she heard the god's voice come from the chamber, and Bria had to investigate.

"Guess what! The male carries the baby," Cindy Lou announced. "Did you know that? I did not know that? Who knew? No wonder he dies, huh? That's a little place to shoot a galaxy out of. The key to surviving is don't stick around and cuddle. It's just empty calories anyway. When he starts to blow up like a balloon, just lock his naked booty in the coffin, launch it into space and zip the hell out of there in your stolen shuttle." Then she started laughing and said, "I didn't even have to say I'd call him in the morning! Can you believe it?"

"I don't know who you are, Ma'am," Perkins started. "But you need to leave before I have you escorted out."

"You're a bit daft aren't you," Cindy said. "We sleep together. Not like you of course." She pointed at the wall, and suddenly a bigger-than-life image of a young Perkins screaming the name of some guy named Paul appeared. It disappeared. Then she turned back into Shade's assistant and elbowed him. "You know what I mean, right, Mr. Prime Admiral?"

Then she was back to her usual Cindy Lou self again, and her demeanor fell.

"But I've gotten away with myself," she said. "You want to get rid of her and give the job to Shade. Why?"

Perkins snapped her fingers towards security.

Cindy snapped her fingers at them too.

"Think they can take me, Shade," she asked.

Shade merely wagged his head at Senator Perkins, and she called off security.

"Smart," Cindy said. "Never piss off a god." She squared herself toward Perkins now. "Now, I asked you a question. Why do you want to rob her of her reward and give it to Shade?"

"I don't answer to you," Perkins said.

Cindy chuckled. "You already have been." Then her face dropped all emotion. "Now, answer me or I'll bury you where you sit!" Cindy's voice boomed and caused the very framework of the chamber to crack right above the admirals' heads.

"He's the most qualified—," Perkins began to answer.

"Since when," Cindy cried.

"It goes without saying that he has an impeccable record—

"Including the time he ignored his most valuable captain's warning about this war, imprisoned him and then gave his ship to a bunch of traitors?"

"He's decorated."

"So is a sparkly vibrator," Almma announced.

"That's a good point," Cindy agreed. "A sparkly vibrator is pretty decorated. I know! You could make him prime dildo!"

Perkins tried to issue another warning, but Cindy held up a finger that was far more intimidating. That finger extended out towards Bria.

"She's a hero, who risked her life for you," Cindy said.

"Real heroes have the decency to die," Perkins yelled. She leaned over the front of her bench of gathered senators. "The survival of the human race shouldn't hang in the hands of retarded people like her!"

"Oh," Dawn said, now rising from within the front row of the audience. "Fuck you!"

"Yes," Almma erupted. "Yes!"

"Lady," Cindy said, drawing Perkins's attention back to her. "From where I stand, this whole race is retarded. You smug people most of all."

Perkins's brow sharpened, and she straightened up to declare her supremacy in the chamber.

"Why else do you think I chose this race," Cindy asked. "It was the only one stupid enough to turn over their resources to build me a ship just so I could get laid. You idiots all made it a priority too, and all I had to do was say I was a god."

"You don't seriously expect us to believe that you went through all this time with Earth simply to get a ship," Shade spoke.

"Did you really think I was going to trust my survival to you morons? Look at how you treat the people who protect you," Cindy replied. "I had planned to steal your ship on its maiden voyage, but then you went and got attacked, and I got the wrong crew. I almost convinced its commanding officers to abandon it, but then the people in this room insisted on fighting back with probes, and they beat the hell out of the enemy. So, I thought, 'why not?' This could be entertaining."

Cindy shrugged apologetically to the row of witnesses and watched as only Bria seemed to understand what she had just confessed to.

"I gave them a hopeless situation," Cindy said. "And they destroyed tractor beams with twentieth-century heavy metal music. Your race was never supposed to endure because of its collective ego, but those people came back with an alliance with the Maridamarak, military discovery and destruction of the Kag'tak. Any other crew, and you'd all be slaves, and I'd have my own bachelorette pad."

Perkins opened her mouth to speak.

"You don't get to call my friends retards," Cindy said. "And you don't get to say who crews my ship."

"We don't make anything without fail safes," Perkins stated through a poorly hidden smirk. "The Onyx belongs to us."

"Oh," Bria burst with realization. "Oh!" She broke out laughing. "Merrecci would have loved this!"

"Ma'am," Kellick asked softly.

"You don't see it," Bria asked.

Kellick didn't, but then erupted with, "Oh!"

On that note, Bria ordered her crew to return to the Onyx.

Over the objections of Perkins, the members of the Onyx crew continued to clear from the hearing chamber.

Then the chorus of robots all presented an image of Senator Perkins from her youth, in her full naked splendor of bad acting and phony voice stating, "I'm Senator—uh. Uh! Perkins! Vote for me for douche bag."

Then the robots began clearing out of the chamber and bumping into each other on purpose—and each time they did, the holographic Senator Perkins moaned in prostitutional ecstasy. The carnage continued out of the chambers and down the exterior hallways.

Perkins soon sat, overlooking half an empty room and a bench of abandoned witnesses.

"I find it obvious that we have an even bigger obligation now to strip Bria Leonard of her rank and allow the admirals to return command to Prime Admiral Shade," she said.

The committee voted and spent an hour entering their ruling. When the findings were announced, the committee, admirals and some of the observers applauded.

"The fleet is yours, Prime Admiral Shade," Perkins said. "Please do us a favor and get it under control."

The committee stood. The admirals too. They congratulated Shade and wished him luck.

"Thought for a moment we'd have to actually report to that faceless clown," Admiral Shade said. "God or not. It's our ship."

After several more adulations, he decided to give his first order.

"Earth Franchise Vessel Onyx," he transmitted. "This is Prime Admiral Shade. Transcend me to the bridge at once."

To those filling the chamber, Shade rose into the air, never fully disappearing entirely as he appeared to melt through the ceiling and exit the room.

Moments later, Shade stood on the bridge of the Onyx. He found Bria sitting in the command chair and wished he could tell what kind of beaten expression she had on her face.

He turned to Almma.

"Issa, get this thing off my bridge and out of my sight before she makes me puke," Shade ordered.

"Dreslin Shade," Bria spoke. "You are under arrest for impersonating a Franchise officer, attempting to overthrow a member of the governing body of the Franchise and attempting to use Franchise vessels for unauthorized civilian use."

"Stand down," Shade erupted. "You have been stripped of authority by the Earth Senate."

"Incorrect," Onyx answered. "Franchise Coalition does not recognize the authority of Earth Senate to remove life-long command postings such as Prime Admiralship."

"As I said," Bria reiterated. "You're under arrest."

"You hideous little shit," Shade roared. "Do you know what one word from me can do to you?"

He stepped for Bria and drew his baton, but found Almma's in his face first, and not just hers. Every baton of each bridge member held aim upon him.

"Check your shoulders, Mr. Shade," Bria said, and she stood from her command chair.

Shade looked and found them blank.

"No Mr. Shade. Why don't you tell me what your word can do to me," Bria said.

She peeled shade's baton from his grip. Then she instantly plunged the butt of that baton into his gut. He buckled to his knees.

"Sorry. Merrecci's orders," Bria said, kneeling before him. "Now get off my bridge."

Almma signaled for two guards to escort Shade away.

Bria turned to Nandy.

"Captain, will you make that other call for me and then join us in my office," Bria asked before exiting.

Nandy opened a channel.

"Attention all Earth admirals," Nandy announced. "This is Captain Adrigga Nandy, first officer aboard the Onyx. By order of the Prime Admiral, you are hereby ordered to report immediately to diplomatic fleet carrier Vandenbutcke for debriefing and reassignment. Failure to do so will be considered to be your resignation and cancelation of your pensions. That is all."

While Nandy was issuing the prime admiral's requests, Bria had let herself sit against the edge of Merrecci's desk. Even though it was hers now, she felt it somewhat disrespectful still to sit on the other side.

"It's been a weird way to get here," Kellick said. "But it's definitely been a way, Prime Admiral."

"Truthfully," Bria asked.

"Yes, there's some sting," Kellick said. "But it wasn't as much as having to sit in here while you established your authority out there. I really wanted to see it."

"Do you think I'm making a mistake going out to investigate the former Kag'tak space now," Bria asked.

Kellick appeared to think a moment.

"Merrecci was right about how it's the people who've traveled the least distance who think they know how the universes work. That committee on Earth was proof of that," Kellick said. "I think it's not only the right idea, but also necessary in your case. They may not have succeeded today, but even admirals like me always have someone questioning if we're needed. Some day, they may find a valid way to revoke your position. If you're out there doing this work, it's going to be your name people learn. That should help you."

"In that case," Bria said. "I've been doing some research, and it seems I'm in my right to appoint an ambassador in my absence. I'd like to appoint you to that position and, with it, the title of vice-prime admiral. I'd be grateful if you'd accep—"

"Yes, Ma'am," Kellick replied. "I'd be honored to act in your name."

The door clicked, and Bria allowed Nandy, Almma and Cindy entrance.

Nandy took one step in, slumped her shoulders and stopped.

"You're not going to change this office either, are you," Nandy asked.

Bria shook her head.

"I need him to still be here," she said.

"Why," Nandy asked, bewildered, and perhaps disgusted.

"Because he saw me," Bria answered.

"So, name a ship after him," Kellick suggested.

"Not even your ship's big enough for his name," Bria said.

"God, everybody on it would be haunted by six inches of ego," Almma stated.

"At least change the bridge," Nandy said. "I hate baseball."

"You hate it? Did you see me almost break my back out there when we were fighting the Kag'tak," Almma asked. "Oh no, you didn't. You were unconscious."

The door clicked again. This time, Prilla entered with Dawn and was carrying a box.

"Well, I've packed him up," Prilla said. "I just wanted to say good luck, and thanks."

"I wish you'd stay," Bria offered one last time.

"No," Prilla replied. "These ships take everything from you."

"Not me," Dawn said. "I got a car!"

"I tried to get Charity to stay," Bria said. "But she won't answer my calls."

"She needs some time to be pissed off with the rest of her family," Prilla explained. "And it's probably best you're not around for that. I'm sure you'll hear from her when it's over."

Bria nodded her understanding.

"That's somewhat what Drinker said too," Bria replied. "He left first thing this morning with the Compass."

"What's he doing with the Compass," Prilla asked.

"It's classified," Bria said. "He's been assigned to Jossel and Fram's new lab on Earth."

"Good for him."

"I'm going to race," Dawn said, beaming. "They have this thing called crash derby clubs. You're supposed to kick each other's ass." Then she frowned. "Take care of Mike."

Bria promised she would.

Prilla's finger began waving around the room.

"You going to change this," she asked.

Bria shook her head.

Prilla nodded hers, but more disapprovingly. Then she reached into her box and rifled through its contents before pulling out a baseball that was sealed inside a plastic cube.

"He'd want you to have this," she held the ball to Bria.

"William E. 'Dummy' Hoy," Bria asked reading the signature. "Who is William E. 'Dummy' Hoy?"

"You should look him up," Prilla suggested.

After a few goodbye gestures, Prilla and Dawn left the ready room.

"Dummy Hoy," Cindy dug deep from her memory, and she sided up to Bria and sat on the ledge of the desk as well. "I remember him."

"My final advice," Kellick said, wagging his finger between Bria and Cindy. "This—you two—doesn't happen in here. We all need to respect what the commander of this ship does in here and out on that bridge. You're the examples still. You'll give her opponents ammunition so don't change the rules."

"Right," Cindy said, and she thought about making a joke as she turned to caress the side of Bria's face and suddenly stopped. "Between you and me and everybody else in this room who knows we're doing it, don't ever put a mask on this face. It's far too beautiful for that."

Bria attempted to hide.

"Aww," Nandy said. "She's blushing!"

"What did I just say about this room," Kellick asked.

The others, even Cindy, sobered up.

"Ma'am," the communication operator's voice entered Bria's ready room.

"Yes?"

"We're receiving a weird transmission," she urged.

"Can it wait? I need to speak to some admirals," Bria explained.

"Why," Nandy asked. "Make them wait."

"Might as well," Almma said. "Let them enjoy their last few moments celebrating their superiority before you take it away."

"You know they're going to try to mutiny at some point, right," Nandy said.

"Won't happen," Bria replied.

"With respect, Ma'am," Almma said. "You don't know that."

"Yes, she does," Kellick replied then he turned to Cindy as if waiting for her to speak.

"Oh, fine," Cindy surrendered. "I'm Onyx. Happy now?"

"Come again," Almma stated.

"Ma'am," the communication operator's voice intruded once more. "I must insist you hear this message now."

"I'll take it in here," Bria finally acknowledged and tapped her finger on the desk to allow the transmission to start.

A thorny head appeared.

"Solar system Obptahr Twelve," the head bellowed. "You have insulted our race without regard to consequence. You thought we wouldn't find your destruction of our benefactor world criminal."

Cindy's holographic head suddenly appeared, hovering above the desk.

"We have tracked this offender to your system. Do not prepare for war. There will be none. You will die now. Pursuant to Luool Convention Rule Krupp-two, you are duly warned."

Bria played the message again.

"What is this about," Bria asked.

"I have no idea," Cindy replied.

"I'm not familiar with this race," Kellick said.

"You don't know the Ascalade," Cindy asked then suddenly fell into an old, almost forgotten memory as she mewed out, "Oh."

"What is 'oh'," Bria asked.

"It's been so long, I didn't even remember," Cindy said. "Before I even came to Earth." She drew deeper into realizing her own logic and what she'd forgotten from so long ago. "They must have detected Cha giving birth to a galaxy and likewise detected me. Man, they have a long memory if they're coming this far, and believe me, you do not want them coming here."

"Who are they," Kellick asked.

"Umm," Cindy said. "They're the ones the Kag hired to destroy my world. They're much worse."

"Worse," Bria burst. "Worse is coming here?"

"Prime admiral to the bridge," an announcement came to Bria's office as it suddenly filled with yellow alarms.

Bria was through the doors and into the bridge before anyone else and asking for reports.

"It just appeared," the newly promoted Ensign Basil from astrometrics replied. It was her first day of bridge duty.

"Show me," Bria requested.

The holo turned into an image of the Milky way. Some sort of object raced past Neptune's orbit.

"I've seen this before," Cindy stated.

"What is this?"

"It seems like I should know this one. It's been so long, but I can't remember," Cindy informed then urgently erupted with, "Order the fleet to Maridamarak space."

"What? Why," Bria asked.

"Just do it," Cindy insisted then turned to Admiral Kellick. "Get to your ship, now and do the same."

"What's going on," Kellick asked.

"Don't ask, just go," Cindy said. "Now!"

The object on the holo was speeding through Saturn's orbit.

Kellick called to his Maridamarak fleet carrier Vandenbutcke and through Maridamarak technology transformed into a what a more ignorant person might consider a lightning bolt and zapped away.

"Attention all fleet," Bria announced. "This is Prime Admiral Bria Leonard. Focus all fire on the unidentified incoming ob—

"You can't stop it," Cindy interrupted. "It will destroy us all."

"Cancel that order," Bria announced. "Quickly recover any personnel you can and rendezvous in Maridamarak space. Repeat, quickly recover—

"There's no time! Remember your original mission," Cindy recalled. "This is it, and I mean this is it!"

Nandy found herself suddenly summoning a holotab over her wrist.

"Cancel that," Bria said, demanding silence with a snap of her finger. "All fleet are ordered to the Maridamarak system now."

"Hold on," Nandy said. "I need a second."

"No," Cindy replied sharply.

"Again," Bria stated and then repeated her last order. "The highest ranking officer on your bridge is authorized to give the command to jump your ship to Maridamarak space now. Anyone else hearing this message—if you can, get out of the Milky Way now!"

"One second," Nandy demanded.

"No," Cindy yelled. "Go!"

"We can't," Nandy screamed. "I just need—

*   *   *

The projectile raced through where Mars might have orbited with a bit of adjustment in the solar system, and Bria gave the order to jump the Onyx.

The object sped straight towards Earth. As it drew nearer, it began to spin. Upon entering Earth's space, several orbs flew out of the main body. They activated a tractor coupling system that locked into the strange mix of energy weapon and missile. It appeared as a comet now. The large core continued to throw out the smaller orbs that attached themselves to the body and each other. The moment the strange device entered atmosphere, the central cylinder stopped its approach, but continued coughing out its orb-like contents.

Once it had finished emptying its insides, the smaller spheres all suddenly blasted towards the Earth and dug deep into its crust. Once each orb had anchored itself into the blue planet, they instantly retracted their tractor couplings.

The core of the weapon snapped right down from its orbit, punched into the Earth, initiating an impact that immediately pressed Japan straight to the bottom of the ocean. Frightened waves retreated over the face of China, Hawaii, the Americas, and Australia, all in less than two seconds.

Less than three seconds later, the device had punctured through the core and broken through the other side of the planet. The device sped off as though no obstacle had been in its way in the first place. In less than another minute, it entered Earth's sun. The giant star turned black and then burst apart in waves of molten fire.

As the Onyx sped towards Maridamarak space, the bridge watched the milky way slowly get swallowed into darkness.

Kellick's head appeared in the battlecron.

"Prime Admiral," he said. "Are you okay?"

Bria reported her crew were alive but found twelve of her fleet had not responded to her orders. This is when she found Nandy still invested in her holotab.

Just then, Prilla and Dawn came storming back onto the bridge.

"What the hell is happening," Prilla demanded. "Our shuttle was about to leave."

Nandy suddenly broke out swearing.

"What are you doing," Cindy asked.

"Get off," Nandy snipped back, her focus tight on her holotab. Sweat bubbled from her brow, she held her breath.

"Nandy," Bria asked.

"I'm busy," Nandy replied.

Prilla posed her question again.

"Earth's gone," Almma reported in amazement.

"The crash derby too," Dawn asked.

"Everything is gone," Bria reported with some difficulty as she turned to Prilla. "There's not even a star left in our system."

"So now what, Ma'am," Kellick's holographic head asked.

"Now," Bria answered, trying to decide for herself. "Now." And found herself looking over her crew for answers until her eyes fell on Dawn, her sharp brow, and clenched fists. Dawn's shoulders heaved deeply. Before Dawn could let it loose, Bria answered, "You're God damned right!"

Visit
davidfairchild.com
to learn more about the author, his
other works and news regarding his
forthcoming books.

Thank you for reading.

Printed in the USA
CPSIA information can be obtained
at www.ICGtesting.com
LVHW090822221023
761503LV00005B/78/J